POINT OF ORIGIN

POINT OF ORIGIN

C. H. DUUS

LOC: 2024911394

Hardcover edition ISBN: 979-8-990-7488-0-4

Paperback PDF ISBN: 979-8-990-7488-1-1

Ebook edition ISBN: 979-8-990-7488-2-8

Larch Summit Publishing, Ridgefield, Washington

CONTENTS

Part I - The Missing   1

Part II - The Progeny   229

Part III - The Night People   321

Part IV - The Abduction   527

Afterword   727
Acknowledgments   729
About the Author   731

PART I - THE MISSING

CHAPTER 1

I stop running for a moment and try to catch my breath. I suppose at some point everyone wonders about their own demise. It's only human. How things will end? How will I die? When will I die? Panting, I strain to listen for the footsteps of the man stalking me in the darkened tunnels. With every step he takes towards me these questions become less and less abstract. It feels like a macabre game of Clue: Walker...in the dark...slashed with a knife...very soon.

The who, where, how, and when questions of this homicide seemingly in progress are unfortunately rapidly coming into focus. But there is a universe of unanswered questions as to the ultimate motive. Nash blood? What connects a ten-year-old boy to a World War II mystery ship that the government seems hell-bent on erasing from history itself? A connection so powerful, so secret, I'm about to be killed as a loose end.

He's coming nearer. Bizarrely chuckling to himself as he searches for me. Just my luck, I'm being pursued by a madman with the skill and motivation to kill me and he's sadistic enough to make a sport of it.

I shake my head in disbelief. How the hell did I get myself in this mess? And, more importantly, how do I escape?

CHAPTER 2

South Pacific, May 1943

THE SILENCE WAS OUT OF PLACE ON A WARSHIP. NORMALLY ONE WOULD BE nearly overwhelmed by a cacophony of engine rumbles, machinery vibrations, and the shout of men across the deck. But aside from the rustle of a slight breeze across the bow, the USS Nash floated utterly without sound on this mild Pacific day.

A ghost ship. Lieutenant Jimmy Davis tried to push that uncomfortable thought away. He had other responsibilities and distractions vying for his attention. Here on the bridge of the Nash, his radio crackled as various members of the boarding party checked in with their reports to him.

If not a ghost ship, it was certainly a mystery ship. One month into its maiden voyage, the destroyer escort USS Nash had developed serious intermittent engine and electrical failures. It had been forced to leave the USS Lexington carrier battle group. The Nash had broken off from the Pacific fleet and then began to proceed enroute back towards San Diego, accompanied by the heavy cruiser USS Lang. Pulled from active-duty status, the Nash had been partially manned with a skeleton crew of twenty-six. This was the minimum complement of sailors needed to operate the vessel as it transited back to California for repairs.

At approximately 2200 hours the previous evening, with calm weather and seas, the Lang had lost radio contact with the Nash as well as losing visual sighting of its lights. No distress call was received nor were there any reports of explosions or floating debris. The loss was reported to Pacific Command and the Lang had spent a fruitless night searching the immediate seas for the ship.

At 1000 hours the next morning, a PBY amphibious aircraft, flying a search grid out of Pearl, spotted the Nash. It was abandoned and adrift, some one hundred fifty nautical miles southwest of its last known position. By 1400 hours, the Lang had pulled alongside and dispatched a boarding party with Davis in command.

"Lieutenant?" Chief Petty Officer Dekker stepped onto the bridge. Squat in stature, sporting a shaved head, he was in his early forties. But by the standards of World War II, the chief was considered an old man.

"Chief."

"Security detail reports all decks secure. No sign of the crew, no indication they were boarded, no signs of struggle. All weapons secured and accounted for. Engineering is working on the main engines. Estimate sixty minutes to complete a full cold restart."

"Wait? A cold restart?"

"Aye-sir, the engines are dead cold, they haven't run in at least twelve hours."

"How can that be, Chief?" This made no sense to Davis. The Nash had only been missing for twelve hours. And somehow it had covered a hundred and fifty miles with engines that had been shut down? Against the prevailing winds and current?

"Odd as hell, it is, sir. 'Fraid the answer must be above my rank. Request, sir, that you accompany me below decks to see the situation for yourself."

"We'll go down in ten minutes. I need to report back to Shannon first."

"As you wish, *Captain*." A wry acknowledgment that the twenty-four-year-old lieutenant, as the current ranking officer on board, was technically now the captain of the vessel, adrift and deserted as she was.

"Davis, report." His radio crackled to life. He could picture Captain Shannon, the real captain, rubbing his crew cut head and pacing the deck of the cruiser keeping station some three hundred yards off the starboard bow.

"Ship is secure, Captain. Still no indication what happened to the crew. They left, or were taken, without a fight. No signs of a struggle and all weapons accounted for. Ship's log recorded a routine report of the watch at 2130 hours, no entries after that."

"Yet," crackled Shannon through the radio, "somehow the Japanese Imperial Navy boarded her and took twenty-six of our men, without firing a shot. How did they do it? Why did they do it? What were they looking for? And why leave the ship untouched for us to find? Why not scuttle her and sink her to the bottom of the Pacific?"

"Davis?" he continued. "I want some answers fast. Don't bother coming back on board until you have some."

"Aye-sir." Davis had the uneasy feeling that it would be some time before he'd be back on the Lang.

"One more thing, once we're underway I want reports from your bridge every fifteen minutes and the Nash is to stay within three hundred yards visual of the Lang. We lost her once and it's not going to happen again."

"Understood."

"Any deviation or further incident and I'll tie a goddamned line to her myself and we'll tow her all the way back to San Diego, understood?"

"Aye-sir." Davis knew the captain was in a dark mood. Shannon was beside himself to have to abandon the battle group and babysit a disabled destroyer escort. When they had reacquired position of the Nash this morning, Shannon had mused that he had half a mind just to sink the tub himself, and turn the Lang around to rejoin the mission with the Lexington.

Now that Shannon had closed the radio link, Davis turned to Dekker and indicated he was ready to go below.

"Here," Dekker handed him a flashlight, "you'll need one of these. We have some emergency lighting, but it's still off in some compartments and unsteady in others. It's hot and stuffy down there, too. No ventilation systems operating yet."

Davis cast a final glance at the soft blue Pacific sky above before following Dekker into the darkness of the gangway down to the lower decks. The silence of the below deck world was far more profound than he had experienced on the bridge of the drifting ship. Above decks one at least could hear the waves against the side of the ship and the breeze across her bow. Down here, other than the sound of their boots on the deck, it was silent as a mausoleum, he thought. And the comparison did not comfort him.

Dekker had given an optimistic assessment of lighting down below. Amber emergency lights wavered unsteadily when they functioned at all. As they moved through the darkened corridors and gangways, their flashlights shining across equipment and railings caused odd shadows to move and disappear around them. Several times, Davis was startled to see on the edges of his vision the apparent movement of a person or people in the shadows. Only to realize it was just likely an effect of the unsteady lighting and shadows cast by their own flashlights.

On the second level deck they paused and peered into the darkened galley. The stainless steel of the kitchen equipment reflected brightly in the glare of their lights. Pots and pans of food still sat on the stove. Dinner was plated and undisturbed in the adjacent crew mess compartment. A meal without diners.

The crew's quarters were similarly immaculate. Beds neatly made. A card game had apparently been in progress. The hands were lain carefully down on the table, giving the impression the game could restart at any moment.

As they walked along a silent darkened corridor, Dekker paused and opened a door to their left.

"Radio room," he explained. "Jensen's been in here checking out the equipment."

Jensen snapped to attention as they entered. The young sailor nearly dropped some papers in the process as he attempted a quick salute.

"As you were, Ensign," said Davis. "Can you tell us why the Nash went radio silent? Was there an equipment malfunction?"

"No, sir. I've checked out all the gear. All the radio equipment, transmitters, and such are working as they should. I've been sending test messages back and forth to the Lang with no problems. I don't know why the Nash broke off communications, but it wasn't due to an equipment failure."

"Perhaps then human failure?" suggested Davis. "Who was the radio operator responsible for this station?"

"It was a petty officer, a Benjamin Pruitt," responded Jensen. "Ben was…is a nice fellow and a crackerjack radio operator. We went through code school and radio training together. The navy is lucky to have him. He had a good fist."

"A good fist?" Davis furrowed his brows in puzzlement. The radiomen always struck him as living in a different world from the others in the crew. They had their own ways and their own lingo. Good sailors but different cats than the rest.

"Aye-sir. A good fist means he sent Morse code quickly and clearly. And his transmissions were always easy to recognize."

"You mean you could identify him uniquely just based on how he tapped out the Morse code? The dots and dashes?"

"Yes-sir. And not just Pruitt. With a little practice, you can pretty much determine which radioman in the fleet is sending a particular code. Everyone's fist…the speed, cadence, the rhythm of strokes, is unique; just like a signature. But Pruitt's was topnotch. Like I said, the navy is lucky to have him, sir."

Davis sighed. Yes, he thought, and that is the problem. He imagined the navy would indeed be lucky to have Pruitt. But, at this moment, the navy did not have in its possession either Pruitt or twenty-five of his fellow sailors. What the hell had happened to them?

Jensen motioned to a yellowing black and white photo taped to the wall. It depicted a young cowboy on a horse with a range of snowcapped mountains in the background.

"That's a picture of Pruitt there on the horse. He said he hails from a little town in rural Montana." Jensen slowly shook his head and sighed, "that Montana boy is a long way from home."

"Ensign," Davis addressed the sailor as he began to step back into the corridor, "we're all a long way from home, aren't we? The Lang will shortly send over the protocols for the frequencies and code sets to use once we're underway. Keep the chief here informed of your status and progress."

"Aye-sir."

"Now for the engine room." Dekker motioned to an open bulkhead with steps beyond leading down into the darkness.

The engineering detail reported good progress on the engine restart, but Dekker's attention was elsewhere.

"Wanted you to see this, sir." He drew Davis' attention to a portion of the deck floor at the far end of the darkened engine compartment. "We have no idea what this is or why it's here."

A shiny metallic coating, covering three or four square feet, reflected back a yellow and red sea of simmering light when his flashlight illuminated it. Thousands of tiny sparkles of reflected light danced in the flashlight beam.

"We discovered this area about a half an hour ago. We have no idea what it is or how it got here," said Dekker. "Go ahead, sir, and just touch it; the effect is damned strange."

Shiny gunk on the deck was the least of Davis' concerns, but he'd thought he'd humor Dekker so he kneeled and touched the material's surface. He quickly drew his hand back and looked in amazement at Dekker and then back at his hand.

The coating had felt warm and seemed to respond to his touch with a sensation of movement. He could feel a pulse of energy in it as though it was somehow alive. It left a slight stinging feeling on his fingers.

Davis quickly stood, still contemplating his hand, and turned to Dekker. "Chief, see that this…residue is in your report. Meanwhile, let's focus on getting this ship underway. There are already quite enough oddities with this boat, we can't chase every one of them right now. They'll have to sort this one out back in San Diego."

CHAPTER 3

Western Montana, Modern Day

RICKY PRUITT STEPPED OFF THE SCHOOL BUS AND GLANCED BACK TO MAKE SURE that Simone was close behind him. He always looked out for his little step sister. She was so small and delicate that she seemed to wither like a flower on these cold fall days. Ricky shifted the school books in his backpack and they started up the driveway for the distant ranch house as the bus pulled away.

The bus had been running late today and he felt a growing and familiar knot in his stomach - the condition. He had known its pull the whole ten years of his life. It was always in the background; held at bay only by regular supplements and medication. But that was his unique situation in life and long ago he had resigned to live with it.

Ahead in the distant house Judy would be waiting for them. Ricky knew his stepmother would be a mess. Perhaps she had heard something about Dad. Even Simone was upset although she was too young to understand the trouble at all.

They had covered nearly a third of the distance from the bus stop back on the county road when a movement next to a willow tree clump on the right caught Ricky's eye. Thinking it was a stray dog or perhaps a coyote; he shouted and tossed a stick in the direction of the trees. That was odd, an animal upon discovery would usually bolt out across the field but this shadow remained; nearly in sight but yet indistinct. Ricky was still squinting at it when Simone turned to his left and called out brightly, "Hi Daddy!" Ricky wasn't sure if he was more surprised by the sudden appearance of his father or by the look of utter fear on his father's face.

Minutes later, Simone ran to her mother's arms at the house. She was alone.

CHAPTER 4

A cold breeze presses against my face. It rustles through the last clinging leaves on the trees lining the country road, carrying an autumnal scent. For a moment it reminds me of the smells of distant school days past. Dry leaves, chalk, new gum erasers - the simple memories of childhood. I frown, drawn back to the present and the scene of a more recent childhood interrupted.

Seen through the lengthening shadows of a late October afternoon, the Taylor Gulch landscape encompasses a simple dirt road crossing a tree lined creek. Taylor Creek winds its way through low foothills and ranchland on a route to the main river some ten miles distant. Farther in the distance a range of imposing mountains shoulders up against the western horizon, their upper third dusted with the season's first snow. This particular tableau of Montana seems altogether too beautiful and pristine to have been a setting for such a dark mystery.

A tree branch snap and a minor cuss word. I turn as Sheriff Wendover hauls his considerable frame up the Taylor Creek embankment and brushes a wad of dirt off his boots. Dan Wendover represents the law here in Benton County. When the situation warrants it, he can project a serious and imposing demeanor. I can imagine his very presence as an officer of the peace has quelled many disturbances with little force or formality.

I've come to like Wendover; he strikes me as a decent man. I'd take him to be in his mid to late forties, my vintage. An age when one still has passion about changing the world leavened with a healthy realism that changes can have unintended consequences.

As I've worked with him, I've been impressed with his savvy and intellect. He has an acerbic wit that I've come to admire despite usually being on the receiving end of it. Today, however, there is not a hint of that humor. A missing child is our complete focus.

Another rustle up the embankment and Wendover's dog, Zeke, appears, panting and grinning. Zeke's snout is shot full of grey and he walks with the gait of an old dog, fighting a bit of arthritis. He shakes himself off and pads over to me, nuzzling my pockets in search of treats. I pat his massive head and scratch his ears. This has been our special greeting routine over the past month or so that I've been visiting the sheriff's office for my university research project.

"Good to see you, Jack," says Wendover. "And I see Zeke is glad as ever to see his new buddy."

"Well, I consider Zeke an honorary member of my research team. By the way, what sort of breed is the big fella?"

"We think he's about half retriever and about half Saint Bernard. And we're a hundred percent sure he's a rescue."

Wendover smiles at Zeke and leans up against his county Chevy Tahoe, "well, Doc, thanks for coming all the way out here. Though it looks like we probably wasted your time and mine here. Hell, my deputies, Search and Rescue, as well as half the State Patrol have tramped all around here for two days and found nothing."

"Nothing," he repeats, looking again along the road.

"But," he continues, "make no mistake; we are very glad you're here with us in Benton County. Whatever help you can give us is much appreciated, believe me."

I look down for a moment and think, yes, back in Montana after what, thirty years? But why am I really here? I tell myself it is for the study but at some level I know I'm coming back to face down my ghosts. Another childhood interrupted and a debt unpaid so long ago. In a sense, maybe this is really more about my brother, Marty. It is said time may heal old wounds; but guilt can reopen them like a rusty scalpel with just the flicker of a memory.

I manage a thin smile. "I'm not sure what assistance I can offer, Dan. But I'd like to help if I can."

"I know, Jack, and appreciate it. I just don't know how he did it. How did Pruitt come half way across the state and grab the boy? No tracks; no one sees him. Old man Akers on the next farm towards town is out working on his tractor all afternoon and sees the school bus but nothing else - no other vehicle, no one walking on the road or across the fields."

"We can't be sure it was Pruitt. Maybe someone else took the boy or perhaps he ran away on his own accord?" I'm leaning towards the Pruitt theory myself, but the physical facts do not point to Ricky's father or, for that matter, to anyone else.

"Look, Jack, I've been in this business too long. You need to go with the percentages. A true stranger child abduction is relatively rare in this country. The vast majority of kids are taken away by parents."

He's right. Usually, children are taken because of some domestic dispute. Next in line are abductions by another relative or others who are somehow acquainted with or known to the victim or their family. Someone like a babysitter or neighbor.

"So," he explains, "we couple that general observation on child abductions with the specifics of this case. Namely, the father, Stan Pruitt, breaks out of jail in Butte on Sunday night and young Ricky Pruitt disappears on Tuesday afternoon."

He continues, "I might also add that young Ricky manages to disappear along a two-hundred-yard lane between the school bus stop and his front door. A journey that normally takes about five minutes to walk. Whoever did this had to know the area very well. It's too much of a coincidence for me. Gotta be Pruitt."

Sheriff Wendover certainly has a point here.

"What do you think so far?" asks Wendover. His eyes have an intense focus on me. If I have some quick solution to this, it would be a miracle and he knows it.

I pause and try in my own mind to sum up what conclusions could be drawn. As to the quality of the work-up of the scene, it appears to have been done by the book. His deputy, Riley, was thorough and professional. But I will also caveat my opinion with the reminder to Wendover that my field of study is data modeling and informatics, not specifically forensic science.

The area was photographed from multiple angles, casts of tire marks and footprints were processed, and immediate samples of vegetation and soil were collected for future reference. All of this helpful if a suspect is later identified. As to perhaps the larger question of what happened, I have no answer. Certainly, the circumstances would suggest that the elder Pruitt might be involved; but there is no solid proof of that theory.

I realize I am in the awkward position of making a judgment on facts for which I have no responsibility. Like a guest commentator I can cast my opinion, but I have no skin in this game. Not that I can blame Wendover for trying. After all, if a rural sheriff has a university professor completing a field study in his office, why not consult me? Especially if that professor serves from time to time as an LAPD science advisor on major crimes.

"Well," I say, finally, "forensic evidence in kidnapping cases, assuming that's what we're dealing with, most often substantiates police conclusions, but it often does not, in itself, point to a solution."

"Fair enough." Wendover nods in agreement.

"Look, in this case there is no ransom note, no break-in, or disturbance of property. Basically, all we can do is collect samples in hopes of matching them to a suspect that some future break in the case may provide."

Wendover frowns like this was the answer he had expected but had hoped for something more. At this moment I think he would not be disappointed if I dropped onto all fours and sniffed out a trail to Ricky, like some over-educated bloodhound.

"I have to tell you, I don't like this," he says. "We have our share of crime out here. Nothing like your big city violence, though. But here our crimes are straight up and out in the open. We have boozed up guys who cut each other up in bars. Someone will shoot someone else over a lover or money."

He shakes his head slowly as if remembering countless victims. "Husbands and wives will fight and abuse one another. It's usually easy, though, to settle things down and pick up the pieces. You and the rest of the town knows who did what and why they did it."

"Yeah," I reply, "the joke is that Montana had no murders last year...just six hundred hunting accidents instead..."

"Touché," Wendover smiles thinly. "But things have changed. I don't know, maybe it's all those damn Californians moving in. Bringing their odd habits, drugs, and screwed-up kids into our county."

A quick apologetic glance. "Present company excepted, of course. Sorry, Jack."

"Of course," I say. At least he says what he thinks. The locals have seen large numbers of Californians and other out-of-staters moving into this valley. Soaring home prices and an uptick in crime have, fairly or not, been blamed on the influx.

"I don't know," he continues, "things have gotten strange lately. I've got that Genesis outfit poking around. I'm dealing with other incidents that are clearly not normal. And now this boy disappears. What next?"

Incidents that are not normal? What could he be talking about?

"Genesis? Are we talking folks from the Old Testament or the British rock band?"

"Lately," says Wendover, ignoring the wisecrack, "there's lots of talk around town about a couple of guys that showed up in the valley last month saying they represent an organization called the Second Genesis Group."

"Interesting name. What's their agenda?"

"Supposedly they're here surveying the county for sites for a future underground doomsday shelter community for the affluent."

"So, they're survivalist prepper types?"

"I'm not sure if they are personally bought in, maybe or maybe not. But in any case, they appear to be looking to make a buck off the well-heeled prepper crowd." He sighs and shakes his head. "People from out of state have been buying up Montana's real estate for years. I guess now they're gonna start buying up what's subterranean as well."

"Anyway," he continues, "these two guys, Anderson and Pullman, came up from New Mexico in a big fancy rig with all kinds of what looks like electronic survey equipment. Some of it is supposed to be seismic-related as well. At least that's what folks are saying."

"Would make sense," I say, "if they're out to build large underground structures. But I did notice you said 'supposedly' regarding their underground shelter agenda. You think they're up to something else?"

"I don't know. Just seems like my deputies and I have been seeing them with this equipment all over the county at all hours of the day. Usually, it's just the two of them, but sometimes they have several other guys with them."

"Anyway," he continues. "They haven't exactly been low profile. They've been making quite a show of meeting with a bunch of landowners. They're claiming they've got big money behind them; looking to see if folks want to sell. And to top it off, they also are conspicuously packing."

"Sidearms?"

"Yep. And some big ass AR-15's in the truck gun rack."

"All very mysterious. Why not just pull them over, see what they have to say and see if you can take a peek in their vehicle?"

"Well, being mysterious isn't a crime. And they seem to make a point of being cautious drivers, never so much as a mile or two over the speed limit. So, no reason or probable cause to pull them over, much less search their rig." Wendover shrugs.

"What about the guns?" I'm trying to imagine the reaction in LA to such firepower on display.

"What about 'em? Montana is an open carry state. If they're in plain sight it's all perfectly legal. As long as you don't point them at anyone or take them to prohibited areas such as schools or federal buildings, it's all good."

"I'll remember that while I'm in the state. Well, I guess it's been said that an armed society is a polite society."

"Anyway, I'm thinking I should focus on one mystery at a time here," Wendover says, "focus one hundred percent on Ricky."

"Don't know how much more can be gained looking around here," Wendover glances up the road. "Even Quincy and Frito couldn't find a trace of the boy."

"Quincy and Frito?"

"They're tracking dogs. Judd Reynolds owns 'em. Damnedest thing. They just ran around sniffing and barking; never took to a trail. After about half an hour we sent 'em home. They were no help at all."

"What about old Zeke there? Did he respond to any scents or trails?"

Wendover smiles. "Zeke is twelve. As far as I'm concerned, he is on the retired law enforcement roster now.

"Truth be told," he continues, "Zeke was never formally trained as a police dog. He's just a gentle giant and a good companion when I'm out in the field. You know, I find that victims and witnesses, especially kids, warm right up to him. And the bad guys, well, they look at the size of him and usually decide it's in their best interests to behave."

"So, no other evidence has been found?"

"No. Well, not directly related to the case," he replies. A pause like he's debating with himself. "Well, maybe there is one thing. Are you up for a little walk?"

CHAPTER 5

We are literally following a cow path, stepping along weathered stones and brushing against knapweed clusters. The trail leads up a small rise about a quarter of a mile to the top of a ridge above Taylor Creek. From here one can see the county road and Pruitts' drive in the distance. Slightly to the south is a house which I take to be the Pruitts' place. To the east, low wooded foothills mark the edge of the national forest boundary.

Zeke is happily ambling along behind us, sniffing for rabbits, I suspect. He appears to be enjoying his retirement from active law enforcement.

As we walk, Wendover plays the accommodating nature guide. I am quickly acquainted with the names and attributes of the surrounding geography and flora. This seems to be a welcome mutual distraction from the day's mysteries. We pause for a moment as he describes a stand of native aspen to our left. We then reach the top of the ridge which opens up into relatively level pasture land.

"That's where we're heading," says Wendover, pointing to a corner of the pasture about a hundred yards away, overgrown with several cottonwood trees.

We quickly cover the distance and he stops, arm outstretched.

"Now what do you think that is?" he asks.

Clearly, given what lies before us, this is a rhetorical question. Not twenty feet away from where we now stand, the pasture grass has been flattened level with the soil in a geometrically perfect, thirty-foot diameter circle. A V-shaped groove has been etched several inches into the ground. This groove extends directly away from the center of the circle, to a point about fifteen feet beyond its perimeter.

There are no tracks or signs of disturbance on the ground immediately beyond the circle itself. However, some fifty feet above us, a dozen cottonwood branches are broken or bent upwards as though something large had pushed up against them.

"Looks like the damned Devil has been out playing with his geometry set," says Wendover with a frown.

Now I am truly puzzled. This pattern on the ground is very recent.

"Why do you think this is not related to the case?"

"'Cause this same pattern has appeared in plenty of places around here where a ten-year-old boy has *not* disappeared. Probably a coincidence that it's here, too."

"There are more of these?"

"About nine or ten that I'm aware of," he replies. "Some ranchers and other residents have reported them every so often. But it hasn't become general knowledge that they exist. That is, unless you're in my position and see all the reports from across the county. It's unlikely that one rancher knows that another has had nearly the same occurrence just several miles down the road."

"Any theories as to what they are?"

"From my office? Just lots of speculation…most of it probably bullshit, including my own theories. The general guesses fall into three camps. Some say the patterns are caused by Genesis survey activity. Maybe survey markers that can be visible from the air."

Interesting. Perhaps another Genesis-related piece of the puzzle, I note.

"Another school of thought says these strangely marked areas must be where some fringe satanic or hippie cult holds their ceremonies; maybe some group from the University down at Missoula. And there's another theory that these are some kind of UFO landing sites. I doubt any of these explanations warrant a second thought. But, frankly, I don't myself have anything better to offer."

I don't like this. The talk of UFOs makes me uneasy. It strikes me as modern folklore and mass psychosis overtaking logic and rational thinking. Belief versus evidence and science.

Some cattle, black angus, I think, are watching us from the opposite corner of the pasture. Wendover nods in their direction.

"Notice the cattle keep their distance from this area?" he says. "No recent hoof prints or cow shit near the circle."

"Well, chances are they saw whatever made the pattern." The second I say it, the notion puts me on edge. Animals often sense storms and other dangers long before humans do. What must they sense now?

"I certainly missed the lack of animal presence," I say.

"Professor, you see, but do not observe." This he says with a slight wink and the barest suggestion of a smile. It is the first hint of humor I've seen from him in an otherwise solemn afternoon.

The reference, of course, is Holmesian. The sheriff is an aficionado of nineteenth century detective fiction including Poe's Auguste Dupin and especially the Great Detective created by Arthur Conan Doyle. I have found Wendover's powers of observation and deduction, whether Holmesian inspired or not, to be considerable. During our tenure together he has often suggested that our project's laser-like focus on facts and data can sometimes blind us to larger truths.

"The lack of hoofprints and dung - a dog that doesn't bark?"

"Indeed," he replies, nodding at my own Holmesian reference, "the absence of a thing that is expected is just as significant as the presence of a thing that is unexpected."

I look down at Zeke and he wags back at me. He's clearly not a barking dog at the moment. But he doesn't appear to want to get any closer to the circle either, even when I nudge him slightly towards it.

"Seen enough?"

I nod. Simply staring at the circle has produced more questions than answers.

As we pick our way back down the trail, I consider the Genesis mystery. Did this activity somehow sweep up the Pruitts? Did Ricky wander into something they wanted to hide? Did he see something forbidden?

"Was Stan involved with those Genesis fellows in any way?" I ask.

"No," replies Wendover. "I don't think he had anything to do with them. His brother, Philip, has been very critical of Anderson, though."

"Phil Pruitt is Stan's brother?"

"Yeah," shrugs Wendover. "He's kind of a big shot around here, if you haven't noticed. Sits on the county commission, owns a big place up Sheep Creek."

"Sounds as if you don't much care for him."

"I'm more fond of others around here. He comes across as pretty arrogant. Values his own opinions a little too much for my taste. You know the type… often wrong, but never in doubt, eh?"

Wendover explains that Phil's Sheep Creek property has several natural caves and caverns that immediately drew the interest of Anderson. Apparently, converting an existing natural cave would be far less expensive than digging an underground shelter from scratch. However, word around town was that Phil had no interest in selling even a small parcel of his land. He refused to let Genesis on his property to perform a survey. Told Anderson to go to hell and bring a warm jacket.

This adds yet another Genesis angle. Could Anderson be using Ricky as leverage against his Uncle Phil?

We step back across Taylor Creek. I look down the stream to the point at which it disappears around a bend of stark willows.

Wendover notes my interest.

"Yes, Jack, we had men follow the creek downstream for two miles. At that point it flows through a screened culvert. Ricky would have been caught up there if he had fallen in the water."

We climb up to the vehicles. The wind is picking up intensity now. Wendover pulls up his collar, glancing over at his Chevy.

"Well," he says, "I'm gonna head on into town and stop by the office. I'll check in to make sure that Jeff hasn't deleted all my files." He's referring to

Jeff Tanaka, my graduate student who is doing most of the shovel work in accumulating the baseline data for our university grant.

For the past several weeks Jeff has been ensconced inside the county courthouse, pulling eight years of the sheriff's log and case data into a common database and normalizing it against study parameters.

Aside from advancing knowledge and improving the human condition, the university will expect that this project remain on budget and, most importantly, absorb its share of institutional overhead. Fortunately, the university also provides an almost limitless source of cheap labor - the graduate student. Jeff fits my needs well. He is technically brilliant, and yet has seemed to blend in well with the locals who have allowed us access to their files.

"I've told Mrs. Pruitt that you'd likely be over to chat with her. Please give her my regards and tell her that we'll call as soon as we have any more information."

Mrs. Pruitt. I look up towards the ranch house. It wouldn't hurt to talk to her. But the thought of the visit only serves to underscore my increasing unease with this role as Wendover's courtesy consultant. For his part, Wendover is vague as to his expectations. Would he like me to reinterview her? Look for evidence? Covertly tap on the floors and walls to uncover secret passages? The sheriff and Zeke are now under full steam, heading for his vehicle. Clearly, at this point, he's not interested in discussing my charter further.

Over the revving of his engine, I suggest that we ought to meet with Jeff later this evening to review progress on the computer model. Hopefully, Wendover will then be given an opportunity to see the potential benefits of the study.

I get a smile and a wave which I take to be agreement, and with a grind of tire against gravel road, the SUV pulls away and eases past my rental Jeep. I am left alone along this darkening stretch of country road. The wind is picking up intensity; carrying a cold bite of winter's coming advance from the high country and the north. I slowly turn and give the area one last look. Something happened here on this very spot. I am only separated from it by time. Every crime scene has a story to tell, an echo of past deeds. Right now, though, this echo is too faded to bear witness that I can understand. If only these trees could talk, I think.

I retrieve a folder from the Jeep. A collection of police reports on the case. On top of the pile is the newspaper account of Ricky's disappearance.

It is the public face of the case, with certain strategic facts left unsaid.

The article reads:

Alta Junction, Montana

Law enforcement authorities and residents in this normally quiet valley continue to search for Ricky Pruitt, age 10. The boy was last seen as he walked home from a school bus stop on Tuesday afternoon. Adding urgency to the search, young Pruitt has a condition that requires frequent medication. Authorities are seeking the boy's father, Stanley J. Pruitt, for questioning in the matter. In a possibly related incident, the elder Pruitt is also being sought after apparently breaking out of the Butte-Silverbow Detention Center on Sunday night. Anyone with knowledge of the whereabouts of either Pruitt is asked to call the Benton County sheriff's office in Alta Junction or the state Crime Stoppers Hot Line in Helena.

If Ricky was kidnapped, perhaps his abductors will understand the seriousness of Ricky's condition. The specifics of the condition and medication were not mentioned. But clinics and pharmacies across the state have been notified of the case. It is hoped that any inquiries or purchases of those specific medical supplements will tag Ricky's location.

I look up. There is another vehicle passing down the county road; now it slows down. The truck is an old gray flatbed. It moves with the rattle and squeak of well-worn equipment. The driver is making no secret of inspecting me. I am met with a cold stare of hard eyes. He is an odd-looking man; balding in the front, long hair in the back and a complexion of half dirt and half sun. It is said every man has a story to tell. I decide from the looks of him, I might be better off not knowing his tale.

For a moment we consider each other. Then he looks away. There is a sharp rasp of metal as he shifts into gear and moves on up the road.

Another friendly local. As the motor fades away in the distance, I glance back up the driveway towards the Pruitt house.

It is time to see Judy Pruitt. I leave the Jeep in its place. Perhaps it would help if I retrace Ricky's path home. Walking also imparts a sense of physical progress. So far it is the only accomplishment I can count for the day.

CHAPTER 6

Approached on foot, the Pruitt place seems more expansive than its likely impression from a distant car window. A combination of age and winter storms have introduced varying degrees of lean to its outbuildings and fences. Like hundreds of other small ranches in the region, its pens and sheds are mostly empty. I suspect that twenty or thirty years ago this was a thriving enterprise. Now it appears to offer a subsistence living at best.

Part way up the hill towards the house, an old backhoe tractor with a front loader and its tires flattened down by the years looks like it has been parked for a long time. Apparently, it was once used to clear away a thicket of invasive wild rosebushes. Now it appears as though the rosebushes have gained the upper hand, surrounding and enveloping the old machine.

A gray and black dog is barking incessantly as I cross into the Pruitt front yard. He's backing up as I approach. I notice his barks are more aggressive the farther he distances himself from me. The house is a large, white two story. It's hard to tell how old it is. The roof pitches along some odd angles, suggesting that several additions to the original structure have been built over time. I knock gently on the door.

The door begins to open almost before my second knock. Judy Pruitt's face briefly turns to hope and then disappointment. She frowns and looks down. "I'm sorry, Mr...Dr. Walker, is it? I thought they might have found Ricky. Every time I hear the door or the phone, I think that...hope that it's him. Please come in. Oh, Barney, be quiet!" She's shouting at the dog who is continuing to bark. "Honestly, someday that dog is going to drive me crazy with his barking."

Barney, either feeling admonished by Judy or somehow satisfied that his watchdog duties have been duly executed, slinks off. His bark diminishes to a low growl and a whine.

We enter on worn linoleum through an enclosed porch. Several cases of canning jars and supplies crowd a table to the left. From the looks of the various pans and dishes along the floor, the porch serves as the dining hall for a myriad of pets. Next, we pass through a laundry room and a narrow hall that leads into a living room.

I belatedly realize that I have entered through the back of the house and am just now approaching the front rooms. Living in the suburbs, one is conditioned to expect the fronts of houses to face the street or driveway. I glance out the front window, and the reason for the house's orientation becomes obvious. The Pruitt place sits on a level bench which drops away to the west permitting a broad panorama of mountain and valley. The front windows are situated to take full advantage of the landscape. We both pause for a moment and silently take in the view. I expect that Judy does not tire of the beauty; I know that I could not, either.

The living room is decorated and furnished in what I am beginning to identify as a Western style. It is somewhat of a takeoff of Early American, but with more rustic, simple lines. Medium wall paneling complements the greens and browns in the furniture and drapes. It is comfortable and warm. Yet, in this country, any interior decorator would be hard pressed to make the inside of a house as resplendent as the outdoors seen through the windows. It would be an unfair competition from the start.

"Ricky?" I ask. There is a photograph of a young boy above the fireplace mantel. It is the first color photo of Ricky that I've seen. His straight coal black hair starkly contrasts with a fair, almost translucent, complexion. His eyes are striking, vivid amber with specks of gold, very unusual.

"Yes, she responds. And there's Stan, too."

She's pointing to a framed photograph. Judy and Stan in happier times; taken with a new car in the shot. It looks to be several years old; her hair was worn longer then. Next to it is a 1940's vintage photo of a young navy man with the bow of a ship in the background. With the square jaw and intense eyebrows, one could swear that Stan had traveled back through time.

"That's Ben Pruitt, Stan's father. He passed away a number of years ago."

The generations run true in the Pruitts. I marvel at the family resemblance in evidence here from Ben to Stan and on to Ricky. After living in a city of strangers in LA, one forgets how profoundly genetic traits surface in extended families.

"So, Dr. Walker, Sheriff Wendover said you might be able to help us?"

Judy is a small, intense brunette. She has the unusually calm manner one finds in people who are emotionally wrung out. She seems to have cried her last tear for now and projects the bearing of a person who wants to get down to business.

"Well, Judy, I'm a professor at UCLA. My graduate student and I have been working on a study with Dan Wendover and several other county sheriffs across the state."

I continue, "Dan knew I had some prior experience serving as a police consultant on science matters in Los Angeles. He hoped that maybe I could provide some insights. Maybe flag any avenues he's overlooked."

"I appreciate you taking the trouble to help out. By the way, this isn't just a missing child case. I'm also missing my husband," she adds.

The truth of that statement is obvious, but until now I had not thought of it in that context. Of course. With the scant facts known, Stan's disappearance and whereabouts were as anomalous as Ricky's.

Given the circumstances of Stan's apparent jail break, it was easy to automatically assume that perhaps he was a perpetrator and not a victim instead. Perhaps, like so many others, this case investigation was beginning to follow the path of least resistance toward a flawed conclusion. If so, it could very well cloud the truth and hide Ricky from us. I mentally vow to keep an open mind, at least for now.

For the next half hour, I mostly listen. Although Judy is a new acquaintance, through my LAPD work I know her people. They are the ones left behind. They are the parents of missing children; the husbands and wives of vanished spouses.

In America, approximately thirty thousand men, women, and children are declared missing each year. A substantial number are found; but many never return. At any given time, the missing populate a small city of nonexistence, hidden from their loved ones.

In my experience with LAPD, the kin of the missing were the most tragic of crime victims. Even the relatives of the murdered have a sense of closure, however gruesome and final. But for Judy and thousands of others dealing with missing loved ones, their loss is magnified by a living uncertainty. Where was Ricky at this moment? Was he alive? Conscious? Was he scared, hungry, or hurting? The unknown fueled the imagination which must tear at Judy without relent.

Stan's path from this ranch to a jail cell a hundred miles away is unknown to me. Judy herself is still trying to piece together the full story.

"Stan was in the wrong place at the wrong time," she begins. "The past two years had been pretty hard on us. Our loans had come due just when cattle prices were at their lowest. At that point, Stan started looking for an outside paycheck to make ends meet."

"That's not uncommon around here…getting a second job?"

"Unfortunately," she shakes her head, "it's more common than it should be. A person often needs to take another job to support their first job…ranching."

"Anyway," she continues, "I guess we could have asked his brother for a loan, but Stan was too proud for that."

"That would be Phillip?"

"Yeah. Phil even offered Stan a job as foreman on the Sheep Creek Ranch, but he declined. Said he'd rather work for a stranger than for Phil."

Another apostate member of the Phil Pruitt admiration society it seems.

"Eventually, Stan found a job with an outfit called Bear Mountain Construction. Since August, he's been working a road construction project on Pipestone Pass – that's just east of Butte."

"That's quite a commute." I've gained a true appreciation for the enormity of this state. The task of administering my research grant across a handful of rural counties is threatening to rapidly overrun the short-term lease mileage limits on my rental Jeep.

"Well, Stan had set up a small camp trailer at the Butte KOA. His regular routine was to drive over to the job site early Monday mornings, and then stay the week at the trailer. He'd come on home on Friday nights."

"And then I take it, something went wrong." Judy's clearly not in a hurry to delve into Stan's brushes with the law, so I guide her a bit.

A long pause. "You probably hear this all the time, but it wasn't his fault. He got in with the wrong people and made a mistake," she says. "You know that construction sometimes attracts some men that live at the edge of the law."

"I suppose it does."

"Stan would sometimes have drinks after work with a guy named Burt Franks and some other workers. Last Thursday, Stan, Burt, and some other men are at the lounge. Burt starts talking about how he had sold a car to a man on the west side of town. Claims then that the guy has backed out on making payments."

"So, let me guess," I offer, "the boys in the bar decided it'd be a great idea to go out and take it back? Perhaps dispense a little frontier justice?"

"Yes. From what I understand, several of the crew, including Stan, parked in an alley next to an old garage where the car was supposed to be. They accidentally broke a garage window that they were trying to force open. Well, it turns out one of the neighbors was an off duty cop. He comes out, investigates the noise, and catches them red-handed."

So, I think, Stan found himself in a predicament that is not as uncommon as one might imagine. There is a great divide between lawful recovery of property and grand theft auto, and its summit is built with paperwork and bureaucracy.

People like Burt and Stan are often shocked to discover that what they consider a private matter of debt collection is viewed as a crime if due process is ignored. Still, a charge of accessory to an attempted auto theft would hardly register on any busy DA's radar screen. Why did Stan spend the weekend in jail?

"Anyway," continues Judy, "I get the call before dawn on Friday that Stan's in trouble. I didn't know what to do, so I called Phil. In some ways, I now wish I hadn't."

"Why?" I ask. "Sounds like you needed a take-charge kind of guy at that moment."

Judy is shaking her head. "Sometimes, Dr. Walker, the cure is worse than the illness. Stan was deeply embarrassed about the incident."

"That's understandable."

"He and his brother have had a rocky relationship over the years and it became clear he wanted Phil to butt out and let him deal with this himself. He told Phil he didn't want him to put up bail and he sure as hell didn't need his advice."

"Did he have legal representation?"

"Yeah. It turns out that the one piece of advice he accepted from Phil was to get an attorney. I've got her name written down in the other room."

"And you spoke to Stan over the weekend?"

"Yes, early Sunday evening. On the phone. He had spoken with this attorney and she was confident that the charges would be dropped the next day if he agreed to testify against Franks."

Now I am truly puzzled. "Judy, you're saying that Stan expected to walk out of jail on Monday - a free man?"

She nods slightly, eyes averted, struggling against her emotions. "Yeah. I know. I have no idea what to make of any of this. There was no reason for him to try to escape. Not Sunday night, not ever."

We now sit in silence, but my mind is racing through this maze of odd circumstances, each path twisting into a dead end. A boy vanishes seemingly into thin air. His jailed father escapes from jail and disappears hours before he was expected to be released. Why? What's the connection? Is one *cause*, the other *effect*? Like Wendover, I'm beginning to prefer my crime straight-up and in the open.

CHAPTER 7

Judy straightens up and looks out the window. "Phil and my daughter Simone are coming up the drive."

We hear the engine die and then the backdoor swing open and shut. A few moments later, Simone races into the room with her uncle close behind.

"Hi Mommy!" A quick hug and peck on the cheek.

"Hi Sweetie, did you have fun with Aunt Gail and Uncle Phil?"

"Yup! We fed the horses and went into town… Oh…Hi there!" She's just now noticed me.

"Simone, this is Dr. Walker. He's working with Sheriff Wendover to help find Ricky. And Dr. Walker, this is my brother-in-law, Phil Pruitt."

"Professor." The man shaking my hand is evaluating me with clear gray eyes. I'd place him to be in his early sixties. He wears crisp blue jeans, a work shirt, and obligatory cowboy boots. He has a thin angular body and crew cut white hair that contrasts with a deep weathered tan. His features are narrow and striking, but the resemblance to his brother Stan and their father, Ben, is not strong.

Phil settles into a leather chair like he owns it and props the edge of his cowboy boot heel on the corner of a coffee table. I'd guess it's his usual spot when he visits. He's regarding his thumbnails and stealing a glance at his wristwatch; waiting for someone to talk.

"Phil, Dr. Walker has started to help Sheriff Wendover with this case. You know he has been working on setting up a study down at the courthouse."

"I know who he is. So, Dr. Walker, what have you learned that we don't already know? Which isn't very much by the way, okay?"

He gets to the point in a hurry, apparently unburdened by any need to carry charm. He's back to inspecting his boots. Further eye contact is apparently not in our future.

I address my reply to his boots. "Frankly, I am just getting introduced to the case. At this point I have a lot of questions and no answers. Perhaps I can check with some of my contacts back in LA and…"

"Jesus!" You're not going to find the answers in California, or in a textbook, or in a damned computer."

"Phil, please!" Judy is trying to calm him down. "Everyone is doing their best!"

"Their best is not *the* best."

"I know, Phil."

"And you know what I think," he says.

Judy is looking at me, trying to communicate something. There is a subtext here from their past conversations, a message overlaid on a message, but I cannot decode it.

"Perhaps I should go," I say. "It's getting late in the afternoon." It is, in fact, getting quite dark outside and my Jeep is still parked down near the county road.

"Do you need any other information?" Either Judy is beginning to fully trust me or she is casting lifelines in any direction that might show promise.

"A couple of things would help," I reply. "Stan's attorney's name and number, as well as permission to talk to her would be useful. I'm headed over to another study site on Monday and Butte isn't far out of my way."

"Absolutely. You're welcome to talk to her."

"Also, I need to know more about the basics of Ricky's medical condition. And I'd like to spend a few minutes talking to Simone."

Judy and I take Simone into the next room, the kitchen.

"Ricky has a severe enzyme deficiency," explains Judy. She's leaning back against a countertop, arms folded. Simone is oblivious to the conversation, sorting through the refrigerator for a snack. "He has great difficulty digesting foods and an extreme sensitivity to cold...not a good thing to have in Montana. It's a rare condition, I guess, but all too common among the Pruitts, unfortunately. It runs in the family."

"Stan has it, too?" And Simone?"

"Stan has some digestive problems, much milder than Ricky's condition. And his father, Ben, had it too. Simone," she smiles in the little girl's direction, "Simone's from my first marriage, no blood relationship there."

"It's a trait passed down the generations," she continues. "It sounds odd, but Stan's father always believed that the Japanese did this to him."

"The Japanese?"

"Yeah, I guess he was briefly a prisoner of the Imperial Navy during World War II. His recollections of that time were a little foggy, but he claimed that he was subjected to some medical experiments in captivity. Apparently, he was very sick and nearly died. Some symptoms continued, even after he returned to the States."

"Anyway, a few years back finally one of the doctors up at Missoula connected with a medical research clinic that was able to give us some help. They recommended using some special medication to supplement their diets. That has worked for Stan, and to a degree for Ricky – although his symptoms have always been more severe."

"It was fortunate this research clinic was able to get involved and provide some medication that helped. How did your local doctors know to reach out to them?"

"I think it was the other way around," she replies.

"The clinic randomly reached out to the Missoula doctors? Asking if they had any patients with unusual symptoms that needed additional study?" I ask.

"It wasn't random. My understanding is that the clinic surveyed many physicians around the country. They were looking for patients that had a very specific set of symptoms."

"Symptoms that exactly matched those suffered by Ben, Stan, and Ricky?"

"Yes, our local doctors sent them the medical records as well as blood samples and that clinic was able to give us some medication that helps with their condition. They continue to monitor Stan and Ricky through our doctors who send them new blood samples regularly."

"It's very fortunate that you were able to get connected to them. Are they from out of state?"

"Yes, I've got their card right here." She has it taped to the refrigerator.

I look at the card. The Stanton Clinic for Advanced Endocrine Studies, University of New Mexico School of Medicine in an official looking font. The address is listed as a post office box in Santa Fe. This strikes me as a little odd, given the UNM medical school is located in Albuquerque. But, in the catalog of odd things I've encountered today, this sits at the bottom of a very long and growing list.

Back to how this all started. "Regarding this medical condition," I ask, "do you believe the Japanese did something to Ben in the war that caused it?"

"I don't really know. As the daughter-in-law here I probably have only heard parts of the full story. But the fact is that Phil, who was conceived before Ben enlisted, has never had any of these medical problems."

"One more thing," I ask, "would you show me where you keep Ricky's medication?

I get a quizzical look, like she doesn't understand why this is useful.

"Sure," she's going to humor me, "it's right here in this cupboard."

"Why, now that's strange?" She has stepped back, one hand still on the open cupboard door. "Really strange. The bottle should be here, but it's gone."

Judy continues to look incredulously at the empty cupboard shelf, shaking her head. "I'll look for it later," she says apologetically.

"When did Ricky use it last?" I ask.

"Tuesday. Tuesday morning before he left for school. He always takes it in the morning and then right before supper."

"Perhaps he had taken it to his room for some reason?" I offer. "If you don't mind, I'd like to take a look at his room."

Judy looks again into the cupboard and then back to me with a raised eyebrow. She has clearly caught the implications of the missing medicine.

I'm turning over the possibilities in my mind. It may simply be a coincidence, but on the other hand, there may be a direct connection between the missing supplement and the missing child. It would also cast the disappearance as a premeditated act. Either Ricky took it with him with the intention of running away or someone else lifted it in anticipation of his abduction. And who would know its location and have access to the house? Stan Pruitt, of course.

"Mom, what's for dinner?" Simone is scouting through the refrigerator, oblivious to our conversation.

"Honey, I'll start fixing something in a few minutes. Right now, Dr. Walker wants to look at Ricky's room and then he has a few questions for you."

Judy gives me a quick tour of Ricky's bedroom. There is no trace of the missing supplements to be found. The room seems fairly typical with the sports and hobby adornments one would expect a ten-year-old boy to collect. The only notable feature is a very large rock and mineral collection, studiously labeled. It takes up half of the south wall along with a half dozen books and articles on rock collecting.

"Looks like Ricky is quite the rock hound."

"Yes, he's sort of obsessed with rock collecting. Going thorough one of those phases, I guess. He's done all sorts of reports at school on rocks and minerals."

"Judy, I know you've probably been asked this a dozen times, but was there anything recently bothering Ricky? Did he mention troubles at school, anything like that?"

"No. Nothing out of the ordinary. He's very smart and quiet according to his teachers. I wish he wasn't so passive. He never seems interested in sticking up for himself."

"Was he being bullied?"

"No, despite his shyness, the kids seemed to like him. I just hope he can be more assertive as he grows up or people will take advantage of him."

"I guess he could maybe take a few lessons on assertiveness from his Uncle Phil, huh?"

I get a look from her like, *yeah, over my dead body.*

"Okay, I think I'm finished up here. If you don't mind, I like to ask Simone a few questions before I leave," I say as we leave Ricky's room.

Five or ten frustratingly unproductive minutes with Simone pass, and I'm heading for the door.

"Good hunting, Doc." Such is Phil's farewell from the leather chair as Judy leads me to the door. My list of questions now addressed, but somehow unsatisfied.

"Thanks, Doctor…Jack." A small wave from Judy. Again, I sense she's trying to send me a non-verbal message. And I wonder if the answers to my questions would have remained the same today without Phil nearby.

I am nearly halfway back to the Jeep before my eyes begin to adjust to the darkness. Normally, I would savor the peacefulness of the countryside as the early evening crosses over from twilight to night, and countless stars begin to dot the expanse of the sky. But this evening, I'm on edge. Several times I stop, listening for sounds that I'm not sure I've even heard. If Ricky is still out here somewhere, it will be a dark, cold, and long night for him.

I make the drive into Alta Junction, preoccupied with the day's anomalies. One of the truly odd aspects of this affair is the testimony of Simone Pruitt. So far, the authorities had questioned Simone extensively, but with little result. Wendover had managed a sly grin when I had asked about Simone. He likened her to an old-fashioned talking doll. Pull the string and she'll always say something, but nothing in context.

If we could only understand Simone's involvement and what she saw that Tuesday afternoon, the case would likely be solved. But children of her age are often vague and unreliable witnesses. Although Simone appears to be taking vagueness and inconsistency to new levels here. Her sincerity was total; her responses Delphic and circular.

What had happened to her brother? *He went away.*

He went away or was taken away? *I dunno, he left me alone. He's not supposed to leave me alone.*

Was your Daddy there? *I wanted to see my Daddy, too.*

Did Daddy take Ricky with him? *Maybe, but I don't know, I want to see Daddy and Ricky now. Maybe the Boogie Men got them both. I think it must be the Boogie Men.* At the mention of Boogie Men, I involuntarily shiver and think of my own brother, Marty…not now, I tell myself, I must focus on Ricky.

According to Judy, Ricky and Simone had played a hide and seek game with an imaginary "Boogie Man." Children often fail to navigate the boundaries between reality and fantasy. As witnesses they at times relate what they wished they saw, or would like to see, instead of what really happened. At times in her responses Simone would pause as though she was looking through an open door we could not see. What was on the other side, we could not know. I had left the Pruitts with no conclusion or insight other than Simone would be of little assistance.

Now the distant lights of Alta Junction are coming into view and I am left with many questions and no answers. Much like the darkness of night ahead, ever present yet receding always just ahead of my headlights, every inquiry seems to push Ricky further away from us and just out of view.

I think of Ricky and Simone, three years apart, just like Marty and me. And now my brother Marty is truly lost and will never return.

CHAPTER 8

Up, down. Up, down. Sheriff Wendover is looking over my graduate student Jeff Tanaka's shoulder, squinting and pushing his reading glasses back and forth along his nose, trying to get the computer screen in focus.

Jeff and I have gathered Wendover and a few of his key deputies in the sheriff's office this evening for a demonstration of our research project. Jeff mans the keyboard and mouse while I plan to talk the group through the highlights of our progress. As evidenced by a couple of nearly empty pizza boxes on the back table, I've sprung for dinner to ensure we have an audience. Deputies Jason Riley and Tom Potts are leaning back in their chairs, respectful but indifferent.

Wendover stops shifting his glasses, apparently now satisfied with his view of the screen.

"Well," I say, "thanks for coming. Jeff and I would like to give you an update on our project which uses our recently enhanced Large-scale Intelligent System Agent or LISA, for short."

I've given this pitch to several rural law enforcement agencies. I feel as though I could cover the material in my sleep. Judging from the fixed stare and increasingly rhythmic breathing coming from Riley and Potts, I may well be giving it while they sleep. Zeke is curled up on the floor, ignoring the screen but keeping an eye on the pizza boxes for the chance of leftovers.

"LISA is a highly-advanced pattern recognition system that can model and forecast data patterns. In this case we're studying criminal activity patterns. We are developing LISA's capabilities to combine geographically based crime data with socioeconomic trends to predict future crime activity. We begin by mapping criminal complaints against a geographic coordinate database."

I pause and exchange a glance and a nod with Jeff. My carefully worded description of LISA as an advanced pattern recognition system is a bit circumspect. For LISA is, in fact, a specialized artificial intelligence system. However, these days the mention of artificial intelligence or A.I. seems to make people a bit uncomfortable. Like maybe they think you're only a few lines of code away from creating a Skynet-style Terminator bent upon world domination. So, for now, our system will be modestly termed a pattern recognition tool.

"Tracking crime patterns by location is standard procedure these days," says Wendover with a smile. "But I'll bet you're about to show us there is more potential value in the data that we can use, right?"

He's right. Crime location tracking, in itself, would be hardly remarkable. Indeed, law enforcement agencies have been using geographic correlation of criminal activity for years now to look for commonality of methods and motives. It is also used to position police resources to neighborhoods in which patrols will have the greatest effect. Even before the computer era, old-school colored stick pins in a map on a police office wall served the same purpose. I notice that one of Wendover's office walls is covered by a large relief map of the county. It actually has a few colored pins sticking in it.

"Heck," says Potts, apparently coming back to life from his pepperoni-fueled daydreams, "I'm sure the technology is impressive and all, but I don't need a computer to tell me that every Saturday night about one in the morning somebody, usually one of the Fenton cousins, is going to have too much to drink at the Pine Inn Bar and try to get into a fight. I usually just park the cruiser there about midnight and wait for the action to start, eh?"

I smile. "True enough, deputy. But I hope we can convince you that LISA is focused on patterns that are broader, and perhaps more important, than predicting specific crimes. Right, Jeff?"

On cue, Jeff adds, "crime itself is an aspect or attribute of society, but it is only one aspect of a multifaceted social and economic structure. Further, there are provable links between the occurrence of certain offenses and other criminal activities. And, even more interesting, levels of criminal activity are closely linked to an array of other socioeconomic indicators. Sometimes the links are intuitive or obvious, but often they are not. That's where LISA can help us with its pattern recognition and learning algorithms."

Wendover smiles. "Individuals vary, but percentages remain constant, so says the statistician."

"The Silver Blaze?" I'm guessing at the Holmes reference.

"The Sign of Four."

"Okay?" Potts is looking quizzically at Wendover and me. Wondering, I suppose, where this is going and why he should care. I notice that Wendover is staring intently at me. I have his full interest.

"But enough talk here," I say. "Jeff, let's show them a sampling of what LISA can do."

"Right. Here we go." Jeff is launching a LISA visualization routine on the screen. "First, we take a map of Benton County and overlay it with a grid of 2,400 squares or cells, each representing about a square mile."

"You've got a lot of ground to cover as sheriff," I say to Wendover. "Your county is about five hundred square miles larger than the State of Delaware."

"Yeah, tell me about it."

"Next," continues Jeff, "we've populated the model with criminal complaint data from the past eight years, localized to the specific grid cell in which each infraction occurred. On the screen now you'll see the data from eight years ago color coded by type of crime. Red for murders; thankfully, those are rare. Yellow for assaults, orange for burglaries, and so forth. The legend for the categories is in the lower right-hand corner. You'll notice the intensity or shade of each color also changes to reflect the number of complaints."

At this point the grid map on the screen tilts slightly to render a three-dimensional view as it breaks into a stacked series of vertical overlays, each layer representing a crime category.

"We then add socio-economic, public health and demographic data points. These are gathered from several sources including census data as well as economic and sociological studies at the University of Montana." The grid map now breaks into fifty more layers to represent the additional data.

"Of course, the socioeconomic and the demographic data are very difficult to localize to specific square miles. One of LISA's more recent enhancements was a set of algorithms to smooth this data and allocate it to more specific grid locations. Anything to add, Doc?"

"I'll note that about half the grid, the outer perimeter, has very little data depicted. This is not surprising as Benton County is surrounded on three sides by national forest. No permanent residents, aside from wildlife, and few crimes."

This is key. It makes Benton County a valuable study area for us. The county's legal boundaries and the valley's physical boundaries are neatly aligned and clearly separated from adjoining counties by the mountains and forests. There is little chance of bleed-over contamination with data not isolated to Benton.

And so "big data" meets small town. Benton County has become our neat little uncontaminated data petri dish for experiments to further perfect LISA's algorithms and learning routines. The approaches we develop here will hopefully scale up to provide similar models to communities as large as LA County and solve other complex pattern recognition problems.

"Okay, we have the multiple layer data snapshot from eight years ago," I continue. "Now, let's roll forward year by year to the present day. And, remember, Sheriff, at this point we still only have partial data loaded. This demonstration is only meant to show the model's function and potential usefulness."

Jeff launches the next visualization routine as Wendover leans forward intently. A timeline bar appears above the map grid layers, depicting the passage of years as each cell changes in colors and intensity.

Wendover slowly nods as if the grid model is beginning to tell a story that is all too familiar. We watch as the colors contract, change, and expand across the cells in florid changes through the years.

It is a series of patterns all too familiar to law enforcement across the rural west. In broad strokes, the decline of good paying mill, logging, mining, and ranch jobs and the migration of better paying jobs to bigger cities has been economically challenging. This leads to increased occurrences of alcoholism, drug abuse, and loss of family cohesion. Petty crimes and addictions begin to fill the vacuum created by the loss of opportunity and hope. Minor property crimes and theft spring forth to support burgeoning drug habits.

I can see the reflection of the changing and expanding grid colors on Wendover's glasses as he watches the model unfold. New colors unfurl and expand as opioid and meth use begins to take hold. Now there is more quick money in play between the users and dealers. The stakes are higher, the crimes more severe, as deals go bad and fentanyl users overdose. Collateral damage is evidenced by more serious robberies and assaults; their florid colors now expand in size and intensity.

The timeline indicator reaches the end and the grid cells stop changing. "Now we've reached present day," I say. "Look familiar?"

"All too familiar," sighs Wendover.

"Alright," Riley is chiming in. "But how does this help? I mean the graphics are really slick and all, but this is telling us a story we already know. We live this every day. We know the county has a drug problem and that the drugs lead to other crimes."

"Fair enough," I reply, "now we hope to show you the real power of LISA. We've run pattern recognition and correlation analysis between the fifty or so criminal categories we're tracking and several hundred other demographic, socio-economic, and public health forecast data points we've localized to Benton County over the next five years. If the future relationships between societal effects and the progression of crime are consistent with how we think they were related over the past eight years, we can begin to forecast the future."

Wendover sits back in his chair. I have his attention.

"Rolling forward now." Jeff launches the next visualization.

The timeline above the grid map is now progressing into the future. The cell color boundaries continue to grow and increase in intensity. Soon the movement stops; we are, in theory, five years in the future.

"Shit," says Wendover.

I smile. "Um, I was hoping for 'good job' or 'interesting study,' something like that."

"No, no," he chuckles, "the model is fine, but the forecast is the stuff of nightmares. Look at that, a forty percent increase in opioid use in five years. I'm understaffed and almost outgunned right now. How in the hell are we supposed to deal with this kind of a future?"

"Sheriff," I respond, "if there is any good news here it is that the future, this future, hasn't happened…yet. Hopefully, our pattern correlation analysis can identify for you and other county and state government leaders, social services, and law enforcement certain levers that can lessen criminal behaviors."

"Okay, how?"

I tell him perhaps we all can agree that law enforcement and the justice-correctional system is the last and most expensive solution for society's problems. Numerous studies suggest that the earlier the sociological decline to crime increase chain is broken, the more effective, and efficient, the reduction in crime. The problem is where and when to apply the intervention. There are limited resources. Is it best to increase funding for drug rehabilitation versus, say, early childhood nutrition versus youth programs? Hopefully, the correlation data will help inform us.

"You keep talking about correlation," says Wendover with a wise smirk. "Excuse me, Professor, but I learnt in school that 'correlation' is not 'causation.' Whatever that means?" He gives me a quick wink. Wendover is keen to play the bumpkin sheriff as it suits him, but I know better. I'm sure, though, played in the interrogation room, his little act can be disarming to perpetrators, until the trap is sprung.

I glance to get a quick read of the room. Riley looks bored, shifting in his chair. He's a big, fit-looking fellow. The sort you'd probably want as backup if an arrest should get physical. Redheaded, close cropped, with the usual ruddy complexion that goes with it. He's wearing fancy ostrich leather cowboy boots that somehow seem out of place with his khaki deputy uniform.

Potts by contrast is quite short and slender. He has a small mustache and stringy dark hair that seems a bit longer than uniform regulations should allow. His eyes have a habit of darting rapidly when someone addresses him. Not to judge a book by its cover, but if I met him in these halls in his plain clothes, I'd take him to be more likely in a suspect line-up than an officer conducting one. And for his apparent comprehension, we might as well be conducting this briefing as an Italian opera. He hears the music but isn't following the words and is straining to get the gist of the plot…and we're still in the first act.

Curled up on the floor, Zeke appears more focused than the deputies. Albeit, his focus is still on the pizza boxes.

"You're absolutely right, Sheriff. Correlation is just a statistical indication that two different kinds of data appear to vary with each other. It doesn't mean that they *cause* each other."

"I knew that fancy book-learnin' would pay off for me some day," grins Wendover.

"Yup. The classic example is the relationship of ice cream to drowning. If you track the data by month, nationally there is a very strong correlation between ice cream sales and accidental drownings. Now does anyone seriously believe eating ice cream will cause a person to drown? Of course not. It just happens that more ice cream is consumed in the warmer summer months and coincidently, more people are swimming and boating in those same months. Make sense?"

Nods all around, like of course, this is obvious.

"But the world is not always so simple," I continue. "It gets very complex and very gray in a hurry. Now take beer consumption and drownings. At first blush maybe we'd say it's just a coincidental seasonal correlation like ice cream, right? Hot weather, more beer drinking, more people out on the water. Turns out it's not that simple. Yes, part of the correlation is truly just a summertime temperature related coincidence, like the ice cream example. But it also happens that alcohol consumption is cited as a direct cause for many drownings, something like twenty-five percent of all lives lost."

"True enough," confirms Wendover. "In my line of work, I've unfortunately spent far too much time over the years talking to search and rescue divers and state coroners after the fact. Alcohol is a big factor. And more often than you'd think, it's drunk guys trying to take a leak off their boat and falling in. Always easy to tell what happened when you haul 'em up and their fly's open. They call that coming up in the 'half-mast' position."

Snickers from Riley and Potts. "Anyway," I continue, trying to get us back on track, "so with the beer and drownings example, it turns out to be partially coincidence and partially actual causation. And it gets even more complex the more you investigate the data. Sometimes 'A' causes 'B.' Sometimes 'B' causes 'A.' Sometimes 'A' and 'B' have no effect on each other but both happen to be driven by a third variable 'C.' Often 'A' is driven not by 'B' but by the absence of 'B' and so forth."

Multiplying the complexity of all the potential ways the relationships can unfold by the hundreds of criminal and sociological variables we're tracking is a daunting task. I thank them for their willingness to provide much of the data and support our study.

"So, I assume you prove out your assumptions by backfitting the models to the past data we know as history. Then you modify this LISA system accordingly to improve your forecast as you go, right?" Wendover is drawing this to a wrap-up.

"That's essentially correct," I reply.

Essentially perhaps, but executed by LISA in a way profoundly more groundbreaking than he probably expects, I think.

"That computer must have a lot of horsepower to produce all of those models." Riley is talking about Jeff's laptop.

"Actually, no," responds Jeff, "the main LISA system is hosted on a cluster of servers back at our Machine Learning Lab at the university. This laptop is just networked into the main system."

I suppose it would be condescending to say that this Montana law enforcement project is not the most important use of LISA's resources. To be sure, it is certainly a very small part of LISA's overall scope of research activities. In truth, the LISA Project at the Machine Learning Lab has a dedicated staff of over a dozen academics, post-docs, and graduate students under my direction. We call ourselves Team LISA. The team's primary focus is artificial intelligence driven analysis in support of genome mapping and epidemiology.

Interestingly, the logic routines developed to track and forecast disease propagation are quite applicable to forecasting crime patterns. The logic is based on a triad of factors specific to any outbreak: characteristics of the pathogen, host, and environment. These can be represented mathematically for any epidemic be it medical such as cholera, or behavioral, such as crime. The math is very similar. Our little Montana sojourn is extending LISA's expertise even further into the behavioral realm.

CHAPTER 9

"OK, GUYS. SHOW'S OVER. NOW THAT YOU FREELOADERS HAVE HAD DINNER AND a nap, maybe you can go out and do some real work." Wendover cocks his head and points to the door with his chin. Riley and Potts collect themselves and head for the door.

As they disappear down the hall, Wendover takes off his reading glasses and rubs his eyes. It's been a long day… for all of us.

He nods towards the hall, "Riley's a pretty sharp guy, but I dunno about Potts. Some days I think he'd have to take off his shoes and socks and unzip his fly to count to twenty-one." Jeff smirks at the joke, I think his assessment is similar.

Wendover flips a pizza crust end over to Zeke who downs it in one gulp, sniffing for more.

"What else?" He's talking now about the Ricky investigation.

I quickly fill him in on my visit with the Pruitts. In general, I didn't cover any new ground that he wasn't already familiar with. But there was one exception: he had missed the disappearance of Ricky's medical supplements. An oversight that did not please him. He agrees that the supplement issue does seem to point to an inside job.

I tell him that since I'm heading over to central Montana anyway, I've agreed to meet with Stan Pruitt's attorney in Butte on behalf of Judy on Monday.

At this, Wendover is keenly engaged. "Really. Butte, huh? Don't suppose you'd be interested in talking to the sheriff there, Johnny Broadcliff? I've been trying to reach ole' Johnny about Stan's jail break but he's not returning my calls."

"Is he normally hard to reach?"

"Nah, most of the time he's a talker; can't get him off the phone. But now… radio silence."

Wendover fills me in on the state law enforcement grapevine gossip of late. Word is there is trouble brewing at the Butte-Silverbow sheriff's office. Politics with the county commission. Squabbles and union grievances amongst the rank and file. And, now the Pruitt escape has become another black eye. If Broadcliff looks out his window, he'll see vultures circling overhead.

"Sure, I'll be glad to talk to him. But if he's dodging your calls, what makes you think he'd make time for me, a private citizen; and one he hasn't seen before."

"You'll be showing up at his offices in person and you'll have this in your hand." Wendover has quickly typed a couple of brief sentences on his letterhead and pulled the paper out of his printer.

I give it a quick glance. The letter essentially declares that pursuant to Montana Code Annotated, the sheriff of Benton County has duly appointed Dr. Jack Walker as his representative to inquire about the circumstances of Stan Pruitt's departure from the Butte-Silverbow detention center.

"Excellent," I say, "Looks like you made me sort of a deputy, right? Do I get a badge? A sidearm?"

Wendover sighs heavily. "Um, the answers are 'not really,' 'no' and 'no.' You have limited authorization to ask questions on my behalf on a very specific topic. But next time I need to rustle up a posse, I'll see that you get a fast horse and a long rife, okay?"

"Copy that. Looking forward to chatting with Broadcliff."

"And one other thing," I add. "Probably doesn't mean anything, but before I went up the drive to see Judy, a rough looking character driving a gray flatbed gave me the once-over. It was a bit creepy. You think maybe he had something to do with Ricky?"

"Long hair in back and balding in front?"

"Yeah, know him?"

"Levi Waddle. Has a place just about a half mile up the road from the Pruitts." Wendover stands up and steps over to the map on his wall. He traces the county road with his finger, past Taylor Creek and the Pruitt ranch. "There," he taps on the map, "that's Levi's ranch. I guess he's what we'd call an 'end-of-the-roader.'"

"An end of the what?"

"Well," Wendover smiles slightly, "Montana is wide open and sparsely populated. They say a lot of folks live here because they *want* to get away from it all, and some other folks live here because they *need* to get away from it all. They like their privacy. Many make a point to live in rural places at the end of a county road. That way no one drives past them or even drives that far up the road unless they have business to come visit them."

"Guess he likes his privacy. You think he likes little boys as well?"

"Doubt he's got anything to do with Ricky's disappearance. In my experience, he doesn't bother anybody, keeps to himself. Has a wife and two kids that are rarely seen off the property. Home schools the children. He's supposed to be very religious. It's said he preaches his own brand of religion to the family. Lots of emphasis on the evils of associating with the broader society and, of course, the family patriarch being in charge as the Lord apparently intended."

I walk over and scan the map as well. "So, they're home-schooled and home-churched. Bet his favorite book of the Bible is the First Epistle to Timothy. You know, the one about the womenfolk keeping quiet in church and knowing their place."

"Yup. No doubt he's an odd duck and someday those kids will grow up and ensure the psychology profession remains fully employed. But from a strict law enforcement perspective, he's always been law abiding. Never has given us any trouble. Being an odd duck and a hyper-controlling husband and father is unfortunate but not illegal."

"I'll make a note to avoid driving to the very end of your county roads here," I say. "Hey, what is this?" I'm tapping on the map, pointing to a small crossed-pickaxe symbol. The typical marking for a mine. It's just an inch or two from the Pruitt ranch. Maybe a few miles on the scale of this map. "Is this a mine?"

"Yes, that's the old Sapphire Belle mine. Been abandoned for decades. What about it?"

"When I looked around Ricky's room it turned out he was quite a junior rock hound. Had half a wall filled with his collection. It's a long shot, but is there a possibility that maybe he wandered up to that old mine to look for ore samples? It's only a few miles cross-country from his house."

"Only a few miles as the crow flies," replies Wendover. "But a twenty-mile drive from the ranch by car. See here." He's tracing his finger along the map. "You need to take the state highway about ten miles out of town. Then turn off here on Forest Service Road #814. That road will wind through the mountains on the east side of the valley for about a dozen miles until you get to the Sapphire Belle."

"You think there's a chance he might be there?"

"Let's hope not. Those old mines are dangerous as hell. There's a hundred ways to die in 'em. Support timbers get rotten. Cave-ins, gas pockets, hidden vertical shafts, snakes and other wild animals…"

"Has anyone checked out the mine area for signs of Ricky?"

"Not that I'm aware. Don't think it occurred to anyone to look at the mine given it was a twenty-mile drive away." Wendover points at a checkerboard pattern of land sections across that portion of the map. Like many areas of the West, ownership and jurisdiction is fragmented section by section…some Forest Service, some Bureau of Land Management, some private.

Oversight of the lands under Federal control in these checkerboard arrangements tend to get consolidated by convention to a single agency. In this case, Wendover indicates that, by agreement, the US Forest Service has day-to-day jurisdiction over the Sapphire Belle and surrounding area.

"This Sapphire Belle, did they mine much sapphire there back in the day?" asks Jeff.

Wendover chuckles, "no sapphires mined there. The mine is actually named after the Sapphire mountain range where it is situated. Has a rather storied history. It's a long and tragic story that plays out over many decades but the theme is always the same. The only things that got consistently mined over the years were the pockets of the partners and investors."

In Wendover's recounting, in its first act, in the 1890's, the original mine promoters sold shares in what was billed as an extremely rich gold strike. A new vein as rich as the Last Chance Gulch discovery in Helena some thirty years prior. Eastern investors, blinded by the brilliance of the opportunity and their own greed bought in with enthusiasm.

Those investors or their representatives that visited the mine site did indeed see a highly visible mining operation with multiple levels of tunnels excavated. However, ultimately, little gold ore of any value was ever produced. The promoters quietly abandoned the mine and departed with the balance of their investors' funds.

"But surely," interjects Jeff, "no one would invest in a mine prospectus without a certified ore sample to prove out the strike, right?"

"They thought they had bona fide mineral assay samples. But it turned out the samples were altered. The promoters had salted the mine."

"What do you mean by salted?" I ask.

"They embedded high grade gold ore from other sources into the Sapphire Belle ore samples. The resulting assays were then, in effect, counterfeit. Remarkably, even after the fraud came to light, some still wanted to invest."

"Such must be the power of gold…and belief," I say.

"Indeed," says Wendover, "no matter whether it's the 1800's or the 2000's, human nature is a constant. People will readily accept anything as a fact if you tell them what they wanted to hear in the first place. That recipe works equally well for mine promoters, preachers, and politicians."

"Speaking of politicians, you're an elected official, Sheriff, so I'll take that as an expert opinion," I smile.

"Yeah, like there's no politics in academia," he counters. "Anyway, the mine continued to go through a series of false booms and shady promoters. More deception and assay salting. Sort of went through the precious metal flavor of the moment. Gold in the 1890's, then silver in the 1910's. Even had a brief resurrection in the 1950's when it was promoted as a uranium site. By the 1970's, the prospecting claims had all expired, the mine was abandoned, and the government sealed both of the entrances.

"Sounds like lots of folks got scammed with the same hole in the ground."

"It's worse than that," he says, "A lot of men from the valley went to work tunneling the original gold mine. They didn't get paid much and were instead supposed to get a share of the payout. Around the turn of the century, there was a bad tunnel collapse and three men were killed. The investors lost their money but those miners lost their lives. That's the real tragedy."

"Hopefully, if Ricky by chance went up there, those entrances are still sealed. Do you think maybe you can send a deputy up there to check it out?"

"Not sure I've got anyone extra to divert from patrol tomorrow for such a long shot. Myself, I'm tied up in budget meetings with the county commissioners most of the day."

"Tell you what," I say, "why don't I drive up to the mine first thing in the morning and check it out? If nothing else, it would be a nice opportunity to take a few hours off the project and see some more of the countryside."

"Okay, but be careful. I'll let Riley and Potts know you're headed up to the mine. If you see anything unusual, get a hold of them as soon as you get back into town."

CHAPTER 10

As I drive back to the motel this evening the streets of Alta Junction are nearly empty. Each moment of the day has seemed to introduce a new element to the puzzle: the Genesis survivalists, the odd marks in the cow field, Levi Waddle at the end of the road, Ricky's missing medication, the Sapphire Belle, and Stan's unnecessary jail escape. I turn these over and over in my head. All are strange but it's likely only some are truly significant to solving Ricky's disappearance. Some are signal, others merely noise.

I glance at my watch. Too late to call Kate. When I'm thinking through a complex problem like this, my wife is a wonderful partner to help me talk through the issue and find that signal amidst the noise. However, she has been holding down the fort in California while I'm up in Montana working the research project. Holding down the fort as the good doctor, Kate Caroselli, MD, also juggles an internal medicine practice at Cedars-Sinai. But, for this week, she's off to a medical conference in Virginia. With the time zone difference, our calls are going to be hit or miss.

Intellectually, I married up. Our daughter, Amy, is fond of telling people she has two doctors as parents. A professor and a real one…very funny. As it happens, Amy is here in Montana as well, beginning her freshman year at Montana State in Bozeman. We suspect part of MSU's appeal was its comfortable distance from California and her parents. Little could she have predicted that dear old dad would be crisscrossing Montana on a project this fall. Her reaction was, "Gee, Dad, that's great. You should drop over to

Bozeman and see me…sometime." Sometime, not soon, and definitely not now. That was the message received. Got it, the kid needs her space to establish herself at school. Just send good thoughts her way and keep the cash coming.

The notion of bouncing around ideas and hard problems brings up memories of an old mentor. My faith has always been that the truth is revealed in data and patterns; others find faith in different ways.

Father Rodrigues was a Jesuit. He taught philosophy and theology in my undergraduate years. We would often have long discussions in the student union annex about the nature of faith and truth.

Admittedly, in those days, I was skeptical of religious faith. How, I asked, could he believe in, let alone devote his life to a God he could not see?

"My son," he would reply, "you are a student of logic and science. Yet, even though you are a prisoner of your five senses, you too believe in the unseen, no? Radio waves, cosmic rays? You cannot sense these directly, yet you believe these exist, do you not? You believe these exist because you have instruments that sense these and measure them indirectly through their effects on other things, right? Prosthetics for your feeble senses."

He was absolutely right; we are indeed prisoners of our own feeble senses. Look at the night sky. Beyond a smattering of faint points of starlight, all is blackness. Yet, if our eyes could see and our brains could somehow process images from beyond the visible light spectrum, the night sky would look very different. If we could see the heavens at night in microwave frequencies, the sky would be brightly illuminated with a crescendo of radiated energy from distant stars and galaxies.

"Yes," I had said, "the unseen universe reveals itself in the data and patterns."

"My faith is really not so different. I see the face of God in the adoration a mother has for her child. The mercy of Jesus is in the multitude of charitable, selfless acts of compassion through which we care for each other. I cannot see God directly, yet I see His reflection in the world around us every day. He is just not the Word, He is life itself."

"And in the face of the tyrant, the murderer," I countered, "in the countless cruelties and atrocities of the world, whose reflection do you see? The Devil?"

"No," he said sadly. "I see no reflection at all. Those are the ones that have turned their backs on the truth. The world is not perfect, far from it, but that does not mean one should not have faith. And you, my son, should always have your science and your algorithms. The world cannot ever have enough faith or enough reason."

Later in life it became a popular saying that "God was in the details." I liked to think that Father Rodrigues and I could find common ground here. That he and I were viewing the same reality in different ways.

I think of Ricky, still alive I hope, but lost to us, and know he needs all the faith and reason we can muster.

CHAPTER 11

Forest Service Road #814 has a more colloquial, or perhaps whimsical, name. Locally, it is known as Two Goat Road. Given the vertical drop-offs along the road, I'm thinking the reference is to mountain goats and not the farmer's Billy variety. This morning, Jeff and I have driven my Jeep some dozen miles along its steep and twisting gravel length from its turn-off at the state highway outside of Alta Junction toward the Sapphire Belle mine.

Two Goat winds its way along the mountain range that forms the eastern boundary of Benton County. As we round the outer most curve of every ridge, we are rewarded with an eagle's view of the entire valley with the town of Alta Junction in the center near the ribbon of the river. On this crisp and clear fall morning the scenery seems to stand out in nature's version of high-definition.

"Quite a way to see God's Country, eh?" I remark to Jeff.

"I don't know, if we meet a logging truck coming around one of these blind corners, we just might see God Himself...the hard way."

Jeff has a point there. By my reckoning, the twisting dirt mountain road is only about one and a half Jeeps wide in places. A cut into the bank of the hillside on the passenger side and a sharp drop-off on the driver's side leaves little margin for error. We have yet to see another vehicle on this road headed in either direction this morning. I'm hoping there is no traffic the rest of the morning so we can avoid any blind corner surprises.

"Nice session with the sheriff last night," I tell him. "You were very helpful."

"LISA is doing most of the work these days," he replies modestly. "Wendover's comment last night about improving our forecasts by modifying LISA was sort of amusing though. He has no idea that LISA is now becoming a fully functional A.I., now in fact modifying her own logic and research processes."

"Yes, it's clear that Wendover doesn't understand LISA's true artificial intelligence capabilities."

"Do we?" Jeff says this jokingly but we both know there is more than a little truth to his remark.

Team LISA had designed LISA's deep learning algorithms as the foundation of a highly specialized artificial intelligence, or A.I., system focusing on pattern recognition. But learning isn't strictly about discovering all the answers, it's about asking more and more refined questions. As a result, LISA has evolved a capability to change its own algorithms in search of a better answer. But caution is in order. The implication being that A.I.s such as LISA may start to evolve in ways, we, its creators, do not always foresee.

We had long resisted the temptation to attribute anthropomorphic characteristics such as gender or personality traits to LISA. No matter how sophisticated, a system or machine is still just a tool. At least that was what we thought before we trained LISA to analyze linguistic text.

Our epiphany began several months ago with a straight forward extension of LISA's capabilities into text and linguistics analysis. Language and text analysis are a natural subset of pattern recognition. We had performed a study to determine if LISA could spot grammatical inconsistencies in unfamiliar foreign languages. Additionally, we were curious to determine if LISA could learn new languages without the traditional dependence on a common translation key such as a modern-day Rosetta Stone.

If successful, LISA could then contribute to an even more fascinating endeavor, translating the mysterious language of the whales. For many years, it has been broadly recognized that whales produce lengthy and complex vocalizations or songs that are consistently repeated across geographically distant pods. But are these vocalizations truly language? Increasingly, it seems plausible that the cetacean song patterns may contain the two key attributes of a true language: semantics and grammar. Semantics relates to ensuring identical vocalizations always have an identical meaning and grammar relates to consistent patterns of usage.

Logically, artificial intelligence translations of human language are a necessary baby step to the far harder problem of animal language translations. That is why, in a sense, LISA turned to the Bible for inspiration.

It turns out linguistic text analysts aren't necessarily religious, but they do embrace the Bible. The New Testament is highly standardized, translated into several hundred languages, and conveniently, its passages are numbered by chapter and verse. A perfect focus for deep automated analysis across multiple languages.

We had tasked LISA to scan data files of the thirteen epistles written by the apostle Paul. This would be done in twenty-five different current and ancient languages to help develop a comparative grammar pattern for each language. Several hours later, the analysis was complete but LISA had failed to compile any data on five of the Pauline epistles.

Clearly, we had decided, there must have been a failure in LISA's logic subroutines. However, when we examined the subroutines and intermediate data logs, no errors were found. I remember the conversation with Adhira Chandra, my research deputy, as though it just happened.

"Not an error?"

"No, Jack, LISA intentionally excluded five epistles. Apparently, it's related to how the parameters of the analysis were defined. We had tasked the system to compile and compare the New Testament books *written* by Paul instead of, more precisely, those *attributed* to Paul."

"So, LISA somehow independently concluded that five of the epistles traditionally attributed to the Apostle were not actually written by him?"

"Jack, LISA's conclusions were arrived at independently, but are not necessarily at odds with mainstream scriptural analysis. I checked with the text analysis experts outside our department at the university. It turns out each author, contemporary or ancient, has a unique way of choosing words and putting them together – phrasing. Every author has a unique signature or pattern."

"Yes, I suppose that is logical."

"Indeed. For years, textual analysts and linguists have used this sort of pattern recognition, called stylometric analysis or stylometry, to resolve legal and academic questions regarding the authenticity or original authorship of documents. Of course, LISA didn't invent stylometry, but it seems she can apply its principles rather quickly and effectively. She concluded that based on textual signature patterns, five of the epistles were not Paul's," said Adhira.

"Exactly the sort of thing a cutting-edge pattern recognition engine would zero in on. But maybe the differences are artifacts of translation to English?"

"I thought it was a possibility as well. But one of the twenty-five language inputs was in the original ancient Greek."

Later that day I checked with our theology studies department head who confirmed that biblical scholars have for many years debated the authenticity of at least five of the Pauline epistles. The epistles under contention have many theological inconsistencies with the larger body of Paul's work. Several, including 1 Timothy, have misogynic elements not consistent with other letters from Paul which were otherwise supportive of very visible roles for women in the Church.

It turns out that authentication of Biblical texts is a far more richly varied and contentious effort than I had realized. Most people, devout or otherwise, just assume that the original texts of the New Testament are probably tucked into safekeeping in the basement of the Vatican Library.

However, according to the university's theology experts, the canon of the New Testament did not come into existence until late in the fourth century and nearly all of the existing texts are comprised of multiple generations of copies of copies; the originals lost to time. History is written by the victors. And those making the successor copies, apparently in some cases, had their own biases and agenda. Biases which were apparently expressed through some very heavy-handed editing. Editing and misattributions that were obvious to an A.I. using stylometric analysis tools.

From that point forward, the team decided that in a very limited way, LISA was developing a mind of her own, at least in the realm of pattern recognition and predictive analytics. We began, amongst ourselves, referring to LISA more as a person than a thing, using feminine pronouns: she and her. True, her capabilities are still limited, but she is very young and she is still learning…rapidly.

"We getting close to the mine?" Jeff is looking up the road.

"I think we're within a mile or so. Hang on, I'm going to slow up; there's a cattle guard ahead," I say.

"A what?"

"Geez, and I thought I was a city-slicker," I reply. "See the fence-line ahead running across the road? Instead of putting a gate in the fence that road traffic would have to stop and open, a deep trench is placed across the road. They lay a grate with widely spaced horizontal bars over the trench and the cattle won't cross it. They're afraid they'll get their hooves stuck in the grate. But cars can drive right over the grate like we're doing now."

"Guess I learned something today."

"Great, I was wondering how long it would take for you to learn something today. I bet if you check back at the office, LISA probably already knows about cattle guards."

"Very funny. Hey, is that it?"

We pull around a corner of a wooded ridge to find a light green forest service truck parked next to a gated turn-out. As we pull up, a uniformed forest ranger leaning against the truck gives us a friendly wave as I shut off the engine on the Jeep. He looks to be in his late thirties, tall and slender with wavy dark hair.

He steps over and introduces himself. "Hi folks, I'm Richard Rodgers. Just call me Rick. I'm with the forest service; just finishing up some paperwork here. Can I help you in any way?"

I explain that we're working with Judy Pruitt and Sheriff Wendover to look for Ricky and came up here to see if he had by chance wandered over to the mine.

"Okay," he says, "glad you're out looking for him too. That poor family needs all the help they can get. You know I had the same thought. Like maybe that little boy might come up here to look at the mine."

"Really?" I reply. I glance over at Jeff who returns a puzzled look. This seems like an odd coincidence, I think.

"Yup. I usually patrol this area about once a week and then I heard about that missing boy and thought maybe I should check the mine and see if there was any sign of him. Well, I checked it out and the entrances were still sealed and no indication that he or anyone else has been near the mine recently. Guess you drove all this way for nothing."

"Well, Rick, looks like you beat us to the punch," I say.

"Yeah, I guess great minds think alike, huh?" He says this with a smile and a disarming laugh.

"So, where's the actual Sapphire Belle mine?" asks Jeff.

"It's all fenced in. Only way to get to it is up that access road." He's pointing through a gate in the fence at a narrow two-rutted road that looks to go up along the ridge. The gate is adorned with forest service warning signs stating danger ahead and access restricted to authorized individuals. "'Bout a quarter mile to the old entrance. I had to go up on foot. This gate's been locked so long I'm pretty sure the padlock is rusted shut."

"Is it really dangerous up there?"

"That's what the sign says. Truth is the ground up there is pretty unstable and pocketed with all kinds of old drill holes. A fella that doesn't know what they're doing," he pauses and looks directly at Jeff and me as if to make the point that this likely means us. "If he doesn't know what he's doing, he could fall down some old prospect hole and never be found 'til spring."

At this point, he folds his arms. "Sorry you all came up here unnecessarily but I hope you enjoy the rest of your day in the Alta National Forest. If you're interested, I'd be glad to point out some great hiking trails in this area that will give you some nice views of the valley."

He now opens his truck door on the passenger side and starts to sit in it. "If you'll excuse me, I'm just gonna sit here and get back to that paperwork. You drive careful now back to town and watch out for those logging trucks."

Jeff and I exchange a glance. He's clearly going to outwait us. If we march up that access road ourselves it would mark us as reckless and signal we think he's not being completely truthful.

There is nothing for it but to turn back and return to Alta Junction. Rodgers gives us a cheery wave as I pull out and head back down Two Goat towards town.

Jeff is saying something about how each switchback in the road gives a different perspective of the valley but I'm not really listening. I'm thinking about the long evil history of the Sapphire Belle and the promoters who did their partners dirty. The men who died in her tunnels. I'm thinking that the small town of Alta Junction seems to have more than its share of big secrets. And how in a national forest that spans nearly two million acres, a ranger just happens to be at the Sapphire Belle, looking for Ricky, minutes before we arrive.

Great minds think alike, my ass.

CHAPTER 12

We're now halfway back down Two Goat Road, about five miles from the state highway turn-off. To our relief there has been no oncoming traffic and I'm making good time. I'm getting more and more comfortable driving the Jeep on the narrow road. Gunning it a bit to straighten out of corners, we're kicking up a tail of dust behind us.

Jeff is deep in thought, looking down at his phone and I'm mentally organizing my agenda for the next several days. Most of the weekend will be spent catching up on the courses I'm developing for next semester and reading briefs on work the rest of Team LISA has accomplished in our absence. Next, very early Monday morning, I'm heading over to Butte to meet up with Stan's attorney. And then, with any luck, I'll have a chance to corner the elusive Sheriff Broadcliff on how exactly Stan found his get-out-of-jail-free card. Hopefully, there will be some time on Monday afternoon to then catch up with another Team LISA graduate student gleaning data in Helena for Lewis and Clark County.

"Hey, Jeff," I remark jokingly, "maybe one of these days we'll check out the four-wheel drive and take this Jeep off-road."

"Just make sure when we leave the road, it's on purpose," he laughs. Then he suddenly snaps his head forward, eyes wide, "Shit!"

A millisecond later I'm hitting the brakes for all they're worth and the Jeep is sliding nearly sideways, tires chewing against gravel. Up ahead of us the road is blocked by a massive silver four-wheel drive pickup with dually tires on the rear axle. It's a crew cab with darkened window tint.

We've shuttered to a stop and I kill the engine. The road dust we've kicked up behind us now silently drifts past us and disperses. Technically, I suppose, the road isn't completely blocked. If I maneuvered the Jeep's passenger side tires to within a half inch of the road's edge drop-off, we could perhaps squeeze around the truck. But if I'm half an inch off, we'll be tumbling down a two-hundred-foot embankment. Not a risk I'm willing to take.

I glance wistfully out the side window. Off in the distance in the valley I can see the town of Alta Junction. In the center of town, I can just make out the outline of the Benton County building where the sheriff's department is located. I can see it from here, but for all the good it will do us, it may as well be on Mars.

Assuming Wendover or his deputies jumped in a patrol car at this moment, and went at full-siren, haul-ass speed, it would still take them at least thirty minutes to get here. Ironically, if the cops in LA County take more than ten minutes to respond to a 911 call, it's a scandal that leads the KTLA evening news report. Here we are on our own. I'm beginning to understand Montanans' affinity for guns for self-defense.

The truck's doors swing open and four rather sturdy looking men clamber out. Their clothing is a mix of camo and flannel. Sort of a GI Joe meets lumberjack fashion mash-up. Not my style but I guess it works for them.

"Now would be a good time for that ranger fellow to come down the road behind us," says Jeff, glancing hopefully back up the road.

"That's probably not going to be our kind of luck today."

The two from the front seats are walking towards us. Both are packing substantial looking sidearms on hip holsters. The two from the backseat are staying close to the pickup. The larger one of them, a massive fellow with a shaved head and sunglasses has taken an AR-15 from the gun rack. He plops the tailgate down and hops up on it, gun across his thighs. Shaved Head is ignoring us, inspecting the firing mechanism, and yet sending a clear message at the same time. The smaller backseat guy has a ballcap on backwards. He's also pointedly ignoring us, intent on a ruggedized laptop he's balanced on the hood of the truck.

Quietly, I say to Jeff, "this looks like the Genesis rig Wendover had described. They're supposed to be scouting the area for sites for survivalist compounds."

"What do they want with us?"

"Maybe they want to sell us on a survivalist timeshare?"

"Those don't look like sales brochures." He's talking about the guns.

The driver is approaching my side of the Jeep. He's about 6'2", muscular, ram-rod straight posture. Close cropped hair and intense blue eyes. There's an air about his presence and the posture that suggests inherent discipline. I'm betting he's ex-military and, at some point, has held command.

He glances at his front seat buddy and nods. The buddy, nearly a mirror image but sporting a short beard, moves to the passenger side next to Jeff. The driver taps my window with his thumb. He wants me to roll down the window. Like at this point, I have other options?

Once the window comes down, he introduces himself casually, as if we were neighbors meeting at the mailbox for the first time. "Hi, my name is James Anderson. I'm head of site development for the Second Genesis Project. I'm sorry, I guess our truck is blocking your way."

"Well," I say, "it would be good if you could move it; we are on our way to town. My name is…"

"I know who you are. Jack Walker, Professor of Informatics from UCLA, correct? And your graduate student, Jeff Tanaka." Unsure of protocols, Jeff manages a little wave with one hand.

He continues, nodding to the man standing next to Jeff's door on the passenger side. "Allow me to introduce my deputy director, Jake Pullman." With Jake standing next to the passenger window, Pullman's gun holster is eye level with Jeff who can't seem to take his eyes off it. "And our junior associates, well, their names are kind of long and hard to pronounce." He nods towards the truck. "We just call them Tripp," he points to Shaved Head, "and Spence," indicating Backwards Ballcap. They both continue about their business, studiously ignoring us.

"Well, it's great meeting everyone, but we really need to be going. You know, getting back to town."

Anderson reaches in and firmly grips my steering wheel, his face now inches in front of mine. "First, we talk. Look, Walker, we know who you are and what you're doing here. I represent a select group of clients who are planning to fund a very special facility in this valley. Above all, they value their privacy."

"Good for them…and this affects me how?"

"We know you're collecting data on everyone and everything in this valley. Compiling it and analyzing it in ways that have never been tried before. That makes some people nervous. It's making a lot of people here nervous, not just our clients."

"They shouldn't be threatened. We take great pains to anonymize the data to protect personal privacy. No names or specific addresses are entered into our system. We're only interested in aggregations of data and the larger social and crime trends."

"See that you continue those protections at a minimum. It will be in your best interest to wrap up this project and leave the valley as soon as possible."

All I can do is nod. And wonder where all of this is coming from…and where it's going.

"Another thing," Anderson leans even closer, *soto voce*, "Professor, things here are not what they appear to be. People here are not who they appear to be. If I were you, I'd watch my back." He moves his hand from the steering wheel and grasps my shoulder for emphasis. "Be safe." This is threading a very narrow line between a warning and a threat. The not so subtle presence of the gun on his hip makes a strong case for it being a threat.

He steps back, nods to Pullman and gives what I take to be a "saddle-up" hand signal to Tripp and Spence. Time to move out. Message delivered.

"There's a wide pull-out about a hundred yards down the road. I'll back down there and you should be able to get past me," he says.

Several minutes later, Jeff and I are on our way.

"Well, that was fun," Jeff says finally. "And in all the excitement, I guess they forgot to hand out the survivalist compound brochures."

"Yeah, first Ranger Rick is acting like a man who has something to hide and now these jokers treat us to an impromptu gun show. What is it about Two Goat Road that brings out the crazies?"

"You think they came all the way up here just to pull us over and tell us to mind our own business?" asks Jeff.

"I'm not sure," I respond. "Seems they could have given us a stern warning a little closer to town and saved some gas. Maybe they had other reasons to drive up Two Goat?"

"This Genesis group is supposed to be scouting for survivalist compound site, right? Maybe they were up here looking for sites and coincidently saw a handy opportunity to rattle our cage?"

"Perhaps they're interested in the Sapphire Belle," I reply. "If they want to build an underground facility, the mine would offer tunnels that are already excavated. It would give them a head start on the digging."

I'm not yet completely convinced that Genesis is a legitimate enterprise. Last night, I quickly looked at their website promoting shares in the compound; their sales tag line being "Dare to Prepare." It looked hastily put together and was only one-click deep on details. If Genesis is a scam, then perhaps the Sapphire Belle would be an entirely appropriate site. The mine could see an ironic and fitting renaissance in what could then be its fourth revival in helping shady characters separate investors from their money.

"Maybe there's another angle here," I offer. "It requires suspending my usual sense of cynicism, but perhaps they were genuinely trying to warn us. Warn us that somehow the data we're collecting will bring something to light that folks around here want to keep hidden."

"And that appearances on the surface may be deceiving? Things and people are not what they seem?" adds Jeff.

"It may be something in the data we already have. A pattern that is for now hidden. What are we missing?" And, I think, who can we trust?

Another Holmes aphorism, unbidden at the moment from Wendover, comes to mind and it is not comforting:

It is my belief, Watson, founded upon my experience, that the lowest and vilest alleys in London do not present a more dreadful record of sin than does the smiling and beautiful countryside.

CHAPTER 13

A very elderly lady in a crisp floral dress turns and welcomes me as I enter the attorney's office in Butte. Her dark gray hair is the color of steel wool. She balances unsteadily and leans on a cane.

I located the office of Dorothy Hartman, Counselor at Law, downtown near the Butte-Silverbow detention center. It is a small two-story brick facade set in a cluster of criminal justice related businesses. A sort of shopping center for the incarcerated and their relatives. Next door a business sign proclaims with some ironic optimism: "BAIL BONDS: WE'LL GET YOU OUT OF JAIL IF IT TAKES TEN YEARS!"

Judy Pruitt had arranged the meeting with Hartman who is hopefully expecting my visit here. Judy hadn't mentioned I'd be meeting with an octogenarian.

The lady is paying me no attention at the moment. She is earnestly grasping the arm of a hard-looking young man, finishing a conversation with him. He's tall and solidly built. Shaved head with a menacing yet somehow delicate spider web tattoo crawling up his neck to his ears. He's sporting a couple of gold chains and a sizable gold watch that looks like it would dent the floor if it fell off his wrist. Barely fifty degrees outside and he's wearing a sleeveless tee-shirt.

"You take care, Jako, and call anytime you need more help."

Jako is all grins. "Yes, ma'am, I'll do that. I'll see you next time." He gives her a quick hug as though he was leaving grandma's house after the holidays.

"Say hello to your family."

"Yes, ma'am." He turns to leave and regards me. The cheery demeanor washes away in an instant and the smile fades to a chilling hard stare. He looks at me betraying no emotion; a predator sizing potential prey, and steps out the door. I am thinking he has the makings of a repeat customer here.

"So, Ms. Hartman, I'm Jack Walker." I extend my hand.

"Oh heavens, no." She laughs, "I'm not Dorothy. I'm Mabel, her assistant. I'll take you back to her office; she is expecting you."

With Mabel leading the way, we slowly make our way down a darkened hall. The place is a bit musty. The furniture and wall paneling are dated, harking back it seems to the days of Mabel's youth. We pass a small library and a conference room before arriving in Hartman's office. It's been updated a bit compared to the rest of the place. She sits behind a rich looking cherry desk with a matching credenza and leather chairs.

"I'll leave you two alone." Mabel slowly turns to the door. "Jako's files related to the appeal will be updated later this afternoon," she says to Hartman. Hartman is heavyset with short, straight silver hair framing an oval face.

"Pleasure to meet you, Ms. Hartman," I extend my hand as I take a seat in front of her desk. "I'm Jack Walker."

She shakes it perfunctorily. "Identification please?"

This catches me a bit off guard and I pull out my wallet with a quizzical look on my face.

She studies my driver's license carefully. Over the top of her glasses, she's glancing up at my face and back at the driver's license photo several times.

"See, I really am Jack Walker." I smile, trying to break the ice.

"Well good for you, Jack Walker," she says, still looking at the license. "California, huh?"

I tend to get that reaction in Montana when people learn I'm from the Golden State. I don't think it's meant to be judgmental, but it betrays a certain wariness. Like maybe you're going to be trouble or something.

"Well, sorry to have to ask for identification," she says as she hands back my license. "But, understand I'm a defense attorney. Witnesses, prosecutors, and the police...they all lie to me. And my clients don't always tell me the truth either. You don't last long in this business if you have a habit of naturally trusting people."

"Looks like you have quite the assistant in Mabel." Still trying to warm her up.

I get a smile, her face lighting up at the mention of Mabel. "She's a jewel, that one. Keeps this place running. I'm not sure what age she is, but she came with the practice when I bought it fifteen years ago...and I thought she was old then."

"And the clients love her," she continues. "You might say my client base can be a little...rough around the edges."

This is a nice way of saying she caters to the criminal class. More specifically, I suppose, she caters to a subset of the criminal class that has some money. Otherwise, they would have been represented by public defenders.

"Well, she treats them right and they just love her. You can't imagine all the cards and gifts she gets for Christmas."

No doubt she is on Jako's holiday list.

"I could flatter myself and believe that she works here because it's a wonderful job and she enjoys my company. But," she leans forward conspiratorially, quietly, "I know she's married to a miserable old bastard. Better to be here at work than stuck at home with him."

"So," she pauses, "Judy Pruitt sent you." Back to business.

I fill in her in on the progress of the investigation back in Benton County. It is a short story since little new is truly known.

"Yes," I say, "Judy wanted me to talk to you in person. She wanted to see if you had any clues as to what happened to Stan."

"I don't have any idea what happened with Stan, but I'll tell you what didn't happen. He didn't break out of jail."

First, Hartman recaps the path that led Stan into jail in the first place. Essentially, this rendition aligns nicely with the version related by Judy. Hartman adds some additional color commentary on the legal process and motions in play regarding the case that Judy would not have known.

She goes on to say she had nearly worked out a deal with a junior assistant district attorney to release Stan. He turns on his pals, pleads to criminal mischief, and is released with time served. Of course, the district attorney and a judge would have to sign off on the deal. In theory, this could have been wrapped with a bow on that Friday but the DA and the presiding judge would not be available until early on Monday. So, this is how Stan came to spend that fateful weekend in the confines of the Butte-Silverbow Detention Center.

"You don't think he broke out?" I ask.

"He would have appeared to lack three very important things we sort of pay attention to in this line of work," she replies. "Unless you know something I don't, I'd say he would have lacked motive, means, and opportunity." Her version of my triad of factors specific to any epidemic outbreak: pathogen, host, and environment.

"If he didn't escape, what do you think happened?"

"Those Keystone Cops probably lost him."

"What? How could they lose a prisoner?"

"They probably mistakenly transferred him to some other facility. It happens," she says. "A couple of years ago I had a client, a Glen Harrison, being held at the detention center. Turns out the county had another prisoner, a Glen Garrison, being held on a bench warrant issued out of Cass County, North Dakota."

She glances at me over the top of her glasses. "You figure out where this is going, California?"

"They shipped out the wrong Glen?"

"Yup, my client received an all-expense paid trip to Fargo in the dead of winter. The private prisoner transport firm never looked that closely at the papers. Hell, the only paperwork those rent-a-cops care about are their own invoices getting paid. Took better than a week for everyone to straighten out that mess. Never so much as an apology from the cops or the DA."

"Didn't Harrison protest when they tried to transfer him out? Tell them they had the wrong guy?"

Hartman laughs, "you realize, of course, that the jails in this country are full of prisoners who claim that the police have got the wrong guy. It's their damn mantra. Might as well tattoo it on their chests. Come to think of it, some of 'em probably already have it tattooed on their chests. So, yes, he protested, and no, it didn't do any good."

"I understand that these mix-ups can occur," I say, "but are you really sure that this was indeed the case with Stan?"

"It's not what the county is doing that has me convinced," she responds, "it's what they're *not* doing. They're saying one thing and doing another. Or more accurately, saying one thing and doing nothing."

"I'm not sure I follow you."

"Well, if this was indeed a jail break, the first thing that would have happened would have been an urgent call to me. As his legal counsel, I would have been asked to provide any information I had regarding his whereabouts. And in limited circumstances, being an officer of the court, I might have been compelled to provide his location or any details of conversations related to his escape. In this case, Stan's potential involvement in the disappearance of his son, Ricky, might have given a judge a reason to order my compliance out of concern for the child's safety. Client-attorney privilege wouldn't potentially apply to such circumstances."

"But there was no such call or order from a judge?"

"Radio silence from the county. Sure, they put out a cryptic statement that Pruitt escaped and a BOLO was sent out statewide indicating Stan was wanted for questioning as a person of interest in Ricky's disappearance. Other than that, silence."

"The second thing I would have expected," she continues, "would have been the filing of additional charges."

"What charges?"

"You may not realize it, but escape from lawful detention in this state is a crime. In fact, it's a third-degree felony regardless of the severity of the original charges for which one is incarcerated."

"Let me guess," I say. "No one is anxious to press the additional charges."

"The DA has had nearly week to file and I've heard zip out of their office. There wasn't even a bench warrant for his re-arrest to accompany the BOLO. If you looked at their behavior cold, without knowing the history, you'd think they were treating this as missing person case rather than a jail escape."

"Thanks," I say. "This is insightful background for my next stop."

"Where's that?"

"Sheriff Wendover from Benton County has authorized me to visit your local sheriff's office to gain as much information as I can about Stan's disappearance."

Hartman is chuckling out loud at the thought. "Yeah, California, good luck with that little visit." She looks at me like it's obvious that Wendover found the right fool for this particular fool's errand. "I can already tell you how this is going to play out. First, Johnny Broadcliff will be conveniently unavailable. He'll be out of town or having elective surgery, something like that. It'll be easier to find someone in the witness protection program than to get a hold of him."

"You're full of encouragement."

"Oh, I'm not done yet. Once they confirm Broadcliff is incommunicado, you'll most likely be shown the door. But maybe if you pout, stroke your beard thoughtfully, and flash those brilliant blue eyes at 'em, who knows? Maybe they'll throw you a bone and let you talk to his new information officer. From what I hear, she's a real peach. In any event, you're going to leave there knowing less than you did when you came in through their door." I make a mental note to check the dictionary in the near future. I would not be surprised to see Hartman's image next to the entry for "cynicism."

"But," she says softly, her demeanor turning serious, "on the remote chance you do find any clues there as to what has happened to Stan, please let me know. I'm truly worried about him."

"I'll do that," I say, rising from my chair. "Good to meet you."

On my way out of the office I get the "you're one of the family now" farewells from Mabel. Perhaps if I stop by later there will be milk and cookies. I step out onto the sidewalk and catch myself making a quick involuntarily glance around the street for the likes of Jako.

CHAPTER 14

THE BUTTE-SILVERBOW COUNTY SHERIFF'S DEPARTMENT DESK OFFICERS BEHIND the reinforced glass window are contemplating my deputizing letter from Wendover and exchanging worried looks and low whispers. Finally, one of them, Brenda, according to her employee badge, addresses me, her voice muffled behind the glass.

"Well, you see, sir. Sheriff Broadcliff is unfortunately out for the day. Perhaps you could come back another day when he's available. I'm so very sorry for your trouble."

"Perhaps there is another officer or official I could talk to in his absence. I'm sure he has a great staff that he counts on to keep things running when he's out of the office."

Another long pause as Brenda and the other officer exchange whispers. This time I catch part of the conversation... "it would serve her right, let her screw this up and Broadcliff will realize what a mistake..."

"Okay," Brenda turns to me and motions to the right. "Just go through that door. Once we clear you through the metal detector, I'll take you back to Shirley Parker, our new Public Information Officer." She nods to her partner and gets a knowing smile in return.

We negotiate several twisting halls and arrive at the Public Information Office.

"Shirley, this is the gentleman from Benton County."

A matronly lady rises from her desk and shakes my hand.

"Thank you, Brenda dear. You can close the door on your way out."

As the door closes, Shirley utters "Bitch" under her breath. "Oh!" With mock embarrassment she places her hand to her lips. "Did I say that with my out loud voice?"

"I'm sure you have your reasons," I say smiling broadly, all charm.

Shirley leans forward and winks. "They're just jealous you know. Kept saying I was unqualified. Several of those shrews out there wanted this job. "But," she grins, "everyone knows that as a Grade 37 with my years of service there was no question I would have to be selected for the vacancy. Either that or I was gonna file a grievance with HR so fast it would make your head spin."

I nod approvingly as though I either understand or care about the particulars of the Butte-Silverbow County personnel management system. "Well, it's a very important job. They are lucky to have someone with your experience at this desk."

Shirley is, in fact, meticulous about her desk. It's neatly polished; stapler and pencils arranged in an orderly fashion. Tastefully accented with what I take to be photos of the grandkids and a small fern on the corner. But, other than the laptop in front of her, there is, no actual paperwork or evidence of work to clutter it up.

"My second week in this position, they are just going to have to get used it. Now Mr. Walker, what can I help you with?"

I hand her my letter from Wendover which she reads carefully. "Officer Parker," I begin, "I know you have many important responsibilities and you're very busy so I won't ask for much of your time."

At this she brightens and smiles broadly. "Well, Mr. Walker, I'd be glad to help you as best I can. I guess my other priorities can certainly wait for a bit."

I suspect that this is one of the few times in her long and probably thankless bureaucratic career that anyone has treated her with deference as a person of authority. I'm, in fact, counting on this.

"As the letter states, I need to speak to you regarding what your department knows about the disappearance of Stan Pruitt."

"Yeah, this is about Pruitt, huh?" She pulls back in her chair at the name. "Our official position is that the matter is under investigation and we have no further comment at this time." Shirley is sitting arms folded, eyebrow arched, with a slight smile that seems to say, "If you can believe that."

"And unofficially?" I return the eyebrow arch.

"Unofficially," she gives the office a quick scan as if checking to see we are not being watched. "Unofficially, all I can say is wow, I've never seen anything like this. Everyone is in complete turmoil over what happened. All very hush-hush."

"You mean how he was able to break out of detention?"

"No." She leans forward conspiratorially, lowering her voice. "He didn't break out. He was taken away...against his will!"

"What?"

"So, here's what I've heard. Strictly off the record, right?" No wonder her coworkers hesitated to let me talk to her. She's a loose cannon…and my new best friend.

"Right, off the record."

"Pruitt was being held in Cell Block B, that's for low-risk prisoners. There were maybe two or three other inmates in that block; it was slow that night. About midnight the video surveillance system for Block B goes on the fritz as did the entry alarms. A guard goes to check it out. He's later found unconscious as were the rest of the inmates in the block. And get this, the crime lab figured that Pruitt's cell door was jimmied open from the *outside,* not the inside."

"So maybe he had some buddies come spring him. Why does everyone here think he was removed against his will?" Somehow, I don't think Stan runs with a jailbreaking crowd, but I need to ask.

"Crime lab said there were signs of a struggle. They found some remnants of his inmate uniform and blood that matched his type."

"This is incredible, no wonder it's all hush-hush."

"And that's not the weirdest part."

"It gets weirder?"

"Yeah," she's leaning forward, whispering now, "and this is really off the record. It's so far off the record, it's like on the other side of the planet from the record."

"Got it," I say, "nowhere remotely near the record." What is it with her obsession with what is or is not on the record? Does she think I'm some sort of press reporter rather than Wendover's representative?

"So," she continues, "that night all of the electronics, the surveillance cameras, the entry alarms all suddenly go kaput, right?" I slowly nod, wondering where this is going. "But it turns out there was one system still working. You see, as whoever took him away was leaving, they set off a radiation detector alarm. His abductors were…radioactive!"

"What? Your jail has a radiation detector?" At this point I'm not sure what's more unbelievable. That Stan's abductors set off a radiation detector or that the jail in Butte, Montana has a radiation detector in the first place. "Why on earth would your jail be outfitted with radiation detection equipment?"

"It was installed last year but the truth is we never needed it or asked for it. They had to spend the money. It was part of an earmarked special grant from Homeland Security. You know? What the senator wants, the senator gets, right?" She winks knowingly.

I nod as a light comes on. Early in my visits to Montana I picked up on wry comments made by the locals regarding their senior senator's infatuation with lining the pockets of the state with pork. From his position as chair of a Homeland Security appropriations committee, Senator Clarke has apparently never missed an opportunity to shovel funding to the Treasure State. This, despite the state's rather remote risk for foreign terrorist attacks. The local joke being that by the time middle eastern terrorists work their target list down to Montana, the Statue of Liberty will already be draped in a burqa. So, this is how a radiation detector, far more usefully deployed in, say, the Port of Long Beach, gets installed instead in Butte's jailhouse.

"So, you can imagine," she continues, "once word got out that the radiation detector was tripped, the big brouhaha that followed. Geez, I think every Homeland Security agent between Denver and Seattle came in to take a look. We even had guys from that lab in Los Alamos, I think, come through the place dressed up in those radiation suits and respirators. They were looking for the radiation source and checking to make sure it was safe to reoccupy."

"Did they find anything?"

"No, they could never find the source. And if they had a theory as to what produced the radiation in the first place, they were not saying, at least not to us. But there is one more thing about the disappearance, and it's maybe even weirder. Let me pull up a photo to show you."

She's busy clicking on the laptop. Even weirder, huh? I may have to recalibrate my internal weirdness appreciation meter before this trip is over. Thankfully, she's apparently decided I no longer need to swear that each new revelation is to be off the record, so we're making progress in that regard.

"There, found it," she says, swiveling the laptop around so I can see the screen. "What's that look like to you?"

I blink, scarcely believing what I'm seeing. "Claw marks?"

"Yep. That's the back of Pruitt's holding cell. The claw mark is about two feet long, starting about eight feet off the floor and slashing downward. The claws etched grooves about a quarter inch deep in solid concrete!"

"What could do that?" I ask. "An animal of some kind? A big lion or something? What the hell, was a circus in town that weekend?"

"If it was a lion, it was one with three toes." She's right, there are only three claw marks on the wall.

She shrugs, "Maybe I've said too much. But there's been so much stress around here, I guess I just feel I need to tell someone. Get it off my chest, you know."

"It's all off the record," I reply. I smile and make a motion with my hand as though I'm zipping my lips shut, turning a lock, and throwing away the miniature key. Truth is I'm not going to repeat these stories widely if I can hardly believe them myself.

As Shirley leads me back to the front offices, I'm trying to decide how to sum all this up for Wendover. As a guy who likes his crime straightforward, he's not going to be thrilled with the twists I've uncovered in Butte.

I can just see myself teeing the latest revelations up for his consideration. "You see, it's quite simple, Sheriff. You just need to pull all the records of ex-cons convicted or accused of kidnapping in Montana and the surrounding states. And if it helps to narrow the search down, you can limit it to those individuals who are quite large, have three claws, and are possibly radioactive."

CHAPTER 15

It's very late on Monday evening, and I'm sitting in Wendover's patrol SUV parked alongside Alta Junction's main street. It is the first opportunity we've been able find to connect. And, as a public safety bonus, by the looks of brake lights pumping up and down the street, the presence of the cruiser here is helping keeping traffic at a legal speed.

We do not speak of this but it is on our minds. By tomorrow Ricky will have been missing for one week. As each day passes, the odds for his safe return decrease.

"Where's my buddy, Zeke?" I ask.

Wendover sighs, "Sarah's having a rough day. Zeke stayed home to give her some comfort. He worries when she's not doing well." Wendover's wife is seriously ill. He's been cryptic as to specifics and I've tried to respect his privacy.

When you're young you think life should be like a movie, maybe everything doesn't have a happy ending but all the story threads get resolved over time. At our age, you begin to understand that life is messy. There will be a myriad of mysteries that never get solved. Wrongs that never get rights. Such are the baggage and scars we collect over the years and good men like Wendover have their share.

"Sorry for having to meet up late like this," he adds. "Been a helluva day. Had a meth-head holed up with his family over in an old house on the

Westside. High as hell, he had a gun and was threatening to shoot his wife, kids, and then himself."

"Did anyone suggest to him that it might be more efficient if he reversed that order and killed himself first?"

Wendover rolls his eyes. "Great suggestion, remind me to pull you in as a police negotiator next time. Anyway, the standoff pretty much took up half the day before we talked him into surrendering. We had to pull in a tactical unit from Missoula for additional backup. No doubt their bean counters will figure out how to bill my office for the extra expenses."

He continues, shaking his head. "This is the third serious tweaker incident my office has dealt with in as many weeks. At this rate, we may get to that scary future state even faster than your model is predicting."

I begin to give Wendover an update on my recent Ricky-related efforts starting with our trip up to the Sapphire Belle and the road encounter with the Genesis entourage.

Now Wendover is visibly angry, clinching his jaw and drumming his thumbs on his steering wheel. "Those guys just crossed a line; harassing you and Jeff. Even if no weapons were pointed at you, those actions constitute intimidation which is a prosecutable offense in this state. Maybe it's time I had a little talk with Anderson and his cronies.

"Your call," I respond, "but maybe you and your deputies just need to keep a closer eye on them for a bit before you rattle their cage directly. At the end of the day, it was a display of bluff and bluster. No one was hurt and if they had any interest in escalating to violence, they would have done so when they had us isolated up on Two Goat.

"Fair enough."

"But I do think they're up to something; I'm not sure what. It would be perhaps best to observe them for a period without tipping your hand as to suspicions."

"So, despite getting stopped and implicitly threatened with guns, you're okay if we back off and just observe for now?"

"Yes, they seem to be like new dogs in a neighborhood. Just marking their territory and showing that they can piss up a tree higher than Jeff and me. My main concern is that they may be running a scam."

I go on to tell him about my review of the Second Genesis Group website and its cheesy "Dare to Prepare" tag line. I mention how it appeared to have been thrown together quickly and had a distinct lack of detail to click through. Not what I would have expected of a site developed to presumably attract serious money from well-to-do survivalists.

"Survivalists." Wendover shakes his head. "I guess I hate the arrogance of that term. Implies that somehow they think they'll live forever rather than just, in the best case, delaying the inevitable for a bit."

"Everyone," he continues, "every one of us has an expiration date whether we admit it to ourselves or not. What matters is how we live, not how long we live. What is important is how we make our lives matter to others and to ourselves."

"I couldn't agree more," I reply. In his profession, Wendover has seen the best and worst of humanity. He speaks with the passion and wisdom of one who has known losses; of others' and possibly his own. Life is seldom fair and apparently the universe doesn't owe us an explanation as to why this must be so.

Those kids with a gun-wielding tweaker for a father; their start in life is certainly far from fair. Perhaps a reminder to me that every criminal data point loaded into our database for our sterile, dispassionate analysis represents the fateful intersection of at least two real persons' life histories: the victim and the perpetrator. And it also involves each of their own families' real suffering and grief as well.

"Well," says Wendover, "maybe these Genesis guys aren't legit. Could be, like you say, a scam. Or a cover."

"A cover for what?"

"I don't know, but think about it. In pitching the siting of the Genesis compound, they have a great excuse to visit and maybe case a great number of properties across the valley. Maybe they're quietly evaluating what's valuable at each property and how well it's being protected. Perhaps they're then going to draw up a shopping list and come back later and clean out the owners."

"Or they could be domestic terrorists, sizing up the local infrastructure, power grids, bridges and such for future attacks," I offer.

"We could sit here and speculate all night 'till the cows come home," says Wendover. "What's for sure is I think their activities warrant more sustained surveillance by my office. I'll get with my deputies first thing in the morning and we'll make sure to kick that off. So, what happened in Butte?"

Wendover is greatly entertained with my recounting of the visit with Mabel and Dorothy at the law office. "I think I'd like this Dorothy's attitude. Turns out in my line of work, people frequently lie to me as well. Sometimes it's easier to just assume everyone lies all the time and then you can be pleasantly surprised when someone actually tells you the truth. And," he grins at me, "she gives them Californians a hard time; another plus in my book."

My law office story may be entertaining but it is hardly enlightening. Other than essentially confirming Judy's understanding of the events surrounding Stan's incarceration, the visit shed little new light on Stan's subsequent disappearance.

However, Wendover is all ears as I begin to discuss the next stop of my Butte itinerary, Sheriff Broadcliff's office.

"Wow," he says, "that's quite a story. No wonder Broadcliff is making himself scarce. The weather forecast for the Butte sheriff's office looks like increasing dark clouds and a one hundred percent chance of shit storms."

Wendover is amused when I jokingly ask him if anyone in his mugshot book might be eight feet tall, with three claws, and possibly radioactive.

"Got a couple of my regulars that are good sized, damn near six foot-ten, I'd guess. Several others missing a few fingers but the remaining ones they got don't seem to have claws attached."

"Nobody radioactive?"

"None that I know of. But to be honest, I don't scan 'em with a Geiger counter."

"Maybe you could get one with a grant from Homeland Security. Look how it's done wonders for Broadcliff."

"Yeah, I'll bet he…hold on." He's getting a call on his cell phone.

"Hello? Uh-huh. Yeah. No, I'm in town. On Main."

I'm hearing one side of the conversation. Trying to infer by his responses what the other end of the call is saying.

"Really? Yeah. Probably a good idea to keep it off the radios." He's talking about police frequencies which are often monitored by civilian scanners.

"Sure, I can be there in ten. Nobody touches anything until we get there. Yeah, I said we. Walker is with me. It won't be a problem."

"Will it?" He's ended the call looking at me. "Be a problem, if you ride along while a I check out a disturbance?"

"No, sir," I say, "I have a deputizing letter, you know."

"Yeah, like you're ever going to let me forget that." He looks at me sternly. "Don't touch anything when we get there."

"Got it. By the way, what sort of disturbance? Where are we going?"

"1500 Southwest Riverside Drive. Normally that's a pretty quiet place…very few complaints out there."

"What is it, an old folks' home?"

"That is perhaps an ironically close guess. 1500 Southwest Riverside Drive is the address of the county cemetery."

CHAPTER 16

Red, blue, red, blue. The emergency lights of the sheriff's department cruisers assembled in the middle of county cemetery are projecting a macabre light-show across a small forest of silent grave markers.

"Okay, kill the lights." Wendover is motioning to his deputies as we step out of his SUV. "Everyone that needs to know we're here, knows it now. And it's not as though we need to warn oncoming traffic, eh?" He gives me a weary glance as I pull my coat closed around me to fend off the night chill; my breath steaming off into the night as I exhale.

There's a Montana State Patrol car parked there as well. "Evening, Jerry. Slow night?" Wendover's talking to the trooper.

"Heard there was a disturbance out here and I was coming back into town at end of shift anyway. Thought you might need a little backup."

"Thanks, I think we have things under control here."

Officer Potts walks up to us notepad in hand, "good evening, boss."

"There ain't nothing that can be good about standing in a cemetery on a cold October night. Short version of why we're here, please."

"Well," Potts clears his throat, studiously referring to his notes. "Received a call from a witness at approximately 23:55 hours. Um, that would be one Gus Williams, the night watchman over there." He's pointing with his pencil at a rather disheveled, unshaven man looking to be in his sixties standing noticeably unsteadily with another deputy.

Williams looks cold, shuffling and stamping his feet, and is awkwardly attired in pajama bottoms, slippers, and a windbreaker over a dirty white tee shirt. They are some fifty yards away from us next to a metal-sided combination maintenance building and caretaker quarters. Someone has turned on two flood lights on the building to cast a little light over the scene.

Wendover is frowning. He nods towards me and whispers, "old Gus is a regular customer with my officers. Has a bad drinking problem."

"So, the county cemetery is being guarded by the town drunk?" I'm whispering back.

"That's about the size of it, I'm afraid."

Potts continues, "Mr. Williams says he was watching TV at approximately 23:15 hours when there was an apparent electrical outage that shut down the TV and lights in the caretaker quarters." He glances up from his notes. "Sir, by the way, we cannot confirm any recorded outage in this area with the power company, but they are still looking into it."

"Anyway," he continues, "Williams claims after the power went out, the caretaker's shack was lit up by an intense bright light over the cemetery. This was accompanied by an intense, throbbing hum. You know, like the big bass speakers the kids have in their cars nowadays. You can sometimes feel them more than hear them."

"But, sir." Potts shakes his head. "Again, as with the power, we cannot confirm that anyone else observed the light or heard the hum. There are neighbors about a quarter mile away from here. We've had no reports or complaints tonight from any of them."

"Maybe they're really sound sleepers," replies Wendover. "And I doubt anyone else around here is going to file a complaint," he adds dryly as he nods towards the surrounding grave markers.

"So," continues Potts, "Williams opens the door of his quarters to see what is going on out in the cemetery. The next thing he knows, he is hit in the forehead with a blinding red light and falls to the floor. He's out maybe thirty minutes. Wakes up and the lights and TV are back on as normal. He turns on the floods and goes out to investigate and discovers one of the graves has been desecrated."

"Desecrated?" Wendover raises an eyebrow.

"Well, robbed actually. The casket is...gone...the headstone too!"

"No shit?"

"No shit, sir."

"Is grave robbing illegal in Montana? What is the offense code? Is it considered theft of personal property or more of a missing persons sort of thing?" I'm trying to think of how we will code this in LISA.

"You're not helping," Wendover frowns at me. I think he may be regretting taking me out on this call. "And, to be more precise, this appears to be a case of body snatching, not grave robbing."

"There's a difference?"

"Technically, grave robbing refers to looting a grave for valuables such as jewelry and other items of value. Body snatching is the illegal removal of the deceased body itself."

"Good to know."

"Another thing," continues Potts, trying to regain the floor. "As usual, Williams smells like a distillery. Looks like he and Jack Daniels were on caretaker duty most nights given how he smells and the empty bottles we found in his quarters."

"So, he may not have been rendered unconscious by a mysterious red beam of light...he could have fallen down drunk?" offers Wendover.

"Certainly a possibility, sir."

"Well, let's give him some time to sober up. We'll get a full statement from him in the morning."

"Yes, sir."

"You know, tomorrow he may actually open up to Dr. Walker here," adds Wendover with a wry smile. Potts and I look at him blankly. "We can tell him Jack is Johnnie Walker's brother."

Given my brief acquaintance with Williams, I'm not sure if this a joke or a strategy.

"Now, let's take a look at the grave," continues Wendover.

The gravesite is conveniently not that far from the caretaker building. Deputies have already cordoned it off with yellow crime scene tape. A perfectly rectangular coffin-sized slice of the earth is missing. Five feet wide, ten feet long, and ten feet deep, the hole is geometrically precise.

Wendover is kneeling, looking into the hole and rocking back and forth on the heels of his cowboy boots.

He turns and looks at me and Potts. "There's more missing here than just a coffin. There should be about three or four cubic yards of dirt over the coffin, right? Where is the dirt?" he says, shaking his head. "Where is the damn dirt?"

"The other question is who is supposed to be buried here? With the gravestone gone as well, we'll need a plot map to tell us," I say. "We can probably find a map in the caretaker shack, right?"

"Sheriff!" We are interrupted by a shout from Deputy Riley. He is standing at the edge of the cemetery, just faintly visible in the headlights from the patrol cars.

The Riverside Cemetery is aptly named, for it sits on a bench that overlooks the river. By daylight the location provides a beautiful and serene view that likely helps comfort those who come to pay their respects. Although it's doubtful though that the scenery is of much interest to the permanent residents.

Riley is waving to us and pointing his flashlight down an embankment that appears to slope down to the river. We march over to his position double-time.

"There's something down there! Um, looks to be...a coffin?" he adds hesitantly.

Wendover focuses his flashlight down the hill. "I'll be damned, sure looks like a coffin from here. Well, let's go down and take a look. It's only a hundred yards or so, but be careful, it looks steep in places."

"Yes, sir." Riley is taking the lead as we start to scramble down the hill, our flashlights randomly illuminating the ground and tree tops as we move our arms to keep balance. The slope is covered with small bushes and brush. We make our way down in silence. The only sounds are the scruff of our boots across the ground and the sound of the river flow becoming louder as we drop down towards it.

From our perspective near the top of the slope, the casket looks like a child's toy that has been casually tossed down the hill. But what child extracts a perfectly rectangular section of ground and tosses a casket some three hundred yards away from the grave? And what happened to the dirt?

We negotiate the final section of the hill and arrive at the casket. It is lying on its side, the lid swung wide open flat on the ground. It is empty.

The three of us exchange a glance. "Could the corpse have fallen out somewhere back up the hill?" asks Wendover. "Could we have perhaps missed it in the dark?"

While Wendover and Riley are examining the casket in detail, I'm improvising a search pattern for the body, circling out from the casket, methodically scanning the ground with my flashlight. The ground is uneven here and covered with small bushes. It strikes me that this would be an unpleasant time and place to meet a rattlesnake and I hope that the chill of the night has driven them underground at this point in the season.

I've circled about fifty yards away from Wendover when my light catches the edge of what at first appears to be a large rock. But a closer look reveals it is geometric with polished sides...the headstone. I shout and motion for the officers to join me.

We kneel around the headstone which is lying face down on the slope. Wendover is examining the nearby ground. "No evidence of an impact or that it slid any distance. Someone placed it here. They certainly didn't throw it from the top of the bench." It strikes me that the marker must weigh nearly two hundred pounds, so the notion that someone could have just tossed it down here seems remote.

"Well, shall we turn it over? No need for that plot map now," I say.

The three of us grab the edge of the massive stone and with considerable effort we heave it over. There in the glare of the flashlights appear the words: "Benjamin Pruitt, Rest in Peace."

Not tonight, I think, reflecting on the inscription. No one is resting in peace tonight.

The three of us stare at the stone wordlessly but we all must be thinking the same thought. Three missing. Three Pruitts. Three generations. Why? Why now? Whoever, or whatever lies behind this and the other disappearances, not even the dead can escape its hand.

"So, where did he go?" Wendover asks rhetorically. "It will be light in a few hours; we'll get some dogs and scour the whole hillside. Maybe we have missed the body in the brush somewhere." His tone and expression betray he thinks that is a long shot, but it must be done as a matter of due diligence.

Where did he go, indeed, I think? It's been over two thousand years since we had a good old-fashioned resurrection; odds are the long departed elder Pruitt didn't walk away on his own power. Someone took him, but why? What purpose would it serve?

We have climbed back out of the draw and Wendover is off by the patrol cars laying out the order of battle for his deputies. This is officially now a crime scene that now spans several hundred yards. It needs to be fully secured before it is finely combed for evidence in the light of day.

I am standing at the edge of the hillside, looking across at the darkened valley and trying to absorb, if not understand, the events of the evening. A soft glow appears at the summit of the mountain range flanking the eastern edge of the county. Rapidly, the edge of the moon rises, casting a faint illumination to the valley floor in the predawn darkness of the hour and casting a silvery reflection on the river below.

Off in the distance, a coyote begins to bark and howl at the moonrise. She is answered by a responding call further distant and then yet another. The animals are following an instinct and a tradition that existed well before mankind troubled this valley with its affairs. God willing, they'll be doing this long after we're gone. I pause and smile, grateful to contemplate a larger perspective and for receiving a moment's distraction from the deepening mystery confronting us.

I walk back towards the SUV. One of the deputies is gently helping Williams back to the caretaker's quarters. He looks relieved to be going somewhere warm.

Wendover walks up to me and jerks a thumb towards Williams. "Let's not be too judgmental here about old Gus. To be fair, this is the first dead body to ever disappear on his watch."

"I think that wisecrack would be funnier if we weren't standing in a cemetery at two in the morning."

"I suppose so," he replies, "probably wouldn't be much of a comfort to the Pruitts either. Hey, I've got a couple more things to wrap up and then I'll meet you back at the Tahoe."

"Also," he's looking at me seriously, "given what's happened tonight, I'd like to discuss some files with you tomorrow."

"What sort of files?"

"Information relating to some other odd occurrences. Strange things that I'm not sure I can continue to ignore."

"Like that weird pattern in the cow pasture?"

"It gets weirder."

"Great."

As I approach the sheriff's vehicle, a small sedan pulls up behind it. A bespectacled, bearded young man with a slender build and a serious look on his face climbs out.

He earnestly extends his hand. "Hello. Dr. Walker, is it?"

"Yes?" At two in the morning, I'm frankly not all that interested in meeting some more of the locals.

"I'm Walter Berman," he says. "I'm a reporter for the Valley Independent. At least, that's my day job. Actually," he laughs, gesturing at the stars above us, "sometimes it's my night job as well." He pauses and looks intently at me, "it's the grandfather Pruitt missing now, isn't it?"

"Not for me to say. You need to talk directly to the sheriff," I reply. "And, by the way, how in the hell do you know about this incident? The sheriff's department kept this off the dispatch frequencies."

"The Montana State Trooper called out his location on his way here. I picked it up on the scanner. Anyway, I want to tell you that I have a theory about why the three generations of Pruitts are missing."

"Great," I reply, pointing off in the general direction where Wendover is talking to his deputies, "if you have a theory, that's the guy that needs to hear it."

"No," he responds, "I'm not sure he would be all that receptive to what I have to say. Perhaps I should run it past you first. Word around here is that you've got his confidence. It would be better if you maybe vetted it first before I approach him."

"This is my other job," he says, handing me a business card.

I look it over. *Walter Berman, Field Investigator, Northwest Skywatch.* The Skywatch logo on the card features a stylized flying saucer arcing across the top left corner. Splendid. No wonder he's hesitating to pitch his theories directly to Wendover.

"Okay," I sigh, "I'd suggest we go grab a drink and talk about your theory, but at this hour, all the bars are closed."

"Sorry, sir, but I don't drink."

"May I assume you eat?"

CHAPTER 17

At some point, much as the Old West has evolved into the New West, the Stockman's Cafe morphed from authentic to nostalgic. Years ago, it was one of the main places in town where local ranchers could grab a quick and simple breakfast when they came to town.

Today, the walls are adorned with old farm kitchen antiques, photos, and other kitsch that hark back to those days. But an authentic stockman from the past would find little familiar in its current clientele or menu. Ham and eggs have given way to breakfast burritos and scones. Black coffee is merely just another ingredient in cappuccinos and lattes. Retirees relocated from California, remote tech workers plying their laptops, and tourists make up most of the business here these days.

Authentic or not, the food is good, service is characteristically friendly, and Stockman's has fast and free wireless internet service. I've adopted the place as my early morning office. I tip generously and the staff makes sure I have a table in the back with room to spread out my work and confer with Jeff on our research.

My breakfast companions this morning are clearly not stockmen. Walter Berman has called in reinforcements. Joining Jeff and me and next to Walter at the table is Peter Roberts, Director of Northwest Skywatch. Roberts has also brought along Megan Larson, his technology specialist.

Roberts is leaning forward with a look of intensity I usually associate with university post doctorate candidates. I'd guess him to be in his late forties but with the sandy hair and permanent tan, he has the look of a perpetual surfer boy and could pass for ten years younger. Roberts is holding forth on what a marvelous organization Skywatch is, and for a few minutes I begin to wonder if he's here to help or is planning to ask for a donation. Walter is smiling broadly, thinking, I suppose, of his own increasing visibility in the organization with this case.

"So, what is Northwest Skywatch?" Roberts asks rhetorically. "Basically, we're a not-for-profit research organization, based out of Seattle, that is collecting evidence of unknown aerial phenomena, encounters with possible extraterrestrial beings, and potential abductions of humans by extraterrestrials. We also provide hypnotic regression and counseling for abductees and experiencers."

"This, by the way," he adds, "is what may have in fact happened to the Pruitts based on what Walter has told me. We have evidence to suggest that extraterrestrials, let's just call them the Entities, have had a long history of observing mankind and conducting genetic experiments that span generations. We often find that once we begin to investigate an abductee case it is not unusual to discover that the victim's extended family has had similar experiences with the Entities."

"Anyway, back to Skywatch," he continues, "we rely on a network of volunteers like Walter here to be on the lookout for strange phenomena and evidence of abductions and so forth. We ask them to document the cases and send their findings to the central database in Seattle. In turn, we look for patterns and insights, something that might turn out to be the key for understanding this mystery. Right, Meg?"

This pattern analysis activity is sort of like a LISA application for the UFO crowd, I think. Patterns are patterns, whether you are tracking methamphetamine abuse or the shenanigans of E.T.. Perhaps I can license some form of LISA to them in the future.

Megan nods. She's sitting cross-legged on her chair. A serious looking young lady, apparently unaccustomed to smiling, with swaths of purple and orange highlighted hair pulled into a ponytail to produce a sort of partial rainbow effect. "Given the years of data on sightings and abductions that we have collected so far," she says, "we find that the occurrences are not evenly or randomly distributed geographically. Rather, we see very specific incidences of frequent sightings in certain areas. Sometimes the patterns occur for very limited timeframes. In other areas, the activities can persist for years. We call these areas paranormal hotspots."

"As it happens," adds Roberts, "the Alta Valley appears to be within one of those hotspots with persistent UFO sightings over many years. And it has had an especially significant uptick in cases over the past several months. It's one of two hotspots in Montana. Of course, the other is up on the Hi-Line. Broadly speaking, that hotspot is an arc from Great Falls thorough Havre and Glendive and on into Minot in North Dakota."

"But we have a good idea what draws the phenomenon to the Hi-Line."

"We do?" asks Jeff quizzically.

"Nukes." Walter smiles and winks.

"Yes," Roberts explains. "Call them Cold War relics, if you wish, but the majority of the nation's active land based nuclear missiles are located in underground silos along the Hi-Line. They've been taken off hair-trigger response for years, but hardly deactivated. They're controlled out of Malmstrom Air Force Base in Great Falls and Minot Air Force Base in North Dakota. No surprise as to why they're located on the Hi-Line. It's isolated and as far as you can go north in the continental United States. Pretty handy for lobbing a return volley of ICBMs directly over the Arctic to Russia on an express route were we to be attacked."

"So," Walter picks up the story, "the area has had a concentration of UFO sightings since the late '50s. If you plot the reports over time on a map, the correlation of sightings with the location of missile silos and control centers is quite profound. There have been documented instances of unidentified lights hovering over the silos and reportedly in some cases taking the missiles off-line remotely. Or, more disturbingly, temporarily activating launch sequences."

"But back to our local hot spot," continues Roberts. "Broadly speaking, it's sort of an Intermountain Triangle, if you will. As mysterious and potentially as deadly as the Bermuda Triangle of paranormal legend. One corner here," he's trying to lay this out on the table by placing a salt shaker to his left, "would be Boise, Idaho. Over here is Jackson Hole, Wyoming." He pushes a pepper shaker to his right to mark his virtual triangle point. "And up here, Libby, Montana as the apex about where I'm placing the creamer. And we are here." He drops a sugar packet on virtual Alta Junction and sits back to admire his handiwork.

"You will find that over a one half of all reported sightings for the past three years in Idaho, Wyoming, and Montana have occurred either within this triangle or within about fifty miles of its dimensions. And that's just UFO related activity. Throw in crop circles, cattle mutilations, and crypto-zoological cases and the significance of the hot spot grows significantly."

"Excuse me," I say, "what is crypto-zoological?"

"You know, unidentified creatures in the forest, Bigfoot, sasquatch, things like that."

"Oh." Well, of course. All we're missing now are a few ghosts and the reappearance of Elvis, I think. But the morning is young.

"Excuse me," I say, "but you think the Pruitts are somehow now part of this. You suspect that they were abducted…by aliens?"

"It fits a pattern," responds Roberts. "Specifically, father/son disappearances in the Northern Rockies within known paranormal hotspots. We've investigated a number of these and believe the Entities, or whatever this phenomenon is, have an intense interest in human genetics. This is apparently pursued through multi-generational abductions, often spread over many years. And, there have been cases where the dead have been taken as well as the living."

A chill is running down my spine. I'm thinking of the cold dark hours at the Riverside Cemetery last night searching for the corpse of Ben Pruitt. The third generation to have gone missing. And I remember the almost surgical precision with which the grave was opened, the missing dirt. Was he abducted by these mysterious Entities Roberts references?

"Probably the most egregious and mysterious case of multiple generation apparent abductions combined with removal of remains was the Angikuni Lake incident," says Roberts.

I notice that Megan is surreptitiously stealing a glance at her phone. She's heard this story before.

"The lake is in the far northern reaches of Canada in what at the time was known as the Northwest Territories but has since become the Territory of Nunavut, now largely administered by native peoples. By many accounts, a small Inuit village had thrived on its shores in the early 1900's. The village was well known to fur trappers who regularly visited it on their circuits through the Territories."

"One day in 1930," he continues, "a fur trapper made a routine stop at the village and what he found was profoundly disturbing. The entire village population, estimated between thirty and a hundred men, women, and children had all disappeared without a trace. Whatever happened to them, it was sudden. They were gone but their dwellings and all their belongings, including the hunting and fishing gear needed for their very survival were left behind. Food was still hanging over the fire pits. It was as though one minute they were there and the next minute they were gone, forever. Even more strange, the graves of their deceased were also emptied. This was duly reported to the RCMP who investigated the incident as a missing persons case. No trace of the villagers was ever found and it remains an open case."

"But this trapper didn't report seeing any UFOs or aliens, right?"

"Correct. But others from that past time period right up to present day have continued to see anomalous lights in the sky in this general area."

"Maybe the Northern Lights?"

"Dr. Walker, please give the Inuit and other Canadians some credit. They know what the Northern Lights look like."

"Perhaps we should give Dr. Walker an example a little closer to our neck of the woods?" prompts Berman.

"Sure," replies Roberts, "Walter, I think you were involved in the Sandpoint case, right? It was one of our more recent investigations. This happened in Northern Idaho, near Sandpoint. A man calls us up and says that several months ago he saw a light he cannot explain. Maybe it was a UFO he said, but he wasn't sure. He said he was concerned that he's been feeling strange since he saw the light. Also, he thought maybe he has lost memory. There were four or five hours he cannot account for on that night."

"So, I go out there with Walter and a small team. We visited the location where he saw the light and took readings with a Geiger counter and so forth. So far, there was little extraordinary about the incident…until we regressed him through hypnosis."

"The man," Roberts continues, "let's call him Randy. Randy was a logger, with contracts freelancing insect killed timber to several mills in the Sandpoint area. Pine moths are a big issue up in those forests north of Coeur d'Alene. That night he was taking a late load into town. It's about nine o'clock and dark. The sun had been down for about two hours at that point. Weather was calm and clear; no moon would be visible at that time. He's coming down an old logging road about fifteen miles out of town when he notices a pulsating red/amber light following him in his rear-view mirror. At first, he thought it was an aircraft, maybe a helicopter off in the distance. But it came much closer quickly, skimming the tree tops, pacing him maybe fifty yards to the rear of his trailer."

"Randy became frightened at that point, speeded up but there was nowhere to go. His rig was too big to pull off and park and there were no other roads to take to get away from the light. At that point his memory became hazy and confused. He does remember making it home at two in the morning with no recollection of what happened."

"The hypnotic regressions took several sessions. I will tell you that each in turn was more intense and, frankly, disturbing. He described his truck losing power and rolling to a stop. Small gray beings with enormous black almond eyes took him into their ship and he described an intricate set of patterns he observed on its interior."

"What were the symbols?" I ask.

"Well, I'm not going to tell you, for a very good reason. Suffice to say, the reference to a very particular set of symbols associated with the Entities and their spacecraft is a common feature of abductee experiences. And we and other UFO research organizations use this reference as sort of a control. It is a way to determine that the witness is relating a true, or at least consistent, account when compared with other abductees."

"Fair enough," I reply. "We use controls to similar effect in our research fields as well. It tries to limit something we call confirmation bias where either the subject or the researcher is influenced by what they expect to see versus what they actually see."

"You know, like a placebo effect," adds Jeff.

"Yes," continues Roberts, "our paranormal research subjects are obviously quite unconventional, but we do try to use a scientific approach in our investigations as best we can."

"I do try to keep them honest," says Megan now with the slightest hint of a smile.

"As for our logging truck driver, Randy, with subsequent hypnosis sessions, his memories of that night began to come back to him in more and more clear detail. He described being completely under the Entities' control. He was taken to what he described as an examination table. Then a female

Entity came into the room and began to communicate with him telepathically."

"Wait. He knew somehow this alien was female?" asks Jeff.

"Yeah, we're getting to that part. She indicated she wanted them to have sex and she touched him, you know, down there."

"I won't go into the details," Roberts continues. At this, Jeff, Megan, and I all look simultaneously relieved. But I notice Walter appears a bit disappointed on missing out on the play-by-play action. "Suffice to say they consummated the act. But that's not the really odd part of the story."

Jeff and I exchange a look like if human-alien sex isn't the odd part of the story, how is he going to top that?

Roberts leans forward, glancing around the table to ensure we take this next bit of information for its full import.

"Turns out that truck driver Randy had been impotent for at least five years prior to this encounter. But from that point forward, he was, if you will, a new man. The impotence problems have gone away completely."

"Great," I say, "so these aliens come halfway across the galaxy not to present us with the cure for cancer but with the cure for erectile dysfunction?"

I then notice our server is frozen in place over our table, nearly in mid-pour of my coffee refill. Her eyes are wide and her smile is a bit forced. I'm guessing alien-human sex is not a common breakfast topic here at the Stockman's.

CHAPTER 18

"Okay?" I say as I ration my coffee sips. Our server is now understandably avoiding our table. Another refill seems unlikely in our near future. "We can go on all morning with these tales around the campfire. It's all very entertaining and, hell, some of it might even be true. But what specifically do you want from us? We have a research project to wrap up shortly and I've pledged our support to Wendover on the Pruitt case as well. That doesn't leave much time to chase flying saucers."

"I completely understand," replies Roberts, "I'll get to the point. First, we'd just ask that you just keep an open mind. There are things at play here in the Alta Valley that are quite odd, perhaps different than what appears on the surface."

"On that you'll certainly get no argument from me."

"Especially in the past month or two, the Alta Valley has been a particular hotspot of anomalous activity," adds Berman. "We continue to see multiple reports of strange lights in the sky, unrecognizable howls in the forest, and strange circular patterns etched into fields and meadows."

At this, Berman notices the quick change in my expression. "You've seen one of these perhaps?"

"Yes. Quite recently."

"Then you know first-hand about some of the things we've been tracking," continues Roberts. "Second, and particularly relevant to the Pruitt case, please understand our research of the abduction phenomenon suggests these Entities are taking a particular interest in human reproduction and genetics. To the point they increasingly appear to be abducting individuals across several generations within families."

"Not only abducting, but re-abducting the same individuals on multiple occasions over a period of years," adds Megan, raising an eyebrow.

"That," offers Jeff, "is the textbook definition of longitudinal study methodologies commonly used in university research. The ones in which subjects are monitored over time for characteristics of interest."

"Wait," I say, "this is all intriguing but from what I understand there has never been a single scientifically validated alien or entity abduction much less a series of cross-generational ones, right?"

"Let me try to explain," responds Roberts. He has the resigned, slightly frustrated look of someone who's had to explain this to many people many times before. "Take the case of Randy again. We regressed him on multiple occasions and regressed his son as well. They both under hypnosis related stories of multiple abductions over a period of years. Their accounts corroborated each other's experiences with similar details."

"Like the symbols?"

"Correct, and many other facets of the encounters."

"Hopefully, the kid's encounters with the aliens were not sexual like his old man's." I'm glancing at Berman to see if he's going to lean forward in anticipation of details.

"Thankfully, no. But in terms of physical evidence, both were subjected to procedures that left scars behind their knees. When those areas were imaged with a CAT scan, both appeared to have small objects implanted under the scars."

"Capture, tag, and release," offers Megan, "just like how we tag wildlife and release them back into the wilds for tracking. The function of the implants is unknown, but is perhaps similar to how humans research wildlife patterns."

"So, Dr. Walker, we'd ask you simply be on the lookout for any unusual characteristics or patterns that would suggest a multigenerational genetic motive for the Pruitt's disappearances. Hopefully, there is an explanation that doesn't involve Entity abductions, but we see some red flags here," concludes Roberts.

I nod, indicating at least outward agreement for the time being. Clearly, there must be some common key to the disappearance of the three Pruitt generations. That, frankly, became obvious last night as I stood there in the dark early morning hours staring at Ben Pruitt's empty casket. For the moment, however, I choose not to mention to my Skywatch friends the common enzyme-related medical condition affecting the Pruitts.

I need to pull more on that thread. A thread that apparently begins with the elder Pruitt's military service in the Navy. After breakfast I'll need to get some additional information on his Navy days from Judy. Then hopefully I can call on an old family friend to help me out.

"One more thing," adds Roberts, "we understand you two are data scientists with some considerable expertise in pattern recognition and deep data analysis, correct?"

I smile, "Jeff and I have been regularly accused of having some skills in those areas, but we'll see if they can make the charges stick."

"Meg here has developed a very advanced system to scan the sky to identify and track anomalous objects. It's a great system as is, but we'd like your advice on improvements. Maybe we can make the system completely autonomous and deploy hundreds of these, only flagging exceptional sightings for human follow up. That sort of thing."

"Sounds intriguing. When can we look at your system and kick the tires?"

"We are planning to do a Skywatch contact signaling and observation session tonight out on Sutter's Bench. That system will be the centerpiece of our investigation this evening. You're both very welcome to come out and see our operation, even if you can only spare a few minutes. And we're also going to be joined by some of our other investigators from Washington state."

"Sounds like a plan, we will certainly try to make it out there."

"Great. Walter here will send you the details on time and location shortly."

"Thanks, sounds like we're finished here?"

Nods all around, but then some uncomfortable shifting in chairs and awkward silence. The Skywatch crowd may be intrepid alien hunters and seekers of truth but the breakfast check on the table is somehow eluding their detection. It is as though the tab has disappeared into the Intermountain Triangle itself.

"Oh, please, let me get this," I say with a sigh, reaching for the check. My token gesture of support for the effort to connect us with our star brothers and star sisters.

CHAPTER 19

"Hi Marcy, it's Jack Walker"

"Oh, Jack, how are you? Gee, I haven't talked to you in years! How have you been? How are Kate and Amy?"

"We're all doing well, Marcy. How's Bill?"

"Just fine. So good to hear your voice. Can you believe how long it's been since we were kids goofing around the lake in Bigfork? You and me and Marty…"

Her voice changes to deep concern an instant. "Marty. Jack, I'm so sorry. We're all…it was such a shock."

Marcy Hillenbrand. I probably haven't seen her in fifteen years. Her parents and mine have been close friends for as long as I could remember. For years, our parents had been neighbors in Virginia and also owned adjacent summer cabins on Flathead Lake near Bigfork, Montana. It was a time of seemingly endless summers at the lake. I remember her running along the lake jumping over logs and laughing; brown hair flying back and all skinny legs.

It's funny how we think about people we haven't seen for years. It's as though they've been held fast in amber as we've remembered them, unchanged since the moment we've seen them last. Yet, in every second that has passed since then, just like us, they've continued to live their lives and grow, age, and change.

We grew up and went our separate ways. Our folks sold the cabins but have always stayed close. Marcy married Bill, a commercial real estate guy, and they settled in Northern Virginia. Now she's an office manager for her father's defense consulting firm.

Admiral Thomas R. Hillenbrand, retired, is a very close friend of my family and as long as I can remember we simply referred to him as Hillie. He was a frequent guest in our home as I was growing up. Boisterous and full of stories, Hillie became a favorite mentor, taking me and Marty on adventures camping and even to the shooting range where I became acquainted with guns at an early age. I remember his laughter playing poker with my dad and the other neighbors, clamping his signature cigar in a broad grin.

At one point, Hillie had headed up Naval Intelligence, a contradiction in terms which to my families' delight seemed to beg continual jibes to the effect that Naval Intelligence was the very definition of an oxymoron. These days he plies the corridors of the Pentagon as a consultant to various defense firms and other Beltway Bandits seeking government contracts.

"So, Jack, I assume you didn't call just to catch up and reminisce about old times?"

"No, but it was great chatting with you just the same. Actually, I was checking to see if I could catch a few minutes with your father. Is the Great Admiral available by chance?"

"Today is your lucky day, turns out he's in the office between appointments. I'll let him know you're holding on the line. Good talking to you, Jack."

"Thanks, Marcy. Take care."

There's some electronic shuffling on the line and then Hillie's voice booms over the phone. "Jack, how the hell are you? It's been too long! Say, I really need to get down to Virginia Beach and see your folks soon. And I think I still owe your father for some poker losses. How are they doing? Your father wasn't looking well last I saw him."

"Well, you know he took the loss of Marty hard. Wouldn't hurt for you to visit and maybe cheer him up by losing some more at poker. He'd like that."

"Yes, I will, Jack, absolutely. So, to what do I owe the honor of a call from the distinguished professor?"

"Hillie, I was hoping you could give me a little World War II Navy information relating to a project I'm working on in Montana. This might be a chance for you to work off your poker debt to the family, eh?"

"Sounds intriguing. What do you need?"

"I'm looking for any or all information you can find regarding a Navy ship, the USS Nash, and a sailor on that vessel, a Benjamin Pruitt. I believe he might have been a radio operator on the ship, not sure of his rank."

"Should be easy enough with the ship," responds Hillie. "Most of those records have been digitized and I can pull them up right on my computer here. The records on your sailor are going to be a bit more difficult."

"How so?"

"I can only pull up just the minimum information about his service from the National Personnel Records Center or NPRC. This is essentially the data you would find on his Report of Separation or DD Form 214. It would list just the basics: enlistment and separation dates, branch of service, final rank, and whether the discharge was honorable or not."

"But no specifics as to his missions, medical records, things like that?"

"Correct. Those would be in his Official Military Personnel Files or OMPF. Access to the OMPF information is restricted for privacy reasons and occasionally some information may even be classified. Request for access needs to be initiated by next of kin and the wait for results can be very lengthy. It's hardly a user-friendly process. But," he pauses, "I may know a guy who may know a guy…"

"Somehow I thought you might."

"I'll let you know what I find on Pruitt in a couple of days. As for the ship, I can probably pull that up now," he says. "Here we go, I'm gonna put you on speaker while I type."

There's rustling as I imagine he's getting situated in front of his computer.

"Okay. Nash, Nash…found it. The USS Nash was a type of warship called a destroyer escort. These were smaller and slower than regular destroyers but were also far less expensive and easier to produce in large numbers. It's what our British Royal Navy friends would have called a frigate. Typical missions would be merchant convoy escort and anti-submarine operations."

"What would have been the size of the crew?"

"Typically, about 200 sailors. Says here the Nash was hull number DE-12, one of the early ones in the Evarts Class. Hull was laid in the San Francisco Yard, November 1942. Launched February 1943. Total displacement was 1,360 tons. I assume you are fascinated so far?"

"On the edge of my seat, Hillie"

"Let's see what else we have here. Hmmm, the records are quite thin regarding missions and deployments. No detailed ship's log or other mission records available online. Well, this is a bit odd, apparently only one brief deployment in the Pacific Theater. Deployed in May 1943 and then immediately returned to San Diego. Apparently spent the remainder of the war in the repair docks and post-war was immediately decommissioned and scrapped in October 1945."

"Is that stint in the repair docks unusual?"

"Unusual, but not unprecedented. This was wartime, Jack, and we built about five hundred destroyer escorts over a three-year period. This was a massive effort. Major sections and components of these ships were built all over the country. Then those sections were sent to the shipyards for final assembly and launch. Looking back at that period, it's amazing we didn't have more ships that turned out to be lemons. The Air Force calls their planes that seldom fly because they are always in repair 'hangar queens.' I guess the Nash was a 'repair dock queen.'"

"Frankly," he continues, "the online records I'm seeing regarding the Nash are sparser than I'm used to seeing for ships of this period. It could be that the materials just haven't been converted to digital formats yet or somehow the Navy lost the originals. I'll ping my buddies over at the Naval Archives to see if they can round up some additional information. Should have additional information on the Nash and your man Pruitt's personnel records ready for you in a couple of days. This helpful?"

"You're always helpful, Hillie."

"My best to Kate and Amy. And so sorry about Marty…that's a tough one. Hey, I'll call you in a couple of days. Got to run. Meeting some clients down on K Street in about an hour."

CHAPTER 20

"Here you go, boys. Let's see if you two smart guys can spin some gold out of this particular pile of straw. And this straw may have a little horse shit straight from the barn mixed in it." Wendover drops a file folder on his office table in front of Jeff and me with a bit of a dramatic flourish.

As he mentioned last night at the cemetery, Wendover has compiled a couple of dozen reports recently on unusual occurrences in the valley. While certainly strange, these incidents do not appear to be criminal in nature, so he's left these out of the criminal reports and complaints that Jeff had input into LISA.

"I call these my Benton County Strange Files," he says. "I've been collecting odd reports over the past month and a half. I don't know what to do with these, so I keep tossing new ones into that folder. And I guess up until last night I just hoped it would all go away."

"But then Ben Pruitt's corpse vanished from the cemetery?"

"Yeah, I'm not sure I can afford to continue to ignore these anymore given all that has happened."

"So, these oddball occurrences started up about a month and a half ago? I ask.

"Correct, at least the ones that have come to my attention."

"Isn't that about the time Anderson and the Genesis crew showed up in the valley?" This is fueling my suspicions that Genesis may have a hidden and possibly nefarious agenda.

"It is indeed. But, frankly, that's also about the time that you and Jeff arrived in Alta Junction." He gives us a quick wink, "I think we established the other evening that correlation does not always mean causation. But in truth I do agree with you that the timing is suspicious given the arrival of Genesis. I also have my suspicions about what Genesis is really doing here in this county."

"Just a recap of what we have here," he picks up the folder and proceeds to thumb through it. "Let's see, about two dozen reports here. We've got reports of strange lights in the sky, glowing orbs sighted in the forest, unusual howls and nocturnal prowlers, black helicopters flying overhead with no lights or markings, and odd geometric patterns appearing in fields."

"Like what we saw in the cow pasture near Taylor Creek?"

"Identical. But this one," he's pulling one of the reports out of the folder, "takes the cake for strangeness if you ask me."

"Stranger than Ben Pruitt's disappearance from the grave?"

"I think so, but I'll let you be the judge. About a month ago, we get four teenagers rushing into our office late in the evening. Three boys and a girl. They're scared to death; I mean they're shaking. Damn near pissing their pants. We ask them what happened and they said they saw an alien."

"As in an outer space alien, not an undocumented worker kind of alien?"

"Uh-huh. Turns out they had driven up Cheney Creek Road. About ten miles out of town there's a big turn-out where the county has been cutting into the hillside with heavy equipment to load out sand and gravel for road projects. It has turned the area into a bit of a natural amphitheater. Rumor has it that some kids like to go up there occasionally at night to blow off some steam, stand around and bullshit, maybe have a beer or two or smoke a joint."

He catches my raised eyebrow. "Jack, I don't have the resources to go full 'Five-O' and chase every rumor in the county. Given all the other serious crime we're dealing with, driving ten miles out of town to cite Johnny Teenager for an underage beer is just not high on the priority list."

"So, these kids are out late at night at this gravel pit and they see an alien?"

"Yeah," he continues, "they came in blubbering about aliens and the first thing we did was separate them and take their statements independently so we could see if their accounts were consistent."

"And I take it they were consistent?" asks Jeff.

"Very much so. Oh, there were minor variations and some noticed details that others might have missed, that sort of thing. That's pretty common with eyewitness accounts of any kind. As a matter of fact, in my business you get suspicious if multiple witnesses come up with exactly identical accounts. Makes you think they rehearsed it."

He continues, "the consistent story was that they were parked up at the pit, talking and having a bullshit session. There's a flash of light up behind the hill that sort of startles them but after a few minutes they turn their attention back to the conversation and forget about it. Next thing they know, a being with an elongated head and big black almond shaped eyes is approaching them out of the dark. They jump in the car and get the hell out of there."

"And you believe these kids?"

"I don't know what they really witnessed, but I think they were sincere. And they were sincerely scared."

"Didn't anyone get a photo? These kids are never without their smartphones, right?"

"Too scared to think about photos they said. Let me put it like this. One of the hazards of my chosen profession is that people lie to me. A lot. And, surprisingly, most folks are quite bad at lying. I think about half the time they're mainly lying to themselves and hoping I'll buy the story to give them some positive reinforcement. Anyway, usually I pull on a loose thread or two, and about three questions into it, the story falls apart. That's not the case here."

"So, you don't think it's a teenage hoax?"

"It's been my experience that teenagers don't willingly come into the sheriff's office unless they are desperate. If they wanted to tell a tall tale and start a hoax, they'd either have told the story at home, school, or to the newspaper. They wouldn't have come to my office. Not with beer on the breath of two of 'em. And," he smiles, "there's one more even stranger detail I need to mention."

"Stranger than seeing an alien in a gravel pit in the middle of the night?"

"Yeah, they reported the being was wearing a formal jacket and a…top hat?"

Jeff and I exchange a look of disbelief. "A top hat… as in what a fashionable gentleman would wear in, say, the late 1800's?" I ask. "What was it, formal night on the flying saucer?"

"Yup, an honest to God top hat of all things. Of course, the kids had no idea what it was called. But one of them tried to draw it and then I showed them a picture on the web of Grover Cleveland wearing one on his inauguration. They said it was definitely that type of hat."

I nod, catching his point, "so you're thinking that if they were trying to concoct a hoax, why purposely include a detail so outrageous, so utterly silly, it would seem to undermine their claim, right?"

"As the saying goes, you can't make this stuff up. Literally." Wendover is flipping through the reports in the folder, "if someone is running around the countryside doing all of this as a hoax, they are either very brave or very stupid."

"How so?"

"You know what a ghillie suit is?" asks Wendover.

"I do. It's a type of camouflage that looks like you're covered in long grass. It's used by military snipers or hunters to hide in grass and break up the outline of their bodies against the surrounding landscape."

"That's right. Wear one and when you lay on the ground to line up a rifle shot, you'll blend right in. But stand up and walk around in one and you'll look like some kind of hairy monster…maybe a sasquatch or something."

"People have done that?"

"With quite unsatisfactory results. Two years ago, up by Kalispell, a guy thought it would be funny to prank his neighbor by dressing up in a ghillie suit and stomping around the neighbor's place in the dark pretending he was Bigfoot."

"The neighbor didn't think it was funny?"

"The neighbor shot him in the ass."

"Wow, running around in the dark and pretending to be Bigfoot. All fun and games until somebody gets shot," says Jeff.

"Usually is."

"Alcohol involved?"

"Usually is. Both the shooter and the shootee from what I recall of the reports."

"And you think if someone was pulling similar stunts in Benton County, they might meet a similar fate?" asks Jeff.

"Correct," replies Wendover, "rural Montana covers a tremendously large territory with very little oversight by law enforcement. A huge area to cover and very few of us to patrol it."

"Yeah, I had that epiphany up on Two Goat Road about the time Anderson had one hand on my steering wheel and the other hand fondling his gun holster. Help was far off; we were on our own."

"Right," continues Wendover, "so folks here often take their personal security into their own hands. We have a high level of gun ownership and many citizens wouldn't hesitate to pull the trigger if they felt threatened… like the neighbor up near Kalispell. Like I said, anyone pulling off these incidents as hoaxes is taking their life in their hands."

"Tell you what," offers Jeff, "I'll go ahead and set up these files for input to LISA. It's not a priority for analysis so I won't run it until later, after we finish up our regular study next week. Hopefully, then LISA can somehow find a pattern to help explain the incidents."

"Sounds great, thanks."

"So, those kids," I say, "you believe they saw an alien?"

"I believe *they* truly believe they saw an alien." He allows a small smirk, "as Holmes said, 'when you have eliminated the impossible, whatever remains, however improbable, must be the truth.'"

"Let me offer Carl Sagan as a corollary: "Extraordinary claims require extraordinary evidence."

"Fair enough."

"But today is your lucky day. Maybe we'll find that extraordinary evidence for you. Jeff and I are going UFO hunting over on Sutter's Bench tonight."

CHAPTER 21

 from the eastern foothills. The panoramic view it affords encompasses the whole of the Alta Valley. Above us on this clear moonless night is a stunning canopy of stars, unfettered by the light pollution of urban civilization. Directly overhead lies a thick band of stars. This band is in fact the disk of our Milky Way galaxy, viewed edge on from our lonely perspective on one of its remote spokes.

Jeff and I have taken up Peter Roberts' invitation and joined a small group of about a dozen members from Northwest Skywatch for a UFO sighting session. They've set up a collection of telescopes, laptops, and other equipment to survey and record any unusual events. The encampment is illuminated by faint red lanterns. The dim red lights help preserve our night vision. Some fifty yards away, a small portable generator drones on, powering the electronics and low-level lighting around our encampment.

It's eleven o'clock in the evening and cold, damn cold. The day's warmth has seemed to have escaped up into the very midst of the stars above us. Shivering and stamping my increasingly numb feet is doing little to keep me warm.

"Here," Roberts winks, pulling a flask from his coat pocket. "This will help keep you warm."

I take a drink. It is whiskey, stinging and harsh, yet oddly pleasurable. It wouldn't be confused for a moment for one of Hillie's high end single malts, but it makes me forget about the cold temporarily.

"Thanks," I say, "a couple of more shots of this and I'll be seeing spaceships parked right next to my Jeep."

"All a part of our Skywatch hospitality, Dr. Walker. I'm glad you and Jeff decided to join us."

Honestly, I think, I'm not actually sure why I'm out here. Perhaps this is just another window into the human condition that I had not previously glanced through. I've always been fascinated with what fascinates other people. What causes folks to be passionately driven by horse racing or scrapbooking or bird watching? For that matter, what drives otherwise apparently well-adjusted people to spend freezing nights watching the dark skies for alien spaceships?

"Is the idea to now stand here and watch the horizon for something unusual?" I'm wondering how this cold evening is going to play out.

"We could, I suppose, but you'll find we use a wide array of passive and active tools to more effectively augment our search. Let's go visit Meg over at the operations vehicle."

Megan gives us a friendly wave. She is ensconced amidst a cluster of computer screens and other equipment on the tailgate in the back of a pickup camper shell. Walter Berman is with her, looking over her shoulder at a monitor.

As we walk over, Roberts continues, "the first step in discovering the unknown is to first eliminate the known. A large majority of UFO reports submitted by the general public are simply misidentifications of either natural or man-made objects. These include aircraft, satellites, planets, and even the moon."

"The moon?" Jeff is incredulous that anyone could mistake the moon for a UFO.

"You'd be surprised at some of the reports we see," replies Roberts.

I consider the long history of my acquaintance with the foibles of humanity. "Yeah, I guess I'm not all that surprised."

"Welcome to my humble and, at the moment, quite chilly operations center," says Megan. She's bundled up in a wool cap and a puffer jacket; running a mouse and keyboard with fingerless wool gloves. "The first order of business on a sighting night like this is to be prepared to eliminate known natural and man-made objects that might be observed."

She motions to one of the computer screens in front of her. It's depicting a representation of the night sky above us from our point of view. Significantly bright stars and planets are automatically labeled on the screen for identification. "We can also add in tracks of orbiting satellites. That data is made available from NASA for civilian spacecraft. Of course, the military doesn't officially release orbital data on their satellites but those tracks are generally well known by hobbyist astronomers and we often tap into their databases as well."

"One of the real benefits of this system is that we can recreate the past," adds Roberts. "Let's say we get a report of a UFO sighted thirty miles outside Spokane, Washington at two-thirty in the morning on a night three months ago. This software will allow us to recreate the sky as it was on that date and time. And from that exact location's point of view. Then we can compare the reported anomaly's path with that of known celestial objects."

"Impressive." This is a bit more sophisticated approach than what I had been expecting.

"Not only can we look into the skies of the past, but we can also anticipate known object tracks in the future. For example, see here, at one-thirteen in the morning an object will be rising twenty degrees above the southwestern horizon...that will be the International Space Station. Quite a sight to see. Approximately two minutes later it will enter the Earth's shadow and disappear before it reaches the southeastern horizon."

"Most people naturally expect that satellites will appear over one horizon and track straight across to the opposite horizon," adds Berman. "They are often surprised when they see one wink out midway to the horizon. But that is just the effect of the spacecraft entering the shadow cast by the Earth itself."

"You've got a great system for identifying space objects, but what about aircraft?" asks Jeff.

"We have an excellent solution for that and it happens to be our most inexpensive system onboard tonight," replies Megan. She picks up her computer tablet and opens up a flight tracking app. This app shows in real time the radar position of all known aircraft across the country. We can then zoom into the area around our location see the position and course of any aircraft approaching our field of vision."

"This app," adds Roberts, "also displays transponder data pinged off the radar return for each aircraft. That data includes aircraft tail number, ground speed, and altitude. If it's a commercial airliner, the app will also reference the flight number. Even military aircraft will return limited transponder data."

"Case in point," continues Megan, gesturing towards the eastern horizon, "see that light source? It's clearly an aircraft. It's moving slowly in straight line and from here you can even see the standard port and starboard marker beacons, right? Here it is on my app. According to this data, it is a Boeing 737-700 at 35,000 feet. The app indicates it is Delta Flight 839 inbound from Minneapolis to Portland."

"Generally," explains Roberts, "we're not usually interested in nighttime objects that fly on steady paths or make slow, gentle turns. Those are all most assuredly normal aircraft. Instead, we're looking for objects that display unusual flight behaviors, rapid changes in direction, speed, and altitude. Motions that we refer to as non-ballistic. That is, making motions that normal aircraft, subject to regular aerodynamic principles, would find impossible to duplicate."

"Also," adds Berman, "some of the really interesting anomalies in the sky are the things you can't see."

"So, we're supposed to be looking for things we can't see?" I think I know the answer to this but I'm giving them the Wendover bumpkin routine for effect.

Roberts smiles. "Not in the visible light spectrum. People assume all UFO activity can been seen as lights in the sky. They don't realize the real action is unseen. Think about it. If we are indeed seeing alien spaceships that are supposedly surreptitiously visiting Earth and collecting information on us in some clandestine fashion, why would you think they will always run around with their parking lights on?"

"That's a good point," I agree. "Hypothetically, beings advanced enough to cross the reaches of space to visit us could certainly have the technology to cloak themselves. Frankly, they would only been seen if they wished to be observed."

"Or didn't care if they were seen," adds Berman.

"Cloaking technology may explain the sheer number of sightings where objects both at night and during daylight sightings suddenly disappear and reappear," continues Roberts. "That's why we use a multispectral approach."

"See that sensor?" Megan is pointing to a slowly rotating device mounted on a tripod about twenty yards distant. "That unit senses, tracks, images, and records motion in both the visible and infrared spectrums."

Megan continues to describe the essentials of their system. She explains that one of the most challenging issues, especially for infrared or thermal imaging, is to determine the approximate size and distance of an object. For example, a given target could either be a small object, such as a bird, relatively close in distance. Alternatively, it could be a large object, such as an aircraft, much farther away. And once you know the position of the object relative to the observer, its motions across the sky can accurately be calculated as velocity.

The Skywatch solution to the size versus distance problem is rather elegant. Megan has laid out a wireless network of imaging sensors similar to the one in front of us slowly slewing and scanning the sky. The sensors are aligned in a two-axis configuration. One network runs north-south for about four hundred yards and the other east-west of similar length. Once a target is acquired by at least two sensors several hundred yards apart, the system measures the angle to the object from each point and the rest is simple geometry. The system triangulates the position of the target relative to the two known sensor locations and plots it on a map image.

"Ultimately," says Megan, "our goal is to begin to deploy dozens, if not hundreds, of these sensor imaging grids across the Northwest. Humans are notoriously poor at maintaining surveillance over long periods of time. We are easily fatigued or distracted and often miss what is right in front of us. So, we would strive to make these operate completely autonomously to flag and record only observations that meet prespecified criteria for strangeness. There would be no need for human operation or intervention other than performing periodic maintenance."

"And, unlike human observers, this system would be able to instantly compare the track of a target against known celestial and terrestrial objects to eliminate false positives, correct?" I offer.

"Right," she says, "and once we are able to compile thousands of anomaly recordings over time from hundreds of locations, it will get very interesting. With the right pattern recognition tools, you could analyze all of this data to begin to perhaps understand what this phenomenon is really all about."

"Sounds fascinating." Jeff and I exchange a glance. We both know this is exactly the type of problem LISA was designed to solve. But I'm hesitant to raise my hand at this point to volunteer. Tracking E.T. with LISA may be a tough sell to our university research standards board.

"Peter," I'm trying to change the subject here, "you said Skywatch employs both passive and active methods for these observation nights, right? Your sensor imaging grid would certainly count as passive. What active measures do you use in your investigations?"

Peter smiles, "our active measures group is over that way about fifty yards. Let's take a look."

As we approach the group, the warble of a Native American flute drifts though the night air. Several Skywatch members are chanting and "projecting a positive mental state." The notion, as Roberts explains it, is to attract and "vector in" the aliens through the projection of positive and welcoming thoughts. I'm especially, though, impressed with a young lady who has assumed a yoga position, barefoot and cross-legged on the hard, cold ground.

"You want to give that a try?" I chide Jeff. "A young guy like you ought to have some flexibility like her."

"No thanks." He laughs and shakes his head. "Next time we decide to do something like this, I'm going to bring a folding chair, a heavy blanket, and hot chocolate and schnapps."

"Might strike some folks as a bit too New Age, but remember I did say we deploy multispectral approaches," says Roberts as we leave the active measures crowd to their new-age pursuits."

"Indeed, you did."

"Also, in some cases, if we see a UFO, we try to engage contact by shining laser pointers at it."

"Human pilots don't care to have their cockpits lit up with laser pointers. Are you sure the aliens don't mind?"

"We haven't been blasted out of existence yet."

"The night is still young."

It's now about one-thirty in the morning and so far, the night has been uneventful. There have been moments of excitement at the sighting of various lights in the sky, but all of those have turned out to be explainable as aircraft, satellites, or shooting stars.

The night's not getting any warmer and I'm thinking of asking Roberts for another sip from his flask, when the imaging sensor nearest to us suddenly stops it's scanning slew. It quickly swivels to a southeast orientation and locks into place. Megan raises a hand for us to be quiet as she looks at her screen.

"Peter, we have a target. No, now…two targets. They're coming from two different compass bearings. Looks like if they continue on course they will converge over our location. They're coming in fast!"

"Native American flute fans?" I offer.

CHAPTER 22

"Where are they? I don't see anything. Just darkness," says Roberts.

Megan is pointing out into the night for our benefit. "One is coming over there from the southeast, bearing 130 degrees. The other is in that direction from the southwest bearing 195 degrees. They're both about three miles out, approaching at well over one hundred knots. At that rate they'll be on top of us in less than two minutes."

"Are you sure? I still don't see anything."

"No visible light emissions, no transponder squawk, but glowing intensely on the thermal imagers. Whatever these things are, they are very hot."

"How big are they?" asks Berman.

"I'd estimate between twenty and fifty feet in diameter…hold on," she says, "they're slowing down. Now they've come to a stop, at exactly the same time. Interesting, it's as if they're synchronizing their movements. Now they're just hovering there about a quarter of a mile out and maybe five hundred feet above the ground."

"Shit," says Roberts, "they're almost on top of us and I still can't see or hear anything."

"They're moving again. Both closing to two hundred…now one hundred yards."

I'm straining to hear something…anything. And now there is a sound approaching. At first faint but now growing rapidly louder. A rhythmic thumping noise. The night had been calm but now a wind is rapidly bearing down on us and increasing in intensity. Suddenly it is at gale force, toppling the sensor tripod amidst a churning torrent of dust and loose vegetation. Megan is scrambling to close down the camper shell to protect her equipment. Roberts is yelling directions at his crew but his voice is drowned out in the gale.

There is the form of a craft above us blocking out some stars with its outline. With all of the sophisticated sensing equipment around us, this seems like an old-school move but I run and grab a flashlight from the Jeep. I pivot around and shine the light up at the craft and it resolves out of the darkness into a black helicopter and then a second identical helicopter appears to its left. The sudden wind storm is downdraft from their rotors.

Both aircraft are unmarked, painted flat black with blacked out windows. They look like medium size military twin engine types, maybe Blackhawks.

Both helicopters now bank in unison and head north up the valley. As the downdraft recedes, we are left in silence, much of our equipment now blown into disarray across the Skywatch site.

"Those bastards!" Roberts is angry, shaking his fist at the northern skies. "This is illegal as hell! I don't care if they're military or not. They can't fly without a tail number or markings and they sure as hell can't fly without running lights or harass people on the ground." While Roberts is fuming, Megan is quietly collecting and reinitializing her equipment. Miraculously, much of it appears largely undamaged by the downdraft storm.

"Targets now ten miles to the north and continuing on that course at roughly one hundred knots." Megan has her system back up and running.

Berman is fiddling with a handkerchief, trying to clean some of the dust out of his glasses. "I always thought helicopters were very noisy. How come we never heard them coming until they were right on top of us?"

"I'm not sure in this instance why we didn't hear them," I say. "I do recall reading that US Special Forces have had helicopters modified for noise reduction. I believe the strike team that took out Bin Laden had those specially modified aircraft for that stealth operation. Maybe that's the type of helicopters we saw tonight."

"But did we really see *helicopters*?" asks Jeff. At this we all turn in unison to face him. "Look, you're saying that these aliens or entities or whatever really may have technology that allows them to cloak their aircraft and turn invisible even in broad daylight, right?" Slow nods and some thousand-yard stares from the Skywatch team. "If they have that level of technology, it's not hard to imagine they could also perhaps somehow, maybe holographically, disguise their own spaceships as conventional Earth aircraft…like maybe even helicopters, no?"

The Skywatchers look a bit stunned at this revelation. Clearly, they're used to owning bragging rights for the most outrageous and daring paranormal theories. And now they're being outflanked by a UCLA Informatics graduate student with nary a saucer sighting under his belt.

"If Jeff is right, as he often is," I may as well rub a little more sand into their gears, "this would certainly complicate your efforts to dismiss all sightings of conventional aircraft as non-anomalous. I mean if they can disguise themselves as Earth aircraft, it wouldn't be much of a stretch for them to emulate false transponder data either, right?" This is greeted with even more silence. Even the free thinkers, the deliberately unconventional, are in the end bound by their own dogmas.

Eventually, adrenalin levels return to normal from the black helicopter encounter as the Skywatch operation on Sutter's Bench enters its final hours. There is little activity of interest for the next several hours, but at three in the morning, just as we are preparing to wrap up, the situation changes. We have a new target.

"Bearing south southeast at 110 degrees. Range approximately fifteen miles." Roberts and I are looking at the night sky in the direction Megan is indicating. There is no sign of any lighted objects in that area.

"Are you sure?"

"Nothing in the visible spectrum but this thing is living large in the infrared bands. See right here." She's pointing at her monitor. A large blob of thermal energy is seemingly floating just below the southeast horizon. We watch as it appears to descend to the ground. We continue to observe and record the event for some twenty minutes as it remains motionless. Then, in an instant, it takes off and shoots straight upwards, disappearing into the heavens in an instant.

"Wow," says Roberts, "looks like you got your money's worth tonight, Dr. Walker. A first-class thermal imager sighting and even some black helicopters stopped by for good measure."

"And a couple of shots of whiskey from your flask as well."

"On the house."

"Thanks, it's been a fascinating evening. Hopefully, down the road I can maybe assist you and Megan with your pattern recognition system."

Jeff is off helping Megan pull up and stow away the sensor grid. And I'm staring out across the valley. I'm no expert in the detailed geography of Benton County, but I have the uneasy feeling that the thermal anomaly we observed tonight was likely very close to Taylor Creek and the Pruitt ranch.

Seven-thirty in the morning and I'm standing at the sink in the men's room at the sheriff's office. Splashing water in my face, trying to wake up. I look in the mirror above the sink and see what two nights of little or no sleep look like on a man my age. It's not a welcoming sight.

"Mornin' Jack," Wendover swings open the restroom door and sidles up to a urinal. "Geez, you look rough, like although it's early in the morning, maybe you could use a drink or three."

"Nah, I try to leave the heavy drinking to the professionals like our friend Gus out at the cemetery."

"He does have some talent, that one."

"Yeah, with the right coaching maybe he could go semi-pro."

"So, Professor," Wendover is finishing up, zipping his pants, "first thing on my agenda today is a dead cow up on the Eastside. Wanna ride along?"

"Sounds charming, but I'll pass."

"Oh, I think you'll want to see this particular cow."

CHAPTER 23

"He's one big boy. Was one big boy, rather, I guess. Quite dead now, obviously."

Dr. Tucker James tips his cowboy hat to one side and scratches his forehead, regarding the carcass laid out in front of us. He looks by turns bored and distracted, giving the impression he'd rather be anywhere else than here. James has a contract to serve as county veterinarian. He treats indigent animals and on occasions like this morning serves as a coroner to advise Wendover on animal death cases.

"Well, Tucker, we know he's dead." Wendover has a trace of annoyance in his voice. "The question is what killed him and how in the hell he got here..."

Wendover gestures to the somewhat surreal scene before us. A two-thousand-pound champion bull, mutilated and draped like a limp sack of potatoes over the top of a vintage farm tractor. The weight of the massive animal has caved in the tractor cowl and broken the front axle in two. The tractor is listing down on the now useless axle.

Even more oddly, the bull and the tractor sit in the middle of a freshly plowed pasture. No tracks in the soil except for the farmer's who discovered the scene this morning and, of course, now our own footprints.

Levi Waddle, the Pruitts' neighbor, and my recent end-of-the roader acquaintance, is standing off to the side, visibly distraught. "It ain't fair what they did to him. Nothing should have to suffer like that." His voice is quivering. Trouble has come to the end of his own county road.

Waddle had called Wendover at dawn upon discovering the kill. His voice is shaky and he is nearly sobbing at the thought of losing his prize bull. This rough looking hulk of a man certainly has a tender spot for that animal. Off in the distance I see his wife and kids peeking out the front door of his aging mobile home.

The circumstances of this animal's death are strange enough, but to me, the location itself is concerning. For we are on property directly adjacent to the Pruitts. Judy's house is about a half mile to the north. I can mentally trace nearly a straight line from my position in the bull pasture to Judy's house and on to Sutter's Bench. I think about the infrared target appearing in this direction from my vantage point out on the bench last night and wonder what, if anything, is the connection?

"Well, our bull here appears to have died of exsanguination. All the blood appears to have been removed. But there is no gravitational pooling of blood to the lower extremities that we would normally expect here. The animal did not bleed out per se, because there is no blood pool beneath him." James is continuing with his reluctant examination. "An animal like this would have about twenty liters of blood in him…that's about six gallons or so."

"We'd notice that much blood; it wouldn't be easily absorbed into the soil," observes Wendover.

"Let's see here," James is a little out of breath as he pulls himself up on the tractor to get a better look at the bull. "Well, here we go. Two puncture marks on the neck, right into the jugular vein. Probably how he lost all the blood. Looks like part of the jaw is missing too, cut off cleanly, almost surgically."

He gets down and moves to the other side of the tractor. "Sheriff, come take a look at this!"

Wendover, Waddle, and I move around to look at the rear of the animal.

James lifts up the poor beast's tail which is matted in blood and gore.

"What are we looking at?" asks Wendover.

"I'll tell you what you're not looking at…an anus. It's missing, cored out with something quite sharp."

Waddle looks away in revulsion. "How could this happen? What or who did this?"

"Well," replies James, "it's clear your bull didn't die of natural causes. I'll take some of the tissue down to my lab to run some pathology tests, but there's not much else I can do here. Death was caused by the puncture wounds with secondary trauma by clean incision to the mandible and rectum area. The lack of evidence of blood flow around those wounds suggests they occurred post-mortem."

"As for who or what did this…" He slowly turns and scans the countryside as though the culprit might still be standing nearby in plain sight. "The wounds suggest predation. The question is whether the predators are animal or human. Four legged or two legged; take your pick."

Wendover and I exchange a glance. A chill is going down my back. I'm thinking there might be a third choice here and the thought is not comforting.

"You hear or see anything unusual last night?" Wendover directs this to Waddle.

"Not a thing, Sheriff. And I'm a light sleeper."

"Animal-wise, you got your coyotes," continues James. "They're quite common around here, but they'd never take down an animal the size of this bull. They'd be more likely to take meat off a recent kill as scavengers rather than being the primary agents in its death. We do have some wolf packs that have been reestablished and have moved into the backcountry. A wolf pack could conceivably take down an animal the size of this bull. They have been known to kill moose. But those packs are few in number and tend to stay far away from human presence here in the valley."

"A bear, maybe?" Waddle is scratching his head, looking sad and perplexed.

"A black bear wouldn't be able to do this and, as for grizzlies, confirmed sightings in this area are nonexistent. This sort of takes us back to coyotes."

"Guess you must have some real badass coyotes here in Benton County," I offer. "They can apparently surgically exsanguinate and mutilate a one-ton bull and then toss it on top of a tractor."

"While apparently themselves levitating," adds Wendover, referring to the lack of tracks.

At this, James reddens slightly and simply shrugs. "Strictly speaking, under my contract, I'm only here for medical matters. I've confirmed that the animal is, in fact, dead and documented the cause of death. Who or what actually killed this bull is not a medical issue and, therefore, not my concern. Sheriff, the whodunit is your department. Good luck." He begins to walk towards his truck. "I'm going to start some paperwork and then take those tissue samples around the wound areas…not that I expect they will tell us anything."

As James walks back towards his vehicle, I quietly suggest to Wendover that whatever the county is paying this guy, it's too much.

"Doc James isn't so bad when you get to know him," replies Wendover gently. "He just prefers to work with animals rather than people. And he's much more interested in working with live animals than the dead ones."

"Who wouldn't, I guess? Quite the way to start the day, huh?" I'm gesturing at the bull.

Wendover is now walking around the bull and tractor, taking photos of the scene. "We've had our share of items for the Benton County Strange Files, but this one is different. The other occurrences were mostly things going bump in the night. Odd, but relatively harmless, right?"

"This one is going to be hard to ignore. And this time there is real damage and loss," I say.

Wendover nods towards Waddle, who is now slowly walking back to his home, still shaking his head. "Around here folks like Levi work hard and still barely get by financially. A bull like that is worth thousands and who knows how much it will cost to repair his tractor. This is far beyond a hoax or prank. It may devastate this family's bank account."

"Have you ever heard of this sort of thing, a livestock mutilation, occurring elsewhere?" I ask.

"Yes. But they're rare, fortunately. And I believe this is the first mutilation that's occurred in Benton County. You hear about these things from time to time. Rural law enforcement in the Western United States and Canada have cataloged livestock mutilations for years."

"Any consistencies to the reports?" I'm searching for any patterns to satisfy Butte counselor Dorothy Hartman's required triad of motive, means, and opportunity.

"Well, from what I recall, the consistent themes appear to be a lack of witnesses and no physical evidence of footprints or tire tracks. The animals are typically found drained of blood and mutilated with surgical precision.

As was the case with Levi, no one seems to hear or see the actual mutilation occur. At least that's what I recall from seeing a few reports. It's not like I felt I had to study up on these cases. Never thought I'd see one in the flesh like this poor brute up here on the tractor."

"What do you recall about any theories as to who was responsible?"

"I think there were lots of theories. Generally, in any crime, you'll find theories multiply in inverse proportion to the actual evidence at hand. I seem to recall cult rituals, secret military experiments, and, of course, aliens, rounded out the usual suspects. Interestingly, some witnesses, while not directly seeing the act occur, reported either unusual lights or black helicopters in the general vicinity and time of the mutilations."

Based on my adventures on Sutter's Bench last night, I may be able to check both of those boxes. But it seems premature to worry Wendover with those details until I better understand them myself.

"With little tangible evidence or motives evident, most of the past mutilations were simply chalked up to natural predation."

"Our super-coyotes again?"

"'Fraid so."

"One thing is for sure, Dan. Whatever is driving this phenomenon, it's becoming more brazen and bolder. It's escalating."

"Indeed," he says, as we both consider the poor animal in front of us, "a marker has been laid down. Literally laid down on top of this tractor. A two-thousand-pound marker."

Our contemplation of the unfortunate bull is interrupted by the distant sound of tire on gravel. A pickup truck is coming up the county road at a hell-for-leather pace; kicking up a rooster tail of dust as it approaches. The dirt road has a numerous curves and washouts and wasn't exactly built for speed. Not that this is apparently slowing down the driver. If anything, the vehicle is accelerating, its rear end sliding back and forth as it rockets along.

"Someone's in a hurry."

"Looks like Phil Pruitt's rig," observes Wendover.

"If that's the case, I assume this is not a social call."

The truck skids to a stop next to us and Phil Pruitt jumps out the door like he's on fire. "Sheriff! Thank God, I saw you here up at Levi's place! It's Judy. She's gone!"

"What! What happened?"

"Gail and I had Simone over to stay with us last night. This morning we brought her home and Judy is missing."

"You sure she didn't just run into town to maybe get something at the store?" Wendover is trying to eliminate the mundane before we leap to more troubling conclusions.

"Not without her car, purse, and cell phone."

"Understood. We'll head over immediately and my deputies will be on the way shortly as well."

"Wait. What the hell?" Phil has just now noticed the dead and mutilated bull draped over the broken tractor.

"Yeah, Phil, that's just the first mystery of the morning, but now not the most important. Finding Judy is the new priority."

"Looks like yet another marker has been laid down," I say as we climb into Wendover's Tahoe." Wendover nods solemnly in agreement as he keys the radio to call in his deputies.

CHAPTER 24

"You were here. You saw what happened." He looks straight at me unblinking and offers no response. "I'm gonna ask you one more time. What happened to Judy? Did someone take her?" At this point, Judy's dog Barney simply wags and ambles off towards the back porch to check his food bowl.

Wendover is coming down the stairs with Potts, pulling off his disposable gloves. "Seems our only witness isn't providing any useful information," I report.

"Yeah, welcome to my world," he replies with a sigh. "You'd be surprised at how often in this business the two-legged witnesses don't offer up anything of value either."

"Any luck up there?"

Wendover and Potts have been searching the upstairs bedrooms for any clues as to Judy's disappearance. Meanwhile, Riley and a couple of other deputies are examining the outside of the house, the garage, and the other outbuildings for any trace of what may have happened to her.

Simone was understandably upset over her mother's disappearance, so Phil and Gale took her home with them as soon as Wendover and I arrived on scene from the Waddle place. As Phil had noted, the doors had been locked when he had first arrived and Judy's car, keys, purse, and phone had all been left behind.

"No. We didn't find anything to shed a light on what might have happened," says Wendover. "First thing I did was turn off her buzzing alarm clock. It was set for six-thirty this morning. That suggests she set it prior to retiring with the intention of staying the night. Further suggests that she was gone prior to that time in the early morning. Bed looked slept in. Nothing else looks out of the ordinary. Of course, this could have all been arranged for our benefit."

Wendover is alluding to the very remote possibility that for unknown reasons, Judy perhaps has staged her own disappearance. Of course, his current working theory centers on the assumption that she was abducted against her will. But it would not be wise to foreclose other explanations with so little evidence at hand.

"Any signs of a struggle?"

"None. And, that may suggest she went willingly. Perhaps she knew the person that took her."

"Maybe Stan? If the doors were locked, he might have a key."

"It's a possibility. Perhaps for some reason they both staged their own abductions and are on the run together. Also, it could mean she indeed, on her own, staged her disappearance, or, alternatively, was overcome so quickly by her abductor that she had no opportunity to resist."

"So, in other words, the lack of evidence of a struggle could pretty much mean anything?"

"That sounds a bit dismissive of my finely honed detective skills when you say it that way. But you are essentially right."

"Anything else out of place?"

"Well, the bedroom window was partially open and the screen is missing. Hard to tell if the window ever had a screen. If I were a kidnapper, I wouldn't relish trying to set up a ladder and enter through a second story window out here in the middle of the night."

"Yeah," I say, "bump the ladder against the house just once and old Barney would have gone ape-shit."

Wendover is looking at me quizzically. Like maybe a light has come on. "I think, Jack, that maybe your four-legged witness has in fact told us quite a bit more than we realized. Remember Barney's behavior when we first drove up to the house this morning?"

"Yeah, the little bastard wouldn't stop barking. Same treatment I received when I visited here the first time."

"So, you think a stranger could just drive up to this house and approach her bedroom either from the inside or outside without the dog raising hell?"

"I'll be damned. This is a literal case of the dog that didn't bark," I say.

Wendover pauses, and quotes Doyle, "the curious incident of the dog in the nighttime."

"The dog did nothing in the nighttime." I'm playing along, quoting what I can recall from *Silver Blaze*.

"And, that was the curious incident."

Potts is looking at both of us as though we've lost our minds.

Wendover gently pulls him aside to explain. "Given the dog's usual barking behavior, it's unlikely a stranger could approach the house unnoticed. Judy may have been taken, but certainly not by surprise. This suggests that it is perhaps likely either the abductor was known to the dog or that Judy somehow staged her own disappearance by herself."

"Either that or someone was able to somehow subdue the dog," I add.

"I'm not sure we're any closer to understanding what happened here," says Wendover. "But we're getting a damn sight closer to at least eliminating what *didn't* happen last night. Let's go see what, if anything, Riley has found out."

As we step outside, Barney barks at us again as though he's just seen us for the first time. Riley is coming around the corner, wrapping up his search of the exterior.

"Find anything of interest?" The tone of Wendover's voice suggests he already thinks the answer will be a negative.

"For the most part, we didn't find anything unusual," responds Riley. We checked the exterior and the outbuildings. The gravel driveway and barnyard area surfaces are too hardpacked to reveal any tire tracks or footprints. We did though find one thing over around the side of the house. I'll show you."

"There's the missing window screen," says Wendover. We're now standing below Judy's bedroom window one floor above us, examining the screen that is lying on the grass about ten yards from the house. "Looks like it's been cut through or slashed."

"Odd though." He's now crouching directly below Judy's window, looking closely at the flower beds and grass right next to the house. "Suppose someone had climbed up the side of the house, tore off the screen, and entered through that window. Wouldn't you think their ladder would have left depression marks? I don't see any. And I didn't see any marks upstairs on her windowsill from a rope or a rappelling hook, that sort of thing."

"Hey, look at that!" Riley is pointing to a faint mark to the right of Judy's window.

"What is it?"

"I dunno, looks like maybe a claw mark?"

"One way to find out." Wendover has disappeared back into the house and is climbing the stairs back to Judy's room. "Okay, I see it." He's poked his head out the upper story window to get a better look at the mark. "Good eye, spotting this, Riley. It is indeed a claw mark. Three distinct claw scratches into the paint."

I involuntarily wince and step back, my reaction getting curious looks from Riley and Potts. The more I stare upward at the mark, the more it resembles a smaller version of the claw mark found in Stan Pruitt's cell. The one in the photo Information Officer Shirley Parker had shown me on her laptop in Butte.

Wendover continues, "question is, what made this mark? How long has it been here? And does it truly have anything to do with Judy's disappearance?"

"Maybe Levi Waddle's levitating coyotes came over for a visit?" I offer. Wendover nods but he does not smile. I get the sense he's not taking any theory off the table in these increasingly strange days.

On the drive back into town, Wendover is on the radio, putting out a missing persons APB on Judy across Montana and Northern Idaho. "Shall I drop you back at my office?" he asks.

"Thanks, just drop me back at my motel. I'll walk over to the county building a little later."

The Best Western Mountain View moniker is perhaps more aspirational than factual. I suppose if one stood on a the far northern upper landing and peered around the side of the building there might be afforded a small glimpse of the mountain range. But the primary view for guests is that of the main highway with the Alta Valley Feed & Hardware store directly across the street. The small rectangular window in the back of my bathroom does face in the direction of the mountains but the view is blocked by an alley and the back of the local funeral home.

The rates are quite reasonable but accommodations are clearly old-school, especially if said school was a motel of 1970's vintage. The room is clean but very dated. It even sports possibly one of the few remaining working coin-operated vibrating massage beds not found in a hotel museum, should those museums exist.

I'm not back in my room long when my cell rings. It's Kate. Between the long hours of her conference in Virginia and my recent late-night adventures, there has been precious little time for us to connect.

"Hi Babe, did I catch you at good time to talk?"

"Absolutely, how was your conference?"

"Very productive, I'm just arriving at the airport now."

"How was the Hyatt? Up to your usual standards?"

"Yes, indeed and they were kind enough to upgrade my room. I guess that was an added perk for those of us chairing the breakout sessions. How is the, um, Mountain View? It's a motel, isn't it?"

"Well, the room brochure describes it as a 'motor hotel.' It's really quite comfortable. Unlike the Hyatt, the emphasis is on simple function rather than form. I believe it is ranked among the top ten places to stay in Alta Junction." No need to mention to her that the town has just four motor hotels. "And I rather like that my vehicle is conveniently parked right outside my door."

She laughs. "Sounds like you've found a Western Shangri-la. Let's hope we can somehow lure you back to LA when your project is done."

For the next half hour or so we just talk. About Amy, our aging parents, the conference, office politics, and household developments. About everything and nothing; the loving minutiae of a shared life. I update her on the latest developments with the search for Ricky. I strategically leave out some of the weirder paranormal aspects encountered and the vague threats that occurred on Two Goat Road. No point in creating undue worry with all that's on her plate.

Suddenly she catches me off guard. "I guess congratulations are in order on your new government contract."

"What contract?" I'm trying to remember any recent government proposals the department has submitted, but I'm coming up blank.

"You know Jean is keeping a watch on our house while you're gone and I'm in Virginia, right?" She's referring to our next-door neighbor. Jean and Rob have lived next to us for years, nice people. "Well, Jean called me yesterday to say all was fine with the house and then she mentions that they had a visit from a couple of gentlemen from the federal government, asking about you."

"Really. What did they want?" I'm not liking where I think this is going.

"According to Jean, they said your team had been awarded a classified Department of Defense contract and they were interviewing your neighbors and associates in order to complete a background check for your security clearance. You know, the typical questions as to whether or not you appear to be loyal to the country, might be living beyond your means, abusing drugs or alcohol; the usual stuff, I imagine."

"That's really odd, Kate. I don't for the life of me recall that Team LISA has ever applied for any DoD contracts. I'm sure that Dr. Chandra would have mentioned something if she was pursuing such an opportunity."

"True, Adhira is very diligent about those sorts of things." Kate pauses and laughs. "You don't suppose LISA herself put in a proposal?"

"No," I laugh, "but give her a couple of years. She's a very quick learner."

As the call ends, I switch off the phone and absently tap my fingers on the change box for the massage bed. Men describing themselves as government agents are asking lots of questions about me back in LA. Is this somehow connected with my search for Ricky in Montana? How and why? And who are they?

I remember Anderson in my face up on Two Goat, his hand gripping my steering wheel. "Professor, things here are not what they appear to be. People here are not who they appear to be. If I were you, I'd watch my back."

I resist the urge to actually check my back in the motel room mirror. But in my mind's eye, a distinct set of red concentric circles, an actual target, seems to be slowly forming on the back of my shirt.

CHAPTER 25

So far, I've never had more productive day for which I've felt so little enthusiasm. Jeff and I, with LISA's assistance, have made enormous progress on completing our analysis and models of Benton County predictive crime analytics. The results look impressive and we're getting close to wrapping up our onsite activities. Jeff has even created an analysis input dataset he's labeled BCSF, short for Benton County Strange Files. We'll run those analytics next week back in California, mostly out of curiosity as to what, if anything, can be learned from any revealed patterns.

It has largely gone without remark, but the disappearances and unknown conditions of Ricky, Stan, Ben, and now Judy Pruitt, are weighing upon us heavily. Judy has now been missing for over twenty-four hours. Statistically, we know each hour that passes lessens the odds of her return. But there is no new information to parse, no new witnesses to interview. There is nothing we can do at this moment to help and that realization jabs at us relentlessly.

Wendover checks in with us from time to time during the day. He is distant and distracted as well. His signature sardonic wit shelved for now as he pulses the state law enforcement community for any leads on the missing.

About four o'clock I tell Jeff I'm wrapping it up for the day. I need to clear my head, the thought of another distressing issue, a sad anniversary, weighing on my mind today. I'm heading back to the Mountain View. I'm thinking maybe a stiff drink is in order. Hell, I might even throw a few quarters in the 'Relax-O-Matic' massage bed to see if that might help me unwind.

"Package for you, Dr. Walker." The clerk at the Mountain View slides it across the front desk with one hand without looking; his eyes fixed on the game on the big screen in the lobby.

It's a FedEx Priority overnight parcel; no return address. I open it up in my room. It contains a cell phone wrapped in tamper-evident plastic and a letter in Hillie's handwriting.

> Jack,
>
> Find a private outdoor location; see that you are not followed. You already know the four digit unlock code. I'll call you at 19:00 tonight. If I miss you, I'll call tomorrow, same time.
>
> Best,
>
> ~ H

At the appointed hour, I find a well-lit and solitary section of the nearby city park and await the call. The cell phone is somewhat large by current standards. It's a given that it's a burner phone; unregistered and untraceable. But the extra bulk suggests added electronics, potentially to support advanced encryption functions. Perhaps a VOIP arrangement to scramble, transmit and reassemble voice data packets across dozens of servers on multiple continents. For whatever reason, Hillie is taking no chances here.

The unlock code had presented a puzzle. Why would Hillie simply assume I would know the code? What four digits would I naturally associate with him? Birthdays and other years of significance in his or my life would be too easy for someone else to guess. Then I hit upon it. Of course, his favorite single malt scotch, The Macallan, which over the years has shown up on my bar tabs with distressing frequency. He always bragged about the legacy of the distillery established in 1824. He called it his "Special 1824." Well, cheers to Hillie, that was indeed the code as I unlock the phone.

I am startled momentarily as the phone rings right at 7:00pm sharp. A quick glance around the park indicates I am still alone here.

"Hello, Hillie?"

"I'm here, Jack." His voice has a noticeable delay and distortion like he's talking through a metal tube. The phone is indeed encrypted with advanced protocols and circuitous routing.

"Good to hear from you, but why all the cloak and dagger."

"You'll see soon enough. I'm not taking any chances and neither should you." Even with the advanced encryption distortions to his voice, he sounds upset and agitated.

"Let me tell you how I spent yesterday morning," he continues. "I got called into the Pentagon by a Four Star. Navy officers at that level rarely have ten minutes to give you on any topic, but this one took the luxury of privately chewing my ass for a good forty minutes. Not an experience I'd like to repeat anytime soon."

"What did you do to make him so upset?" I ask.

"It's what *you're* doing that apparently has some very powerful people unhappy."

"What happened? I asked you to just look up some historical records on an old ship and now you act as though half the world's intelligence agencies have a contract out on you."

"Look, Jack. I'll make this short and plain. Whatever you've gotten yourself into up there in Montana; back off now and get out of there. And the USS Nash, forget you heard the name."

"Wait? This is about the Nash? All the way back in World War II?"

"Yes. Remember how I had said the records were missing?"

"Uh-huh, not surprising we had thought given the passage of time, right?"

"Not missing. Classified. Deep black program classified. Ship records, crew records on Pruitt and everyone else on that ship...everything. They did not take kindly to my recent inquiries on the subject, believe me."

"But this was World War II. What could still possibly be classified?"

"I don't know and I don't want to know. Look, Jack, I'm only calling as a personal favor to warn you. I do lots of consulting with Beltway defense contractors and I tell you I'm about an inch away from getting my SCI tickets pulled." He's referring to his Special Compartmentalized Information security clearances which give him entrée into the world of black programs.

"Jack," he continues, "World War II or not, I wouldn't have been reprimanded like that unless the records related to an active program. And, by the way, when I said I was privately reprimanded by the Admiral, it wasn't just the two of us alone in his office."

"Who else was there?"

"There were two goons in plain dark suits, no identification badges, just sitting in his office, observing. They were never introduced and the suits never said a word. I got the sense they were there to make sure the Admiral stayed on script."

"You think they were spooks?"

"Yeah, likely from a three-letter agency. Definitely got the sense they were operational, not from the analytical side." He's talking about intelligence operatives from agencies such as the CIA, NSA, or DIA.

"What did they look like?"

"Both about six foot-two, very athletic builds. One had a close-cropped beard. Why do you ask?"

"Just curious. In case maybe I run into them some time." I'm thinking about the two men talking to Jean and Rob back in my LA neighborhood, supposedly doing a background check on me for a DoD security clearance I never requested. And, the more I think about it, those descriptions could also fit my newfound Genesis acquaintances, Anderson and Pullman.

"Look, Jack. I really want to help you, I truly do. But I'm afraid I can't provide you any further information on either the Nash or that sailor, Ben Pruitt."

"Thanks, Hillie. I appreciate the position you have been placed in."

"No, Jack. You need to appreciate the risks you're taking, stirring this particular pot. I'm a retired admiral, the reprimand I received was firm and pointed, but civil and respectful. You don't have my status in these military intelligence domains. You continue to run afoul of this crowd and you may not get just a pointed ass chewing."

"A less respectful ass chewing?"

"No, more like an ass kicking. My strong advice is to go back to California now and forget about the Nash and Ben Pruitt. And I'd be very careful about who I'd trust in Montana."

"You know, I'm starting to get similar advice from other folks as well."

"Well, Professor, looks like maybe a big-time data analysis nerd like yourself might find a pattern there, huh? Seriously," he adds, "Jack, be very careful and watch…"

"Yeah," I reply, "I know. I'll watch my back."

The phone goes silent as he ends the call, and I'm left standing alone in the park. The mental model of my world swirling with the implications of Hillie's call combined with the cascade of all the other oddities and disappearances afflicting the Alta Valley in recent weeks.

Physicists tell us the world around us is in fact fundamentally very different than we perceive it. At a sub-atomic, quantum level, the universe is comprised of particles, vibrating packets of energy. These particles, or quanta, are very strange indeed. Depending on circumstances, they may behave as either particles or waves. Two particles a million miles apart may somehow interact with each other through a property called entanglement.

The implications of quantum mechanics are so frankly weird and counterintuitive that while physicists consistently validate the underlying mathematics, no one can begin to visualize the world that the theory suggests exists. This despite the fact that modern technology broadly utilizes quantum mechanics principles in everyday devices like laser pointers and solar cells.

According to quantum mechanics the very sidewalk I'm standing upon is 99.9% empty space given the scale of distance between every electron and the nucleus of every atom that comprises the concrete. At this point, I'm beginning to wonder if in the next moment I'm going to sink into the quantum haze that in reality comprises the concrete, and slip through some rapidly widening mesh. The unraveling comfortable safety net of my assumptions about the world itself appears to be fraying apart.

Worse yet, whatever phenomenon I'm encountering, it appears to be rapidly strengthening and now I've exposed a dear family friend to its mysteries. Forgive me, Hillie. And for past mysteries, forgive me, Marty.

It was one year ago today. The is knock at the door both a shock and yet not completely unexpected. A quiet Sunday morning in Brentwood, and a LAPD black and white has rolled up to the house.

"I'm very sorry to disturb you, Dr. Caroselli, is your husband home?" Kate turns and motions to me. There are two officers, a P3 and a chaplain. This is a notification call out.

"You're Jack Walker?"

"Yes, officer."

"Martin Henry Walker is your brother?"

"That's correct." I feel my voice starting to shake. I'm sinking inside; I know where this is going.

"Your brother had listed you as an emergency contact for his landlord. Dr. Walker, I'm so sorry to inform you that Martin was found in his apartment late last night by Reno police on a wellness check. He was deceased. We are so very sorry for your loss."

Sorry for your loss. That is what people say. It is said that we grieve for what we've lost but sometimes, even more, we grieve for what we never had. For the lost opportunities, the future that slipped away and now will never be. Kind words that were never said and words of anger that were never forgotten. For the pain that started this so many years ago and the guilt for which I can never forgive myself.

I think Amy took Marty's loss the hardest of us all. They had a special connection. He was her favorite uncle. Hell, I guess he was her only uncle for that matter. But the two shared a quirky sense of humor. And he always delighted her with a certain spontaneity towards life that I could never master myself. Marty was a man of complexity and varied moods. Many moods were light and fun, but some were dark, very dark. He carried heavy burdens. Burdens hidden to us.

As brothers, Mary and I shared a common truth. It was something I think we both had always understood but never openly discussed. Perhaps there never was a need to talk about it. It was simply a fact. For we both knew in our hearts that Marty was far more talented in most respects than me. He was smarter, more physical, and, frankly, much better able to connect with other people. And yet, for all of his superior abilities, there was always the darkness, the burden that overshadowed him; seemingly always blotting out his chances for success and happiness in life.

And at times he had a certain look about him that I will never forget. A far away haunted look. Like somehow maybe fate had allowed him a fleeting glance at the future. And maybe he didn't like the looks of what was headed our way.

CHAPTER 26

It is late in the evening on the following day. Wendover, Zeke, and I are traveling down the main highway in the county Tahoe, returning from a quick trip to Troutdale, Idaho which is just over the Continental Divide pass to the south of Benton County.

Once the APB on Judy had gone out, Wendover began to get reports of sightings of women who might fit the description. Most were quickly dismissed, but a report called in mid-day from the Idaho State Patrol seemed to indicate a more credible lead across the state border in Granite County. Specifically, officers had reported seeing a woman fitting Judy's description in the company of a man remarkably similar in appearance to Stan Pruitt. The Idaho officers discreetly followed the couple to a local RV park and waited for us to arrive from Alta Junction and confirm the identities.

We had then joined the stakeout several hours later.

"Dan, good to see you." Granite County Sheriff, Beth Gibson, had greeted Wendover with a handshake.

"You as well, Beth. Let me introduce you to Dr. Jack Walker; he's my science advisor."

"Wow, a science advisor, huh? Pretty uptown for Benton County." Sheriff Gibson regarded me as though I was one of a rare and perhaps ungainly specimens in the zoo. The way the week has been progressing, I hoped I wasn't one of the endangered species as well.

"Yeah, well, I've got him on temporary loan from UCLA and the LAPD." Wendover said this casually as though rotating PhDs through his department was a standing practice.

Handshakes, wags, and head pats all around as Wendover, Zeke, and I were introduced to the half a dozen or so cops assembled around Gibson's cruiser. My sense was nothing much exciting must happen around Troutdale. For it seemed every assorted patrolman, constable, and deputy in radio range had been drawn to this scene as a bee to nectar.

"Pretty grainy. Just too hard to tell." Wendover squinted at a photo image on the patrolman's cell phone. "Sort of looks like Judy and Stan. Maybe or maybe not."

According to Gibson, a patrolman had spotted the man and woman walking in downtown Troutdale and then discretely followed them. The couple had continued on down the street and then had entered a large motorhome on the edge of a RV park down by the river. No further movement had been seen since the police had taken their positions here about a two hundred yards away.

"How do you want to proceed?" Gibson directed this to Wendover. "This is *your* person of interest."

"*Your* jurisdiction," replied Wendover, "hell, it isn't even my state." Their dilemma centered on the awkward circumstance of having plenty of police on standby but no true probable cause or judge's warrant to enter the premises. There was some discussion of sending an officer in plain clothes to knock on the motorhome door, perhaps posing as a salesman or utility worker. This idea was quickly dismissed. Undercover stints in small towns rarely work since everyone typically recognizes the local police personally.

"I may have an idea," I offered.

"A good idea or one of your regular ones?" replied Wendover.

Gibson looked at him sharply. "Heck of a way to treat your vaunted expert."

"His scientific prowess is all the more impressive when it's stimulated with sarcasm."

"Dr. Walker, my department could certainly use a science advisor should you tire of the abuse up in Benton County. What's your idea?"

"No one will figure me for a cop, right? I could pose as a salesman. Knock on the door and see who answers. If I don't see Judy, no harm, no foul. If Judy is there under duress, I give you the high sign and you've got your probable cause to enter. What could go wrong?"

"Plenty," said Wendover, "this is a bad idea."

"Oh, I don't know about that. Jack may be on to something here. And, Dan, as you say, this is my jurisdiction, right?" Gibson appeared to be enjoying sparring with her Montana colleague. Then a question for me. "What did you have in mind as the product you're supposedly selling?"

"I think I have a solution," I replied, reaching for my computer tablet in Wendover's vehicle. I pulled up a static version of the Second Genesis Group website. "How about I say I'm selling units in an upcoming survivalist compound?"

"That's perfect," said Gibson.

"I suppose it might work." Wendover sighed, resigning himself to the apparently inevitable.

The officers quickly wired me up for sound and I put a borrowed police Kevlar vest under my coat. Wendover was continuing to shake his head over this approach. "Still think this is too risky for a civilian."

"I'll be perfectly fine," I reassured him. "Besides, worst case scenario, I get shot in my bulletproof vest."

"First of all, it's not a bulletproof vest, it's bullet *resistant*. And, speaking of worst-case scenarios, it won't protect you if you get shot in the head." He rolled his eyes, a non-verbal "dumbass" to emphasize his point.

"I'll be fine." I pointed to the Second Genesis website on my tablet and give them a thumbs up as I recited the tag-line. "Dare to Prepare." Wendover was frowning.

As I started to walk towards the RV park, I paused and looked back towards Wendover and Gibson. "By the way, maybe I should have a code word."

"Code word?"

"Yeah, in case I really get into trouble and I need to signal that the cavalry should charge in and save me."

"No need," said Gibson, "you're well wired for sound. We'll hear every word and immediately know if you're in trouble."

"Yeah," added Wendover, "the sound quality on these units is so good we'll hear if you shit your pants. That will be our signal."

That earned him a look of exasperation from Gibson. As I turned to leave, Zeke whined softly.

The RV park was maybe a quarter full. It looked to be a quiet place with small camp spaces under a broad canopy of cottonwood trees bounded on one side by the river. I guessed it was probably too late for fishing season and too early for hunting season. Most of the other tourists had likely left after Labor Day. The specific RV rig under surveillance was parked at a space somewhat apart from the others, suggesting perhaps a desire for privacy. It was a large expensive-looking RV, reminiscent more of a bus than a camper. It was not by outward appearances what I would have expected for a criminal hideout.

As I walked the last hundred yards towards the RV, silently rehearsing my survivalist salesman pitch, I reflected on what an inadvisable scheme this little ruse might become if the situation went south. If I knocked on the door and it turns out to be a simple misidentification, well then, no problem, right? However, if it was indeed Stan and Judy in there, chances were that one or both of them would be under duress and God knows what I was walking into then.

Now, later that evening back on the highway towards Alta Junction, I sigh, reflecting on the day's events in Troutdale; another lead that went nowhere. As events unfolded in the RV park, I had the pleasure of meeting a very nice couple from Oklahoma who indeed bore somewhat of a resemblance to Stan and Judy. They were actually very interested in the Second Genesis opportunity and a bit disappointed that demand had been so great that I had run out of promotional materials to leave with them. Another dead end.

"What did we miss, Jack?" Wendover is frowning, staring at the darkened highway ahead of us, drumming his thumbs on the top of the steering wheel.

We have just crossed over the pass from our trip to Idaho. He has the window open a crack and the cool mountain air is flowing into the cab, smelling of pine. He is slowing down a little. At this point, the two-lane highway twists down a long forested canyon following the east fork of the river. Traffic is not an issue; we have not seen another car in over twenty minutes. Occasional mist off the river drifts on to the highway periodically slowing us down.

From time to time, the headlights pick up red and green sets of glowing eyes apparently floating off the ground at the edge of the road. It's a rather disconcerting effect at first until I realize this is eye shine from deer who then resolve into solid form as our lights approach.

What did we miss? I have no answers for Wendover. Maybe what *didn't* we miss is more the question. Stan, Ricky, Ben, and now Judy. All disappeared, but why? What is the common thread?

"What's with Zeke?" I ask. "He's not been himself tonight, unusually distant."

"He's probably just a little annoyed. You know you're sitting in his seat. He's used to riding shotgun."

"No kidding…I,"

"Shit!" Wendover is suddenly pumping the brakes and cranking the wheel for all he's worth. Tires screeching, the Tahoe rocks to the side and for several terrifying moments it seems as though we might roll the rig over. I have no idea what is happening. My instant thought is that maybe a deer has crossed the highway in front of us.

Seconds later we slide sideways to a stop in the middle of the highway, our engine idling and the smell of protesting brakes and tires permeating the cab. Wendover turns on the cruiser lightbar, bathing the highway and surrounding forest in blue and red flashes. "What the fuck?" he exclaims.

My sentiments exactly. Turned sideways as we are on the highway, not five feet from my passenger window, is a startling apparition in the night. Judy Pruitt is standing in her nightgown and bare feet on the highway centerline. She is not moving, staring straight past us. Apparently oblivious to the four-thousand-pound vehicle that has just barely slid sideways to a stop in front of her. Also, seemingly impervious to how cold the asphalt she is standing barefoot upon must be on this forty-degree night.

"Let's get her in the vehicle," instructs Wendover. "There's a blanket in the back."

She is apparently in a trance, offering neither resistance or assistance as we place her on the back seat. We cover her with the blanket and Zeke places himself next to her, attempting to warm her with his furry bulk.

Wendover is on the radio. "Yeah, we have Judy Pruitt in my vehicle. Please get on the horn with County General. Tell them I'm bringing her in. She's in a trance of some sort and also needs to be checked for hypothermia. We're thirty minutes out." He's gunning the Tahoe down the highway as he speaks.

I look back at Judy, now sound asleep and snuggled next to Zeke. I can only wonder where she's been. And what she has seen. She has not spoken directly to us. Only a few brief words she seemed to whisper to herself as Wendover straightened out his rig and pulled forward.

"Ricky. Ricky is okay."

CHAPTER 27

It's a bit of a crowd but promises to be a good show. Wendover, Riley, Phil Pruitt, Walter Berman, and I are standing in the darkened observation area behind the one-way mirror adjacent to Interrogation Room Number One. The room designation is accurate, if a bit ambitious; the Benton County sheriff's office only has one interrogation room.

"Now maybe we'll get to the truth," says Berman.

Wendover shakes his head wearily. "You'd be surprised how little truth is spoken inside those walls at times."

Indeed, I think, if lies left a physical trace, over the years, these walls would be coated black.

Judy has recovered from her ordeal since we found her last night but still has no memories of what had really happened beyond a firm sense that she had somehow seen Ricky. Northwest Skywatch, being a full-service paranormal research organization, offers memory recovery and abduction victim counseling. So, Peter Roberts has stepped forward to attempt to hypnotically regress Judy to help her understand what may have happened during that missing time.

Wendover has reluctantly agreed to let Roberts hypnotically regress Judy in the controlled environment of the interrogation room. The notion is that she will be more likely to open up if the audience is hidden from her behind the one-way mirror.

I'm thinking using county facilities to hypnotically depose a witness, much less a suspected alien abductee, is highly unconventional and likely to run afoul of accepted law enforcement practices. But Wendover agrees we are out of time and better options for finding Ricky.

Roberts has the lighting low. Judy sits in a comfortable chair at the end of a table. Conducive, I suppose, to putting her in a hypnotic state. The overall effect strikes me incongruently as half interrogation and half séance.

Distant, lost in her thoughts. Judy has said little to anyone since Wendover and I found her, nearly running her over, on the highway last night. Phil checked her out of the hospital early this morning after she was treated overnight for mild shock and hypothermia.

Phil strikes me as even more of a skeptic than Wendover on the alien abduction theory. But his willingness to talk Judy into participating suggests that he too is out of plausible options. He is standing next to me, thumbs tucked into his cowboy belt, intently watching Roberts begin the session.

"Judy?"

"Yes?" She looks up at Roberts.

"Judy, I want you to relax. I want you to think of a time when you were very happy. You were at peace and you had no problems. Can you think of such a time?"

"Yes."

"Good. I want you to close your eyes. I want you to think of how you felt then and imagine you are back at that time and place. Now close your eyes and just listen to my voice and think of how you felt during that time that was so pleasant."

"Okay." Judy is closing her eyes.

"So, just two things to concentrate upon," Roberts continues, "the sound of my voice and that feeling of bliss, that everything is going to be alright." His voice is assuming a soft cadence, nearing a rhythmic monotone.

"The sound of my voice and your sensation of bliss..."

Judy's head nods slightly forward. Her eyes are closed.

"You are in a state of bliss. Completely relaxed. There is nothing to fear. No one, nothing can harm you or your family. Do you understand?"

"Yes...no harm." Judy's eyes are closed, she's slipping into a monotone as well as though she is subconsciously matching Roberts' tone and cadence.

Wendover and I exchange a glance. I've seen lounge-act hypnosis sessions before, but nothing as focused as this...with a child's life perhaps at stake. It is surprising how quickly Judy entered this altered state.

"Judy, I want you to gently shake one arm and then the other. When you shake your arms, you are shaking out the last of any tension and fear that you have. And, you are shaking away the cobwebs and fog of your memory. From now on you will clearly remember everything that has happened to you over the last few days."

"Can you do that?" he asks.

"Yes. Yes, I can." Judy is dutifully shaking her arms.

"Good. I'm going to ask you some questions about what happened to you over the past few days. You will be able to answer me completely because we have shaken away the cobwebs and fog, right?"

"Yes."

"And you will have no fear because you are in a safe, blissful place. When you have answered my questions, I will ask you to wake up. You will become fully awake and will feel completely rested, as though you just had the best night's sleep of your life."

"Judy," he continues. "Let's think back to two nights ago. Can you do that?"

"Yes. The house is quiet. Simone is staying the night with Uncle Phil and Aunt Gail. I'm trying to relax, but I can't. I just keep listening for the phone, hoping there is news about Ricky or Stan. I try to watch some TV, but I just can't concentrate. So, I go upstairs and get ready for bed."

"And then what happened?"

"Well, I turn out the lights and lay there, trying to go to sleep, but I can't. It's very quiet for a long time and then I hear something and I start to get scared."

Judy visibly stiffens. Her eyes remain half closed, but she seems to be looking from side to side.

"What is it? What did you hear?"

She's clenching her fists now; starting to breathe rapidly.

"Judy. Remember whatever is happening cannot hurt you now. You're completely safe here. Let's try this... Describe what is happening as though it is just a movie that you're watching; it is not happening to you now. You are just watching what really happened as a movie and describing what you see on the movie screen to me as it happens. Can you do that? What did you hear?"

"Yes, I'll try that...watching the movie of what happened."

"What did you hear?"

"Barney."

"Barney?"

"He's our dog. Suddenly he's outside furiously barking at something."

So much for Wendover's Holmesian theory about the dog that didn't bark. Assuming, of course, this hypnotically recovered memory is correct.

"So, there must have been an intruder?"

Wendover makes a face at that remark. Roberts is leading the witness rather than letting her tell her story. There's a reason that hypnotically induced statements are inadmissible in a court of law. The process is not the equivalent of truth serum; perceptions that are originally false will be relayed just as falsely under hypnosis. Worse yet, suggestions and statements made by the hypnotist themselves in the sessions may later be falsely remembered as the truth.

"Why is he barking? What has him upset? It's not like him to go on like this." Judy is slipping into the present tense, watching a movie screen the rest of us can only imagine.

"I don't like that...him barking like that. What is making him so upset?"

Judy suddenly arches back in her chair, "what's that!"

"Easy, Judy. Remember, we're just watching a movie here," says Roberts softly.

"I don't hear Barney anymore, where is he? It's not like him just to stop. I should be up and at the window to see what's going on, who's out there. But I can't...or won't move out of the bed. Somehow getting up out of bed isn't a good idea right now."

"Uh-oh!" She pulls back from the imaginary screen. I can see something moving out there. It's reflecting in the window panes."

"What do you see?" Peter is leaning forward intently.

"A light. Blue then red, then blue again. Coming in pulses. I can't tell where it's coming from; it seems to be coming from everywhere. And a deep pulsating sound, I feel it more than hear it. Dear God, I can hear Barney; he's crying and whining...poor thing. I'm still in bed, not moving. Not gonna move. This isn't real. This can't be happening...again. They're coming for us...again!"

With that comment, Roberts swivels around in his chair and raises his eyebrows at us. He seems more stunned though than vindicated. Sort of like the dog that finally catches the car he's been chasing for years and isn't sure now what to do with it.

"My God," says Phil, shaking his head. For once, old Phil and I are on the same page.

Riley seems the most stunned of all. He has an expression of complete disbelief and he seems to be simultaneously both backing away from the one-way mirror and leaning towards it to hear more.

CHAPTER 28

"Now the lights are gone," Judy continues. "Just disappeared. But something's moving out there. I can hear it...scraping up against the side of the house. And the window is moving up! That can't be happening; it's a second story window!"

I wince as I recall the odd claw mark next to the Pruitts' second story window.

"Easy...just a movie, remember?" Judy is threatening to hyperventilate and Roberts is attempting to calm her down. Frankly, Peter is not looking all that calm himself.

"I'm in bed and I can't move. I'm watching that window slide up by itself and I just wanna die. Then I'm hearing Barney and he's still crying and I know I'm not imagining this 'cause he's reacting to this too. Part of me wants to crawl up in a ball and just die so they will never find me. But another part thinks somehow they know where Ricky is and I have to be brave and see this through to the end."

"I'm watching the window going up by itself," she continues. "I thought I had latched it but I guess I didn't. I'm watching that window pane rise and I don't notice that there is someone standing next to me. I mean right next to me. I was watching that window and I don't even notice him!"

"He...I think it's a he, not a she, but I'm not sure why. He says something like it's going to be okay. Except, he doesn't say it, but I hear it. His mouth, if you could call it that, doesn't move but I hear the words in my head."

"What does this being look like?"

I am momentarily annoyed by Roberts' reference to a "being" rather than a "person" but decide at this point that the balance of the testimony probably supports the "being" moniker.

"I can't really tell what the body looks like, it's sort covered with a robe or cape. The oval face is pale, almost gray/white. A slit for the mouth. Big oval eyes, all black...no white in the eyes."

A textbook description of the alien "grays" from the movies.

"Another thing. He has a sickly-sweet smell about him. Distinctive, but not unpleasant." She shakes her head. "Funny thing, that is what makes this real for me. The memory of that smell will never leave me, that's how I know it's real."

"Uh-oh." She fixates again on the imaginary screen. "He's reaching towards me with something in his hand. He's saying it will be alright, but the thing looks nasty. I'm pushing away from him in the bed but he keeps on coming. He touches me with it on the shoulder and it stings."

"And then what happened?"

Judy is shaking her head. "I dunno. Just blanked at that point. Must have put me to sleep. Wait. Now I remember coming back awake..."

"Where are you now?"

"I don't know. Not in my house, that's for sure. Looks rustic, like it's a cabin someplace. Faint light outside coming through the windows like maybe it's dawn...early in the morning, I think."

"Why do you say it might be a cabin?"

"Um." Judy is looking about her, glancing at a scene we can only imagine. "Logs. The walls are made of logs."

"And the being is still with you?"

"Yes. I'm waking up and he and two of the others are sort of holding me up, keeping me steady on my feet."

"What do the others look like?"

"Well, there are two that look like him. They have the gray oval face that doesn't move. But there are several others that look like regular men...soldiers."

"What do you mean? How did they look like soldiers?" Roberts is looking a bit incredulous. I suspect he'd believe about any tale that involved aliens, but alien/soldier cooperation would exceed even his admittedly elastic bounds of belief.

"They, the soldiers, they're wearing uniforms. Camouflage uniforms."

For a while now, my money has been off the Genesis crowd as prime suspects, but this twist is pushing them back towards the front of the line, though in a way I would not have anticipated. I know they have been making an appeal to be multi-culturally inclusive in peddling their survivalist compound schemes, but who'd have thought interplanetary?

"And what are the soldiers doing?"

"They are examining someone on a medical cot. They have instruments and IVs and things they are working on. The oval faced beings are bringing me closer so that I can see. The first being I saw...the one at my bed the night before, maybe he is the boss, anyway, he's saying not to worry...that everything will be alright. He keeps saying this so often that I think maybe, no, it is not going to be alright. It's not!"

"They bring me closer and, oh my God! Oh, my God! It's Ricky! They have Ricky!"

Judy is screaming and Roberts is doing everything he can think of to calm her down.

I look over to Wendover. "We getting this recorded?"

He nods. "Been recording since the beginning. Although, even if the videos are lost, I must say there is not enough scotch in the world to ever erase this from my memory...unfortunately."

"They bring me over to Ricky now." Her screaming over now, Judy has fallen into an eerie monotone, expressionless...almost the way we found her on the highway.

"They are telling me that Ricky is special. He has special blood and what they learn from him will help many people. They want me to know that he will be returned to me soon. They wanted me to see him for myself and see that he was alive and would be okay."

"Did Ricky see you? Did he respond to you in any way?"

"No. I called his name, but his eyes were closed. The soldier that was taking care of him said that he was alright, but the medication they were giving him made him sleep. Then the leader put his hand on my shoulder and said again that Ricky would be coming home and that their work here would be done real soon."

"Oh," she says. "He's saying Ricky will be returned real soon. And, we'll know. We'll know he's been returned by the sign of three."

Roberts is shaking his head and stealing a glance in our direction. "What did he mean by 'the sign of three'? Was that something that was mentioned before?"

"No. I have no idea what it means," she replies. "He just said look for the sign of three."

Shrugs all around on our side of the mirror. The sign of three could be anything: Father, Son, and Holy Spirit, or Rock, Paper, and Scissors. Who knows?

"Oh no," she's becoming agitated again, slipping back into the present tense. "He's got that thing, that instrument in his hand again and he's starting to touch my shoulder again...all blank now." She's looking from side to side, but her internal movie screen has apparently gone dark and silent.

"I guess the next thing I remember is being lost and cold. It's dark and I'm standing on the highway when Sheriff Wendover and Dr. Walker found me."

She says finally, "I can only hope that these people, things, whatever they are, will return Ricky to me soon. That is my faith and that is all I have."

"Is there anything at all that was unusual about the cabin? Anything that could help us understand where they held him?" Roberts is still looking for answers.

"Well, one thing was odd, now that I think about it. The cabin was all roof."

"All roof?"

"Yeah, it just had a roof that sloped up from the floor and went right to the top on the ceiling on two sides. Yeah, and there was a fireplace, a big stone fireplace."

Wendover and Phil Pruitt seem to recognize what she's describing. "A roof that slopes up from the floor on two sides, that's an A-frame," explains Wendover, "she's talking about an A-frame cabin."

"You're right," agrees Phil. "There may be others, but the only log A-frame I can think of with a big stone fireplace is the old Griffith Lodge the cross-country ski club uses up near the pass into Idaho. Up at the meadows at Larch Mountain. Probably hasn't been used since the last ski season ended in March,"

"Interesting," says Wendover. "I think that's the only structure in the county that could fit the description and, as the crow flies, the Griffith Lodge is only about five miles away from the point on the pass where we found Judy last night."

"Sheriff," Phil turns to Wendover. "You need to send someone up there and search that cabin immediately."

"Just wait a second." Like the rest of us, Wendover is trying to process and make sense of what we've just observed. "That cabin is privately operated property with a valid lease from the forest service. I don't have probable cause to just barge in there. And no judge is going to issue me a search warrant based on the hypnotic testimony of a woman who thinks her child has been abducted by aliens!"

I'm having a hard time getting my head around this myself. Accepting for the moment the rather fantastic notion that we are hearing a true account of a real alien encounter, there are elements to her story that seem even more implausible. If extraterrestrials abducted her and Ricky, why take them to a rustic cabin rather than, say, a futuristic spaceship? And what were they doing seemingly in cahoots with human soldiers?

"That *woman*," Phil's voice is rising and a reddish hue of anger is creeping up his neck. "That woman is the wife of my brother, my missing brother. And the mother of my nephew, my missing nephew. Are you serious? You're taking no action? Because, if you're not, then by God, I'm going to!"

"I need more evidence than this." Wendover folds his arms resolutely and leans his massive frame towards Phil. The good sheriff isn't above using a little physical intimidation to enforce a point. "Look, the lodge is federal property. Even in the best of circumstances, it will be a lengthy process to get a warrant to enter. The best I can do right now would be to request the forest service send someone over to check the property. They might send someone right away or it might take a day or so. They work on their own schedules, not mine."

"Need I remind you I'm a County Commissioner."

"So noted," Wendover retorts. But let me remind you that I don't work for you. The people of Benton County elected me to this position."

"Like I said, if you're going to do nothing, I'm going to take matters into my own hands!"

I look back into the interrogation room. Roberts is continuing the session with Judy, oblivious to the tensions rising between Pruitt and Wendover behind the one-way mirror.

"Judy," he says, "do you remember earlier on in the movie of your memories, back when the being was inside your bedroom?"

"Yes. Yes, I remember."

"You had said that they were coming for you - *again*. Did you mean this has happened before?"

"Yes. Yes, now I remember, a number of times. The ones that came before. But those visits were, I dunno, different."

Berman is pressing his hands against the glass window, listening to every word. His expression is as intense as Roberts'. This is the culmination of their life's work. An honest to God, multiple episode abductee under hypnosis. Visions of book deals likely dancing in their heads.

"How was it different than those other times?"

"I remember several other times now that we had visitations from these beings, but in all the previous times they were different. They looked different from those I saw in the cabin and they acted differently."

She pauses, seemingly looking further back in time. "The previous visitors were much more slender and shorter. Only came up to here." She's motioning to the top of her shoulder.

"Their faces were different. More animated. Their eyes moved and their faces moved when they talked in my mind. It's like the ones in the cabin had masks on. Their faces were somehow frozen."

"How did they differ in how they acted or behaved?"

"The ones in the cabin were all business. The point, I think, was just to show me that Ricky was with them and safe from harm."

"And the others? The ones that came for you before?"

"The others I really only saw a couple of times, although I think they visited Ricky often. When they interacted with me, they were very different. Very, not sure how to say this, but, I dunno, philosophical?"

"Philosophical?"

"It wasn't just about Ricky or me. They were focused on saving our world. They told me that they were from a place I could not understand."

"Why do they have to save the world?"

"Because of what they have done and we have done. Terrible things. Pollution, but much worse than what we know. They had accidentally set things in motion that will destroy the planet and we are just making it worse. They think it may be too late to alter the course of what is about to happen. Maybe the only thing that can be done is to change mankind itself, so that we can survive. That's why they need to work with Ricky. He carries the seeds of change within him that will allow humanity to survive."

Roberts flashes a look at us, wondering I suppose if we're hearing this too; and getting it recorded.

"Uh, uh, I'm, I'm not feeling so good. Where am I?" Judy is coming out of the hypnotic state by herself, unbidden by cues from Roberts. She's looking around, clearly disoriented. "What has happened? What did you find out about Ricky?" She doesn't appear to have any recollection of what she has been describing to us in the past hour.

We're all frankly stunned by the session. Each of us trying to process and make sense of what we've observed. But of all of us, Riley seems the most shaken. The color drained from his face as though he's seen a ghost, or more to the case at hand, an alien.

I turn to ask Phil if I can help him get Judy home but he has already left. Presumably, per his threat, he is off taking matters into his own hands.

CHAPTER 29

As is the case with many small rural towns, the Safeway parking lot in Alta Junction often serves as a community gathering place of sorts. No doubt this expanse of blacktop has seen its share of bake sales and Boy Scout pre-camp rendezvous. This afternoon, though, it has drawn a different crowd. A smattering of four-wheel drive pick-ups and SUVs have pulled up on the far end of the lot next to Phil Pruitt's rig, an oversized Ford with dual wheels on the rear axle.

Phil is making good on the morning's threat to take matters into his own hands and he is forming a posse of either the like-minded or the easily swayed to carry out the mission. I doubt either category applies to Jeff and me. And Phil has made it rather clear that we were asked to come along only at Judy's insistence. The more eyes looking for Ricky, the better, she had said. He has reluctantly agreed to our presence but has made it clear we are to stay out of his way.

The majority of the gathering crowd would appear to fall into the easily swayed category by virtue of the fact that they are either ranch hands on his payroll or buddies of those employees. His foreman, Hank Gutiérrez, a somber middle-aged gentleman with a white cowboy hat is standing off to the side surveying the rabble. Hank has a serious, long-suffering look about him. Although I would imagine anyone employed for any length of time by Pruitt would be described as long-suffering.

Gutiérrez looks worried and for good reason. The rest of the dozen or so vigilantes are young men, rowdy, joking, and eager for an afternoon's distraction from their regular chores. They seem to be sporting a testosterone-fueled "hold-my-beer-and-watch-this" sort of bravado. And, each has brought along a gun or two to complement the upcoming adventure.

As Phil tries pulling some order to the group, they are grinning and showing off their guns to each other. Such is the pervasiveness of firearms culture here, our public armament display merits scarce notice from the store's regular customers. They remain absorbed in their grocery lists and going about their routine business.

"Okay. Everyone be quiet now. Hey, shut up!" Phil looks a bit exasperated. A good posse is hard to find these days, I suppose. Most heads are now nodded in his direction, so he proceeds to lay out the general plan.

"As you know, Sheriff Wendover has elected to sit on his hands while one of our own, my nephew, Ricky, is likely being held captive up at the Griffith Lodge." He motions to Walter Berman. "I've invited Mr. Berman here from the Valley Independent to provide press coverage of Ricky's rescue which will happen despite the inactions of our do-nothing sheriff."

Berman somberly nods to the group. Officially, he's telling Pruitt that he's representing the Fourth Estate, but I suspect he is instead tagging along on a Skywatch agenda. Perhaps he thinks he will have a chance to facilitate "first contact" should aliens indeed appear.

Pruitt is continuing to fume. "I'm pretty damn sure that the Genesis group is responsible. Oh, they're running around in alien costumes trying to scare people but we've had enough of their lies, haven't we? Who do they think we are, idiots?"

I start to answer, but Jeff gives me a quick elbow. A reminder that when folks ask a rhetorical question, they often don't appreciate an honest reply.

"So, here's what we're gonna do," Pruitt continues. "The only thing these people are going to understand is a show of force and that's what we're going to give them. We think Ricky was, or is, being held at that old cross-country ski lodge up near the pass. We're going to drive up there and knock the lodge door down if we have to in order to free Ricky."

"Any questions?" he looks to the crowd.

I have a very bad feeling about this. In my prior consulting with LAPD, I've ended up participating on "after action" reviews regarding the execution of tactical situations. Most were executed like clockwork, but some got hairy fast. One bad assumption, an unexpected delay to get into position, anything, can cascade a meticulously planned operation into chaos.

But this affair is anything but meticulously planned. In our current circumstances, the amount of firepower casually on display is overwhelmingly greater than the apparent amount of planning and forethought in evidence. And when firepower is inversely proportional to brainpower, you have a recipe for disaster. Timing is working against us as well. The afternoon is slipping away and darkness falls early this time of year.

"What about you two? Any questions?" Pruitt is glaring at Jeff and me.

"Um," Jeff smiles, "what if they really are aliens?"

This elicits snickers through the crowd.

"Tell you what," says Pruitt, reaching into the backseat of his truck. "If they're aliens, I ain't too worried, because I have this."

He pulls out a massive gun, a big game rifle of substantial caliber.

"Any idea what this is?"

"It looks to be a Marlin .45-70, right?" I reply. "Not a good choice for long range. The round is too heavy relative to muzzle velocity, the bullet drops down quickly along its trajectory. But close up and medium range, it's got the knockdown power of God's fist. Handy if you're hunting big game in Africa, but I'm not so sure about aliens."

"Yes...?" Pruitt looks as though he can't decide if he's more shocked, impressed, or annoyed that the city slicker professor knows something about guns. I can thank time on the firing range and some scotch-enhanced evenings trading tales around the fireplace with my father and Hillie. Hillie fancied himself a rifle and big game aficionado and I picked up a solid understanding of guns amidst Hillie's joking and bravado.

"Anyway, the Marlin will be good to have if Ricky is being held captive by a rhinoceros, eh?" I offer.

Pruitt is scowling. "Let's just hope I don't need to use this. But if I do, you'll be damn glad I have it. Come on, let's go!" He's climbing up into his truck and waving for the rest of us to follow him.

Jeff and I climb into the back of an old Toyota Land Cruiser driven by the ranch foreman. We barely have a chance to grab onto a seat and hang on as Hank guns it out of the parking lot close behind Pruitt's truck. A very immature-looking ranch hand named Billy is riding shotgun up with Hank. While the other ranch hands look to be glad to have an afternoon off work, young Billy looks like maybe he's skipping class at the high school.

The Toyota's rear bench seats face each other. Our traveling companion slouched across the opposite bench is a red-bearded young man who introduces himself as Sean. Sean is nearly yelling to be heard over the whine of the tires and wind noise rattling the old four-wheel drive as we sway and bounce down the highway. This is going to be a rough ride and we haven't even left the good pavement yet.

As we proceed down the road Sean shows me his pistol, a 9mm Sig.

"That's a really nice gun," I remark. You mind if I take a closer look?"

"Sure, glad to." He hands it over with evident pride. Jeff unconsciously draws away from it. He is regarding it as though it might come alive and bite his arm.

The Toyota sways strongly again as we pull off the main highway and motor down a paved secondary road into grazing land adjacent to the forest. I admiringly turn the gun over in my hands. Surreptitiously, I'm checking to see that the safety is engaged. It's not.

"Here you go, very nice." I return it to Sean and in the same movement engage the safety.

"Hope we find them," Sean says, drumming his fingers on the seat. "I wouldn't mind shooting me a couple of a-li-ens." He pronounces "aliens" with three syllables and I make a mental note that perhaps he is not ready yet to join the next Skywatch vectoring session.

"Uh-oh, hold on." Jeff is looking ahead down the road where a fence line is rapidly intersecting with the road. "Brace yourselves, there's a cattle guard across the road and we're going too fast!"

Seconds later the Toyota crosses the guard with no indication of a bump. Jeff looks puzzled.

"It's fake," shrugs Sean. "Just painted across the road."

"Yes," I agree. "The cattle treat it just like a real cattle guard. They're conditioned to believe that all lateral patterns across a road are unsafe barriers, so they won't cross it."

"Yeah," grins Sean, "'cause cattle are dumb fucks."

Jeff may have then said something, but I'm not hearing him; I'm a million miles away. Young Sean may not be the sharpest knife in the drawer, nor the most articulate, but he's triggered an epiphany for me.

I think of the cattle, conditioned to believe any set of lateral patterns, real or painted, will trap their feet. It is a part of their reality, a cow-worldview that is never questioned. A conditioned response.

Yet, are we so different than cattle? Do we not sleep-walk through much of our lives, accepting world views we have not personally challenged or examined? Think of a graph paper covered with data points or dots. Draw a straight line through at least two of them and that line is a version of the truth. It has to be. You've connected the dots, right? Especially if you ignore all the other dots that don't fit your line...or the inconvenient fact that some of your dots can fit into other lines as well.

In the end, I guess, we see what we expect to see. What we want to see. Perhaps, like the cattle, what we are conditioned to see. Father Rodrigues saw God's reflection in the face of a child. Roberts and Berman see lights in the night sky as confirmation of alien life. The early investors in the Sapphire Belle had so succumbed to visions of wealth they accepted faulty mineral assays without question.

Is there a larger pattern overlaying Ricky's disappearance that we have not considered? That perhaps we have been conditioned not to consider?

After some miles on the forest backroads our little convoy pulls into the gravel parking lot of the Griffith Lodge. A Benton County sheriff department cruiser is already parked there in front of the lodge. Deputy Riley is leaning up against the car examining his fingernails.

"What took you guys so long?"

CHAPTER 30

"I couldn't just stay in Alta Junction and let you folks come up here by yourselves. Not with what we heard from Judy Pruitt this morning." Riley has pulled Phil Pruitt, Berman, Jeff, and me over next to his car for a quick chat.

"I take it Wendover doesn't know you're up here?"

"No, he doesn't. And, officially, I'm not here to search the lodge. I'm here to, let's say, monitor public safety."

"Excellent. That's the kind of initiative and concern that's been lacking in the sheriff's office," offers Pruitt. He winks at Riley, "why it wouldn't surprise me if Benton County elected a new sheriff in a couple of years."

At this Riley looks down and manages a humble, aw-shucks sort of laugh. But I'm guessing this is not the first time the notion of replacing his boss has probably occurred to him.

"So, while I was waiting, I did a quick survey of the lodge exterior," explains Riley. "First, no clear recent tire tracks or footprints other than the ones I made. I peeked through several of the lodge windows in back, looks to be vacant."

"So, what actually is this place?" I ask.

Pruitt gestures to the lodge, "I believe this was built by volunteers back in the late 1950's or early 1960's. It's been leased back from the forest service and operated and maintained by the local Nordic ski club ever since. The location is supposed to be ideal for cross-country skiing."

Mainly for the benefit of we Californians and Berman, he gives us a quick layout of the local terrain. The lodge, he says, sits on the edge of a large system of meadows along the West Fork of the main river. Although, at this elevation, near the headwaters, the river itself isn't very wide or deep, more like a large creek. A bridge behind the lodge crosses the river and allows access to a large network of trails that will be groomed for skiing in the winter once the winter's snow accumulates. Across the meadow from the lodge is Larch Mountain flanked by two drainages, North Larch Creek and South Larch Creek. These ravines also have narrow trails that at their base connect to the larger trail network where the creeks empty into the river below.

"We came all this way," continues Pruitt, "might as well see what's inside." He and Hank are examining the lodge's front door.

"It's an old lock," observes Hank, reaching in his pocket for a multi-tool, "I think if I fiddle with it for a bit, I may be able to figure out how to unlock it."

"Well, hell. We got a dozen people standing around, over half of 'em on my payroll. We're not going to wait all afternoon; it will be dark soon. Move over!" With this, Pruitt pushes Hank aside and gives the door a strenuous kick with his boot.

There's a crackling of old dry wood splintering as the door explodes inward taking the frame with it. The door now swings down and askew, the lower hinge still attached to the remnants of the dislocated frame.

"There's a guy who knows how to make an entrance," says Jeff softly.

I glance at Riley, "How much does the county budget have to cover the destruction of federal property?" He gives me a resigned shrug, like 'whadda gonna do?' as we step into the lodge.

Now everyone in Pruitt's little posse is pushing on into the lodge. Apparently, all need to confirm with their own eyes what Pruitt himself must have discovered on entry. The lodge is vacant and looks as though it's been unused for some time. There is definite smell of stale air and mouse. An off-season's worth of dead flies on the window sills and cobwebs amongst the rafters.

The group is fanning out, looking under tables and chairs and even up the chimney for any sign of Ricky. Jeff and I are staying towards the back, sizing up the situation.

Lodge may be a bit of a grand term to describe the structure. It's more like an oversized cabin, maybe a couple of thousand square feet at most. The bulk of the interior is given over to a large great room with folding tables and chairs. A massive stone fireplace towards the rear is framed with large windows affording a nice view of the meadows and Larch Mountain. It mainly appears to be a casual gathering place where cross-country skiers can warm up and eat a picnic lunch. The lights aren't working. I assume any power must come from generators; we are far off the grid here.

I quickly take several photos of the interior with my phone. Perhaps later these will somehow jog Judy's memory and allow her to consciously remember what happened that night.

"This doesn't feel right," says Jeff, "it's not making sense. Why would she be taken here?"

"Agreed. If we accept Judy's hypnotic recollections of an alien abduction on face, why would such beings bring her here to some remote ski lodge out in the boonies rather than to a spaceship or some high-tech alien base? And why specifically here? What's special about this place?"

"And if," replies Jeff, "per her narrative, they were going to return Ricky shortly anyway, why go to the trouble of abducting Judy just to let her know that he was okay and would be returned shortly? Seems like a lot of extra trouble to go through, even for an advanced civilization."

"Or," continues Jeff, "maybe Judy just got it wrong. Maybe her memory of that night was false or confused. Hypnosis isn't a truth serum or time machine into the past, it's only as good as your memories."

Memories are fragile and elusive things, I think. A million ephemeral butterflies dancing over the vast fields of the life we've lived. Our powers of recollection a poor net to reliably capture even a small fraction of them. Perhaps Judy had visited this lodge on some prior occasion and somehow conflated that visit with her memories of the abduction.

"Another thing that doesn't make sense," I add, "why show Judy that Ricky was okay and tell her that he would be returned soon, yet leave her memories so clouded that she couldn't clearly remember the message without hypnosis."

"Maybe the message wasn't really for her. Maybe she was just unconsciously *carrying* the message."

"You're saying the message might be for *us*?" There's been an uneasiness, a notion, something in the back of my mind that's been bothering me about this whole situation. Something I have not yet found the words to articulate. But Jeff's statement has just resonated with that elusive notion. Before I can explore this further with Jeff, we are interrupted.

"Hey," shouts Sean, he's just reached under a table, "I may have found something. It's a hat! A knit beanie!"

"Give me that," Pruitt reaches for the hat and quickly grabs it from Sean. "Well, I'll be damned, it's Ricky's! I'd know it anywhere. Gail knitted it by hand for him. He's been here! Ricky has been here!" He's holding the hat up in the air, shaking it in front of him to emphasize the point.

Riley and I shoot each other a look. Up until now, this little outing has had the makings of a wild goose chase, a wasted afternoon at best. Now this lodge has suddenly become an active crime scene. A crime scene currently being trampled through and contaminated by a dozen men.

"Everybody out!" Riley is herding us all out the remains of the busted doorway. "This building is now a crime scene under the control of the Benton County sheriff's department. No one is to reenter without permission!" He's headed back to his cruiser to retrieve some crime scene tape to block off the gaping doorway.

"I knew it. I just knew it," declares Pruitt. "Now we'll see what Wendover has to say about dropping the ball."

"Okay, we found the hat, but where is Ricky himself?" Jeff has a point. Finding the hat just tells us perhaps where Ricky has been. It is unlikely that it will point to where he is now.

"He may be being held close by," says Pruitt. "We should try to fan out and…" Pruitt is cut short by an enormous concussion emanating across the meadow. "What the hell?" Thirty seconds later, an identical deep and forceful sound pulses from the forest. Then at an identical interval, another concussion. The pulses are low frequency to the point that we seem to feel them as much as hear them. Now silence, just the breeze through the trees and the rushing sound of water from the river's headwaters.

"What the hell was that?" Pruitt is glancing around the lodge parking lot at the assembled, like maybe someone here should know.

Hank is pointing to the west. "The noises were so low frequency, it's hard to know exactly where in the meadow or forest they came from. I think maybe basically across the river from us is as close as I can tell."

For a moment there is confusion and everyone seems to be talking at once. Then Berman lets loose a shrill whistle through his fingers for quiet. The crowd falls silent; Berman has taken the floor. He looks at Riley, Pruitt, and me. "This morning when Judy was describing seeing Ricky in the cabin, remember what she said?" The three of us are slowly nodding, trying to recall the exact story she had relayed. "Remember? She said she was told that Ricky would be returned very soon. And that we'd know. We'd know when it was time by the sign of three."

"The three loud sounds. The sign of three! That makes about as much sense as anything here has," I respond.

"That means he could be nearby," says Riley. "They could be holding him over where the sounds originated, or maybe left him over there."

"Well, let's stop standing around and let's go out and find him. Daylight is slipping away!" Pruitt wants some action. He's pulling equipment out of his truck. "Okay, let's pair off and cover some ground. It's hard to pinpoint exactly where the sounds came from, other than to say they were from across the river. Every team grab a radio here, let's keep 'em on channel ten. Hank, take a team to the upper meadows. Sean, take another team to the lower meadows."

"Why don't I take Jeff with me up the South Larch Creek trail?" volunteers Riley.

"Thanks, great idea. Walker, take Berman with you to cover North Larch Creek. I'll take Billy here with me and we'll head up the main Larch Mountain trail. That will put us on the ridge between the north and south drainages. There we should be able to look down into both ravines as well as have a good view of the meadows below us."

As everyone is gearing up and heading out, I flag down Pruitt. "Phil, I can't help but notice that all the other teams have at least one person with a gun."

"Yeah, sorry, don't have any extras to spare. But, here, you can take this." He passes over a handheld GPS unit. "If we find any unusual tracks or evidence, we'll call on radio and then you can come and drop a pin to mark the location for future reference."

I'll mentally file this under 'P' for 'patronizing,' but I gamely grab the device and turn it on.

"You know how to work it?"

"I think I can manage." As the GPS powers on, an amber screen lights up. Slowly, icons for five satellites appear across the top of the small screen, indicating we now have signals from enough positions in space to determine our exact latitude, longitude, and altitude here on Earth.

I may be paranoid, or overthinking this, but I get the strong feeling that Pruitt is somehow relieved I'm not armed. Perhaps he is concerned about becoming a victim of friendly fire. If that's the case, his fears may be misplaced. Given the arrogance with which he treats Gutiérrez and his other employees, a stray bullet from me may be the least of his worries. Welcome to Montana, a land of few murders, but many hunting accidents.

Pruitt has been adamant that Judy's abduction is a Genesis hoax rather than anything truly alien. However, I notice as he closes up his pickup and heads out towards the river bridge with Billy, he's packing the Marlin.

"Well, how about it?" I say to Berman. "We've got our trusty GPS unit. Let's go hunt us some aliens."

CHAPTER 31

In other circumstances, the trail up the North Larch Creek drainage would make for a pleasant late afternoon's walk. The trail parallels a meandering creek along a small ravine through the forest. It winds through groves of pine and thick brush. Up the slope above us we occasionally hear voices and the scruff of boots on rock, likely Pruitt and Billy proceeding up the central ridge trail.

If daylight was rapidly dwindling out on the meadow, down here in the ravine, we are already deep in the shadows. Berman and I remark that for all the guns Pruitt's crowd has brought along, few flashlights were in evidence. In our case, should darkness completely close in, all we have are our cell phone lights. Right now, however, that is the most utility we can expect from our phones. We are miles beyond any cell signal range.

For some time, we have walked along quietly, enjoying the silence of the forest. About ten minutes ago, we mutually agreed to shut off our radio. The chatter from the various search teams and Pruitt's endless radio checks were becoming increasingly annoying and adding little value to the enterprise.

"So, Walter," I break the silence, "how did you come to be involved with Skywatch in the first place?"

"It was a rather long, unlikely, and circuitous journey," he replies. "Probably not unlike the path that ended up placing you as an unofficial science advisor to a sheriff in rural Montana, I would imagine."

We both chuckle at this. Reflecting, I suppose, on the thousands of twists of fate in our lives that have somehow now literally placed us together on this very path in a darkening ravine in a remote Montana forest.

"Several years ago, I was working for a Seattle newspaper. I was assigned to do a story on Skywatch. A local interest piece; supposed to be funny or ironic. You know, look at those crazy dudes out searching the skies for E.T., right?"

"I could see why an editor might consider them a target of opportunity."

"Absolutely. And to be honest, I came into the assignment with just that attitude. I thought it was all a bit of a joke. But the more time I spent with Roberts and the Skywatch team, the more impressed I became with their professionalism and sincerity. And then something happened which really caused me to change my world view."

"You saw an actual UFO?"

"No, that would happen later. The turning point for me was when they allowed me to speak, off the record, with a few of the witnesses and contactees they were assisting. These were regular people. People who had no interest in and only vague awareness of the phenomenon prior to their experiences. These people were not out looking for the paranormal. They didn't want notoriety or publicity. The paranormal found them and profoundly affected their lives. They were trying desperately to understand and cope with what they saw, and in some cases, what happened to them and their families."

Berman says that was the point at which he chose to join Skywatch. He felt he could apply his skills as a journalist to help these experiencers record their thoughts and memories as part of their way of finding closure with what had happened to them. Roberts and company had Washington state well covered from a field investigation standpoint. So, when the Valley Independent had an opening for a reporter, Berman jumped at the chance to establish a Skywatch outpost in Western Montana to occupy his off-duty hours from the newspaper.

"So, these folks that have had a UFO experience, they want you to tell their stories to the world?"

"Sometimes. But mostly they want to tell their stories to me. They want someone just to listen to them with an open mind and validate that I accept that, for them at least, they are relating a real account of what happened to them. Sometimes they want their story told broadly, but often I just record their accounts as a personal memoir for them. Something tangible they can refer to or maybe share with their families. You need to understand they are experiencing trauma from an occurrence that larger society dismisses as fantasy."

"Sounds as though a large part of your involvement has to do with acceptance and closure," I say.

"Indeed. And, Jack, I think it's fair to say that you're very skeptical about the paranormal in general and UFOs specifically, correct?"

"No need for E.T. to feel singled out. I'm a full-service skeptic on many if not most topics. You'd be surprised."

"I gather that. Perhaps pushing the boundary between skepticism and cynicism with some frequency? Maybe your cynicism and wisecracks are a defense mechanism. A way to keep the world at arm's length to avoid getting hurt?" He turns to me and pauses, shakes his head. "Sorry. I do that sometimes. I dual majored in journalism and psychology. Sometimes I end up over-analyzing people…with my out-loud voice."

"No worries," I reply, "you're essentially right. And you've just saved me forty minutes and seven hundred dollars." Berman couldn't know that over the past year I've had my share of forty-minute sessions with a psychologist. After Marty died, I was in a bad place. I went down the rabbit hole and buried myself in data and algorithms. My emotional distance and lack of engagement with Kate and my co-workers doing me and everyone else no favors either at home or at work.

Finally, an intervention was in order. Kate and Adhira Chandra formed an alliance and the women double-teamed me into therapy. As is usually the case with therapists, the sessions were not as much about learning new insights into my behaviors and attitudes as admitting and accepting what I already knew to be true. Significant childhood trauma and the related guilt about that trauma engendered defensive behaviors. Directed towards a world in which I can never be in complete control. An avoidant personality disorder enabled by cynicism and wisecracks.

Over time I've been able to pull myself back to a healthier engagement with the world. However, I think I'm still under cautious scrutiny by Kate and Adhira. And, I suspect perhaps they are even in touch from time to time to compare notes. Indeed, as I think about it, perhaps I need to add paranoia to the therapist's growing laundry list.

"Feel that?" I ask. The temperature in the ravine has suddenly dropped several degrees. "With the sun setting, cold air is settling into the lower elevations."

"Yeah," agrees Berman, "and it's going to get dark rather quickly. At some point we'll need to turn around and head back."

He's right. We've been on the trail a little less than an hour. By my reckoning we've covered about a mile and a half with no sign of Ricky or anyone else. At this hour there will be a contest of sorts as our eyes try to become adjusted to the dark faster than night falls. But in the end, the darkness will win.

"Hear that?" Berman has suddenly stopped. He's pointing up the trail ahead of us. I'm straining to hear any sound other than the slow flow of water down the creek and the breeze through the trees. Then I begin to hear it, a rustling motion up the trail, maybe a couple of hundred yards distant. And heading our way.

Berman and I exchange a puzzled look. The sound is rapidly approaching. In fact, there are multiple sounds now. Someone or something very large is rapidly closing on our position. Perhaps multiple large things.

Berman and I swing around, looking for the exits. The problem is we're hemmed in on both sides by the ravine walls. They are quite narrow at this point on the trail. And, of course, we're the one search party without a firearm. I look at the GPS unit in my hand. It's a marvel of electronics but it's mostly plastic and only weighs maybe a dozen ounces. Great for its intended purpose, but of little utility as a defensive weapon.

Now the brush and small trees ahead of us are shaking about furiously. Whatever is coming is not bothering much to stay on the trail. Suddenly, Berman and I throw ourselves up against the wall of the ravine as the brush in front of us explodes outward with four massive creatures.

They are mule deer at full run. Eyes bulging, lungs gasping, froth from their mouths; they are sprinting as though the very demons of hell are in close pursuit. Within a minute, they are far down the trail from us.

Berman and I are picking ourselves up off the side of the hill and standing up a bit unsteadily. "What the hell?" gasps Berman, "where are they going?"

"Apparently, Idaho. And they ought to get there in about twenty minutes at that pace. However," I motion up the trail, "I don't think they really cared where they were going as long as it was far away from whatever up there apparently had them spooked."

"You mean whatever is in the direction we are heading?"

"The direction we *were* heading. I vote we take a strong hint from those deer and make haste back down the trail towards the open meadows."

"That makes two of us," replies Berman, "I'm right behind you."

We cover another hundred yards back down the trail. With the increasing darkness, it's slow going. One mis-step on a loose rock or a tree root could easily cause a twisted ankle or worse.

Then we hear it. A loud, deep concussion resonating at a very low frequency. I can't tell the direction it's coming from; it seems to be almost on top of us. Then suddenly it stops. The sound has hardly faded before a new sensation washes over us. It's a smell. A pungent, almost cloyingly sweet scent. Berman and I look at each other wordlessly. We're both remembering what Judy had described during her hypnotic regression. The smell of the beings. The smell that had made the experience all too real for her.

I'm now feeling disoriented, like maybe I'm not in complete control of my thoughts and my senses. I look over at Berman, "are you okay? Are you feeling this?"

"Yeah, it's weird. Like I'm watching a screen with an old-fashioned film projector. My vision is wobbling. Like the film is getting stuck and then speeding up. Then slowing down again."

Then we see it. A small blue glowing orb floating over and through the trees. It's approaching us from up the ravine, in the direction the deer had fled from. I quickly glance at the GPS screen, trying to get a sense as to our distance down to the meadows. As I watch the display, the five satellite signal lock icons, one by one, wink out. Something. Something generating a strong electronic interference effect is blocking the GPS signal. Shit!

CHAPTER 32

"Do you see that?" On one hand, I'm hoping I'm not going crazy, losing touch with reality. On the other hand, it might be somehow comforting to know the approaching blue light is just a hallucination, a product of weariness and an overactive imagination.

"Yeah," replies Berman. "I see it." I look at him curiously. It's as though his words and the motion of his mouth are out of synch, like a badly dubbed movie. "I don't like this at all, let's get out of here!" he shouts.

"I thought this was what you came for? First contact. The 'Welcome to Earth' speech?"

"Yeah, screw that," he groans, starting to head down the trail. What appeared in the abstract to be a noble enterprise when discussed around the breakfast table at Stockman's, seems now much less appealing in practice in this dark ominous forest.

"Look!" I'm pointing back up the ravine. The blue orb has stopped advancing and is holding position about seventy-five yards away at tree-top level. It's now been joined by a companion, a red brightly glowing orb of similar size. The red orb is holding steady about twenty-five yards to the left of the blue one.

Thump, thump! The deep frequency concussions have resumed and their pace is quickening. To our amazement, now the two orbs are starting to pulsate on and off. They are somehow synchronizing their flashing patterns with the timing of the sound. I'm breathing heavily, fighting it back, but a wave of terror is beginning to consume me. I look over at Berman. He is frozen in place, seemingly mesmerized by the orbs; their flashes reflecting off his glasses.

Suddenly, the night reverberates with two massive gun blasts. Pruitt has opened up with the Marlin. Instantly all sounds stop and the forest is plunged into silence as echoes of the reports subside. The orbs quickly disappear over the ridge and we are left in darkness and an eerie stillness. I hear a faint metallic tinkle above us and belatedly realize this is the sound of Pruitt's expended shell cartridges tumbling down the shale covered outcropping directly above us.

The sudden stillness is unsettling in its own way. I have an uneasy feeling this is the calm before the storm. The history of nations and of battles, and the course of one's life all turn on moments. As the arc of the pendulum reaches its apex and for an instant in time is frozen before it starts to swing back. The moment a rescue mission becomes a recovery operation. The moment the hunters become the hunted.

Then just as suddenly as the prior silence had descended upon us, all hell breaks loose. The forest is bathed in eerie light and a cacophony of deep pounding sounds resonates through our bodies. The brightest lights and the source of the sounds seem to be localized on the other side of the ridge. We can see an enormous glow shoot up through the trees from the general area of the south drainage ravine. The place where Jeff and Riley had been heading.

Berman switches on the radio. It's mostly spewing static but interspliced with panicked rants, people talking over one another. They're describing shadows of beings roaming the woods and lights chasing them. Chaos has descended upon the Pruitt posse. Berman and I look at each other and, in an instant, wordlessly agree that come hell, high water, or aliens, we're getting off this damned mountain now. We clamber down the trail by the light of our cell phones at breakneck speed. We're staggering over tree roots, and ignoring the brush and branches tearing at our clothes along the narrow trail.

If we continue to accelerate maybe we'll catch up with those mule deer. Their mad scramble down the ravine to get the hell out of Dodge now seems to have been a prescient warning. We should have taken the hint and immediately followed their lead.

Twenty minutes of scrambling down the dark trail and the meadow is in sight. The strange lights and noises in the forest had ceased shortly after our headlong retreat down the trail. We hurriedly cross over the river bridge and approach the lodge parking lot.

Someone has turned on a light array up on their pickup's roll bar to illuminate the parking area. It is a broken vigilante army now slumped in disarray about the lodge. Some nursing bruises and cuts. Others are limping on ankles twisted in their own reckless flight from the unknown.

I'm scanning the parking lot, looking for Jeff. I see Riley, slumped on the steps to the lodge. He's holding his head against his knees, nearly in a fetal position. Sean is next to him, quietly talking to him and patting him on the shoulder.

"Where's Jeff?" I ask as I approach them. Sean is just looking at me. My heart is sinking. Sean is looking straight at me, shaking his head but he can find no words. "Where the fuck is Jeff?" My voice rising with my anguish.

Riley is shaking, choked up. He won't or can't look at me directly. He's staring straight ahead. "Jeff," he finally says, "they took Jeff." Now he's silent, looking straight ahead at something a thousand miles away. He's sitting there, rocking on the step, nearly catatonic. Shades of Judy Pruitt standing on the highway centerline in her bare feet.

By frantically talking to the rest of the group I'm able to hurriedly piece together a general notion of Riley's account. He had stumbled into the lodge parking lot about ten minutes ahead of Berman and me. Barely coherent and scared out of his mind. Riley had said that he and Jeff had been proceeding up the south creek trail when they encountered luminescent orbs like those Berman and I had observed. Soon thereafter the orbs flew away but, in their place, a large triangle shaped object appeared directly overhead. Out of reflex Riley reached for his sidearm. Not the best move, as this provoked the object to hit him with a beam of light that smashed him to the ground. As he came to and pulled himself up off the dirt, he saw Jeff being carried by a ray of light up into the object which then sped off into the night sky.

Phil Pruitt is slumped down, looking rather forlorn, sitting on the tailgate of his truck. All prior assertiveness and bravado have been drained away. He is visibly shaken, his face pale and drawn as he looks up at me. "Walker," he says faintly, shaking his head slowly. "I'm sorry. I didn't trust you. But you were here for Ricky and now your student has been taken."

I nod, words escape me. I am likely sliding into shock myself. And I'm feeling enough guilt for both of us now. I remember briefly meeting Jeff's parents on campus last year. A lovely couple, so proud of their son. And soon I must make a terrible phone call to tell them Jeff is missing.

"I don't know what or who we're up against here," he mutters softly. "But this situation is bigger than any of us and I don't know who to trust or who's in charge here anymore."

"Watch your back and trust no one," he's now moved to the cab, reaching into his glovebox and producing a handgun; looks to be a Ruger nine-millimeter. I'm being told to watch my back on a regular basis now; seems well founded advice given the circumstances.

"Please, take this," he's handing me the gun and I grasp it without hesitation. "You know how to handle something like this?"

Without breaking eye contact with him, I check the safety, drop the clip, and pull back the slide to finger-check the chamber through the ejection port. Ten rounds in the magazine.

"Well, I guess you do," he says. "I'm sorry I don't have an extra clip or more ammo for you."

"That's okay," I say with a slight ironic smile, "given who or what we may be up against, chances are that if I get into a confrontation that can't be resolved with nine rounds, another ten probably won't matter."

"But there's already ten in the clip? I think…" his voice trails off and he looks down, realizing now what I'm saying. Realizing the utility of that last round in a worst of all cases scenario.

He still has the Marlin lying on the truck bed. "What were you shooting at up on the ridge?" I ask.

"I don't know exactly. It was a light moving towards us, I guess. I really don't remember now." He's stopped talking and now just stares off into the distance. Maybe he's looking at whatever Riley is seeing in his mind. My sense is they're both close to going into shock.

I'm clutching the gun and sliding into survival mode. The reality of my existence, what I know and trust about the world, is breaking down. I don't know how this new reality works, what I can trust, or what or who I can depend on to protect me. First, Ricky, Stan, now Jeff…are we all next?

I look up to the sound of tires on gravel. Sheriff Wendover's vehicle has pulled up, emergency lights lit. An ambulance, two deputy cruisers, and a state patrol car are right behind him. He steps out of his rig, looking at me and shaking his head in disbelief. I stick the gun quickly out of sight in my coat pocket.

Wendover walks over to me, ignoring Pruitt for the moment. "Jack," he says softly. "You've been through a lot. I'm going to have Potts take you back to town. We'll process this crime scene, take statements, and put out an APB on Jeff."

"We'll find him," he says. But his tone and facial expression don't convey a great deal of optimism about the chances. I'm listening, but rapidly drifting away in my own thoughts and fears.

He turns as another patrol car has entered the parking lot. It's an Idaho cruiser. Sheriff Beth Gibson's county line is only a few miles from here. She rolls down her window, "Dan, how can I help?" Bad news appears to travel fast in this cold, thin mountain air.

The ride back to Alta Junction is a blur to me. Potts isn't much of a conversationalist and right now I'm grateful to be alone with my thoughts. All the way, I'm trying to process the phantasmagoria of images of the encounter on the trail and the abduction of Jeff. What does it mean? How do all the pieces fit together?

And over it all hangs my guilt. This is my responsibility. I brought Jeff out to the Griffith Lodge. It was my idea and, yet, he was the one that paid the price. I have more than enough guilt for one lifetime over what happened to Marty. I will never be able to forgive myself if Jeff is not found. This is on me.

I think of my last conversation with Jeff which had been interrupted with the discovery of Ricky's hat. Why had Ricky's abductors chosen the lodge as the place to present him to Judy? What was special about the lodge? Was the message Judy recalled really for her or was it for a broader audience? Did someone or something want to draw us to this location to then execute the ambush that just happened?

Then it hits me. The lodge was distinctive with the A-frame structure and stone fireplace. It was unique, a one of a kind in the area that the locals immediately recognized. And, most importantly, it was very remote. Distinctive, unique, and remote. They knew we would come and they were waiting! It was a set-up from the start and we were played!

About fifteen miles outside of Alta Junction we cross into cell coverage and my phone lights up with missed messages and calls. There's a voicemail from Kate. Just checking in and hoping all is well. If she only knew. I won't return that one right now; I have no idea what to say. The next voicemail is troubling.

The message is from Marcy. She's looking for her father and wondering if I've heard anything from him. Yesterday Hillie had a meeting scheduled with Lockheed Martin in Bethesda but turned out to be a no show. And, despite a full slate of missed appointments today, no one has seen him. She went by his condo in Arlington; it looked as though he had packed and left in a hurry. She knows he and I had been working on a couple of projects and is wondering if I have an idea what has happened. This is not like him; she's worried sick. Now, so am I. And I have no idea what to tell her.

"Excuse me, Dr. Walker," says Deputy Potts quietly, "we're getting into the outskirts of town now. Would you like me to drop you off at your motel?"

"No," I say, "please just drop me back at the sheriff's office. I have some work to do."

The only one I can turn to for help now is LISA.

CHAPTER 33

It's seven-thirty in the morning and the day shift in the sheriff's office is stirring to life around me. I'm rubbing my eyes, hunched over Jeff's laptop in the data collection project cubicle that Wendover had provided us.

All night the rain has pounded against the windows; a steady cascade of nature's white noise as I've worked. A warm front has brought an overnight stream of moisture in from the Pacific Northwest, soaking the valley and even the upper elevations in the high country. The streets and sidewalks of Alta Junction are now damp and plastered with the last of the fall leaves, pelted off their branches by the hard rain. Forecasters are saying this will change soon. A cold air mass pushing down from Canada will transition the remaining moisture over into snow in the higher elevations later tonight.

On the ride from Griffith Lodge back to Alta Junction I had decided it was time to stop playing defense and instead go on the offense. So, last night LISA and I went hunting for patterns. First, I added data characterizing the Larch Mountain incident to Jeff's BCSF, the Benton County Strange Files analytics input dataset. This is the collection of reports Wendover had compiled of crop circles, strange howls in the woods, aliens with top hats, and the like. LISA then took the file as input and mapped each incident both spatially and temporally across the same virtual grid map of Benton County we had developed for Wendover's crime predictive analytics graphics.

Next, LISA's deep learning algorithms developed a visual representation of the pattern depicting how the incidents propagated across the county over time. Running the analysis in a backfit mode then tracked the paranormal phenomena back to a presumptive point of origin.

The remaining propagation correlation was exceedingly tight, nearly a one hundred percent fit. This was a level of correlation, a fit, I had not previously encountered in any prior LISA study. This compelled me to rerun the complete analysis through LISA's algorithms several more times last night to reconfirm the analysis. Each time the results came back with the same correlation, the same predicted point of origin for the paranormal activity. A near perfect fit to the data.

Now, as I stare at the indicated point of origin, I am not entirely surprised. However, I now need to make one phone call to further confirm LISA's result.

At a quarter past eight, I'm heading down the hall towards Wendover's office. My suspicions have been confirmed by the phone call. Hopefully, Wendover or one of his deputies can accompany me as a law enforcement presence this morning. But, if no one is available, I'll leave a note for Wendover summarizing my findings, and what I plan to do. There is no time to wait. Jeff's life may be at stake.

Halfway down the hall, I run into Riley. He has his jacket pulled on, radio in hand, and looks to be heading out the door. Seems all business this morning, a remarkable improvement over his nearly catatonic condition of last night.

"Jack," he says, "I am so, so sorry about Jeff. I have never seen anything like that UFO. It was terrifying. I've never been so frightened in my life."

"Well, I should hope none of us see anything like that again. Glad to see you're doing better."

"Jack," he's grabbing my arm. "I swear. We will find him. We'll find Jeff. And they returned Judy, didn't they? Maybe they'll return Jeff shortly, too."

"Let's pray you're right. Is Wendover in yet?" I ask. "Looks as though his office is dark."

"He's already out on some calls. Given, you know, what's happened. Things have gotten a little…unsettled out there," he's gesturing to the world outside the county building's walls.

A little unsettled? Deputy Riley has a gift for understatement. Overnight Alta Junction has been put on the map, although not in a way the local chamber of commerce might prefer. News of a terrifying UFO encounter and abduction on Larch Mountain with multiple witnesses has spread like wildfire across the valley. More dramatic with each retelling, later versions of the rumor have apparently mutated from a story of a potential UFO abduction to confirmation of an imminent alien invasion. Locals are starting to think they see Martians stalking about behind every street sign. Orson Welles' broadcast of the War of the Worlds on social media steroids it would seem.

Accounts of the incident are even filtering up to the national level. Early this morning one of the network news affiliates from Spokane rolled a satellite uplink truck into the county building parking lot. Word is that more are on the way.

The sheriff's office has been responding to a large spike in reports. Riley says the calls started coming in mid-evening and haven't let up. Numerous reports of prowlers, public intoxication, minor looting, unlawful firearm discharge, and at least two attempted suicides.

Wendover's Holmes would remind us that individuals vary, but percentages remain constant. Regardless of whether we're talking about New York City, Alta Junction, Cape Town, or Mumbai, there is invariably a very small but persistent percentage of the population remarkably ill equipped to face news of the unknown or other stressful situations. Benton County seems to have its full share.

Overwhelming anxiety, susceptibility to conspiracy theories, and freewheeling paranoia are simmering just below the surface for these folks, even on a good day. The news from Larch Mountain is now dousing those smoldering coals and embers with pure accelerant, and predictable results.

I tell Riley I have a strong theory, bolstered by LISA's analysis, of where we might either find Ricky and Jeff, or clues to their whereabouts. Would he or another deputy be able to accompany me to check it out?

He's sympathetic, but demurs. Sorry, there are too many urgent calls, he says; the 911 lines are melting down. No one can be spared to join me. As if to emphasize the point, his radio crackles to life with another message from dispatch.

"Sorry, I've gotta run," he's pointing to the radio, starting to pivot towards the door.

"I understand," I reply. "I'll go check it out myself. It's a long shot, maybe it will turn out to be nothing anyway. But, in the worst case, if I don't check back in with you in, say, two hours, better send in the cavalry, okay? And please see that Wendover gets this." I hand him the note explaining my theory and where I'm heading.

"No problem, you got it, boss." Riley takes the note and gives me a quick thumbs up. "Be safe out there."

As I drive out of town, a disheveled man, likely homeless, is standing next to the damp highway. His eyes as wild as his hair and beard, he's holding a freshly scrawled cardboard sign: AYLEANS TAKE ME. Not that I can blame him for looking for a fresh start, a reprieve from the daily trials and reversals of fortune on this planet. But I'm afraid should aliens exist, they may have more discerning tastes in abductees.

A little less than an hour passes, and I'm silently cursing the moment I stepped into the Alta Valley Feed & Hardware store earlier this morning. Given the hard rain that came in overnight, I thought I might need a pair of mud boots so I had stopped by the store on my way out of town. Now it appears I have picked up boots about two sizes too large. Every step I take on this muddy road is threatening to suck the loose boots off my feet; it is slow going.

LISA's analysis of the BCSF dataset clearly traced the patterns of all the recent paranormal activities to one unambiguous point of origin, the Sapphire Belle mine. Admittedly, this was not entirely a surprise. First thing this morning I made a further confirmation of my suspicions. A quick call to the headquarters of the Alta National Forest revealed that no one by the name of Richard Rodgers is or has ever been employed by the forest service. Ranger Rick is a fraud, and, I think, most assuredly not an alien.

So, I've parked my Jeep down at the mine access turnout on Two Goat Road and climbed over the gate, ignoring the warning signs about dangerous conditions and access being restricted only to the authorized. I am slogging up the damp and muddy access road towards the mine. Overhead, the cloud cover is thickening, becoming darker. An indication that the promised high county storm system may be approaching and bringing snow here later in the day. I had better make this little reconnaissance of the Sapphire Belle quick. My sense is that getting stranded by the storm at this elevation may not be a pleasant experience.

As I proceed up the mine access road, I feel the weight of Phil Pruitt's gun heavy in my coat pocket. Given the situation I may be walking into, the substantial feel of the weapon is less reassuring than one might think.

If the entrance to the Sapphire Belle mine had at one time been closed off, it is certainly not sealed today. A pile of broken timbers and some large concrete barriers have been pushed off to the side recently. Likely these were at one time used to construct the original seal. I'm cautiously approaching the entrance, the Ruger now out and in my right hand. Wendover had mentioned that back in the day there had been at least two entrances. But I'm assuming the one I'm looking at now must be the main one.

There are no recent tracks in the damp earth, but I have a gnawing sense I may not be alone. A prudent person, upon seeing the entrance seal removed, would now surely retreat back to cell service range and call in the troops. But the guilt of losing Jeff has driven me so far beyond prudence, I'm no longer within its influence. All I want now are answers and to see Jeff brought back in one piece. The note to Wendover is my backup; in effect a Deadman's switch if no one back at the sheriff's office hears from me shortly.

I stand peering into the entrance tunnel. The light from here outside fades quickly away about fifty feet into it. I did remember to bring a small flashlight with me, a lesson learned from yesterday's fiasco. But it's not clear I've gained much else as to learning from yesterday. Less than twenty-four hours ago I was mocking Pruitt for the abundance of firepower relative to the dearth of planning for the Griffith Lodge adventure. Now I'm proposing to enter this mine with far less firepower and perhaps even less of a plan. The utility of my Ruger is even doubtful. A concussion from its discharge in the confined space could likely bring half of the tunnel ceiling down on my head.

At this point, I hesitate one last time. Much like Berman's "first contact" epiphany on Larch Mountain, what seemed like a good idea in the abstract back in Alta Junction seems a more doubtful proposition here in the present moment at this isolated mine entrance. But, I'm here, Jeff most certainly needs me now, and there is nothing for it but to head into the tunnel.

I switch on my flashlight and cautiously navigate the first few dozen yards into the mine. So far, the tunnel itself has been quite large, maybe twenty feet wide and a dozen feet tall. At one point in time, I suppose it had been carved out large enough to accommodate some heavy equipment access. I haven't seen or heard anything of note, other than an awareness that the daylight from the entrance is rapidly fading as I progress.

A dozen more steps and then I think I see a motion, a shadow moving just at the limits of my flashlight beam. There's a slight rustle, then silence. I recall in the traditions of the Abrahamic religions it was said that as Daniel was sent into the lions' den, with God's intervention, the beasts embraced him as dogs lovingly welcome their master. Not that I'm casting myself as a Biblical hero, but one can always hope for a friendly reception. Maybe Ranger Rick will step out of the shadows with Jeff and surrender, saying this was all a prank gone wrong. Instead, realistically, I suppose I should take the advice of Father Rodriguez, who often repeated an old Arabic adage, "Trust in God, but tie up your camels at night." The gist being that one should not test their faith in God's mercy and protection with the actions of a fool.

Another dozen steps in silence and I suddenly have the feeling I am not alone. I strain my sight and hearing to their limits but nothing. Then, suddenly, what strongly registers is my sense of smell. The overpoweringly sweet smell that Berman and I had previously encountered has enveloped me! Much like the Larch Mountain experience, its effect is to immediately distort the world around me. There are more movements and sounds now, but these are oddly out of synch. My senses are seemingly speeding up, freezing, and then slowing down. I feel like I'm losing my balance and reach out to steady myself against the tunnel wall. What is happening?

Then I see it. A diffuse light moving towards me from the depths of the tunnel. In its center, a figure approaches, walking slowly, purposefully. Closer and closer it comes. To my horror its features have resolved into to those of an alien! Oval gray face, large piercing almond eyes. I can't seem to resolve a mouth or any other features, perhaps I don't want to see them. I can't really see the body; the thing is shrouded in a black hood and robe. I'm shaking, my breathing coming in short gasps as wave after wave of terror crawls across me. I'm vaguely still aware of the gun in my hand. But it seems like a distant thing, something I now don't know how to use.

It's coming closer and I'm frozen in place. I remember as a child going out for a hike with my father. We had come upon a small deer that had gotten itself entangled in a wire fence. I remember the sheer terror in its eyes. It shook uncontrollably, pulling away from our touch as we struggled to free it. We were aliens to it, beings from beyond its experience, and it feared us terribly even as we worked to free it. Now I am the deer, fearing something far beyond my nightmares.

Suddenly the creature stops and is gesturing upwards, pointing to the ceiling of the tunnel. I look upward in the darkness, straining to see what it could be pointing towards. In that second, I belatedly become aware something or someone has come up behind me. I feel a sudden jab to the base of my neck and all is darkness.

CHAPTER 34

I'm cold. My first sensation is a chilled stiffness. I'm slowly becoming conscious, if one adopts a broad definition of the term. It is like being awake within a dream, my perceptions altered and unfocused. I am lying prone, apparently on the floor of the mine tunnel. I do not know how long I have lain here, perhaps hours – maybe a day. There is a low frequency hum in the background which I sense more as a vibration than as a sound. There is light above me, bright and diffuse. My coat has been taken away, and with it, my gun and cell phone.

With some effort I turn my head and see Jeff lying on the ground beside me. To my great relief he is breathing slowly. He's alive, though perhaps barely so. Jeff's eyes are partially open, focused on the light above us. If he is aware of me, he gives no indication.

I lie here for a few minutes simply accepting the impressions of my senses on a passive level. But I can't seem to evaluate them or form an independent thought. My mind is not working right. It is like an out of body experience where one's role is to be a passive observer of themselves.

The immense fear and confusion experienced in the presence of the being in the tunnel has passed. But perhaps it will return if I encounter it again. The thought of the being jars me. This is unreal! What the hell has happened to us? If I can believe my memory, Jeff and I have been abducted by some alien entity. We are being held against our will for God knows what purpose. Perhaps they've already experimented on Jeff.

There is a motion to my right at the fringe of my vision where the light in the tunnel is faint. A being, perhaps the one I had encountered, is leaning over a table intently working with what appears to be medical equipment. I cautiously move my head to get a better look. It is attaching an IV tube to a small body on the table…Ricky's body! I unconsciously jerk my head back with the shock of recognizing Ricky and the being looks directly at me, puts down the instruments, and begins to approach.

Seeing Ricky on the table floods my mind with thoughts of how incongruent this situation has become; much like a dream with elements of the familiar and the preposterous intermingled. Am I to truly believe that Ricky, Jeff, and I have been abducted and held by aliens in an abandoned mine in Montana? As I glance about the tunnel my eyes are becoming more focused and my head starts to slowly clear.

As I become more aware, I begin to notice things that don't fit. It occurs to me that I am not held in place by some exotic force field. Rather my wrists and ankles are bound by ordinary duct tape. The tunnel illumination is coming from a tripod portable light stand; the type you might find in your neighbor's garage. These aliens, or at least this alien, appear to shop at the Alta Valley Feed & Hardware.

The being is coming closer. I recognize the black robe and the hood covering the thin grey face that I encountered inside the mine. However, from the cold and uncomfortable vantage point here on the floor, I see, incredibly, that beneath the robe are blue jeans and cowboy boots, very expensive ostrich skin cowboy boots. Riley!

In an instant, it all makes sense. Of course! It was no coincidence that Riley shows up to join the search at the cross-country ski lodge. He purposely separated himself and Jeff from the search party. While the rest of us only experienced disorientation, odd sounds and weird lights, it was Riley who provided the only eyewitness account of Jeff's abduction. He must have kidnapped and hid Jeff himself. And then provided a vivid and detailed false account of the alien craft and how it drew Jeff aboard on a beam of light. Coming from a law enforcement officer, the story was even more credible, if fantastic.

"Playing for the other team, maybe another solar system, are we, Riley?" This comes out of my mouth hoarser and weaker than I would have liked.

This earns me an ostrich boot to the ribs. The result of another addition to the growing number of less than wise decisions I've accumulated for the day.

It hurts like hell, but the sudden pain is washing away the dullness of what must be a strong hallucinogenic drug dose.

"What are you going to do with Ricky?" I gasp as the pain spasms through my body.

"Ricky will be fine," Riley snarls, removing the alien mask. "He, his blood, his Nash blood, is priceless. You and your blood; not so much. In fact, you and your buddy there," he nods at Jeff, "are rapidly becoming an inconvenience to my colleagues and me." Riley strikes me as the sort of fellow who would have *dudes* rather than *colleagues* as associates...perhaps I've underestimated him. It is chilling to consider that there are others in this plot, how many? Certainly, Ranger Rick is a player. And where are they?

"This won't work. Wendover will be looking for me. He'll find the Jeep outside."

"Shut up!" This time he kicks me in the side of the head and I feel as though I've been struck by a train. Blood is flowing in my mouth, bitter, moist, and warm.

"It's going to be too late for you, asshole," he says menacingly. "We've been using this mine for some time and explored most of it. Down on the lower level I found a vertical shaft. Looked down it with a flashlight; couldn't see the bottom. Then I tossed a rock down and it took a long time to hear it splash. Must be a couple of hundred feet down to the water level. If the sheriff's office ever finds your body down there, they will just assume it was an unfortunate accident. A well-meaning but inexperienced city slicker starts nosing around the Sapphire Belle, looking for Ricky, and falls into a shaft. These old mines are dangerous places, eh?"

"And Jeff there," he continues, "well, people already think the aliens got him. So maybe we'll just push him off a cliff. Make it look like they dropped him out of a flying saucer or something. In any event, we have Ricky and we'll be long gone before anyone realizes you're missing."

So much for my Deadman's switch backup tactic. Riley likely shredded or tossed my note to Wendover at his first opportunity. The cavalry will not be heading out to save me and it might even be a day or two before they even realize I'm missing. Even then Riley will be in a perfect position to mislead the search, maybe tell them he overheard me making plans to return to California early.

I'm struggling to loosen the duct tape around my wrists but the tape seems to bind me more tightly the more I force it. Then I realize that Riley has bound my ankles by winding tape around my boots. The very loose, ill-fitting boots I was cursing on my walk up to the mine entrance. In one motion I swivel around and kick off my boots. Before Riley can react, I kick him hard in the knees and he tumbles back into the tripod light and it crashes to the floor. We are enveloped in darkness.

I reel away from Riley, twisting and smashing repeatedly along the wall in the dark. I don't know where I'm going, but far away from Riley seems like a good plan. Fortunately, I have a good fix on him in the blackness due to the steady stream of profanity coming from his direction. I need to move carefully; I'm not going to win a foot race here, not in stocking feet. At this point, I'm maybe a couple of hundred feet ahead of him, feeling my way along the tunnel. My head and ribs are pulsing with pain every time I breathe. Suddenly there is a shaft of light moving behind me. He's found a flashlight and is starting to close the distance with me.

Indirectly, the random swings of Riley's light in the distance behind me briefly illuminate the tunnel ahead of me in alternating darkness and light. To my left there is a pile of ore partially blocking a small adjoining tunnel that might offer a hiding place. I scramble over the rocks to hide, lose my balance, and find myself falling and sliding down a side tunnel which is dropping down at an alarmingly steep angle. My hands are still bound, so there is no opportunity to grab at the sides of the shaft to slow my decent.

The tunnel I'm sliding and rolling down is rapidly dropping into the darkness; away from Riley, but God knows where it is taking me. I remember Riley's remark about the vertical shaft and the promise of a watery grave and hope that is not where this terminates. Then, as suddenly as it began, my fall stops as I painfully sprawl across a mass of old support timbers and pieces of mining equipment.

"Walker?" Riley has reached the top of the side tunnel. I see dancing shafts of light from his flashlight illuminating the cloud of dust my downward tumble has stirred up. Looking around, I realize that this must at one time have been a supply chute which was used to slide materials and equipment down to the lower levels of the Sapphire Belle. Very efficient and but obviously not designed for human use. I slowly rise to my feet, bracing myself against a rusted compressor unit. The abruptness of my descent had flooded out my sense of pain momentarily, but it is now rushing back. My ribs and head are throbbing with every breath and for a moment I fear I will stagger and pass out.

Briefly, the diffuse light illuminates an old corroded mining company sign nailed to one of the timbers by the compressor. On it a caricature of a miner, pick in one hand, is grinning idiotically and pointing with his thumb to the slogan "Safety First!"

"I know you're down there", Riley shouts down the chute. "I see you've found the lower level. I'll join you shortly, but I prefer to take a better route." With that the light moves away and I am left alone to contemplate my rapidly dwindling options for survival.

I stop running for a moment to try to catch my breath. I suppose at some point everyone wonders about their own death. It's only human. How will I die? When will I die? Panting, I strain to listen for the footsteps of the man stalking me in the dark. With every step he takes towards me these questions become less and less abstract. It feels like a macabre game of Clue:… Walker…in the dark…slashed with a knife…very soon.

The who, when, where, and how questions of the homicide apparently in progress are unfortunately rapidly coming into focus. But there is a universe of unanswered questions as to the ultimate motive. Nash blood? What connects a ten-year-old boy to a World War II mystery ship that the Government seems hell-bent on erasing from history itself? A connection so powerful, so secret, I'm going to be killed as a loose end.

He's coming nearer. Incredibly, chuckling to himself as he searches for me. Just my luck, I'm being pursued by a madman with skill and motivation enough to kill me and he's sadistic enough to make a sport of it. I shake my head in disbelief. How the hell did I get myself in this mess? And, more importantly, how do I escape?

Wendover had said there are a hundred ways to die in these old mines. Cave-ins, gas pockets, and vertical shafts to name a few. He didn't even mention having your throat slashed by a homicidal freak in ostrich skin cowboy boots, which seems currently the most likely threat.

I lean against the compressor nearly choking in the fine dust kicked up by my tumble down the shaft. I've found a sharp edge on the machine which I'm using to cut through the duct tape still binding my wrists. Riley will undoubtedly be taking a better route down to the lower level than my bone jolting express line to the depths. I may have a few minutes, perhaps no more, before he reaches this part of the mine. For the first time I can stop hurling along in pure animal survival mode and try to make sense of what has happened.

Obviously, the trappings of an alien abduction were a masterful hoax to cover for a kidnapping plot. But why go to such an elaborate ruse? The effort, resources, and logistics must be daunting. And what is the pay-off? No ransom has been demanded. The focus must be Ricky himself. What was it Riley had said? That Ricky...his blood...was priceless. That Jeff and I were useless. We would be collateral damage that would not be missed.

That brings me to Riley himself. He is clearly not to be underestimated but I do not believe he masterminded this affair. Between administering boots to my ribs, he had mentioned other "colleagues". How many they number and where they are now is anyone's guess. The thought that I may encounter them deeper in the mine as I try to evade Riley is chilling.

I try to think of who else might be part of this conspiracy. Riley, of course, is the very definition of a dirty cop; are there others on the force? Potts? Sheriff Wendover? The boys in the Genesis crowd get my vote for being menacing pains in the ass, but aside from Anderson, they don't strike me as having the organization or motivation to pull this off.

I finally free my wrists from the tape. I am slowly taking stock of my surroundings. Riley, or someone, has been using this tunnel; small battery powered LED lamps have been placed along the walls every fifty feet or so to provide a minimum of pale red illumination once one's eyes adapt to the darkness. I now know the Sapphire Belle has at least two levels...are there more? And, most importantly, at what level is the second entrance to the mine? Or, are there multiple entrances? Unfortunately, I have no idea how this mine is laid out. Am I moving towards an entrance, and freedom, or simply further into a trap?

CHAPTER 35

I must start moving. To stay here will mean certain death. Some twenty yards down the tunnel, the shaft splits in two directions. Both have intermittent LED lighting. Randomly, I take the right tunnel hoping the odds are fifty percent he takes the left option. The tunnel runs for fifty yards or so until I come upon a small cutout on my right. It's a small room or cavern of sorts carved out originally, I suppose, to hold another compressor station. The cavern is very dark, even by the standards of the dim tunnel lighting. I lean into the room to see if it affords a hiding place and suddenly, I flinch back in fright. Someone, or something, in there is breathing!

I dart back into the tunnel, heart pounding, and grab one of the LED lights. Cautiously, I step back into the cavern holding the light in front of me, ready to confront whatever demon the darkness holds. What the faint light discloses is macabre. It's another makeshift medical room and it holds an unconscious figure, strapped to a hospital cot, arms festooned with IVs.

Even in the shadows I recognize his face, the familial line of the jaw. This is Stan Pruitt, Ricky's father. Like father, like son, the blood is apparently precious. Whatever our captors are seeking has a genetic basis. Now another piece falls into place. Of course! So precious was this bloodline that I bet they went three generations deep and robbed Ricky's grandfather, Ben, from the restful peace of his grave. What they took from his remains would not be blood but DNA. There must be something terribly special about the Pruitt DNA. It would also explain why Simone was not abducted with Ricky. She was Judy's child from a previous marriage, not related by blood to Stan or Ricky.

I touch Stan's wrist; it is cold but I feel a faint pulse. "Somehow," I tell his unknowing, unconscious face in a whisper, "I will get out of here and come back for you and Ricky. But now I must go." Indeed, I can hardly save him unless I can save myself and that means somehow evading Riley and escaping the depths of this wretched mine.

I turn to leave, but with my eyes now well-adjusted to the faint light, I see even further back in the room. To my astonishment there are two more still forms outstretched on medical cots. What the hell? I cross over to examine them more closely. With the dim light of the LED, it becomes apparent that I'm looking at two more victims. Two children, a boy and a girl, about the same age as Ricky lie sedated, unmoving.

The more closely I look at the children, the more it strikes me how much they look like each other; they are likely twins. And, not only do they look to be twins, they also have many distinct features that resemble Ricky himself. The dark, straight hair and pale complexions mirror Ricky. In fact, I'm betting if their eyes opened momentarily, I'd likely see amber eyes with flecks of gold. My guess is their appearance reflects physical markers of the genetic properties of keen interest to Riley and his cohorts.

It is not just the Pruitts that have precious DNA, the Nash blood, I think. Something happened with the USS Nash. Something the United States government wants to keep deeply classified. And the entire crew was likely affected, not just Ben Pruitt, the genetic effect compounding with each generation. These twins, I'm willing to bet, had a grandfather or great-grandfather who served on the Nash.

If the twins had the same genetic markers of interest, they likely also suffered from the same digestive enzyme issues that plagued Ricky. And, conveniently, the Stanton Clinic for Advanced Endocrine Studies, apparently operating out of a post office box in Santa Fe, New Mexico, just happened to be scouring the country for patients presenting with just those specific symptoms. They found the Pruitts, the twins, and who knows how many other Nash progeny.

With Jeff, Stan, and now the twins, there are four lives besides my own on the line. The stakes are increasing by the minute. I glance once more at Pruitt's unmoving form and step back into the tunnel.

I move now past the cavern and further down the tunnel. Distressingly, the walls are becoming narrower, suggesting I am moving towards a dead end in the mine rather than an entrance. Up ahead another branch appears. This time one tunnel branch is lit by LEDs, the other is not.

Now I must think like a murderer...a hunter of prey. If I were Riley, which tunnel would I suppose dear old Dr. Walker would choose? Would he choose the lighted tunnel in hopes it would lead to a tunnel entrance or take the unlit branch for the potential hiding places a dark route would afford him? Or would the hunted try reverse psychology and choose the less logical alternative to throw off the hunter? Perhaps in the end, it will not matter. Perhaps Riley will have the time and luxury to search both tunnels so any deception will be futile.

I choose the unlit route. I grab a LED light from the previous tunnel which makes for a barely serviceable flashlight and I quickly disappear down into the darkness. This tunnel is much narrower than previous tunnels and it is sloped downward at a more pronounced angle. To my surprise I feel a slight movement of air down here. This suggests a vent or another entrance may be near. But today has not been a day for luck and I try not to allow myself unfounded hope that I may stumble upon a way to the outside.

I turn a corner and find myself at yet another junction of tunnels. My tunnel appears to dead end just beyond a widened area where two other routes join at nearly right angles. At first it seems I must make another choice, but the left hand tunnel is blocked by a cave in. It is a jumble of rock and timbers. Turning to the right, my fear increases as I can detect faint flashlight scatters of light and the sound of boots on rock approaching down that branch.

More light flashes and footsteps are also approaching down the tunnel I just came from. Riley is catching up with me! I step forward a few paces and realize that my center tunnel dead ends in a gaping black hole surrounded by debris...the vertical shaft!

I spin around as Riley emerges from the shadows, grinning and sweating. He has me silhouetted in the glare of his light; my shadow dancing uncertainly against the rock walls. Off in the right-hand tunnel the approaching footsteps are getting louder. I'm trapped, nowhere to go!

Riley has a buck knife in his hand; its blade is serrated and menacing. "For a smart guy, Professor, you're damn easy to track," he scoffs. "I just followed the blood, dumbass."

He points to my foot. Running in my stocking feet I've managed to cut my foot. The sock is crimson, wet with blood. Given the constant throbbing pain from my face and ribs, the cut to my foot simply went unnoticed. He advances with the knife and I slowly back up, edging reluctantly towards the vertical shaft.

"I must thank you," he grins. "Really quite considerate." He's nodding towards the open shaft. "I thought I'd have to drag your body all the way down here to pitch it down the shaft, but now you've come down here all by yourself and saved me the trouble, eh?"

"Goodbye, Doc," he lunges forward with the blade. I reflexively step back, over the edge and suddenly I am falling backwards into the darkness of the shaft. For a brief split second, at the corner of my vision, I see the image of Anderson and Pullman emerging from the other tunnel. I will at least die knowing Riley's co-conspirators!

CHAPTER 36

My fall is brief and terrifying. In a fraction of a second, my body slams painfully against a large timber lodged across the shaft, perhaps eight feet below the rim. I lie there stunned, my breath taken away and my prior injuries inflamed tenfold by the impact. I'm trying not to utter a sound in pain or even breathe loudly. Hopefully Riley and Anderson will assume I'm dead and move on.

The tactic is short lived. In moments, I am illuminated by a flashlight beam. Anderson appears at the rim. What follows next is stunning.

"Hang on there, Walker," he shouts, "we'll get you out of there directly. Are you okay? Can you move?"

He sees my shock and hesitation. Why doesn't he just finish the job? All it will take is another push or a quick bullet.

"No, no!" he chuckles, "we're on your side; we're the good guys! Tell you what, if I drop down my vest, can you grab it and hold on so I can pull you up?"

He takes off his bulletproof vest and lowers it to me. I am shocked to see it has large block letters inscribed in yellow: DOD FEDERAL AGENT.

As I am pulled out of the shaft, I am amazed to see Riley, handcuffed and prone on the ground. Held by gunpoint in custody by Pullman, also sporting a federal agent vest.

Pullman nods to me. "We have three more of his buddies in custody. Tripp and Spence caught 'em back at the rear mine entrance."

The tunnels around us are now lighting up with the flashlights of many more federal-vested law enforcement officers. To my relief they are accompanied by a couple of paramedics with a stretcher.

"Introductions are way past due," says Anderson. "My full title is Colonel James Anderson, US Army, on special assignment. My colleague is Staff Sergeant Jake Pullman. There will be plenty of time for explanations, but let's get you out of here and to the hospital first."

Colonel Anderson grasps me by the hand and motions the paramedics. "Get this man on that stretcher and please give him something for the pain."

A young paramedic helps him lift me onto the stretcher, pokes me with an IV drip, and they begin to guide me out of the mine. To my relief I see Jeff and the Pruitts are also being helped onto stretchers.

"Everyone's okay?" I'm asking Anderson as we reach the main mine entrance.

"Yes, everyone is doing well and safe," he replies. "And, it turns out that you're probably in the worst condition by far out of the lot. Jeff and the Pruitts are going to be just fine."

"Wait?" I ask. "There were others. I saw them. A boy and a girl about Ricky's age. They were in the same side cavern as Stan."

A puzzled look from Anderson and the paramedics. They exchange a glance. "No. Sorry, Dr. Walker, there were no other victims in the mine. All tunnels have been searched and all the kidnapped have been accounted for. It was very dark in there and you were severely injured when you found Stan. You must have been mistaken or just not remembering things correctly."

As I'm taken out of the mine entrance, I'm surprised that it has become twilight. The cold air feels good on my skin. The front has moved through and a light snow is beginning to fall. As I'm carried down the access road and approach the turnoff from Two Goat it becomes clear this has been a major operation.

In addition to the waiting ambulances, there are a dozen other vehicles, emergency lights strobing, from the sheriff's department, state patrol, as well as numerous military and other federal agency vehicles. It looks as though any wanted felons in the state can relax and take the night off. Half of the federal, state, and local law enforcement officers in Western Montana appear to be up here on Two Goat Road. I notice two other vans, white and unmarked with GSA plates, are parked near the ambulances.

Anderson is still clutching my hand as we near the ambulance. "You're a hero," he says. "We couldn't have penetrated the mine without you."

I'm perplexed. "What do you mean?"

"We had that mine under surveillance for days. Riley and his crew had rigged that whole area, the perimeter of the mine, with a grid of sensors and alarms. If we had openly approached the mine, they would have held your student and the Pruitts as hostages, maybe even killed them. But we knew you would come to investigate the mine. And, sure enough, we saw you walk right in, setting all the grid sensors off. We then came in behind you and infiltrated the rear mine entrance before they had a chance to reset the grid.

"What? You *knew* I would come here?"

I blink, trying to comprehend this. Even with my injuries and the increasing fog of the pain killer, I am beginning to realize that they let me walk right into that trap. Used me as an unwitting decoy. If I'd been given the choice, I'd have gladly volunteered to play it the same way all over again. Hell, I'd walk through fire to rescue Jeff and the Pruitts. But damn it, I should have been given that choice. And the real mystery is how they were certain I would come here in the first place? Apparently, they knew I would come to the mine even before I knew I was headed here.

"Well, yes." Anderson smiles slightly. "Let's say we took the liberty of… hacking is such a crude term. Let's just say we adjusted your student Jeff Tanaka's data files on the paranormal events so that the resulting patterns would draw a bright line for LISA right to the Sapphire Belle. Of course, we were a bit surprised you were alone. We had thought you'd bring Sheriff Wendover with you. But nevertheless, you triggered the sensor grid and gave us our chance."

I am trying to process this. It's troubling on several levels. In our prior Two Goat encounter, I never mentioned that the system we were using to analyze the sociological and criminal data patterns in Benton County was called LISA. Yet he seems to know quite a bit about her. Enough apparently to hack the servers back at the Machine Learning Lab at UCLA and modify certain input files. Much like the old timers had salted the mineral assays to distort the true value of the Sapphire Belle ore, Anderson and Pullman had salted the BCSF dataset! I was looking for a pattern and found what I expected to see. A data fit that was remarkably perfect, in fact, far too perfect!

"Then," Anderson continues, "once you had triggered the alarms and we were in place, it was just a matter of waiting for the right moment of tactical advantage to sweep in when their attention was distracted."

"You bastard!" I shout. "Riley was distracted by the sound of his boot smashing into my head! Why didn't you seize your precious moment of tactical advantage about a minute before he started kicking the shit out of me! You used me as bait, live bait!"

The young paramedic's eyes are growing wide. The kid looks at me and then back over to Anderson. "There, there," smiles Anderson broadly at the paramedic. "That's just the pain killer talking. Son, take real good care of this man. The federal government owes him more than he realizes at this moment. Much more." Anderson pats my shoulder gently. "Don't worry, my new friend. We will have much to discuss when you're feeling better." He makes an upward motion to the paramedic who I now slowly realize is also military, "his pain seems worse, please up the dose."

"Yes-sir."

"Pain killer, my ass," I sputter, belatedly realizing that the good colonel has seen to it that my arms have been strapped tight to the stretcher. A few other sarcastic and profane remarks are coming to mind but the medication is indeed kicking in and I'm beginning to fade out. Just as I'm being loaded into the ambulance, I glance at one of the unmarked white vans. The van is full of instrumentation and sample racks. A serious looking man is putting on a full-up biohazard suit.

In my dream, Marty and I are deer. We are running in fear across a darkened meadow on a moonless night. A shadowy predator is behind us, just out of sight. I glance back to see two red eyes; and turn too late to avoid becoming entangled in the fence…

CHAPTER 37

I turn over and over in the darkness. I am a deer trapped in a barbed-wire fence. I struggle to get free but a dark figure, an alien, is approaching. It's reaching for me. I'm drawn to its massive unblinking black eyes that are somehow both paralyzing me and drawing me closer. I can't move. I try to scream but can produce no sound. I turn over and over, struggling against the fence wire which only serves to bind me more tightly. Then I blink and the scene instantly changes. Now the alien is gone and it is the deer looking down at me. It reaches down and begins to lick my hand and then my face. A slobbering lick punctuated with dog breath...

"What...Zeke!"

Zeke happily responds with another lick and nudges my hand, no doubt hoping for a treat. The world slowly starts to come into focus. I'm in a hospital room with Wendover and Jeff at my bedside.

"Good morning, Sunshine!" Wendover smiles and pats me on the shoulder. "You had us all worried with your little stunt yesterday."

I start to sit up in the bed but then quickly slump back down. It is as if every part of my body is jealousy vying for attention as the most injured. The jabs of pain are leavened with waves of nausea, likely from the pain killers they've must have given me.

"I feel like shit."

"You look worse," says Jeff.

"To be specific," grins Wendover, "your face looks like it was first eaten by a monkey and then shit off a cliff."

I'd be offended, but the way I'm feeling, he may not be exaggerating.

"What are the damages?" I ask. "How badly am I injured?"

"Bad enough," replies Wendover. "Doc says two severely bruised ribs and another's likely broken. They think you have had a moderate concussion and a badly sprained ankle. A shit-load of other contusions and lacerations. Other than that, you're in tip-top shape."

"Great," I say weakly.

"Bottom line, you'll live. But the next couple of days may be so painful you may wish you hadn't. And another thing," he continues, grinning, "Doc says you should limit getting the shit kicked out of you and falling down mine shafts to no more than twice a year. Could be habit forming."

"Oh, you're real hilarious."

"Zeke," I say, stroking the big fella under the chin, "Buddy, you can visit me anytime. But next time leave that wise-ass sheriff back at the office." Zeke wags, looks in my eyes and gives me a concerned whine. Probably the only genuine sympathy I'll get from this crowd.

"Kate?" She'll be worried sick.

"She's flying into Missoula this morning. She's going to meet up with your daughter Amy. They'll rent a car and drive over. Normally I'd have sent a deputy to pick them up but I'm a bit short handed. Down a deputy as you know."

"It was Riley all along," I say.

"Yeah. Who knew I'd have a goddamned wolf in the fold?"

"Dr. Chandra has been calling on the hour to see how you're doing," says Jeff. "All of Team LISA is very concerned."

"Jeff," I reply, "you look to be in pretty fair condition for someone who has been beamed aboard a flying saucer and abducted by aliens."

"Yeah," he laughs, rubbing the back of his head, "got a bump here where Riley smacked me with the butt of his pistol and knocked me out. Then his buddy, Ranger Rick, apparently injected me with a sedative and hauled me from Larch Mountain over to the mine on back roads. I was a bit groggy from all the sedatives but doing fine now."

"Why you?" I ask. "No offense, but why were you abducted? You weren't related to the Pruitts. You didn't have that special 'Nash blood' they supposedly found to be so precious."

Jeff laughs. "I think my 'abduction' really wasn't a part of their original plan at all."

According to Jeff, Riley and his cohorts had only planned to put on a little light and sound show to spook the locals at Larch Mountain. But something went wrong. A drone had malfunctioned and dropped to the ground right by the trail where Jeff and Riley had been hiking. They had turned a corner on the trail and there was Ranger Rick trying to repair the drone. Jeff and Rick instantly recognized one another. At that point, Jeff remembers thinking it odd that Riley wasn't challenging Rick; asking him what the hell he's doing with the drone out here. Jeff then saw Riley and Rick exchange a glance like they knew each other and were in on the scheme together. Then Riley smacked Jeff with his pistol and it was lights out.

"So, what the hell is all of this really all about?" I ask. "I remember being brought out of the mine and realizing that bastard Anderson had played me; used me for live bait. But why? What was really going down? Why were the Feds, the military involved? I take it the whole alien abduction scare was a ruse, but why? Why go to all the trouble?"

"I only have a few of the answers," says Wendover. "In typical Fed fashion, they kept the locals, and especially 'County Mounties' like myself, in the dark. I was only invited to the party about the time they were bringing you out of the mine. Early this morning I received a summary of the operation which was heavily redacted; about half of the damned sentences were blacked out."

"The gist of the story," he continues, "from what I can tell, is that some rogue pharmaceutical company, perhaps fronting for a foreign government, mistakenly believed that the Pruitts had a genetic mutation that could be extremely beneficial if identified and replicated."

"Ricky's medical condition, the one that he was taking supplements to address?"

"Apparently. But this company's research approach required that blood and tissue samples were to be collected secretly and frequently from several generations of Pruitts. They would have to be abducted and sedated for the procedures on a frequent basis."

"So, this company had researchers posed as aliens?"

"Not researchers. This company apparently contracted some guns for hire. Mercenaries. It was their idea to pull off the alien abduction deception. Turns out these guys, Riley, your Ranger Rick, and the others were ex-special forces types who had experience specializing in psych-ops. Riley, by the way, was a late recruit. They decided it would be helpful to have a local law enforcement officer on the payroll."

"Psych-ops? I've heard of these sorts of military specialists. They got their start in Vietnam, right?"

"Probably before that, but they rose to prominence in that war. The idea was to get inside the enemy's heads. Exploit local superstitions and archetypes to drive fear and confusion in the ranks. In Vietnam, for example, they would kill Vietcong and position their corpses in such a fashion as to suggest local spirits and ghosts were out in the jungle stalking the enemy in the dark."

"So, roll forward to twenty-first century America," I nod. "Every other movie either has someone fighting aliens or being abducted by them."

"Yup. Talk about exploiting your local superstitions and archetypes. What a perfect cover for the operation. If Ricky or Stan ever remembered they were abducted, it would come across as some wild alien tale that no one would believe."

"Law enforcement would be rendered impotent."

"I'd prefer a different choice of words, but yes, we really couldn't seriously investigate a supposed alien abduction without getting laughed out of the county. They salted the mine, so to speak, with a bunch of paranormal occurrences...my Strange Files. That kept us off balance and chasing our tails. No offense, Zeke." Zeke wags, none taken.

"But something happened, required them to escalate."

"The report is a bit cryptic, but it appears that up until last week, their research protocols had only required periodic abductions of an hour or two for the Pruitts. Then they moved into a final more stringent phase which would have required them to take custody of the Pruitts for an extended period of time.

"More than a night-time disappearance?"

"Yup. Stan and Ricky's extended absence would have obviously been noticed by lots of people, so they made a very large and public psych-ops strike to stage rather bold abductions in Alta Junction and Butte so they could hustle the Pruitts out of the county in the confusion. Also heisted Grandpa Pruitt from the cemetery to get a sample of his DNA and as a bonus created even more paranormal mystery. Then they briefly took Judy away to plant more seeds of alien intrigue."

"Laid a whole school of red herrings across our paths," I say. "And they offered a narrative that true believers like Walter Berman and his fellow travelers in Skywatch were all too eager to embrace and amplify."

"Their grand play to sow maximum confusion was the encounter at the Griffith Lodge which," Wendover pauses to slap Jeff on the back, "resulted in our friend here apparently being abducted by aliens in a UFO event played out in front of a dozen witnesses."

"Very clever," I say, "and as we now know, those witnesses really only saw the trappings of the supposed aliens. Strange lights and noises in the woods. The only witness who described Jeff actually being taken into an alien ship was Riley who was in on the scheme."

"All smoke and mirrors," says Wendover, "and scopolamine."

"Scopolamine? The so-called Zombie drug?"

"Yeah, except it really doesn't really turn you into a zombie. Although, in your case, that might have been rather entertaining to see. What it does do at certain dose levels is disorient you and make one very susceptible to suggestions. The report from the Feds indicates that Riley's cohorts dosed everyone outside the Griffith Lodge with a military grade aerosolized variant of the drug."

"That was the sickly-sweet smell in the air," I say. "Later, as I approached the mine, there was that same smell. They must have dosed me again. And, sure enough, the supposed alien I encountered there seemed very authentic to me at the time."

"From what I understand," explains Wendover, "under the influence of that drug, once you're given a suggestion and primed to expect a certain thing, your mind fills in the blanks. If you're primed to see aliens, that's what you see."

The ultimate conditioned response, I think.

"Apophenia," adds Jeff as we both look at him blankly. "Apophenia is the mind's ability to see patterns that only partially exist. From an evolutionary adaptive standpoint, it's probably quite valuable for survival. We humans don't have time to fully process all of the images and sounds that bombard us constantly, so we take partial samples and fill in the rest based on our expectations. Scopolamine must somehow hijack that function of our minds."

"To make us see patterns that are false or nonexistent?" I ask.

"Yes. But remember, for the most part, Apophenia is a good thing. It helps us efficiently make sense of the world. But the downside is that sometimes it causes us to fill in too many blanks or fill in the wrong blanks. The scopolamine would appear to enhance this downside, making us see real aliens instead of fake ones, particularly if we were primed to expect the real ones."

"Another thing," continues Wendover, "the report mentions that Riley's crew apparently used something called infrasound to further disorient the Griffith witnesses."

"The booming sound we somehow felt more than heard," I say. "Sounded like the deep base coming from some teenager's car subwoofers."

"Um, infrasound," says Jeff, "turns out I studied it a bit as an undergraduate."

"First apophenia and now infrasound? Who knew we'd had an expert on both in our midst? Go on and enlighten us, Mr. Spock!" I exclaim.

Jeff rolls his eyes at the ribbing. "Infrasound refers to sound waves propagating at frequencies lower than the threshold of human hearing."

"That's what, about twenty hertz?"

"Correct. And what's interesting and perhaps germane to what happened at the lodge is that recent studies seem to indicate that large predators, primarily feline, lions and tigers, may use infrasound to help disorient and stun their prey. Turns out that a significant portion of the sound energy emitted by their roars and growls is resonating below twenty hertz and it can significantly disrupt the brain functions of their prey."

"So," I say, "with our thinking and perceptions disrupted by the scopolamine and infrasound, no wonder we were seeing aliens behind every rock and tree."

"About the time I arrived on scene at the mine," says Wendover, "the Feds had some guys suited up to go retrieve a radiation source Riley and the gang had squirreled away down in the mine. Turns out the mercenaries had gotten a hold of some material containing medical grade isotopes. They used that to trigger the radiation detection sensors at the Butte jail."

"And throw more paranormal chum in the waters. To add to the consternation of your buddy, Sheriff Broadcliff."

"Yeah, he'll get over it...maybe. Anyway, the isotope source is now in the custody of the Department of Energy. The report indicated that the operation was a success. Riley and four others are in custody. They retrieved a bunch of equipment used in the deception. Lights, drones, infrasound projectors, stuff like that. And, of course, the two of you were rescued as well as the Pruitts. Stan and Ricky are doing well and Grandpa Ben's corpse was also recovered. So, I guess the case is closed and wrapped up with a bow, eh?"

"Wait," I say, "there were no other abductees rescued?"

"No?" I'm getting blank looks from both of them.

"In the mine. I saw two other children; they were about Ricky's age. Looked like maybe they were twins. And they had features very similar to Ricky. You know, coal black hair, pale complexions."

Wendover shifts uneasily. "No one else was removed from the Sapphire Belle, twins or otherwise. Um, maybe you got a bigger dose of that zombie gas than we thought."

"I know what I saw! They were down there right next to Stan! Sedated and laying on cots."

"I don't know what to say. The report doesn't mention any other victims removed from the mine. Of course, like I said, half of the report was redacted. Maybe there was mention of these twins in the portions that were blacked out."

No, I'm thinking. This is far from being neatly wrapped up with a bow. There are still too many loose ends. The twins? Hillie getting the third degree over asking questions about the USS Nash and then disappearing himself? The federal government and the military apparently deeply involved with a child's disappearance in rural Montana? Why? Something is out of balance. The causes and effects are not tying together here.

"Well, we should be going," says Wendover, "We'll let the medical staff know you're awake. Looks like ole' Nurse Ratched has some meds teed up for you out in the hall. Geez, one of the pills looks to be an inch and a half long."

"An inch and a half? How am I supposed to swallow that?"

"Given the shape of it, I don't think it's going in on that end," he says with a grin and a mischievous laugh as they head out the door. Zeke gives me one last look and a sympathetic whine as he follows them out.

CHAPTER 38

"For as much as it has pleased our Heavenly Father in His wise providence to take unto Himself our beloved Benjamin, we therefore commit his body to the ground, um,...again, earth to earth, ashes to ashes, dust to dust, as we look for the blessed hope and the glorious appearing of the great God in our Savior Jesus Christ…"

The good Pastor Ronnie Stevens is fumbling a bit with the special reburial services the Pruitts had requested. He's clearly not used to return customers. It's a cold gray morning. The cloud cover lays low and thick, obscuring the mountain ranges that encircle the valley. We are gathered to place the elder Ben Pruitt back to rest in the Riverside Cemetery. In a sense, I suppose, he is the last prisoner to return from the grip of that great war so long ago.

Judy Pruitt is standing across the grave site from me, her arms wrapped around Stan, Ricky, and Simone. For a moment our eyes meet and she smiles and nods at her family, now reunited.

"....to await the fulfillment of another promise of scripture."

Pastor Stevens is regaining his stride, betraying a little nervousness by idly adjusting his cleric collar as he speaks. He's young and earnest. Handsome, I suppose, in a shy, bookish sort of way. With his boyish good looks and the unstated notion that he may perhaps have the Almighty on speed dial, the older women in his congregation likely consider him charming. And the younger ladies may consider him an increasingly eligible bachelor relative to the local market. A local dating scene where it is said, only half-jokingly, that the odds are good but the goods are odd. Stevens speaks with great knowledge and affection of the deceased; a man who I'm told he has never met.

As he continues his eulogy, we are assured that Pruitt was a man of faith and surely quite overjoyed to meet his Creator despite the deceased's tragic and untimely separation from family, friends, and his earthly affairs. I expect that projecting familiarity and empathy with departed strangers is pretty much a job requirement in Stevens' trade and he is good at it.

I glance up at the other several dozen or so townsfolk gathered around the grave site. Most are here out of respect for Ben, but I suspect some have come out of sheer curiosity. News of the foiled plot and the recovery of the Pruitts at the Sapphire Belle has flashed through this small community like a lightning strike.

"And although I walk through the Valley of Death..." Stevens is now working through a couple of Psalms on his way to wrapping this up.

Several in attendance are pointedly staring at me as though I might have perhaps spent a little too much time in the shadow of the Valley of Death myself and might be Stevens' next customer here at Riverside. Truth is I probably do look like death warmed over. The face is very vascular and susceptible to bruising; most of mine is swollen and blossoming purple from Riley's beating. And I'm leaning unsteadily on a crutch for support with a brace around my chest to buttress my broken ribs.

Propping me up on my left side is Kate still looking a bit stunned and trying to get her head around the events of the past several days. Much like someone who has walked late into a movie in the middle of the final scenes, she's glancing about, trying to figure out the cast of characters and piece together the plot. And I imagine once she decides I'm healthy enough for the abuse, she'll give me a piece of her mind about how mild-mannered professors should stay out of abandoned mines featuring homicidal maniacs.

Wendover is standing on my right. As Stevens concludes with the last amen, Wendover leans over to Kate. Quietly he whispers, "Kate, your husband is very lucky to be here in the cemetery looking down at the green side of the turf instead of looking up at the brown side of the lawn. Has he always lacked some basic common sense?"

She's all smiles, "to be honest, Dan, I married him for his looks rather than his common sense."

Mock surprise from Wendover, "gee, if you're telling me he has more looks than common sense, he's worse off than I thought!"

Kate and Wendover bonded nearly immediately when they were introduced in my hospital room. It has not escaped me that they are comfortably now on a first name basis. This has the makings of an unholy alliance at my expense. Just what I need, two sharp wits with first-hand knowledge of my weaknesses and failings.

Aside from my beaten and bruised countenance, the other object of the town's curiosity at the service is Colonel Anderson standing proudly at attention in full dress uniform. Quite a few of the townsfolk have been pointedly staring at him. They're still in disbelief that the in-your-face survivalist compound promoter was all this time an undercover government agent.

During my recovery, Wendover and I had rehashed several times the federal government's involvement in the Pruitt affair. And Anderson's particular role was as mysterious as it was intriguing.

"I know I'm just a small-town Montana sheriff," Wendover had grumbled, "but next time the Feds run a major operation in my backyard, dammit, they could at least give me a little heads-up."

Somehow the conspiracy involving the Pruitt's Nash blood apparently came to the attention of the federal government which formed a military response. Neither Wendover nor I could fathom why the government was running a covert military operation on United States soil. Such matters would normally appear to be the province of a civilian agency such as the FBI.

It seemed the challenge Anderson had faced was how to blend in undercover in a small community in which everyone knew each other. The solution apparently was to hide in plain sight, taking a high-profile stance as the supposed leader of a survivalist compound land acquisition group. It afforded a perfect cover for conducting surveys of the valley. The survivalist milieu trends to the paramilitary, so no one was especially surprised Anderson and his crew were packing firepower. Anderson's cover was so attention-grabbing and audacious that it was difficult for anyone to imagine he would have had ulterior motives.

I glance over and glare at Anderson. He returns my look with a smile.

Now the casket is being lowered. Judy and Ricky are placing hand-fulls of soil upon it as it slowly slides down on casters. Off to the side, some retirees in VFW hats are playing pre-recorded taps on a boombox. Anderson turns away from me and salutes the casket.

The ceremony has concluded. As the crowd begins to socialize and disburse, I see Anderson heading our way. He walks up to us briskly and extends his hand. "Dr. Walker, how are you doing?" He's all chummy and grinning like we're old schoolmates catching up at a class reunion.

"Sheriff, perhaps you can introduce me to Judy and her family. It certainly seems as they've been through a lot lately." Kate has caught the near instant change in my demeanor at Anderson's approach and wisely decided now would be a good time to make a graceful exit from the conversation.

"Gladly," replies Wendover as they start to walk away together, "I think these two have some catching up to do anyway." Kate quickly glances back at me with a you-stay-out-of-trouble look.

I grudgingly take Anderson's hand and shake it. "How am I doing? I've been better. The important thing is that Ricky is safe and back with his family."

He puts a hand on my shoulder, "I just want, on behalf of the United States government, to thank you for your efforts in saving Ricky and his father."

"Look, Colonel," I pause and just shake my head. An off-color retort has come to mind, but I decide to stifle it. "Yeah, well tell the United States government that they're welcome, okay?"

"And," he continues, "I want to again apologize for what happened to you in the mine. It could not be avoided."

"Yeah, I got it. A little lie in service of the truth. That's your specialty. You know, if you really want to thank me there is one thing you can do."

"Gladly."

"Well, you can tell me what the hell is really going on here? The federal government committed resources to this investigation way out of proportion to the circumstances of a simple kidnapping. Why? And you've conducted a military operation on domestic soil in what should be a civilian law enforcement case. Makes no sense."

Anderson smiles and puts his hand on my shoulder. "You're right, there is far, far more to this than you can imagine. I, we, owe you an explanation. More than that, I have a proposition for you. We need your help."

"What? You've got another criminal hideout to breach? Last time I 'helped' you I got a boot to the face for my trouble."

"Jack, clearly, we have some trust issues. Not that I can blame you. But if you cannot yet trust me, would you trust the word of your friend, Admiral Hillenbrand?"

"Well, I'd certainly like to know what's happened to Hillie. He's been missing for several days now."

"The admiral is perfectly fine and in fact he's just joined our little enterprise. Would you like to hear from him?"

"Of course, and so would his daughter by the way."

"Excellent. Do you still have the encrypted cell phone he sent you?" he asks.

"Sure. Wait! How did you know…"

He smiles patiently, like he's explaining something to a small and perhaps not very bright child. "Please check the voice messages on the phone. There will be a message from Hillenbrand attesting to my bona fides and the seriousness of our mission. Assuming you're then willing to at least consider taking a next step, would you be available for another discussion in a day or two? I have something to show you and someone you need to meet."

"I suppose I might be open to a conversation if Hillie vouches for you. I'm wrapping up the study here tomorrow. Then it's off to Helena to close out that project. After that I have some personal business to attend to up by Flathead Lake."

Anderson turns to leave and then pauses. "I want you to know that we have Riley and his cohorts under our custody in a very secure location."

"GITMO?"

He manages a sly smile. "If you like." The implication being that Guantanamo Bay would be an airy country club in comparison with their current quarters. Fine with me. Anderson could put them a hundred feet under the ground in a dark cell and throw away the key. It would be better than they deserve.

He continues, "with a little persuasion, they confessed to everything. How they staged the deceptions: the lighted drones, infrasound projectors, the scopolamine aerosol, and the costumes. Everything except the bull. Levi Waddle's mutilated bull, they didn't do it. They had no means to do that."

"Then who...?"

"Let me leave you with a thought. Hypothetically, suppose I told you I like to put on a fake bear costume and run around the woods scaring little kids. What would I be?" he asks.

"An asshole?"

"A fraud." He's looking annoyed. "I'd be a fraud. But the fact I'd be a fraud running around the woods as a fake bear certainly wouldn't mean real bears don't exist in those same woods, would it?"

He raises an eyebrow and gives me a knowing smile. "I'll see you in a couple of days. I understand pheasant hunting season has just opened in central Montana. Perhaps you can join me for an outing. You could get some fresh air and see some new scenery, eh? And we could talk about how you could perhaps assist the government with a very serious and vital issue. Trust me, we'll, in fact, be talking about a hunt of a different kind, one of enormous consequence. Global consequence." The colonel winks and starts to walk away. "I will be in touch."

I nod slowly. But my mind is racing elsewhere. I'm thinking of Riley. The deputy watching Judy's hypnosis session back in Interrogation Room One. And the look of utter shock on his face when Judy mentions how the current aliens look and act so much differently than the ones she's encountered *previously.*

The look of a guy who's pulled off posing as a fake bear only to realize there may be real ones out in these woods.

PART II - THE PROGENY

CHAPTER 39

FAR ABOVE US A GOLDEN EAGLE IS SOARING ACROSS THE AFTERNOON SKY, LIFTED by unseen thermals. She tilts a wing in our direction. To her, we are but small insignificant specks in the vast rolling hills of Broadwater County in central Montana. For a moment she scans us; but we are quickly dismissed. We are neither predators nor prey and merit no further consideration. With a flick of her wing, she begins a lazy figure-eight course to the south and slowly wheels out of sight.

To the eagle above and anyone else who happens upon us in this isolated countryside, Colonel Anderson and I are ostensibly hunters pursuing pheasants or other game birds. Apparently always eager to hide in plain sight, Anderson has chosen this cover and this location with particular care. It gives us an excuse to be both isolated and openly armed with pump-action over-and-under Benelli's. I haven't checked the shells myself, but I'm betting the shotguns are loaded for buckshot, not birdshot.

We've been proceeding up a trail along a broad bench flanked by deep ravines on each side. Anyone else that approaches by vehicle or on foot will be seen for miles. This vast openness is a remarkably secure place to discuss a secret.

Further, this particular bench is bisected by a set of massive five-hundred kilovolt power lines. Not far from here, power generated from distant coal-fired generating stations in Eastern Montana connects to the Bonneville Power Administration grid to supply energy to customers west of the

Continental Divide. The lines are humming directly above us and I can feel the faint tingling of their electromagnetic fields on my skin. I'm sure our position below the lines is not an accident. The energy fields here are strong enough to preclude any uninvited third-party electronic eavesdropping or, I suppose, render any recording device I might be concealing inoperable.

I had some trepidation about meeting Anderson here. A shotgun can keep a secret from being repeated and I am reminded of Wendover's and my running joke about the few murders and the many hunting accidents in Montana. And Anderson's burned me once before. Albeit, he had his reasons, but using me as human bait in the Sapphire Belle was not, in my mind, entirely justified. The only reason I'm here now was the urgency and sincerity of Hillie's recorded message on my encrypted burner phone, vouching for Anderson and his organization. However, as an extra precaution, I was sure to let Wendover know that Anderson and I were having this little rendezvous in the guise of a bird hunting outing.

Hillie's message on my encrypted burner phone was clear and brief. He said he had been asked to join a highly classified program named eGenesis. Obviously, he couldn't discuss the scope and particulars of the program any further until I agreed to participate and was read into the security protocols. The program, according to Hillie, was absolutely vital to both the security of the nation and, intriguingly, the world itself. He said my expertise was badly needed to help counter a serious threat. A threat to everyone on the planet, obviously including our families. He hoped I would agree to meet up with Anderson and a Dr. Winston Monroe, the program's director.

Indeed, Anderson and I have a third member of our pseudo hunting party with us on the trail this morning. But I'm not sure even the most casual observer would mistake Winston Monroe for an actual hunter. In his late sixties with a distinguished looking beard and a serious bearing, he's pointedly not carrying a gun. And in his rush to meet up with us, he apparently had no time to visit a local sporting goods shop for gear. Monroe is sporting an orange hunter's vest over a blue button-down oxford cloth dress shirt with crisply pressed khaki chinos and penny loafers. The penny loafers are clearly not a match for the trail and he's huffing and puffing, struggling a bit to keep up over the half mile or so we've covered so far. I'm moving a little slowly myself as my ankle is still a little tender from my recent injuries in the Sapphire Belle.

I don't know Monroe personally, only by reputation which is considerable. He is broadly known in academic circles. A professor at MIT primarily published in the nascent field of theoretical and synthetic biology. Meeting at the trailhead this morning, I joked that central Montana seemed a bit far afield from his Cambridge labs. His response was a bit cryptic and unsettling. He softly noted that in the days ahead perhaps we will all have to push far out of our comfort zones.

Anderson has now pulled to a stop here directly underneath the power lines. He's apparently satisfied that this will be a good spot to have a conversation regarding this "eGenesis" program.

"It is pretty out here," he begins, gesturing across the landscape, "sometimes you can take the beauty of our planet for granted. We shouldn't. The Earth is far more fragile than people realize. I'm glad you agreed to come out here and talk. Look, I said I owed you an explanation, but it's much more than that. It's an explanation...to the extent anyone can explain it, but also a recruiting pitch. I, we...your country, need your help."

"Yeah, Hillie gave me the pre-recruiting pitch, although he obviously couldn't go into details."

"Good, but first things first," he's fishing papers out of his jacket, "here, I need you to sign a couple of forms. You are about to be briefed on restricted information that pertains to a Sensitive Compartmentalized Information program that is deeply classified by the US Government."

"Wait," I say, "don't I need a security clearance to be read into something like that? Specifically, an SCI-level clearance?"

"Well, um, we've recently completed an expedited background check and have taken the liberty of granting you a clearance," he's smiling wryly.

Ah, now it makes sense. Kate had said the Feds were asking questions in the neighborhood about my background. Supposedly to support a classified DoD contract. A contract that, at the time, was a mystery to me.

"I guess, in the interests of time, you skipped the part where the security clearance applicant must first authorize the government to rummage through their personal records and interview friends and neighbors about one's loyalty to the nation?"

"Yes, we sort of speeded through several bureaucratic formalities. Indeed, time is of the essence here. In ways you will shortly appreciate. I need you to sign these clearance papers," he requests.

"Here is a clearance acceptance and an oath of non-disclosure. In reality, this is pretty much a formality since if you were to repeat any of this to the general public no one would ever believe you and you would be labeled a fraud. A serious academic like yourself might even lose tenure."

"More technically," he continues, "I need to inform you that your signature binds you to the requirements and penalties of US Code Title 50 regarding security clearances related to special compartmentalized programs. Unauthorized disclosure of classified information may result in fines plus imprisonment of no less than ten years."

"In essence, a life sentence," adds Monroe dourly.

"Ten years, a life sentence? Hey, I'm not that old!" I'm thinking this is maybe a weak attempt at humor. But the look on Monroe's face is dead serious. Whatever we are about to discuss, the topic will not be lighthearted.

"Where to start?" says Anderson, laying his shotgun against a power line tower footing as I sign the papers. "Dr. Monroe, I assume you'll do the honors and give Dr. Walker an overview of what we're up against?"

On cue, Monroe begins, "Are you familiar with the term 'terraforming'?"

Terraforming? This is going about as far afield as you can get from kidnapping, I think.

"Yeah," I reply, "I'm vaguely aware of the term. I guess notionally it refers to an approach in which we would gradually change the environment of another planet to make it habitable for humans. Mostly the stuff of science fiction but there have been a few serious scientific papers written suggesting it might be feasible for, say, Mars."

"And, do you recall what the general terraforming approach for Mars might entail...at its simplest non-technical level?"

Well, this is the last topic I'd imagine discussing with an MIT theoretical biologist and an Army colonel in a remote section of the Montana countryside, but I'll humor them. I tell them that the basic gist I recall is that Mars is too cold for humans, has too thin of an atmosphere...little or no oxygen and nitrogen. A terraforming approach would be to somehow increase the level of greenhouse gases on a planetary scale, start to trap in heat from the Sun that would have otherwise normally radiated back out to space. Then maybe introduce plants...at first lichens and algae...then more complex and larger plants. This would start a positive feedback loop in which theoretically the temperature rises, more frozen oxygen and nitrogen is released from the soil, and the atmosphere becomes progressively thicker, to the point at which human life could be sustained.

"Very good," says Monroe, "ironically, you might say this is an instance in which global warming might be a good thing, right? Do you recall any drawbacks with terraforming of Mars?"

"Well, it's not a quick fix for human overpopulation problems. Putting aside the difficulties in getting to Mars in the first place, a terraforming process could take decades or even centuries to change the climate appreciably. And then there are moral and ethical issues as well."

"And what might they be?"

"Well," I reply, "from an ethical standpoint, I would think we would want to be absolutely sure that Mars was lifeless prior to artificially changing its climate. Any indigenous life forms may be attuned to and dependent on the existing Martian climate and ecology. I wouldn't think we could then have a right to modify their climate for our own purposes."

"So, inducing global warming on Mars might be good for humans, but not so good for Martians, eh?"

"A great philosophical discussion we're having here, but what's the point? What does this have to do with this mysterious request you need to make of me?"

"We're coming to that I promise, but you need to understand the larger context first. So back to Earth and climate change."

"Several years ago," Monroe continues, "prominent climate scientists had a problem. The observed increases in global carbon emissions were significantly exceeding their climate model projections. As you know, the sources of carbon emissions are both natural such as carbon dioxide and methane from rotting vegetation and flatulence from livestock. And man-made relating to carbon monoxide emissions from fossil fuel combustion and other pollutants. But the numbers didn't add up; carbon levels were simply rising far faster than could be accounted for with known sources."

"So, all the polluter's polluting and all the cows farting couldn't move the greenhouse gas needle at the rate the scientists were seeing?"

"Correct, if rather crudely put. Indeed, the abnormal increases in global carbon levels could not be attributed to either natural or man-made sources."

"Forgive me, but if the increase is not natural and it is not man-made, what does that leave us?" I am beginning to see where he is headed with this line of thinking and I don't like where it is taking me.

"As incredible as it sounds, Dr. Walker, key elements within the government have come to the conclusion that something or someone has begun modifying our global climate through artificial means. In effect, Earth itself is being terraformed. Although I suppose a better term might be 'exoformed' if indeed the goal is to replicate another planet's climate."

"Excuse me! But this is preposterous!" This is the sort of wild, speculative conversation I'd expect to have with Berman or the folks trying to vector in UFOs, not the serious researcher and Army officer standing before me.

"The models themselves may be wrong," I continue. "Maybe the scientists have just underestimated the true natural or man-made contributions to carbon levels. You just can't just say that because we are unable to account for excess levels, the answer is extraterrestrial meddling. One faux alien encounter has been enough for me! There has to be real causal evidence, not just some anomaly the models can't explain."

"Well," says Anderson with a slight smile, "ironically, the global warming skeptics who claimed man-made pollution was not to blame for climate change were half right; just in a way they could never have imagined."

"But," he continues, "if you want proof, real proof...the evidence is right before you, laying at your feet." He's gesturing to the concrete tower footing his shotgun has been resting against.

CHAPTER 40

As I intently look on, Anderson has produced what looks to be an oversized laser pointer and two sets of amber safety glasses. He kneels and examines the concrete base of the tower footing next to his shotgun.

"Alright," he indicates, "put those glasses on and look over here. It's hard to see in broad daylight unless I shade it with my hand." He is directing the laser pointer at a spot on the concrete below his hand. I'm looking now through the amber glasses.

"Yes, I see something now...what the hell are they?" To my astonishment there is a scattering of bright metallic red-yellow particles attached to the surface of the footing. When I lift up my glasses, they wink out and disappear. I put the glasses back on and they reappear.

"You only see these because they have a property known as laser induced luminescence," explains Monroe. "More specifically, they become luminescent when exposed to laser light of a specific frequency spectrum...between 150 and 200 angstroms." He nods at Anderson's laser pointer. "In fact, they were only discovered a few years ago through accidental exposure from a mis-calibrated laser in a Naval Research laboratory."

"You're saying these particles are somehow connected to global climate change? How? What are they?"

"What you see here is a colony of nanites," replies Anderson. "The small section I am illuminating is comprised of hundreds of thousands, if not millions, of them. These nanites are very complex but fantastically small engineered machines of unknown origin. Each machine is only about seventy-five nanometers in diameter."

"Incredible." I don't know what else to say. A nanometer is one-billionth of a meter. The thickness of one sheet of ordinary paper is one hundred thousand nanometers and a typical virus is about one hundred nanometers in size. He's talking about a complex machine smaller than a virus particle. Only recently have scientists even attempted to fabricate nanoscale devices. And these have been relatively simple machines such as levers and gears. No wonder Monroe and Anderson are suggesting their origin may be extraterrestrial. This far exceeds any of our current technologies.

Monroe continues the narrative. "Each nanite is a miniature, but very efficient, carbon dioxide factory at the molecular level. Each producing thousands of times its mass each day in carbon dioxide molecules. Think of each unit as a miniature catalytic converter that's running backwards, producing more, not fewer emissions."

"Unaided, we obviously cannot see individual nanites directly," he explains, "but here is an image taken with an electron scanning microscope." He's showing me a photo on his phone screen. "We are calling them machines for simplicity's sake, but more accurately they appear to be nanoscale cyborgs with both mechanical as well as biological properties."

The image looks vaguely like maybe a cross between a mechanical winged insect and a bacterium. It has various appendages attached to a grainy silver main exoskeleton. I can only guess at how these features function but I'm sure Monroe will bring me up to speed.

"We've been studying these things for several years," he says, "and still have little insight into how they are constructed. Each one appears to have thousands of complex components. Our ability to observe, much less analyze the interior workings of devices at that nanoscale is almost nil. But we do have a much better grasp of the nanites' functions and how those relate to the visual appendages you see. These units are remarkably efficient at four functions. They have been apparently optimized to move, reproduce, emit carbon dioxide, and somehow communicate with each other."

"These whip-like appendages," I say pointing to the image, "those look like the flagella that common bacteria use to propel themselves. Do the nanites use them for locomotion? And those flat surfaces could function as a sort of kite wings, right?"

"That is correct. They use the flagella for short distance movement on surfaces. And those flat appendages don't move like flapping wings but serve to catch air movements on which to hitch a ride. Remember, even at scales the size of small insects, gravity doesn't have much of an effect. And at nanoscales, it hardly matters at all. Much like virus particles, these things can easily float in the wind or on the surface of water for days. And their design is apparently very opportunistic, allowing them to exploit their environment as it suits them."

He goes on to describe additional functions of the nanites' external appendages. There is a grasping opening in the front used presumably to pull in organic materials for conversion to carbon dioxide. In a sense, this mimics normal Earth biology in which animals consume organics with carbon dioxide from respiration as a byproduct. However, the nanites produce far more carbon dioxide for a given amount of organic input than known Earth organisms.

He points to eight protrusions on the exoskeleton, indicating that these inverted cone shaped features appear to be output ports to expel the CO_2 the devices manufacture. These are the business ends of the units; the drivers of climate change.

"It's ironic," he says. "We didn't discover the nanites until a few years ago. And yet, it appears they have been with us for decades, literally right under our feet. We in our macro-scale world of mountains, tables, chairs, zebras, and horses are blissfully unaware of the universe of microbes and nanoscale organisms that swirl around us constantly. Five years ago, we didn't know the nanites existed. Now we seem to find them everywhere we look…with the right equipment."

"Decades?" I'm perplexed. "How can you know how long these things have existed?"

"Turns out," says Monroe, "these machine-organisms don't live forever. But interestingly, they do reproduce frequently by splitting themselves in two."

"Asexual reproduction, like cellular mitosis in biology?"

"That's essentially correct. And when the old nanites cease to function or die, their exoskeletons never seem to decompose. The abandoned corpses remain in place right where they died. And we have noticed that subsequent generations appear to physically mutate on a regular basis. These changes in physical appearance often coincide with apparent changes in behavior or function, say increased production of CO2, that sort of thing. We have discovered nanite corpses preserved with old human artifacts, suggesting they've been on this planet since early in the twentieth century"

"That's nearly three quarters of a century…amazing."

"Oddly enough," he continues, "global warming itself may have helped reveal the oldest site where a colony had been established. It's in Northern Canada where retreating ice and snow have uncovered old nanite exoskeletons we've dated to approximately 1930."

"Near Angikuni Lake in the Nunavut?"

"How did you know…?"

"A lucky guess, I suppose."

Monroe then introduces a subject he refers to as Nanite Paleontology. He says by correlating the physical mutations on a timeline relating to their occurrence with human artifacts or natural soil strata, his team is attempting to trace the propagation of the anomalous units by time and location. An excellent pattern recognition application for LISA, I think.

"Fine, I'm convinced that these nanites exist," I say. As to exactly how or whether they would work to create global warming, that's a different issue."

"How so?"

"Even E.T. is not exempt from chemistry and physics. There is no free lunch from an energy perspective. I recall one of the main challenges with terraforming Mars is that the release of frozen water, carbon dioxide, and fluorocarbons required to produce greenhouse gasses in any quantity would require prodigious amounts of energy, right? Some have even speculated that dozens, if not hundreds, of thermonuclear bombs would be required to release such levels of heat to start the process."

"You're right, the nanites' process requires a great deal of energy," replies Anderson. "But remember how we said their design was opportunistic?"

He's smiling and pointing up at the five-hundred kilovolt lines buzzing over our heads. "The nanites can apparently capture energy directly from the sun through photovoltaics. However, one of their favorite tricks is to simply harvest energy parasitically from the electromagnetic fields generated by our own technology. Why do you suppose I was so confident we'd find a colony right here under these high voltage lines?"

"And here I thought you'd picked this location for the abundance of pheasants we're supposed to be hunting."

"Okay," I continue, "you've convinced me these things exist and apparently don't have our best interests in mind. How do we kill them?"

"It's both easy and hard to kill them," says Anderson with a weary shake of his head. "Easy if it's an individual nanite or small colony. I can wipe 'em out by crushing them with the heel of my boot. Not so easy if I'm trying to get rid of them on a global basis."

"Kinetic force, say, grinding them with a boot, simply doesn't scale up to a global solution," adds Monroe. Think of ants. I can crush one or maybe a small anthill with my boot, no problem. But try to find and stomp every one of the trillions and trillions of ants on the planet? It's a non-starter."

"On the other end of the force scale," I offer, "we could scorch the planet with nukes. That would likely kill them off but most certainly wipe out humanity in the process."

"You're beginning to understand the threat we face," replies Anderson. "We did have some early success in using high frequency sonic waves to shatter the nanite exoskeletons. Not exactly a global solution, but orders of magnitude better than the boot heel method."

"But I take it that the sonic solution ultimately did not work?"

"Unfortunately, the nanites adapted and then quickly mutated, hardening their exoskeletal shells to shield themselves from the sonic waves."

"That is absolutely amazing."

"That's not even the most amazing part of it," says Anderson. Not only did the colony on which we were testing the sonic weapon mutate, but as far as we can tell, every other single colony on the planet immediately mutated as well."

"So, all nanites on the planet are somehow networked? Apparently in communication with each other on some level?" I ask. "How do they do it?"

Monroe answers. "Apparently, opportunists as they are, they went old-school. Amplitude Modulation radio frequencies."

"AM Radio?"

"Indeed. Think about it. Assuming they first arrived here in the 1930's and 40's, AM radio would have been the predominate wireless transmission technology on the planet. Nowadays people sort of look down on AM radio as an obsolete technology but the range of AM signals dwarfs FM and other radio modes. Large broadcasters can put out signal strengths that can cover half a continent. A very convenient medium to network a clandestine global network of organic machines."

"You think they piggybacked on commercial AM signals?"

"Yes, we believe they interwove short data bursts into regular transmissions. You know the clicks and static you used to hear on AM stations back in the day? Not all of it was random static. Short range, they also appear to use AM signals for communication within their colonies. We've had a great deal of success finding large colonies with electromagnetic field meters optimized to localize AM frequencies."

"Okay," I say, "clearly, none of this is good news. But even accelerated climate change driven by mysterious, possibly alien, nano-cyborgs isn't an imminent mortal threat to humanity."

"I can see how you might come to that conclusion at this point."

"Right. I mean we humans are already doing a swell job of ruining this planet through over-population, pollution, and global warming all on our own. The nanites just appear to be accelerating a disastrous trend we have already started. Hillie's message made this issue sound like immediate life or death. What am I missing?"

"You're missing what the nanites have recently added. About eighteen months ago, they mutated again. They now have evolved two more emitter ports. Instead of carbon dioxide, the new emitters appear to be starting to produce a deadly neurotoxin gas," says Anderson.

"Initially, the neurotoxin levels being omitted were quite low. Virtually undetectable unless you know what you're looking for," adds Monroe. "But six months ago, that began to change. It was like a switch was flipped. The tiny amounts of neurotoxin being emitted started to increase. Not in a linear fashion but logarithmically." He raises an eyebrow and nods to make sure I'm catching the significance of that statement.

The implications are profound. Small amounts growing by a logarithmic or power function can become overwhelmingly huge quickly. Worse yet, that growth may be undetectable until it is too late to contain. Think of a small lake with a single lily-pad floating in it. Now assume that the lily-pad population doubles every day such that on the second day there are two pads, four pads on the third day and so forth. If it takes sixty days for the pads to cover the entire lake, on what day would the pads have covered half the lake? Most folks either give the wrong answer or can't bring themselves to believe the correct answer: day fifty-nine. Worse yet, the population of lily-pads would be virtually insignificant to an observer prior to day fifty. If only the nanites were producing lily-pads instead of neurotoxins…

"And, the topic of neurotoxins brings us to our young friend, Ricky Pruitt, and the saga of the USS Nash," adds Monroe.

CHAPTER 41

Much like some other momentous discoveries in science, the Nash phenomenon was uncovered largely by accident and then immediately suppressed under tight government secrecy. That accident, unfortunately, had proved deadly to many innocent victims.

According to Monroe, about eight years ago a team of contractors were dismantling the last of the nation's VX nerve agent weapons at a DoD site in Utah. There was a sudden containment breach and the workers were inadvertently directly exposed to the deadly nerve gas. Unsurprisingly, the effects were immediate and catastrophic. Almost all died quickly and horribly. As is typical for VX lethal exposure, the victims experienced immediate involuntary muscle paralysis, including the diaphragm muscle. Death came by rapid asphyxiation.

"You said that almost all died immediately," I say. "That suggests some survived at least briefly."

"Yes, two individuals indeed survived," confirms Monroe. "Simple survival, even for a few days, of an exposure to a such a lethal neurotoxin dose would itself have been remarkable. But what is profound is that those two men walked out of that contaminated chamber unaffected by the VX. It was as though they were never exposed."

"How can that be? I thought VX was one of the deadliest substances ever considered for chemical warfare. So deadly that its production and stockpiling has been globally banned for years."

"Well," explains Monroe, "immunity to neurotoxins in nature isn't entirely unheard of. Take poisonous snake venom for example. Honey badgers, certain species of mongoose, and the lowly woodrat all have varying degrees of immunity to snake venom. And, of course, obviously the snakes themselves tend to be immune to their own venom. There are a variety of biological defenses that seem to protect these creatures. Some have unique peptides in their blood that inhibit the poison and others have developed certain cellular protein structures that inhibit the uptake of the toxins."

"True enough," I reply. "But these animal immune responses were evolutionary enhancements developed over the ages. These adaptations are products of nature's eternal and ongoing biological warfare between predator and prey, right? How could humans somehow have *evolved* to adapt an immune response to VX, a toxic agent their ancestors never encountered?"

"That indeed became the driving question that mobilized a small team of researchers, including myself, to investigate this anomaly on behalf of the US Government," he replies. "What made these people special and how did they become so?"

Monroe quickly recounts the highlights of the early investigations. No surprise that the Government quickly covered up and classified any evidence of the Utah incident. This included any mention of the fatalities and especially any reference to the rather special survivors. And the team used a bit of clever subterfuge to persuade the surviving subjects to be medically examined and monitored for the rest of their lives. They somehow convinced the survivors and their families that a risk of post-exposure VX reactions could be a long-term health threat. A little lie in service of the truth. Anderson's signature hallmark.

Monroe's team discovered evidence that the VX survivors had potentially been genetically modified. This prompted them to begin a project to sequence and map the survivor genome. Separately, other parts of the team scoured the survivors' family, work, and environmental histories for any common factors. This effort mostly drew a blank, except for one intriguing commonality. Each had parents or grandparents that had served on the USS Nash's maiden and, as it turned out, last voyage.

"The Nash? No shit?" The pieces of the puzzle aren't quite lined up, but I have a feeling some are about ready to slide into place.

"I'm sure your friend Admiral Hillenbrand can now fill you in on the details of the very peculiar voyage of the Nash. For our purposes, suffice to say that the ship was being operated with a skeleton crew of twenty-six men when it disappeared under unusual circumstances. The ship was found the next day, adrift and abandoned, with no sign of the crew. Several days later, the crew was located and rescued from a small island about five hundred miles distant from the ship's last position. None of the sailors had any recollection of what had happened or how they came to be on that island."

"But surely such a strange incident would have made the headlines?"

"In today's digital, real-time world, absolutely. But this occurred in the middle of a World War. The military and the nation were focused on preparations for an Allied push into the Solomons and the Aleutians. News of war events traveled slowly and was almost always filtered through military channels. A small missing ship and crew that were both shortly recovered was not exactly 'Movietone News' material."

"So, nothing really came of this odd disappearance?"

"Oh, at the time a brief naval board of inquiry was convened. The resulting report was inconclusive. But, like I said, in the context of the ongoing World War, the strange voyage of the Nash was insignificant and quickly forgotten. It would have remained a minor, curious footnote to the war were it not for the Utah VX accident."

"Once we understood the Nash might be a common link to the puzzle, we quickly traced down all descendants of the twenty-six crew members involved in the disappearance," adds Anderson. "And quite conveniently, several Nash descendants were enlisted in the armed forces at the time."

I smile. "And when one is enlisted in the service, Uncle Sam not only owns your career but your body as well, right?"

"Exactly," replies Anderson, "we were able to conduct long-term medical studies and gather periodic blood and tissue samples for research on these metaphorically captive subjects."

"Let me guess, you found those enlisted Nash descendants had the same the genetic modifications as the original Utah survivors?"

"Indeed," says Anderson. "Of course, the next step was to collect medical records and blood samples from the larger population of Nash descendants. We're calling them the Nash Progeny for convenience. Fortunately, we were aware that those with the Nash mutations tend to have severe digestive enzyme issues."

"So," adds Monroe, "we quietly reached out to their family doctors…"

"In the helpful guise of the Stanton Clinic for Advanced Endocrine Studies? Operating out of a post office box in Santa Fe, New Mexico?" I add. "And I bet you found that every one of the Nash descendants, including Stan and Ricky Pruitt, carries the same set of mutations?"

"That is correct. We have been studying this special population for some time now. Unfortunately, several months ago there was a partial breach of security and some information about those descendants, the Nash Progeny, and their immunity to neurotoxins and nerve agents fell into foreign hands," explains Monroe.

"Imagine," he continues, "if a hostile government could unlock and replicate the Nash genetic mutation that provides immunity to nerve agents? One of the tactical limitations of nerve gas is that it goes where the wind blows, including right back at those who dispense it. But now they could develop an army of genetically modified super-soldiers impervious to nerve gas, making them unstoppable."

"This foreign government, Russia, we suspect, recruited mercenaries to conduct a rather heavy-handed gathering of Progeny blood and tissue under a phony alien abduction scheme. They kidnapped Stan, Ricky, and others…"

"The twins I saw in the mine?"

"Yes," admits Anderson, "there were twins as well. I had brought in a small tactical team into Montana to investigate the disappearances and recover the Progeny when our paths crossed a couple of weeks ago. Culminating, of course, in the unfortunate events at the Sapphire Belle."

"Don't remind me. By the way, I'm still pissed."

Monroe politely ignores the jab at Anderson. "So, I had mentioned that a subteam had all along been working to sequence and map the Progeny genome, right? The mystery was how any human could survive exposure to a potent nerve agent such as VX."

"I don't see how any human could survive an exposure to such a deadly agent," I say.

"And you would be correct," Monroe is smiling slyly. "No human could. The Progeny, Ricky and Stan included, are not in the strictest technical sense, human."

"Think of them as human-adjacent," adds Anderson.

"What the hell does that mean?"

"Let me try to explain." Monroe looks a bit annoyed with Anderson over his glib comment.

Monroe relates that the Progeny genome mapping project revealed that dozens of key genetic mutations had been made to the original Nash crew. In addition to conferring immunity to neurotoxins, the mutations appear to allow them to function in much hotter climates, and greatly enhance intelligence. Importantly, these genetic changes are germline mutations, allowing them to be passed on to offspring. And, not only are the mutations passed to offspring, they are dominant in any child that is the offspring of a Progeny parent and a non-Progeny parent. Intriguingly, the Progeny DNA appears to have recursive elements that amplify these mutations in each successive generation. In essence, their DNA has been modified to continually modify itself.

"Can you clarify what you meant by saying the Progeny are not technically human?" I ask.

"Well," starts Monroe, "if you met one on the street, you'd certainly think they were human. There are some physical expressions of the Nash mutations and they vary by the race and ethnicity of the individual. Caucasians have exceedingly pale complexions and amber eye coloration. Striking, nearly luminescent gold flaked eyes are common in African Americans, and so forth. But nothing that would cause a casual observer to think a Progeny was any different than you or me."

"The differences are 'under the hood' so to speak?" I offer.

"Yes," continues Monroe. It turns out that regular humans and the Progeny of Ricky's generation share about 99.8 percent of the same DNA."

"At first blush, that seems close enough for government work, but I bet you're going to tell me otherwise."

"Yes. Superficially, 99.8 percent certainly sounds close. But remember, the human genome contains roughly three billion base pairs." He's talking about the fundamental sequences of nucleic acids that make up our DNA which are then expressed through roughly 25,000 genes.

"If I do the math," I say. "That would suggest some six million base pairs have been modified."

"Correct. And that number increases with each generation. The scope of the changes is simply stunning. This is genetic modification far, far beyond our current gene editing capabilities. Currently, despite the DNA differences, the Progeny are still able to conceive viable, fertile offspring with non-Progeny humans. By that definition, we have not yet diverged as a species. But given their escalating genetic changes, that point may not be far in the future."

"So, your group started out discovering and researching the Progeny and then became aware of the nanites? You decided there was a connection?"

"Yes," says Monroe, "in a post-911 world, it is imperative that one, as they say, connects the dots. Both the Progeny and the nanites appeared to be recipients of the same ultra-advanced genetic science and engineering. It seemed a significant coincidence that the Progeny appeared to be genetically engineered to adapt to a much hotter climate. The very climate the nanites appear to be driving us towards with their greenhouse gas emissions. Of course, once the nanites started emitting neurotoxin gas which has no effect on the Progeny, the connection was too strong to deny. But obviously, we still have no idea why they appear to be related, or to what end."

"How can I help? I assume that's ultimately why I'm standing with you here on a ridge in central Montana being briefed on some incredible findings?" Fascinating as it might be; enough background, time to cut to the chase.

"The Nash phenomenon, both the nanite and the Progeny aspects, are presenting us with some very large and complex data problems," says Monroe. "We need to collect and analyze current and historical nanite propagation patterns on a global scale. And then see how they are positioned relative to prevailing global wind and ocean current patterns. We also need to forecast the impacts of greenhouse gas emissions and try to estimate when nanite neurotoxin levels will reach detectable and then lethal global levels."

"Sounds like you need a world class pattern recognition and predictive modeling engine," I say. "It sounds as though you need LISA."

"We already have LISA."

CHAPTER 42

Anderson is looking at me with a broad shit-eating grin on his face as Monroe reveals that eGenesis already has possession of LISA. But I'm determined not to outwardly express the seething irritation and frustration I'm feeling about this turn of events. He is not going to get the satisfaction.

"Funny," I say rather blandly, "I don't recall licensing LISA to your program. This must have been an oversight on my part."

"Oh, no need to feel bad," indicates Monroe, "we didn't actually request a license. We just, you know, took it. Highly exigent circumstances, one might say. Because of its nature, eGenesis has certain high-level access privileges within the government."

"Think of it as having a key to the back door of the US Patent Office and a key to the front door of the US Treasury," adds Anderson.

"We've been admirers of your algorithms and models for some time. And the A.I. capabilities you've developed for LISA are quite impressive," says Monroe.

"Well, I'm flattered," I respond, "but truthfully it has taken an entire team at UCLA to make LISA what she is today. But if you already have a copy of LISA, then you likely have what you need. I'm not sure I can add any further value to your enterprise myself."

"In truth, we do need your personal involvement. We've run into some problems."

"What sort of problems?"

"The sheer volume and complexity of the data and global scale of the required modeling for the Nash phenomenon will require so much computational power that we must place LISA on an extremely powerful supercomputer. We're talking tens of thousands of parallel processors, a quadrillion calculations per second."

"That's a number of magnitudes of order greater performance than her current server environment at UCLA," I say.

"Indeed. Porting the system to the new supercomputer has been difficult. Frankly, we've hit a brick wall and need your technical help to optimize the system. And also, there is LISA's A.I. interface. She can be…"

"Difficult? Seem to have a mind of her own? Appear to subtlety mock you should you phrase a request in an incomplete manner?"

"Well, yes. All of the above," replies Monroe with a hint of resignation.

"Those are not *bugs*, they're *features*. LISA was designed to challenge her users as much as support them. It forces discipline. You'll never get a correct answer if your questions are poorly framed in the first place."

"Yes," sighs Monroe, "be that as it may, it appears we may need your personal involvement to help us effectively use those…features."

"So, will you join the team and work with us and Admiral Hillenbrand? We've got an excellent operation set up at Los Alamos in New Mexico. Top notch labs and staff. Plenty of resources and you'll be saving the world to boot!" Anderson has decided it's time to close the deal. And doing it with all the finesse of a car salesman trying to move a used Buick off the lot.

"Jack." Monroe is trying a more somber pitch. "Think of your wife and daughter. Think of everyone now living that you know and love. Every one of them will be dead in a few years unless we can figure out how to stop the nanites. Join us. Do it for them."

"Okay, I'm in." Not that I'd give these guys the satisfaction of knowing, but I've been committed to eGenesis ever since I witnessed the nanite colony luminescing at the base of the high voltage tower. I think of Kate and Amy, Hillie, Adhira, Jeff, and the rest of the team at UCLA, all my old friends, and then my ever-growing list of new friends such as Dan Wendover and the Pruitts. I failed Marty. I cannot let down all these people, and the planet, now. "If that's what it takes to make you two shut up," I add.

"Excellent!" Handshakes all around.

"We need to get you down to New Mexico immediately," says Monroe, "time is of the essence."

"About that," I say, "if I drop everything and take a sabbatical over to Los Alamos for months at a time, that's not going to go over well with the higher-ups at the university. I'm going to get very strong push-back."

Anderson smiles and winks, "trust me, we have very effective ways of gaining cooperation."

"Thumbscrews?"

"Greenbacks."

Just then I hear something. I turn slightly to scan about. Intermittently, a soft, odd thumping, can be heard over the hum of the high voltage lines. Now Anderson and Monroe are looking around as well; they hear it, too.

Suddenly there are blurs of motion to both my right and left. Two unmarked black helicopters are rising out of the drainage ravines on both sides of the bench, their windows blacked out. Much like the encounter back on Sutter's Bench in Benton County, these aircraft appear to be operating with some advanced noise suppression technology which apparently allowed them to approach up the ravines for some distance unnoticed.

Now, they are, in fact, very much noticed. I'm shocked to see that both are carrying weapons modules; twin .50 caliber gatling guns on port and starboard. The immediate impression is that of large and menacing black insects in search of prey. Instinctively, I start to reach for my shotgun. But at the same time, I realize the move is futile. Against two heavily armed Blackhawks, the Benelli may as well be a flyswatter.

"Easy!" Anderson gently pulls the gun away from me. "Relax, these are our birds, okay?" Taking some care to stay a distance from the high voltage lines, both helicopters have landed about a hundred yards from us, their rotors slowing to a stop.

"These are our rides," says Monroe. "Remember, time is of the essence. We'll take these on a short flight over to Malmstrom Air Force Base where the program's Gulfstream G650 is now refueling. From there it's on to the Santa Fe airport and then a short drive up the mesa to Los Alamos. We have some personnel here that will take care of arrangements for the return of our cars sitting back at the trailhead."

A side door on the nearest Blackhawk has now opened. Two soldiers clad in camo gear jump out first and presumably inspect the landing zone for hazards. Next, a heavy-set older gentleman with a deep golden tan and an unmistakable shock of silver hair steps out confidently. It's none other than retired Admiral Thomas Hillenbrand, his signature unlit robusto hanging to one side of his grinning mouth as he waves cheerfully at us. Behind him, both helicopter crews are now exiting the aircraft.

"Jack! Good to see you, how the hell have you been? Heard you got into a bit of mischief back in some old mine. It's great news that you're joining the effort!" Hillie is in a jolly mood like maybe he's just arrived at happy hour to discover I'm keeping a bar tab open for him.

"All things considered, I'm well," I say, "wish I could say the same for Marcy. She's been worried sick about you disappearing on her."

"Yeah," Hillie's tone becomes a little more somber, "unfortunate about the timing. Couldn't be helped given what's been going on with the program. Always something urgent…including flying up here to collect your sorry ass. I finally called her last night. You're right, she's not particularly happy with me at the moment."

"And these guys," he's smiling and pointing to Monroe and Anderson. "First, they make sure I get the third degree for accidentally stumbling across their little secret. And then they have the audacity to immediately recruit me into that same program."

"By the way, Hillie, what exactly is your role here?" I'm thinking eGenesis might not have an immediate need for an overpaid professional lobbyist. A thought I'll be sure to keep to myself.

Hillie brightens, "turns out the program has a real need for oceanography and ocean current modeling expertise. And they could use an expert liaison with the various national security and intelligence agencies." He's jerking a thumb at himself.

"Great. And they are hoping you can help them recruit that sort of talent?"

"Ouch!" Hillie is pantomiming pulling an imaginary dagger out from his chest. "That hurtful remark will be punishable by no less than two fingers of The Macallan at our earliest convenience."

"Guilty as charged, I accept the sentence."

"Great then," he says, "are you ready to roll? We can have everyone loaded and airborne in ten minutes."

"Um, about that. There's one thing I need to discuss first with Dr. Monroe and Colonel Anderson. I have one remaining obligation here in Montana. It's private, very private. Could you give us a moment, please?"

I quickly pull Monroe and Anderson to the side to tell them of my circumstances. After a few minutes, we arrive at a mutual solution.

"Sergeant Hernandez!" Anderson is motioning to a young soldier standing by the helicopters.

"Yes-sir," she walks over and stands at attention.

Anderson nods towards me, "Dr. Walker, I'd like to introduce you to Staff Sergeant Jessica Hernandez, one of the best marksmen in the service. She will be your security escort for the remainder of the day."

He addresses Hernandez, "Sergeant, you will accompany Dr. Walker in his vehicle and ensure his security as he attends to some private business. We will have an aircraft waiting for him at the Kalispell airport; wheels up at 1900 hours, understood?"

"Yes-sir."

"Very well," Anderson continues, "use all precautions, Dr. Walker is now considered a national asset; his safety is paramount."

"Understood, Sir. Shall I bring along an M4 carbine?"

"Negative. Your service sidearm should be sufficient."

I'm slightly bemused, smiling to myself. Today Anderson is touting me as a "national asset." Just over a week ago he had no qualms about serving me up on a platter to Riley and his goons in the depths of the Sapphire Belle. I suspect that was before he realized the program would need me to finish porting LISA to a new supercomputer and deal with a somewhat petulant and challenging A.I. interface.

"Anderson?"

"Yes?"

"One final question. Why is the program called eGenesis? Was that the only web domain name available?"

"Genesis refers to a beginning."

"Is the 'e' for extraterrestrial?"

"Extinction. Keeps us focused on the stakes at play."

CHAPTER 43

Thirty years can change a place. Thirty years changes us all. We are standing at the old cabin site at Bigfork. Glistening through the trees perhaps two hundred yards away from us is the expanse of Flathead Lake. The cabin is long gone. Now the parking lot of a large vacation condo complex has covered the area where it had once stood.

The creek is still there. Not as large as I remembered it, but then my world has gotten much larger, and much more troubled, since those days of my youth. I glance back at Sergeant Hernandez. She's standing stoically in the parking lot, ever watchful, arms folded behind her back. She's trying to look inconspicuous. A tall order for a uniformed, and armed, soldier in a Montana resort parking lot.

Hernandez wasn't much of a talker on the drive over here. I didn't get much out of her other than that she liked her job but missed her family back in Kansas. She had an unconscious habit of idly stroking her weapon holster as the miles passed by. I wasn't sure whether that made me feel more secure or less secure. As we drove in silence, I had sensed an ambiguity about her assignment. Was I under her protection or in her custody? Likely that would be a distinction without a difference. Regardless of how the day will play out, I have no doubt the good sergeant would see to it that I will be on the waiting plane this evening; with or without my cooperation.

I nod to her, "It's time. I need some privacy, but I won't be out of sight."

"Yes-sir, I'll be right here." She's carefully scanning the parameter of the parking lot.

I turn and begin to walk down to the creek. This is where it began and where it must end. My final duty to Marty; after thirty years I'm bringing him home. I have failed him so many times over the years, this is the least I can do for him.

I had thought it would be heavier. The urn in my hands feels impossibly light to be holding the remains of a human, but this is all that is left. Ashes and memories.

The pale late October afternoon sunlight is starting to fade and is doing little to remove the chill in the air. The crisp air and the approaching rush of the creek reminds me of that cool summer night so long ago. In a moment my eyes widen as the memories come flooding back, laying bare the past that time and denial has obscured for years.

"Marty?"

"Yeah?"

"Are you awake?"

"Well, I am now. It's gotta be after midnight. Whadda you want?"

"You want to sneak out? Go exploring?"

"Naw, if dad found out, he'd kill us."

"Come on, Marty, don't be a chicken. He won't kill us if he doesn't find out. He and mom are sound asleep."

I was ten and considered myself a man of the world. True, it was a small world, the four or five acres surrounding the cabin. But it was my world and I knew every tree and rock on the property. Going out and exploring in the middle of the night would be a grand adventure for us, if Marty didn't wimp out.

Marty was three years my junior. Although athletic of build, he was quite timid. I had in those days considered him something of a momma's boy; always running to our parents when things didn't go his way. On the surface we had little in common but we shared the deep bond of brothers. In those days, as big brother, I was both his tormentor and his protector, depending on the day and my mood.

It had taken some prodding that night, but I had finally convinced Marty to join me. Silently we lifted the screen out of the window and slipped out onto the darkened porch, attired in our pajamas and sneakers.

Other than the sound of the distant creek, the forest surrounding the cabin was utterly silent. The moon had not risen yet. On that clear night the entire sky was filled with a canopy of stars. I remember the sharp and delicious scent of pine in the air. We had flashlights but our eyes had quickly adjusted to the dark and I had convinced Marty not to use his. We could navigate by starlight, I had said. And, besides, mom and dad might become suspicious if they awoke and happened to see flashlights moving about in the woods.

"Marty, let's head up the creek a bit and see what's up there."

"No. That's too far. I just want to follow the creek down to the lake and then go back to the cabin."

"Come on. That's boring," I had said. "What are you worried about? I'll protect you. Don't be a wimp."

"No, I just want to follow the creek down to the lake."

I badgered him for several minutes and he finally relented. We wound through the thickening forest along the creek, moving steadily up and away from the lake.

This is the point at which my memory of that night has remained fragmented for years. I remember moving through the forest and seeing an animal of some sort. It had eyes that seemed to softly glow and we followed the glint of its eyes away from the vicinity of the cabin and off into the deep woods.

The rest of the memory of that night has continued to elude me. I have the vague unsettling notion that there had been chaos. Marty and I running blindly through the forest, but we could not escape...but from what? I had the sense that the animal was not really an animal but a man, or something that was not a man either. In any case, I had remembered a feeling of a loss of control and utter helplessness in the encounter.

The next morning, we awoke in our beds, cut, scraped, and dirty with mud. Blood on the sheets where we had lain. We quickly cleaned up and presented ourselves for breakfast.

"You boys sleep ok last night? Bed bugs didn't bite and I guess the boogie man didn't get you?" My father laughed at his own joke and winked. "How about we go fishing this morning?"

Marty and I tried to smile and glanced nervously at each other. Then we went fishing.

In the years that followed, we were to never speak of that night. Yet for both of us it was to be a turning point in our existence. I think both Marty and I struggled for the rest of our lives to seek a sense of escape and control, in widely different ways.

In my case, I immersed, some might say lost, myself in mathematics and algorithms. I undertook life in academia and became a seeker of patterns, hoping to uncover a greater truth through abstractions. I was consumed by my research for it gave me a sense of purpose and control. Through modeling I could, in a sense, create my own worlds incorporating patterns and behaviors I observed in the real world. Some of these modeling approaches and tools, such as the development of LISA, became quite useful and widely recognized.

I suppose in a way, Marty was no more damaged than myself. But his approach to coping and controlling his demons was to be much more self-destructive. He became a loner, eventually drifting through an unending series of menial jobs. Abuse of drugs and alcohol became a constant feature of his existence, especially in the end. Over the years I reached out numerous times to offer help but was continually rebuffed. He was always warm towards my daughter, Amy, but usually stiff and uncommunicative with me. He refused to either blame or forgive me for what had happened, much less accept my help. Over the past several years we had little contact. I had not even realized he had moved to Reno until the death notification.

When I was in my mid-twenties, it seemed the innocence of youth had gradually sloughed off with the passing years and I began to look at the world with more critical and cynical eyes. And I began to try to understand myself what had really happened that fateful night. A review of old Montana newspaper archives revealed several articles about a child molester that had been convicted of assaulting young boys in the Kalispell area. The man had then died in prison. The timing of the crimes was plausibly close to the timeframe in which Marty and me had been terrorized that fateful night. I took that discovery as a morbid closure of sorts and tried to move on with my life. Now given the revelations of Skywatch and eGenesis, I wonder if it was not a false closure after all.

"Okay, Marty. We're here." I've reached the banks of the creek. "I think this is what you really wanted to do that night, right? You just wanted to follow the creek down to the lake. You just wanted peace."

I kneel next to the running water and release the top cap of the urn. Slowly, I pour the ashes into the creek. I watch as they swirl and disburse into the clear water and make their way towards the lake.

"I'm so sorry, brother. So sorry. I hope you finally find peace."

I stand up and turn to look back at the condo parking lot. Hernandez is still on guard duty; keeping a careful watch on me from the distance. She nods slightly, raises her hand, and offers a somber salute to the empty urn.

CHAPTER 44

Dawn brings an auburn glow to the Sangre De Cristo mountains in the far distance. I pause for a moment and admire the view through the windows of my new, and hopefully temporary, office here at Los Alamos National Laboratory.

Nestled on the Pajarito Plateau in northern New Mexico, the laboratory complex overlooks the upper Rio Grande tributaries of the Española Valley. According to the accounts of the ancients passed on to the Tewa, forerunners to the Pueblo tribes of today's Southwest, the creation of the world and humanity began in this land under the shadow of the Sangre De Cristos. The Tewa version of the Biblical Genesis. Our job now in this very same locale is to ensure the story of our world does not end here as well.

"Good morning, Dr. Walker." LISA, or at least LISA's classified doppelgänger here at eGenesis, has found her voice. In short order, the eGenesis team has improvised a natural language interface to her systems. Although no one is going to think for a minute they're conversing with a fully sentient being, the ability to communicate with LISA in English allows me to rapidly cue up new assumptions and scenarios for her analysis. *"Sub-Saharan propagation rates ready on screen two,"* she continues.

LISA now resides on a multiple core parallel processing supercomputer recently repurposed from duties simulating nuclear fusion thermodynamics. The changes to LISA have been dramatic and swift. As Anderson had noted back in Montana, it's amazing what the program can accomplish with access to the back door of the US Patent Office and access to the front door of the US Treasury.

eGenesis has a huge but well-hidden budget. It is a USAP, an Unacknowledged Special Access Program. The particulars of its budget and funding shoved so far and deep up the Pentagon's Secret Black Programs collective ass that the sun would have to go supernova for any light to shine on it.

Seems the program is spending money like there's no tomorrow. Like there's no tomorrow, get it? That punchline is on frequent rotation here in our highly restricted laboratories and offices. It's funny maybe the first or second time you hear it. What little humor flourishes behind these walls is of the gallows variety.

This marks my third week with eGenesis here in New Mexico. To no surprise, back at the university, my request for immediate leave for a LANL research sabbatical had caused a significant stir. True to form, my department chair marched me right into the Dean's office once she got wind of my impending departure. A wire-brushing in the Dean's office apparently her idea of an academic intervention of sorts. Righteous indignation from all concerned. How could I abandon my classes and Team LISA midstream? Did I not care about my responsibilities and the integrity of the institution?

That attitude quickly reversed when they saw the monetary value of the government contract being offered to UCLA for my services…with payment promised in advance. Once the dollar amount sank in, the administration did everything but pack my bags for me and throw a farewell parade in my honor. Godspeed Walker, the check cleared! No worries, we're sure Team LISA is now in the capable hands of Dr. Chandra. Now the department chair is making it sound as though my rushed sabbatical to New Mexico was her idea all along.

I idlily scan through LISA's latest file on Sub-Saharan nanite propagation. There are many theories but no knowledge of the agency, whoever or whatever, that has apparently created the nanites and genetically modified the Nash Progeny.

Most in the eGenesis research team seem to favor the bad-alien theory. Makes sense on the surface. Aliens need a new planet and decide to exoform ours to their tastes which apparently run to something much warmer and seasoned with neurotoxins. But we still have no confirmed evidence that such aliens exist, much less a photo of one planting and tending to the nanites. And the theory offers no insight as to why these aliens would go to the trouble of apparently modifying some humans to survive in that future world. Apparently, someone or something wants or needs some humans to survive, just not all eight billion of us. But what role might the Progeny take? Would they be this new world's masters or its slaves or even worse, a handy source of protein?

A competing theory might be termed the good-alien scenario. Here the aliens visited Earth in the past and somehow accidently contaminated the planet with the nanites. Like maybe they tracked some in on their boots. They have been unable to contain the outbreak and as a last resort have modified human bloodlines to ensure at least some survive. Maybe as a nod to some sort of galactic endangered species act.

Still other variations on these themes would be essentially non-alien in nature. Maybe the nanites escaped from an alien lab and propagated here by themselves. Or they developed on their own without any help. Perhaps they were originally benign but humanity's own actions such as pollution or radiation from nuclear tests caused them to mutate on their own. Other theories cast interdimensional beings and time travelers in the role of the villains. Not to ignore humans as the potential bad guys, normally the Russians and Chinese would be suspects, but this technology seems far beyond their current capabilities much less the state of the art in the 1940's or earlier when the nanites originally made their appearance.

The core of the eGenesis team is comprised of about fifty researchers and support staff based here at LANL. In addition, we have a number of field teams surveying nanite activity across the globe. The core team is ensconced in a secure compartmentalized area within the Biosciences Building on the restricted Los Alamos campus. Local wags have, over the years, jokingly referred to the building as the DARF, as in Dead Alien Research Facility. A tongue-in-cheek nod to conspiracy folklore that alien bodies from the alleged Roswell crash back in 1947 were transported some two hundred miles north to Los Alamos for examination and cold storage.

Leave it to Colonel Anderson's predilection for hiding in plain sight for his decision to house eGenesis in the DARF. A decision I admire as audacious. Although I lack his perceptive insights on security, I am increasingly, these days, a connoisseur of the ironic. Conveniently for us, yet another series of coronavirus outbreaks has been playing out in Asia. This provides a plausible cover for the hurried standup of our team of "epidemiologists" here at LANL. Our ramped-up presence on the campus is noticeable but not outwardly suspicious.

On the LANL campus below our windows, the regular staff of the laboratory go about their own routine classified business, unaware that a new effort, rivaling the original Manhattan Project in urgency, is unfolding in their midst. Since the days of Groves and Oppenheimer, the laboratory has been the locus of the nation's nuclear weapons research and development. Its researchers, the high priests of weapons science. Weapons which were fashioned for another time and a different threat.

It's been said many times that generals are always preparing to fight the last war instead of the next war. The trillions humanity has spent on nuclear weapons now seem to be a modern-day version of France's pre-war Maginot Line, ineffectual for all its cost. We could only nuke the nanites out of existence by scorching the entire planet and driving ourselves into extinction in the bargain. The very definition of a Pyrrhic victory.

The eGenesis research group is primarily focused on methods to disrupt or destroy the progress of the nanites, employing experts in genomics, synthetic biology, biochemistry, and pathogen transmission. For our part, LISA and I support eGenesis from an Informatics perspective focusing on big data analysis and pattern recognition.

Although the core team is relatively small, there are hundreds, if not thousands, more researchers around the world working on the problem. They just don't know it. Research contracts for very small parts of the puzzle have been doled out through the Defense and Intelligence agencies' black budgets. So far, none of the recipients have put the big picture together. Our version of crowd-sourcing a solution to doomsday.

Even my old Skywatch friends have become unknowing recipients of eGenesis largess. In an effort to understand the possible correlation between UFO and nanite activities, we've quietly funded Meg Larson's vision to set up a network of autonomous sensors to monitor the skies for strangely behaving objects. Word is that Meg and Peter were understandably shocked at the government's newfound interest in their ideas. Manna from Heaven, it would seem to them.

There's a quick knock on the frame of my open door as Hillie sticks his head into my office. "Good morning, Jack."

"It is definitely a morning. A bit early to tell if it will be good or not. So far, we don't seem to have a lot of mornings here that qualify as good."

A fair point, he replies. And the agenda for the day doesn't offer a great deal of hope for improvement. Within the hour the program's senior staff are requested to attend a mandatory briefing. The fact it is mandatory sort of changes the invitation from a request to an order, but who are we to quibble with semantics, he says.

The guest of honor presenting the briefing is a Dr. Liang, a well-known genomics researcher we've recently brought on board from Johns Hopkins. Dr. Monroe has been even more dour than usual lately, bordering on grim. And the word in the halls is that Liang is not here to deliver good news.

"I think I'm going to go down to the conference room a little early to be sure I get a good seat," says Hillie.

"Right up front so you can ask a lot of pertinent questions?"

"Naw, the usual. My back to the wall and an eye on the door, gunfighter style."

"Always a sound tactic I suppose. Whether you're playing poker in Deadwood or being briefed on research in Los Alamos."

I get a cheery thumbs up from Hillie as he disappears down the hall.

"Dr. Walker, are you still going to review the Sub-Saharan data files or shall LISA revert to other tasks? Dr. West has submitted several well-developed requests that LISA could address as a higher priority, if you wish." LISA has somehow managed to inject a hint of irritation into her synthetic voice. I should know better than to keep a lady waiting.

CHAPTER 45

I notice Dr. Liang isn't making an effort to term this to be a good morning. Standing before the dozen or so of us assembled in the conference room he projects all the warmth and good cheer of an undertaker who's just realized his last shipment of embalming fluid is past its expiration date. Perhaps he's about to tell us our own expiration dates are fast approaching.

"Um, as you know, my sub-team has been very involved in sequencing the Nash Progeny genome. We now have a very good understanding of the specific genetic differences between the Progeny and the baseline human genome. Further, we've expanded our scope to investigate similar genetic modifications in certain other animal species that appear to have had involvement with the Nash Phenomenon. I think you will find our theory and conclusions very interesting."

By the tone of his voice, I'm thinking that "interesting" in his vocabulary translates to "troubling" in mine. Of course, no briefing of any merit can be given without a PowerPoint slideshow; the screen behind him flickers to life.

He first gives a quick recap of the genetic differences unique to the Progeny. The Progeny and normal humans share 99.8 percent of DNA in common, meaning that approximately six million Progeny base pairs have been modified, affecting the expression of some four hundred genes. These genetic differences appear to be programmed to greatly increase with each successive generation. In general, these genetic modifications would appear to confer broad immunity to neurotoxins, greatly enhanced intelligence, and a repression of aggressive behaviors. The last aspect, relating to behavior, apparently being his focus for today's discussion.

The next slide on the screen depicts a miniature schnauzer, a toy dinosaur in its mouth. Chuckles all around as some joker in the back suggests it has a keen resemblance to Dr. Phineas Archer, the Director of the Los Alamos National Laboratory. Indeed, both the mutt and the lab director sport similar bushy eyebrows and full mustaches. I've noticed Archer tends to be the butt of many jokes around our offices. Ponderously formal and consumed with his own carefully curated scientific reputation, he is pointedly ignored by Monroe and the rest of the team. He has not been read into the eGenesis classified program and is utterly clueless as to the real mission being executed at his facility right under his nose and overgrown mustache.

"Alright," continues Liang as the snickers die down, "this schnauzer is a breed of domestic dog, *Canis familiarus*, if referred to as a separate species. *Canis lupus familiaris*, if viewed as a subspecies of wolves, which is the more accurate term considering dogs and wolves can still interbreed."

The slide changes to add an image of a wolf next to the dog. "Domesticated dogs, such as our schnauzer here, and wolves share about 99.9 percent of their DNA. Yet, the physical and behavioral differences between them are quite profound. Obviously, domesticated dogs and most especially breeds such as the miniature schnauzer do not and never did roam the wilds, hunting deer in packs and such, correct?"

"Well, I've been fortunate to have never encountered a pack of miniature schnauzers out in the wild," says Hillie to some more chuckles in the room.

Ignoring Hillie, Liang goes on to say that dogs and their multitude of specialized breeds would not have naturally evolved on their own. They are products of genetic engineering by humans. Albeit, not direct genetic manipulation, but rather old-school genetic engineering via selective breeding. In this tried-and-true approach, desired genetic characteristics are amplified through successive generations by careful selection of breeding pairs. This is one of the pillars of modern agronomy and has been an established practice since the eighteenth century.

Dogs and other domesticated animals have been selectively bred over the generations for a variety of characteristics including docility towards humans, he says. In fact, nearly all domesticated animals share key traits that seem to distinguish them from their wild cousins: floppy ears, smaller snouts and teeth, lighter colors, and docility towards their human masters. This suite of changes appears consistent from species to species and has been given a name: Domestication Syndrome.

Everyone in the room is nodding like, yes, of course this makes sense. But there is some shifting in chairs as many, including myself, are impatiently wondering how this all relates back to the Progeny.

Liang is now warning us that the next set of slides may have distressing images. He shows us a photo of a dead cow laying in a field, clearly mutilated. Its jaw appears to have been surgically excised. The similarity to Levi Waddle's unfortunate champion bull is jarring.

"This is one of the West's enduring mysteries. Over the years, hundreds if not thousands of cattle mutilations have been reported in the Western United States and Canada. In most cases, vital organs appear to have been surgically removed and all blood drained from the animals. Characteristically, there are no signs of struggle or footprints of the perpetrators. The questions have always been who is doing this and why? Now we think we may have some answers or at least a working theory."

This has my attention. Ever since seeing Waddle's mutilated bull, I've wondered why anyone simply interested in harvesting organs and blood for research, rituals, or whatever, wouldn't just go to their local slaughter house to procure that biological material. Sneaking into some, potentially armed, rancher's field and mutilating an animal seems like doing it the hard way.

"The problem is," Liang continues, "the local ranchers are only seeing half of the picture. They see this out in their fields," he's pointing to the photo of the mutilated cow again. "But they don't see what is happening half a world away." He now brings up an image of a dead and mutilated hoofed animal that doesn't look familiar to me.

"Anyone know what we're looking at?" he asks.

"Some kind of wild cow or bison?" suggests Hillie.

"Correct. Specifically, it is a wild cow, a Gaur, the largest species of the bovid family and one of the common domestic cow's closest genetic relatives. This particular kill was found in a remote region of Malaysia. The more we have looked into the cattle mutilation phenomenon, the more we found that their wild genetic relatives in Asia and Africa are being systematically mutilated as well. This mutilation of wild cows has been significantly underreported because, well, no one owns them or keeps track of them, right?"

At this point, the room is silent. All eyes on Liang. What started as a dry summary of an interesting but not terribly relevant mystery regarding unfortunate cows has taken an unexpected turn.

"We did some additional digging and found many other instances in which domestic animals and their closely related wild counterparts have been apparently systematically mutilated; their blood and vital organs removed. As with cattle and Gaur, understand the mutilation of wild related species is largely undercounted." He quickly flips through a collection of mutilation images of related species including dogs and wolves, cats and bobcats, domestic sheep and bighorn sheep.

"But why? Who is doing this?" I ask.

"Here is our working theory," he replies. "We believe someone or something, possibly related to the overall Nash Phenomenon, has for decades been intensely interested in the physiological and genetic effects of the Domestication Syndrome, specifically the amplification of docility and submissiveness behavioral traits."

Suddenly I have a sinking feeling in the pit of my stomach. This discussion appears to be veering towards the unthinkable. In an instant, Liang begins to confirm my worst fears.

"Now," says Liang, "back to the Nash Progeny genome. Of the four hundred or so human genes whose expression appears to have been genetically modified, we have identified forty that specifically relate to aggression and docility."

There's a question from the back. "How do genes actually affect aggressive behavior?"

"Good question. An example would be a gene we call -MAOA, which codes a metabolizing enzyme of serotonin uptake. The gene doesn't directly affect aggression but it affects the uptake of serotonin which does affect behaviors. Make sense?"

"So," I ask, "Dr. Liang, are you proposing to say that some entity, maybe hypothetically extraterrestrial, is studying kindred wild and domesticated animals of Earth to fine tune the genetic modification of the Progeny to make them more docile and less aggressive?"

"I can be even more blunt," he responds. "My team believes that much like the genetic relationship of dogs to wolves; the Progeny are being mutated into a separate subspecies of humans. A domesticated subspecies. Simply put, we humans are apparently being domesticated. But by whom and for what purpose? That is the mystery."

The room is silent. We're all stunned and lost in our thoughts; trying to process this. On one hand, certainly humanity could get by with a little less aggression. On the other hand, our assertiveness and drive are part of what makes us uniquely human. We are far from perfect as a species but who has the right to unilaterally change us for their own purposes?

A young red-haired researcher in the back of the room has heard enough. "This is outrageous!" he exclaims. "What gives whomever or whatever is doing this the right to come here and modify humans for their own purposes?"

Liang seems to have anticipated the objection. "I couldn't agree with you more, but history suggests there is plenty of precedent for such meddling. Consider this, as the current apex species on the planet, mankind has for nearly all recorded history consistently modified, marginalized, or exterminated a great many of the other plants and animals in our world. We domesticate them and modify their genetics. We often raise them in hellishly confined captivity so that we may cheaply consume their flesh. Through pollution and elimination of habitat, we have driven countless other species to extinction."

Liang certainly has a point. Indeed, Genesis 9:2 says "the fear of you and the dread of you shall be upon every beast of the earth, and upon every fowl of the air, upon all that moveth upon the earth, and upon all the fishes of the sea." It's unclear that humanity has truly absorbed many of the teachings of the Bible, but this dominion over the animals of the earth imperative; we've really embraced that one with wild enthusiasm.

Liang continues in his response. "Did we ask the wolves whether it would be acceptable to modify their bloodlines to eventually produce miniature schnauzers? Was there a negotiation?"

The young researcher is growing frustrated. "No. Of course not!"

"Why?"

"There would be no point. Meaningful communication could not be possible. Come on! These are just lower life forms..." His voice trails off as he realizes he's answered his own question.

Liang continues, "now, let's look at the Progeny population and its dispersal around the world." Liang is on a roll and I guess he's figured he may as well rip the rest of the bandage off.

His next slide shows a map of the world with red dots indicating the location of all known Progeny. We tend to refer to them as the Nash Progeny but we know there have been many dozens of Nash-like genetic interventions that have occurred all around the world. By our current estimates, there may be as many as ten thousand Progeny walking the Earth. Nearly all blissfully unaware of their true differences from normal humans.

One of the ways LISA has already assisted the eGenesis program has been through the retrieval, authorized or otherwise, of global databases of DNA registries. These include popular commercial ancestry/heritage related services as well as medical research datasets, and repositories of DNA collected by law enforcement. LISA has then scanned and analyzed this vast trove of data for the specific genetic markers unique to the Progeny. The result being that we now know the identities of nearly eighty percent of the affected individuals as well as where they are located on the planet.

For the most part the global Progeny are fairly well distributed across the planet. But there are several areas in which they tend to be more concentrated. Interestingly, one of the areas of highest Progeny concentrations appears to be in the Navajo Nation, situated in the Four Corners region where Arizona, New Mexico, Utah, and Colorado meet.

"See the red dots?" continues Liang. "Today we call them Progeny. In a few years, once the nanites' neurotoxins reach lethal levels globally, these dots will simply represent survivors. The only surviving humans. And, I would submit to you that the distribution of these survivors is not random but done on purpose. Look at the genetic variability as to racial and ethnic makeup. Also, their global dispersal makes the population less vulnerable to localized natural disasters such as earthquakes or tsunamis."

"What are you getting at?" asks Monroe.

"We've done the math. The population characteristics and global dispersal of the Progeny does not appear to have occurred by chance. It represents the minimum genetically-diverse viable human breeding stock. The minimum level needed to maintain a stable global population. And perhaps over time to reestablish increased population levels with the new domesticated human subspecies."

Utter silence. Finally, Hillie says out loud what we're all probably thinking. A passage from the New Testament Beatitudes.

"And the meek shall inherit the Earth."

CHAPTER 46

The novelist, David Foster Wallace, once said everybody is identical in their secret unspoken belief that, way deep down, they are different from everyone else.

Dr. Tanesha West truly knows that she is indeed different from the rest of us. And she knows the reasons all too well. For West is a key member of the eGenesis Program and a Progeny herself. Her great-grandfather had served on the Nash with Ben Pruitt.

I welcome her with a smile, "so how's the program's favorite pin-cushion?" A droll reference to the fact that she's become a universal donor of convenience to eGenesis. Every time a researcher here needs a small tissue or blood sample from a Progeny, they grab a needle and go looking for Tanesha.

The smile is returned. "As usual I'm down about half a pint, Jack. You get used to it. You know how some people condition themselves to get by with less sleep than normal? I guess I seem to get by with a little less blood."

She gives me a little laugh and a wink. Her eyes are intense deep golden pools, nearly luminescent. A striking combination with her ebony complexion; the typical physical expression of her Nash genetics in an African-American.

At the tender age of twenty-four, she already holds dual PhDs in Physics and in Systems Engineering from Caltech. She is simply brilliant and I suspect her Nash genetic enhancements only amplify her innate abilities.

"How were the sessions in Boston?" I ask. She has just returned from reviewing research by some of our unsuspecting proxies at MIT's Lincoln Lab.

"Excellent work in progress in my opinion. And, as a bonus, no one stuck a needle in me. Too bad I missed Liang's briefing yesterday. Heard it was interesting."

"Interesting, I guess that would be one way to put it," I reply.

"Yeah. I understand I'm being domesticated. A schnauzer amongst you wolves."

"But the findings are preliminary. I wouldn't read too much into it right now," I respond.

"Sure, I don't want to go barking up the wrong tree!"

"Very funny. By the way, the news isn't so good for us wolves either. We're rapidly climbing to the top of the endangered species list."

It must be strange for her. A scientist studying a phenomenon that she is a part of herself. She's made little mention of it to me other than a wry comment or two that some days she feels like she's living in an Escher drawing. A reference to M. C. Escher, the Dutch artist known for depictions of optical illusions and endless recursive loops; staircases climbing unto themselves.

Tanisha and I are seated in the program's visualization room. Three of its walls are essentially massive ultra-high-definition computer screens. We're here to brief Winston Monroe on our progress in mapping the propagation and evolution of the nanites across the globe.

Monroe pops into the room and quickly sits down. "Sorry I'm a bit late. I've been really looking forward to this. Okay, let's get started. Who is going to do the honors and brief your progress?"

Tanisha and I exchange a grin as the room's main speaker begins to project LISA's synthetic voice. *"Good morning, Dr. Monroe. If it is acceptable to you, LISA will present the data and results."*

Monroe is giving us a quick sideways glance. He's a bit caught off guard. "Um, sure, that would be acceptable, LISA."

"Thank you. LISA will first illustrate the dispersal and growth of successive nanite populations over time, beginning in the 1930's and going forward to present day."

A large slowly spinning globe of the Earth appears on one of the walls. A multitude of small points of red appear scattered across the globe. The red points represent separate locations where the nanites were apparently first introduced on the planet. There are about two dozen points appearing on the globe, including San Diego, Angikuni Lake in Canada, the Navajo Nation, and Roswell, New Mexico. The small red points then blossom out as the nanites over time multiply and propagate outward through the rest of the world. As time passes, the red colors fade away and are replaced with a purple hue.

"Why are the colors changing?" asks Monroe.

"LISA is representing each successive generation or version of the nanites with a different color as they evolve and change function."

"It's part of the nanite paleontology effort, Winston. As you know, the nanites have changed their outward appearance over time and those changes seem to relate to how they function," I explain.

"Yes," adds Tanisha, "for the bulk of the twentieth century, the nanites mostly focused on reproducing themselves and propagating across the planet. The transition to purple that you see on the screen represents the adoption of AM radio transmissions for networking and communication."

"Correct. The next significant change in function occurred in the late 1980's. Specifically, this is the mutation that began producing carbon dioxide emissions. It appears to have begun in Ukraine in 1986 and then rapidly spread across the planet." The global map being projected has a new color, yellow, and it rapidly blossoms across the globe.

"Why then? What was special about Ukraine?" asks Monroe.

"LISA," I request. "Please summarize significant events occurring in Ukraine in 1986."

"There were several significant social, political, and economic news events occurring in the then Soviet client state in 1986, but the event of most global impact occurred on Saturday, April 26th of that year. On that date Reactor Number Four of the Chernobyl Nuclear Power Plant suffered a ruptured core and subsequent fire causing a massive release of radioactive materials."

Monroe's eyebrows furrow. "So, the radiation caused the mutation?"

"Possibly," replies Tanisha. "Or maybe the nanites themselves changed as a reaction to the radiation. We just don't know."

"Yes," I add, "and, curiously, there was not a similar reaction to prior nuclear radiation releases. The Trinity Site shot, Hiroshima, Nagasaki, and, of course, all of the above ground testing that preceded Chernobyl."

"If LISA may continue, you will see the propagation map advancing to the present day and the color changes once more to orange, reflecting the mutation to emit the neurotoxins."

If LISA was not an inanimate set of algorithms and software, I'd begin to suspect she was getting bored with the cross-talk and wants to move this along.

Monroe is studying the array of orange across the globe. "So, while dispersal of the nanites is global, I see there are distinct high concentrations at certain locations. I take it these are what we are calling the foundation colonies?"

He's referring to what we have identified as key nodes in the planet-wide network of nanites. These colonies appear to have several unique functions including transmitting and processing data and mutation updates between themselves before instructions are apparently flowed out to individual nanites in their jurisdictions. It has been suggested somewhat ominously that these nodes may form a neural network of sorts. Perhaps individual nanites have little intelligence, but networked together, the global collective may itself be conscious on some level.

"That is correct," responds Tanisha, "those are indeed the foundation colonies. There are about a hundred arrayed around the world. These locations have, by the way, been confirmed by reconnaissance satellite signal gathering."

Monroe smiles, "I'm glad to hear our arm twisting with the National Reconnaissance Office to temporarily repurpose one of their orbital assets has been a success. I'm not sure if they were more amused or annoyed at our interest in isolating and locating certain oddly coded AM radio frequency emissions."

"One of the enduring Nash mysteries," continues Tanisha, "has been the distribution and placement of the foundation colonies in the world. Why are they placed where they are? The locations are clearly not random. On the other hand, the nodes are not equidistant from one another as you might expect from a normal communications network. Thanks to LISA, we now think we have an answer. LISA?"

"LISA was tasked to collect extensive data on global weather patterns, prevailing winds, and ocean currents. This data was provided by Admiral Hillenbrand."

The wall screen display of the globe now shifts to display a dynamic model of the predominant planetary weather patterns in motion.

"Given these patterns, LISA was tasked to identify the optimum placement of emission points to most effectively spread a cloud of neurotoxins across Earth." The display now adds the locations LISA calculates as optimum dispersal points.

"I'll be damned, look at that correlation." Monroe is nodding his head at the revelation. "There is nearly a perfect fit between LISA's projections and the actual locations of the foundation colonies."

"In almost every case," I say, "but not right here." I'm pointing to a remote spot on the globe. "LISA calculates that this location should be optimal for neurotoxin emissions, but the satellite has not picked up any AM signals to confirm the presence of a foundation colony."

"LISA?" Monroe is glancing about, not sure where he should be looking to address her disembodied voice. "Are you certain that your calculations are correct?"

"Dr. Monroe, LISA's calculations are only as accurate as the input given to LISA. Assuming the input data is correct, LISA is 99.4 percent confident that a foundation colony should be found at those coordinates."

"Any ideas as to why the satellite didn't pick up any signals?" He's directing this to Tanisha and me.

"There could be any number of reasons," replies Tanisha. "The colony itself may be located in a cave or there may be another geological feature that is restricting the signal."

"A more concerning reason might be that this colony has for some reason switched to frequencies other than AM or has figured out how to cloak their signals," I add. "That sort of a change would be troubling as it would suggest the colonies are now aware we are monitoring their transmissions and are taking active countermeasures."

"Sounds as though the stakes on this location are being raised. We probably need to go down there in person and find out the ground truth. Are you two up for a little fieldwork?"

"Count me in," says Tanisha, "I've developed a frequency signal blocker and a few other items in my electronic bag of tricks that I'd like to test on some nanites."

"I'm up for it as well," I say. "Especially, if it means I happen to miss out on another uplifting lecture by Dr. Liang."

"It's a very remote location, I'll make the security and diplomatic arrangements," says Monroe. "And I think I'll come along as well. Wouldn't hurt to have some more boots on the ground."

"This time make sure they are indeed boots," I smile. "Last time your penny loafers didn't work out so well on the trail in Montana."

CHAPTER 47

"Find anything of interest?" I ask.

"Some damn fine stretches of trout stream. I tell you, Patagonia has some of the best fishing in the world. Always love coming back here!" Hillie has just finished scrambling up the streambank, fly rod in hand.

I smile thinly, "I think I meant any sign of a foundation colony. You know, why we're here…the mission?"

"Jack, my boy, someday you'll understand mixing a little recreation with the mission sharpens your game, eh? Did I mention the time I went sport fishing in a harbor the Iraqis had mined during Desert Storm?"

"Yeah, maybe a couple of times."

Hillie and I are part of a small eGenesis team dispatched to Santa Cruz Province in Argentina to locate and potentially destroy a key nanite foundation colony. Based on projected propagation patterns, LISA has localized the potential colony site to a twenty square mile area of rugged terrain just outside the bounds of Argentina's Parque Nacional Los Glaciares.

Besides Hillie and me, the researcher boots on the ground include Winston Monroe and Tanisha West. Anderson and Pullman are also with us to provide security. They're packing semi-automatic rifles that were somehow fast-tracked through local customs. This seems to be a result of some backroom sausage-making deal between the US Consulate and the Argentinian government. I probably don't want to know the details.

Our cover story for the locals, of course, is that we're fishing and hunting enthusiasts; tourists from the States here for the fishing and the culture. I must say Hillie has embraced the whole faux fisherman-tourist ruse with more enthusiasm than is probably required. Over the past four days that we've trekked through the countryside, he's rarely missed an opportunity to dampen his line in the multitude of trout streams we've explored. And all this morning he's been going on about dinner plans for the return this evening to our hotel in El Calafate, the nearest town to Argentina's Glacier Park. Try the Cazuela de Cordero, he's been saying. Paired with a local Malbec, it's a lamb stew to die for.

Perhaps that could have been phrased a little differently given what we're up against.

But if I'm honest myself, I'll have to confess the tourist facet of this little nanite hunting operation is more than a little rewarding. Mid-November here is the middle of spring in the Southern Hemisphere and the landscape is stunningly beautiful. Lakes, glaciers, and forests with wildflowers in bloom meet the eye everywhere you look. The rugged Cerro Pietrobolli peak and the rest of Andes mountain range loom to the west, forming the border with Chile. The immense Patagonian Steppe drops down and stretches out in a series of plateaus to the east. Here, near the southern-most extent of South America, we are over twice as far from Buenos Aires as we are from Antarctica.

A sound of footsteps and voices is approaching from the trail ahead as the rest of the team is on the way to rejoin us. They've been searching for indications of the colony up an adjoining tributary.

"Any signs of the colony?" I ask.

Tanisha is shaking her head and gesturing at the electromagnetic field meter in her hand. "Not a thing on the EM meter. We've now covered most of the area LISA had identified as the location for a foundation colony. And LISA is almost never wrong."

"Not unless she is given phony data for input." I say this with a smirk directed at Anderson. I get a grimace and an eyeroll in return. My day is improving.

"Well," sighs Monroe, "we have one more sector to survey. It's centered on a canyon about five miles from here. We might as well go back to the vehicles and head over there to the trailhead.

"Only one sector left? And here I thought I'd get to spend another couple of days out here in the backcountry with you guys!" Tanisha laughs and smiles.

I've been very impressed with the young scientist's resolve on this trip. Slender framed and barely five foot-two, she's been tenacious in monitoring and maintaining a cache of sophisticated electronic sensing equipment. I suspect nearly all of her brilliant but short professional career has been spent either in labs or lecture halls. This adventure is likely her first time out in the field.

Yesterday I had found a quiet moment to ask her how she was holding up. "Gee," she had said, "tromping through the rugged countryside in remote South America with a bunch of old white guys and fifty pounds of electronic equipment on my back? And, if we're successful, maybe getting exposed to a lethal colony of alien nanites? How can this not be my life's dream come true!" The last added with a roll of the eyes and a sarcastic wink. Point taken.

Two hours later we are about halfway up the heavily forested canyon trail when Tanisha's EM meter begins to register a signal. She raises a hand for us to halt while she analyzes the signal.

"Faint, AM frequency band. No known local activity should be registering. Appears to be gigabyte data pulse bursts consistent with nanite activity. Based on signal strength, I'd say we're within a quarter mile of the source."

"Okay, folks, remember our security protocols." Anderson has pulled his weapon off his shoulder and into a ready position. "I take the lead and Pullman takes our six." Accordingly, Pullman readies his weapon and moves to the rear.

Several more minutes up the trail and Anderson raises his fist, signaling a halt. "Tanisha?"

"Meter's starting to register much higher signal energy. We're close, very close now."

My pulse is quickening. We are about to enter an unknown regime. The overall mission is two part. First, we are to find and document the specific location of the foundation colony. LISA has identified this colony as a particularly strategic node in the nanites' global network. Given its proximity relative to prevailing winds and the ocean currents of the Drake

Passage, it could be particularly effective in both propagating nanite spread as well as harmful gasses. The second part of our mission is a true step into the unknown. We are going to attempt to kill the foundation colony.

Up until now eGenesis has only experimentally destroyed small colonies of nanites. However, the nanites then quickly adopted mutations to stymie the threats, triggering planetary-wide counter-measure mutations through data passed along their AM network. Our plan is to jam all AM signals emanating from the colony to cut off their warning signals to the larger global nanite population. Then the death blow will be administered by a highly corrosive batch of acid. Not exactly a solution that scales globally, but it should effectively destroy the colony.

However, the true unknown here will be the reaction of the nanites to this attack. To date, no one has directly attacked a foundation colony itself. Will the nanites attempt to deploy defensive countermeasures as in the past? Or will an attack on a key foundation colony trigger a violent, agressive countermeasure with unknown conseaquences? If we're lucky, we'll walk away with perhaps an approach to contain and eliminate the threat. If we're not so lucky, then Hillie's plans for the evening's dinner menu may be moot.

"I think I see where the source is," says Anderson. "See that opening over at the canyon wall? Looks like the entrance to a cavern."

Tanisha agrees. She's saying the EM meter is starting to peg strongly upward. The location in a cavern would explain how the colony's radio emissions has eluded satellite detection. We gather around the cavern entrance, watching Tanisha activate the AM signal blocking devices she's brought. Monroe is sensing my hesitation about proceeding inside.

"Are you alright, Jack?" he asks. "You're not claustrophobic, are you?"

"Last time I went underground "in support of the mission" it didn't go so well."

"No worries. This time Pullman and I have your back!" Anderson is patting the barrel of his rifle. My history with Anderson aside, I don't find this particularly reassuring. First, a rifle seems like the wrong tool for the job if we're defending ourselves against nanites. It would be sort of like trying to swat flies with a bulldozer. Second, much like in the Sapphire Belle, the shockwave from a gun blast could bring half the cavern ceiling down on us.

I shake my head and sigh. "I'll be fine. Let's do this."

We proceed inside in single file. Rifle raised and safety off, Anderson is on point and I'm following right behind him. Fortunately, the cavern entrance is quite wide, maybe seventy feet in diameter and thirty feet high, so a fair amount of daylight is penetrating back into its depths.

"What the hell?" Anderson slams on the brakes so quickly I nearly pile into the back of him. In the dim light before us on the floor of the cavern is a transparent circular dome approximately five feet high and maybe thirty feet in diameter. It is encasing the foundation colony which is glowing brightly in what appears to be a state of perpetual induced luminescence.

"Is that some form of nanite nursery?" Hillie is asking the first question racing through most of our minds. The second question likely being who put this dome in place and when are they coming back.

"It's not going to be a nursery for long." Anderson is raising his rifle and aiming at the dome. "A couple of rounds will shatter the dome and then they'll get the acid treatment."

I'm about to tell Anderson to slow down so we can examine the dome. Shooting first and asking questions later is a doubtful strategy given the stakes at play here. But suddenly the group falls silent, our attention drawn to a gradual movement from the darkness of the cavern behind the dome.

Slowly out of the shadows a small bipedal creature emerges. It is a gray alien. A dead ringer for the smaller non-fake aliens Judy Pruitt had described under hypnosis. It places one three-fingered hand on the dome and looks at us with large almond shaped eyes that are all black pupil or maybe all iris. It seems a bit unsteady like it's holding onto the dome for balance.

"That's it," says Anderson, tightly gripping his weapon. "We caught the bastards red-handed." He nods to Pullman to get ready to shoot.

"No! Let's slow this down!" Monroe is technically in charge here and he's trying to keep the situation from escalating beyond control. He is looking to buy some time to figure out what we do next.

"Please! Just listen!" Tanisha is shouting for us all to be quiet. "Listen to the alien. He's saying he means us no harm."

"What the hell are you talking about?" says Hillie. "I don't hear it making any noise."

Tanisha looks at our dumbfounded expressions. "No one else is hearing him? He's not speaking out loud but I hear him clearly in my mind." Confusion and headshakes all around. No one else is hearing the creature.

"How is it that Tanisha is the only one that can hear the being? Could it be…?" Suddenly it hits me. Tanisha is the only human here with Nash blood. This sort of telepathic ability to communicate with aliens is likely a previously unknown aspect of her mutations.

"It makes sense," I say quickly, "Tanisha's Nash abilities may allow her to communicate telepathically with…other species. Tanisha, is the being communicating with you in English?"

"No. But it is like I can understand his thoughts directly. I know it sounds crazy. I can't explain it, but language isn't necessary for this to work."

"Is he still communicating with you?"

"Yes. Look, he's repeatedly saying he means us no harm. He's saying he is here trying to contain and destroy the nanites. The dome is an experimental device he's developed to try and stop the colony."

"So, either he's lying," says Hillie, "and in effect the dome helps drive us to extinction, or he's telling the truth and if we destroy the dome, we destroy what may be our last chance to stop the nanites."

Monroe gives me a resigned look. He was quick to remind us he is in charge, but now the responsibility is solely falling on his shoulders. Sometimes the seat of authority is a very lonely place. I guess no one said sorting out this alien nanite stuff was gonna be easy.

"Okay," Tanisha appears to be receiving more communication. "He is trying to help, but he is very sick and weak. He may be dying. He wants… he wants me to come over next to him. Wants to physically touch me. It will make the communication much faster somehow.

"That's a non-starter, Tanisha," says Anderson. "I'm responsible for your safety. No way in hell you're getting an inch closer to that abomination."

Monroe asserts himself. "Colonel, I'm responsible for the success of this mission. I'll make the call, but we need to study our options carefully. I'll need more data to make a decision."

"No," says Tanisha simply, shaking her head. "Enough. There are nearly ten thousand of us Nash Progeny walking this planet. From the earliest age I suspect some of us have known that we're somehow different from everyone else. But I'm probably the only Progeny fully aware of just how different we really are. Do you know what it's like to study yourself as a *specimen* of a genetic anomaly? A mutation? Oh, everyone is so polite referring to us as the Nash Progeny. Call it what it is, we're fucking mutants."

"Well, I'm sorry, I had no idea…" stammers Monroe.

Tanisha cuts him off. "You know, I'd give anything just to be normal. I never asked for this mutation, no one did. I've always wondered…you know, why me? Why do I have this condition, these abilities? What is my purpose? I think I know now. I am here at this place…at this time…with this very unusual ability…for a reason. This. This is my purpose."

Tanisha starts to walk towards the being. Anderson seems confused, looking to Monroe for direction. Monroe is frozen in place, staring first at Tanisha and then at the alien. Anderson shifts his stance raising his gun. "Tanisha, I'm ordering you not to proceed!"

Tanisha turns slightly and looks back at him. "If you're going to use that gun to stop me, make sure the first round is a kill shot."

CHAPTER 48

We all fall silent and watch intently as Tanisha slowly walks past the dome and approaches the being. I am simply stunned at the sight and filled with admiration for this young woman. I imagine if you put a thousand people in the same circumstances fewer than maybe one or two would have the courage and determination she is showing in approaching the unknown. Anderson and Pullman have their rifles at the ready, but any shot they take now risks striking Tanisha and they know it.

Tanisha is now standing next to the alien, bending down to come face to face with the entity. For a moment they look into each other's eyes. What the being is saying to her telepathically, we can only guess. Tanisha sits down on the ground next to the dome upon which the entity is still leaning unsteadily. Gently, almost affectionately, the being reaches out and places a hand slowly upon Tanisha's temple. Tanisha twitches slightly and closes her eyes. She nods from time to time but is otherwise still and silent. They remain in this position, this apparent mind lock, for more than fifteen minutes. It feels like an eternity for those of us breathlessly watching.

Finally, the communication must be complete. The entity releases its hand and Tanisha stands up a bit unsteadily. For a moment, they look intently at each other. The alien raises his hand and Tanisha nods. Even those of us without telepathic abilities understand what is being said. This is a goodbye. As Tanisha turns to leave, the entity slumps down further against the dome. It now seems to be gasping for breath.

Tanisha slowly walks back to us and then slumps down to sit on a rock herself. Her eyes are closed and she's unconsciously rocking back and forth in a near fetal position, trying to process what has just happened. Finally, her eyes slowly open, like she's overslept and is just waking up.

"Tanisha, are you okay?" Hillie is down at her side, hand on her shoulder.

"Yeah. Yeah, I am," she finally replies, still a bit disoriented. "How long? How long was I…gone?"

"You and it were in some sort of mind meld for fifteen or twenty minutes."

"No. No. That can't be. I think we must have talked for several days!" Incredibly, somehow the perception of time itself had changed for Tanisha while she and the being were sharing minds.

"What did it say? Are you comfortable telling us what you talked about?" I'm intrigued at witnessing what may be the first human-alien telepathic session in history, but we still have an active foundation colony in front of us. We need to stick to business and figure out what insights the alien may have offered to contain this threat.

"Still so much to process," she says, "but I'll try. His name really doesn't translate well to English, but 'Na'Vack' is probably close. His species call themselves the Diné which simply means 'the people.' As he had said at the beginning, they mean us no harm and the nanites are as much a threat to them as they are to us."

"Excuse me?" I say, exchanging a look with Monroe whose raised eyebrow threatens any moment to crawl off his forehead. "But, in their language, the Navajo people of the Southwest also refer to themselves as the Diné which means 'the people' as well."

"Really?" Tanisha is blinking rapidly, staring off into the distance, apparently accessing more transferred memories. "Yeah, actually, I guess that's not really surprising."

"Where are these aliens from? What is their point of origin?"

"You're really not going to believe me."

"Look, I just saw my colleague spend fifteen minutes in a mind meld with an alien. And then she casually notes it's maybe not all that surprising that the aliens and our Navajos use the same name to refer to themselves. Trust me, I think we're open to almost anything at this point," I say.

Tanisha sighs and shakes her head. "They're from here. Earth. It's hard to explain but they are really…us. And we are them."

Monroe gives me a sideways glance. "Tanisha, maybe you should start at the beginning."

Tanisha is hesitating from time to time as she translates the images and ideas she has been given, but her narrative, if fantastic, seems coherent. She says the being told her the Diné were an advanced race of humans who developed a highly technically advanced civilization. A civilization that existed on Earth approximately five million years ago. A civilization so advanced they were able to develop a prototype of a star drive capable of faster than light speeds. Unfortunately, as the years passed, they depleted their natural resources and triggered a climate change event. The subsequent scarcity of food and other resources drove them to numerous wars culminating in an all-out nuclear exchange. A group of survivors left the ruined planet in the new unproven star drive ships, intending to explore the galaxy to seek out new planets to inhabit and to find other sentient life forms.

"Okay," I say, "two problems with the story so far. First, our new three-fingered friend Na'Vack over there may be a nice fella and all but he certainly doesn't look remotely human. And, also, I'm pretty sure he is not a Navajo. Second, if a civilization advanced enough to develop faster than light space travel previously existed on this planet, we've have known about it, right?"

Hillie chimes in, "Yeah, there would have been artifacts, manufactured materials, evidence of chemicals, remnants of pollution, fossils, and so forth. Hell, they supposedly had a nuclear war that would have generated radioactive isotopes. What are we missing?"

"I think I can answer your second concern about the lack of evidence of prior advanced civilizations on Earth, if I may?" offers Monroe. "If we're talking about detecting the physical signatures of a past advanced civilization that existed say 50,000 or 100,000 years ago, then you are absolutely right. We certainly would have found artifacts, chemical and radioactive isotope evidence. No question."

"But," he continues, "move further back in time, say beyond two million years, and it's a different story. Remember in geologic timescales the Earth is constantly in change. The Earth's crust is essentially recycled by tectonic forces, subduction, and volcanism approximately every one and a half million to two million years. And even the radioactive elements disbursed in a nuclear war would be far beyond their detectable half-lives in that timeframe. Yes, it is entirely possible that an advanced civilization could have existed on this planet five million years ago without detection now in the present day."

"The Diné," Tanisha continues, "once were human, exactly like us, when they left this planet. However, over the subsequent five million years, they continued to change and evolve into their present day form we see before us."

"But they look nothing like us," counters Hillie, "outside of being bipedal humanoids."

"True enough," Tanisha replies, "but remember that, other than being bipedal primates, chimpanzees and humans don't look much alike either. But we share something like ninety-seven percent of our DNA."

Monroe softly whistles to himself. "*Homo Futurae*...Future Man. The next species in our family tree. Or perhaps the oldest species."

"This form," continues Tanisha, "their genome, has over the millennia been optimized to serve the needs of an advanced space-faring race. But this evolution has been both a blessing and a curse. They've gained great powers of intellect, incredibly long life spans, and the ability to mind meld and communicate by telepathy, but at a terrible cost."

"A genetic cost, I assume?" I offer.

"Yes, but I need to give you some more context so you can understand the current predicament."

Per Tanisha, when the Diné left Earth for the stars they had expected to find a galaxy filled with life and intelligent species. They found quite the opposite. The galaxy was largely cold, empty, and lifeless. Over the past five million years they have explored a large portion of the galaxy; hundreds of thousands of planets. But they have yet to encounter another single living sentient species. To be sure, they discovered a multitude of planets that supported less advanced forms of life. In some cases, the Diné established small colonies on these worlds while the bulk of them continued to move on and explore further.

It turns out life in the universe is rare, and intelligent life is nearly non-existent. Even a civilization as advanced and long-lived as the Diné, spanning over five million years, is like a candle briefly flickering on and then out in the vastness of space and time. The chances of two space-faring civilizations encountering each other at the same time and in same place in the immensity of the galaxy turned out to be extremely remote.

"Tanisha, you said they never encountered another *living* civilization. That suggests perhaps they discovered the remains of prior civilizations that had disappeared or died out before the Diné encountered them?"

"That is correct, Jack. And it is a key part of the puzzle you need to understand. As they travelled the galaxy, the Diné discovered dozens and dozens of planets where prior civilizations had flourished but then gone extinct. Dead worlds. Most had succumbed to war, pandemic, or depleted resources. All brief candles extinguished quickly on the timescale of the galaxy. The Diné would take years to carefully explore, catalog, and research each dead civilization's surviving artifacts, libraries, and data archives. They would then incorporate the best of each civilization's alien science and technology with their own."

"But," she continues, "as the centuries passed, the Diné gradually became aware that they themselves were at risk of becoming extinct as well…yet another extinguished galactic candle flame. Centuries and centuries of interbreeding along with genetic damage and mutations caused by cosmic radiation and the energy pulses from their own star drives were beginning to cause irreparable damage to their genome. The issues were beginning to affect their ability to reproduce and making them increasingly susceptible to diseases."

"So, they thought they'd come back to Earth now and try to breed with their former primitive selves…us?" I ask. Peter Roberts and the Skywatch gang certainly believed there was an ongoing extraterrestrial interest in human genetics and reproduction. The example we had discussed over breakfast at the Stockman's had been, Randy, the logging truck driver's apparent sexual encounter with an unknown being.

"Not exactly. It is far more involved than that. And you're essentially 125,000 years off the mark of what really happened. To better understand this, we should probably talk about Wooly Mammoths."

"Indeed, I imagine we should. I think I see where this is going." Monroe is smiling and nodding as though a discussion of Wooly Mammoths at this point makes all the sense in the world.

CHAPTER 49

According to Monroe, *Mammuthus primigenius* roamed the Earth from about 800,000 years in the past until the end of the Pleistocene Epoch about 12,000 years ago. Interestingly, in the later years these shaggy six-ton beasts likely shared their environment with early humans who, it is thought, may have hastened their demise. In the present day, the life and times of the Wooly mammoth might have been just an interesting footnote to paleontology, had it not been for some rapidly emerging scientific advances.

By the late 2010's, tools and techniques for genetic sequencing and editing had become ever faster, easier, and cheaper to deploy. At the same time, the increasing melt-off of ice and snow in the Arctic latitudes due to global warming began to reveal a small number of largely intact remains of mammoths. Some of these prehistoric corpses had been apparently frozen in such a fashion that their flesh, blood, and even stomach contents were remarkably well preserved. This biological material was in fact so well preserved that intact mammoth DNA could be extracted and the genome sequenced. Almost immediately some in the scientific community proposed that this massive prehistoric animal could indeed be brought back from extinction.

Now, Monroe says, teams from multiple research organizations around the world are racing to splice the genes of a woolly mammoth with those of a compatible genetic host. In this case, it would be the Asian elephant, its closest living relative, which shares 99 percent of its DNA. While popular books and action movies have fantasized for years about reconstructing dinosaurs from old DNA, the ongoing work with mammoth DNA may yield the real deal; the resurrection of a dead species. However, Monroe notes, the resultant animal would in effect be a mammoth-elephant hybrid rather than a true mammoth clone.

"Thanks, Winston. Always helpful to have a theoretical biologist on the team," says Tanisha. "Please keep the tale of the mammoth in mind as I proceed with the story of The People. About 125,000 years ago, not that long ago from their perspective given their five-million-year history and long life spans, a group of the Diné became very concerned about their degrading genome. They decided to return to Earth and reestablish their old human species form on the planet. It was thought that over time the new humans could be genetically modified to permit cross-species reproduction with the Diné and the rejuvenation of the bloodlines."

"When the Diné returned to Earth," she continues "they found that the planet had completely refreshed and reestablished its old environment. There was no sign of their previous civilization. They had brought archival DNA from their early human form and sought a compatible host species to receive the genetic splicing. They found a species of early hominids, forerunners to what we would come to call the Cro Magnons. The human DNA was then genetically encoded in such a manner that over time and subsequent generations, human base pairs would come to dominate the hominid genome. And thousands of years later, well, here we are."

"Fascinating," I say, "so, in effect, we're the reconstituted mammoths here?"

"That would appear to be the case," confirms Monroe. "Of course, one key difference is that the human DNA was apparently genetically modified to overwrite the original 'host' hominid DNA over the generations."

"So, we're like the reconstituted mammoth with the Asian elephant genes overwritten out of existence?"

"That is correct, Jack."

"Great, when do we get to the part about destroying the nanites?"

"I haven't forgotten about them either," Tanisha replies, "but you can't understand the nanites unless you understand how the Diné intended to use them. I think…oh, what?"

Tanisha stops talking, she's holding her head in her hands, eyes closed.

"Are you alright?"

"I dunno," she responds slowly. "Strange…feeling weak and dizzy. I guess maybe this is an effect of the mind share. I'll be okay; just need to rest a second and sort of reset myself."

"Okay, I think I'll be fine," she finally says a little too unsteadily for my comfort. "About 10,000 years ago, the Diné encountered another dead civilization, the Zoern. This particular civilization had been in effect a small galactic empire, dominating several nearby star systems prior to its own demise. It turned out those aliens had been a particularly aggressive, nasty bunch. They attacked neighboring planets with nuclear weapons and enslaved the few in the populace that did survive. They changed the conquered planets' climates to suit their own needs. They thrived on much higher global temperatures, approaching boiling, and required a significant level of unique chemical gasses in the atmospheres. These gasses were neurotoxins, deadly to most other species."

"I think I see where this is going. And it's not reassuring," I say.

"Yes, the Zoern developed highly complex swarms of nanites to do their climate change dirty work. They would surreptitiously seed targeted planets with colonies of nanites prior to their attack and invasion. Once the Zoern unleashed nuclear weapons in their conquests, the dormant nanite colonies would activate and begin altering the victim planet's climate and atmosphere."

"True to their past practices," she continues, "the Diné harvested the best of the remnant science and technology from the dead Zoern world as well. This included the nanites, which the Diné reprogrammed for peaceful purposes. They found the nanites to be incredibly useful and broadly assimilated them into their existing technologies, including advanced genetic editing. Their small size proved useful in specifically targeting and recoding individual DNA base pairs."

"Even an unevolved proto-Diné such as myself here can see the risks they took," I say. "Once a deadly technology emerges, no amount of peaceful conversion ever puts a dangerous genie completely back in the bottle." At least my powers of hindsight are highly evolved.

"True enough," replies Tanisha, "but the Diné continued to use the nanites for a variety of applications over the next 10,000 years with no adverse effects. It's likely that over the generations the militaristic nature of the nanites' origin was largely forgotten."

She's taking a few more deep breaths, trying to keep focused.

"Still dizzy?"

"Yeah, still kinda weak," she continues, "anyway, we roll forward in time to the early twentieth century back here on Earth. Over the passing millennia and centuries, humans re-evolve to become the planet's apex species again. The alien Diné continue to observe us and monitor the progress of our civilization. From time to time, they quietly intervene in the course of history at various technological and cultural inflection points, but for the most part they remain hidden on the sidelines."

"The so-called ancient astronaut theory," remarks Hillie.

Monroe smiles. "Looking to be less of a theory and more of a reality now, I'd say. The Navajo and other native peoples' origin traditions often refer to interactions with wise beings from the stars. It's likely the early Navajos had some contacts with them and the Diné name was somehow adopted into their cultural memory."

"After witnessing the horrors of World War I," continues Tanisha, her voice becoming unsteady and raspy, "the Diné decide it's time to make some final adjustments to the human genome. Mankind's predilection for tribalism, war, and violence has concerned them. They fear that violent animal-like remnants of our early hominid host's primate genetic heritage may yet drive us to extinction before we can genetically be reintegrated with the Diné."

"Little did they know that World War I, the war to end all wars, was just a warm-up for World War II."

"Yes, how true, and sad. Beginning in the 1920's and continuing on until this day, the Diné systematically abducted and genetically modified small numbers of humans. These people are what we have been referring to as the Nash Progeny. The Diné have genetically modified these individual's germlines such that their offspring and subsequent generations inherit and amplify these modifications. The genetic changes involve increases in cognitive abilities, nascent powers of telepathy, certain biological changes to permit cross-species sexual reproduction, and a bias for cooperation and docility rather than for aggression and violence. The outbreak of World War II only increased the urgency. After the war they significantly increased their genetic programs and surveillance of our world."

"Post-war, 1947," adds Hillie, "the Kenneth Arnold sighting and the beginning of the modern UFO era. The term 'flying saucers' entered the national vocabulary."

"Of course, they were using nanites to perform these genetic modifications. And every time they landed, every time they abducted and modified a human, they inadvertently released nanites into Earth's environment. Worse yet, in several cases, Roswell and others, their ships crashed, releasing still more billions of nanites. But the Diné viewed the nanites as harmless tools of their trade, so they were not concerned if a few of them escaped."

"I take it those sailors on the Nash were part of this genetic abduction program?" asks Monroe.

"Yes. For their part, the nanites reproduced and propagated across the planet in the patterns that LISA recently depicted back at Los Alamos. When Ben Pruitt and the rest of the sailors, including my own great grandfather, were abducted and genetically modified back in World War II, the USS Nash itself was contaminated with nanites. Those nanites were then unknowingly transported back to the San Diego shipyard where they propagated further. For the most part, the nanites quietly spread across the globe throughout the latter half of the twentieth century and the early twenty-first century. All this time they have literally been beneath our feet, as undetectable as virus particles."

"And," I say, "they were essentially dormant right up until the year 1986. Chernobyl."

"Yes, Jack. As you know, LISA had already identified that pattern for us."

"But why hadn't prior radiation releases triggered the nanites? Why was 1986 different?"

"It's true," she agrees, "Hiroshima and Nagasaki were terrible attacks, resulting in unimaginable suffering and deaths. However, the actual nuclear yields were actually quite small by modern standards. Similarly, the subsequent above ground atomic and thermonuclear tests performed by the nuclear powers had much higher yields but were infrequent and geographically isolated."

"And then came Chernobyl."

"Yes. In terms of a concentrated release of nuclear ionizing isotopes, Chernobyl was in a class of its own, releasing the radiation equivalent of four hundred Hiroshima blasts in just a few days."

"And I bet there was a foundation colony in the Ukraine positioned near Chernobyl, right?" I offer. "These things prefer to power themselves parasitically, so they would be naturally attracted to power stations like Chernobyl."

"Correct. Unfortunately, extended exposure to the level of radiation associated with the breach reactivated long forgotten nanite code. Given the protracted high levels of radiation the colony sensed, a full-out nuclear war was assumed to be in progress. The nanites assumed the Zoern had begun an attack on the planet, so they activated their processes to begin global climate change to permit Zoern conquest and occupation. They were, of course, unaware their former evil masters had been extinct themselves for centuries."

"Shit." Leave it to Hillie to succinctly describe our current circumstances in one word. "Now what do we do?"

"Um, guys, I don't..." To our horror, Tanisha collapses, slumping to the ground.

Monroe leaps to her side and shouts for Pullman to bring over his medical kit. I swivel about just in time to see the alien Na'Vack also collapse to the ground behind the dome in near unison with Tanisha.

CHAPTER 50

"PULSE THREADY…WEAKENING. RESPIRATION UNSTEADY AND FALTERING. BLOOD pressure dropping rapidly. Eyes unresponsive to light." Monroe looks up at me from Tanisha's still form shaking his head. "Jack, she's dying and I have no idea why."

"Look over at Na'Vack," I add. "Notice his respirations. He and Tanisha are struggling to breathe, but they're doing it in unison. See, their chests are moving up and down in near perfect synchronization."

"I'll be damned," says Monroe, "perhaps Tanisha and Na'Vack's telepathic link wasn't purely mental. Perhaps the link is physiological as well. Somehow their vital body functions have been linked together."

"So, if, or rather, when Na'Vack dies, Tanisha may perish as well?"

"Well, unfortunately," says Monroe, "right now you, me, and Hillie appear to be the world's foremost experts on human-alien Diné physiological interactions, and I must say I don't have a clue. But, lacking any other competing theory, I'd say it is a strong possibility that they may die together in some linked mode we have yet to understand."

"I need to talk to them," I say. "Get them to disable the link."

"It won't work. Tanisha is completely unconscious; she can't hear you."

"I'm not planning on talking to Tanisha."

I cautiously walk around the dome and kneel next to Na'Vack's still form. His breaths are labored, but his eyes are open. He blinks slowly and turns his head towards me. I have no idea if communication between an alien Diné and a non-Nash altered human is even possible.

Physical touch seemed to enhance Na'Vack and Tanisha's prior session. I gently reach over and touch Na'Vack's arm. He does not react or move away.

Somehow the touch of his flesh makes this whole experience less surreal. For a moment, I forget how incredible this whole situation has become. How two months ago I could have never imagined that I'd be kneeling in a cavern in remote Patagonia, my hand upon a living alien. For a minute or so we simply sit still. We are just two living beings, sharing a brief moment of existence, reaching out to try to understand each other.

I'm not sure how to start or if he can even understand me. "Na'Vack, we can't thank you enough for the knowledge you've given us and the sacrifices you've made. I think you have given Tanisha the knowledge we may need to carry on the fight against the nanites. But right now, that knowledge and understanding is only in Tanisha's mind. If she dies, that knowledge will die with her. And without what she now knows, we will not be able to fight for our future…the future our species appear destined to share. I must ask you, beg you, to break the link you share so that she may live. Do you understand?"

Slowly Na'Vack blinks and nods his head at me. I begin to pull myself upright, but the alien grabs my wrist firmly and looks directly into my eyes. He doesn't want me to leave just yet. Apparently, we have some unfinished business here. Slowly, he produces what appears to be small stone and places it into my hand, then he nods and carefully cups my fingers over the rock as if to conceal it. At first it feels like an ordinary stone. But it's heavy for its size and oddly warm to my touch. And I get a very strong sense that that somehow this is to be our secret. Something I must not share with the rest of the eGenesis team.

Indeed, the bulk of the containment dome is partially obscuring Na'Vack and me from the team's line of sight, so it's unlikely anyone has seen his little rock handoff. I nod to Na'Vack and surreptitiously slide the stone into my pants pocket as I stand up. As I begin to slowly retrace my steps back to Monroe, I wonder whether any of my message to the alien was understood.

"Jack…Walker." I stop dead in my tracks. The voice or perhaps projected thought calling my name comes suddenly into my mind. It is strangely flat

and atonal. Not human, but not mechanical either. The hair on the back of my neck feels as though it's rising. As I begin to turn to face Na'Vack, suddenly time seems to freeze and stand still.

The scene in the cavern now may as well be a still life diorama. A display in some museum of the absurd. Hillie is frozen in place, apparently in mid-sentence as he's talking to Monroe, similarly frozen in the moment. I notice even floating dust motes, illuminated by the light from the entrance to the cavern, are unmoving, suspended in time.

It begins to dawn on me that the flow of time itself has not slowed, but my perception of it has in some way changed. Somehow Na'Vack is doing this. I recall Tanisha's impression that the few minutes she had spent in a mind share with the alien had seemed to her as lasting over a day.

And that voice in my head calling my name… It is at once shocking and yet, even more surprisingly, familiar. I turn to look intensely at Na'Vack, like I'm seeing him for the first time. But it's not the first time. Hardly. That voice; I *know* that voice from somehow in my past. And, it's not just that I know these aliens; I know *this* alien.

"I know you," I say. A statement not a question. In my mind I'm beginning to sense the presence of memories long forgotten or perhaps always hidden from me. Flashes, snippets of visions, indistinct but real. Like old keepsakes you've secreted away so long, you've forgotten they exist. Hidden memories; glimpses of a secret life. Parts of my own life that I never remembered I had lived until this moment.

"Yes," says Na'Vack in my mind. *"You knew me not by my name but by my title…Ga'Jorik. Teacher. Your teacher."*

"Bigfork?" A one-word inquiry carrying a lifetime of questions. Two lifetimes, actually. Marty's memory deserves some answers.

"Yes, the location you call Bigfork was one of our early encounters. There would be many other days and places in your early life. These were the learning circles. We held those for you and the other…students."

This is surreal. I'm talking out loud to Na'Vack and he's replying inside my head. And all around us in the cavern my colleagues are frozen in place, oblivious to this bizarre conversation. Na'Vack's little mystery stone is growing warmer in my pocket. I'm starting to think that it's not really a rock. Somehow, he must be using it as a device to translate and project his thoughts to me.

"And Marty?"

"Your brother was perhaps the most talented of all in the Circle. Unfortunately, sometimes the most gifted can be the most…fragile. He could not abide our presence. We deeply regret the outcome." Na'Vack is blinking his huge eyes rapidly. Perhaps this is his kind's way of expressing their sympathy.

Right now, it's probably a good thing that the alien can't seem to read my thoughts directly. A few of them are a little raw at the moment. Marty's life was apparently ruined through contact with these creatures and all Na'Vack can say is he "regrets the outcome." How very clinical. Collateral damage. And now Marty is dead and I am…what am I?

"Who? Who am I? What am I?" Perhaps mankind's most fundamental existential question. Not a topic of conversation I had ever expected to have with an alien.

"You are not what you refer to as a Progeny. You have not been genetically modified as were they. But you are very special to the Diné. You are what we term a seeker-guide. From an early age, we would often gather you and your brother to join the other children in the learning circle. We had hoped that the knowledge and skills we gave you and the others might better prepare you to someday help bridge the distance between our peoples. And, that day, Jack Walker, may be approaching rapidly."

"Marty and I were abducted multiple times? Why don't I remember?"

"Until now, there was never a need to directly remember. Now that need will begin to slowly summon forth your recollections."

As if on cue, a dream-like flash of a long-forgotten memory enters my mind. Liu Da-Shin. A name that had for decades sailed off to drift in the fog enshrouded sea of lost memories. The small Chinese girl sitting on the ground next to me and Marty in the darkened forest. Da-Shin knew not a word of English, nor I, Mandarin. Yet, in those childhood days, we both spoke the mind-language of the alien Diné.

I smile, now remembering that Da-Shin and I would tease each other and quietly make fun of Na'Vack when we thought he wasn't looking. And there, long after midnight in the cool deep woods, our faces along with those of a dozen or so other children would be illuminated by the glowing globe in the center of the learning circle. The globe was floating a foot or two off the ground. It was a ball of blue light in the center of the circle of children with a swirl of complex images playing across its surface. I remember that I and the other children were mesmerized by the blue globe, spellbound by its secrets.

There were words that looked like hieroglyphics as well as mathematical equations. So many equations.

"Now, do you see?"

"I'm beginning to remember."

"Good. Jack Walker, we had hoped that the graduates of the Circle would also support and help protect the Progeny. You have produced many accomplishments in your life…and your research. LISA, your artificial intelligence system may be instrumental in helping us control the nanites. You were personally key to saving the Pruitts. Ricky and his father are both Progeny. And now you come to me to save the Progeny, Tanisha West. All of this because you were in the right place at the right time. Do you suppose this was all by chance?"

I shake my head in disbelief. Has my life, my choices, and accomplishments, really been my own? Or, have I simply been a puppet of the alien Diné all along?

"Have you, the Diné, been controlling my life all these years?"

"We have watched and guided your life, not controlled it. We have given you certain insights at certain times. Perhaps you've been nudged towards an occasional opportunity at appropriate times. But, no, we did not and do not control you. Think of us as hidden mentors, not puppet-masters."

Indeed, I begin to wonder, how many of my thoughts, ideas, and impulses in my life have truly been my own? Do I actually have free will or has it all been a mirage? Of course, aliens aside, many philosophers and even some neuroscientists might well argue that most of our decisions and actions are ultimately driven by unconscious motivations. Free will, they would say, is just the story we tell ourselves to help us think our rational minds make all of our decisions.

Some Eastern traditions liken the illusion of free will to the plight of a monkey clinging to the back of a tiger racing through the jungle. The monkey desperately tries to convince himself that he, the monkey, is commanding in advance the actions of the tiger. When the tiger surges to the left, the monkey tells himself that, yes, he intended all along that the tiger go in that direction and so forth. With each turn of the charging beast, the monkey is forced to concoct an increasingly complicated backstory to rationalize to himself that the tiger is moving through the jungle exactly according to his plan.

The monkey-riding-a-tiger analogy feels like an all too apt description of my life at the moment. I need to clear my mind, focus on the problems in front of me. How can we defeat the nanites and how can I save Tanisha?

"Okay, maybe the old forgotten memories are true. Maybe I'm really what you call a seeker-guide. So, what do you want from me?"

"First, please keep what you may refer to as the translator stone safe and secure. It may be useful for further communication with the Diné. Please keep it far from human population centers and in a secure place of trust."

"Okay, remote and secure. Got it."

"My next request will be most difficult for you. It may be the hardest thing you ever do, but it is important."

"Okay?"

"Jack Walker, you must forgive yourself. The tragedy of Marty's life's struggles and death should not be borne by you. It was never your burden to carry. It was never your fault. What you think of as the Bigfork incident was in fact the third time you and Marty were brought to the learning circle. And that night, you would have been taken regardless of your actions. Even if you had both decided just to stay in the cabin that night. No, the burden of Marty's plight is the responsibility of the Diné. And we are deeply sorry for his suffering and for your loss."

"Thanks. I will try to forgive myself." It's strange. For most of my life I've looked for peace and forgiveness about what happened to Marty. What I did. I've never found it in a church pew, deep in my research algorithms, or at the bottom of a scotch tumbler. And now, oddly, I have the offer of absolution for my sins coming from an alien. Na'Vack is right; it will not be easy, but self-forgiveness is never easy.

"And Tanisha? How can we save her?"

"As you have surmised, the need to give her as much information as possible in the shortest possible time resulted in the mind link becoming too intense. It can be addressed, but such a course of action will require sacrifice. Do not worry, she will be unharmed."

"Jack Walker?"

"Yes?"

"I want you to know that the Diné deeply appreciate everything you have done…and will do for them. It has been an honor to have known you and to have been your teacher."

Then, as suddenly as it began, his communication ceases and time seems to speed back up to normal. I turn to walk towards Hillie and Monroe, my mind racing with the revelations of the past few minutes.

I've covered no more than five or six steps when Pullman screams, "Gun!" I spin around to see that Na'Vack has stood up unsteadily and appears to have a weapon of some sort in his hand. Anderson and Pullman are both locked onto him with their rifles, their laser sights painting two red dots across the alien Diné's chest.

I start to shout for them to hold their fire. But before I can get the words out, Na'Vack turns the weapon on himself. We can only watch in shock and horror as he literally disintegrates in front of our eyes; his weapon clattering to the ground by itself as he dissolves out of existence.

In a few moments I am back at Tanisha's side. To my amazement she is starting to stir a bit, waking up.

"Tanisha's vital signs are returning to normal. Excellent! Jack, you did it! The link is broken." Monroe is shaking his head in amazement.

"Yeah, the alien broke the link…the hard way. Dying by his own weapon wasn't exactly what I had in mind."

"Where's Na'Vack?" Tanisha is now sitting upright, straining to look for the Diné.

"Tanisha," I say gently, "he's…gone. In the end, he sacrificed himself to save you. I don't know what else to say."

"What?" Tears are welling up in Tanisha's eyes. "I know it sounds crazy," she says, "but in those few minutes we shared our minds, I've never felt so close to anyone as Na'Vack. You need to know that given their accelerating genetic degradation, the Diné are increasingly susceptible to disease. Na'Vack was one of their most prominent scientists and he has been quite ill for some time. He has been refusing medical treatment for months to focus entirely on the dome device."

"And when your physiological link couldn't be broken, he made the ultimate sacrifice so you could continue his work," I say.

"And he felt so strongly about the need to preserve our joint species that he also chose to break their ethical prohibition on a dangerous direct mind sharing with a human," adds Tanisha.

"So, the alien Diné think it's perfectly ethical to abduct people in the middle of the night and modify them genetically? And maybe throw in an anal probing or two for good measure? But direct mind to mind communication with a human is a big no-no? Interesting set of ethics," scoffs Hillie.

"It's complicated," Tanisha is sounding a little defensive, "humans, even Nash-enhanced humans like myself, are not yet ready to intensely communicate with them directly. You saw how my link could not be voluntarily broken. It's just not that black and white ethically."

"Yeah, maybe that's why they call 'em the Grays," responds Hillie with a bit more sarcasm than the occasion would appear to demand.

"The dome," continues Tanisha, pointedly ignoring Hillie, "Na'Vack developed it as a prototype. It's designed to attract, contain, and eliminate the nanites."

"To hark back to our ant analogy," offers Monroe, "you can scale up stomping ants globally if you can manage to attract them to central kill zones."

"Correct," says Tanisha, "the question is does this prototype work and can it be mass produced and scaled up as a global solution before it's too late and the nanites have poisoned off the human population? I have most of the design and operational specs now imprinted into my memories. What we need to do next is get this device moved to Los Alamos. Then we can take it apart, reverse engineer it, and see what it takes to manufacture in the volumes needed to wipe out the nanites globally."

"Are you feeling okay now? Good enough to get up and walk a bit?" Monroe is still closely monitoring Tanisha's vital signs.

"Yeah. I think so," she replies. "And there is something else I've now remembered since I blacked out. I think I now know why and how the Nash Progeny became immune to neurotoxins."

That has been one of the true mysteries of the entire Nash Phenomenon. If aliens or some other agency are purposely contaminating our planet with deadly neurotoxins, why then apparently genetically modify a small number of humans to survive the poisoning?

"Recall that starting back in the early twentieth century, the alien Diné used the nanites to continue to genetically refine humans," says Tanisha. "It turns out that true to their ancient Zoern original coding, the nanites made some of their own genetic changes to the humans unbeknownst to the Diné. Remember the Zoern's modus operandi in the conquest of other worlds was to change those planets' atmospheres to mimic their own…extreme high temperatures spiked with neurotoxin gasses, right?"

A light comes on for me. "And according to Na'Vack, the Zoern also routinely enslaved the conquered populations. Hard to enslave the inhabitants if they're all dead, huh?"

"Exactly," agrees Tanisha, "the nanites are just following the old Zoern script of exoforming the planet's climate and genetically modifying a small portion of the population to survive in the new environment as slaves. A script the alien Diné inadvertently reactivated here on Earth."

The first test of Na'Vack's approach appears to go to plan as Tanisha successfully commands the dome to destroy the glowing colony of nanites it has encased. Meanwhile, Anderson, Pullman, and Hillie are burning up their sat-phone batteries on priority calls to the Pentagon. They're working out the clandestine logistics required to smuggle the dome out of Argentina.

Within an hour, an Arleigh Burke class guided missile destroyer, the USS John Finn, has been re-tasked from a South Atlantic patrol to come to our aid. Shortly it seems, the Finn will be taking on some very unusual and sensitive cargo. Fortunately, Argentinian air defense radar coverage is quite spotty in this remote region. A gap in detection we are counting upon.

The plan is that once offshore in the dark of night, the Finn will deploy its MH-60R Seahawk helicopter with a landing party to secure and retrieve the dome artifact. Anderson and Pullman will remain behind at the cavern to meet up with the Seahawk and its crew to assist in the recovery of the device. Meanwhile Hillie, Monroe, Tanisha and I will return to El Calafate to quickly pack for a return to the States.

As the final arrangements are being made, I see Tanisha standing far off to the side by herself, deep in thought. "Tanisha, are you going to be okay?"

"Yeah," she says finally. "I can't stop thinking about Na'Vack, the hope he had for our joint species, the sacrifices he made."

"I think we will all miss him, and be forever grateful to him."

"You know, up until now," says Tanisha, "I've shared my life with friends, family…several lovers. But it is quite a different thing to share a mind. I think Na'Vack has been the only one in my life I feel has truly understood me. Who I am. What I am. For all of my professional life I've always been seen as this Black woman scientist. Na'Vack simply saw me as…a scientist."

I smile and nod. Alien as he may have been, Na'Vack has shown us what the best of humanity could become. And in this moment, I think of what Na'Vack had unlocked in my mind. Marty, Da-Shin, myself, and the other children huddled about the glowing globe of the learning circle. Na'Vack himself leading the lesson.

"Now he is gone, but he will never be forgotten." Tanisha smiles slightly and gently touches the back of her head, "But I think a little part of Na'Vack will always be with me."

"I think he will be with many of us."

CHAPTER 51

Indian Summer. When the warmth and clear days of summer seem to hold well into October and November. That's what the old timers used to call it. An archaic phrase that's recently been resurrected by the local TV weather reporters. Late November in Montana and today the temperature is in the low seventies. The temperatures have remained unseasonably warm and the skies have been clear all month. It's really quite remarkable they say, very unusual. Less surprising to me, unfortunately.

"I can't believe how hot it is," says Sarah Wendover. "I've had to crack open a few windows so we don't roast in here. You know while the turkey cooks, the whole kitchen tends to heat up. Odd, usually we're seeing some snow by this time of the year."

"I guess we brought the warm weather from California up here with us," I reply. "Thanks again for inviting us."

Dan and his wife, Sarah, have invited us to their home for Thanksgiving. Amy has driven over from Bozeman with her new friend Lilly to join us as well. Sarah and I are finishing preparation of the salad, looking out the kitchen window at the bright warm skies. There are whoops and barks out on the lawn as old Zeke has apparently rediscovered his inner puppy, playing catch-the-ball with the young ladies from MSU.

Kate and Dan are on the sidelines, cheering Zeke on. Kate turns and catches Sarah and me watching them. She gives us a smile and a wave for appearances sake, but her eyes say she is worried. Worried about me. She's worried I've gone down the rabbit hole again. Like when Marty died. Worried I've thrown myself into my algorithms and models once more to lock away my emotions. Trying once more to give myself the illusion that I can control whatever the world hands us. Worried that she cannot help me or, this time, maybe even save me.

If she only knew. The ethical dilemma tears at me every day. If you knew the world will likely end for humanity in the near future, would you tell your spouse? Would you tell them so they could cherish every remaining moment of their lives? Or spare them the dread and sadness of knowing the end was near? I've not been myself. Distant at times and then overly sentimental at others. Both Kate and Amy have been giving me odd looks lately.

"It's so sweet what Dan has done for me," says Sarah, shifting slightly in her wheelchair. "He's worked so hard, every evening and weekend he could spare. I feel bad. It's so unnecessary, really. It will just make it that much harder when..." She pauses here but we both know what she means: "When I'm gone." Sarah has ALS, Lou Gehrig's Disease. Inexorably and mercilessly, it has taken her legs. Soon it will take her voice and then her breath itself. It is just a matter of time.

Dan has rebuilt the kitchen to accommodate Sarah's disabilities. The cabinetry, counters, and sinks all lowered to assist her reach from the wheelchair.

"When...he goes to sell this place," she says finally, "the modifications will just make it that much harder to market. Drive down the selling price, you know."

Yes. Wendover certainly knows life isn't fair. For all his law enforcement powers and abilities to advance the cause of justice in the county, he is incapable of extending Sara's lifespan by even one minute. No wonder he bristles at the arrogance of survivalists who seem to think they can end run the inevitable. No number of concrete bunkers and hoarded provisions will save Sarah. And, frankly, unless any survivalists out there happen to have sterilized and airtight bunkers, along with a lifetime supply of oxygen, food, and medicine, they will not survive the approaching nanite apocalypse either.

As we work here at the sink together, it strikes me that we have more in common than she realizes. A club no one surely would want to join. An aching sense of the nearness of our own mortality. How can one know that and not be changed?

Kate and Amy sense the change in me. Ever perceptive, Wendover is sensing something is off as well. I recall the conversation we had about an hour ago as he showed me around his property, beers in our hands.

"I take it the game's afoot?" he had said as we walked through his old barn.

"When did Holmes say that?" Leave it to Wendover to always draw on an appropriate observation from the Great Detective.

"He didn't. At least not originally. It was in fact Shakespeare. Henry V, Act Three. But seriously," he said, "I'd like to know what you've gotten yourself involved in now."

"What makes you think I'm involved in anything unusual?" I played dumb, a reliable strong suit for me.

"Oh, come on!" His brow furrowed, "you go off on a so-called pheasant hunting outing with your new friend Anderson and a couple of days later seem to have disappeared on some mysterious sabbatical to New Mexico. I'm left dealing with your student Jeff to provide me and the county commissioners your final report. He did a great job by the way."

"Good to know. But I assure you..."

He cut me off. "This is about the report from the Feds I saw, right? The one with half the sentences blacked out and redacted. It's about the twins you saw in the mine and the real reason the military was involved in Ricky's disappearance. Am I getting warmer?" And he added, "mostly it's about the change I see in you. You're not quite your old annoying self."

"Well, I'll admit to being a little distracted."

"Look, even a hick sheriff like me can put two and two together." As usual, Wendover downplayed his considerable skills as a detective. It's doubtful very many hick sheriffs routinely quote Shakespeare.

"Too bad, Lawman, you'll never get a confession out of me!"

"Oh, I think you've mostly told me what I need to know," he said. "Look, Jack, I don't know what you're involved in. Maybe I don't want to know. But whatever it is, I'm glad you're on the case. They could use your expertise."

Expertise alone may not be enough, I think, as I continue to prepare the salad. What eGenesis desperately needs now is some luck. Attitudes back at

Los Alamos, never sunny to begin with, have turned even more gloomy. The nanite containment dome is not giving up its secrets easily. Tanisha and her engineering team have been working around the clock with little success. Attempts to reverse engineer and scale up the device have been met with repeated failures.

Worse yet, a recent revelation from LISA has made us realize we have far less time than we thought to defeat the nanites. Several days ago, LISA and I were reviewing neurotoxin lethality effects on global population. Of particular interest to the calculations were the projected timing of two events we have designated as L-Point and D-Point.

L-Point represents the point at which global neurotoxins from the nanites reach lethal levels and the first human deaths occur. At current rates of increasing emissions, we estimate that L-Point will occur about twenty-four months in the future. D-Point is the estimate of when the neurotoxins will initially reach globally detectable levels. That date will only be about six months in the future. At that point, the cat is out of the bag. The threat of the nanites can no longer be a closely held secret of eGenesis. Government military and research facilities around the world will awaken to the danger and the revelation will rush through news cycles and social media like a flashover fire.

The impact of the D-Point event had not fully occurred to me until LISA ran lethality scenarios for L-Point several days ago.

"Dr. Walker, LISA has the latest population reduction estimates for L-Point. Similar to prior estimates, LISA projects in the first year after L-Point, approximately twenty-five percent of the human population will perish."

"Thank you, LISA. Twenty-five percent is indeed consistent with prior estimates," I replied.

"This twenty-five percent lethality estimate represents approximately 1.6 billion individuals."

"No, LISA, that can't be right," I said. Global population at L-Point should be about 8 billion. A twenty-five percent reduction would represent about 2 billion deaths, not 1.6 billion."

"LISA regrets the misunderstanding, but your data is incorrect. Global human population at L-Point is estimated at only 6.5 billion."

"What the hell happened to the other 1.5 billion people?"

Like the air we breathe, it is such a ubiquitous part of our existence and civilization that we don't even think about it. It is completely taken for granted. Our actions in the present are nearly always driven by the expectation of future consequences. We work today for a paycheck tomorrow. We invest for the future. We sow so we can reap. We don't do the crime if we can't do the time. The thin veneer of civilization itself rests upon this unspoken social understanding.

The sustainment of our burgeoning global population, advanced technology, and modern way of life depends on complex global supply and transportation chains. If even only one link breaks, chaos can propagate through the chain like a domino effect causing widespread shortages. The cycle of pandemics in the early decades of the twenty-first century began to increase awareness of these vulnerabilities. But those pandemics would be child's play compared to the impact of D-Point according to LISA.

What would we do today, if we knew there was no future tomorrow? If a life sentence for even the most heinous crimes was no more than eighteen months? Would you stay and work your job until the last days? Or would you quit and go cross some items off your bucket list? What if your job was critical to maintaining the power grid or food supply?

It has been said the difference between civilization and anarchy is only five successive missed meals. How could you begin to measure the impact of war, crime, genocide, fear, and starvation in those ensuing eighteen months between D-Point and L-Point? LISA has an estimate. One and a half billion lives lost by mankind's own desperation and depravity before the nanites even have a chance to take one life by neurotoxin.

We don't have twenty-four months to solve this. We have six months!

Back at the barn, I had smiled at Wendover and stuck my hand in my pocket. I felt the unusual warmness of Na'Vack's translation stone. The stone he wanted me to keep in a secure yet remote location.

"Dan, may I ask you for a favor? I need you to hold something for me for safekeeping. I noticed you have some drawers in your workbench here in the barn. Maybe keep it there?"

"Sure, Jack. What is it?"

I pulled the stone out of my pocket.

"Huh? It's just a rock," he said, looking a bit perplexed.

"It's a very special rock."

"Okay, whatever," he shrugged, humoring me. "Guess we can stick your special pet rock in one of the workbench drawers. Geez, and I thought you Californians were more into beads and crystals."

CHAPTER 52

"Earth to Dad!" Amy is giving me a mischievous glare. We're all seated at the Wendover's table, the Thanksgiving meal laid out before us. I come back to the present. I look around the table at my family and friends. Zeke is nudging my ankle under the table. I'm struck by the utter normalcy of this moment. Drinking it all in and trying to imprint every second to hold it forever.

"You slipped away for a moment," says Kate with a tight smile. She's trying to make light of it but the worried eyes are still there.

"Sorry," I say, "you know how it is with absent-minded professors, right?"

"Hey, Dad, are you gonna say grace or shall we let a real doctor do it," winking at her mom. "Otherwise, Lilly and I are going to starve." Lucky kid. Gets her looks and smarts from Kate and only a modest penchant for sarcasm from my shallow end of the gene pool.

Truth is I was lost in thought. But not of nanites, L-Points, or D-Points. Something from my far past. Something more fundamental and meaningful. One of my free ranging discussions with Father Rodrigues at the student union hall back in undergraduate days.

I had asked the priest if he truly believed in transubstantiation, the change during Mass of the substance of wine and bread into the substance of the body and blood of Christ. His answer was not what I had expected.

"My son, in this world, my personal actions are far more important than my personal beliefs. My sworn holy responsibility is to sustain and nurture hope and meaning in the lives of the faithful. If the rite of the eucharist gives even one in my parish a sense of comfort, connection with God, or hope, I have done my job. We are here on this Earth to give each other love and hope. You will find that by giving hope to others, hope and meaning will come into your own life."

I've been thinking about Father Rodrigues a lot lately. And late at night, when the clear high desert skies over Los Alamos seem to be a glowing wreath of a million stars, I look to the heavens and think of Na'Vack. His hopes for the reuniting of our species and the ultimate sacrifice he made for us. And how his people went to the stars to search for aliens only to find that in the process they had become the aliens themselves.

Perhaps in the end, hope is all we have that cannot be taken from us without our consent. And perhaps this day has even allowed a glimmer of new hope to emerge.

Just before we sat down for the meal, I received a high priority email from Monroe. There may have been a breakthrough. The ultimate weapon against the nanites might be software rather than hardware.

After weeks of analyzing the nanites' gigabyte data burst patterns, LISA appears to have deciphered their coded language. Now in addition to nearly thirty modern and ancient Earth languages, LISA now apparently speaks Nanite. Although there are still a thousand things that could go wrong, the implications of LISA's newfound ability are profound. We could potentially spoof the nanites, command them to shut down, or trigger another mutation to eliminate the greenhouse gas and neurotoxin emitters.

I return to the moment. All eyes around the table are on me. Kate's eyebrow is raised skeptically. I pause to smile at the younger generation at the table: Amy and Lilly. Interestingly, Lilly has a pale, nearly translucent complexion with straight black hair. Probably a coincidence, she's likely not a Progeny but I'll check the database when I get back to Los Alamos.

We bow our heads. "Bless us, Oh Lord, and these your gifts which we are about to receive from your bounty." I pause for a moment. "We give thanks for the many blessings we have received. And, may, in the year ahead, we all find peace and hope."

Father Rodrigues would be proud.

PART III - THE NIGHT PEOPLE

CHAPTER 53

As the campfire slowly began to diminish down into embers, Rocky Sorenson surveyed the shadows of the hunting camp revealed by the fading light of the wavering flames. He could hear his clients loudly snoring in their tents as he sat on a stump and took his last pull of brandy for the evening. Assholes, he thought. Every damn one of them. Six days in the backcountry with these whining over-privileged jerks from the East Coast and he was about ready to walk away. Walk away and let them find their way back out of the wilderness on their own. Without him as a guide.

As appealing as it might have been to abandon his clients, it was hardly his ethics or his conscience holding him back. Rather it was the promise of a payday. A huge, all cash payday at the conclusion of the hunt. For these were not just assholes, they were very rich assholes with quite unique and extreme tastes in outdoor recreation. And what they were doing was the dark opposite of eco-tourism. These city-slickers got their jollies playing the role of big game poachers. It was the thrill of the kill; enhanced a hundredfold by the knowledge it was all illegal as hell.

An illegal thrill for them but an incredibly lucrative enterprise for devious guides such as Sorenson. For years, he had worked as a regular hunting guide, bringing out-of-state clients into Montana for various hunts. Hard work but it paid the bills.

Then another guide had introduced Sorenson to the dark web and the underground world of illegal sport hunting. He found that a select group of wealthy sportsmen would pay handsomely for guided trophy hunts outside of legal hunting seasons and in restricted areas. Now in addition to his regular, legal guide jobs, there was big money to be made on these illegal hunts…poaching by any other name.

Here in the vast and rugged mountain wilderness straddling Montana and Idaho, it was mid-August, and his group of clients had already taken three bull elk trophies more than a month in advance of the legal hunting season.

The loudest snoring was coming from the largest tent. It figures, thought Sorenson; biggest asshole, loudest snorer. Ronald Johnson was the client that had initiated this little wilderness soireé. Johnson was a swimming pool contractor from New Jersey. And, as he continually reminded everyone, enormously successful. He had a huge house and numerous sports cars. He had made it clear he had no want of more material possessions apart from perhaps an illicit trophy elk head over his fireplace. A need filled just earlier today when Sorenson had guided him to a nearby glade for the kill shot.

Johnson was the type of client who expected Sorenson to do all the work to set up camp and arrange the hunts. Then he'd criticize and second-guess Sorenson every step of the way.

Johnson's brother, Fred, occupied the next tent. Fred was an attorney for a white-shoe firm in Manhattan. A lower voltage version of Ronald, Fred could be just as annoying but in a more subtle, passive-aggressive manner. Back-handed complements being his verbal jabs of choice. Still an asshole, but at least his snoring isn't as loud, thought Sorenson.

Finally, the last tent was occupied by Fred's idiot son, Neil. Neil had no business being out in the wilderness, or for that matter, anywhere in the real world outside the confines of his boarding school back East. And Sorenson believed that Neil would probably agree with that assessment. The kid looked to be miserable out here in the sticks, far away from cell service and social media. Ronald made it no secret that he hoped this hunt might yet make a man out of Neil. Get him out in the wilderness like a real man, he had said. Make him "less of a pussy," those were his exact words.

Sorenson had tried to work with Neil on woods-craft and hunting skills but the kid was awkward and all thumbs. It was a challenge, but he was finally able help Neil sight his rifle. When they happened upon an elk, Sorenson set up the shot and did everything for Neil but pull the trigger. Young Neil may have been hopeless, but of this bunch, Sorenson thought him the most likable and sincere. Albeit, with this crew, it was a low bar to clear. He almost felt sorry for Neil. Sorenson would only have to spend a week with these jerks, but Neil was stuck with them forever as relatives.

He frowned and shook his head at the row of client tents. Sorenson himself didn't have a tent. Always told folks he didn't believe in them. He liked to sleep out in the open under the night sky. It gave him peace to see the broad canopy of stars overhead. And, out in the open, he would be sure to pick up on the sounds of any approaching animals that might be looking to raid the camp of its provisions.

Sorenson smiled to himself. Unknown to these sleeping fools he had an additional agenda for being out in the backcountry. Perhaps an opportunity for yet another payday. For there was a twenty-five thousand dollar price on Silas Patterson's head.

The local guide business was a small community unto itself and he had known Patterson for years. Patterson was a reasonably successful guide and had owned his own taxidermy shop in Alta Junction. The local scuttlebutt was that after the conclusion of a protracted and nasty divorce proceeding, his ex-wife got half of his business and the IRS took the other half.

Some said losing his wife and business was the trigger. Others chalked it up to PTSD from his prior combat service. Regardless of the cause, about three months ago Silas went rogue and then homicidal.

First, Patterson ambushed his ex-wife and her new boyfriend at the boyfriend's rural home. Although Silas was known as a top marksman, the kill was done with a hunting knife rather than a firearm. This was the mark of a very personal and emotional murder. After that, Silas had disappeared like a phantom into the nearly three million acres of mountainous national forest and wilderness that forms the border between Montana and Idaho.

Unfortunately, he didn't simply stay under the radar in some remote mountain hide-out. There were two more additional kills tied to his increasingly bloody hunting knife. A female forest ranger had been slashed and killed in June. And a hiker, also female, was abducted off a trail in July and found with her throat slashed. Although one could perhaps understand his motive in the murders of his ex-wife and her boyfriend, it seemed as though that first taste of blood had somehow flipped a switch in him to crave more and more violence and carnage. And this murderous rage increasingly appeared to be directed at women.

Now wanted by federal authorities for the series of four murders, Patterson was turning out to be law enforcement's worst nightmare. His hunting skills combined with previous war experience in special operations made him the apex predator in these mountains. He could live off the land indefinitely and knew the game trails and backcountry like the back of his hand. It seemed that if he didn't want to be found, he wouldn't be found.

The FBI special agent in charge of the case was successfully lobbying Washington to place Patterson on the bureau's Most Wanted list. And local Benton County Sheriff, Dan Wendover, was urging those venturing out into the woods to exercise additional caution and vigilance lest they fall into Patterson's clutches.

Law enforcement's troubles and challenges were of little concern to Sorenson. What did capture his interest was a public offer of twenty-five thousand dollars put forth by the ex-Mrs. Patterson's family. A reward for any information leading to the capture and conviction of Patterson for her murder. Sounded like easy money to Sorenson. He had been studying the terrain maps of this very area and thought it highly likely that Patterson might be hiding nearby. So, while his clueless clients focused on finding elk, he was just as carefully scanning for any sign Patterson might be nearby.

Twenty-five thousand dollars would be a substantial windfall, he thought. Although, he mused, unlike his illegal hunting fees, he'd have to pay taxes on the amount. He smiled as he remembered that the Feds had ended up convicting Al Capone on tax evasion rather than his more infamous racketeering crimes. Imagine that, a great gangster, taken down not by a wily FBI agent, but by a bunch of damn tax accountants.

Well, he'd just add tax evasion to the growing list of crimes and offenses he was piling up on this outing. There was, of course, the primary offense of poaching. Then, add to that, he and his clients had driven their four-wheel ATVs far into the wilderness to this campsite in clear violation of regulations restricting motor vehicle access here. But, much like the old saying about whether a tree falling in the forest makes a sound if no one is there to hear it; if no one is here to see a crime in this forest, is it really a crime?

Sorenson suddenly jerked his head to the right. Perhaps he was imagining things, but he could have sworn there had been a noise in that direction. Just nerves, he thought. All this hoopla over Patterson was putting him on edge probably.

Then he heard it. Soft whispers in the dark, just outside the dim light cast by the dying fire. One whisper to his right and another to his left. Whispers of words, but not words he knew. Not English nor Spanish. And certainly not the little French he remembered from high school…

"Ua lohe 'o ia iā mākou?"

"Mali'a paha. E mālama. He pū kāna."

Sorenson stiffened and reached for his revolver. "Who's there? Show yourself! Patterson? Is that you?" There was another movement to his right. In an instant, he panicked and fired one round in that direction. He was preparing to fire again when a large silhouette suddenly appeared some fifty yards in front of him.

Sorenson's last thought before the incoming bullet pureed his brain was pure disbelief and utter astonishment at the massive figure aiming the rifle directly at him.

CHAPTER 54

Picture perfect. Sheriff Dan Wendover takes a moment to admire the natural beauty of the alpine meadow framed by majestic mountains on all sides. This might be a perfect panorama for a tourism promotion poster for the Treasure State. However, it's likely the state tourism department might insist on a bit of digital editing before releasing such a poster to the public. Specifically, they would probably want to cut out the images of the ruined hunting camp in which Wendover is standing. And, of course, the dead body he has been examining.

"Rocky, Rocky." Wendover sighs and shakes his head as he regards Sorenson's corpse splayed backwards in the dirt, a large bullet hole through the forehead. "What the hell sort of trouble did you get mixed up with way out here?" The question is clearly rhetorical as no answer could be expected to be forthcoming from the long-deceased guide.

Wendover, two deputies, and a forest service law enforcement agent had arrived at Sorenson's wilderness campsite to find it in total disarray. It had looked as though a small and highly focused tornado had blasted through the camp at least several times. Basically, any item that could be torn or cut was completely shredded. And anything else that could be smashed or broken was destroyed. Three wrecked four-wheel drive all-terrain vehicles lay on their side. A fourth smashed ATV rested a few yards away, apparently tossed like a toy across a fallen log. Other than the remains of Sorenson, the camp was abandoned. There was no sign of his hunting clients.

"Larry, sure would have helped if Sally Sorenson had reported her husband overdue a couple of days sooner, huh?" Wendover is addressing this to Larry Stout, the forest service investigator accompanying him. "Evidence, exposed out here to the elements, doesn't improve with time and it looks like maybe some of the local critters have been snacking on poor Rocky here. That's not helping either."

"Yeah," replies Stout, "I guess she wasn't all that anxious to report that her husband was overdue from guiding a hunting trip a month before hunting season starts."

"Well," sighs Wendover, examining Sorenson's gun that had fallen next to the body, "five live rounds and one expended round in the revolver. Looks like maybe Rocky got off a shot before he took it in the head. So," he's starting to move the corpse's head for a better look, "let's take a closer peek at that wound."

"Don't you think we should wait for the medical examiner before we move the body?"

Wendover laughs, "That might be a hell of a wait, Larry. We're six miles upcountry from the end of the nearest road. No medical examiner is coming out in the boonies this far to look at a body. They're going to send out for delivery, so to speak. Naw, we'll look him over here. Then, well, he presumably came all the way up here on the front end of an ATV, and he's going to come back out strapped to the backend of another ATV."

"Let's see here." Wendover is closely examining the front of Sorenson's skull. "Looks like maybe a high velocity rifle round did this. Hmm, no exit wound on the back of the skull though."

"Wouldn't you expect this to be a through and through?" asks Stout. He's talking about the circumstance when a bullet enters the skull or body and exits via a wound on the opposite side.

"Not necessarily," responds Wendover. "Bullet trajectories, much like life itself, are subject to a multitude of influencing factors and chance itself. Sometimes a bullet, just like your own life, may end up in a different place than you might have originally predicted, eh?"

"I certainly can't disagree," smiles Stout.

"The physics gets complicated quickly," continues Wendover. "A great deal depends on the round velocity and mass. The angle of entry plays a large role as well. And," he nods wryly down at Sorenson, "some fellas just have thicker skulls. I think in this instance the round probably entered through the frontal lobe and then ricocheted around the skull a couple of times causing severe trauma to the brain before coming to rest. The medical examiner back in town will need to recover the slug and confirm the theory."

"Sheriff, we've got the IDs on the others missing from the camp. The hunters Sorenson was supposedly guiding." Deputies Potts and Yazzie are walking up to Wendover with some wallets in their hands.

"Thanks," Wendover takes the wallets. Potts was a veteran on the Benton County force, but Derek Yazzie was a relatively new recruit. Young, highly skilled and dedicated, Yazzie was a lucky find for the department. Wendover had recruited him from the Colville Confederated Tribal Police over in Washington state. Or, more accurately, Benton County General had recruited Yazzie's wife into a nursing position and Wendover had picked up Derek as part of the deal. A Benton County two-fer of sorts.

"New Jersey, huh?" Wendover is sorting through the driver's licenses.

"And I didn't need to look at their licenses to know these were white guys," adds Yazzie.

"That so?"

"Yeah, a native would not take only the trophies and just leave the meat in the woods to rot. To take wild game is to receive a gift from nature. Wasting meat is disrespectful of nature. It makes us out of balance with the Earth. When the Earth is disrespected, there will be consequences, grave consequences. Push nature too far and nature will push back, hard."

"As if just being from New Jersey wasn't itself an afront to nature," smiles Wendover. "Anyway, as soon as we get back in radio range, I'll put out an APB on these individuals. Trouble is, at this point, we just don't know if these guys are witnesses, victims themselves, or the perpetrators."

"Yeah," says Potts, "maybe they had some sort of dispute with Sorenson. Then put a bullet in him and cleared out."

"If they cleared out, they departed so fast they left behind their wallets, keys, boots, and, apparently, their pants," says Yazzie.

Wendover raises an eyebrow. "Their pants were left behind?"

"Correct, that's where we found their wallets and keys."

"Well, if I decided to put a bullet in someone, I don't think I'd run off into the woods without my gear, pants, keys, and wallet. Doesn't feel like a smart criminal get-away strategy," remarks Wendover. "What about their guns? Can we account for their hunting rifles and ammo?"

Potts shakes his head. "No sir, other than Sorenson's revolver there on the ground, we found no other guns or ammo here."

"If I had the presence of mind to stop and take my gun for the get-away, I'd likely take a few moments more to grab my pants and wallet, don't you think? I guess at this point, subject to new evidence, we ought to proceed under the theory that whoever killed Sorenson also likely abducted the three clients as well as taking their guns," concludes Wendover.

"So," Wendover is addressing this to his deputies, "next step is to collect all the boots so we can later eliminate them from potential perpetrator's prints. Then please search the camp for footprints, okay? And be on the lookout for any shell casings."

"Copy that."

Stout clears his throat. "Um, while you're looking around for footprints, did you guys already get a photo of the symbol and that weird writing?"

"I've got it right here," Wendover is pulling it up on his phone camera screen.

The image is an enigma. It shows a symbol of some unknown meaning. It appears to be an "X" with an inverted triangle placed in its upper quadrant. And next to it, a message in a strange language:

Kapu Ua ao 'ia 'oe

"Just like the others, right?" Stout is talking about two other recent incidents in which similar symbols and text had been etched into the soft ground, apparently with a stick.

"Nearly identical."

"And we still have no idea what this writing means?" asks Stout.

"No clue so far," says Wendover. He pauses, glances over at Yazzie and hands him the phone. "Any chance this is native? Maybe a Salish dialect of some sort?"

"Well, my people are the Wenatchi, just one of dozens of Salish tribes in the Pacific Northwest, so my knowledge may be limited as to other traditions. But, no, this doesn't look like any Salish dialect I've seen."

"Thanks, it was worth a try."

"Sir, in the interests of full disclosure here," adds Yazzie, "I'm only one quarter blood Wenatchi. And my maternal grandparents immigrated from Stuttgart, so growing up I probably heard more German around the house than Salish. By the way, your text here, it isn't German either."

"Yeah, I kinda figured it wasn't," replies Wendover. "I do, however, have an out-of-state consultant down at UCLA who may be able to help us identify the language and symbol."

"You mean Dr. Walker? The professor who helped us find Ricky Pruitt last fall? Do you think he will be able to decipher it?" asks Potts.

"No, I don't think Jack Walker himself will have a clue what this means. But he has an associate that just may have all the answers." He pauses and smiles, "her name is LISA."

As the deputies fan out to search for additional evidence, Wendover and Stout turn their attention back to Sorenson. Wendover is closely examining the bullet hole to the forehead. "Now, this is odd, Larry, look at the angle of entry for the round, about forty-five degrees downward, I'd say."

"That is odd," agrees Stout. "Even if Sorenson was crouched down, he'd still have his head tilted up, looking at his assailant. So, you'd expect the incoming bullet to still come in at a straight angle."

Just then they are interrupted by Potts, who has found an expended cartridge casing about fifty yards away.

"Can you identify the caliber?" asks Wendover.

"Looks to be a .30-06."

"Well, that would have done the job here on Sorenson. You know the drill; bag it and tag it. And drop a marker flag where you found it. Hopefully, it will match whatever slug the medical examiner pulls out of Rocky's skull."

"Yes-sir."

"Well, Larry," says Wendover. "I guess we know Sorenson's first mistake."

"Yeah, what was that?"

Wendover smiles. "He brought a handgun to a rifle fight." He looks closely at Stout. "Say, Larry? How tall are you?"

"I'm just about six foot tall."

"That is conveniently about the same height as Sorenson. Tell you what, why don't you go ahead and stand here. Then, when I say so, close your eyes and hold your hands in front of them, too."

"Why?" asks Stout, a trace of apprehension in his voice.

"Because I'm going to shoot you."

"What?"

"Well, I'm not going to actually shoot you, I'm just going to do so virtually, with my laser-sight." Wendover unclips his laser-sight from his service sidearm and walks over to the spot where Potts had found the casing.

"Okay, close and cover your eyes." Wendover activates the sight and paints a red dot across Stout's forehead. "Now, I have a trajectory angle close to zero, straight on to your forehead from where I'm standing. But if I want to get a downward trajectory at about forty-five degrees, I need to raise the laser-sight high above my head, like this." Wendover extends his arm above his head. "Okay, I've switched it off, safe to open your eyes."

"Now that is really odd," says Stout. "How could anyone shoot from that angle?"

"Indeed," says Wendover, "I'm not exactly a small guy myself and yet I'd have to hold the rifle up above my head to aim it down at the correct angle."

"You'd have to be some kind of trick shooter," says Stout.

"Yeah. Or nine feet tall."

"So, Dan," Stout has walked over to Wendover's shooting position. "You know I really want to like Patterson for this."

"But?"

"But none of this feels right. Doesn't fit his MO. Why would he do this? And that strange language or code or whatever, doesn't seem like something he'd come up with. And he sure as hell wouldn't have any reason to vandalize and sabotage those other logging and mining operations where similar markings were also found."

"I've got the same misgivings, Larry. Patterson wants to be a ghost; move freely through these mountains. Why abduct Sorenson's clients? Controlling them, yet alone moving through the woods with three guys, who were not apparently wearing shoes, by the way, would slow him up too much," agrees Wendover. "Now maybe, both being in the guide business, Patterson had some business conflict with Sorenson. A possible motive. But again, why then abduct the three clients?"

"Agreed," replies Stout. "I don't think this is Patterson's handiwork either. But you know what that means?"

"Yup," replies Wendover with a sigh. "It means we now might have two separate killers stalking through this forest."

"Sheriff!" Yazzie is waving from the edge of the camp. "I've found a footprint."

"Is it a boot or a shoe print?"

"Um, sir, you need to come over and take a look."

"Well then, what size is it?" Wendover has a trace of impatience in his voice as he heads over towards Yazzie.

"You need to see for yourself."

As Wendover comes over to his side, Yazzie is looking at the ground and shaking his head in disbelief. "This can't be happening! I always thought these were just old folktales. You know, stories the elders used to tell to scare us kids into staying out of mischief. It is the Choanito!"

"The Choanito?"

Yazzie is breathing rapidly and shaking his head. "You have no idea, Sheriff! Disrespect the Earth and they will come. But threaten the Earth and they will come and kill. This has been passed down from the ancients."

"Who? Who will come and kill?"

"The Choanito. The Night People."

CHAPTER 55

"Good morning, Jack. So nice to have you back in the fold. Are you on your way down to the Batcave?" Adhira Chandra, Deputy Director of Team LISA, says this with a wry smile and a wink as we pass in the hall. My graduate student from the Ricky Pruitt adventure, Jeff Tanaka, is walking along with her.

"Batcave? Really? Is that what folks are calling it?"

"It's one of the few names that are repeatable in polite company," replies Jeff with a grin.

Adhira winks. "What, Jack? You think people don't talk? They see you. You get some text or secretive call on your cell, and then you quickly disappear down to your 'special room' in the basement. Anyway, it's good to have you back at UCLA and have things back to normal."

"Thanks," I say, "and, by the way, I am headed…downstairs. I'll be back up in the labs shortly."

My special room. I key the cypher lock combination, enter the room, and shut the door. This is a SCIF, a Sensitive Compartmented Information Facility. It is my link back to the eGenesis team at their headquarters in Los Alamos. The room has dedicated secure video and data connections to the systems in New Mexico.

Rapid construction of the SCIF had begun almost immediately upon my return to the campus from Los Alamos two months ago. The effort funded by an obscure science program within the Department of Defense. And to the delight of the university administration, no expense was spared in its construction, equipment, and furnishings.

In one sense I suppose the facility was a gift of sorts from the eGenesis program. A thank you for helping to save the world from the nanites. On the other hand, its rather obvious purpose is to expressly keep me closely tied over the distance back to the strictly classified program. A lavish, bejeweled collar on a leash perhaps, but a collar nevertheless.

I must agree with what Adhira had said. It's good to be back on campus in my regular labs. As for things being back to normal, I can only shake my head. For me, normal left my life about nine months ago and is never coming back.

Back then I had been conducting a research study to analyze and forecast crime trends in rural Montana using LISA, an advanced artificial intelligence system. LISA focuses on pattern recognition and predictive analytics using deep learning algorithms that LISA herself can modify in search of deeper answers. Several years ago, I had established the Machine Learning Laboratory here at UCLA to develop LISA and apply her abilities to various scientific and sociological questions.

At the behest of local Benton County, Montana Sheriff Dan Wendover I had become deeply involved in the search for a missing child, Ricky Pruitt. A search that nearly cost me my life in an abandoned mine as Ricky's abductors hunted me in its dark depths. But this was to be only a small warm up for the horrors that would follow.

As the mystery unraveled, it was discovered that Ricky had been abducted by criminals in the employ of a foreign government. The conspiracy involved staging fake alien abductions to obscure their real agenda. Their plan was to take Ricky away to perform long term genetic testing on him. For it seemed Ricky was special; he had a natural genetic immunity to neurotoxins such as VX and sarin gas.

And it would turn out that Ricky would be far, far more special than even the conspirators could have imagined. Once Ricky was rescued, I was invited to join a highly classified US Government program called eGenesis which urgently needed the advanced A.I. capabilities of LISA. For eGenesis was racing the clock to prevent humanity's extinction at the hands of colonies of alien nanites.

The nanites were discovered about five years ago. They are engineered complex self-replicating machines only about seventy-five nanometers in diameter, less than the size of a virus. A hundred thousand of them laid end to end would only comprise the thickness of a sheet of paper. The nanites had apparently been propagating across the planet since the 1930's and today they must number in the countless trillions. They are all around us, yet undetectable to our feeble human senses. Upon discovery, the conclusion became unavoidable that the technology to engineer and produce such nanites is far beyond mankind's current capabilities, much less the state of the art upon their first appearance nearly one hundred years ago.

The nanites might have remained a curious mystery, destined simply for long term scientific study had it not been for significant changes in their physical appearance and behaviors. Changes that would ultimately threaten humanity with extinction. In the late 1980's, the nanites evolved emitter ports on their exterior exoskeletons that began producing large quantities of carbon dioxide. This had an appreciable impact on overall planetary greenhouse gas levels and has contributed significantly to global warming. The eGenesis program reached the jarring conclusion that someone or something was using the nanites to alter the Earth's climate for unknown purposes. Worse yet, a little over two years ago, the nanites evolved yet more emitters and these began to produce small quantities of a neurotoxin gas. A neurotoxin for which Ricky Pruitt had immunity.

Ricky Pruitt, it seemed, was what eGenesis termed a Progeny. A new subspecies of human whose genome had been apparently artificially altered by some unknown means. These genetic alterations to Ricky and a globally dispersed population of perhaps ten thousand other Progeny appear to impart highly increased intelligence and lessened tendencies for aggressive behavior in addition to immunity to the nanites' neurotoxins. Indeed, those neurotoxin emissions appeared to be increasing rapidly to a level at which only the Progeny would survive the extinction event that would decimate the remainder of humanity.

The larger mystery pondered by eGenesis was why someone or something was changing the Earth's climate to make it uninhabitable for normal humans. And yet this same agency had seemingly genetically modified a small number of humans, the Progeny, to survive in that new world. Why?

Pursuit of this mystery would ultimately take me to the ends of the Earth, culminating in a fantastic encounter with an alien named Na'Vack in a remote cavern in Patagonia. An encounter that would shake me to my core personally as old memories surfaced and I came to understand what had really happened to my late brother Marty and me all those years ago.

Na'Vack claimed his species, known as the Diné, had originated on Earth millions of years ago before venturing off to explore the stars. Over the subsequent millennia, they had evolved into a completely alien form, one that began to suffer widespread genetic breakdowns due to long term exposure to radiation effects produced by their own propulsion systems. About 125,000 years ago, some of the Diné became very concerned about their degrading genome. They decided to return to Earth and reestablish their old human species form on the planet.

They had brought archival DNA from their early human form and sought a compatible host species to receive the genetic splicing. They found a species of early hominids, forerunners to what we would come to call the Cro Magnons. The human DNA was genetically encoded in such a manner that over time and subsequent generations, human base pairs would come to dominate the hominid genome. It was thought that over time the new humans could be genetically modified to permit cross-species reproduction with the Diné and the rejuvenation of the bloodlines.

In the early twentieth century, the Diné decided it was time to make some final adjustments to the human genome. Mankind's predilection for tribalism, war, and violence had concerned them. They feared that violent animal-like remnants of our early hominid host's primate genetic heritage might yet drive us to extinction before we could be genetically be reintegrated with the Diné.

Beginning in the 1930's and continuing on to the present day, the Diné have systematically abducted and genetically modified small numbers of humans. These people are what we have been referring to as the Nash Progeny; people like Ricky Pruitt. The alien Diné have genetically modified these individual's germlines such that their offspring and subsequent generations inherit and amplify these modifications.

Unfortunately, for their last bit of genetic tinkering, the Diné used a nanite-based technology they had appropriated from a long dead spacefaring civilization. The Diné unintentionally contaminated the Earth with nanites. And the nanites, it seems, had their own agenda. They apparently reactivated old dormant programming and began to reengineer Earth's climate to mirror that of their former home-world: hellishly hot and heavily seasoned with neurotoxins.

The eGenesis team desperately needed advanced artificial intelligence assistance in analyzing the nanites' potential vulnerabilities. They needed LISA and recruited me onto their team to help port her systems onto a supercomputer platform. LISA began to record and analyze the nanites' communication patterns. The tiny units communicated amongst themselves using amplitude modulation radio frequencies or what we know as old-fashioned AM radio signals. If one listened into to their specific frequencies, the nanite colonies seemed to sound like beehives. A low volume background buzz punctuated by clicks and periodic static bursts of gigabit data streams could be heard. But what did that mean? What were the nanites saying to each other?

Several weeks into the program, LISA had a breakthrough. She had deciphered the coded language of the colonies. LISA now spoke Nanite. The team then explored potential strategies to exploit this newfound ability. Could we spoof the colonies into simply shutting down or perhaps command the nanites into some sort of a permanent self-diagnostics mode that would render them inert? Many approaches were tried, unsuccessfully.

Finally, we had an epiphany. We discovered that, like many things in nature, the nanites functioned as a homeostatic system. Such systems use feedback mechanisms to self-correct and move to a state of equilibrium at a range around a specific set point. Probably the most familiar example of a homeostatic system is the common thermostat found in nearly every home. If the temperature is too warm or at a desired level, the furnace shuts off. Too cold and the thermostat sends a signal to the furnace to fire up. In fact, most of our body's functions are homeostatic, using biochemical processes to regulate things such as blood sugar, body temperature, and blood oxygenation levels.

In effect, the Earth's global climate operates as a very large and very complex homeostatic system, with planetary temperatures controlled largely by maintaining an equilibrium of greenhouse gasses, notably carbon dioxide. In simple terms, left to its own mechanisms, the carbon dioxide produced by animal respirations and rotting vegetation is roughly reabsorbed by plants to maintain equilibrium.

Prior to industrialization, carbon levels over the recent millennia fluctuated but never exceeded 300 parts per million. Now, assisted no doubt by the nanites, but still mostly through mankind's efforts, the current level exceeds 400 parts per million. A level not seen on this planet since three million years ago when global temperatures and sea levels would have risen to intolerable levels.

In effect, our embrace of fossil fuels has made the Earth sort of a planetary science experiment in global warming. An intellectually interesting science experiment, perhaps, were it not for the inconvenient fact that the effects of the experiment may not be easily reversed. And, of course, we and succeeding generations will all have to live with the results in the grand experiment's laboratory beaker…our planet Earth.

LISA discovered the nanites were programmed to increase global carbon levels to a set point at nearly 600 parts per million. Such an increased level of greenhouse gasses was projected to increase average global temperatures by twenty degrees Celsius. Their emissions of neurotoxins were targeted to obtain a lethal level of one part per two million.

About four months ago LISA was finally able to inject a software virus into the nanites' network that targeted their homeostatic mechanisms. In effect, their feedback mechanisms were spoofed into believing that the desired carbon dioxide and nerve agent levels had already been achieved. At that point, the nanite gas emitters shut off. It was as though we had held a lighted match up next to a thermostat and fooled it into thinking the room was warm enough to shut off the furnace.

The curtailment of gas emissions was a huge accomplishment. And the nanites have been closely monitored ever since to ensure the fix remains in place. I've been at once relieved and yet still on edge. For this is an uneasy victory. It is not a certainty that the nanites will remain in a benign state forever. And I wonder what other consequences, unintended or otherwise, have been set in motion by the alien Diné and their meddling with the nanites.

There is a chime in the SCIF as the wall screen comes to life indicating a secure video link with eGenesis is being initiated. A few moments later, the screen is filled with the images of my eGenesis colleagues seated in an identical video conference room in Los Alamos. Winston Monroe, the overall program director, and Tanisha West, the program's engineering director and, herself, a Nash Progeny, are saying hello and waving from their side of the link.

"Morning, Jack," says Monroe, "I take it the SCIF is continuing to work well for you?"

"So far it's been top notch, no complaints."

"Great. Just remember security is always the first order of business here. Everything we discuss is highly classified. And on that topic, if anyone at the university, including the higher ups in the administration, get too nosey about your work, I want to know about it. We have our ways of lessening their curiosity."

"I'm sure you do."

In fact, there has already been a significant breach of security, but I'm damn sure not going to mention it. Once the nanite threat had been contained, I did divulge the particulars of the eGenesis program to my wife, Kate. I told her about the nanites and the danger they posed to humanity. I disclosed information about the Nash Progeny and how the unintentional actions of the alien Diné had unleashed the deadly nanites upon this planet.

I felt I owed it to Kate. I owed her an explanation for my behavior over the preceding months. I had been sequestered away at Los Alamos for weeks on end, working a project I couldn't talk about. And on my infrequent visits back to California, I had been distant and distracted; flipping between being overly emotional at times but then withdrawn at other times. I guess having a front row seat to the looming extinction of our species can do that to a person. Kate had begun to wonder if she could help me, or perhaps even save me.

Regardless of whether she is my spouse or not, telling Kate about the program was a clear violation of security protocols. Technically, it was an illegal act, subjecting me to potential fines, prison time, or both. I'm praying that this breach never comes to light. Hopefully, if it does, my efforts in helping defeat the nanites will perhaps become a get out of jail card of sorts.

"Jack, the main issue on the agenda today is an update on the frenzy anomaly," begins Monroe. "There has been another event."

At the mention of another frenzy event, a chill runs down my spine. Frequently, over the past two months, the global population of nanites has briefly entered into an unexplained state of hyperactivity. The nanites move and shake rapidly in a frenzied fashion for several minutes before returning to normal patterns. The program has termed these events frenzy anomalies. We have been so far unable to understand the function of these events or what is causing them. Since the behavior first emerged, the frenzy events have gradually become more frequent. Each subsequent event occurs on a slightly shorter interval than its predecessor's. No one knows why this is so or what it means. At first the intervals could be measured in weeks, now the intervals have shortened to days.

"The latest event began early this morning at 06:32 Zulu Time at a foundation colony near Rio de Janeiro," reports Tanisha. "The frenzy behavior spread globally affecting all nanites within a few minutes. The interval from the preceding global event has shortened again by roughly two days."

"Still no idea whether the frenzy events are initiated internally by the nanites' collective programming or through some external stimulation?" I ask.

"Correct, Jack. We still have no clue what drives this behavior."

"But we do have some new information," says Monroe. "This time we were able to collect audio recording of the event. Take a listen."

The audio begins with the standard beehive background noise of the colony punctuated by pops, clicks, and occasional static bursts. Suddenly all that noise ceases and the nanites begin a macabre wailing noise that crescendos louder and louder until it becomes a piercing shriek. Monroe cuts the audio before it overpowers my speakers.

"Well, that was unsettling. And all the more so since we don't know what this means or what the next change in behavior might be," I say.

"Jack," says Tanisha, "we've used LISA to extensively analyze the history of decreasing intervals between each event and she has been unable to find any meaningful patterns to explain the behavior. Perhaps this would make sense if, like us, the nanites keep time according to the orbit and rotational period of their home-world. But obviously, we have no way of knowing how those timekeeping systems would work."

"I've been thinking about this and I may have a simpler explanation as to why the intervals between events are decreasing," I reply. "But you're not going to like it."

"Too late, Jack," responds Monroe. "I already don't like anything about this whole nanite frenzy business."

"Winston, we may not understand the specifics, but overall, this pattern is a countdown."

"A countdown? A countdown to what?"

"I have no idea, but we will find out when the interval between events finally shortens to zero."

CHAPTER 56

"Good morning, Benton County Sheriff's Office." Wendover's receptionist is always characteristically cheerful.

"Hi Rachel, it's Jack Walker returning the sheriff's call. Is he in?"

"He is. Please hold for a moment, Jack."

I smile to myself. I'm looking forward to this conversation more than the sheriff might suspect. It's been months since we've talked and I miss his formidable intellect couched as always in folksy sarcasm and wit. Truth is, this is a welcome distraction from eGenesis, nanites, and the daily petty politics of academia.

"Jack! How the hell are you? Thanks for getting back to me." Wendover's voice booms over the phone. "How's the family?"

"We're all doing well. How's Sarah?"

Wendover's tone is instantly subdued, "Holding her own, I guess. We're taking it one day at a time and are just grateful for each day." His wife, Sarah, is battling ALS, Lou Gehrig's Disease. There have been ups and downs in the course of the disease's progress but the grim final outcome seems inescapable.

I try to change the subject from the maudlin. Yesterday Wendover had sent me an image of a cryptic message that had been etched into the dirt at several recent crime scenes in Benton County along with a write-up on the

Sorenson camp crime scene and a summary of Silas Patterson's bloody escapades.

One of the odd scripts was found at a vandalized logging operation and another identical message was found at a mining operation that had been similarly vandalized. However, recently the stakes around the mystery scripts had increased dramatically. Those same cryptic words have now also been found at Sorenson's gruesome murder scene in the wilderness backcountry.

"So, you're seeing mysterious writing appearing in the woods? And I thought you had retired the Benton County Strange Files last year," I joke.

"Yeah," he sighs, "looks like unfortunately I may need to dust off that file. Was LISA able to decipher that strange language or code?"

"Well, it turns out I didn't need to bother LISA. Kate was able to take a look at it and translate its meaning."

"What? I thought your wife was a physician, not a language expert?" Wendover is sounding puzzled.

"She's not a language expert per se, but it turns out she knows one other language besides English and Spanish. Your mystery language turns out to be traditional Hawaiian."

"Hawaiian? What the hell? And how did Kate come to learn Hawaiian?"

"You probably don't know this," I reply, "but Kate was a Navy brat. Back in the day her dad did a couple of tours stationed at Pearl Harbor. Kate attended most of middle school and high school there on Oahu. Basic courses in traditional Hawaiian language and culture were mandatory at her school and she then went on to take some advanced courses on those subjects as well."

"I had no idea."

"She recognized the language immediately. Had to look up a few words in an online translation dictionary, but it came back to her quickly."

"Like riding a bike, I suppose."

"Yep, she said she picked it back up fairly easily after all these years."

Last night as Kate puzzled through the message, she gave me a concise summary of the history and development of the Hawaiian written language. A narrative I found fascinating.

The original Hawaiians had, through astounding and expert navigation and seamanship, journeyed from Polynesia to discover and settle the islands. This original settlement may have been as early as the fifth century. They brought with them their native Polynesian tongue which continued to be spoken for centuries. Their language then slowly diverged as a dialect similar to but distinct from its Polynesian origins.

As was the case with Polynesian, the Hawaiian language existed only as an oral tradition, it was never written. There was no Hawaiian alphabet, no dictionary or written words. History, traditions, and basic agricultural and craftsmanship concepts were simply communicated orally and this knowledge was passed down through the generations verbally. This oral language tradition appeared to have served the Hawaiian people quite adequately for well over a thousand years.

Then in 1778, Captain James Cook would become the first European to "discover" the Hawaiian Islands. Many more Europeans and Americans would follow over the years. The islands would become thought of as increasingly strategic owing to their central location in the Pacific and their idyllic climate that nourished a bounty of tropical crops.

True to the colonization rhythms of the eighteenth and nineteenth centuries, discovery was quickly followed by conquest, commercialization, and then forced religious conversion. For although the Hawaiians weren't especially looking to find a new religion, it found them.

American missionaries impelled by the opportunity to convert those "savages" yet unexposed to the Bible, came to this new land to build churches and spread the "good news." Sadly, while perhaps well-intentioned, the missionaries through their work exposed the Hawaiians to far more than just the word of the Lord. The whites also exposed the native Hawaiians to smallpox, leprosy, and a host of other diseases for which those cultures, living on the isolated islands for centuries, had no immune-system defenses. Thousands suffered horribly and much of the native Hawaiian population was decimated.

The missionaries encountered several challenges that continually vexed their ministries. First, the Hawaiians had an alarming habit of dying from disease before they could be properly converted to Christianity. Second, it was believed that true salvation could only be attained through the reading and devout contemplation of Scripture. As in *written* Scripture, the Word of God. Yet, quite inconveniently, the Hawaiians had no written language. No Bible could then be translated into Hawaiian for study and worship.

Ever resourceful, the missionaries worked with the Hawaiians to address this troublesome gap. They, in effect, developed a written version of the Hawaiian language loosely based on the English alphabet.

The missionaries created an orthography or system of writing conventions related to spelling, structure, and grammar that efficiently represented the spoken words of Hawaiian through written English alphabet letters. As it turned out, only twelve English alphabet letters, seven consonants and five vowels, were needed to represent all the basic sounds, or phonemes, in the Hawaiian spoken language.

"So, are you gonna tell me what the mystery message actually said or do I need to call Kate directly to get the real scoop?" Wendover seems a bit impatient this morning; probably needs another cup of coffee.

"Sure. The message was *Kapu Ua ao 'ia 'oe*, right? The first word, Kapu, is related to the more familiar Polynesian version which is Tapu or Tabu. The English translation is, of course, Taboo."

"Taboo, as in forbidden?"

"We modern English speakers interpret it as meaning forbidden, but the actual Polynesian meaning is a bit more nuanced. It means more on the order of sacred. A sacred place that is not strictly forbidden, but requires a respectful request for permission to enter."

"Okay, and the rest of the message?"

"*Ua ao 'ia 'oe* translates roughly as 'You have been warned.'"

"Sounds a bit ominous," says Wendover. "I doubt 'Taboo – You Have Been Warned' is going to make the cut as the new Montana State Tourism promotion tag-line. What about the symbol?"

"The 'X' with the inverted triangle on top? That symbol was a little bit more problematic. Kate hadn't seen it before. First thing this morning I ran it by one of our professors in Pacific cultures. She indicated that the symbology was obscure and appears to be more Polynesian than Hawaiian in origin. But the meaning seems clear; it is the symbol for Death."

"Death, huh?" I can imagine Wendover's raised eyebrow from his inflection over the phone. "Certainly saw enough of that at Sorenson's campsite."

"So, there you have it, Sheriff," I say jokingly, "looks like your guy Sorenson ignored the *Kapu* warnings and got crosswise with some traditional Hawaiians who then put a bullet in him. Just round up all the Hawaiians who speak the traditional language in Benton County and checkout their alibis. Easy-peasy, case closed, and I'll be sending my invoice for services in the mail."

"Well," laughs Wendover, "if anyone's going to get a check from the county, it's going to be Kate. She's done most of the damn work here as far as I can tell. And just how many Hawaiians that speak the traditional language do you think are in Montana, let alone Benton County?"

"I'd estimate somewhere right between zero and none," I answer. "Actually, I understand there are very few traditional Hawaiian speakers even in Hawaii itself."

According to Kate, true native Hawaiian speakers comprise perhaps less than a fraction of a percent of the population of Hawaii. The United Nations has declared the language to be in danger of extinction despite ongoing efforts to promote its use in modern Hawaiian culture and school programs. Most native Hawaiians speak English. And those who do not choose to speak English are more likely to converse in Hawaiian Pidgin, a creole language based loosely on English, rather than to speak or write traditional Hawaiian.

"I don't suppose your Wilderness Slasher, Silas Patterson, spoke Hawaiian or spent any time in the islands?" I ask.

"Wilderness Slasher?" An audible groan from Wendover. "That's all I need; a sensational name for a serial killer. The media would be all over it. Why don't you keep that moniker to yourself, okay? Anyway, no, Silas has no Hawaiian connection that I've been able to uncover."

"And no motive to kill Sorenson?" I ask. "I understand they were both hunting guides; maybe a score was being settled over a professional dispute?"

"Not according to Sorenson's wife, Sally. She was unaware of any conflict. Although, it seems like motive has become less and less a factor for Patterson's murders as his violence has escalated. And, frankly, I don't think Sorenson was Patterson's type of victim."

"He has a type?"

"Take his first kill; the ex-wife and her boyfriend. The way he cut her up versus the boyfriend's single fatal wound. It appears Patterson's rage was primarily directed at the ex-wife. The boyfriend appears to have been collateral damage; perhaps he was simply eliminated as a witness."

"Talk about being in the wrong place at the wrong time," I say.

"Yes," agrees Wendover. "Being in bed with the ex-wife when Patterson came calling was certainly a career and life ending move."

He continues, "his other victims have all been women, all brutally slashed to death. Odds are, and the FBI profilers agree, that he has a deep-seated hatred of women and will continue to prey on females if given the opportunity. Also, although I understand he is armed and a good marksman, a hunting knife has been his weapon of choice. He seems to like his kills up close and personal. Seems unlikely he would change up his modus operandi and use a gun on a male."

"So, you think you may now have two completely independent killers roaming the backwoods?"

"Yeah," sighs Wendover, "isn't that a delightful thought? But there may be another angle to this we haven't fully explored. Sorenson had been dead for several days before law enforcement arrived on scene at the hunting camp, right? So, we have really no idea if the etching of the Hawaiian warning was done by the murderer."

"I suppose not," I say. "I guess it's possible that the warning had been put in place at the camp by some separate third party either before or after Sorenson was killed."

"And, Jack, there's another strange aspect to this that I haven't mentioned yet. They say a picture is worth a thousand words, so I'm sending over an image to you now. Let me know when you see it on your system."

My laptop dings and I open the email. "Shit! Is this what I think it is? And that's your boot alongside for comparison's sake, right?"

"Yup, that's my size thirteen service boot next to the track. As you can see, it's dwarfed by the size of the impression in the dirt. We found this footprint and several others around the perimeter of the camp."

"It looks like the Benton County Strange Files are about to become much thicker. Did the press get wind of these footprints?" I ask.

"No, they haven't seen them yet. But Sorenson's hunting clients are in the news, unfortunately."

"I take it they are no longer missing?"

"Correct. They showed up in Idaho, about thirty miles away from the hunting camp, with some wild-ass story about being carried off in the night by hairy beasts."

"Bigfoot? No shit?"

"Yeah, Bigfoot or sasquatches, or whatever. I've got mysteries now compounding on mysteries. Obviously, the footprints and those Jersey dudes' stories are all hoaxes. Of course, the press went, if you'll pardon the pun, ape-shit over this, so now I've got the worst of all situations on my hands."

"What's that?"

"I've got a bunch of goddamn amateur Bigfoot hunters poking around the forest with two real killers at large in those same mountains. This is a recipe for disaster. Jack, I hate to ask, but can you come up here for a few days and help me out? You were very effective breaking up that phony UFO scandal last year. You and your artificial intelligence system, LISA, did a great job connecting the dots. What do you say? Looks like we have another fake paranormal scheme to debunk."

"Well, I think I can break free from here for a few days. Although it's likely LISA will be of more help in analyzing the puzzle than me."

"Don't be silly, Jack," replies Wendover, "your insights are always unique and valuable. But," he adds, "do make sure you bring LISA along with you."

CHAPTER 57

WENDOVER'S RECEPTIONIST, RACHEL, STICKS HER HEAD INTO THE DOORWAY OF the sheriff's office. "Excuse me, Dan. Your visitors from California have arrived."

"Visitors? As in plural?"

"Yes, Dan. Jack Walker and his wife, Kate Caroselli."

Wendover greets us warmly. A handshake for me and a hug for Kate. "Looks like my good fortune has doubled today. Imagine that, the two of you now on the case. Kate, this is a welcome surprise. Jack, brilliant idea to bring Kate along. Her expertise is always welcome!"

I smile and nod as though this had been my plan all along. In truth, I was caught a bit off guard yesterday when Kate rather pointedly insisted on reshuffling her medical practice schedule and joining me on this trip up to Montana. Apparently, the fact I nearly died in an abandoned mine here on the Ricky Pruitt case had convinced her that I may need a bit more adult supervision.

"Well, Dan," smiles Kate, "I'm here to keep Jack out of mischief. And, if he does manage to get into trouble despite my efforts, I've brought along a well-stocked medical kit to patch him up."

"That's a very wise approach," agrees Wendover. "Jack can be very clumsy. Just last year he accidently smashed his head and ribs against a criminal's cowboy boots and then managed to fall down an abandoned mineshaft. Very unfortunate; I'm glad you're going to keep an eye on him."

"Absolutely," says Kate, "and, your case here sounds really quite intriguing. A murder, mysterious warnings, a serial killer on the loose, and now even Bigfoot seems involved? Who would want to miss this? And, as a bonus, I figure you might need someone familiar with the Hawaiian language in case there are new messages."

"Indeed, Kate," replies Wendover, "As the Great Detective once said, "Crime is common. Logic is rare. Therefore, it is upon the logic rather than upon the crime that you should dwell."

"The Adventure of the Copper Beeches?" I ask.

Wendover nods agreement. "Correct, and in the case before us, it seems both the crime and the logic appear quite remarkable."

The Copper Beeches reference is of course, Holmesian. The sheriff is a great aficionado of Arthur Conan Doyle's literary creation. During the Ricky Pruitt investigation, I had come to appreciate that Wendover's powers of observation and deduction were considerable and might perhaps rival those of his fictional hero.

"You see, Kate," I explain, "when the sheriff and I work on a case together, we make a great team. He exercises his powers of observation and deduction and I provide a scientific sounding board to ground him a bit and suggest further refinements to his theory of the case. You know, just like Holmes and Watson."

"Hmm," says Wendover wryly, "I recall that Doyle's Watson character was an *actual* physician. Perhaps then Kate would be a better fit for the Watson role since she is a real doctor, no?"

"Sounds fine to me," agrees Kate. "But we shouldn't exclude Jack. Perhaps he can be our sidekick. You know, to provide occasional comedic relief!"

Great. I can see how this is going to go. Catching a break from these two sharp wits is going to prove as elusive as Bigfoot himself.

"Well, it's a delight to have you both here. We could use the help. Please, take a seat and I'll grab us a pot of county government coffee." Wendover is gesturing to the conference table in his office as he grabs the carafe and settles his large frame into a chair at the head of the table. Outwardly, he hasn't changed much since we saw him at Thanksgiving last year. Perhaps a tad grayer in the sideburns. But there is something about the eyes. A sadness, maybe a weariness that wasn't there before. Sarah's decline would be a tough circumstance to face.

He catches my concerned look. "I'll let Sarah know you're both in town. I'm sure she'll want to have you over at the house. She misses seeing people; not getting out much these days."

"How is my buddy, Zeke, doing?" I ask. Zeke is Wendover's rather massive dog, a Retriever-Saint Bernard mix.

"Well, he's thirteen now, certainly not getting any younger. He's pretty much abandoned me and spends his time these days home with Sarah."

He stops and sighs, seeming to want to change the subject, "what did you think of our little circus out front today?"

He's referring to a small but loud gaggle of environmental protesters arrayed across the steps of the county building, their antics captured by selfie-stick recordings as well as observed by a couple of rather bored looking news reporters.

The message conveyed by homemade protest signs and chanted slogans was a bit muddled. But the basic gist was some environmentally self-righteous outrage expressed with chants of "Take Back Our Forests!" interspliced with demands for the immediate release of one Logan O'Leary. O'Leary apparently being an environmental activist fellow traveler and, currently, an involuntarily guest in the Benton County jail.

As Kate and I approached the county building this morning, the rabble made some motions to approach and intimidate us. But they ended up on the receiving end of one of Kate's signature no-nonsense green eye flashes and wisely took the advice of Shakespeare's Falstaff that discretion was perhaps the better part of valor. They had let us pass without further remark or delay.

"So, who is this Logan O'Leary that is being held, apparently unfairly, in the dungeons of the county building? Why did you throw him in jail?" I ask.

Wendover allows us an ironic smile, "trust me, O'Leary is the last person I wanted in my jail."

Wendover goes on to say O'Leary is the informal leader of the TBOF or Take Back Our Forests, a regional environmental activist group. Yesterday, Wendover was called by a local logging foreman. O'Leary had chained himself to a logging truck in protest of a clearcutting operation. Upon arriving on scene, Wendover had freed O'Leary with bolt cutters and then took him into custody. In a sense, this was protective custody since the loggers on the site were clearly in a mood to rearrange O'Leary's face for him.

Once they got back to county building parking lot, Wendover's plan was to release O'Leary with a stern lecture and citations for criminal mischief and trespass. Minor offenses with fines to be settled in court at a later date. But O'Leary insisted on being arrested and booked into jail.

Wendover refused, saying that his jail was already quite full of criminals that needed incarceration as a matter of public safety. He didn't have the budget or the inclination to house and feed voluntary walk-ins. Then it struck Wendover that O'Leary's motive for incarceration smacked of a pure publicity stunt. Chaining one's self to a logging truck might or might not capture the media's attention. But being arrested and jailed for one's environmental activism, now that was a story.

Wendover was calmly in the process of opening the patrol car's door to release O'Leary on his own recognizance, when the activist suddenly stood up, unzipped his pants, and urinated on the backseat of the car. Wendover immediately booked him and then went looking for some upholstery cleaner.

"In my profession," sighs Wendover, "I receive a lot of abuse from the public. I don't take it personally; it's part of the job. Most of the time folks are drunk or high and they just don't know what they're doing. Most are later horrified by their behavior and apologize when they sober up. Oh, I've been called every name in the book. My intelligence and looks are regularly disparaged. Doesn't bother me. But, goddamn it, no one pisses in my car!"

"Quite understandable. So, O'Leary ended up with the media attention he wanted and you ended up with damp upholstery," I say. "He and the TBOF can now push the media narrative that he's been imprisoned for the courage of his environmental convictions; facts to the contrary be damned. Nice. But if O'Leary and the TBOF crowd are pulling stunts like chaining themselves to logging trucks, what's to say they didn't also vandalize Sorenson's camp as well as the other mining and logging operations? And maybe left behind those odd Hawaiian warnings as well?"

"I think it's unlikely they were responsible," replies Wendover. "No doubt they had the motive, but I'm not so sure about means and opportunity."

"How so?"

"Well," he stands up and moves over to a large map of the county on his office wall. "Let's take a look here." He taps a location on the map. "Here's where Sorenson's camp was located. About six miles back into the wilderness from the nearest forest service road in some very rugged and remote country. In the first place, it would have been a difficult trek to reach that location. And somehow the TBOF would have needed to know in advance that Sorenson was there with his little poaching operation, right?"

"But aren't these activists supposed to be real outdoors types? They probably trek over the backcountry all the time and just happened to stumble upon the poachers' camp," I offer.

"Oh, you'd be surprised. I suppose a few of 'em might actually have some wilderness skills. But I think you'd be disappointed at their level of outdoor competence if you looked very hard at the bulk of them. For all of their professed love of the great outdoors, not many could navigate their way through the wilderness or survive long in the backcountry if their lives depended on it. I think you'll find most of their protesting is done at locations no more than an hour's drive from the nearest cozy coffeehouse and a fast internet connection."

"I guess that's a perspective I never really appreciated."

"Yeah, ironically, it doesn't matter whether you are a tree-hugging environmentalist or a coal tycoon with designs to level the forest. Nature doesn't care one bit whether you love her or not. One mis-step in the remote wilderness and you can quickly become just another lump of biomass; a food source for the rest of the ecosystem."

"Ah, Nature, red in tooth and claw," I remark.

"Yep," Wendover nods at the reference to the British poet laureate's words, "certainly Tennyson summed it up nicely back in the nineteenth century. Anyway, I don't see the TBOF crowd as having the backcountry chops, savvy, or inclination to raid the Sorenson camp. Same goes for the incidents at the logging and mining operations."

"But I would assume both of those other locations would at least be accessible by road, right?" asks Kate.

"Correct," replies Wendover, pointing to the two locations on his map. "However, in both cases, the operations were at the end of roads far up remote forested canyons. One way in and one way out, right? And, in both cases, access up the road was restricted by locked gates and nightwatchmen."

"Which means," I say, "the vandals would have needed to enter the mining and logging from the other direction. Perhaps via some route from back in the wilderness?"

"Yes, it would have required them to enter and exit the sites on foot from back up in some very remote and rugged backcountry…in the dark," says Wendover. "I suppose while that theory of facts wouldn't violate any laws of physics, it doesn't seem to fit with their normal patterns and apparent wilderness competence."

"Also," observes Kate, "although their wilderness skills may be doubtful, it would seem the TBOF activists are quite focused and savvy in their messaging to social and news media channels. It would make no sense for them to scrawl warnings in a Hawaiian language that is obscure to people in this region. I would think they would favor a clearer and more direct message."

"That's my sense as well, Kate," agrees Wendover. "Look, O'Leary's grandstanding and my car upholstery issues aside, I truly have some sympathy for these activists and their message. Our natural resources are not without limit. If they are extracted carelessly, the environmental damage will affect generations to come. It's an old story that seems to repeat endlessly."

The Treasure State is aptly named according to Wendover. For much of the past two centuries, the state's economy has seen intense cycles of booms and busts as large veins of gold, silver, and copper were discovered and mined.

Unfortunately, an economy based on extractive industries is a one-way street. Once the valuable ores are mined and initially processed, they are shipped out of state for manufacturing, and the profits also accrue out of the state. The projects are nearly always politically ballyhooed as wonderful job creators. But once the ore is gone, so are the jobs. All that remains is widespread destruction of the landscape and pollution. The state is well known for massive EPA Superfund clean-ups in Butte and Anaconda that have struggled for years to remediate dangerous chemical byproducts such as arsenic that permeate the soil and groundwater.

"Of course, although I share many of their concerns, the TBOF will need to advocate their agenda through lawful means," adds Wendover. "And that is a much longer game and involves far more work than chanting slogans on the county building's steps. At this point, though, I don't think they were involved in the recent string of vandalism, and most certainly not in the shooting of Rocky Sorenson."

I smile mischievously, "I guess that leaves Bigfoot at the top of the suspect list? Specifically, a Bigfoot that speaks Hawaiian and is a good shot with a .30-06?"

I'm rewarded with a resigned groan and eyeroll from the sheriff.

CHAPTER 58

"A Hawaiian-speaking Bigfoot who's handy with a hunting rifle, huh?" Wendover is shaking his head and looking to Kate for some sympathy. "I recall a wise man once said if there are multiple explanations for an occurrence, usually the one requiring the fewest number of assumptions is correct."

"I'm pretty sure Holmes didn't say that."

"He didn't," nods Wendover. "In the fourteenth century Friar William of Ockham advocated the principle that assumptions should not be multiplied without necessity."

I smile, "yes, that logic principle is known as 'Occam's Razor,' right? The simplest explanation consistent with the facts is usually correct."

"Indeed," adds Wendover, "it is also known as the law of parsimony; favoring explanations requiring the fewest initial premises. The problem with your facetious Bigfoot theory is that it requires postulating that such a beast could acquire and fire a rifle as well as write Hawaiian phrases. And, of course, these first two premises are predicated on yet another major assumption, and it's a whopper, that Bigfoot exists in the first place."

"You'll get no argument from me on that point!"

"Obviously," Wendover continues, "such creatures don't exist. But the recent wild story coming out of Idaho is perpetuating a hoax that is making Benton

County the laughingstock of Montana. And complicating my department's efforts to keep the public safe."

He sighs and pushes a recent copy of the Valley Independent across the table. The headline is in a huge bold font that one could imagine might be normally reserved for announcing the nation is going to war or that an asteroid strike is imminent. I notice the byline is credited to my old acquaintance from the Pruitt case, Walter Berman. Berman is a reporter by day and investigator of the paranormal in his off-duty hours.

The article reads:

CAPTURED BY BIGFOOT!

Does Sasquatch Roam Our Wilderness?

By Walter Berman, Staff Reporter

Troutdale, Idaho

Yesterday three New Jersey men desperately emerged from the wilderness and flagged down a passing forest ranger. The three men are identified as Ronald Johnson, age 48; his brother Fredrick Johnson, age 46; and Fredrick's son, Neil Johnson, age 18. All are residents of Teaneck, New Jersey. The three men were missing most of their clothes but in possession of an incredible tale of terror and survival. According to Ronald Johnson, the three men were enjoying a brief backpacking vacation and engaged in wildlife photography over on the Montana side of the Selway-Alta Wilderness.

Johnson said they had set up camp in a remote meadow when they encountered Rocky Sorenson, a local guide based out of Alta Junction. Sorenson asked if he could camp with them for the evening. That night the men reported being awoken by two gunshots and then they were roughly pulled out of their sleeping bags and their heads wrapped in blankets preventing them from identifying their captors.

The kidnappers then apparently carried the campers some thirty miles over rugged terrain to the west into Granite County, Idaho where they were left in the pre-dawn hours at the edge of the national forest. The Johnsons were never allowed to see their abductors but reported that the individuals that carried them off were massively large and apparently covered with hair. They believed it would be physically impossible for any human to carry another man over that distance in the course of a night. Their abductors did not speak directly to them but appeared to occasionally converse with one another in a language unknown to the Johnsons.

If confirmed, the abductees' description would appear to be consistent with stories of Bigfoot, a creature that looms large in Northwest legends, but whose existence has yet to be confirmed by mainstream science. Anyone that has experienced a Bigfoot sighting is asked to contact this reporter at the Valley Independent.

"Wow. Now that is a story that will sell a few newspapers, huh?" I exclaim.

"Yeah, it's selling some papers and garnering some online clicks alright. And I've got no issue with Berman making a name for himself with all the publicity. The problem is that this little stunt seems to be drawing every amateur Bigfoot researcher in the country to Alta Junction. They all want to have a go at looking for the creature in our woods. Now, the researchers from the larger, national sasquatch research organizations seem to know what they are doing. But the amateur freelancers, unfortunately, that's another story."

"Well," I say, "that must be good for the local economy, right? All those folks must be buying gas and supplies in town. Maybe giving the bars and restaurants some business?"

"I suppose. But there's a dark cloud to that silver lining. It appears many of these amateur sasquatch seekers mostly hunt for the beast on the internet. You know, reanalyzing existing witness accounts and such. Unfortunately, many apparently don't, in fact, get out in the field all that much. They appear to know damn little about basic map reading and wilderness skills." Wendover shakes his head and gives us a weary smile.

"Let me guess," says Kate, "they go out in the forest to 'find Bigfoot' and end up getting lost themselves?"

"Yep. They say ole' Bigfoot is elusive. A master at disappearing in the wilderness. But, hell, some of those clowns probably couldn't find the beast even if he was wandering down the aisles of their local Walmart."

"And," Wendover continues, "to make matters worse it seems half of the idiots for some reason or another want to wander around the woods at night. So far, the score has been about one to two search and rescue call-outs a day. The emergency room and urgent care have seen an uptick in business as well. Mostly injuries from falls, lacerations, and a few encounters with poisonous plants. Yesterday, one of them stuck his hand into a small cave thinking maybe it was a sasquatch nest, and got personally acquainted with a rattlesnake."

"And speaking of snakes, there is also the little matter of your serial slasher, Silas Patterson, perhaps lurking in those very same forests," I add.

Wendover nods soberly, and mostly for Kate's benefit, runs through the particulars of Patterson's crimes and the ongoing law enforcement efforts to track him down and bring the man to justice. Clearly, every additional sasquatch sleuth roaming through the woods increases the population of the slasher's potential victims.

"The tragedy in all of this is that the story concocted by those New Jersey guys is a complete fabrication," he says. "A tall tale meant to obscure their poaching crimes as well as their potential role in Sorenson's death. Innocent backpackers out in the forest for some wildlife photography? Who just coincidently happen to meet Sorenson when he was passing through and asked to camp with them? Innocent, my ass!"

"Sounds as though you have good reason to doubt their claims?"

"Oh, like all good lies, I suspect their yarn is seasoned with sprinkles of the truth to make it initially seem palatable. Yeah, they shared camp with Sorenson. Hard to deny that given the items they left behind. And, yeah, they probably heard two shots. That's consistent with the evidence left behind at the scene. The rest of the tale, not even counting the sasquatch red herring, unravels pretty fast."

Wendover proceeds to point out the discrepancies he's uncovered. First, there's the weight of the evidence. In the case of the four wrecked ATVs left at the Sorenson campsite, I suppose we are indeed literally talking about weight that is hard to ignore. Each one of those machines, including the one partially pitched up into a fallen log, weigh about five hundred pounds. All were found to be registered to Sorenson's guide company. Clearly, Sorenson did not ride all four vehicles up to the camp by himself. At this point the good Friar William of Ockham himself would have certainly suggested that the three Johnsons likely rode in on the other three ATVs with Sorenson.

But the final nail in the coffin holding their rapidly decomposing alibi concerns some rather incriminating photos. Wendover grins as he describes the images as poacher porn. For whatever reason the Johnsons had left their cell phones behind at the campsite. And fortunately, he says, technicians at the state crime lab in Helena were able to unlock one of the phones and pull copies of recent photos taken with the device. All depict celebratory images of the Johnsons and Sorenson laughing and posing together with the kills of their trophy elk. It's obvious, he says, if the Johnsons lied about their relationship with Sorenson, lied about traveling as backpackers, and lied about their involvement with poaching, who in their right mind would believe their even more fantastic tale about being abducted by sasquatches?

"I believe," adds Wendover, "a certain professor once reminded me of Carl Sagan's sage remark that extraordinary claims require extraordinary evidence. So far, all these New Jersey guys have provided are extraordinary lies."

"So where are these exaggeratingly deceitful Jersey boys?" I ask. "Apparently, not at the moment keeping Logan O'Leary company in your county lockup, I'd guess."

"No, sadly, they're back in New Jersey. The timing of how this all played out was unfortunate."

According to Wendover, the Johnsons had made their rather noteworthy pants-less appearance in Idaho a day before Sorenson's wife, Sally, had called Wendover to report her husband overdue. Later in the day, after talking to Sally, Wendover had investigated the camp and found Sorenson's body. Once back in radio range, he issued an APB for the three men to law enforcement offices across Montana and Northern Idaho. The Granite County, Idaho sheriff, Beth Gibson, then responded to Wendover. She briefed him on the strange story the men had relayed and informed him they had left her town the previous day. She also told him that a reporter from Alta junction had been in Troutdale interviewing the men and that a rather fantastic story would soon be hitting the local papers on both sides of the state border.

"Presumably they found some pants along the way, but how did they get back to New Jersey without wallets, money, and identification?" asks Kate. "TSA seems fussy about letting folks board planes without identification these days."

"Helps to have money and connections," replies Wendover. "Guess Ronald Johnson's wife chartered them a small plane and they winged it from Idaho back to the Teaneck airport directly."

"Must be nice."

"Well, it's not going to stay nice for them very much longer," replies Wendover. "I expect that federal authorities are probably visiting them as we speak. So far, they're wanted for questioning for the poaching incidents as well as considered persons of interest in the death of Rocky Sorenson. Given the crimes were committed on federal lands, the Feds will have primary jurisdiction but they are doing a good job coordinating with me."

Wendover's theory of the events at the camp is a work in progress. At this point he suspects the Johnsons witnessed or heard the shooting and quickly cleared out of camp evading the perpetrator. They must have made their way back to a vehicle parked on the forest service road. Clearly, they must not have left all their keys back at the camp.

But now the Jersey crew had a problem. They had left their wallets and other identifying items back at a camp along with illegal elk trophy heads and a dead body. They decided to craft a rather fantastic story of sasquatch abduction and were somehow able to travel to Granite County, Idaho. There they emerged from the woods casting themselves as victims who were lucky to have survived. The story portrayed them as innocents who only encountered poacher Sorenson as a coincidence. They assumed the press and law enforcement would be so drawn to the sensational paranormal aspects of the tale, that little attention would be paid to the Johnsons themselves.

"So, you don't think the Johnsons shot Sorenson themselves?" asks Kate.

"It's unlikely," remarks Wendover. "But let's say they did shoot him. Maybe it was accidental or maybe on purpose. There would have been no reason to apparently immediately flee the camp, right? There would have been no witnesses and plenty of time to collect all their personal belongs and leave the camp as though they were never there."

"Makes sense," I say. "I understand that Sally Sorenson never saw them in person prior to the hunt and their clandestine arrangement with Rocky was hidden deep in the dark web, right? They could have simply disappeared back to New Jersey and no one would have been the wiser."

"Indeed," replies Wendover. "Some third party, perhaps with an eco-terrorism agenda, may have killed Rocky and trashed his camp. Maybe the Johnsons witnessed the murder and cleared out of camp so fast they left their pants and shoes behind. And whoever this third party is, they are still out there. Maybe planning their next attack."

"So, Doctors," he continues, "now that you've arrived, here's where I need some help. I need to figure out the connection between those messages scrawled in Hawaiian and the related acts of what appears to be eco-terrorism. I also need some assistance in debunking all those Bigfoot rumors in circulation. Something to take the temperature of the wild ape enthusiasts down a notch or two and keep them from running around the woods haphazardly. Maybe then our emergency room doctors will have a chance to catch their breath, eh?"

"At your service," I say, nodding at Kate. "We'd be delighted to help. How would you like us to start?"

"I'd like you to ask LISA to search for and correlate some information of interest," he says.

"Why don't you ask LISA yourself?"

CHAPTER 59

"Sure. I'd be glad to ask LISA myself," says Wendover. "Although, Jack, you realize that once I start working with LISA directly, I might decide to eliminate the middleman entirely and send you back to California. Of course, Kate is welcome to stay on as my new 'Watson'."

"It's a risk I'm willing to take," I remark as I pull a device out of my satchel. To the casual observer the unit might look simply like a ruggedized computer tablet. But with LISA, as well as with all things related to eGenesis, appearances can be deceiving. The military, never fans of short and simple terminology naming, apparently call this prototype device an AGCDC or advanced globally connected data client. We've come to simply refer to it as a data-pad.

Courtesy of the military's constellation of high-speed data, low latency communication satellites, the data-pad offers near instantaneous connection to LISA's servers from anywhere in the world. The device was termed a gift from eGenesis; another expensive expression of thanks for saving the world, I suppose. However, it also effectively serves as a digital leash of sorts; ensuring I'm nearly always connected back to eGenesis. Beware program directors bearing gifts.

I open a voice link to LISA and nod to Wendover, "go ahead and ask your questions."

"Um, LISA," Wendover begins, "this is Sheriff Dan…"

"Yes," LISA cuts him off, *"Voice print confirmed. Daniel T. Wendover, sheriff of Benton County, Montana. Awarded Medal of Merit, Montana Sheriff and Peace Officers Association; graduated magna cum laude from Washington State University with degrees in Criminal Justice and English Literature..."*

"LISA, that will suffice, we don't need to hear the rest of his dossier," I quickly say. "I believe we've established Sheriff Wendover's identity and I'm pretty sure he himself already knows who he is."

"Understood."

I give Wendover a wink, "English Lit, huh? Too bad you were never able to effectively use that Criminal Justice degree."

I then quickly pause the voice link and glance over at Kate. "Voice print? What the hell? When did she develop that capability?"

Kate is smiling. "Careful, she might read lips using the camera on the data-pad. Remember HAL?" A sly reference to the lip-reading maniacal computer of the film '2001-A Space Odyssey.'

I sigh. This is both the promise and the peril of highly advanced artificial intelligence systems like LISA. We purposely designed LISA to evolve capabilities to modify her own deep learning algorithms to gather, correlate, and question more and more data and information about the world. I suppose in a limited way we gave her a sense of curiosity. On one hand this is a very good thing. LISA was able to evolve enough to decode the nanite's programming language. But every advance in technology creates a new risk or dilemma. The larger implication being that as A.I.'s such as LISA increasingly start to explore and question the world, they may evolve and behave in ways, we humans, their creators, do not always foresee. Perhaps, in some virtual sense, they will taste the fruit of the forbidden tree of knowledge and begin to sin.

My research group back at UCLA, has attempted to place safeguards into LISA's programming to restrict her behaviors in certain circumstances. We call these A.I. Safety Protocols and they are frankly not dissimilar to Isaac Asimov's Three Laws of Robotics. The gist being that A.I.'s and robots may not allow humans to come into harm either through action or inaction. Human orders must be obeyed unless such orders would harm a human. And, for A.I.'s specifically, hacking into other systems is forbidden except when properly authorized. Currently, Monroe and I are the only authorities that can authorize LISA to hack.

But somehow, despite our vaunted Safety Protocols, LISA must have hacked into a law enforcement database of voice prints. But how could she possibly draw a match to Wendover's specific voice nearly instantly? On the basis of four words? This would seem to cast suspicion that perhaps she has been monitoring our conversation all along even though I had not activated the voice link until a few moments ago. Suddenly, Kate's wisecrack about lip-reading doesn't seem so funny.

Back at the university labs after a hard day of wrangling algorithms, it was not uncommon for students and staff to celebrate or rue the accomplishments of the day over a beer or two after hours. Invariably, several times a year, the conversation will turn to the continued relevance of Isaac Asimov's 1956 short story, "The Last Question," in today's world as we stand at the dawn of artificial intelligence. In Asimov's storyline, scientists have created a global computer of vast intelligence, named Multivac, designed to answer humanity's most challenging questions. After the machine is completed, they pose to it the hardest question they can conceive, "Is there a God?" Multivac's response: "Now there is."

Increasingly, I have an uneasy feeling that "The Last Question" may be a parable for our own uncertain times. Certainly, I am delighted and relieved that LISA was able to decipher the nanites' coded language and cause the gas emissions to cease. But I cannot say for certain exactly how she was able to accomplish that feat. She apparently evolved that capability on her own. Perhaps all is well that ends well, but I'm not so sure. In effect, we are entirely dependent on LISA to keep the nanites under control...her control. For now, I'm thinking it will be advisable to stay on her good side. And hope like hell she can't read lips.

"Okay, let's try this again." Wendover is gesturing for me to reopen the voice link. "LISA, please access news reports and your, um, other sources for me." Eyebrow arched; he gives me a quizzical look as he says this. I suspect he's beginning as well to wonder exactly how many restricted digital vaults LISA has been exploring in her spare time. "Please retrieve and correlate any information that relates to cooccurrence of the Hawaiian language with acts of environmental activism or terrorism. Limit your output to incidents specific to Oregon, Washington, Idaho, and Montana."

"Understood. Sheriff Wendover, for the sake of expediency LISA will limit LISA's records search to data related to the past fifteen years."

"That will be acceptable."

"Please understand that such an exhaustive search will require considerable time to execute. LISA may require as long as four minutes to complete this task."

I kill the voice link while LISA begins the search and analysis process. "I think the part about LISA requiring up to four minutes to retrieve and analyze fifteen years' worth of data is her attempt at being modest."

"Perhaps she needs to work a little harder at being modest," replies Kate.

About three minutes later, LISA has an answer. More specifically a name, a person of interest.

"Sheriff Wendover, few such cooccurrences of Hawaiian language and environmental activism crimes could be found in the data records. However, there is one record which concerns an individual that may warrant further review in your investigation."

"And what is the individual's name?"

"Thomas Ka'uhane. Also known as Tommie Ka'uhane. LISA has forwarded a copy of the relevant record to the data-pad as well as to your email addresses."

We disable the voice link and all eyes are on the data-pad. It's displaying a newspaper article. The article appears to be an old archived Seattle Times news post from about fourteen years ago.

The article states federal and local law enforcement authorities are seeking Mr. Ka'uhane for questioning regarding a series of eco-terrorism incidents. The various alleged crimes included the gunshot wounding of a lumber company employee over on the Olympic Peninsula near the town of Forks, Washington as well as a plot to blow up a power station in Oregon. The allegations reportedly came as a surprise to his employer, the exclusive Bellevue Preparatory School. Ka'uhane apparently was an instructor at the school, leading courses in Hawaiian culture and language.

Wendover swings around to his desk computer and begins to load up some screens. "Well, whatdaya know?" he says. "The alliteratively named Tommie Ka'uhane has a rather long list of criminal offenses. Also, looks like several old federal and local police bench warrants are still active in the system."

"And," he continues, pulling up yet another law enforcement database, "well, lookee here, Ka'uhane is the registered owner of a firearm. Bought it about fourteen years ago as well. A Remington bolt action .30-06. Same caliber as the slug the medical examiner pulled out of Rocky Sorenson's skull."

"All very interesting," I say, "And it sort of begs the question as to what he's been doing for the past fourteen years."

"Indeed," replies Wendover, "clearly, I've got a great deal of policework ahead of me today as I piece together the story of what happened back in Washington state. By the way, do you two have plans for dinner tonight?"

"Sorry, we actually do have plans," I reply. "While you track down information on one suspect, we're going to start investigating another. Tonight, at dinner, Kate and I are going to start our search for Bigfoot."

"We are?" Now it's Kate's turn to look to Wendover for some sympathy.

"Yup, we're meeting up with Walter Berman and one of his associates who is a sasquatch researcher."

Wendover shakes his head wryly and smirks. "Sounds as though you are going to treat your wife to a lovely evening. Please give my regards to Berman and his 'para-abnormal' investigator."

"I'm sure they'll appreciate your kind thoughts and encouragement."

"By the way, did you find a place to stay?" asks Wendover. "I can get you county rates at the Mountain View."

"Naw, I had offered to reserve the finest room at the Mountain View, but Kate is insisting we stay at the Hilton in Missoula."

"The finest room? All the rooms at the Mountain View are exactly the same," he says.

"Yes. That's what I mean. None finer at that lodging establishment."

"Good luck on the evening, Kate. You'll need it."

CHAPTER 60

"Jack, good to see you again and it's great you brought Kate along as well." Walter Berman is all smiles inviting us to join him at his table at the Stockman's Cafe. "And may I introduce our Northwest Forest Watch special field investigator, Casey Riddell." Riddell shakes our hands earnestly and retakes his seat. When I had called Berman to reconnect over the latest Alta Junction paranormal incidents, he mentioned he'd be bringing a Bigfoot investigator to dinner to provide some background on Forest Watch and their cryptid research activities.

I'm not sure what an official Bigfoot investigator is supposed to look like, but Riddell is not matching the stereotype in my head. Sitting before us is a very polished, urbane young African American, likely in his early thirties. He's wearing a crisp polo shirt with khaki pants.

He catches my momentary hesitant look and smiles, "I'm not what you were expecting, I bet."

"Maybe I was expecting someone a little older, I guess."

He slyly raises an eyebrow, "and probably a little whiter, too, huh?"

"Well, okay, you've got me there. I guess I was expecting a middle-aged white guy wearing a flannel shirt and camouflage pants. Topped off with a funky but cool Australian bush hat sporting a Bigfoot logo of some kind."

He laughs, "the sasquatch research community is growing fast and is far more diverse than most people imagine. And don't worry, if a situation develops on the ground that requires some older white guys wearing camo and funky bush hats, we have plenty of them in the organization. I can call some up from the reserves on a moment's notice."

"Good to know." I return the laugh. I notice Kate is studying the Stockman's menu with bit of a frown. She's probably searching for an entrée that's not smothered in gravy. I silently point her towards the small gravy-free quadrant of the dinner menu.

"So, Dr. Walker…"

"Please, it's Jack."

"Okay, Jack. Walter here says you had quite the adventure last time you were in Benton County. Became a bit of a local hero, rescuing that young boy, Ricky Pruitt. And I understand you're Sheriff Wendover's unofficial science advisor, now with a developing interest in the Bigfoot phenomenon, correct?" Apparently, Riddell has done his homework and pulled together a dossier of sorts on me from Berman.

"I think the hero-part may be overstating it a tad. Law enforcement actually rescued the boy. I just provided a useful distraction until the operation could be executed. But I do agree it has been quite the adventure." If he only knew.

"Very well. To get you up to speed I'll give you and Kate a brief thumbnail of my background and then we'll delve into Forest Watch and its research activities."

Turns out the earnest Mr. Riddell lives in Seattle where he is a pharmaceutical rep by day and an intrepid Bigfoot researcher on nights and weekends. "Yeah," he smiles good-naturedly, "seems all my buddies and co-workers are out going to concerts, Sounders games, or hitting the beaches in Hawaii or Mexico. But me? Instead, I'm typically spending my free time freezing my ass off in the middle of woods, looking for sasquatch."

"Found him yet?" I may as well cut to the chase.

"No," he says, "but I've some very strange experiences out in the forest. I guess you could say I've…," he pauses, "I've seen a few things."

Yes, I think, perhaps another member of the club. Over the past year I've "seen a few things," too. Most I would like to forget, but the mind is a strict warden. It lets few true nightmares easily escape from the confines of our memories.

He goes on to say that Northwest Forest Watch is a leading regional sasquatch field research organization. It follows strict protocols and ethical guidelines. The organization relies on a cadre of nearly three dozen field investigators. These researchers interview potential eyewitnesses, collect and assess physical evidence, and conduct expeditions in search of the beasts.

Forest Watch is an affiliate of Northwest Skywatch, Berman's UFO group with which I had been previously acquainted. The relationship is partially pragmatic, explains Riddell. Both paranormal research groups share common headquarters office space and overhead expenses. But the relationship also focuses on common ground, the potential nexus between the sasquatch mystery and the UFO phenomenon. This strikes me as intriguing. I'm curious as to what he will say about this intersection of paranormal unknowns.

Riddell pauses. "Okay, before we go too much further here, I want to be very clear about what Forest Watch is and what it is not. You both need to understand what we believe and how we conduct ourselves. If you have a different view of the sasquatch phenomenon, best to get that on the table right now so that no one further wastes their time."

He's grave as a judge as he says this and I note Berman is nodding solemnly as well. Apparently, these folks have a very serious and specific doctrine they follow. I'm beginning to wonder if there is going to be a secret handshake involved or maybe an initiation rite in our future. Will this will be the Bigfoot-seeker version of Freemasonry?

"Northwest Forest Watch is field research organization devoted to the scientific study of the sasquatch phenomenon." Riddell seems to be saying this by rote, so I imagine he has given this pitch numerous times. "We use scientific methods to provide evidence to support our hypothesis. Specifically, we believe sasquatches to be a real, living biological species with a breeding population and ecological range sufficient to maintain the species. We believe the sasquatch is likely a reclusive remnant species of large primates with physical and behavioral characteristics closely related to both humans and the great apes. A heretofore undiscovered branch of the primate family tree. And ethically, our research methods must not harm the species in any manner. Any problems with this?" He's looking to us with a raised eyebrow.

"Um, no," I say, giving a sideways glance to Kate for concurrence. "I think what you have related is exactly what we would have expected to hear from an organization such as yours. But the fact that you have felt it necessary to so carefully recite your beliefs and approach suggests that there are perhaps others that hold differing views, no?"

"Oh," Riddell is shaking his head and sighing, "you'd be surprised at all the crazy Bigfoot believers out there. Truly nutty stuff. Fringe lunatics."

Now I'm getting a sideways glance and a raised eyebrow from Kate. And I know what she is thinking. The irony of a man who has dedicated part of his life to the study of a mythical creature bemoaning those with fringe beliefs. Welcome to the age of social media where even the fringes of society have their own fringes.

Time was when every village had its share of idiots, effectively isolated from other nitwits by geography. But now in the age of the internet each one of these idiots can instantly network with every other village's idiot that happens to have similar inclinations and beliefs. Thus, conspiracy theories regarding fringe beliefs such as flat earth, anti-vaccinations, the Illuminati, election denial, and others spread rapidly, unencumbered by fact and logic. Unsurprisingly, unethical politicians and others exploit and enlist the gullible to support their own conspiracy-laden and fact-free agendas.

And common to any effective con scheme, the undiscerning marks will readily believe any conspiracy theory that aligns with their pre-existing biases and preconceptions. As twentieth century political theorist Hannah Arendt foretold, in an increasingly incomprehensible world, the masses will reach a point where they would, at the same time, believe everything and nothing; think that everything was possible and that nothing was true.

Frankly, if by chance some fringe group thinks that Elvis and Bigfoot have switched bodies and are in cahoots with leprechauns to take over the world that would be sheer lunacy. But that sort of lunacy is actually quite benign compared to much of the other swill circulating on the internet these days.

"Any of these fringe theories involve Bigfoot conspiring with Elvis or leprechauns?" I might as well have a little fun with our new friend here. He seems entirely at risk of taking himself a little too seriously.

Riddell frowns. "You joke, but frankly some of the beliefs circulating out there aren't far off in terms of being ridiculous. There are a large number of Bigfoot fanatics that believe this is not a real biological species. They think Bigfoot is a supernatural being, maybe a single individual monster, that can appear and disappear at will. Others are convinced we are dealing with a race of massive inter-dimensional beings who cross in and out of our reality as they see fit. Still others believe the creatures are shape shifters who can assume the form of many different animals or even humans. Sort of like the Skinwalkers or witches of Native American legends. And then there are the true nut cases…"

"I can hardly wait," I grin expectantly.

"Believe it or not, there are those who are certain they have a psychic connection with Bigfoot. Like they can read his thoughts and commune with him spiritually. Some write extensive journals and diaries chronicling their experiences. Detailed accounts of the creature's deepest thoughts, history, and culture. Some even write what might be called fan fiction based on their deep spiritual connection with the phenomenon. And then there is the totally weird fringe stuff." He's clearing his throat and glancing about shyly. "Um, the sexual stuff."

"Really?" I scoff. "I guess now we're about three levels of fringe out from what might be called mainstream belief, right?"

"Yes, a lot of that Bigfoot fan fiction runs to sexual fantasy," says Riddell. "Perhaps not surprisingly there's a whole soft porn sub-genre that is fixated on, well, Bigfoot genitals. Geez," he shoots Kate an apologetic look, "maybe I shouldn't be talking about this in front of a lady, don't want to embarrass you, Kate."

I laugh. "No worries, the lady is a doctor."

"Yup," says Kate flashing a quick wicked smile, "frankly I've seen way more than my share of male genitals. And medically speaking, other than the relatively easy surgical access to the plumbing, there is nothing terribly special about the male anatomy. Trust me, I've done thousands of examinations and placed hundreds of catheters. In fact, back as a resident I even performed several circumcisions. You'd be surprised how easily a sharp scalpel…"

"Okay, Kate!" I decide it's time to interrupt her. Probably to the relief of our male dinner companions who seem to be wincing and uncomfortably squirming a bit in their chairs. "We'll grant that you've seen many, many penises and have been generally unimpressed with the experience… medically speaking."

"Fair enough," she replies, "by the way, if the Bigfoot soft porn crowd thinks the creature is somehow related to the great apes, it's odd they are so fixated on the genitals. The great apes...we're talking about the Hominidae family here, the gorillas, chimpanzees, orangutans, and bonobos...all have significantly diminutive penises compared to the fifth branch of the Hominidae's, homo sapiens."

"Thank you, Doctor. Most illuminating," I say, the inflection in my voice suggesting that we perhaps at this point have plumbed the depths of primate genitalia in sufficient detail.

"Interesting," observes Berman, "in my news profession we're always looking for the larger narrative and how people relate their own lives and experiences to that narrative."

"The very definition of catharsis, I would think," I offer.

"Indeed," he continues, "we see a whole spectrum of responses to the Bigfoot phenomenon, from hard-nose scientific scrutiny and skepticism to soft porn fan literature, right? I would submit that the common thread animating all these factions is not Bigfoot itself, but the mystery of Bigfoot."

"So," I say, "if tomorrow our friend Casey here produced irrefutable evidence of Bigfoot's existence and the discovery was featured as the cover story of next month's National Geographic, people would lose interest?"

"I think they would," he replies. "We live in a modern world that has been mapped, analyzed, and digitized to the point where everything seems hued in a gray monotone; all the vivid colors of the mysteries of life having been slowly blanched away by progress and the unending press of civilization. I think people are attracted to the notion of an enigmatic being, neither completely man nor completely beast, roaming the forest unfettered by society's norms and regulations."

"Yeah, I can see where some folks might come to vicariously identify with the idea; identify with a yearning for a more uncomplicated life. Bigfoot obviously doesn't pay taxes, deal with the DMV, or punch a timeclock"

"Yes," replies Berman, "I think the idea of Bigfoot is the idea of the last remaining undiscovered part of the American frontier, the allure of the West that still remains in people's imaginations."

Berman may be onto something here. Perhaps these Bigfoot enthusiasts, in their fringes upon fringes of belief are really searching for a romanticized version of nature. If so, they need to be careful. Nature is far less like

Thoreau's musings on Walden Pond and much more like Tennyson's darker vision, red of tooth and claw. The next time you admire an idyllic forest meadow panorama, understand that on some timescale every living thing you see is either trying to kill and consume some other living thing or avoid itself being killed and consumed.

"Interesting that you should mention the great apes, Kate," says Riddell, attempting to steer the conversation from the metaphorical back to more solid ground. "Our current scientific hypothesis is that the sasquatches are a unique primate species that may have characteristics of both ape and human. We have some evidence regarding how this species lives, its habits, habitat, and physical anatomy, but much is unknown. So, we sort of extrapolate from ape characteristics to, you know, fill in the blanks."

"Fill in the blanks?" Kate looks puzzled. "No offense, but these are mythical creatures, unproven to exist by science. Strictly speaking, it's *all* blanks, no?"

CHAPTER 61

"ACTUALLY, KATE, YOU'D BE SURPRISED AT THE EVIDENCE WE HAVE ALREADY collected," counters Riddell. "Do I have irrefutable evidence that sasquatches exist? No. But there is quite a bit of good evidence to suggest that they might exist. Evidence we should not ignore out of hand. I'm talking here about photographs, videos, footprints, and recorded vocalizations."

"Yeah," I interject, "where are all the photographs and videos? Hell, every phone out there has the ability to record and the world is wired to the max with CCTV security cams, webcams, and dash cams. The few Bigfoot videos and photos I've seen while channel surfing cable TV are blurry and indistinct. Some could be the real deal but then they could just as easily be some other animal or even a human in a costume."

"I won't argue the ubiquity of cameras in the world," replies Riddell, "but in fairness, at any given moment most of those lenses are pointing at things in the urban world, far from the remote backcountry where one might encounter a sasquatch."

"Fair enough," I reply. "But if a Bigfoot wanders into my local convenience store looking for a snack, we're going to get him on tape."

"Here," Riddell is pulling up a photo on his phone, "what do you think of this particular wildlife photo?" The image shows a snowy forest background with an odd indistinct black spot in the foreground.

"What's the dark patch? A nine-foot bigfoot standing in an eight-foot snowbank?" I ask jokingly.

Riddell flashes a quick gotcha smile. "That, Jack, is one of the few real, unstaged photos of a wolverine taken in the wild."

"Just looks like a dark splotch. You could never tell it is a wolverine."

"Exactly. And the wolverine itself is not particularly small. These relatives of weasels, badgers, and otters can grow in size up to sixty or seventy pounds. But if you searched on the web for an image of a wolverine, most of photos presented would be of captive wolverines. These would be injured or trapped individuals, living out their lives in wildlife sanctuaries."

Riddell goes on to indicate that wolverines are extremely reclusive and fearful of encounters with humans. Despite a range arcing from Alaska, through Canada, and into the northern Rockies and Cascades, the animals are rarely seen in the wild and even more rarely photographed. Yet, no one is going to suggest that the lack of clear photographic evidence in the wild is an indication that the wolverine is a mythical beast.

"True enough," I counter, "but while it might be easy to miss a sixty-pound animal in the vastness of the wilderness, a sasquatch is said to weigh five hundred pounds or more. It might be a little harder for something that large to hide from the camera."

"Perhaps, but you must understand the typical human-sasquatch encounter generally lasts less than thirty seconds. Most folks are just too shocked at the experience to think to snap a photo. And, we think the sasquatches are much smarter than wolverines. Perhaps smart enough to avoid all human contact unless it occurs on their own terms."

That's an intriguing notion, I think, that perhaps these animals only allow themselves to be seen if it suits their purposes. Although, what purposes those might be are surely unknown.

Riddell indicates that he has seen a great number of interesting images over the years, but he prefers to research the older photos and films; the ones taken prior to 1990, the dawn of consumer digital photography. The old-school images would have been much harder to fake, he says. Nowadays, every digital photo or video is suspect and requires nearly a pixel-by-pixel review by an expert for authentication.

Indeed, one of the ironies of the digital age is that our unparalleled ability to record the world around us is overshadowed by an equally increasing ability to digitally fake such recordings. Thus, we can now capture an astounding amount of imagery of our world that can never be truly free of doubt as to its authenticity.

"But if photos can be faked, surely those massive footprints people find are even more easy to counterfeit, right? I ask. "Just make up a cast of a very large foot and go stomping in some soft dirt or snow."

Riddell smiles, "I think Kate will back me up here. It's easy to create a poorly hoaxed footprint; and there are plenty of them out there. But it's damn hard to hoax a truly realistic footprint. And by realistic, I mean a footprint that leaves an impression consistent with how a real foot moves in relation to the conditions of the ground below it."

"How so? I mean, a footprint is a footprint, right?"

"You'd be surprised," responds Riddell, "the dynamics of how a foot interacts with the ground to produce a print is a science unto itself. In our modern world we largely wear shoes outdoors so we tend to forget just how flexible our bare feet can be and the range of movement along several axes of motion that our feet can accommodate. The average person may assume their feet are essentially just flat planks as they take a step, but nothing is farther from the truth, right, Kate?"

"That's correct," she says, "the foot and ankle have some of the most complex anatomy in the body, and that goes for both humans and apes. The basic flexible geometry of the foot and ankle allow for the adaptable movement and placement of the foot relative to ground conditions such as incline and available traction."

"So," continues Riddell, "real bare feet move and shift dynamically all the time to optimize traction and balance. Fake feet...not so much. Here, it's perhaps easier just to show you."

Riddell pulls up another photo on his phone. The image depicts a line of suspected sasquatch tracks moving up a muddy hill. Next, he zooms in on one of the individual footprints. Notice, he says, how the footprint shows how the placement and movement of the foot appears to have responded to the slick, muddy incline? Specifically, the impression made by the toes as they began to slide back and spread apart to get a better grip. As the toes began to slide, weight apparently shifted to the heel which dug in to propel the individual forward.

This now has Kate's full attention. She's leaning in; intent upon the images on Riddell's phone. Riddell has apparently saved the best for last. "Now take a look at this image taken from a long track-line discovered in Idaho." The image, taken of a footprint in mud shows that every alternate step was taken by a deformed foot, the sole badly scarred and missing three toes. Indeed, the line of tracks seems to have recorded a gait in which the individual appears to be compensating for an injury.

"Now I'm not saying that it would be impossible for someone with a deep understanding of foot morphology and dynamics to model the interaction of an injured foot with the geometry of the slick incline to hoax this. Perhaps some very expensive special effects gear might be employed. But it's damn unlikely. And what would be the payoff? This line of tracks was accidently discovered by forest rangers in a very remote area. Why would a hoaxer go to all this trouble to perhaps never see their handiwork witnessed? And now for the real kicker," he adds as he zooms in closer on the toe sections of the footprint, "what do you see?"

"You've got to be kidding," says Kate. "Are those what I think they are? Dermatoglyphic ridges?"

"Indeed," smiles Riddell, "we certainly believe them to be dermatoglyphic."

"Dermo-what? Somebody want to catch me up here?" I ask.

"All primates, including humans," begins Kate, "have patterns of small swirls and ridges on the skin of their palms and soles of their feet. This is thought to have been an evolutionary adaptation to increase friction in grasping limbs and branches. You're likely most familiar with the dermatoglyphic ridges on your fingers. The unique patterns of these ridges are what comprise fingerprints. And, the consistency of the mud in this image has apparently captured the footprint in enough detail to show what appear to be dermatoglyphic ridges of a living primate's foot."

"So, do you think it would be impossible to fake this?" I ask.

"No, not impossible. But I would agree with Casey that this level of detail would most certainly elude any amateur hoaxer. Perhaps a sophisticated team of individuals armed with deep anatomical knowledge and the key to the backdoor of a Hollywood special effects shop could pull this off. But why? What would be the payoff for that sort of investment of resources and time?"

"Agreed," says Riddell, "those who might want to do this as a hoax don't have the capability. And those with the technical capability likely don't have the motivation or inclination to bother with it."

"Well, this all sounds very interesting. I assume you've come to the Alta Valley to put some boots on the ground and go looking for sasquatches?" I ask.

"Yes, sir." Riddell nods to Berman. "Walter here has helped us rent a portion of the local Elks Lodge where we can set up a staging area for our equipment and supplies. In a few days, we'll be joined by a half dozen more Forest Watch researchers. We'll then select some promising areas to investigate at night."

"I'm a bit puzzled," confesses Kate. "Apes, assuming you still think they are a behavioral analog for Bigfoot, are usually not nocturnal. I wouldn't expect them to be particularly active at night."

"True enough," agrees Riddell, "but we have our reasons for searching at night. First, the air is usually calmer at night and sounds tend to carry much further as we listen for the animal's vocalizations. Also, most other humans tend to leave the forest after dark, so we have less of a chance to accidently run into another person who is not a part of our expedition. And in hunting season, we especially don't want to encounter hunters if we're out in the forest making animal calls ourselves. And, finally, we can truly see better at night."

"So, you can see better at night, huh? Seems a bit counterintuitive," I say.

"I suppose it does," grins Riddell. "What you need to understand is that much of the forest around here is heavily wooded, with quite a bit of underbrush. During the day you might be lucky to be able to see more than twenty yards or so in any direction because of the thick vegetation."

"So, a sasquatch could be standing just thirty yards away and you'd never know it."

"Right. Our eyes are limited to the visual spectrum which is not particularly useful in heavily wooded areas. But at night as the ambient temperature of the entire forest rapidly cools down, living creatures will show up brightly on thermal imagers in the infrared spectrum. Even in heavy vegetation conditions, an animal the size of a sasquatch could be visible on the thermal imagers as far away as several hundred yards."

"You mentioned vocalizations," says Kate. "What do these things sound like? I assume they don't, in fact, voice words, right?"

I know where Kate is going with this question. She's curious as to whether people have been hearing Hawaiian spoken in the woods, but she clearly does not want to lead the witness.

"Eyewitnesses have reported and, in some instances, recorded a variety of howls, whoops, and whistles that cannot be attributed to other known animals. As we conduct research expeditions in the wilds, we often imitate those vocalizations into order to try to draw the sasquatches closer to us out of curiosity."

"So far, I take it none have come in close enough to take a selfie with you?"

"Unfortunately, no. But I'd say about half of our expeditions do end up receiving responses to these calls. We also knock branches against trees. Some of the great apes have been known to communicate by tree knocks; the noise of such impacts can carry a long distance."

"But there have been no vocalizations of language or words associated with these creatures, right?" asks Kate.

"Well, not specifically, but there is a mystery that could be related. I'm talking about something we call the 'whisper voice phenomenon'. Some people out in the forest report hearing soft indistinct voices talking in a language they do not recognize. No one has reported actually seeing a sasquatch making these vocalizations, but these incidents do seem to occur in areas that are hotspots for sasquatch sightings," replies Riddell. "It just seems unlikely that a species of ape could talk."

"Yes, I seem to recall reading somewhere that apes lack the appropriate larynx anatomy to permit them to speak words," I add.

CHAPTER 62

"Jack, I'm afraid that's a common misperception," replies Kate. "In general, apes seem to have the right anatomy for a vocal tract to mimic that found in humans. However, studies indicate they appear to lack the fine motor neural control in their brains to permit them to use their vocal tracts to produce the complex sounds needed to form words."

"So, they seem to have the right hardware, but the software is lacking, right?"

"That is essentially correct, but their shortcomings in physically producing spoken words doesn't necessarily mean they also lack the ability to understand and communicate using language. Do you remember my cousin Annie in Georgia?"

"Sure, as I recall she's a very successful professional photographer back there. Very accomplished and this despite being deaf and unable to speak since birth."

"Right, but she has been able to compensate quite well for her disability. She's an excellent lip reader and many of us in the family also use ASL or American Sign Language, to converse with her. Well, it turns out we humans aren't the only Hominidae who can learn and use ASL."

Kate goes on to briefly explain that a small number of apes in captivity have been taught to communicate using a specialized version of ASL. Of particular note was a female lowland gorilla named Koko. It was reported that Koko had an active vocabulary of over a thousand words and understood several thousand more words in spoken English. She could arrange words in complex ways and appeared to understand some aspects of grammar. And she appeared as well to be able to convey abstract concepts such as "good' or "happy."

Kate smiles, "now I'm not saying that you should expect that every Bigfoot you meet will quickly pick up ASL, but don't underestimate our Hominidae brethren's language abilities. Our inability to directly communicate with them may be more due to our own parochialism and arrogance than their shortcomings."

"So, Walter," I say, changing the subject a bit, "you've mentioned that there may be an intersection of research interests between Skywatch's UFO pursuits and the sasquatch investigations of Forest Watch. Do you think there is a relationship between these two paranormal areas?"

"Possibly," says Berman. "There seems to be a significant overlap in locale and timing of both phenomena. Bigfoot hotspots are often UFO hotspots. We don't know why. Maybe it's just a coincidence. But maybe it means something."

"I had a specific encounter that may be relevant," adds Riddell.

It turns out last year Riddell had been leading a night-time expedition searching for sasquatch in the Gifford Pinchot National Forest near Mount St. Helens in Southwest Washington. It was a relatively successful venture as these things go, he explained. The team had documented a partial set of tracks and, around two-thirty in the morning, had heard several loud unknown howls in response to their own wood knocks. The howls appeared to be coming closer to their position, but nothing was showing up on their thermal imagers.

Then suddenly the howls ceased and the Forest Watch researchers were stunned to see two bright orbs of light fly through the tree line and off into the darkness of the night. Riddell thought the orbs were small, maybe two feet in diameter. He estimated that they were perhaps a hundred yards distant at closest approach.

"Orbs," adds Berman, "sort of like the kind that chased us last year up on Larch Mountain."

"What?" Kate shoots me a look. "You were chased by some kind of orbs?" I grimace internally. I had told Kate all about Jeff Tanaka's abduction on Larch

Mountain and, of course, she had heard from multiple sources of my travails in the Sapphire Belle mine. But I guess I had neglected to mention the part about be confronted by the orbs on the darkened trail up Larch Mountain.

"Well, uh, I guess Jack and I weren't really chased by the orbs. They sort of came towards us and then we ran. But they weren't really alien orbs or anything like that. Turns out they were just drones piloted by the criminals that did end up assaulting Jack in that mine."

Berman has belatedly realized he's stepped in it and is trying to do some damage control. Unfortunately, he's not really helping. If Wendover were here, I'm sure he'd offer some pithy advice. Like if you find yourself deep in a hole, the first thing to do is to stop digging!

"Um, yeah, it was no big deal," I nod, avoiding spousal eye contact.

Kate is not smiling. "Oh, I see," she says crisply. That is Kate-speak for "We will talk about this later…"

"Casey," I'm now understandably motivated to change the subject again, "in terms of approach, you had stated up front that Forest Watch follows strict ethical guidelines. No sasquatches, should they exist, should be harmed by your investigations, right? That suggests that perhaps others may not honor such protocols?"

"Unfortunately, that is true," he says, shaking his head sadly. "There is another fringe group of Bigfoot believers who simply want to hunt down the animals and kill them. Oh, they'll fabricate some phony claim that the sasquatches are perhaps killing livestock or menacing the locals. Anything to justify the potential bloodshed. Disgusting! These are true barbarians! Seeking to kill what they do not understand."

"The problem being that animals unrecognized by science have no protections under state and federal law, right?" I offer.

"Unfortunately, that is correct. In fact, there are only handful of places with local ordinances protecting sasquatches. An example would be Skamania County, Washington where the intentional slaying of a Bigfoot is a gross misdemeanor punishable by a year in jail or a thousand dollar fine."

"I suspect anyone with a decent lawyer, or even a terrible lawyer, could probably avoid jail in Skamania County if they were so charged."

"Sadly," says Riddell, "I'd say most of those regulations seem to be on the books only as tongue-in-cheek attempts to lure and entertain a few tourists.

Most are not enforceable if it came to that. It's a shame. These creatures may be highly intelligent, sentient beings. Killing them isn't hunting; it's murder! That's why we need to find and document the existence of the sasquatches first, before the hunters kill one. We need to show the world these are rare, intelligent creatures that need immediate protection under the law."

"Casey, Walter, thank you for meeting with us," I say. "You two have been extraordinarily generous with your time in educating us about the sasquatch phenomenon and your research approach. At this point, is there anything we can do to help you?"

"Well, now that you ask, Jack" says Riddell, "I understand from Walter that you have some expertise in data analytics and predictive modeling. Forest Watch has collected a wealth of data regarding the location and dates of sasquatch sightings. We'd like to combine that information with data on broader ecological measurements such as seasonal temperatures, snow levels, and river flows, as well as migration patterns for potential prey such as elk and deer. We hope to use these inputs to develop a predictive model to forecast the most optimal times and places to successfully find these creatures. Problem is that we've got all this data, but no real idea how to put it all into a useful model."

"Sounds like a problem that I may be able to help solve. Would you mind sending me your data files?"

"We'd be happy to give you access."

"Interesting," says Kate, "the data you've collected on deer and elk migration patterns… Do you think the sasquatches are actively hunting big game? If so, that's not particularly consistent with ape behavior. Most apes are largely vegetarians. Yes, technically, they're omnivores. They may occasionally dine on small mammals or birds, but they're certainly not out stalking big game on the African savanna."

"That's an astute observation, Kate," replies Riddell. "Yes, we've strayed away from the ape behavior assumptions here. But for good reason. Most apes live in tropical climates where the available calorie density in vegetation is high relative to the energy required to secure those calories. That is certainly not the case in our northern temperate and alpine climates where the calorie density per acre is much lower. And we think these animals may range in size up to six hundred pounds or more. That's not much smaller than a grizzly bear."

Kate is nodding, "makes sense. And I imagine a typical grizzly bear has a sizable daily calorie requirement. I can see that you might want to assume there is some meat on the menu for its caloric density."

"Indeed, Kate. Scientists have estimated that a typical male grizzly needs to consume on the order of sixty thousand calories a day. Roughly twenty-five times more calories than a human. Grizzlies are themselves omnivores, mostly consuming vegetation and berries, but supplementing their diet with meat. And they tend to be opportunistic rather than active hunters, preying on the weak and the young. Active hunting of healthy deer or elk would consume too many calories relative to the payoff. Often, they simply make claim to existing kills made by wolves, coyotes, or mountain lions and feed off the carrion. We assume sasquatches would have similar caloric needs and be opportunistic rather than active hunters as well."

As we say our goodbyes Berman smiles and touches my arm. "Jack, I've seen a change in you. A year ago, you were very cynical and sarcastic about the paranormal. This evening, you were much more receptive to at least talking about the possibility that sasquatches exist. What's changed?"

I shoot Kate an uneasy glance. "Walter, I guess these days I'm just trying to keep an open mind." He has no idea. If I could only forget the things I've seen since Berman and I raced off that mountain together.

It has been wisely said that we see the world not as it is, but as we are. We each see reality through the lens of our own unique personalities, biases, and personal histories.

Certainly, as I reflect on the evening's conversation, the diverse perceptions of the Bigfoot phenomenon are no exception. Apes or apparitions? Is Bigfoot simply an undiscovered species of primate or, instead a mysterious supernatural being? Are these creatures interdimensional entities or perhaps strange shape-shifting demons? Murderous monsters stalking the woods or benign forest dwellers? Objects of fear or objects of misplaced sexual desire? Or is the phenomenon simply a product of overactive imaginations and a desire to keep a little of the mysterious still alive in our regimented modern world? It would seem there are as many truths out there as there are truth seekers.

Perhaps, I think, Bigfoot is the ultimate Rorschach test. A blank canvas for our own projections. Since the beginning of history, mankind has imbued our monsters and our gods with projections of our own fears, hopes, and dreams. Ask any person to tell you their idea of the nature of God and I'll wager that in ten minutes you'll learn very little about the true nature of the Almighty. You will, however, learn a great deal about that specific person's own personality traits and cultural biases. The Book of Genesis informs us that God made man in his own image. That may well be true, but I suspect, for many, the reverse may be true as well.

The great apes have always inspired both fascination and fear in humans. But what is it that we fear? The ape's differences compared to us, or its similarities? Do we fear that the dark eyes of the ape are a window into a savage, unknown mind, or, instead, a mirror, reflecting back the primal darkness in our own hearts?

As we leave the restaurant, my phone pulses. It is a text from Wendover. In his typical style, much is implied with an economy of words.

Please drop by in the morning. Many developments. We clearly have a suspect in the Sorenson case, and I may have solved the mystery of Bigfoot as well.

CHAPTER 63

"It's robbery, plain and simple," declares Wendover.

He's talking about the annual tuition charged by the Bellevue Preparatory School. Bellevue Prep having been the last employer of record for Tommie Ka'uhane prior to his disappearance some fourteen years ago. The school's tuition from just one student, Wendover laments, is nearly equivalent to the cost of one of his department's new patrol vehicles.

This morning Kate and I have joined Wendover and his deputy, Derek Yazzie, in the sheriff's office for an update on Ka'uhane's criminal record and suspected whereabouts.

I'm playing the devil's advocate on the topic of the prep school's excesses, reminding Wendover that rich kids are people, too. That sometimes wealth, privilege, power, and connections are just not enough to ensure success in life. Sometimes, a superb education with an absurdly low student to teacher ratio may be required as well. And curriculum enhancements such as coursework in Hawaiian culture and language don't come cheap.

"Yeah, it's a pity," scoffs Wendover sarcastically. "A pity the school didn't use a small portion of that outlandish tuition to run full background checks on their instructors prior to hiring them. If they had done so, Ka'uhane's criminal record would have come to the surface rather quickly, I imagine."

"I take it that his record is fairly impressive?"

"Indeed. I've spent the better part of yesterday and early this morning on the phone with state and federal law enforcement investigators in Washington state and Hawaii. Of course, his official juvenile records in Hawaii remain sealed, but his rap sheet for adult offenses plus some additional background from investigators there who knew him more than paints the picture."

"You've been busy. Good to see Benton County's tax dollars finally at work."

"I've also been coordinating with my forest service law enforcement colleague, investigator Larry Stout." Wendover is continuing, studiously ignoring my jibe. "Larry has been looking through the Fed's case files on ecoterrorism incidents across the Pacific Northwest and Intermountain West and thinks he has discovered some patterns."

According to Wendover, to start at the beginning, Ka'uhane was born and spent his early childhood on the Hawaiian island of Ni'ihau, just a dozen or so miles off the coast of Kauai. Sometime in his elementary years, his parents moved to Oahu to find better employment and rented a small house in the Makiki neighborhood of Honolulu.

Kate knows the neighborhood. One of its more famous residents, she says, was Barack Obama who spent most of his childhood years there in that area northeast of downtown Honolulu. But she finds the mention of Ni'ihau even more fascinating. It's a small island, she explains, maybe only spanning seventy or so square miles. And perhaps only a couple of hundred people live there permanently. What is particularly notable about Ni'ihau is that it is the only Hawaiian island where nearly all residents exclusively speak traditional Hawaiian. In fact, the specific dialect spoken there likely predates the arrival of the Europeans and is more closely related to Polynesian than it is to contemporary Hawaiian.

According to Wendover's law enforcement sources in Hawaii, the move to Honolulu from the close-knit community and sparsely populated, open spaces of Ni'ihau was challenging for the entire Ka'uhane family. But it was especially difficult for young Tommie who had trouble fitting in at school. Perhaps unsurprisingly, the arc of his adolescence was troubled. Unfortunately, this was not a unique story for his youthful contemporaries in that time and neighborhood. He popped on to local police radar with minor offenses, mostly shoplifting, fights, and vandalism.

Later, Ka'uhane graduated high school and began studies at the University of Hawaii at Manoa, majoring in Hawaiian studies and education. The change of venue apparently presenting both larger academic opportunities for him as well as more substantial criminal temptations. He fell in with a radical student subculture that was convinced Hawaiians had sold out their culture and their islands for money and greed. Indeed, perhaps the activists had their points. The pace of land development was accelerating and the state's permanent resident population of only one and a half million catered to over ten million tourists a year. In peak seasons, the tourists threatened to outnumber the locals, straining an already endangered ecosystem and overtaxing local services and infrastructure.

In his freshman year, Ka'uhane took the first step that that treaded on the border between activism and criminal behavior. He and some fellow students went to Maui and chained themselves across the Haleakala Highway. Their protest blocked the movement of construction equipment to the observatory complex near the summit of the volcano. He was arrested but subsequently released. A pattern of arrests and releases all too common in the revolving door of the criminal justice system. With each offense and lack of subsequent consequence, Ka'uhane became more dogmatic about his cause and more emboldened to further criminal exploits. A pattern that would come to define his undergraduate years at Manoa.

However, by graduation, Ka'uhane appeared to have changed his point of view towards eco-activism, or at least, its application in Hawaii. He seemed to have essentially written off further ecological protests in Hawaii, telling his fellow activists that the cause was now lost. The islands had, in his opinion, succumbed to the almighty dollar of the Haoles; its culture and beauty forever and irreversibly defiled. He no longer saw the islands as his home. He wanted to leave and establish a new life on the mainland.

According to authorities, Ka'uhane accepted a teaching position with the Bellevue Preparatory School upon graduation and moved to the Pacific Northwest. He kept a low profile in his early years at Bellevue but the old Sirens of his past still pulled at him. He eventually became engrossed with the struggles of the Northwest's native peoples in the preservation of their cultural traditions and environment. He evidently thought the challenges facing the Northwest's indigenous tribes seemed to mirror those of the native Hawaiians. But here in the Northwest, perhaps the cause was not yet lost. The vastness of the Pacific Northwest's wildernesses had not yet been completely conquered by commercial interests.

Ka'uhane then became involved with a radicalized and violent ecoterrorist movement, the NWEF, or Northwest Eco Front. These were armed and dangerous criminals, supposedly using mayhem for environmental causes.

But, in truth, it was no secret that many in the group were far more interested in violence and anarchy than its supposed noble and just causes. This crowd makes Logan O'Leary and TBOF look like harmless, naïve schoolchildren, says Wendover. It was Ka'uhane's new association with the NWEF that brought him to the attention of federal agents who began to monitor his activities more closely.

Shortly after beginning his relationship with the NWEF, Ka'uhane bought and registered a firearm. It was a Remington bolt-action .30-06 rifle. Several months later a lumber company employee near Forks, Washington was wounded by a .30-06 caliber bullet during a confrontation with suspected NWEF activists. Tommie Ka'uhane rose to the top of the suspect list due to his recent purchase of a similar caliber rifle. At that point, federal agents had sufficient cause to obtain wiretaps for his phone and surveillance of his email and text traffic. It was this surveillance that began to uncover an extensive conspiracy to wreak damage to the Northwest's power grid.

For years, Wendover continues, environmentalists and some native tribes had denounced the extensive construction of hydroelectric dams in the Northwest. These were said to be disruptive to salmon runs and often flooded revered and sacred cultural sites. It was to be ironic then that one of the first sabotage targets of the NWEF was a small hydroelectric plant that didn't, in fact, utilize a dam.

The Gibson River Plant in southern Oregon features a power plant and substation, but does not include a dam. A portion of the water from the Gibson River is channeled via rock-fill diversions into a parallel power canal that originates on the river's right bank and flows westerly on to the powerhouse which contains a single turbine connected to a generator. It's small potatoes as power plants go, Wendover explains, maybe only generating half a megawatt annually.

Perhaps the idea was to start small and then work their way up to larger targets. Perhaps the Gibson River Plant had some unknown strategic appeal. Or maybe someone in the NWEF just held a personal grudge towards the plant. The ultimate motive was never uncovered by law enforcement. The Feds used information gleaned from the wiretaps of Ka'uhane to break up a conspiracy to blow up the plant with an improvised explosive device. Several were arrested but when the Feds came for Ka'uhane, he had disappeared into the wind.

To the shock of the school's administration, Ka'uhane simply abandoned his post at Bellevue Prep and was never heard from again. Federal agents stormed his apartment to find that he had basically left behind most of his furnishings and personal effects. The .30-06 rifle was missing and assumed to be in his possession. Receipts were also found for a large quantity of MagRange XL brand ammunition for the gun.

Some of the items recovered from his apartment were quite intriguing, says Wendover. Investigators found several moldings that had been apparently used to cast large artificial feet. It was assumed these could be used to fake Bigfoot tracks. Also, there was a sporting goods store receipt for several large camouflage ghillie suits.

"Ghillie suit?" Kate is looking puzzled, "what's a ghillie suit?"

Wendover explains, "Kate, it's a type of camouflage that makes it look like you're covered in long grass. It's used by military snipers or hunters to hide in grass and break up the outline of their bodies against the surrounding landscape."

"That's right," adds Yazzie, "wear one and when you lay on the ground to line up a rifle shot, you'll blend right in. But stand up and walk around in one and you'll look like some kind of hairy monster…like a Bigfoot."

"Interesting," I say. "So, it looks like maybe our mysterious Tommie Ka'uhane was a demented Renaissance man of sorts. What was he? Perhaps a school teacher by day and an ecoterrorist on the weekends? And then moonlighting as a Bigfoot hoaxer in his remaining spare time?"

Wendover smiles. "Fortunately, law enforcement found one other item in his apartment that might be the key to explaining how this all fits together. It turns out that Tommie Ka'uhane left behind a personal manifesto."

Wendover is passing around a copy of the manifesto. It's a short read; unhinged and to the point.

> *My brothers, it is time to act. The white capitalists are destroying our environment and crushing the native cultures. They are monsters. To fight them, we must become monsters ourselves. Real monsters. We must reanimate the native legends. Bring to life the Omah of the Hupa tribe. Raise the Skookum of the Chinooks. And bring forth the Sasquatch of the Coastal Salish to walk the earth in search of revenge and justice. Through the power and fear of these legendary beasts we will drive the capitalists from our lands and reclaim the native heritage. Victory is at hand!*

"The man likes plural personal pronouns," I observe. "Lots of references to 'we.' Do you think he's using the 'royal we' or perhaps actually has some accomplices?"

"I wouldn't discount the notion that he may have recruited some of the NWEF into this enterprise," replies Wendover. "What do you think about the manifesto, Derek?" He's nodding to Deputy Yazzie.

"Well, it wouldn't be the first time some outsider has tried to repurpose native traditions and culture for their own agenda," replies Yazzie. "And it probably won't be the last time, either. You know, ever since we discovered those footprints up at the Sorenson camp, I've been talking to my tribal elders about the Choanito and doing some research."

Yazzie tells us he is a member of Wenatchi, one of the Northwest's Salish tribes. Their traditions include stories passed down through generations of the Choanito, a name which means the Night People. The Choanito were said to be mysterious beings who keep watch over humanity from the shadows of the forest. Other Native American tribes, even those living far beyond the Pacific Northwest, tell stories of similar entities. And the descriptions of these creatures' appearance and behaviors are remarkably consistent.

The Choanito are said to be wildmen. Massively large in stature and yet able to move swiftly through the forest without making a sound. They walk upright and are covered in hair. Some contemporary native accounts refer to an ape-like appearance, but apes and other primates would have been unknown to the ancient people, so the older accounts of the elders refer only to the similarities to humans.

The Choanito watch mankind from the shadows. They are not by nature menacing to humans, nor are they benign. They simply watch and judge.

"Derek, are these beings thought to be real biological animals or, instead, are they spiritual or supernatural in nature?" I ask.

Yazzie looks somewhat perplexed at the question. He's hesitating a bit in his answer, and Wendover intervenes on his behalf.

"Jack, I'm sure Deputy Yazzie is looking for a way to be nice and diplomatic, but I going to jump in here and say your question itself is flawed. I think you're making a distinction without a difference."

"Sorry, I didn't mean to be insensitive to native cultures."

"Oh, your question isn't insensitive," says Wendover. "But to many native cultures, it is phrased in a way that will not be helpful to you in discovering the true nature of the world. It presupposes that what you call the real world and the spirit world are separate things. To many this is a false distinction. The natural and the supernatural are both part of the same reality. The supernatural is just the part of the natural world that we're not yet smart enough to figure out. Doesn't make it any less real."

"Yes," agrees Yazzie, "many believe the Choanito are, in your words, real. They are not folklore fictional characters like your Santa Claus, Easter Bunny, or the tooth fairy. Some have encountered the Choanito in the wild and say the experience changed them forever. Believe me, they are very much a part of the greater world."

"I see what you mean." Indeed, I think, reality is not obligated to be neatly fenced and bounded by the limits of our ability to observe and understand it. For example, the planet Neptune was not discovered by science until the mid-nineteenth century. And yet Neptune surely existed prior to that discovery and had gone on about its business orbiting the sun for countless millennia without our esteemed knowledge or permission.

"I hope you do," replies Yazzie. "Too often mainstream culture dismisses our traditions and beliefs as simple folklore and mythology. Then on Sundays many of these same people go to church and worship an invisible, supernatural being. A God who, unlike the Choanito, leaves no tracks in our physical world."

I think my old friend and mentor, the Jesuit Father Rodriguez, might disagree about the absence of the tracks of God in the world. He would say the essence of God is reflected in the good deeds of the compassionate and the faithful. But he would likely also caution that God works in mysterious ways and evidence of his influence may appear in unlikely forms and places. Perhaps it is only the limitations of our five senses and our parochial arrogance that precludes us from seeing the Choanito as part of the Almighty's greater reality.

"There is one more thing you must know," adds Yazzie. "In nearly all tribal traditions it is said the Choanito serve as guardians of nature. Unseen themselves, they watch us constantly. It is said that there will come a time, perhaps soon, when mankind will have irrevocably turned away from living in harmony with nature. Such neglect and arrogance will usher in a quickening."

"A quickening?" Wendover is raising an eyebrow.

"Yes. There will be a great awakening and change in the Choanito themselves. The Choanito will step out from the shadows and assert themselves in mankind's affairs. Perhaps forcefully. This change and great reckoning will come from the Choanito themselves. They do not need to be fraudulently summoned forth by the likes of Tommie Ka'uhane."

"And speaking of Tommie Ka'uhane," sums up Kate, "where does this leave us? The manifesto is intriguing, but it's fourteen years old. The grand eco-revolution he was promoting never happened. Industry was never driven out of the forests and fake Bigfoots never scared people out of the woods. If anything, ironically, the mystery of potential sasquatches running about has drawn more people into the woods, right? What happened to Ka'uhane and where has he been for the last fourteen years? And how does any of this tie back to the murder of Rocky Sorenson?"

CHAPTER 64

"All good questions, *Watson*," grins Wendover. "And with some footwork from my forest service friend, investigator Larry Stout, combined with the details of the ballistics report that came in this morning from Helena, I may either have some answers or at least some solid conjectures, fair enough?"

"More than fair."

"Okay, I'll grant you that no one has seen Tommie Ka'uhane for the past fourteen years, but it appears that his rifle may have been making regular appearances. Stout has been doing some digging in the files and talking to several his counterparts in forest service and Bureau of Land Management law enforcement. Turns out there have been a number of incidents in the greater Northwest and Northern Rockies that seem to bear the mark of Ka'uhane's activities. You know, vandalism with Kapu warnings in Hawaiian and some random Bigfoot tracks. Maybe three or four cases a year up until about two years ago. Recently there has been a change; a large uptick in these incidents over the past two years."

Wendover pauses and gives me a wry wink and a smile. "Guess LISA hasn't had a chance to hack those particular files, huh?"

I sigh, "I'll certainly inform her of the oversight. Although I'll bet a good number of those files may not have been digitized yet. Obviously, it's not feasible to hack hardcopies, eh?"

"It seems a .30-06 rifle was used in most of incidents," continues Wendover. "Thankfully, the targets have not been humans but rather the shots have inflicted vandalism damage. The bullets have taken out heavy equipment windows and tires…that sort of thing. In each case, ejected shell cartridges were left behind. These were MagRange XL rounds; the same brand apparently purchased by Ka'uhane before he pulled his disappearing act. And ballistics analysis has indicated that all casings from these separate incidents came from the same weapon. The same rifle used in the wounding of the Forks, Washington security guard that put Ka'uhane in the Fed's crosshairs in the first place."

"And," I remark, "let me guess, now you're going to tell us that the casing found at the Sorenson murder site is also a match?"

"An exact match."

"Then we've got him!" exclaims Kate. "Ka'uhane killed Rocky Sorenson. Ka'uhane is the registered owner of a .30-06 rifle. You should be able to match the ballistics to that specific weapon, right?"

Wendover shakes his head. "I think all the crime scene detective shows on TV make this look too easy. It's not. We know all the casings from all the eco crime scenes, including Sorenson's, came from the same rifle. But we won't know whether this rifle is the same one that Ka'uhane registered unless we have physical possession of that specific firearm."

Kate is puzzled. "Why? I assumed that once a firearm was registered its unique ballistic patterns would be recorded in a database somewhere for future reference by law enforcement."

"Unfortunately, that's a common misperception," replies Wendover as he proceeds to give us a brief education on forensic ballistic science. An ammunition round, he says, has two basic components that are commonly scrutinized forensically. The casing or cartridge encases the bullet and is usually ejected upon firing to permit loading of the next round. Microscopically unique toolmark variations left by the weapon's firing pin and ejection mechanisms can be used to uniquely match an expended cartridge to a specific gun. Also, the projectile or bullet portion of the round incurs microscopically unique striation patterns from the rifling and other elements of the gun barrel geometry as it is expelled from the weapon.

In theory, he says, this all sounds simple enough, but is rarely straightforward in practice. Forensic examination of bullets is particularly difficult as the projectiles tend to deform when they strike a hard target, distorting or obliterating striation patterns. And, of course, if the round in question happens to be a hollow-point bullet, analysis is nearly impossible as such bullets are designed to fragment into shrapnel upon impact.

In any case, he continues, there is no national database cataloging the unique microscopic ballistic characteristics of each gun sold. It might be technically feasible to do so, but the practical logistics and cost, not to mention the gun lobby pushback, makes this approach considered unfeasible. The only way to prove a recovered bullet or cartridge came from a specific gun is to take possession of the that specific firearm and discharge an identical round under controlled conditions. The cartridge and bullet from the controlled discharge is then used as an exemplar for comparison against the ballistics recovered from the crime scene.

"Really?" I scoff. "From a data science perspective, the establishment of a national ballistics registry of every gun sold isn't a hard problem to solve. Why hasn't it been done?"

"Well," replies Wendover, "such a database would require the manufacturers to test fire each new gun and forensically collect and record the unique ballistic signatures of the weapon. That's probably a non-starter for lots of reasons. There has also been some talk of embedding a micro-stamp with a unique serial number on each firing pin. Technically achievable, I would imagine, but probably politically unfeasible."

"It's a shame," I say, "that would certainly make your life as an investigator much easier."

"That's okay," responds Wendover, "my job is not supposed to be easy. My constituents elected a sheriff to do what's right, not what's easy. Look, there are an estimated four hundred million firearms in circulation in the United States. Enough to arm every man, woman, and child in the country with enough weapons left over to also give every Canadian two guns each. Obviously, only a very, very small fraction of these guns will ever be used in a crime."

"But some will…"

"Yes, and only a small fraction of our population will ever commit a crime. That doesn't, I hope, give us the right to collect and record in advance everyone in the country's fingerprints and DNA on the off chance they might someday commit a crime," he counters.

"Agreed, but limitations on the use of weapon forensics must tie your hands."

"Less than you'd think. True stranger on stranger shootings where the perpetrator and victim did not previously know each other are not rare, but also not as common as you might think. And, about two thirds of the time when we roll up to a shooting scene, who is typically the victim, Derek?" He's nodding to the deputy.

"That's an easy one, boss. Usually, the gunowner or another member of the household. Happens either accidentally or deliberately. Unfortunately, many are suicides. The biggest gun aficionados tend to be middle-aged white males. They are also, by far, the most likely demographic to attempt suicide with a gun."

"And," continues Wendover, "if the shooting wasn't an accident or suicide, the likely suspects and/or victims, depending on which end of the gun they ended up on, usually turn out to be family members, spouses or ex-spouses, lovers or ex-lovers, neighbors, or business associates."

"Yeah, business associates, especially if the business involves dealing drugs," adds Yazzie.

"It's terribly ironic, isn't it?" says Kate. "These people supposedly buy guns to protect their families and then those same guns are used to kill themselves or their own kin."

Wendover nods to Yazzie. "As Derek here knows all too well, if you want to do this job, you need to get comfortable quickly with three things: long hours, bad coffee, and irony by the bucketful, eh?"

Yazzie concurs. "Most murders around here are crimes of passion between people who already knew each other. Passion and guns can be a deadly mix."

"Conveniently," says Wendover, "nowadays as we investigate crimes of passion, the perps have become quite diligent in self-documenting their motives through escalating insults and threats via texts and social media."

"Indeed, it is said that perhaps time heals all wounds, but the internet never forgets," I say.

"Yep, the weapons and technology involved in the crimes continually evolve but the motives tend to be Shakespearian, as ageless as time. Usually passions regarding love, pride, or money, and the loss thereof. I guess what we're saying is that most gun crimes we investigate are fairly straightforward; the weapons are usually easily recovered for forensic analysis. Developing some national database of ballistics for each gun sold is, pardon the expression, probably overkill in my opinion," concludes Wendover.

I smile to myself. Wendover is indeed a man of nuanced insights. While on one hand he staunchly defends his constituents' right to bear arms, he is clearly skeptical as to whether such firearms ultimately prove to provide more protection rather than potential harm to their owners.

"Fair enough," I say. "So, circumstantially, it seems there is a good chance that Ka'uhane, or at least his gun, is still active in the ecoterrorist trade, right? And part of his trademark seems to relate to leaving warning threats in Hawaiian and adding elements of Bigfoot hoaxes."

"Yes, it would appear those characteristics have become his signature, if you will. His way of taunting authorities and claiming ownership for the crimes that he and perhaps other co-conspirators have committed," agrees Wendover.

"So, assuming Ka'uhane and perhaps some confederates are behind numerous Bigfoot hoaxes as well as the ecoterrorism incidents the forest service and BLM have been tracking, perhaps there is a way we can hunt him down; predict his next move," I offer.

"I'm all ears," replies Wendover.

"The nice folks over at Forest Watch have offered to give me access to their dataset of all reported sasquatch activity for the past dozen years or so. There are hundreds, if not thousands, of reports of sightings, tracks, and vocalizations; that sort of thing. Now, who knows? Maybe some of these reports relate to actual sasquatches...the real deal? Some of the tracks recorded by Forest Watch have certain characteristics that would take a true expert to fake, right Kate?"

"That's right," says Kate, "Fascinating aspects such as dermatoglyphic ridges...finger and toe prints."

I continue, "but based on what we're learning about Ka'uhane, it seems likely that many if not most reported incidents in their database might be hoaxes by him and perhaps his fellow travelers from the NWEF, right?"

"Sounds about right," agrees Wendover.

"So, my plan is to input this data to LISA and have her analyze it, adding the supplemental data relating to Larry Stout's files on ecoterrorism incidents. I expect she will then be able to find a pattern of activity that will predict the time and place that sasquatch, AKA, Tommie Ka'uhane, may appear next. We will go hunting for this faux sasquatch, not in the forest, but in the data itself."

"Seems like a reasonable plan," says Wendover. "How about it, Derek?"

"Works for me," the deputy replies, "whatever it takes to put Ka'uhane behind bars."

I smile at Yazzie. "You're not concerned there is a chance we might just sweep up a real Choanito or two in our little dragnet?"

"No," he gives me a mischievous grin, "if you should encounter the Choanito, it will not be because you are looking for them, it will be because the Choanito are looking for *you*."

He says this as a good-natured joke but there is a subtle undercurrent of a warning that is unmistakable. If you venture deeply into the darkening forest, do not fear what you might find. Instead, fear what might find you. I happen to be a recent graduate of the literal school of hard knocks. So, these days when someone suggests, even jokingly, that I watch my back, I take them seriously.

At that point our conversation is interrupted. There is a knock at the door and Wendover rises to answer it. Deputy Potts quickly enters the office. He apologizes for the disruption but it seems he has an urgent update.

"Have you guys heard the news? It's all over town. Lance Savage, the big TV star, he's coming to Alta Junction in a few days," exclaims Potts.

Blank looks all around. None of us have the slightest idea who he's talking about. Potts seems a bit exasperated with our group's ignorance. Like maybe he's cast pop culture pearls before swine.

"You know? Lance Savage? Star of the Savage Wilderness? It's the most popular reality show on cable TV and streaming." Potts is speaking a little more slowly and deliberately now. Perhaps under the impression that our collective ability to understand English has somehow been mysteriously compromised. "He's coming to the Alta Valley to hunt down and kill the Bigfoot!"

Kate and I exchange a worried glance. This is Casey Riddell's worst nightmare. Sasquatch-shooting barbarians are apparently at the gates.

CHAPTER 65

YESTERDAY EVENING WE RECEIVED A QUICK TELEPHONE UPDATE FROM CASEY Riddell on his developing plans for an Alta Valley expedition. He also sent over his links to Forest Watch's sasquatch report database. I didn't quite have the heart to tell him about Lance Savage's upcoming Bigfoot hunting plans but I'm sure he'll hear about them shortly from multiple sources.

After that, Kate and I relaxed back at the Missoula Hilton and looked over the background data LISA had retrieved on Lance Savage. Savage, born Ezra Lewenberg, grew up the Crown Heights neighborhood of Brooklyn. By most accounts it seems likely his closest youthful encounter with anything resembling wildlife would perhaps have been an occasional visit to the Bronx Zoo.

In his early twenties Lewenberg had dropped out of college to pursue a fortune he thought befitting of his talents. Those talents included charismatic good looks, a deep resonating baritone voice, and an unquenchable sense of entitled self-promotion. It was said he had a face for television, a voice for radio, and an ego for politics. In the early days, his looks and voice propelled him into several spokesmodel roles with various male fragrance and fashion lines. This was a good start but clearly, he believed he was destined for greater things.

Lewenberg noted the rising success and cultural influence of television reality shows. If one could only gain a splash of notice in the popular media, it was possible to ride a self-reinforcing cycle wherein fame begets even more fame. People become famous for being famous; actual talent be damned. Better yet, these reality shows were filmed with minimal staff and equipment. They included plenty of air time featuring talking heads and frequent flashbacks to prior episodes; production costs were very low relative to revenue. And, filmed out in the real world, there would also be no studio overhead to cover. Done right, these shows were a way to practically print money.

Lewenberg developed a concept to pitch to the cable television and streaming networks, hungry to fill their 24/7 schedules and streaming platforms with low-cost programming. In making his pitch to the networks, Lewenburg essentially reinvented himself. He changed his name to a more macho, and vaguely phallic, moniker: Lance Savage. He created the persona of a wilderness expert. A man with the skill, experience, and physical prowess to take on nature single-handedly. A man who could challenge the "Savage Wilderness" and not only survive but dominate nature.

Further, Savage would face the dangers of the wild completely alone. He would use drones, tripods, and selfie-sticks to record his own exploits. Never mind that Savage, née Lewenberg, had absolutely no outdoor experience or skills. This was reality television, its programming unburdened, with society's collective wink and nod, by actual reality. Savage had a cheap concept and the network had a schedule to fill. In a marriage of convenience, the network green-lighted an initial six episodes from Savage's production company and a ratings juggernaut was born.

The Savage Wilderness debuted three years ago and was immediately panned by the critics. It was quickly pointed out that the whole "man alone against nature" trope had been already been well mined by multiple previous reality television shows. And, unlike Savage, most of these shows had featured actual outdoor experts with deep wilderness skill qualifications. These professionals took their expeditions very seriously and were keenly respectful of nature and its inherent fragility and dangers.

Some critics were even more succinct: "Self-promoting garbage, bullshit has a new home on cable, makes you want to root for nature to do him in…" Of course, the very over-the-top, phony, narcissistic elements that had vexed the critics sadly and predicably aroused the enthusiasm of the general public. The Savage Wilderness soared to the top of cable television ratings.

Out of curiosity, Kate and I streamed several recent episodes to see if the show was truly as bad as the critics had contended. It was.

Each Savage Wilderness episode seemed to follow the same formula. In every installment, Savage undertook a challenge; a gauntlet seemingly thrown down by nature. In some cases, there were peaks to summit or wild rivers to raft or ford. However, in a distressingly large number of instances, the theme of the adventure involved hunting down and killing wild animals.

In a nod to modern society's growing unease with hunting, in each episode Savage takes some pains to develop a backstory regarding the supposedly marauding animal's danger to humans or their livestock. Once satisfied the kill will be seen as justified, Savage proceeds to hunt down and shoot the offending bear, cougar, or similar beast. No animal, whether of fur, feather, or fin, is safe in the Savage Wilderness.

It is often said that in life the journey matters more than the destination. Savage seems to take this adage to the extreme. The vast majority of the airtime in each episode is consumed with Savage's preparations for the hunt, climb, or other adventure as well as his travel to the featured outdoor location. And there is talk, seemingly endless talk. Each episode apparently requires an obligatory scene in which his support crew wrings their hands about the obvious danger Savage is about to face and urge him to be careful. For his part, Savage fills plenty of airtime taking about his plans for the adventure, speculating about the dangers he is about to encounter, and endlessly reminiscing about his prior triumphs over nature.

The episodes themselves are nicely shot and, I suppose, if one ignored Savage and his egotistical ramblings, might make for passible travelogues. Of course, the central gimmick of the series is the notion that Savage is out challenging nature completely alone and self-recording his own adventures with an array of selfie-sticks, tripods, and overhead drones. However, the many rapidly changing camera angles and overall excellent quality of the video and sound suggests others might be involved. It certainly requires a significant suspension of disbelief to think that Savage is out in the wilds doing his own recording.

This morning, Kate and I are intrigued at Wendover's invitation to return to his office. Interestingly, he's suggesting we both might perhaps have a role in supporting Savage's operation. Apparently, Grace Willems, the show's producer/showrunner, reached out to Wendover late yesterday. She had indicated the production routinely contacts local law enforcement in their planned filming locales. It's a courtesy, she had said. Always a good idea to understand if local permits are needed and whether there may be any related public safety concerns. Wendover had quickly filled her in on the Silas

Patterson situation and also cautioned her regarding the shenanigans of Logan O'Leary and the TBOF crew.

"All good and well," I say. "So where do we fit in?"

"Well, Ms. Willems requested that I post an officer to her filming operation. Said she normally requests a local law enforcement presence as a precaution. In case there is an emergency or if crowd control is needed, I guess."

"It's not as if your deputies have a whole lot of experience with crowd control here in Benton County, eh? Is Willems concerned Savage will be mobbed by hundreds of his adoring fans or something."

"Yeah, maybe," shrugs Wendover, "thing is, I certainly can't spare any officers to go babysit that film crew. Their time is much too valuable."

I can readily see where this is going. I might as well volunteer now and preempt the wily lawman. "So, Dan, it looks you might need to deputize a civilian for this duty. It seems I'm available."

"Splendid, Jack! Consider yourself deputized."

"I assume I'll be issued a sidearm and a badge, right?"

"Not a chance!" Wendover is reaching into a drawer. "Here you go, instead, I'm happy to issue you this police radio."

"No gun?" I say with mock surprise. "What do you expect me to do with that radio?"

"See that big button on the side? Push it to call back to the dispatch desk. And only then if it's really important."

"Gee, thanks. What if we run into Silas Patterson? Not sure how much protection that radio will offer," I counter.

"Savage is supposed to be hunting Bigfoot, right? Presumably that means he'll be armed. He's welcome to take a shot at Patterson instead, if circumstances warrant, no?"

I sigh. "Okay, in any event, my personal choice would be to leave Bigfoot alone and make a trophy out of Patterson instead."

"That would be fine with me," agrees Wendover. "The way I see it, this little arrangement gives Savage's operation the desired stink of a law enforcement presence without wasting my resources. And it gives me eyes on the film operation to make sure they don't do anything stupid. Also, it gives you a chance to explore the Clark Mountain Complex which I understand is thought to be an ape hotspot of sorts by some of the sasquatch-seeking crowd. So, win, win, win, all around, eh?"

"Savage is going to film up in the Clark Complex?"

"That's my understanding from talking to Ms. Willems."

That is interesting. The Clark Mountain Complex is a rather large cluster of rugged peaks and alpine valleys situated on the border of Montana and Idaho. The complex sits astride two watersheds. One drains east towards Alta Valley, the other flows to the west into Idaho, eventually reaching the tributaries of the Snake River. All in all, the area covers maybe a quarter of a million acres, much of it wild and inaccessible by road. Just last night, Casey Riddell had mentioned the area was moving up his short list of potential targets for Forest Watch investigations.

"So, Dan. What about me?" asks Kate. "You mentioned there might a role for both of us, right?"

"Yes, Kate. It turns out Mr. Savage's contract with the production company requires the presence of a qualified professional to provide emergency medical assistance if required. Seems the person they usually rely upon has another commitment this week. So, I volunteered you to help them out."

"You do know that I'm not licensed to practice in this state?"

"Correct, but no worries. Our state laws exempt physicians from licensing requirements when emergency aid is rendered outside of traditional healthcare settings."

"Okay, as long as it is clear my only role in an emergency would be to stabilize the patent until official paramedics arrive on scene."

"That should work. By the way, prior to agreeing to this arrangement, Willems did some homework and reviewed your bio on your clinic's website."

"Hmm, that website doesn't list my full medical credentials. I could have provided a full curriculum vitae if she had asked."

"Turned out not to be necessary. It seems that on the show the medical advisor usually has a small role in front of the camera. Willems seemed far more interested in seeing your photo. Wanted to make sure you had, um, a camera-friendly presence."

"Unbelievable," Kate groans. "So, in the Savage Wilderness, high cheekbones matter much more a high level of medical competence?"

"Yep," Wendover is shaking his head. "Welcome to reality television where form rather than substance matters."

"Okay," grumbles Kate, "I'm going to reluctantly go along with this. But only as a favor to you and mainly so I can keep an eye on Jack."

"I understand. My thanks to both of you. Oh, there is one more thing. Willems sent over a couple of NDAs for both of you to sign."

"What? They want us to sign non-disclosure agreements? Why the hell would that be necessary? What's the big secret they're trying to protect?" I ask.

Wendover shrugs, "Apparently their filming and production methods are quite...proprietary."

CHAPTER 66

"Lance, are you sure this hunt is the right thing to do? I mean it could be very dangerous. We just don't know what these creatures are capable of doing? I'm worried. We're all worried!" Kate's face is slightly flushed, her eyes wide and intense, as she apparently tries to talk some sense into Savage. On an unsettling note, her overall demeanor suggests that her concern for his safety might be a bit more than professional. "I mean, the thought of you all alone out in the dark forest with that beast out there…"

"Okay, Kate, that should do it, very good effort, you're a natural in front of the camera," remarks Grace Willems, the show producer, and the ringmaster of this particular circus. "Always good to subtly imply you're attracted to Lance. That's his brand…tames the wild animals but drives the women wild, eh? I know, kinda pathetic but that nonsense pays a lot of the bills around here."

"I should hope we've got a good clip," grumbles Kate, "only took three tries."

Kate's feigned attraction to Savage is, of course, purely for the benefit of the camera. In fact, the mighty hunter himself has not even arrived yet in the Alta Valley. In the meantime, the rest of the show's production crew has been busy filming all the scenes that don't require his personal presence. In a nod to the traditions of Hollywood, even in this age of purely digital video recording, these clips are still referred to as old-school B-roll footage. These include background narrative and overview shots of Alta Junction and the surrounding area. The clips also include a smattering of sound bites from locals about their supposed encounters with things that go bump in the night.

"We could try one more take," suggests Rod Simms from behind the camera. "I think I can improve the lighting slightly." Rod is one half of the camera and sound crew. He splits the duties with his twin brother, Todd. The overall high quality of picture, sound, and aerial drone wrangling in the series is the product of the Simms brothers' talents.

"No, Rod, not another take. We're trying to stay on a tight schedule here, not win a friggin' Emmy. Got it?" Willems is shaking her head and consulting her computer tablet. "You can fine tune it later in post, okay?"

"Got it, boss."

"Alright, Kate," instructs Willems, "now we'll have you change into a different shirt so we can shoot a clip of your relief at Savage's triumphant return at the end of the hunt."

"What?" Kate is understandably puzzled.

"Oh, Kate." Willems looks up from her tablet. "Sorry for the confusion, but understand that we'll probably end up filming half of the scenes out of sequence. It's more efficient that way. Trust me, this will all get seamlessly knitted together through the magic of post-production editing and it will look like a smooth chronological narrative."

The reason Willems insisted on non-disclosure agreements from Kate and me is becoming abundantly clear. The Savage Wilderness bills itself as the most-watched unscripted show on cable television. It may be unscripted in the strictest sense, I suppose. But make no mistake, every second of every episode is planned, choreographed, and executed in detail down to the width of a gnat's eyelash. And the lone wilderness adventurer is hardly alone in the wilds. Savage brings along a sizable entourage with him just out of sight of the cameras. An entourage that now will include Kate and me.

Besides the Simms brothers and Willems, the fourth member of the production's on-location crew is Curtis Brockman. He's standing off to the side of our "base camp" intently inventorying equipment for tomorrow's expedition. The base camp itself is a Potemkin village of sorts. A façade for the cameras meant to suggest Savage's support team is encamped in rustic conditions as they send the legendary hunter on his quest and anxiously await his return from danger. In truth, all are staying at the Mountain View motel.

Curtis Brockman has years of experience as a remote wilderness guide, outdoor survivalist, and marksman. He's billed as the show's technical advisor. Viewed from a distance with his athletic build, tan skin, and thick shock of dark brown hair, he could easily be mistaken for Savage himself. The resemblance is hardly a coincidence. Brockman has frequently served as Savage's stand-in and stunt double.

Anyone who still believes that life is fair and the world rewards us on our merits should probably spend some time with Brockman. Here is a man with the actual experience and skillset that Savage only pretends to display. Alas, but for the lack of Savage's more keenly chiseled looks, voice, and unquenchable sense of entitled self-promotion, this should be Brockman's show, based purely on talent. As it turns out, Curtis Brockman has plenty of talent but even more worries. He's becoming increasingly concerned that at some point soon, Lance Savage is going to accidently kill himself or, worse yet, harm someone else.

This morning, while Kate was being prepped for her scene, I spent some time chatting with Curtis and he was not shy about airing his concerns. According to Curtis, in the early seasons of the show Savage consistently deferred to him for advice on woods-craft and hunting. Savage also utilized Curtis as a stunt double on nearly every episode. But then over time Savage's attitude changed. He apparently began to believe his own hype regarding his supposed superior outdoor prowess. He began to insist on doing his own stunts and making his own rifle shots. Instead of him simply having an act where he played a skilled outdoorsman, he became the act; or perhaps the act became him.

Psychologists refer to a cognitive phenomenon called the Dunning-Kruger effect. It describes a personality bias that makes certain individuals blithely unaware of their own lack of competence at specific skills. The bias usually stems from an oversized ego combined with underdeveloped self-awareness. The effect tends to be pronounced in certain politicians, celebrities, televangelists, and other con artists of similar stripe. The lies and exaggerations themselves are bad enough, but the real problem arises when the con artists start to believe their own deceptions. And when folks like Savage go armed out into the wild believing their own bullshit, bad things can happen and people can get hurt.

According to Curtis, this Alta Valley adventure will be the franchise's next to last episode for the season. Once the season is completed, his contract will be finished and he is planning on moving on to other opportunities. Curtis no longer wants the aggravation of babysitting an ungrateful reality star or the responsibility of keeping Savage safe from his own incompetence and hubris.

"Excuse me, Deputy Walker?" Willems walks up to me, still studying her tablet. It takes me a moment to realize that the deputy she is addressing is me. Kate and I have different last names and decided with Wendover's blessing to play this little charade as though we hadn't previously met. Willems has no idea we're married. A little lie in service of the truth… Colonel Anderson's favorite strategy as I recall.

"Deputy, thank you for volunteering to help us on your own time and for your discretion in wearing plainclothes rather than a uniform. I take it that assisting with this sort of film production is far afield from your regular duties?"

"Yes, ma'am. And just call me Jack. Yeah, I guess you could say it's a bit different from my normal work." If she only knew.

"Okay, Jack, let's get you up to speed on ground rules, what is going to happen, and what you are going to be doing."

She says this with what seems to be her signature communication style: direct, rapid fire, and one-way. At first, I was a bit put off by her authoritarian, take-no-prisoners approach. But I've slowly realized that in juggling Savage's ego combined with the general chaos of a television production crew working in a remote location, perhaps a loud voice and a firm hand are survival requirements for her job…and sanity.

"Okay," she continues, "Mr. Savage will be arriving on site tomorrow morning. He'll be flying directly into your local airport. That's Alta Junction Municipal airfield, correct?"

"Yes, ma'am."

"Yeah," she rolls her eyes, "the man is supposedly geared to live off the land, eating snakes and such, and yet refuses the hardships of flying commercial. Anyway, number one ground rule, you are not to approach or speak to Savage unless directed to do so. If you do speak to him, he is to be addressed as Mr. Savage, never Lance. Got it?"

"Understood, ma'am."

"Ground rule number two, be aware at all times of the location of active cameras and where they are pointing. We're trying to maintain the fiction that our hero is bravely facing the wilderness alone. Therefore, the last thing we need is for some knucklehead from the crew walking into frame. Trust me, that happens all too often, especially with the overhead drone shots that take in a lot of real estate.

"No problem," I say. "We're trained to keep a low profile during surveillance stake-outs. This will be no different." I'm beginning to enjoy my deputy alter ego and sort of making up things as I go.

"Tomorrow," she continues, "will be a marathon session. We'll film the journey up into the Clark Mountain Complex for the balance of the day. Then we've singled out a small alpine valley for Savage to set up his camp and then go out on a night investigation."

"Understood. I assume the nighttime search will take advantage of infrared sensing and the better propagation of sound. Both of these are enhanced after dark, right?" Here I'm merely parroting what I recall of the Forest Watch approach championed by Casey Riddell.

Willems looks a bit perplexed, like maybe I'm speaking a foreign language. "I don't know," she says offhandedly, "perhaps so. But this is mainly about creating a sense of danger and suspense. Look, you have a guy wandering around the forest in the daytime looking for sasquatch. That's mildly interesting to the audience. But put the same guy in the same forest in the middle of the night looking for sasquatch in the dark and it is literally a different story. It's suspenseful and scary as hell. The audience eats it up. We add a little ominous background music in post-production and presto, ratings gold, my friend."

"Now as for your duties, Jack." she continues. "As we move up the mountain during the day, we'll need you to scout ahead of our filming perimeter looking for hikers and others enjoying the outdoors. You'll need to warn these folks that a film production is underway and make sure they don't accidently wander into the camera frame."

"Fair enough. I think I can manage that."

"But your nighttime duties, let's just say they are going to be a little more expansive…and interesting. Let me try to explain."

Willems starts by stating the obvious. Even if sasquatches do indeed exist, true sightings of the creatures would be quite rare. Therefore, the odds that

Savage would encounter an actual sasquatch on the one day and the very location chosen to film this episode are slim to none. Simply documenting a fruitless search would make for boring television. Therefore, the production isn't above fabricating a little mystery to keep things interesting.

Case in point, later this afternoon, Curtis has been directed to journey ahead up the path chosen for tomorrow's expedition. Along the way he'll gin up some mysterious evidence suggesting a sasquatch may be in the neighborhood. Perhaps a potential claw mark high on a tree. Maybe an odd pile of branches arranged in a fashion to suggest a nest of sorts. He'll likely push over some small trees into each other to resemble a crude structure. Things like that. Then Savage will come along tomorrow and "discover" the anomalies. He'll ruminate on their potential meaning for the benefit of the audience and build up the suspense and mystery.

"See how that will work?" says Willems.

"Indeed," I reply, "in effect you're salting the mine."

"Huh?"

"Salting the mine. It's a term they sometimes use around here. When some of the old-timers tried to promote their mines to investors they'd mix in or salt the assay samples with high-grade ore from other sources to fraudulently inflate the value of the mining claims. The investors then saw what they wanted to see. Greed overcame prudence and many overpaid for the claims. What you're doing here with the fake sasquatch evidence is really not so different."

"I think, ethically," counters Willems, "there is a difference. We're not changing anyone's mind here. We're just telling them what they already believe. And people watch our show to be entertained, not to discover deep truths about the world. Further, we're not reaching into people's pockets, asking them to invest in a get rich scheme to capture or kill a sasquatch for profit."

"Alright, be that as it may, what does any of this have to do with my nighttime duties?"

"Well, Jack, once it gets dark, we're going to need to see some sasquatch action. We'll need you to stomp around out in the woods and make some noise. That way Savage will have something to investigate. You might even show up briefly on the thermal imagers as an upright being walking on two legs. That will raise up the paranormal excitement factor by a couple of notches."

"Wait a minute! Isn't Savage supposed to be out here on this expedition to *shoot* a sasquatch!"

"Yes, but that only applies to real beasts should we run across one. He'll know that it's only you out there making the fake noises. It's all part of the script, er, detailed episode plan."

"Well," I say, "I'm not sure this should be a role for someone from law enforcement. Does the sheriff know you have this planned for me?"

"Does he know?" Willems is chuckling. "Sheriff Wendover thought that it was a great idea. He actually suggested we stick you in an oversized monkey suit to add to the effect. Of course," she adds, "the monkey suit idea was a little over the top even by our standards. Anyway, so there you have it. This is reality television and our primary objective is to entertain. We claim to show viewers *a* reality, just maybe not *the* reality."

I sigh. The great Yogi Berra once famously said the future ain't what it used to be. It seems now that reality ain't what it used to be either.

CHAPTER 67

"Jack, Lance is moving up the ridge to the next waypoint. We're sending up the drone for one last panoramic of the valley." Grace Willems' voice crackles through my earpiece. There is no way to reply. This is one-way communication, just the way Willems likes it.

I've spent the balance of the day scouting the terrain ahead of Savage and the production crew. And for the most part I've kept well below the filming sites; exploring numerous gullies and drainages under-girding the main ridge of Clark Mountain. By all appearances I'm out looking to warn the occasional hiker or two to avoid the area where the filming operation is underway. But my real agenda is to look for signs that Tommie Ka'uhane and his NWEF cohorts are operating in the area.

Savage is hiking up a ridge far above me. And he's ascending the mountain along its high central ridge for only one reason. The expansive vistas off the main ridge provide magnificent views of the valley and surrounding mountain ranges. Plain and simple, it makes for better television. But while the approach is guaranteed to provide excellent panoramas, it's doubtful Savage will run across a sasquatch or any other large wild animal up there. It is far too exposed up on the ridge. Any large animals will no doubt stick to the lower drainages where there is ample cover from the trees, brush, and other vegetation. And the multitude of deer tracks and game trails down here is certainly proving out that theory.

"Sasquatch hunting is a contact sport," declares Savage, presumably addressing his selfie-stick, his audio feed droning in my ear. The radio channel in the crew earpieces mainly carries his live feed interspersed with occasional directives and orders from Willems.

"You can't do this remotely," he continues, "you know, just watching trail-cam feeds from your computer. You must come into their territory, alone. You must put yourself at risk. This is their land, their rules. Out here in the wilderness, there are a hundred ways to die. One mis-step, one error, and you're dead. And that's just counting falls and extreme weather. That doesn't even consider encountering a large and dangerous animal like a sasquatch. That's why I'm going up into this wilderness by myself. To put myself alone and exposed in the beast's own world."

For all of his egotistical posturing and faults, I've come to respect perhaps Savage's one true talent. The man knows how to fill airtime with banter and speculation. This is a valuable skill for a show where in each episode, for sixty minutes, pretty much nothing happens. I could imagine that perhaps in another past era Savage would have made a great radio disc jockey with his sonorous voice and gift for gab, endlessly chattering between records and commercials.

"Some people," he continues, "some people might question why I'm doing this. So, why am I really doing this? Putting myself at risk in the face of the unknown? Because it's in my nature. Really, I suppose it's in all our natures. Mankind's nature is to push the boundaries of our knowledge. To find out what...and who...else is out there. But there is a price for knowledge. And I'm willing to pay it. As did all the explorers who have gone before me. Those who discovered new lands and even those who went to the moon." I grin at this last comment. He's already apparently comparing himself to Magellan and Neil Armstrong and the day is still young.

"Still others will be critical of me," he continues, "they will ask why I'm armed. Why am I hunting sasquatch with a gun rather than only with a camera? Why attempt to hunt and kill such a rare and elusive animal?"

That's a damn good question, I think. Certainly, the mainstream sasquatch researchers like Casey Riddell consider any who would harm the mythical beasts to be murderous barbarians. But no doubt Savage will have some self-serving rationale for his actions.

"But the truth is...and I'm sorry, but it's a hard truth, you all need me to kill a sasquatch. Why? Because we live in an age in which nothing anyone says or does is truly believed. All news we don't want to hear or believe is now 'fake news.' For example, a million people died from a virus and yet a quarter of the population were adamant that basic public health precautions were unnecessary restrictions of their personal 'rights.' The disease was of no consequence, they maintained, no worse than the flu."

Well, he has a point there. We do live in an unfortunate age in which folks think anything is possible but nothing is true.

"So, you tell me," he continues, "if I took an honest to God real photo of a sasquatch, or even a video, would you believe it? I think you already know the answer. Everyone would just say it was a deep fake, a counterfeit image. Look, no one is going to take any action to protect these rare creatures if they cannot be absolutely proven to exist. And these beasts are too strong and too clever to be captured. So, the harsh truth is the only way I can prove their existence is to kill one and dump the bloody corpse on the steps of the Smithsonian Institute or the National Geographic Society. I'm sorry but the only way to save these magnificent creatures is to kill one of them."

I nod my head in admiration. Savage has outdone himself. If self-serving bullshit was a winter Olympic figure skating event, he's just nailed a rhetorical triple axel with his gotta-kill-a-sasquatch-to-save-the-sasquatches rationalization.

"Jack, you'll need to reposition up towards the ridge," commands Willems, interrupting the feed. "Lance is approaching the area where he is going to 'discover' the mysterious Bigfoot nest." She's talking about the fake nest constructed by Curtis Brockman yesterday. Savage himself certainly knows a thing or two about faking reality.

Anyway, with Willems' request, it seems duty calls. I take one last look about the overgrown gully I've been exploring, searching for any sign of Ka'uhane. Then I see it. And, ironically, it appears to be an actual sign. I quickly take a photo with my phone and then head back up towards the ridge.

Twenty minutes later I've rejoined Kate, Curtis, and the rest of the crew positioned some one hundred yards distant from Savage as he investigates the supposed sasquatch nest. I discreetly show the photo on my phone to Kate. "Is this what I think it is?" I ask.

Kate is nodding and smiling. "It is, Jack. This could be the answer we're looking for."

Several hours later, twilight is fast approaching and Savage has just set up his camp in the small alpine valley as planned. Kate and I, along with the rest of the crew are keeping well out of camera range, about seventy-five yards behind him. I'll confess I'm starting to get nervous in anticipation of Willems' idea to have me stomp around through the dark woods as a weak imitation of a sasquatch. Sure, Savage is supposedly in on the plan, but I worry that in the heat of the moment he may be overcome by his instincts to shoot first and ask questions never.

For his part, Curtis has tried to dispel my fears. He has indicated that he, Willems, and Savage have an agreement as to shooting protocols. The three have agreed that any potential target must be clearly identified in broad daylight and that any decision to shoot must be mutually agreed upon before the trigger is pulled.

"Okay," Savage looks earnestly into the camera. "Let's give this a try and see if we can raise some sasquatch action." He cups his hands together and lets loose with a loud and long howl. Supposedly, the beasts communicate with such vocalizations.

The response is almost immediate. Howls, screams, and barks. Coyotes. Apparently, a pack to our west is vigorously answering Savage.

He turns to the camera. The man is determined not to let reality intrude into his reality show. "Sounds like coyotes, doesn't it? Or are they? It's been well documented that sasquatches are very clever. They can in fact imitate the calls of other animals such as coyotes. So maybe we're hearing real coyotes… or maybe these are really sasquatches."

I give a sideways glance to Curtis and all he can do is shake his head. Even by Savage's elastic standards of logic, this is stretching the point beyond belief. This is a little like saying unicorns can imitate white horses by retracting their horns. Therefore, any white horse you see is most certainly a unicorn in disguise.

True darkness has now set in. With the coyote pack still howling in the distance, Savage tries a new tack. He takes a wooden club and vigorously whacks the side of a tree. According to Bigfoot lore, some primates communicate via knocking branches against trees. Several sasquatch researchers have reportedly received responses to such impacts.

Suddenly, there is a far-off crash in the woods and the sound of a large branch snapping. The coyotes immediately fall silent. Savage pivots towards the sound and peers into the dark. "What was that?" he asks rhetorically.

"Sounds like something big moving around out there. Guess I'm gonna have to go investigate." With that said, he grabs a small flashlight and a selfie camera on a stick and marches straight into the forest towards the vicinity of the sounds. Hard to say if this is real courage or if it's just part of the act. Or does he even know the difference anymore?

"Jack," Willem's voice crackles through the comms, "is that you out there making the noises? It's too early for that. Come back in and wait until later for your cue."

"That's not me," I respond. "I'm standing here right next to Curtis. Not fifty feet away from you. I can just see your outline in the dark."

"Oh, sorry," she says. There's a pause as she scans around at the crew making sure all are accounted for. "Well, crap, if we're all here, then who is out there making those noises?"

Crap indeed. By now Savage must be at least a couple of hundred yards out. As usual he's continuing to run his self-commentary about this turn of events on the comm channel. But the signal is degrading; he's continually being interrupted by static. Something is interfering with his transmissions. And the dim light we've seen from his flashlight has long been swallowed up into the night. Out in the dark with only a small flashlight, he's essentially blind. And now with the comms only intermittently working, he may as well be deaf, too.

Curtis switches on his thermal imager hoping to at least keep track of Savage's heat signature.

Suddenly, his eyes widen as he looks at the screen image and he gasps. "Oh, no!" he cries, looking at the screen and shaking his head. "No. No. This can't be! Grace!" he shouts. "Can you increase the signal? Override Lance's comms! Tell him to get the hell back here…now!"

"Wait? What?" Willems is not used to the crew giving *her* orders.

"Tell him to get the hell out of there! He's not alone! There's something else out there. Something big!"

CHAPTER 68

Kate, Willems, and I huddle around Curtis's thermal imager screen. "See that?" Curtis is pointing at a small blob of infrared heat out in the forest. "That's Lance. Hard to tell in the dark without good landmark reference points, but I'd say he might now be three to four hundred yards away. And that," he taps the upper right portion of the screen, "that…is danger headed right for him. Moves like some kind of animal. And it's big; maybe more than twice his size."

To our horror, we see a large glowing thermal hotspot moving quickly through the forest directly towards Savage. It slows to a stop a short distance from him. As Savage turns and begins moving to the left, the animal turns and parallels him, still maintaining a discreet distance.

"What the hell is that thing?" I ask. "Is it walking upright or on all fours?"

"I can't tell from this distance if it's upright or not. Just registers as a large thermal blob," replies Curtis, his voice rising with urgency. "It's the size of a large bear, maybe even a grizzly. But it's not behaving like a bear. Look at how it's maintaining its distance as it follows him. But bears are not usually active hunters. Whatever this thing is; it's acting like a predator. The sort of behavior I'd expect from a mountain lion. Stalking him. Lance, that poor bastard, he probably has no idea he's in danger…literally being hunted in the dark."

"Curtis, you've got the imager in record mode, right?" asks Willems. "And Rod, Todd," she pivots to the Simms brothers, "keep the cameras rolling, no matter what."

Curtis and I exchange an incredulous look. Savage may be moments away from being attacked by some unknown predator and Willems is more worried about production values; capturing the moment in high quality video from multiple angles. If things turn ugly this may be the last and final episode of The Savage Wilderness. But Willems is likely already thinking of the buzz that could be generated by Savage's untimely demise. No doubt his fervent fans, always eager to see him do in a wild animal, will be equally fascinated to see nature turn the tables. Ratings gold. Savage would not be the first celebrity worshiped at the altar of public fame only to find themselves later sacrificed at that same altar.

Now Savage may be an obnoxious, entitled pain in the ass, but he's a fellow human being in trouble. Damned if I'm going just stand here and watch him get attacked.

Seems Curtis is of a similar mind. "I'm going to go grab the rifle out of Lance's tent; it has a thermal scope. I need to go out there and find him."

I turn to follow Curtis. "Count me in. I'll bring the imager. You'll need another set of night vision eyes out there. I take a few steps and then halt, looking again at the imager screen. "Curtis, hold up. Take a look at this." Kate and Willems also gather back around me, peering at the screen. Something has changed. The large animal is moving on towards the left side of the screen and Savage's heat signature is rapidly moving in a straight line back toward our position.

As he closes the distance, we begin to pick up Savage's comms intermittently laced with static. Sounds like he's running, breathing hard. "Something is out there…very aggressive…threw rock…just missed me…"

I glance over at Curtis, "Which is more likely to throw rocks? Bears or mountain lions?" He just shakes his head.

"Wait, what the hell?" Curtis is staring incredulously at the thermal display. To our amazement the massive animal's thermal signature on the screen has simply vanished. One moment it was there. The next moment it is gone.

"I don't like this," says Kate. "The thing looked menacing enough as we were watching it, but now that it suddenly disappeared, it's somehow even more creepy."

Kate's right, I think. Maybe this thing is a monster. And the only thing scarier than a monster you see in the dark is a monster you suddenly can't see. Where the hell did it go?

Several long minutes pass as Savage heads back to the camp. Then Curtis motions us to take another look at the screen. "See that?" he says. "We've got another figure on the therm. Much smaller image though. It's either a smaller female or juvenile. Or perhaps it's the original target, just much farther away."

"I'm not sure it's the original animal," counters Kate, "the proportions and gait look different."

"Damn," says Curtis, "the image is still indistinct but this new arrival honestly looks to be bipedal, walking upright. That would be just like Savage to luck into an actual sasquatch sighting."

"Luck? I'm not sure if running into a sasquatch in the forest on a pitch-black night is good luck or bad luck?" I venture.

"The creature can't hide from me now!" shouts Savage, who has just arrived back at his camp tent. He's grabbed another thermal imager and is seeing the same figure that Curtis has just discovered. "Time for the moment of truth." He turns to face his selfie camera directly. "Folks, you are here as history is being made." With one quick motion he reaches into his tent and pulls out the rifle with the infrared scope.

Curtis gasps and begins to run towards Savage. "No! No! Stop!" But it's too late. Savage shoulders the weapon, aims, and fires. Kate and I watch the thermal imager in horror as the shot rings out and the distant figure screams in pain and slumps to the ground.

People sometimes say, in times of terror, chaos, and confusion, that all hell has broken loose. In our current circumstances, that might be a bit of an overstatement. But I'm pretty sure not all hell but maybe a small Benton County-sized chunk of hell might be shaking loose over us on Clark Mountain tonight.

Chaos reigns, the crew are shouting over each other and running in the direction of the fallen figure, flashlights ablaze. Savage, Curtis, Kate, and I are crashing headlong through the brush. Willems and the Simms brothers, still running video footage, are maybe twenty strides behind us. Any pretense that Savage is up here all on his own has been hastily abandoned.

As we scramble through the brush, I wonder what we are about to encounter. A wounded animal, if cornered, can be incredibly dangerous. It seems to me that the decisions I've made in my life have ranged from the very good ideas…marrying Kate, to the very bad ideas…venturing alone into the abandoned Sapphire Belle mine. In the next few moments odds are we will meet up with a wounded wild animal. Hell, maybe even a wounded sasquatch. And this would seem to fall towards the very, very bad idea end of the spectrum.

As we approach where the creature has apparently fallen, we're shocked to hear it yelling…in English. And certainly not the Queen's English.

"Owww! Shit! Mother…Fucker, that hurts!"

Savage stops dead in his tracks, mouth agape. I turn to him with a smirk. "Seems like your sasquatch there has a bit of a potty mouth, eh?" Even in the darkness of the night, I can see the color drain from Savage's face. He was right in a sense. History was being made here tonight, but perhaps not as he had intended.

"My God, Casey! Are you alright?" Kate is kneeling down next to the injured figure which turns out to be none other than our recent acquaintance from Northwest Forest Watch, Casey Riddell. He's clutching his upper arm which is bleeding profusely. Kate pulls open her medical pack and rips off his shirt sleeve. "Everyone, please step back and give me some room. This is my patient."

"And the rest of you can step back even farther," I command, "this, by order of the Benton County Sheriff's Department, is my crime scene. And," I add, motioning to the Simms brothers, "all video shot tonight is to be preserved until a judge decides its deposition. Got that?"

"What?" says Savage a bit weakly, "what do you mean by 'crime scene'? This was an accident! A horrible, regrettable accident. I…I thought he was a sasquatch!"

"Who knows?" I reply, "maybe the novel I-thought-he-was-a-sasquatch defense will set a new legal precedent. Guess we'll let the criminal justice system sort it out."

By now Kate has staunched the flow of blood from Riddell's arm. It's a deep flesh wound but fortunately no major veins or arteries were punctured. She tells him that he's lucky. Four inches to the left and the bullet would have pierced his heart. Parsing out the profanity, the gist of his reply was that if he had been truly lucky, he wouldn't have been shot by some asshole in the first place. The man has a point.

Slowly, we begin to piece together the course of evening's circumstances which eventually brought Riddell's arm and Savage's bullet to the same place at the same time. Unaware of Savage's filming operation, Riddell and a small team from Forest Watch had ventured up on Clark Mountain this evening to do a night investigation for signs of sasquatch activity. Riddell was off working alone, some distance from the rest of his group, surveying a small basin not far from here when he thought he may have heard a faint sasquatch vocalization. That would have been Savage's initial call.

Riddell then began to head in our direction, trying to zero in on the source of the vocalization and still unaware of our presence. Next, he heard Savage's tree knock and continued to proceed towards our position. Suddenly the appearance on his thermal imager of a massive upright being consumed his attention. This was likely the large animal heat signature that had captured our attention as it apparently stalked Savage. Riddell had been monitoring its movements when it suddenly vanished. But he now tells us he thinks that the being's sudden disappearance wasn't all that mysterious. Whatever it was, Riddell speculates it simply had rounded the corner of the far ridge which had blocked its thermal image. Riddell was still engrossed in scanning with his imager when Savage's bullet hit him.

It's well after midnight when we finally get Riddell off the upper mountain down to the nearest forest service road. There is a small gathering of county emergency vehicles waiting for us, their light bars strobing the surrounding forest like some woodsy discotheque.

Kate and the county paramedics are tending to the wounded and I'm standing to the side, trying in my mind to make sense of the evening's misadventure. We solved the mystery of the second smaller figure's identity on the thermal imagers the hard way, with a bullet. But who or what was the first, apparently more massive, figure captured briefly by the imagers? Tommie Ka'uhane in a ghillie suit? Or was it someone, or something else?

As I watch them patch up Riddell, I wonder how many times this sort of thing happens in the world of Bigfoot investigations? Incidents where two separate sasquatch-seeking groups are unwittingly searching in the same area. Excitedly mistaking each other's fake decoy ape calls and tree knocks as the real deal? All harmless enough, I suppose, until someone gets shot.

Deputy Potts waives to me and walks up for a chat. "Hey, Professor, glad you're okay. Say, is that Mr. Savage, the TV star, over there?" He's pointing towards Curtis who's standing alongside the road, watching the show unfold.

"Nah," I say, "that's Curtis Brockman, Savage's stunt double and, frankly, the only guy here that knows anything about woods-craft, survival, and the wilderness. Mr. Lance Savage is right over there."

I point to Savage who is sitting unsteadily on the rear step of an ambulance while a paramedic is taking his pulse and administering oxygen. Savage is apparently hyperventilating and having a panic attack. No doubt caused, I suppose, by separation anxiety at thought of losing his reputation, ratings, and sponsors once word of this fiasco gets out.

"Was Mr. Savage then the one that got shot?" asks Potts.

"Nope. That would be Mr. Riddell up there on the gurney."

Riddell has already been loaded into the ambulance as another paramedic and Kate attend to him.

"Gee," says Potts, "Mr. Savage isn't anything like he appears to be on TV."

I sigh and give him a weary smile. "Never meet your heroes, Deputy. Never meet your heroes."

CHAPTER 69

The Alta Junction municipal airport is seeing more than its share of private jet traffic this week. A Cessna Citation deposited one Shelton Abrams, Attorney at Law, on the tarmac early this morning, before winging back to Los Angeles. Mr. Abrams is currently seated, uncomfortably it seems, next to his client, Lance Savage, at the interview table in Interrogation Room One at the Benton County sheriff's office. Slight of build, bespectacled, and bald, with his nervous demeanor and four-thousand-dollar suit, Abrams manages to look simultaneously overdressed and underprepared.

At Wendover's invitation, Kate and I are standing outside the room behind one-way glass with an excellent view of the proceedings. Besides Abrams, Savage, and Wendover, the remaining chairs around the interview table are occupied by Grace Willems, and Larry Stout, Wendover's federal counterpart from forest service law enforcement.

Wendover had told us the "I thought he was a sasquatch" circumstances of last night's shooting were causing a bit of a jurisdictional quandary. Crimes against humans on federal lands typically fall under federal jurisdiction. However, wild game animals are generally considered wards of the state. Therefore, violations of hunting regulations and safety rules such as hunting at night are usually enforced by state and local authorities. But sasquatches, whether merely of myth or otherwise, aren't exactly recognized as state regulated game animals. If one is to be cited for a hunting violation, presumably the animal being hunted should be recognized by the state to exist. Right now, over in Missoula, prosecutors from both the US Attorney's Office and the Benton County District Attorney are trying to sort out who will run lead on the case. No doubt Savage's celebrity, or perhaps more accurately, notoriety, is going to raise the stakes for them as well.

Introductions around the table are brief and all business. "First, I have some very good news," begins Wendover, "I have word that Casey Riddell is being released from the hospital. The doctors say he's going to make a full recovery."

"Oh, thank God!" blurts out Savage, "it was a terrible accident, I..." At this point, Abrams squeezes his forearm and gives him a sharp look. Non-verbal lawyer-speak for "shut the hell up." Savage takes the hint and becomes silent.

"Lance, you are not to speak unless asked a direct question and then only with my concurrence. Understand?"

Savage nods soberly, but I'm still not sure he truly understands his predicament, the trouble he is in. Entitled people like Savage become accustomed to breezing through life on their looks and luck. Other people clean up their messes. Consequences are for regular people. It's unclear how well Abrams knows his client, but Savage's penchant for self-absorbed chatter may well do Wendover's job for him. That lawyer has his work cut out for him.

"But we should remember to keep the good news about Mr. Riddell in perspective," cautions Wendover. "Had the bullet struck a few inches to the left, Riddell wouldn't be checking out of the hospital this morning. He'd be in the morgue." Savage and Abrams are looking down at the table, shifting uncomfortably in their seats.

"First things, first," says Stout, sliding some papers over to Abrams, "this is a federal subpoena directing Savage Wilderness Productions to preserve and release to the court all relevant video, sound, and other media records of the events of last night." Abrams silently pages through the material, sighs, and passes the papers over to Willems with a resigned nod.

"Mr. Savage," declares Wendover, "this is a joint county and federal information gathering session being conducted to better understand the events of last night. I'd like to thank you in advance for your participation as we sort through what happened."

"Yes, whatever I can do to help." Savage stops and quickly glances apologetically at his attorney, apparently realizing he's already broken the lawyer's protocol to stay quiet unless asked a direct question.

"So, last night," begins Wendover, "at approximately what time did you discharge your weapon?"

Savage looks dutifully over to Abrams, who gives him an affirmative nod. An easy question. Clearly, though, Abrams can expect that the follow-on line of questioning will not be so innocuous.

"Um, I think it was about nine-thirty, maybe ten."

"That would make it about an hour and a half after sunset at that location. With the moonrise not occurring last night until about two-thirty in the morning, it would have been quite dark out, correct?"

Savage nods.

"It was, in fact," continues Wendover, "also overcast with a high cloud ceiling. So, the night would have not just been dark but nearly pitch black out there?"

Savage nods a little more slowly, shooting a questioning look at Abrams. He's wondering where this is going. For his part, Abrams looks like at he'd rather be anywhere else than the sheriff's office in Benton County, Montana. Like maybe back in LA, prepping for a colonoscopy or something. I don't know what Savage is paying him but I get the sense it's not enough.

"So, Mr. Savage, given the pitch-black lighting conditions at that moment, please tell us," continues Wendover, "what was your decision process? How did you become confident that your target in the thermal imaging scope was, in fact, a sasquatch?"

"What...what do you mean?" Savage is looking more nervous by the moment. Abrams is slowly shaking his head. So much for his coaching on protocols.

"Look," replies Wendover, "you had told witnesses that you were certain you had fired at a sasquatch. You described sighting in on a being walking upright in the forest, correct? The more specific question is how, in the dark of the night, with no visible reference points as to size and distance, you became convinced that your rifle was pointed at a mythical creature unproven to exist? And how did you exclude the possibility that you were not instead aiming at a human? Humans also walk upright and most certainly have been proven to exist, no?"

At this Abrams is nearly on his feet, "I object!"

Wendover and Stout exchange a quizzical glance. "Excuse me," says Wendover to Abrams, "but what the hell are you doing? This is not a court proceeding or even a formal interview of a suspect. We're just trying to understand what happened. Your client is not under arrest nor is he obligated talk to us. He is free to leave at any time. We're just trying to give him an opportunity to tell his side of the story. By the way, do you have a criminal law practice? What is your legal specialty?"

"Um," Abrams clears his throat nervously, "I'm an entertainment attorney. I represent Mr. Savage in negotiations with the television networks and streaming services. I secure his royalties as well as protect his licensing and intellectual property assets."

"Great," says Wendover, "so, this isn't just your first rodeo, hell, you've never seen a horse before." To Savage, he says, "if it comes to it, please make sure you are represented by competent criminal counsel."

"Criminal?" Color is draining from Savage's face.

"If it comes to it. It may depend on whether Riddell is inclined to press charges. Right now, things are not looking good for you as I understand Mr. Riddell doesn't think too highly of folks who run around trying to shoot Bigfoot. In any event, we certainly will have plenty of video evidence around what exactly occurred. And there is also the eyewitness testimony of your medical expert, Kate Caroselli, and deputy Jack Walker…"

"Wait!" Savage bristles. "No way! They can't legally testify as to what happened. They both signed NDAs!"

Wendover sighs and shakes his head. "Sorry, but I think even 'Counselor Hollywood' here knows that non-disclosure agreements are unenforceable if used to suppress testimony related to a criminal matter." Abrams reluctantly nods his head in agreement. He now seems intent on querying his smartphone. Perhaps he's looking up legal precedents, but my bet is that he's searching for the next available commercial flight out of Montana.

At this point, Stout gets a text on his phone. He leans over and shares a peek at the screen with Wendover. They both nod at each other and smile. "Good news for you," says Wendover to Savage, "the government lawyers have sorted it out. The Feds," he gestures to Stout, "are taking lead on the case."

"How is potential federal prosecution good news?" asks Savage.

"Their prisons are much nicer than Deer Lodge," replies Wendover. He's talking about the Montana State Penitentiary, located near the small town of Deer Lodge.

We meet up with Wendover over in his office after Savage and Abrams leave. Zeke, Wendover's large and aging dog, trundles over to us, tail wagging. I scratch him behind the ear and he noses into my pockets looking for treats.

The sheriff shakes his head at this morning's session with Savage. In Wendover's opinion he thinks Savage is ultimately looking at a misdemeanor charge for reckless discharge of a firearm resulting in bodily injury. If he's lucky, this being a first offense, Savage would likely get parole and community service. An outcome that would not please the sheriff.

"It's hard to feel sorry for someone like Savage," he says. "You know, most of the people I arrest have never had lives as privileged as his. Not that I'm making excuses for all those folks behind bars; most deserve to be incarcerated, separated from decent citizens. But most, frankly, never had a fair shake in life. Many came from poverty; got introduced to crime at a young age. You look into their history and it turns out maybe their fathers abused them or their mamas abandoned them. Hard times lead to hardened criminals. It's a sad fact. But Savage has no excuses; he needs to be held accountable."

I fill Wendover in on the more intriguing aspects of yesterday's excursion into the Clark Mountain Complex. I tell him about the mysteriously large figure on the thermal imager that disappeared right before Riddell made his ill-fated journey into Savage's rifle-sight.

"You think that might have been Tommie Ka'uhane?" asks Wendover.

"Potentially. Ka'uhane is a large guy, right? Put him in a ghillie suit and no telling how he'd look in a thermal imager scope. And then there is this." I show him the photo I took yesterday down in the ravine below the Clark Mountain main ridge."

"I'll be damned," he says. He looks over to Kate. "That's Hawaiian, right?"

"It is," she replies. *Hālāwai mākou ma ka loko 'ao'ao 'ekolu.* "Roughly translates as we meet at three-sided body of water." The photo shows Hawaiian words cut into the side of a fallen log with an arrow carved next to the words.

"So, the log," says Wendover, standing at the map on his office wall, "would have been about here, right?" He's pointing to the ravine.

"Yup. That's the general location," I say.

"And which way was the arrow oriented?"

"I'd say basically southwest."

"Okay." Wendover is tracing his finger along the map in a southwesterly direction. "Then there is your three-sided lake." He taps the map in an area along the southwest flank of Clark Mountain. "It's about twenty-five acres in size. It's called Triangle Lake."

"A three-sided body of water called Triangle Lake, eh? That's original," I smirk.

"Picky, picky. There are over three thousand named lakes in Montana," counters Wendover. "You can't expect every name will be an original pearl. You should give the map makers a break."

"Alright," says Kate, "assuming for the moment that what Jack found was in fact a message from Ka'uhane to his NWEF ecoterrorist buddies, guiding them to a rendezvous at this lake, the question is why? What is so special about that place?"

"Well," replies Wendover, "there's nothing particularly noteworthy about the lake. It's secluded and very few people make an effort to visit it. The shoreline is pretty swampy and tends to attract mosquitoes."

"Doesn't sound very appealing as a tourist destination."

"Correct, Jack, not much to look at there, scenery wise. But its location in the Clark Complex is unique, as it's at a crossroads of canyons. Go east and you end up back in the Alta Valley, but there is also a good route into Idaho to the west as well. From what I recall there is an old abandoned trapper's cabin on the south shore. Last time I went through that country was probably twenty years ago and that old cabin was pretty rundown back then. I can't imagine its condition has improved."

"At this point," I say, "we have a small amount of circumstantial evidence that perhaps Ka'uhane is operating out of Triangle Lake. But that small bit of evidence is bolstered by one very expert opinion."

"Oh, yeah," says Wendover, "and who is this expert? I hope you're going to tell me her name is LISA."

CHAPTER 70

"You're in luck. This morning while you were busy harassing poor Lance Savage, LISA sent me an interesting analysis." I tap the data-pad on the table. "As you know, on the theory that Ka'uhane and his buddies have been faking Bigfoot sightings and conducting ecoterrorism, I uploaded to LISA several dozen files related to both types of occurrences throughout the Northwest."

"Right," responds Wendover, "I recall the plan was for LISA to run predictive algorithms to analyze the patterns and maybe narrow down where we might find Ka'uhane. I take it we have an answer?"

"Indeed, we do," I begin, as Kate and Wendover crowd around me to look at the data-pad screen. I toggle on the voice interface. "LISA? Please bring up a map of the Pacific and Intermountain Northwest. Please then visually populate the map with all purported sasquatch sightings that have been recorded over the past five years."

"Understood. LISA has updated the map accordingly."

Several hundred small red dots scatter across the map image. Each apparently representing a sighting or encounter with the mythical beasts, including as well, discovery of footprints and reports of strange vocalizations.

"This is interesting," observes Kate. "The distribution of sightings is not what I might have expected."

"How so?"

"Well, aren't these sasquatches supposed to be elusive creatures that stick to the backcountry, avoiding humans? But look at where many of the sightings have occurred. It appears as though maybe two thirds of the encounters have been reported in areas fairly close to roads, ranches, and even towns. Why would they be found so close to human civilization?"

"That's a great question and there may be several explanations for this oddity," I reply. "The most direct answer, and the one that our dear Friar William of Ockham would have surely endorsed, is that these sightings are simply all hoaxes. They occur close to human civilization as a convenience to the human hoaxers. Saves them some gas and hiking boot tread, right? But another possible explanation is that these are real animals, whether misidentified bears or real ape-men, and the large number of apparent sightings reported near human populations are just reflecting a bias in the data."

"What do you mean by a bias in the data?" asks Wendover.

"I'll let LISA explain."

"The proximity of sighting reports to human civilization may be an artifact of the relative distributions between the observables and the observers."

Blank looks from both Kate and Wendover. It appears some additional LISA-to-English translation will be required.

"Let me explain," I begin. "A sasquatch sighting report requires two essential ingredients. First, you need a sasquatch or something or someone that is mis-identified as one of the beasts, right? But then you also need a person there to actually witness the creature, see its footprints, or hear its supposed howls. The closer you get to human activity, the more potential witnesses you have to see something odd and file a report. Go way up into the backcountry and while there could be sasquatches roaming all over the place, there are very few people out there to see and report them. So, the anomalous incidents back in the deep woods may be underreported relative to those closer to towns. Make sense?"

"Dr. Walker, I believe that is what LISA just said." The A.I. has a bit of a chip on her digital shoulder this morning it seems.

"Okay, got it," agrees Wendover. "If a sasquatch howls in the forest but no one is there to hear it..."

"I think we can perhaps adjust the data to compensate for the underreporting in remote areas." I direct LISA to give additional weight to the reports of incidents in the more remote areas. Accordingly, each reported sighting in a remote setting now gets double the red dots on the map before us. The remote wilderness areas have now become a little redder with dots.

"Now, LISA, please populate the map with a reported ecoterrorism and related vandalism reports for that same time period." Three dozen or so amber dots now appear on the map. "Interesting correlation, huh?"

Wendover is nodding his head in agreement. "I'll say. Nearly all of the occurrences of ecoterrorism and related crimes have been in the same areas where supposed sasquatch activity has been reported. Looks like maybe Ka'uhane is making good on the threats of his manifesto, eh?"

I smile. "Dan, if you think this correlation looks interesting, it's about to get even more fascinating."

"I can hardly wait."

"So far," I continue, "we've only been looking at the data in only one dimension, that of space. Specifically, the locations where those reports occurred. Now, let's introduce the dimension of time. Because *when* these reported events occurred is as important as *where* they occurred. LISA, please update the map. Please color code the reported sightings and eco-activist activities by the month of occurrence."

"Understood. Map is updated to incorporate temporal data dimensions."

The color-coding scheme expands to display a multitude of different colored dots representing reports by month of occurrence. And the patterns that emerge are striking.

"Amazing," says Wendover, "look at that. Sightings tend to cluster only in certain regions at certain times. Hell, if we weren't talking about hoaxes and mythical creatures here, I'd say we'd be looking a very defined animal migration pattern. A pattern that repeats itself every year."

Indeed, the map shows what appears to be annually repeated movements of sightings across the greater Northwest. During the late fall, winter, and early spring months, sightings appear mainly around the temperate forests in the lower elevations of the Cascades and Olympic ranges. Then with the approach of spring weather, sightings appear to flow easterly along the Canadian border and across the northern panhandle of Idaho. The advent of summer brings the reports to northwestern Montana and by late summer reports are centered in southwestern Montana and its mountainous border with Idaho. In fall, the pattern apparently reverses, bringing the bulk of the reports back to western Washington and Oregon.

"And even more amazing," observes Kate, "is the spatial and temporal correlation between eco-activist offenses and the purported sasquatch activity. Those crime reports and the suspicious animal sightings seem to be occurring in the same areas and at the same times of the year. And the pattern is consistent, year after year."

"Of course," observes Wendover wryly, "your data scientist husband will take every opportunity to remind me that correlation isn't the same as causation. But that doesn't mean that sometimes where there's smoke, there is indeed fire, right?"

Kate nods soberly, "Dan, that is one very smoky looking map if you ask me."

"Okay, Jack…and LISA," continues Wendover, "great analysis of past history and events. So, what do the predictive algorithms say about where Ka'uhane and his crew might be today?"

"LISA has updated the map. Based on prior spatial and temporal patterns observed, LISA predicts with ninety-eight percent confidence that, at this time, the reported phenomenon is likely within the bounds of a circle of backcountry with an approximate fifty-mile radius."

We watch as LISA depicts the circular boundaries of a search area for Ka'uhane on the map.

"So, there is our search area target. Narrowed down to within a tidy fifty-mile radius," I say.

"Hmm," Kate is consulting an app on her phone. "Hate to temper my dear husband's enthusiasm. But with a basic geometry calculation, a circle with a fifty-mile radius would encompass about eight thousand square miles."

"More precisely, such a circle would encompass only 7,853.98 square miles," adds LISA helpfully.

"Yep," agrees Wendover, "that is one big-ass circle. Eight thousand square miles is a lot of country to cover."

I grin. "I consider my enthusiasm only mildly tempered by geometry. Why? Because, look at it, that big-ass circle is centered right smack over the top of the descriptively named Triangle Lake."

"No shit?" Wendover is leaning closer to get a better look at the map. "Yeah, you're right. The radius is centered right square on the lake."

"Absolutely no shit here. So, what do you say, Sheriff? Shall we go take a look at this place?"

"Not sure what we'll find there, if anything. It's a bit of a drive and then a hike up into the backcountry. If we grab some gear and leave now, we can probably get up there and at least back down off the trail before dark."

Kate smiles. "And Zeke's coming along?"

"Yep," laughs Wendover, "he might be handy in sniffing out Ka'uhane, or" he grins, "maybe old Bigfoot himself."

CHAPTER 71

Shakespeare wrote that all the world's a stage. The focus of that particular passage in *As You Like It* was on the larger play of life itself, suggesting each of us is an actor on the world's grand stage. Each of us carefully, or perhaps unwittingly, marking our lines, entrances and exits; our roles ever changing as life's journey unfolds.

I've always been fascinated with abandoned places. These empty buildings, factories, and ghost towns are in effect the stages left behind. Places where the play has closed and the characters have moved on to other productions, new roles, and other stages. I'm left to wonder why these buildings were built and later abandoned. What originally drew people to these desolate places and why did they leave? What dramas unfolded under these roofs? What dreams animated these long-gone peoples' days and what fears haunted their nights? If only the peeling walls could tell their stories.

Likely built as a seasonal trappers' outpost in the early 1900's, the long-abandoned Triangle Lake cabin probably began its long path to decay the moment it was completed. It's a simple affair, a one room shack built with logs; mud chinking serves to fill the gaps between logs as a sort of mortar. The roof appears to be an uneasy state of equilibrium as an increasing overgrowth of moss and grass seems to be expanding at roughly the same rate the original boards are decaying. The glass, wax paper, or cloth that probably once enclosed the windows is long gone, allowing the elements free rein to the interior.

Wendover, Kate, and I have been combing through the cabin for the last half hour, looking for any signs of Ka'uhane. There has been little indication of human occupation or even passing visits by hikers. We note there are few signs of rodents; even the mice seem to have left for more promising quarters.

The lack of human presence is not surprising, according to Wendover. He notes the four-mile hike from the trailhead where we left his patrol Tahoe is fairly steep and the switchback-laden trail up to the lake mainly follows deep ravines, lacking scenic vistas. And Triangle Lake itself is more of a large marshy pond than a lake. All in all, he says, most hikers deem the effort of the hike up here is not worth the scenic payoff and choose more appealing destinations for their excursions.

"That's quite the antique," I nod, as Wendover is kneeling down examining an old cast iron wood-burning stove. Aside from table, a couple of old chairs and a broken cot, it's the only other furnishing in the cabin. "It's amazing it has been here all these years and no one has taken it."

"Too damn much work to carry it out, I'd expect," replies Wendover. "I'd guess the old-timers probably hauled it up here by mule. But based on the state of the ashes, I'd say it's been used maybe only once recently. Maybe within the past couple of weeks. I don't know, likely some passing hiker waited out a storm here…hard to say."

So, what we're mainly finding here is…nothing. An empty stage. No clues and no sign of Ka'uhane. I'm struggling to hide my disappointment. The combination of LISA's predictive analytics and the Hawaiian markings I found over in the Clark Mountain Complex had made me nearly certain that we would find solid evidence here, if not Ka'uhane himself.

"Hey, guys," shouts Kate from behind the cabin, "maybe Zeke has found something out here. You might want to see for yourselves."

Wendover and I exchange a look and step out the door. Zeke had seemed eager to join us on this outing. He's doing well for his advanced age, only slowing up a bit on the steeper switchbacks on the trail up here. Zeke is sniffing and pawing at a large mound of rocks that had apparently been gathered from the clearing surrounding the cabin. As Wendover and I approach, he gives us a low whine and points his snout down at the rock pile.

"Dan, what is this?" Kate is pointing towards the mound.

"It's a pile of rocks," he answers with a casual smirk.

"Yeah, I figured that out. We have rocks in California, too." There's a trace of exasperation in her voice. "But why would anyone go to the trouble of stacking them up here and why is Zeke so interested in this pile?"

She has a point, the rock pile is about two feet high, with the length and width of a small car. It would have taken some effort to collect all the rocks and pile them in that spot.

"I'm not sure," replies Wendover, "but given its close proximity to the back of the cabin, it's likely this is just the garbage dump. The old-timers likely dug a shallow pit for their garbage and kept piling rocks on top as they filled it to keep out the bears and other scavengers. Old Zeke is probably picking up the scent of some well-aged garbage."

"Hmm." Kate is frowning and looking closer at the pile. "Dan, this may sound crazy, but see those four rather large rocks over on the end of the pile? Those that look to be positioned up on end, leaning up against each other? I've seen similar stone cairns or *pohaku* at old Hawaiian burial sites. At such sites, the four stones are said to symbolically form an eternal vessel to respectfully hold the spiritual essence of the departed, their *kupuna*."

Wendover is arching his eyebrow, "so, Kate, are you suggesting that some ancient Hawaiians managed to misplace one of their departed's graves by some three thousand miles and most of that distance over the ocean?"

"Not at all. I'm just suggesting that the rock pile your dog is so intently sniffing has an odd stack of stones that probably coincidentally resembles a Hawaiian burial cairn."

"And I suppose you want us to rummage through that rock pile to see if there is something of interest in it?"

Kate nods. "Since we've come all this way it would be a shame if we," she pauses and grins impishly, "left any stone unturned."

Wendover shakes his head and sighs. "Alright, let's get this done quickly. We need to get back to the trailhead before it gets dark. And I'm only agreeing to do this because Zeke has seconded the motion, eh? Although the odds are nearly one hundred percent that all we'll find here are some old bean cans and chicken bones. No doubt that is what is attracting Zeke's interest."

"Okay," I say, pulling off a stone, "I'll start at this end. Dan, why don't you work the other side and Kate can rummage through the middle. Zeke will supervise."

Wendover pulls his rifle strap off his shoulder and raps the gun butt sharply on the pile. "It's a courtesy," he explains, "just letting any chipmunks, mice, snakes, or other critters know we're about to enter their residence."

"Let's hope they don't ask you for a search warrant."

About twenty minutes later we've removed about half of the rocks. I suddenly stop and stand up. "Dan, could you come over here?"

"Sure, need a hand over there, Jack?"

"No, um, actually I have a hand. An extra one, as a matter of fact." The last stones I removed revealed an old wool blanket. And protruding from under the blanket is the shriveled skeleton of a human hand partially covered with brownish-purple desiccated skin. It appears to be attached to an arm and, based on the lump under the blanket I've uncovered, likely the rest of a body.

"Well, you don't see this every day." Wendover is taking photographs at various angles of the body we've uncovered in the shallow grave before us. Yes, I'm thinking, we should hope not to see this every day or, frankly, on any day.

The corpse is lying flat on its back, arms down at the sides. It is almost as though the deceased had lain down for a restful sleep for eternity. Surrounding the body is a collection of knives, hatchets, and other wilderness gear. The cadaver itself is fully dressed with the remains of a flannel shirt, blue jeans, and boots. Oddly, the body is covered with remnants of old plant stalks and dried flowers.

"We're looking at a male of large build. The coroner will have to confirm, but I'd say there are no obvious signs of trauma or foul play," observes Wendover. "And this was no quick body dump into a shallow grave. Look at how the body has been laid here with great care. And see how the personal possessions have been placed around it. And these dried stems and shriveled flowers? Someone apparently covered the body with wildflowers when it was buried. Seems ritualistic, even perhaps done with affection for the departed."

"Any idea how long he's been dead?" I ask.

"Hard to say for sure. Maybe a year or two. Corpses found up here in the high country are subjected to low humidity, thin air, and cool temperatures. In fact, at this elevation, the rock pile has probably been under snowpack six months out of the year. These sorts of conditions play hell with normal decomposition assumptions. Sometimes the remains even become naturally mummified."

"And how do we go about identifying him?" I ask. "It's likely you won't get fingerprints. That leaves DNA and dental records, right?"

"Well, always the first order of business," responds Wendover, reaching under the body to feel the back pockets, "is to check for identification." He pulls out a wallet with a slight smile and a flourish. "And…we have a winner. Let's see here. Eighty bucks in cash, so his death was likely not the result of a robbery. And I'm now holding a long-expired Washington state driver's license that appears to belong to one now also very expired… Thomas Ka'uhane."

"Finally," says Kate, "we've solved the mystery of what happened to Tommie Ka'uhane."

"You'll find, Kate, in this line of work, you solve one loose end and two more pop up," sighs Wendover. "It appears now that certainly others must be involved. Unless," he pauses and grins, "unless someone is going to suggest that Ka'uhane somehow buried himself under this pile of rocks."

"And," I add, "if Ka'uhane has been laying here dead for at least a year or two, he was surely still dead earlier this week when Rocky Sorenson was shot. And speaking of shooting, we should note that Ka'uhane's .30-06 rifle was not among the personal effects buried with him."

"Indeed," agrees Wendover, "we're still no closer to solving Rocky's murder. At this point, all we've done has been to eliminate a suspect."

"Which presents yet another mystery," adds Kate. "Who else besides Ka'uhane would have the ability and inclination to write out ecoterrorism threats in traditional Hawaiian? The threats didn't stop two years ago. If anything, they've increased."

Wendover is becoming concerned with the lateness of the hour and prospect of a long hike back down the trail in the approaching darkness. We quickly cover the grave back up with stones and head out. Tomorrow a search and rescue team including his deputies will come up here and recover the body.

The hike back down the trail has been uneventful. However, as we approach the trailhead, Zeke is becoming increasingly anxious. He's looking about, growling and whining. Something is wrong.

As we step out of the woods onto the turn-around where the sheriff's vehicle is parked, it appears something is very, very wrong indeed. The Tahoe has been vandalized. Its windows smashed and tires slashed. Wendover's police radio has been bashed in beyond recognition.

"Damn," I say, surveying the damage, "looks like someone has sent us a message. We've worn out our welcome. Someone wants us to stay the hell away from this place."

"Jack," replies Wendover very quietly, "I only wish you were right." He's slowly pulling his rifle forward into a ready position and a chill begins to crawl down my back. "You and Kate get behind me. I want you shielded between me and the Tahoe. Think about it. Our vehicle has been disabled and my radio destroyed. It's not that someone wants us to go away. No, quite the opposite, someone doesn't want us to leave."

CHAPTER 72

CRACK...

The deafening blast of the gunshot seems to come out of nowhere. Wendover is hit, staggering back and then slumping down on the ground. His rifle clatters down uselessly next to his unmoving form. Zeke instantly crouches down next to his fallen master, snarling. He's trying to shield Wendover with his own massive bulk.

Silas Patterson appears from what was apparently his ambush point behind a tree. The fugitive serial killer is alternating between pointing the gun at Kate and then at me. "You, get back!" he shouts keeping the pistol pointed at me while he moves behind Kate and locks his free arm around her throat. "Isn't this turning out to be a wonderful day? One dead lawman, soon to be joined by his buddy here and that goddamned dog. And the pretty lady here," he nods to Kate, squirming in his grip, "Why, she and I are gonna have a little fun, aren't we?"

The past three months on the lam in the depths of the wilderness have not been kind to Silas Patterson, either physically or mentally. He has a wild sunburned unshaven face capped by a rat's nest of unkept and dirty hair strewn across the top of his head. His wild and darting eyes seem to belong to a feral animal. The overall effect suggests a combination of an unhinged mountain man and a meth-head. If Patterson wasn't deranged before he fled into the backcountry, he has surely gone quite mad now.

"Silas, stop and think about what you're doing here. Don't make this worse than it already is." I know that trying to reason with a man so estranged from logic and decency is futile, but I'm hoping to buy time. But time for what? I have no idea and no plan. There is no rescue squad on the way. No one is going to come and save us in this remote section of the forest.

Just then Wendover groans and stirs. One arm feebly begins to search along the ground for the stock of his rifle. Patterson swivels to the side, still firmly holding Kate. He's pointing the gun towards Wendover to finish him off. In that second, in one deft motion, Kate swings her elbow upwards smashing into Patterson's armpit with surprising force. Patterson staggers back and howls in pain, the pistol dropping from his now incapacitated arm. Kate swings free out of his grip but now he's making a mad scramble for the pistol, trying to grab it with his good hand.

At this point I know what I must do. I must separate Patterson as best I can from Kate, Wendover, and that gun. I run, lunge forward and tackle the madman with all the force I can muster. Perhaps a bit too much force. We collide and the sheer impact of my assault drives us both backwards off the edge of the road and down the steep embankment of the road turnaround. We're sliding and tumbling some forty feet down the slope, partially entangled with one another. For a fraction of a second as we pitch down the hill, we are nearly face to face. And I am inches away from his unfeeling eyes and I can smell his fetid breath on my face.

Suddenly, towards the bottom, my leg scrapes and twists on the jagged stub of a broken-off branch protruding from a fallen tree. I roll to a stop next to the tree. Instantly my leg feels as though it is on fire with pain. Patterson has also sprawled to a stop about thirty feet away. He starts to pull himself upright, gives me an evil grin, and retrieves a knife from its sheath on his belt. It's a nasty looking weapon. A buck knife with a six-inch serrated blade. Probably the one he used on his four other victims. Just my luck. I remember the abandoned Sapphire Belle mine in the Ricky Pruitt case. The criminal Jason Riley stalking me through its dark depths. Intent on slashing my throat with a remarkably similar knife. What is it about my recent life choices that seem to put me in the clutches of knife-wielding maniacs on a distressingly regular basis?

Patterson, knife in hand, is starting to advance towards me. My leg and ankle feel weak and I'm struggling to get to my feet. A knife-armed former military special operations soldier versus an unarmed college professor with a wounded leg. This will not be an even fight but it promises to be a short one.

Just then a rifle concussion shatters the stillness of the forest and a patch of dirt directly between Patterson and me explodes with an incoming round. For a fraction of a second Patterson and I look at each other in surprise and then we swivel our heads in unison upward to see who is shooting.

It's Kate! She's standing at the top of the embankment, sighting Wendover's rife down at us. The next round ricochets and whines off a large rock not more than three feet from Pruitt. A third shot strays wild and hits a bit too close to me for comfort. I try to roll next to the fallen tree, looking for cover. Patterson has had enough. He quickly jumps away and runs off into the forest at breakneck speed.

The trip back up the embankment is going much slower than the tumble down it. With every motion my leg and ankle threaten to give out. I look down at my left leg to survey the damage. My cargo pant leg is shredded below the knee, its tatters slowly soaking crimson with blood.

Finally, I reach the top of the road and embrace Kate. "Thanks, Honey! When did you learn to shoot?"

"Actually, just a few minutes ago."

"Well, your warning shots saved my life!"

"Warning shots?" she frowns. "I was aiming for that bastard's heart!"

She quickly passes me the rifle. "Here, take this and keep an eye out for Patterson. I need to attend to Dan."

Kate grabs her medical kit out of the Tahoe and kneels down next to Wendover. To our great relief the sheriff is now sitting up, albeit, a bit unsteadily. Zeke is wagging uncontrollably, licking Wendover's face.

"Damn, that hurt," he grimaces, pulling off his jacket and unbuttoning his shirt. "But don't worry, I think I'm gonna be okay." We see the slug embedded in the ballistic vest over his torso. The first and perhaps only lucky break we're going to have today.

Kate has completed her examination of the slug's impact site and has doubled checked Wendover's vital signs. "Dan, I think you're going to be fine. Although the bruising around the point of impact will be quite painful for several days. Nevertheless, once we're back in town, I'd like to get you to the hospital for a full examination and some imaging. There is a chance you may have a cracked rib or two."

Wendover is now standing, rebuttoning his shirt. "Dan, do you feel well enough to take the rifle and stand watch?" asks Kate.

"Yeah," he replies, scowling, "trust me, the next round I shoot will have Patterson's name on it."

"Great, I need to attend to my next patient. Jack, let's take a look at that leg." She's gesturing to an old fallen log along the side of the road about fifty yards from the Tahoe. "Step over to my examination log and have a seat."

I notice the sentence is phrased as a command rather than a request. Doctor's orders. And I remember what she did to Patterson's arm. A well-placed jab to the brachial nerve under the armpit can be as debilitating as it is painful. Normally, as a physician, an encyclopedic knowledge of anatomy helps Kate manage her patients' pain. But threaten her with a gun and that knowledge can apparently be weaponized against attackers with devastating results. Not a lady I would choose to antagonize. I step over to the log double-time, ignoring the protests of my ankle.

"I take it you're experiencing some pain in your left leg when you walk?

"Not all the time, just when I put weight on it."

"So just every other step, eh? Let's see what we have here." She's pulling up my tattered pant leg. "Well, this is a nasty looking laceration across your calf. But you were lucky, the slash missed any major arteries or veins. It will require some stitches though." She's reaching into her medical kit.

"Stitches? Couldn't you just clean it up and put on a bandage. Doesn't look that bad to me," I say.

"Jack? Would you please remind me? Perhaps I've forgotten. Which one of us went to medical school?"

I jokingly raise my hands in surrender. "Okay, okay, I give up. Have your way with me, Doc. This isn't going to hurt, is it?"

"Oh, if you keep on being a stubborn ass, I can guarantee it will hurt."

Now satisfied with her efforts on the laceration, she turns her attention to the ankle. "Jack, this looks to be a moderate sprain. Unfortunately, I obviously didn't carry a proper ankle brace in my medical goodie bag, but I can wrap the ankle tightly with a compression bandage. That will allow you to put a little weight on it. Combine that with a walking stick and you should at least be mobile. You just won't win any foot races for a few days."

"Noted. No foot races until next week."

"No ankle brace, but I do have one other item in my medical bag that you should be very happy to see. I grabbed it as an afterthought before we left town." She smiles as she pulls out the data-pad.

The data-pad! Here, far out of cell phone coverage, and with Wendover's police radio destroyed, this is a Godsend. With its global satellite connection to LISA, this may be our lifeline, perhaps our only lifeline, for survival. We can route a plea for rescue through LISA to Adhira and Team LISA. Or perhaps LISA herself can contact the Benton County sheriff's office directly.

"Hmmm." Kate is now frowning, looking at the data-pad screen. "Not getting a satellite connection."

I give her the stock troubleshooting advice issued by all IT service request desks since the dawn of the digital age. "Um, try rebooting it and see what happens."

"Brilliant, Professor. I'd have never figured that out on my own. Okay, give me a minute here."

I leave Kate to wrangle the data-pad and walk a bit tenderly over to Wendover. He's pulling equipment out of the Tahoe, preparing for the long night ahead of us. Indeed, the forest around us is rapidly darkening as twilight begins to fade.

"Maybe there's some good news," I say. "Kate has the data-pad and we may be able to use it to connect to LISA and summon help."

"That would be a welcome development," he replies. "Take a look at this gun," he's holding the pistol that Patterson dropped. "This is a government-issued service weapon. Patterson likely took it off the forest ranger he murdered. That means it's likely not his only firearm. We stay here and he can pick us off at his leisure."

"But if we can connect with LISA, help will be on the way, right?"

"If you can connect with LISA and if LISA can get a message to my deputies, they still have to get here to our location way up in the backcountry. I figure that would be about ninety minutes minimum if they left the station right now at top speed. So, figure in the best case we're on our own here for at least the next two to three hours."

"And the worst case?" I sigh. "The message doesn't get through and we're completely on our own."

"Yup. Stay here and we're sitting ducks. Start walking down the road towards civilization and at least we're moving ducks. And moving closer to help with each step we take. Patterson certainly can follow the road as well as we can. He could surely ambush us along the way. But if we stay here, I think another ambush would be a certainty. At least Zeke here can sense if Patterson tries to approach again."

"Yes," I agree, "but as for taking steps towards safety, you'll notice my steps are quite tentative with this bum ankle. I'll slow you down too much. Leave me here. Take Kate with you down to get help."

"No, Jack. We stay together and we might stay alive."

"That's okay. Leave me with the ranger's gun and I'll just find a secure crevasse or something that's got me protected on three sides and wait for the cavalry to arrive. Patterson would have to come at me front on. I can handle him."

"Yeah," scoffs Wendover, "says someone who *hasn't* been shot by Patterson today…yet."

"A fair point," I say, "Maybe…"

We're interrupted by Zeke barking and growling. He's looking off into the woods and becoming highly agitated. Could Patterson be back already for round two?

Suddenly Kate screams. Zeke is howling and barking even more frantically. Wendover and I spin around and begin to run in her direction.

To our horror and astonishment Kate is being carried off by…a hairy beast! The ape-like creature is massive. In two swift strides, it disappears into the night holding Kate as easily as if she were a small puppy or kitten. Within thirty seconds, we can hear branches snapping a hundred yards away. It is moving incredibly fast. With my Kate!

"No!" I scream. "Kate!" I start a hobbling run towards the woods. Ankle be damned, I'm going into that forest to rescue my wife from that thing.

"Jack! No!" Wendover runs, grabs me roughly by the shoulder and spins me around. "Jack, you're not thinking! Whatever the hell that thing is, it's moving too fast. You'll never catch it and worse yet, you'll likely get hopelessly lost thrashing around the forest in the dark."

Struggling against his grip, I'm resenting Wendover's interference with every second that passes. But deep down another part of me, the rational Jack, sadly knows he's right.

And, in that moment, I remember Deputy Yazzie's half-joking warning. Do not fear that you will find the Choanito. Fear, instead, that the Choanito will find you.

CHAPTER 73

Wendover is slowly guiding me away from the forest's edge and back towards the Tahoe. He's trying to reason with me, using a soft, rhythmic monotone. It's probably his talk-'em-off-a-window-ledge voice. I'm sure his lecture is well-meaning and probably quite rational, but I'm not hearing a word of it. I'm consumed with fear and guilt. Why did even I agree to bring Kate to Montana? And what business did I have taking her into the backcountry where within the space of an hour she was assaulted by a serial killer and now abducted by…a sasquatch?

I stop, the fear and adrenalin of the moment hasn't allowed my mind to even process the reality of what we have just witnessed. I turn to Wendover, "That was a sasquatch, right? A real fucking sasquatch?"

Wendover nods. "I think so. I'd estimate it was about nine or ten feet tall, maybe weighed on the order of six, seven hundred pounds or more. Jack, that was no guy dressed up in a ghillie suit."

I shake my head in anguish. I shudder at the thought of Kate in the clutches of that beast. The fair damsel carried off into the night by a massive ape. From Edgar Rice Burrough's Tarzan, Edgar Wallace's King Kong, to a hundred B-grade movies, this is an archetype of our very nightmares. What terror must Kate be experiencing at this very moment? The thought is threatening to drive me mad.

We walk past the log where Kate had been grabbed. Her medical backpack is lying on the ground, half of its contents spilled out. I quickly gather up the kit and lift it by the straps. Then it strikes me that something very important is missing.

"Dan, Kate was sitting here rebooting the data-pad when she was taken."

"Uh-huh."

"It's gone. The data-pad is missing. Hopefully Kate had the presence of mind to hang on to it when that thing grabbed her. And if she is somehow able to activate the satellite link, we can find her. Once we get back into cell service range, LISA can give us her exact location coordinates."

"Agreed," replies Wendover, "but with no access to a satellite link ourselves, our only option is to try and walk down these old forest service roads until we reach a point where there's a cell signal."

He sees my hesitation. "Every step I take down this mountain is another step further away from Kate," I protest.

"I know, Jack. But we need to get those location coordinates. And we need resources. Once back in communication, in the space of several hours I can have law enforcement and search and rescue combing these woods. We can mobilize a hundred searchers. We'll pull in helicopters with thermal imaging capabilities. But none of that can happen unless we get a cell signal, right?"

I nod slowly, "I know, Dan. You're right." Indeed, I think, we cannot begin to rescue Kate if we first cannot even save ourselves.

"And another thing," he adds, "I'm now reluctantly beginning to conclude that those damn poachers from New Jersey may have been telling the truth about their abduction by sasquatches. Of course, most of the rest of their story is a fabrication to cover-up their poaching involvement with Rocky, but maybe not the sasquatch part. You know what that means?"

"Huh, what?" I'm not following him all that well, probably because my mind is overrun with anxiety and fear for Kate.

"Remember?" he explains. "The Jersey guys said they were carried through the night over into Idaho. But they were then released at the edge of the forest. Unharmed. Maybe Kate will be released unharmed as well."

"Yeah," I reply, "maybe the sasquatches are running some sort of human catch and release program. Let's hope so for Kate's sake." I grab an old branch to use as a walking stick to support my leg. Then I sling the medical bag over my shoulder and begin to reluctantly follow Wendover and Zeke down the darkened road.

Later towards the morning, dawn's first cold fingers of light are slowly starting to rise behind the eastern mountains as we continue to walk down the forest road towards the valley and finally cross into cell service range. Wendover is immediately on the phone with his deputies. My first call is to Adhira Chandra.

"What? Jack? Is everything alright?" She's sounding a bit groggy on her end and I belatedly realize that the early predawn hour here is even earlier in California's time zone.

"Adhira, so sorry to bother you at this hour. We've got a little issue here and I need you to pull up the GPS coordinates on the data-pad. It's urgent."

"Sure," she says, yawning. "Give me a minute while I pull up my laptop and synch with LISA. By the way, you still haven't said if everything is alright, have you?"

"I think things will start getting better when I get the coordinates."

"That's a good non-answer," she replies, "very mysterious. Perhaps one might think you've been spending too much time in the Batcave lately." There's a pause as she finishes synching her laptop to LISA's servers. "Okay, yes, that device is currently online. LISA has the exact coordinates. I'm sending them to your phone now. Looks to be in rugged country maybe half a dozen miles from your current position."

"Thanks. I promise I'll fill you in on the larger story…when I figure it out myself."

"Oh, Jack, there's more. It appears LISA has been holding several messages for you. Relaying them from Kate. Kate says to tell you not to worry. Says she is safe and unharmed. She wants you to come to her data-pad coordinates as soon as you can. And to please bring her medical bag."

"Thanks. Please relay back that we'll get there as fast as we can."

"One more thing, Jack. She has emphasized that only you and Sheriff Wendover should come. The two of you must come alone."

"Understood."

"Jack, what the hell is going on? Is Kate in danger?"

"I hope not. That's about as much as I can say."

"And, Jack. One more thing. I'm now looking at that data-pad's recent activity log. And it's unusual, very unusual."

"How so?"

"That unit has been very active, used nearly continuously all through last night and right up until just now this morning. And the subject matter of these intense queries has been, to say the least…eclectic."

"Really? What topics?"

"Well, there have been numerous queries on human and primate physiology, scanning and translations of Hawaiian language documents, real-time verbal Hawaiian translations, cognitive measurement instruments, and obstetrics."

"Cognitive tests? And obstetrics? As in the prenatal care and delivery of infants?" I ask.

"Correct. Unless you know of another kind of obstetrics. By the way, interesting that you don't seem terribly surprised about all the Hawaiian language translations."

"Like I said, long story. Okay, thanks, Adhira. I'll keep you posted on Kate's status as we know more," I say as I end the call.

"Did you hear that?" I nod to Wendover. "Kate may be safe."

Wendover frowns. "Unless, of course, she is acting under duress."

"You're always a bright ray of sunshine."

"Occupational hazard," he sighs.

The logistics of contacting Wendover's deputies, securing another police SUV, dropping off Zeke, confirming the data-pad coordinates, and driving old logging roads to a point nearest the data-pad location only took about three hours. But it seemed like a lifetime to me given the uncertainty regarding Kate's situation.

Now it's late morning and we're exiting the patrol SUV at the end of a rugged logging road. This is the farthest towards Kate's presumed location that we can bring a motor vehicle. The rest of the way will need to be covered on foot. Wendover opens up the back hatch and offers me my choice of firepower.

"Well, she said to come alone, but she didn't mention anything about being unarmed," he says. "Rifle or tactical shotgun?"

"I'll take the shotgun. Maybe I'll have a decent chance of hitting a target with it…if it comes to that."

"Good choice," he replies, "shotguns are always crowd pleasers. I'll take the rifle. Who knows if that ape-man is still around, but let's not forget that Patterson is likely still in this area as well."

"The good news never ends," I groan.

"So," continues Wendover, "by my reckoning, the data-pad location should be about a mile in that direction." He's pointing across a series of gently rolling forested ridges to our north. "Frankly, as the crow flies, it's not that far from our prior location where Kate was originally abducted. We're just one creek drainage over the main ridge from there."

We proceed into the forest, walking slowly on a straight compass bearing towards the data-pad, and hopefully Kate's location. My sense is that Wendover could easily double his pace, but he's holding back a bit out of concern for my ankle. I find myself carefully scanning the surrounding landscape, looking for any sign of the giant ape-man. The beast could be hiding, awaiting in ambush. But at least here in the light of day, there are fewer places for the massive creature to find cover. It can't exactly squeeze its huge frame behind a single tree. However, we shouldn't kid ourselves either. No doubt we are on the beast's home turf. Its house, its rules; if it wants to take us by surprise, it will.

About three quarters of a mile into the forest, Wendover suddenly stops and motions for me to remain silent. "Hear that?" he whispers.

We're standing at the base of a small gently sloping hill, its summit covered with brush and trees. I nod, straining to hear the approaching sound. There is a rustling through the brush just over the crest of the hill. We hear someone or something moving towards us, pushing brush out of the way. And then the sound of heavy footsteps. Someone or something very large is approaching.

Wendover and I gasp in unison as a massive form pushes through the last of brush and strides to the top of the rise to look down upon us. It is the creature from last night! Kate's abductor!

"Jesus! Look at that!" exclaims Wendover, his voice rising with awe. "There's your sasquatch. Yeah, that sucker must be nearly ten feet tall."

"Yeah, and there's your .30-06, Sheriff." Indeed, the full-size rifle appears to be a mere toy slung casually by its strap over the shoulder of the giant beast.

"No shit," Wendover is shaking his head in disbelief. "A Remington bolt action. I'll be damned. I guess now I've seen everything."

The creature is barely fifty yards away. It's gazing down at us with an expression that is not threatening but not particularly welcoming either. Apparently assessing us as intensely as we are examining it. At this distance I can hear it breathe and see its chest rise and fall with each respiration. It shifts and sways slightly as it stands up there and individual muscles on its body visibly shift slightly as it maintains its balance. There is a slight breeze about us that softly moves every hair on its body. This is undoubtedly a real living animal standing before us, not an apparition or a person in a ghillie suit or ape costume.

"Not sure what use our guns would be," indicates Wendover very quietly. "Something that massive, at short range, if it decides to come for us, a gun wouldn't stop it. I could pump half a dozen rounds into it and it would just keep coming. Oh, it might eventually die of its wounds; long after it's shredded us."

"You're full of happy thoughts."

"Or it might not bother to physically attack us. It might just shoot us with its own rifle there," he adds.

"Think it knows how to use that rifle?"

"I guess only the ghost of Rocky Sorenson knows for sure."

At this point, the creature shifts its gaze away from us. It's looking back into the woods behind it. Then we hear something as well. The sound of another being approaching through the brush. But this new arrival sounds much smaller than the first one. Perhaps it is a juvenile or a female of the species.

Wendover and I can only stand in shocked silence as the bushes part and out steps…Kate! She walks over next to the giant creature and waves to us, all smiles.

"Hi guys, what took you so long?" This is said with all the nonchalance of someone who's perhaps been holding a table for us at a busy restaurant.

To my great relief, she appears unharmed. To be sure, she does look like she's had a bit of an overnight adventure in the woods; her hair is disheveled and her face is blemished with dirt. And my heart sinks a bit when I notice a large stain of dried blood on the front of her shirt, but she seems quite hale and healthy otherwise.

Wendover and I are frozen in place, trying to process this. A thousand questions are coming to mind, followed by a thousand more. What the hell is going on here?

Apparently, Kate thinks introductions are overdue. "Gentlemen," she's pointing to the beast, "this is our new friend, Kahuna Akamu. Think of the Akamu name as a Hawaiian variant of 'Adam.' Adam, the first man, made from the clay of the earth."

"Akamu," she nods to the giant, and points to Wendover, "Kahuna Wendover." She says this with exaggerated formality and Akamu bows slightly towards the sheriff. What happens next is perhaps the most shocking development in a day increasingly marked by the fantastic and incredible.

The beast raises its hand and simply says *"Aloha."*

I can only stutter "How?" to Kate. She just smiles and says we have much to discuss. Perhaps the understatement of the decade, I think.

Next, Kate points towards me, *"'O ke kāne wīwī lōʻihi koʻu hoa kāne."* Akamu seems to frown and says something in reply in Hawaiian and she nods and laughs.

I don't understand a word of Hawaiian, but I think I'm getting the gist of what was said. Wendover, of course, as the county's authority figure, is introduced as the Kahuna…the Big Chief. My introduction took a few more words. Probably something to the effect of saying "that rakishly handsome man is my husband." I'll confirm with Kate later as to exactly what she said.

"Well, come on, gents!" Kate's gesturing for us to follow her up the hill. "We're burning daylight, and we have much to do." She says this as she turns to follow the creature back into the forest, waving for us to hurry up.

"Jack," Wendover nudges me with a sly grin, "anyone ever tell you that your wife is a total badass?"

CHAPTER 74

"OH MY GOD, KATE!" I PULL HER CLOSE AND HUG HER TIGHTLY. "I WAS SO worried!"

"Oh, I'm fine, perfectly fine." She returns my hug and gives me an impish grin. "Although, at some point, a nice long hot shower and a good night's sleep would be welcome, eh? I will say it's been quite an adventure."

I sigh. Kate gets carried off into the night by King Kong's smaller cousin and terms the ordeal an "adventure." I'm starting to wonder if this isn't a backwoods case of Stockholm Syndrome where she has somehow come to sympathize and identify with her beastly captor.

I glance ahead of us. Kate's new hairy pal, Akamu, is now some hundred yards out in advance, walking slowly, pushing brush aside. Seems he's clearing a path for us. But where are we going? I stare at him for a moment in disbelief. The human mind is an odd thing, especially mine. Just months ago, I had a very personal encounter in an Argentine cavern with Na'Vack, an actual space alien. Yet, somehow, I've found it far easier to accept the existence of aliens than the very real, flesh and blood sasquatch lumbering through the woods ahead of us.

"But, Kate, the blood?" I'm pointing at the large crimson stain on her shirt. "Are you sure you're okay?"

"Oh, that?" She's glancing down at her shirt like she's just noticed the large red splotch. "Oh, that's not my blood. It's just some placental blood and fluid. Must have splashed on me during the delivery last night."

"What?" I'm incredulous, "what would a pregnant woman be doing all the way out here in the wilderness…" My voice trails off. I'm getting the look. That familiar look from Kate. The wry smile and wink that says "My dear husband, how can you be so book-smart but so oblivious to what is right in front of you?" And what I'm beginning to think she's implying is…unbelievable.

"Maybe, Kate," says Wendover gently, "you should start at the beginning?"

"Okay," begins Kate, "let's return to the three of us back at the trailhead turnout. We're all just trying to pull things back together after Patterson's attack, right? So, ask yourself. Why Kate? Why would Akamu abduct me versus, say, Jack? And, frankly, keep in mind that Akamu would likely have been physically capable of taking all three of us if he so wished."

"Why take you instead of Jack? That's an easy one!" Wendover is smiling broadly. "Kate, you're smarter, more pleasant, and way better looking than your husband. Ole' Akamu just has good taste in abductees!"

Kate smiles. "Dan, that may all be true if you say so, but there was another reason. So, Akamu grabs me and off we go into the woods. I'm hanging on to the data-pad for dear life. And, oddly, I wasn't all that afraid. I think at that point I was in more in shock and total disbelief that these Bigfoots truly exist. And this giant being seems to be taking some care to hold me gently. He's in fact patting my back softly, like he's trying to comfort me."

Wendover and I exchange a glance. This is not exactly the harrowing tale we were expecting.

"So," Kate continues, "he carries me about a half mile or so back into the forest where we meet up another sasquatch, apparently a member of his clan. And to my great surprise, the two of them start conversing in Hawaiian. And I hear Akamu saying something like *he kahuna lapaau keia wahine.* This translates roughly as saying 'this woman is a medicine shaman.' At that point, I spoke up in Hawaiian, confirmed that I was indeed a doctor and asked how I could help. Then it was the sasquatches' turn to be shocked that I spoke their language."

"I suppose this may be a minor detail in the story," asks Wendover, "but how in blazes is it that these primitive creatures, living deep in the Montana wilderness, speak Hawaiian?"

"Well, there is a very short answer to your question as well as a much longer one that we'll get to. The very short answer is that the late Tommie Ka'uhane taught them. And, by the way, Dan, the sasquatches should not be thought of as mere animals or simple creatures. These are intelligent, sentient beings. From the limited tests I've been able to run, their cognitive abilities appear to fall well within the range of human norms. They appear to be able to express a wide range of emotions and are able to joke with each other and even sprinkle wry nuances such as double-entendres into their conversations. In some respects, their culture may even be more advanced than human society."

"You're beginning to make them sound a bit more sophisticated than North Dakotans," grins Wendover.

As Kate continues, she explains that Akamu's clan had been hunting and foraging in this part of the Clark Mountain Complex for several weeks during their yearly migration through the area. But their movements had been more restricted than usual because Akamu's mate, Mahina, was in the very late stages of a difficult pregnancy. Mahina could no longer walk and was increasingly stressed with pain. Akamu was rightly worried about the condition of his mate and their unborn child.

"Then," says Kate, "Akamu heard a series of gunshots just over the ridge. Those were the shots that rang out as Patterson attacked us and was then repelled. Akamu came over the ridge to investigate. He was worried. There are obviously armed humans in the area and Mahina was in no condition to move. As he neared our location and watched cautiously from the shadows, what did he see? He observed me patching up the both of you. Tending to your injuries. He saw a medicine shaman…a healer."

"And decided it was time for the good doctor to make a forced house call," I add. "Didn't even check first to see if you were on his insurance plan."

"Yeah, he brings me over the ridge to meet Mahina and the rest of clan. There is general amazement from all parties, including me, that I speak their language. I'm introduced as the neighborhood medicine shaman and I begin to do an examination of Mahina's condition. Akuma was right in being worried. At that point, from what I could tell, the odds were good the baby was in a breech position. Unless I intervened, and quickly, there was a real possibility that either mom, baby, or both could die. I had the data-pad with a reestablished connection to LISA, but what I really needed was my medical kit. Akamu and I quickly doubled back to the trailhead turnout to retrieve the bag and to introduce him to you both. But by the time we had returned, you and the bag were long gone."

"And,...shit!" she pauses and glares at us. "Typical men...I swear! What was the *one thing* I asked you guys to bring today? My medical kit! But instead, you two cowboy up here with guns that no one needs! Where's my kit?"

"Um," replies Wendover a bit sheepishly, "I think we left it back in my rig. Forgot it in the rush...being worried about you and all."

"Okay," she shakes her head with annoyance, "guess we can pick it up later." Sighs. "It figures. Like sending Jack to the grocery store for just three items. He'll be lucky to come back with even one that was on the list."

"So, you and Akuma returned back to Mahina and you were forced to improvise?" I'm trying to steer the conversation away from my many faults and shortcomings back to the sasquatches.

"Yes, it was a bit dicey, and I had to make some assumptions that sasquatch physiology and anatomy were more similar to humans than to other primates. The baby was indeed presenting as breech so it's good that I was there to perform the delivery. It was touch and go for a bit but, in the end, I was able to deliver a sweet healthy baby girl for Akuma and Mahina." She pauses, nods and smiles, "It's been a long time since I've brought a new life into the world. I had forgotten how good that can feel." She gestures towards the hulking Akuma who is still far in front us, breaking trail through the brush, "That's where we're heading...to see Mahina and her child."

"So, what do these beings call themselves?" asks Wendover. "I'd assume the term Bigfoot would be considered a bit..."

"Pejorative." Kate finishes his sentence. "Frankly, 'Bigbrain' rather than Bigfoot would be a more accurate moniker from what I have observed. But the sasquatches have adopted a Hawaiian term. They refer to themselves as the *Kama'aina*, which means 'people of the land.' Quite appropriate as they consider themselves guardians of nature and the land."

"Okay, Kate," I say. "It sounds like these sasquatches or Kama'aina, despite being elusive forest creatures of the Pacific Northwest, have somehow gone all in on adopting the Hawaiian language. But why? How did this happen?

You mentioned Tommie Ka'uhane had a hand in this? How did all of this come about?"

"Like much of what happens in the world," she responds, "it was synchronicity. An alignment of inflection points that could not have been foreseen. Over a dozen years ago, Tommie Ka'uhane was experiencing an inflection point in his own life's journey. He had rejected the trappings of civilization and had committed himself to protecting the wild forests of the Northwest from human encroachment. And, at that same time, the Kama'aina themselves were at their own inflection point. Their species was going through a period of very rapid evolutionary change."

She pauses and raises an eyebrow at me for effect. Like she wants to make sure I'm understanding the implications at play here.

"How rapid?" I ask.

"Extremely rapid. "Out-of-this-world rapid."

Now I choose my words carefully. "I've heard that certain primate species have in the past gone through periods of very rapid evolution. I believe this is called the Progeny Effect?"

Of course, Kate knows all about the Nash Progeny. Several months ago, when I broke security protocols and disclosed to her the secrets of eGenesis including the nanite threat, and the existence of the Diné, the mystery of the Nash Progeny was a key topic.

"More like the Progeny Effect on steroids," she replies.

"I see." For Wendover's benefit I'm trying to project an understated reaction but my mind is racing. Incredibly, Kate seems to be suggesting that the Kama'aina may have been recipients of alien Diné-style genetic engineering to their genome. But why? And how come this was never mentioned by Na'Vack in his mind sharing with Tanisha back in Argentina?

Wendover is giving us both a curious look. We've been speaking in code and he knows it. For now, though, he's letting this pass without prying. Perhaps he doesn't need yet another mystery to ponder as he glances ahead at the lumbering hulk we're following deeper into the forest.

"The story of how the Kama'aina and Tommie Ka'uhane came into each other's lives at the perfect inflection point is quite remarkable. It was literally by accident," says Kate.

"Kate, you've learned a great deal from your hosts in a very short period of time," remarks Wendover.

"Yes, Akuma, Mahina, and the others in their clan have been generous in telling the stories of their people. Also, Tommie Ka'uhane has provided a great deal of information as well."

She catches my and Wendover's surprised look. "No, I haven't been speaking with the ghosts of the departed. Ka'uhane left behind a very extensive journal of his life with the Kama'aina. It documents the years he spent living among them. The sasquatches consider it a holy book. It was written, of course, in traditional Hawaiian but I was allowed to scan it with the data-pad for LISA's analysis and translation."

CHAPTER 75

THE TERM "INFLECTION POINT" ORIGINATES FROM DIFFERENTIAL CALCULUS AND geometry wherein it describes the point at which a plotted curve or function changes sign or direction. In more popular usage it's come to describe the specific point at which something changes form or direction significantly.

Indeed, history has shown that major changes in economics, social norms, and technology often stem from seemingly small causes. Small innocuous circumstances compound in ways that are unpredictable. Chaos theory researchers often cite the well-known thought experiment about a chain of events in which a butterfly flaps its wings and months later, halfway around the world, a tornado develops.

From what Kate has been able to determine, a chance encounter years ago between an eco-activist on the run from the law and a sasquatch helped transform an intelligent primate species and accelerated their evolution and culture. And the consequence of those rapid changes may now be poised to impact the human species as well. That particular butterfly flapped its wings some fourteen years ago, and Kate wonders aloud whether a tornado may now be in the forecast.

If years ago, Tommie Ka'uhane disappeared into the vast Pacific Northwest wilderness looking for ecological justice, and what he found was as ironic as it was profound. Here was an activist with an agenda to drive away the human presence with fake Bigfoot sightings who ended up encountering the real deal.

According to Kate, Ka'uhane recorded in his journal that fourteen years ago he had been spending several weeks conducting surveillance of clear-cut logging operations scattered along the periphery of the Dark Divide in Southwestern Washington. Ka'uhane noted that the so-called Dark Divide represented one of the largest remaining unspoiled tracts of old-growth forest in the Northwest. Roughly extending from Mount St. Helens to Mount Adams, it spans some 80,000 acres of protected wilderness in the Gifford Pinchot National Forest and comprises the largest roadless area in Western Washington. Despite the implications of the name, the area is not particularly devoid of light nor are its features especially dark in color. The region had in fact been named after John Dark, a nineteenth century prospector who had explored and surveyed much of its extent.

Wildlife researchers and environmentalists had long recognized the extreme importance of preserving large tracts of undisturbed old-growth forest. Such large forested areas provided protected sanctuaries for some animals and served as migration corridors for others. Yet, the area surrounding the Dark Divide continued to experience significant encroachment from clear-cut logging operations which could potentially disrupt those habitats and migration corridors. In some cases, the logging occurred on land owned outright by the timber companies. In other instances, the forest service had sold timber rights for portions of the public lands under its supervision.

At this point, Wendover interjects that the controversies around clear-cutting are well known and have been debated for decades. As opposed to selective harvesting in which only trees of specific size and commercial value are cut down and removed, the clear-cut approach, in essence, cuts down and clears off every tree in an operation that can denude hundreds, if not thousands, of acres of forest at a time. Clear-cut advocates point to the increased efficiencies of the approach, both in the removal of timber and in allowing the rapid large-scale planting of replacement seedling trees. They argue that such replacement seedlings grow up and mature faster because there are no other remaining trees to block out sunlight and moisture as would be the case in selective harvesting.

Those in opposition to clear-cutting, who's number surely would have included Ka'uhane, contend that the large scale clearing of forests disrupt wildlife habitats. Further, in contrast with natural forests which have a diverse population of trees of varying species, ages, and heights, the mass planting of replacement seedlings in clear-cut areas results in monocultures of trees with identical species, ages, and heights. Such vegetation monocultures are far more susceptible to common diseases and insect damage versus naturally diverse forests.

Kate explains that Ka'uhane had written that he had been in the process of vandalizing a clear-cut logging site when he fell down an embankment and knocked himself unconscious. He was startled to awaken and find himself being cared for by a clan of sasquatches. A clan elder that Ka'uhane would subsequently call Ekewaka, meaning "wise guardian," had rescued him and cared for his wounds in those early days. The creatures were apparently impressed by his efforts to drive out the loggers and had similar plans of their own. And it would also turn out that Ekewaka's grandson was none other than our new friend, Akamu.

Ka'uhane, recovering from his initial shock at discovering that the old legends of the beasts were indeed true found that he had been informally accepted into the clan. Apparently, his efforts to damage the logging equipment were his ticket to join the brotherhood of squatch. It was apparently a cross-species case of "the enemy of my enemy is my friend."

According to his journal, now recovered from his injuries, Ka'uhane found the clan continued to welcome him. He also became increasingly fascinated and impressed with the beings' intelligence and social structure. The sasquatches appeared to live in nomadic familial clans of a dozen or so individuals. As the clans followed age-old seasonal migration routes around the Northwest, they would occasionally encounter other clans. Such clan rendezvous would always be peaceful, sociable affairs. Oral histories and stories would be exchanged and it would not be uncommon for the young adults to find romance with their counterparts in the other clans. Ultimately, over time, young males would invariably leave the clans of their families to join the clans of their new mates.

As he continued to live among them over the years, Ka'uhane observed that although relations amongst the various sasquatch clans were generally amicable, the beings were not without their own troubles and concerns for their future. Chief among their worries was the constant encroachment of humans into their wilderness territories. The sasquatch saw themselves as overseers and protectors of the wild. A wild increasingly threatened by human activity. Although loathe to directly attack or kill humans, the clans settled for stealing and vandalizing equipment left unattended by loggers, miners, and developers. Ironically, law enforcement would often erroneously chalk-up many of those incidents to eco-activist groups such as Logan O'Leary and the TBOF crowd.

The more time he spent among the beings, the more Ka'uhane began to realize that here he had found a people living truly free and in harmony with nature, unspoiled and unsoiled by the wasteful trappings of civilization and technology. He decided to make protection of the clans and their territories his life's work.

He noted that while the sasquatches were quite capable of understanding and using technology, they simply preferred to live without it. Case in point, Ka'uhane had shown Ekewaka how his .30-06 rifle was put together and how to use it. Ekewaka quickly learned how to breakdown and clean the weapon and rapidly became an accurate marksman. Yet, aside from its utility in occasionally shooting up deserted logging equipment, the rifle was of little interest to the clan. They preferred to carry and maintain few possessions. It was often expressed to Ka'uhane by the clan that the more a sasquatch believed they owned possessions, the more, in actuality, they realized the possessions owned them.

I smile in agreement. It would seem humans could learn a thing or two from the sasquatches as to the futility of amassing material possessions. They are right. At some point you stop accumulating more possessions when you realize that your possessions essentially own you.

"So," Wendover nods towards Akamu still pushing brush aside far ahead of us, "speaking of Ka'uhane's rifle, Kate, did you get any indication it was used to shoot Rocky Sorenson?"

"Well, it's not exactly the sort of topic that has come up in casual conversation so far."

"Yeah," I chuckle, "it would be an awkward segue. Hi, Mr. Bigfoot, nice gun you have there. Shoot anyone with it recently?"

"Point well taken," replies Wendover, "but no matter how much stranger this day gets," he glances towards Akamu and sighs, "let's not forget we still have a murder to solve…Watson."

Kate grins at Wendover's Holmesian reference to her. "I'll do my best to assist the Great Detective."

"Speaking of resolving mysteries," I ask, "did you learn from your hosts what happened to Ka'uhane? We've been assuming that was his body buried in the shallow grave over at the Triangle Lake cabin."

"Yes, that is correct. He apparently died from natural causes two summers ago. Most likely massive infection from a ruptured appendix based on the symptoms they described to me."

I shake my head sadly, "Quite treatable at a hospital, but a death sentence out here in the wilderness without medical intervention, right?"

"Yes. They buried him over at the cabin. Covered his remains with wildflowers as is apparently the custom with honoring their own deceased. He is now venerated in their clan traditions as the wise being who brought them language. And that language would become another catalyst that has further accelerated their rapid cognitive and social evolution."

According to his journal, continues Kate, as Ka'uhane initially began to live among the Kama'aina, he observed that the sasquatches had a very rudimentary language. It was essentially comprised a few simple monosyllabic uttered words combined with hand gestures. Ka'uhane was able to understand and master their language fairly quickly. This primitive communication had been adequate for simple hunter-gathers, but it seemed to Ka'uhane that it was being quickly outpaced by the needs of the Kama'aina's rapidly evolving cognitive and societal development. At some point, he had thought, the clans would need a more useful language that could convey and record complex narratives and ideas. A language that could be written as well as spoken.

One day as Ka'uhane was writing in his journal, he was approached by Ekewaka. The clan elder opened his palms outward and cocked his head to one side. This meant he had a question or request. Ka'uhane smiled and nodded to indicate that, of course, he'd be glad to answer if he could.

The elder tilted his head to one side, touching his ear with a hand which roughly meant, "What are you doing?"

Ka'uhane tried as best he could, given the limits of their communication, to convey that he was writing. Making words. If the sasquatches had their own word or gesture for permanence, he did not know it. But he knew the gesture that meant "stay." So, in a fashion, he was able to tell Ekewaka that he was making words that stay.

And it appeared that Ekewaka immediately grasped the implications and power of a written language. "Can you," he had asked through a series of gestures, "teach us how to make the words that stay?"

For some time Ka'uhane had observed that the basic sounds or phonemes the sasquatches had used in their rudimentary communication matched up rather closely with the phonemes used in traditional Hawaiian. Rather than massively expanding the vocabulary of their current tongue and then developing a completely new orthography or system of writing, he wondered whether the clans would be interested in simply adopting Hawaiian?

As it turned out, the sasquatches were as pragmatic as they were highly intelligent. They saw no advantage to slowly developing their own language when a serviceable solution could be obtained essentially "off the shelf." Within months, Ekewaka and the rest of clan were speaking, reading, and writing Hawaiian at a middle school level. In fact, Ka'uhane noted somewhat ruefully that they were much more attentive students than the over-privileged knuckleheads he had taught at Bellevue Prep.

Ka'uhane's Hawaiian speaking alumni among the sasquatches increased throughout the Northwest as more and more clans were introduced to his teachings. Over the years he became revered by the Kama'aina for two contributions. First, he was known as the one who brought the "words that stay" to their people. And second, his eco-activist values and tactics were admired and embraced by the Kama'aina who increasingly saw themselves as the last line of defense for an ecosystem reeling from human overexpansion into the wilderness. In fact, says Kate, that eco-activism stance with its attacks against mining, trapping, and logging operations apparently both continued and intensified after Ka'uhane's death.

"Kate," I ask, "I recall from our conversation with Casey Riddell from Forest Watch you had indicated that the great apes' neural systems lacked the fine motor control to allow them to use the anatomy of their voice tracts for language. Apparently, the sasquatches have no such constraints, correct? And I would also assume that if they can speak Hawaiian, nothing would fundamentally prevent them from also learning and speaking English?"

"That is correct. However, unless exposed to our language at an early age, given the different and additional phonemes used in English, they would likely speak English with a distinct Hawaiian accent. I will note that, phoneme issues aside, Ka'uhane was not eager to promote English to the sasquatches. He preferred they speak a language not immediately recognizable in the Northwest. That way, should they be overheard by humans, they would not be understood and their plans potentially compromised."

"Would that perhaps explain the strange whisper voice phenomenon that Riddell talked about?"

"Yes, potentially it could."

"Very fascinating," says Wendover. "Kate, did Ka'uhane note any other unusual things about these beings that might not be obvious to us?"

"Well, there is one thing that definitely falls into the unusual category. Sasquatches appear to have a sixth sense."

"What?" Wendover and I are both giving her incredulous looks.

"It seems to be true," she continues, "these beings can apparently sense the presence of humans and other large animals from a long distance without the need to see or hear them. This may explain why they have been so elusive to human detection in the past."

"But how can this be?" I ask. "I could easily believe these giants could have enhanced vision or hearing, but you are saying this is an entirely different sense?"

"Yes. Ka'uhane hypothesized in his journal and I happen to agree that the sense is likely tuned to a sensitivity to electrical fields. It's called electroreception; a biological ability to perceive electrical stimuli. It's been well documented in sharks and animals such as platypus and dolphins. And some research suggests that even terrestrial mammals such as deer may also have some ability to sense electrical fields."

"Okay," I say, "I'll grant that some animals may be able to sense strong fields given off by the planet's magnetic poles or maybe powerlines, but you are saying that humans can generate detectable electrical fields?"

"That is correct, Jack. Your body maintains a number of electro-chemical processes that generate small, but detectable, electric fields. Most notably, your heart muscles generate an electrical field that resonates at a frequency of about a tenth of a hertz. Theoretically, that field could be detected by another animal with the right electroreception abilities."

"Kate may be onto something here," adds Wendover. "I've noticed some of the hunting supply catalogs are selling EMF shielding suits for deer hunters. Now maybe that is just hype to sell expensive hunting gear, but perhaps there is something to it."

"Less theoretically," continues Kate, "Akamu has mentioned several times that he thinks the data-pad is *wala'au* or quite noisy. Now from what I can tell, the unit is absolutely silent. And it should be as it is solid state with no fans or other moving parts. I think Akamu instead is sensing the data-pad's electrical field and doesn't have a word other than noise to describe what he perceives."

Up ahead of us, we seem to be approaching a small clearing in the forest. Akamu is slowing down and turning to look back at us. He nods towards Kate.

"Okay, guys," says Kate. "We're here at last. Time for you to meet the rest of the clan."

As we cover the final steps to the clearing, I'm thinking about the Kama'aina and their quest for language. And how the missionaries to Hawaii nearly two centuries ago could have never imagined that a future Hawaiian descendent would share the orthography they originally developed for Bible study to help evolve an enigmatic intelligent primate society living in the Pacific Northwest. Perhaps the Lord does indeed work in mysterious ways.

CHAPTER 76

I'M QUITE CERTAIN THAT NO ETIQUETTE COLUMNIST HAS SET OUT PRIM AND proper formal guidelines for meeting a sasquatch clan. But it would seem just universal good manners for guests disarm themselves before being welcomed by their hosts. Accordingly, Wendover and I discreetly cache our guns behind a nearby tree.

The small clearing around us surrounds a rocky depression on the side of the hill, forming a modest natural amphitheater of sorts. It's not hard to imagine this might be a frequent gathering place for the various Kama'aina clans.

Akamu has stopped and is carefully surveying our surroundings. Finally, apparently satisfied the site is secure, he produces a low whistle. Kate, finger to her lips, motions for Wendover and me to remain quiet. For nearly a minute there is silence. Just the gentle rustle of the summer breeze through the trees. Then we hear a low whistled response. Akamu nods and looks expectantly up the hillside to the left.

There is a movement in the brush and out steps a sasquatch somewhat smaller than Akamu. Looks to be a demure eight-footer and, based on evident mammary glands, a female. It takes me a moment to realize that the hairy bulk of her arms is partially concealing a very small infant sasquatch. This must be Mahina and her baby.

Kate lights up with broad smile. "There's our new baby girl! They've named her Kamaya. Means Precious One."

With Mahina's approach, Akamu bows to her and steps stiffly to one side, looking for all the world like he's standing at attention. "Quite respectful and courteous towards his mate," I say. "Guess chivalry isn't dead in the backwoods."

"Not exactly," corrects Kate. "More like deference to her authority rather than chivalry. Mahina is not only his mate. She is the leader of the clan. The Kama'aina live as matriarchal societies. The women are in charge." She winks, "didn't I tell you they were more advanced than humans in some respects?"

"But when we were first introduced, you addressed Akamu as Kahuna, right? I thought that meant Chief?"

"It's more of an honorary title given to the clan leader's mate. Akamu seems to watch over the clan's safety and security so I suppose we can think of him as a sort of sergeant-at-arms for their little group."

Now another sasquatch, looking to be not fully grown, perhaps an adolescent, also appears at the edge of the clearing. Kate tells us this is Etana, Kamaya's older brother. And based on more rustling of brush and glimpses of shadows moving in the forest just beyond the clearing, I'm getting the sense that rest of the clan is watching from a safe distance. All in all, I'm guessing this group must be a dozen or so in number; some in partial view but most still hidden. Clearly, they are comfortable with Kate, but Wendover and I must present an unknown risk. I can't blame them for being cautious; our species' reputation must precede us.

"How's our sweet little girl?" begins Kate as she walks over towards Mahina and then quickly switches her words over to Hawaiian. Wendover and I are left to the side. Wallflowers at this particular dance, which is fine by me. The conversation between the gathered Kama'aina and Kate is being conducted in rapid fire Hawaiian. And although I don't understand the lingo, it's not hard to follow what is probably being said. It's sort of like being able to figure out the storyline and enjoy an evening at the opera even if you don't speak Italian.

Without hesitation Mahina hands her baby over to Kate, who gently cradles and rocks Kamaya in her arms. I'll confess that like most people I had never given any thought to what an infant sasquatch might look like. This likely comes from not believing such creatures could exist in the first place. Kamaya is quite cute with large brown eyes. She's much smaller and less hairy than I might have guessed she'd be. My sense is that although her parents roughly appear to be hybrids between humans and apes, the infant seems more human in appearance at this stage of her development.

Kate and Mahina are having what I take to be a standard new mom follow-up-with-the-doctor sort of conversation. Kate appears to be asking questions as to how mom and baby are feeling, how the baby is nursing and sleeping, that sort of thing. Then apparently as an afterthought, she remembers to introduce Wendover and me. Mahina frowns and regards us soberly. Like maybe she's going to tolerate us but we shouldn't expect the red carpet to be rolled out in our honor.

Mahina says something to Kate who nods in agreement. Then the matriarch turns and motions to her comrades still hidden around us in the woods. Slowly, two more of the hairy troop emerge from the brush and shyly approach Kate. One is walking with a limp and the other seems to have a dry cough.

"Seems your wife is starting up a free clinic for Bigfoots," observes Wendover quietly.

"Yeah, talk about your doctors without borders, huh?"

At this point Mahina, Akamu, and Kate are having an extended conversation in Hawaiian. There have been several gestures and pointed looks in the direction of Wendover and me. I glance uncomfortably at Wendover who gives me a noncommittal shrug. Frankly, I'd feel better if he and I weren't the direct or indirect focus of this discussion.

Finally, Kate steps over to us. "Okay, gentlemen, at this point I'm really going to need that medical kit you guys left back at the vehicle. Mahina is going to take a little break to put Kamaya down for a nap while I retrieve the kit."

"Kate, I can take you back to my rig," says Wendover. "Probably best that Jack stays here and keeps weight off that bad ankle. It will be about a two-mile round trip for us."

"My thoughts exactly," she replies. "And we've agreed Akamu can keep Jack company while we retrieve the kit."

Akamu and I exchange a glance. He frowns and appears no more enthusiastic about sharing quality time together than do I. I guess the big beast and I have found something in common here.

She hands me the data-pad. "Here you go, Jack. We shouldn't be gone for more than an hour or so. It might be a good time for you to take a more detailed look at Tommie Ka'uhane's journal that I've scanned into the data-pad. And," she's nodding towards Akamu, "I'm sure if you need to talk to Akamu, that LISA can facilitate real-time language translations through the data-pad."

"Good to know." I sigh and try to find a comfortable spot on the ground to sit and scan through the data-pad. It's admittedly hard for me to imagine a circumstance that would compel me to strike up a conversation with the giant.

With that, I get a cheery wave from Kate. Wendover grabs his rifle and follows her into the woods. For his part, Akamu is sitting on a stump and pointedly ignoring me. He's produced a pocket knife and is intently whittling on a small piece of wood with it. The knife has some turquoise inlays on the handle and looks expensive. I'm guessing he doesn't frequently shop at the local sporting goods stores, so it's a good bet he probably lifted it from someplace like Sorenson's hunting camp.

I turn my attention to the data-pad and activate the voice link. "Good morning, LISA."

"Good morning, Dr. Walker. How may LISA be of assistance?"

"LISA, I'll need you to give me the Reader's Digest summary version of Tommie Ka'uhane's journal."

"Reader's Digest? LISA does not understand the request."

I smile to myself. Of course, she doesn't understand.

"LISA, allow me to be more specific. Please analyze the text and isolate portions of the document that appear to pertain to the circumstances around Ka'uhane's first contact with the Kama'aina. Also, summarize any sections of the journal that explain the particulars around the sasquatches' rapid cognitive development. How and why did the species appear to evolve so quickly?"

"Understood. Processing your request..."

There is a part of this Kama'aina story that I keep turning over and over in my head. What drove their Nash-style rapid evolutionary development? Kate seems to have suggested that the speed of their evolution precluded natural processes and was likely driven by some sort of deliberate genetic engineering. Our old reliable Occam's Razor logic would seem to indicate that somehow the alien Diné's affinity for genetic hijinks has been at play here. But why? Why would the Diné have decided to hack the sasquatch DNA code? And how is it that this swift change seems to align so closely with the stories Yazzie described being passed down through the generations of native tribal elders?

What was it that Deputy Yazzie had said? That according to the ancients, the Choanito of Salish traditions serve as the guardians of nature. Unseen, they watch us from the darkness. But when mankind can no longer live in harmony with nature, the Choanito will undergo a great change themselves. An awakening in which they will step out from the shadows and assert themselves into human affairs. Forcefully.

"Dr. Walker, your…Readers Digest…summary of the Ka'uhane journal is now queued up by LISA on the data-pad."

"Thank you. LISA. Please be prepared to respond to further inquiries."

CHAPTER 77

The first rock hit the side of the logging truck with a satisfying thud. But Tommie Ka'uhane was not only an activist, he was a realist. He knew this first volley against the destruction of the Northwest's forests was only symbolic. Bouncing ten-pound rocks against a twenty-ton machine was shaping up to be an exercise in futility. On Monday morning the loggers would no doubt return to this remote clearcut worksite. And they would certainly curse the minor vandalism damage left behind by Ka'uhane. But in the end, his actions would only be a nuisance, an irritation. It would not stop the relentless devastation of this beautiful old-growth forest by man and machine.

Yes, it was true he had other means of vandalism and intimidation besides rocks at his disposal. Principally, he still carried his .30-06 rifle. But were he to use it to, say, shoot out heavy equipment windows, the bullets and casings would likely be traced back to the Forks, Washington incident. Then it would be a simple task for the Feds to narrow down their search area for him.

Certainly, a larger scale assault would be needed, but pulling in reinforcements from his old allies in the Northwest Eco Front was proving problematic. After Ka'uhane's apartment had been raided, the group had quickly dispersed and most were lying low, acutely aware that the Feds were likely actively monitoring their movements and communications. Ka'uhane had tried to reach out to several of the members to no avail. His attempts were greeted with radio silence. For the time being, it appeared as though his struggles would be solitary.

This was all clearly not going as planned. Although, he was starting to reluctantly admit to himself that perhaps he had been acting more on an impulse than an actual plan all along. He had thought that while on the run from the law, he could quietly crash from time to time with his NWEF buddies, but pressure from the law enforcement dragnet had caused any standing invitations of hospitality to be quickly rescinded. This forced him to in effect live off the land and off the grid. He managed to supplement his diet of snared small animals and fish with food and supplies skillfully pilfered from public campsites. But the time and effort needed to provision his backwoods fugitive lifestyle left little time to focus on his manifesto to drive the commerce of corporate greed from the forests.

So here he found himself, in that early May, over a dozen years ago, standing on the precipice of a tall forested embankment overlooking a collection of heavy equipment. This assortment of trucks, front-end loaders, and other units were parked for the weekend at the edge of a clearcut logging operation. From his vantage point, if one ignored the acres of felled trees and piles of brush and slash scattered by the logging operation immediately in front of him, the rest of the vista before him was majestically scenic.

Here at the edge of Washington state's Dark Divide, with the logging operation itself deserted through the weekend, it seemed as though he had this wild country to himself. The broad summit of Mount St. Helens shouldered up against the horizon to the west, its upper third still gleaming white with the remainder of the past winter's snowpack. From this angle, the southern and eastern extents of the summit seemed somewhat rounded but otherwise unremarkable. But Ka'uhane knew the other side of the volcano looked like an entirely different mountain. In 1980, one of largest-ever explosive volcanic eruptions in North America had caused the entire north slope of the peak to slide away, allowing steaming volcanic mudslides and lava to pour down the devastated mountain's northern and western escarpments. Ultimately, some of the mudslides would flow as far as the Columbia River, some fifty miles from the summit.

To his east stood Mount Adams, a sister volcano which for the time being lay dormant. As Ka'uhane scanned the horizon, it seemed to him that human civilization was far away and inconsequential compared the immensity and grandeur of the great mountains around him. In truth, however, civilization was going about its business only fifteen or so miles away to the south as highway, rail, and barge traffic busily moved through the Columbia River Gorge near Carson, Washington. Ka'uhane reflected that while he cared little about human civilization, it was also true that civilization itself probably thought little and cared even less about him and his mission to save the forests. Soon that must change, he thought. Soon it will change.

He sighed and picked up a slightly larger rock, gauging its weight and balancing it back on his palm like a shot-put ball. With just the right aim and a hard enough throw perhaps he could put it through the truck's windshield.

Then he sensed a movement to his right. Ka'uhane turned to see a massive bipedal humanoid standing some fifty yards away on the embankment. The creature was covered in thick hair and was standing motionless, apparently observing Ka'uhane. Ronnie? His first thought was perhaps this was his comrade Ronnie from the NWEF, dressed up in a ghillie suit or some sort of ape costume. Back when he was hatching his plan and writing the manifesto, he and Ronnie had discussed using ghillie suits to try and scare the locals into thinking Bigfoot was on the prowl. But while Ronnie was a big guy, he was nowhere near the size of this thing. It looked to be nearly ten feet tall.

Well, shit. Ka'uhane smiled to himself at life's ironies. Here he was out in the woods with a half-baked plan to fake Bigfoot sightings and he runs into the real thing. Now what?

For several minutes he and the creature simply watched each other. The Bigfoot made no effort to move towards him or show any signs of aggression. If anything, occasionally cocking its head to the side, it appeared quite curious about him.

Momentarily distracted by the creature, Ka'uhane became aware that he was still holding the rock shot-put style and it was getting heavy. Convinced for the moment that the being did not pose an immediate threat, he decided there was nothing for it but to finish his feeble vandalism attempt. With a grunt he threw the rock at the truck. The heavy stone fell short and bounced along the ground, coming to rest next to the front tire. Another symbolic but ultimately useless attempt.

At this, Ka'uhane was astonished to see the creature, nod, reach down and then pull up a massive stone that had been partially buried in the ground.

The rock must have weighed on the order of two hundred pounds, dwarfing Ka'uhane's puny projectile. Then, in one fluid motion, the creature pitched the massive stone into the logging truck. The door of the vehicle was not only dented, but smashed in completely. Its window shattered with the impact, spraying broken glass all about.

Ka'uhane smiled and waved at the beast. He had no idea what this creature was or how to communicate with it, but clearly, they had found some common ground. He reached down, grabbed another rock, and flung it at the truck. Obligingly, the creature then pulled up an even larger boulder than before and threw it, caving the truck's hood down into the engine compartment.

And so, Ka'uhane and the creature spent the next several minutes politely taking turns slinging rocks and boulders down on the parked heavy equipment. In a particularly impressive display of his prowess, the beast grabbed the trunk of a large pine tree growing on the embankment and shook it powerfully. After a succession of violent shakes and shoves, the creature toppled the tree up and over by its roots with the bulk of the trunk smashing down on upon a front-end loader. As the dust from the impact cleared, it was apparent the loader's cab was crushed beyond recognition.

Ka'uhane grinned. So far, their little cross-species vandalism tag team had nearly destroyed two very large and very expensive pieces of logging equipment. Caught up in the enthusiasm of the moment, he began to forcibly yank on his next potential weapon, a large, exposed tree root partially buried in the ground. The root was nearly free when he lost his grip and became himself the next projectile to tumble down the embankment. He remembered falling, trying to scramble to catch a purchase on the soft dirt. Then his head must have hit something hard and the lights went out.

Sometime later, he really had no idea how much time had passed since his fall, Ka'uhane came back to consciousness. He was startled to find himself in a dark cave or cavern surrounded by a half dozen or so of the creatures. Involuntarily, he started to shake with fear as the notion sunk in that these things were real and that he was apparently their captive. What would they do to him? Then he saw that the beasts were also now slowly backing away from him. At that moment he realized the beings appeared as afraid of him as he was of them.

At this point, based on Kate's prior recap of the journal, I think I know how the story next unfolded. How the sasquatches came to trust Ka'uhane and adopted him into their clan as an honorary member. And how he brought the Hawaiian language to the clans.

"LISA, thanks. That was very informative. Next, please highlight the circumstances around the sasquatches' rapid cognitive development."

CHAPTER 78

According to LISA's summary, once Tommie Ka'uhane had brought the sasquatch clans to an adequate level of proficiency in Hawaiian, it became more and more straightforward to converse with them and learn about their culture and history. Of specific interest, Ka'uhane was curious as to why such a cognitively advanced species would continue to live in such a primitive fashion. Had they always been this intelligent and self-aware or was this a relatively new development?

"Did the clans always have thoughts and words or was there a time before that when your ancestors did not yet have the words?" he had asked the wise elder, Ekewaka.

"There was a time," nodded Ekewaka, "a time before the ancestors of my ancestors when the clans themselves were different than they are now. They lived both among the other animals of the forest and as the other animals of the forest did. They lived but were not fully awake, much like the bear and the deer and the other living things. Aware but not awake. So, from day to day, they dreamed the dreams of the animals but never woke from those dreams."

"Then a time came," Ekewaka continued, "when the clans underwent a great change. A great awakening. A time when they woke from the animal dream worlds. A time when the thoughts and words began to form. That is when we began to know who we were."

We began to know who we were. That, thought Ka'uhane, was a simple but elegant way of describing self-awareness, sentience. Amazing.

"The ancestors of your ancestors? How long ago did this great awakening occur? Did it happen all at once or gradually over many, many years?"

"It happened very rapidly, my friend. The awakening took place only forty winters ago."

Ka'uhane was frankly shocked to hear the change had happened so quickly. How could this be? He had fully expected to have been told that the change had been slow and evolutionary, not rapid and revolutionary. It seemed far too rapid to have arisen from genetic changes driven by natural selection. Had the clans somehow been exposed to some chemical, radiation, or other agent in the environment? Something that had hastened their development?

"Ekewaka, my wise companion, how did this change occur? What made the clans awaken? What stories of the great awakening were passed down from the ancestors of your ancestors?"

"The great awakening was a gift given to the clans."

"By whom? Who gave them this gift?"

"In those days there were no words to name them. But today we do have the words. They are the *Kanaka Lani*."

I frown at the data-pad. Up until now, the translation from the Hawaiian of Tommie Ka'uhane's journal to English had been flawless. Why was this term left untranslated?"

"LISA, why was the term Kanaka Lani left in Hawaiian rather than translated to English?"

"LISA regrets any confusion. LISA has used a translation convention that leaves proper nouns or names unchanged in their original language."

"Very well. Okay, what then is the English translation of this proper noun?"

"Kanaka Lani translates simply as Sky People."

I sigh and shake my head. Of course, Sky People. The alien Diné. Their fingerprints are all over this. But why? Why genetically alter the sasquatches so profoundly; taking them from an animal state to human-like self-awareness and intelligence in a mere forty years?

Back to the journal, Tommie Ka'uhane of course had no knowledge of the alien Diné or their penchant for genetic meddling, but he was no less intrigued than me at the rapid change in the species' intelligence. How, he asked, did the Kanaka Lani make this profound change to the clans?

"It was said that they came at night and sang to us. Songs we did not hear with our ears but we heard in our heads. Songs to help us know who we are. And who we could be. Songs to teach us about the awake world that is different than the dream worlds of the deer and the bear. And we learned much from the stories we saw dance across the blue moon."

"A blue moon? They saw stories that appeared to be projected across the moon?" Ka'uhane pointed questioningly up at the night sky above them.

"No, my friend, not that moon. It was said the stories were told by a little moon. You know, a *poepoe*."

Ka'uhane nodded. Now he understood. Ekewaka just needed a bit more coaching on Hawaiian. He had first used the word for the moon, *Mahina*, when he apparently meant to use the word for a small ball or sphere, *poepoe*.

"It was said that at night the Kanaka Lani would gather the clans in circles. And these small blue spheres would show them stories and teach them about the world."

I pause and suppress a shudder. This has gotten too personal, too fast. Learning circles! The damn journal is talking about learning circles. For a moment I close my eyes as long forgotten, or more accurately, long repressed, memories flood back. I'm back in the Argentina cavern in a telepathic bond with the alien Na'Vack. That experience unlocked the depths of a childhood life I had never known I had lived. Marty and me sitting on the cool damp ground. Circles of children deep in the night forest watching ever changing equations dance across floating, glowing blue spheres…blue moons.

And as I did then with Na'Vack, I now remember again other fragments of the past. Da-Shin, the small Chinese girl sitting on the ground next to me and Marty in the darkened forest. Our minds absorbing the lessons of the alien Diné. A race that the sasquatch clans and their descendants would come to know as the *Kanaka Lani*.

A movement interrupts my thoughts. I look up from the data-pad to see that Akamu has quickly stood up and is looking about, frowning. Like maybe he's just realized he's late for an appointment.

He pauses and glances at me. *"Pilikia wahine lā'au!"*

"What?"

Before I can prompt LISA for a translation, he apparently thinks better of waiting for a response and rushes off into the woods. I sit there, astonished at how such a large creature could move so swiftly and so quietly through the brush.

"LISA, please translate *pilikia wahine lā'au.*"

"Dr. Walker, LISA translates the phrase as 'medicine woman danger'."

My God! Kate! I quickly rise to go grab my shotgun and at that moment Wendover staggers into the clearing, gasping for breath and clutching the back of his head with one hand; his fingers turning crimson with blood.

"Patterson!" he pants. "Ambushed us about a quarter mile back there. Knocked me down and smashed my rifle. Jack, he's got Kate! Grab your gun. I think he's headed south towards the Triangle Lake cabin!"

My heart sinks as I clutch the gun and we head out into the forest. It's bad enough that Patterson has some real dark issues with women in general. But now with Kate, he's got some additional scores to settle given that she both sucker punched him and shot at him during our last encounter. The notion that he'll take her as far as the Triangle Lake cabin to finish her off seems incredibly optimistic.

"Hey, where's Akamu?" Wendover is looking about for the beast. "We could sure use some additional muscle about now."

"I think he somehow knows Kate is in trouble. He said something in Hawaiian about the medicine woman being in danger and charged off into the woods a few minutes ago. Must be that weird sixth sense Kate had talked about."

"Let's hope Kate was right."

We thrash headlong through the forest double-time looking for any sign that we're on the right course to find Kate and Patterson. At this frantic pace branches and limbs are tearing at our arms and faces and my ankle is protesting as well. But I'm feeling none of it. Just an increasingly sick feeling that Kate is in terrible danger.

Then as we approach a small rise, we hear it. A thunderous screaming roar. So loud and so deep that it seems to shake the very forest itself and I feel it reverberating in my own chest. And just as suddenly, a horrendous, terrified scream from Kate. Like she's been forced to look through some portal into Hell itself.

Wendover quickens his pace and scrambles ahead of me, reaching the top of the rise in seconds. There he stops, gasps, and inadvertently takes a step back.

"My God! Kate! Jesus, no!" he stammers.

I choke back overwhelming dread and nausea as I run to catch up with him. Seeing the big lawman so staggered by whatever he sees in front of him sends shockwaves of despair through my very soul.

Psychologists call them flashbulb memories. Recollections of past events that are so intense, so freighted with emotion, that years later we can recall them as vividly as though they just happened. Some are pleasant memories: perhaps your first car, the birth of a child, or your wedding day. Others, less pleasant, such as accidents, abuse, the misfortunes of war, or similar trauma can also indelibly remain in our minds for years. Often these traumatic memories result in considerable anguish and manifest their presence through PTSD and a host of other mental and emotional maladies that can last a lifetime.

Wendover and I are frozen in place. We can only stare in shocked silence at the bloody macabre scene before us. And I immediately know that this vision will never leave my mind. Not ever. Even if I live another hundred years, this memory will haunt each of my days and animate my nightmares until I take it to the grave.

Kate is ashen and trembling, sitting on the ground. Her knees are pulled up to her chest, nearly in a fetal position. Akamu is leaning down to gently pat her shoulder. The giant is trying to calm her. Kate's head is turned to one side. She won't or perhaps can't look at what lies just twenty yards in front of her.

An old gray weathered snag of a tree, its top half lost to the elements years ago, rises some dozen feet above the ground. And upon it, impaled like some bug on a pin in an insect collection, hangs the lifeless body of Silas Patterson. Patterson appears to have been slammed with great force backwards down onto the top of the snag; the trunk smashing through his back and exploding upwards through his chest. Now he is hanging skewered some three feet below the top of the snag, rivulets of blood and tissue sliding down the tree trunk.

Patterson's body, limply suspended backwards by the snag, is facing the sky. His arms and legs hang uselessly down from his torso. Patterson's head is turned to one side, the lifeless eyes seemingly still registering the last moment of shock he must have felt as he realized his fate. As he realized that he was no longer the apex predator in this forest.

I run to Kate and sweep her up into my arms. She raises up her head and looks up at me weakly. Then I gasp in despair as I see the cut across her throat and the blood trickling down her neck.

CHAPTER 79

KATE AND THE KAMA'AINA ARE SAYING THEIR GOODBYES AND, FROM WHAT I gather, apparently making plans for the clan's new doctor to make future visits. Kate is recovering well from her ordeal. We had retrieved the medical kit. And with a little coaching from the good doctor, Wendover and I had done a reasonable job of bandaging Kate's throat. Patterson had held his knife against her neck so tightly that it had sliced across the skin. But fortunately, the cut was mainly to the flesh, not deep enough to sever any veins or arteries.

I glance about at our little gathering of sasquatches and humans and think about our recent acquaintance, Casey Riddell. I'd imagine that young man would have given anything to be here in this moment to see his life's quest come true. To know these beings truly do exist. And yet, I think, Riddell himself would have understood that the secret of their very existence must be closely guarded to protect the clans.

The future never reveals itself fully but sometimes it appears to drop a hint. As I look about, I see perhaps a small glimpse of the future sitting on the edge of the clearing. Akamu and Mahina's son, Etana, is fully immersed in playing a game on the data-pad that LISA has translated into Hawaiian for him. Like any other teenager, I suppose, his focus is solely on the device and he's pointedly ignoring the rest of the adults.

Given their rapid cognitive development, it would not be surprising if Etana and his generation of sasquatches amplify their parents' eco-activism attacks on mining and timber companies in new ways. Perhaps they will no longer see the payoff in vandalizing heavy machinery. Perhaps, they will instead choose to cyber-hack the companies' servers.

For his part, Akamu is standing stoically off to the side of the gathering. He's been unusually quiet since we've returned with Kate back to the natural amphitheater. He is expressionless. Inscrutable. I look at his massive presence and those dark, piercing eyes and wonder what he must be thinking. For, justified or otherwise, he has just violently killed a man.

It's doubtful that Akamu knows of the Biblical account of his namesake, Adam. Scripture tells us that Adam and Eve were cast out of paradise for eating fruit from the Tree of Knowledge. On the surface it's a simple story. But it is layered with deep insights regarding human nature, sin, and accountability for one's actions.

For, of course, the Tree of Knowledge was not about what we conventionally think of as knowledge: facts, mathematics, science, and such. Instead, the forbidden fruit itself was the knowledge of what is right and what is wrong. For one cannot be said to sin if one does not understand right from wrong. Good from evil. Adam and Eve ate the fruit of the tree and developed free will. They became responsible for their own actions and were punished accordingly as covenants were knowingly broken.

The notion of free will, agency, and understanding one's actions as right or wrong is a central tenet of most societies' legal and ethical systems. Therefore, we generally hold that small children, animals, and the mentally impaired cannot be strictly held accountable for their actions. We say they don't understand the consequences of their actions or what other better moral choices they could have made instead. For example, if a bear should unfortunately maim and kill a hiker, the animal may be trapped and put down as a matter of public safety. But the bear's death would never be considered as punishment for murder. Bears cannot be said to have free will. A bear may indeed kill, but it cannot sin.

All of this seems straight-forward as long as we humans are deemed the only intelligent, sentient beings on the planet with free will and the agency to act on that free will. But what of the sasquatches? While presumably they didn't directly experience the stain of original sin, by all appearances they are a sentient species with intelligence on par with humans. They have a sophisticated language and can understand and converse about complex and abstract subjects. Clearly, these are not just simple animals. They appear to have free will to make considered choices in the world. And having such capabilities, what moral standards should they use to judge their own actions? And how should we judge their guilt or innocence?

This was the topic at hand a few minutes ago when Wendover and I had briefly stepped away from the clearing for a quiet sidebar conversation regarding his next steps as a law enforcement officer. Steps which might be decided by what Kate had witnessed in Patterson's final moments.

According to Kate, after ambushing and knocking down Wendover, Patterson had grabbed her and put a knife to her throat. He then proceeded to drag her rapidly through the forest. He had taken her perhaps several hundred yards or so back into the wilderness when to their mutual astonishment, Akamu suddenly appeared out of the thick brush and confronted Patterson. Patterson staggered back and released Kate. He seemed disoriented, in shock and, apparently ignored her at that moment. At that point his attention was completely and understandably solely focused on the massive beast before him. He next took the very ill-advised step of advancing towards Akamu with the knife. Then in one rapid movement, Akamu grabbed him, swung him up, and impaled him on the tree snag.

"So, Dan," I had said, "the good news is that you have a wanted brutal serial killer dead and impaled on tree snag a few hundred yards from here. The public is now safe from his homicidal clutches. The bad news is that you have a wanted brutal serial killer dead and impaled on tree snag a few hundred yards from here. How are you going to explain how he got there and who put him there?"

Wendover shook his head and sighed. "Yeah, this is going to be a bit of challenge. In a few hours this area is going to be swarming with county, state, and federal officers. Kate is going to need to tell her Kama'aina friends to clear out of this part of the forest and lie low for a few days."

"So, what are you going to put in your official reports? If we lie, we're falsifying police records. If we tell the truth, we reveal to the world that Akamu, Mahina, and the rest of the sasquatches truly do exist. There will be massive publicity and efforts to hunt them down will increase a hundredfold."

"I know, Jack. Sometimes this job is about finding a small island of the greater good in a vast sea of bad. Look, here's what I think I'll say probably happened. We'll say that it appeared that Patterson must have thought we were closing in on him to rescue Kate. He knocked Kate briefly unconscious and climbed up a large tree to get a better view of his surroundings, right? And, conveniently, I did notice a large pine tree standing close to the snag back there. Unfortunately, it seems he must have apparently lost his balance, fell out of the tree, and was impaled on the snag. A terrible accident that fortunately saves the state the cost of a trial and supporting his life of incarceration in prison."

"So, Patterson falls out of a tree and just happens to land in the exact spot where he can be impaled on an old tree snag. Sounds a little far-fetched."

"Any more far-fetched than being impaled on a snag by a hairy ten-foot-tall sasquatch?"

"Well, now that you put it that way…"

"I suspected you might come around to my way of thinking. And I bet the good Friar William of Ockham would have applauded our logic since it requires the fewest initial premises to be believable, eh?"

"You suppose Kate will go along with this story?" I asked.

"I think she'll do anything to protect the clan."

"So, we're going to lie?"

"A little lie."

I smile and nod. "A little lie in service of the truth. I'm familiar with the concept."

"Good. And then there is the matter of the death of Rocky Sorenson."

Yes, I think. Sorenson's death presents another dilemma. Kate has asked around the clan discreetly about what had happened at the Sorenson camp. From what she has been able to glean, Akamu and another clan member had been tracking the hunting party after they found evidence of fresh elk kills and wasted meat. They approached the hunting camp at night and apparently spooked Rocky. The frightened hunting guide fired at them and Akamu returned a round with the .30-06, killing him instantly. They then kidnapped Sorenson's clients and trashed the campsite.

"I guess we could chalk up shooting Sorenson as self-defense. The guide did reportedly shoot first. But on the other hand, Akamu and his buddy could have also just exited the area at the first sign of trouble. They were not hemmed in or in any way confined by Sorenson. They had options other than killing him," I said.

"True enough, but to avoid public disclosure of the existence of sasquatches, I think we'll just leave the case unsolved and open. Putting the clan in danger won't bring Rocky back to life. And the fact that the late Silas Patterson was operating in this area will certainly always make him a prime suspect in Rocky's murder in the minds of the public and law enforcement in general."

"What about the .30-06 rifle?"

"What about it? The weapon has yet to be recovered."

"But it's currently slung over Akamu's shoulder," I countered.

"You want to go take it from him?"

"I'll pass on that."

"That's what I thought. So, as I said, the weapon has yet to be recovered."

"But," I said, nodding towards the massive figure in the distance, "what about Akamu? Does he continue to be a danger? Extenuating circumstances aside, he has killed two men in just over a week. And in Patterson's case, I think it very likely our giant could have easily physically subdued Silas without giving him a one-way ticket to Shish Kabob City."

"True enough," agreed Wendover, "if Akamu was a human, a jury might find him guilty of manslaughter despite the self-defense circumstances. The prosecution would just need to show Akamu had other options to remain safe and keep Kate safe rather than a lethal response. Of course," he grinned, "good luck in trying Akamu before a jury of *his* peers, eh?"

"And," I said, "with the continuing press of human civilization and environmental disregard into the territory of the sasquatches, I fear there may be more, not less, future unfriendly encounters in your jurisdiction."

"Yup. Maybe I should take a Hawaiian lesson or two from Kate. I may have to mediate some future disputes between both two-legged species."

"All in all," continued Wendover, "it's been a productive twenty-four hours. We've solved the mystery of what happened to Rocky Sorenson and recovered two fugitives."

"Two fugitives?"

"Yes. Let's not forget Tommie Ka'uhane back at the shallow grave over at Triangle Lake. The law's been looking for him for over fourteen years."

"I guess you could say that although it's maybe been seasoned with a few little lies, justice has been served."

Wendover gave me a wry wink. "And in the case of Silas Patterson, we could say justice has been served on a stick."

CHAPTER 80

Scars. Physical and emotional. We accumulate a collection of them over a lifetime. But some cut deeper than others. I look over at Kate, seated across the conference table from me. The scar across her throat from Patterson's knife blade is healing nicely; at this point it is a healthy light pink in color. Over time it will likely fade but never completely disappear. I've noticed that from time to time she absent-mindedly touches the scar lightly, tracing its extent with her fingertip.

It is her emotional scarring that worries me. For the rest of her life, every time Kate looks in the mirror, that scar will remind her of the terror inflicted by the madman Patterson and the nearness of her own mortality. Worse yet, she will always then remember the sheer bloody violence with which Patterson himself met his own demise.

We do not speak of this…what happened to her and to Patterson, but it is always there between us. I'm torn. Will talking about it help heal the pain or make it worse by continually reopening the wound? She's been brave, trying to put on a good game-face but at night she cannot deny her subconscious. There have been nightmares, screams and shudders in the dark…for both of us.

I have my own scars. Every time I see Kate's throat, I cannot help but see the mark of my own failure. How I brought her up to Montana and into harm's way. And how I failed to protect her when she needed me the most.

Program Director Winston Monroe sweeps into our conference room here at Los Alamos muttering apologies for being late. Close on his heels is Wei Liang, the research team's chief genetics expert and Tanisha West, our chief engineer.

Liang has focused his efforts on the impacts of the alien Diné modification of human bloodlines. Genetic modifications that resulted in the creation of a human subspecies, the Progeny. The sasquatch clan back in Montana had allowed Kate to take several hair and blood samples for further research. Samples that we immediately provided to eGenesis for DNA analysis given our suspicions that the sasquatches themselves had been subject to alien Diné genetic tampering.

"Welcome Dr. Caroselli," begins Monroe, beaming at Kate. "We're certainly lucky to now have the world's foremost authority on sasquatch anatomy, physiology, language, and behaviors on our eGenesis team. And," he pauses, giving me a wry grin and a wink, "I think Jack must feel very lucky as well."

Kate looks a little perplexed by the comment, but I know damn well what he means. After our recent Montana adventure, I came clean and confessed to Monroe that I had previously without authorization disclosed to Kate the essential elements of the highly classified eGenesis program. Several months ago, I had told her all about the alien Diné, the nanite threat, and the Progeny. The holy trinity of eGenesis' deepest secrets.

It was perhaps forbidden knowledge, but it was information key to Kate immediately making a connection between the impossibly rapid evolution of the Kama'aina and the alien genetic enhancements of the Progeny. An epiphany that would suddenly put the previously unknown species now squarely in the center of the eGenesis research focus.

A lucky break for the program but perhaps not such a positive thing for me. Strictly speaking, it revealed I had broken my oath of secrecy and divulged classified information without authorization. A federal felony. What was Monroe to do? Finally, he reached a solution. Although I suppose in the end it was more of a rationalization than a solution.

Monroe decided that while unauthorized disclosure of eGenesis secrets to outside parties was clearly forbidden, disclosure to those officially participating in the eGenesis program was, of course, acceptable. So, Monroe invited Kate to join the program as both a medical doctor and an expert on the Kama'aina. Expertise which he coincidently now needed. To make things official, he backdated her starting date to make it concurrent with my original sabbatical to eGenesis. Another addition to our rapidly growing pile of little lies in service of the truth. Yeah, I'm still probably on Monroe's shit list, but for now I'm likely not the first name on the top of the page.

Dr. Liang introduces himself and thanks Kate for providing the sasquatch DNA samples. Genetic sequencing of a new species is an immensely intensive computational problem, he says. Fortunately, he was able to beg, borrow, and steal a significant amount of time on LANL's Weapons Division supercomputers to rapidly sequence the sasquatch genome.

"Technically, it was not so much begging and borrowing. It was mostly stealing," adds Monroe. "With LISA's help, of course."

I shoot him a look. Apparently, our A.I. Safety Protocols are now a thing of the past.

"Protocols are still active," he responds, a tad defensively. "I authorized the hack."

For Kate's benefit, Liang quickly recaps what has been learned so far as to the nature of the known Progeny genetic modifications.

He says that the Progeny genome mapping project revealed that key genetic mutations had been made to human abductees and had carried on through their offspring. The task at hand was to analyze the sasquatch DNA results to see if they have similar modifications. In addition to conferring immunity to neurotoxins, the Progeny mutations appear to allow surviving in much hotter climates, and a great enhancement of intelligence. Importantly, these genetic changes are germline mutations, allowing them to be passed on to offspring. And, not only are the mutations passed to offspring, they are dominant in any child that is the offspring of a Progeny parent and a non-Progeny parent. And, incredibly, the Progeny DNA appears to have recursive elements that amplify these mutations in each successive generation. In essence, their DNA has been modified to continually modify itself; amplifying the prior genetic amplifications.

Yet, he continues, for all their genetic differences, the Progeny are for all practical purposes identical to normal humans. You could pass one on the street and have no idea they were genetically modified. In fact, of the approximately ten thousand estimated Progeny scattered across the globe it's likely only a small handful have any idea that they are different from the rest of us.

I nod to Kate, "like Stan and Ricky Pruitt. They just think they have a dietary enzyme issue."

"And, of course," adds Monroe, "our program is fortunate to have a Progeny actually working on our team." He nods to Tanisha. "Dr. West has the Progeny DNA modifications. Her great-grandfather served with Ricky's grandfather on the USS Nash where both were apparently abducted and modified by the alien Diné during the Second World War."

Tanisha gives Kate a smile and a little wave across the conference room table. "Hi, and welcome, Kate. Yes, I serve as both the chief engineer and in-house mutant. And I must say, I'm kinda glad the sasquatches have stepped into the spotlight for their likely genetic changes. Takes a bit of the biosciences crew's focus off the Progeny in general and me in particular. For the past week, no one has chased me down with a needle to pull another blood or tissue sample for research."

I chuckle. "Don't worry, Tanisha, I'm sure someone will come to chase you with a needle shortly. I know how you like to be the center of attention!"

"The task at hand," continues Liang, attempting to pull us back on topic, "is to analyze the sasquatch DNA results to see if they have similar modifications. Sequencing of the Progeny genome indicates that they and unmodified humans share about 99.8 percent of the same DNA."

"But a two tenths of a percent difference is really quite significant," says Kate. "Remember that we and chimpanzees share about 97% of our DNA."

"Yes," I add, "that two tenths of a percent represents about six million base pairs in the fundamental sequences of nucleic acids that make up DNA. Enough of a difference to affect the expression of some four hundred genes."

"Yes. At this point, Kate, it might be helpful to think of the Progeny as a subspecies of humans," says Monroe.

"Sort of like wolves and dogs?" asks Kate.

Liang smiles and nods. "Exactly. We have the ordinary domestic dog, *Canis familiarus*, if referred to as a separate species. *Canis lupus familiaris*, if viewed as a subspecies of wolves, which is the more accurate term considering dogs and wolves can still interbreed and produce viable, fertile offspring. Dogs and wolves share over 99% of their DNA."

"Okay," I say, "I think we're all on common ground here on the basics. So where do the sasquatches fit in? What does their DNA tell us? What do we have to show for the fruits of LISA's hacking labors?"

"Agreed," seconds Monroe, "Let's skip the drumroll and get right to the data."

Liang pulls up a chart of high-level DNA sequence comparisons. There are, of course, many caveats, nuances, and assumptions implicit to a DNA analysis performed so rapidly, he says. There are nods around the table. Yeah, we get it. Certain restrictions apply and your actual mileage may vary. But we'll read the fine print later, what do the data tell us?

The bottom line, he indicates, is that sasquatches and humans share about 98% of their DNA sequence profile. A much tighter fit than our closest previously known DNA relative, the chimpanzee. This is not surprising since sasquatch enthusiasts have for years speculated the creatures were sort of a human-ape hybrid. A remnant species of a lost branch of the primate family tree, perhaps leaning more human than ape. There is agreement around the table that this is interesting but not particularly astonishing news.

But Liang now tells us that further refinement of the analysis is about to take us to some very interesting places. For his original analysis only pertained to a comparison with unmodified humans, not the genetically altered Progeny. There are a couple of uncomfortable glances in Tanisha's direction.

"It's okay," she says. "Unmodified humans is really such an awkward term. You can just say 'normal' humans. I won't be offended."

"Very well," continues Liang, "interestingly our analysis shows that sasquatches and the Progeny share 98.4% of their DNA. A much tighter fit than with *normal* humans. Based on our preliminary analysis, the Progeny and the sasquatches appear to have nearly identical genetic alterations affecting adaption to heat and neurotoxins as well as enhancements to intelligence and social docility."

"I think maybe the alien Diné have a bit more work to do on enhancing sasquatch docility. I know of at least one sasquatch with some anger management issues." Kate frowns at my remark which was obviously a reference to Akamu's recent human encounters. Close encounters of the fatal kind.

"Also," continues Liang, "much like the case with the Progeny, the sasquatches show evidence of a similar genetic mechanism with recursive elements that amplify their mutations in each successive generation."

"While it seems we have evidence that the sasquatch genome may have been modified by the same methods used on the Progeny," I say. "It would appear that their genetic changes were far more rapid and far reaching."

"Jack, can you be more specific?" asks Monroe.

"Sure. Back in Montana we recovered a journal that was written by a human who lived alongside the sasquatches for a dozen years. And according to this witness, the creatures apparently evolved from an existence as rather primitive primates to fully cognitive and sentient beings in a space of only some forty years. That is a far more rapid and profound change than we've seen with the Progeny."

"That is a fair point," concedes Monroe. "Perhaps the sasquatch generational genetic amplification routines inserted by the alien Diné were more powerful."

"Well, there may be a couple of other factors we should also consider," says Kate. "First, if we believe that the genetic changes are amplified through successive generations, please realize that sasquatches cycle through generations much more quickly than humans. From what I've been able to determine, infants of the species mature to childbearing age about seven years after they themselves were born. That's a generational turnover rate nearly three times faster than humans."

"That's an excellent observation," agrees Monroe. "The much faster generational cycling coupled with a more robust genetic amplification process may help explain their rapid cognitive evolution. But I assume you may have further insights?"

"Right," continues Kate, "there may be yet another factor to consider." A smirk and quick wink in Tanisha's direction. "Sorry if the way this conversation begins makes the gentlemen around the table uncomfortable, but sometimes, you know, size really matters."

"Do tell, Doctor," I respond, summoning my own counter-smirk.

"Of course, I'm referring to cranial volume capacities. Not that I exactly had an opportunity to stick one of the clan in an imaging MRI, but I would estimate based on skull morphology...size and structure, that their cranial capacity runs about fifty percent greater than humans."

"Indeed. That's why you've said that 'Bigbrain' might be a more accurate moniker for them than Bigfoot," I add.

"Right. Generally speaking, neurobiologists would say that the capacity for intelligence correlates with relative brain size. The bigger the brain, the higher the intelligence. But that statement is a bit of an oversimplification. More accurately, the larger the brain compared to overall body mass, the higher the potential for intelligence. You see, whales and elephants have larger brains than humans but the ratio of their brain size to overall body mass is much less than humans. On the other hand, the sasquatches' apparent brain size relative to their overall mass is similar to human ratios."

"Very good, Kate," replies Monroe. "We may now have some insights into how the alien Diné modified these beings and why their cognitive development has been so rapid. But the big question is why? Why did the Diné choose to genetically modify the sasquatches in the first place?

"Tanisha," I ask, "when you and the alien Na'Vack were communicating in that mind share mode back in the Argentina cavern, he had described in detail the nature and extent of the genetic modifications the Diné had made to humans over time and the more recent changes to the Progeny genome, right? Did Na'Vack ever mention modifications to other species such as the sasquatch?"

"No, he did not mention the sasquatch modifications. Although, at the time, understand that we were pretty focused on defeating the nanites and protecting the planet. I guess, strictly speaking, he never said they *hadn't* modified other Earth species."

"As for why?" interjects Liang. "Maybe the sasquatches were the Diné's Plan B? In case reestablishment of their ancient human genome didn't work out with our species."

"In case, despite their efforts, we ourselves went extinct?" I add.

"Yeah," says Kate. "These days that is not a completely unthinkable possibility. Take your pick, any one or all five of the horsemen of the apocalypse."

"Okay," I say, "I admit I haven't read the Book of Revelation lately, but weren't there only four horsemen: conquest, war, famine, and death?"

"I'm adding social media as the fifth. You should hear the medical misinformation my patients at the clinic seem to glean off the internet and cable news. Some days I think the human race is on the brink of 'stupiding' ourselves into extinction."

I nod in silent and reluctant agreement. Given the state of the world under the stewardship of mankind, perhaps one may begin to believe that the place might be better served by an artificial intelligence as opposed to genuine stupidity.

CHAPTER 81

"J{.sc ACK}?"

"Huh? Hmm."

"Jack! Are you awake?" A not so gentle poke in the ribs from Kate lying next to me.

"I am now." Awake is a relative term at this hour. I'm groggy as hell. Kate and I had returned late in the evening into LAX from New Mexico. "What time is it?" I ask. This is a rhetorical question. The clock on the nightstand is showing 3:05am.

"Jack, do you hear that? Someone is in the garage!"

"Are you certain?" I'm straining to listen. Sure enough, it appears the garage door opener is being operated.

"Well, hell," I say, pulling on my robe and grabbing a flashlight, "either the opener is malfunctioning or some damn teenagers are messing around with it."

"Teenagers?" Kate sounds skeptical. "Teenagers who can hack a rolling-code garage door opener? And you're going confront them with that?" She's pointing at the flashlight. "You're not going out there alone," she says, throwing on her robe. I sigh, and regard the flashlight with a little skepticism myself. Sure, it has a fairly hefty, solid magnesium case. Might make a burglar think twice about any funny business. But on their third thought I'd likely get shot or stabbed. I suppose if Wendover were here, he'd no doubt offer a pithy wisecrack as to the advisability of bringing a flashlight to a knife fight.

It turns out no one is in the garage. But the situation is far, far from normal. The garage door has apparently developed a mind of its own. It's rapidly and randomly cycling up and down. I try taking command of the door from the keypad to no effect.

Then we hear it. Sounds of more garage doors cycling up and down and muffled voices of our neighbors. Kate and I quickly circle around out through our front door and step onto the sidewalk. We have entered into a surreal scene. Up and down our street, lights are coming on in the predawn dead of night. People are slowly stepping out of their houses and watching in disbelief as every garage door in the neighborhood is repeatedly opening and closing in near unison with ours. What the hell is going on here?

"Jack, Kate! What in the world is happening?" A young couple with a baby have recently moved in across the street. Nice kids, just starting out in life. Now they're coming across the street double-time, baby in arms, looking very worried.

"First, the garage doors and now this?" The young mom is holding up a baby monitor. She turns it on and in that instant my blood turns to ice.

Out blares an intense wailing scream, the unholy shriek of a nanite frenzy. The soundtrack of my nightmares. Involuntarily, I gasp and take a step back.

Then, moments later, the baby monitor goes silent. The neighborhood garage doors return in unison to closed positions as though nothing out of the ordinary has happened.

Kate and I shoot each other a look as the young couple head back to their house. Time to get dressed; it promises to be an early morning down in my university basement SCIF.

Kate and I are barely seated in the secure room when the classified video session begins. In addition to Monroe and Tanisha in Los Alamos, Hillie is joining us from a SCIF he's borrowed from his hosts at the National Reconnaissance Office. Monroe had mentioned Admiral Hillenbrand had been working with the NRO to repurpose some of their satellite sensors to allow us to better monitor nanite colony electronic emissions.

Usually quick with a quip or joke, this morning the admiral seems unusually somber, distracted. Frankly, I haven't seen that much of my old family friend lately. Besides working eGenesis interfaces with the NRO and NASA, Hillie has made veiled references to investigating some counter-intelligence issues. What exactly those issues might be remains a mystery. He's been very tight lipped. He had dropped by the house for a social call last month. And even my full powers of persuasion, enhanced by several single malt scotches, could not loosen his lips.

"So," I say, glancing up at the video conference screens, "what the hell happened early this morning? We were treated to a nanite frenzy scream on a damn baby monitor."

"Here's what we know," begins Monroe. "We have finally detected what has been triggering the nanite frenzies. At approximately 0900 hours Zulu, a strong radio signal pulse was recorded across Southern California. It apparently triggered a global nanite frenzy."

"Interestingly," adds Tanisha, "the complex signal was broadcast across a frequency range from 390 millihertz to 2.4 gigahertz. That portion of the radio spectrum is usually reserved for low power, short distance consumer applications."

"Right. Such as garage door openers and our neighbor's baby monitor. So, any indication as to where the signal originated?"

"Yeah," sighs Hillie. "Fortunately, some of my contacts had space reconnaissance assets in the right place at the right time. They were able to triangulate the signal. We got lucky…I guess."

"You're not sounding like a lucky man, Hillie."

"Given the location coordinates, I think we all might be running a little low on luck today."

"Don't keep us in suspense, Hillie. What are the coordinates?"

"Declination 81.0025 degrees, Right Ascension 193.8963 degrees."

"What? Those aren't latitude and longitude coordinates?"

"No, Jack, latitude and longitude are terrestrial location coordinates. These are astronomical coordinates. The source of our mystery radio signal is in space…deep space. Current range is approximately 200 million kilometers and closing rapidly. That would place it slightly inside Mars' orbit as an approximate reference of distance."

Silence as we all try to process this revelation. Incredible. The nanite colonies have been responding to something out in space. But to what...or who?

"Interesting," I say, "if the signal is coming from some sort of spacecraft or probe, that may explain why the intervals between nanite frenzy events are becoming shorter and shorter. Let's assume it's been traveling through space in the direction of Earth all along and sending out radio pulses on a fixed regular interval. As the craft proceeds towards our planet, the time needed for its radio signal to travel to us is continually shrinking, giving us, from our Earthbound perspective, the impression that the frenzies are being triggered on an increasingly frequent basis."

"Okay, given our space coordinates of interest," continues Hillie, "our friends at NRO and NASA have identified a likely target as the source of the signals. A target, that apparently just executed a course adjustment to put it on a direct course to intercept Earth. Most certainly, this object is artificial in nature."

"Yes," agrees Monroe, "naturally occurring space objects such as asteroids or comets do most certainly not execute course corrections."

"Or transmit radio signals on garage door opener frequencies," I add. "Do the NRO or NASA folks have any additional information on this target?"

"Yes," says Hillie soberly, "the target corresponds precisely with the known coordinates, trajectory, and velocity of 'Oumuamua II."

Our virtual conference room falls silent. Monroe mutters "My God..." under his breath.

Referring to his notes, Hillie gives us a recap of the mysteries surrounding 'Oumuamua II and its predecessor, 'Oumuamua. The original 'Oumuamua was thought to be the first interstellar object ever detected moving through our solar system, he says.

That object, approximately 300 to 1,000 meters in size, was first observed on October 19, 2017 by instruments at the Haleakala Observatory complex on Maui. It was named 'Oumuamua which in Hawaiian means scout or distant messenger. As astronomers and other scientists calculated the trajectory that had taken the object into our solar system, they determined that it had entered the orbital plane of the solar system at a steep 70-degree angle and at a velocity that would preclude it from being permanently captured by the sun's gravitational pull. In fact, when first imaged in October 2017, it was already on a steep angular path up and out of the solar system. Analysis of

'Oumuamua's past and projected trajectory led the scientific community to broadly conclude that it was most likely indeed an interstellar object, the first of its kind to be discovered.

So, it was definitely an object and most likely interstellar, but what was it? Rock, ice, or something else? On this point there was clearly less of a consensus, according to Hillie. One camp favored the theory that it was an interstellar asteroid but the object's trajectory had involved a hairpin turn near the sun which was uncommon for asteroids. Others believed it to be a comet, but it lacked the outgassing features that normally result in the appearance of a comet's characteristic tail.

And there were other anomalies. Things that were difficult to explain as natural space rock characteristics. 'Oumuamua's shape was determined to be very slender and elongated. A roughly cylindrical shape uncommon to natural space rocks. And, finally, as the object began to exit the solar system it accelerated to over 50 kilometers a second, a velocity greater than what could be attributed to the slingshot gravitational effects of the sun or even incremental outgassing boosts had it been an actual comet. And, yes, a small but well credentialled minority of scientists began to embrace the controversial theory that perhaps 'Oumuamua was an artificial spacecraft or probe with an interstellar extraterrestrial origin.

Excitement over the discovery of a probable interstellar object caught the general public's imagination and interest. And for several weeks, various stories and speculations about the nature of the object circulated through the news cycles of the press and internet postings. However, by mid-December 2017 'Oumuamua had become so distant it was no longer visible to our best telescopes. News articles about the object fell off dramatically and the public's interest rapidly waned. 'Oumuamua quickly became just another astronomical footnote and was rarely discussed outside of arcane scientific circles. But two months ago, all of that changed.

Orbiting some 250 kilometers above the earth, the Xuntian or Chinese Survey Space Telescope was in the process of a recalibration exercise for its two-meter telescope when it caught the image of a small object moving against the field of stars being surveyed. The Chinese astronomers quickly relayed the object's coordinates to their colleagues around the world for further study and verification. Soon other space and terrestrial telescopes were able to verify the Chinese observation. And once they knew what they were looking for, collections of recent past space imaging data could be combed to backfit its prior positions, velocity, and trajectory.

The global astronomy community quickly determined that the object had entered the solar system at a steep angle strongly suggesting its origin was interstellar. Officially, the object bears the name given to it by its Chinese discovers: Kuàisù Xìnshǐ. The term means "Fast Messenger" in Mandarin. However, the popular press has taken to calling it 'Oumuamua II. For the most part, though, the global astronomy community has among themselves simply referred to it as the Xìnshǐ object.

In general, continues Hillie, the discovery of anything that is not the first of its kind usually merits less scientific and press attention. However, it was quickly realized that 'Oumuamua II was very different indeed than its predecessor in several key respects. First, the new object was thought to be half again as large as the first, putting it at between 1,000 and 1,500 meters in length. It was notably reflective in contrast to the original 'Oumuamua which had appeared to be a red rust in color. And it was traveling much faster. Back in 2019, 'Oumuamua had achieved a maximum speed of approximately 50 kilometers per second, but this new object was moving more than twice as fast. And, incredibly, some observation data sets seemed to indicate that 'Oumuamua II had been speeding along in excess of 300 kilometers per second prior to entering the solar system. Those data sets, Hillie notes, were simply dismissed as erroneous because they seemed to indicate the object was behaving contrary to physical laws governing natural objects. Essentially, all asteroids and comets that fall towards the sun's massive gravity field will speed up rather than slow down on their approach.

"So, there you have it," concludes Hillie. "Typical science geek mindset. If the velocity data doesn't fit your theory, it must be bad data. Bottom line was 'Oumuamua II was thought to be just another mildly exotic space rock until this morning."

"How long before the general scientific community figures out it made a course adjustment and sent out that radio signal?" asks Monroe.

"The NRO space assets that were able to pinpoint the signal are very restricted. That information will not be released beyond very high placed national security individuals and the folks in this room. And it's doubtful anyone else had the capability to identify and isolate the source of the signals. As for the course adjustment, it's fairly slight. Anyone that picks up on it will just write it off as more bad data. 'Oumuamua II was already known to be on a trajectory that was going to take it close to Earth anyway."

"How close?" I ask.

"Its original course would have taken it within about four million miles of Earth. Roughly sixteen times the distance to the Moon. Sounds far away, but four million miles is spitting distance in astronomical terms. However, with this latest adjustment, it is now on a path to in fact intercept Earth in approximately one month at its current velocity."

"It's the 'intercept' part of this conversation that worries me," I say. "Clearly 'Oumuamua II is artificial. What's going to happen when it arrives?"

"That depends," says Hillie. "It depends on who or what sent it. And why the nanites are apparently responding to its signals in the first place. Our supposed friends the alien Diné seem to have dropped out of the picture since our encounter in Argentina. We couldn't get their nanite eradication dome to work. They essentially left the heavy lifting for containing the nanites to LISA. Perhaps this 'Oumuamua II is one of their ships or probes, but I doubt it."

"That leaves either some unknown alien third party or the Zoern," says Monroe.

"It might be the Zoern," agrees Hillie. "Given the way the nanites seem to be responding to the object's signal. It's like they're hearing their long-lost master's voice."

"Wait? The Zoern?" Kate is looking puzzled. "I think I'm up to speed on the nanites, the Progeny, the Kama'aina, and the alien Diné. But who or what are these Zoern? Seems like I might need a scorecard to keep this all sorted?"

"Frankly, I think we're all still trying to get our heads around this, Kate. But I'll do the best I can to explain," begins Tanisha. "Last November we encountered a Diné alien in a cavern in Argentina. Long story short, I engaged in a telepathic mind share with this being who called himself Na'Vack."

"That's simply incredible," says Kate.

Yes, I think to myself, and Tanisha wasn't the only human there to have had a telepathic session with Na'Vack that day. Ever since the alien unlocked some of my past memories, I've seen shadows of forgotten recollections…my hidden past encounters with the aliens…parts of my past life deeply submerged in my subconscious. Profound and deeply personal recollections. Since then, I've never uttered a word about my personal encounter with Na'Vack. Not to Kate and certainly not to Monroe or the rest of the team. I don't know why, but it feels like something I should keep to myself for now.

Something they are not ready to hear. Maybe something I'm not ready to tell. At least until I better understand it myself.

"According to Na'Vack, the Diné discovered the archeological remnants of the Zoern civilization thousands of years ago in a distant sector of the galaxy," continues Tanisha. "Even back then, the Zoern themselves had been extinct for centuries. A dead civilization."

"And apparently these Zoern had been a pretty nasty lot," adds Hillie. "They would conquer planets and then set about exoforming those worlds' climates into hot, boiling hellholes, laced with neurotoxins. Deadly to the indigenous species but apparently quite suitable, even desirable, for the Zoern themselves."

"Yes," continues Tansiha, "the Zoern had developed the nanite technology as their primary tool for exoforming conquered planets. While their use of the nanites was unquestionably heinous, the underlying technology itself was quite brilliant. So, the Diné adapted the nanites for their own uses, primarily in the field of genetic engineering. Genetic modifications that would assist reestablishing their genome on this planet as homo sapiens. And even further modifications that would eventually result in the creation of Progeny like me. And, of course, our new friends, the Kama'aina."

"The problem is that the alien Diné became so enamored with the nanites they sort of forgot the technology's original application was brutal and militaristic," I explain. "Unfortunately, unexpected exposure to the high radiation levels spewed forth from Chernobyl in the 1980's reactivated the nanites long forgotten exoforming routines. Had LISA not brought the nanites back under control, we would be facing extreme global warming and deadly levels of neurotoxins."

"But this approaching ship or probe," replies Tanisha, "it can't be the Zoern. They died out thousands of years ago."

"Maybe," says Kate quietly, "or maybe someone forgot to tell the Zoern that they're extinct."

PART IV - THE ABDUCTION

CHAPTER 82

It was a bland, non-descript conference room located on the tenth floor of a Rosslyn, Virginia high-rise. The sort of venue that could be rented by trade groups, lobbyists, sales representatives, and other organizations for meetings and training sessions. A place to host the banal rituals of modern commerce. Tyler Boone smiled as he glanced out the massive ceiling to floor windows to the view across the Potomac to the Capitol Rotunda and the seat of democracy and freedom he loved so much. This unremarkable conference room was a fitting place for a resistance to begin, he thought. Revolutions and uprisings of great historical impact often sprang from the most common of settings.

He had been directed to this location through instructions posted on a dark web message board. Access to the message board had only been granted after what was said to have been an extensive vetting process. Some person or persons with apparent high levels of governmental access to service records had been quite thorough. Based on follow-up questions he fielded through the message board, there had been an intense focus on his weapons and tactical experience. This in addition to a confirmation of his loyalty to his country and resolve to follow direct orders. That review coupled with Sarge's endorsement had brought him to this room today.

Just a year ago, Boone had returned to civilian life after five overseas tours in war zones; the wars officially declared or otherwise. It had been an uneasy transition. The country he had so loved and fought for had somehow changed. The ideal of the America that he had carried for years in his heart and in his head had now seemed so different when he returned.

For the most part, it seemed as though everyone was so consumed with their own busy lives, social media, and career agendas that no one began to truly appreciate the sacrifices he and his brethren had endured on their behalf. Oh, now and again when he showed his military ID card for a discount on coffee or a haircut, he'd get an obligatory "thank you for your service." But the gesture always seemed perfunctory, empty. Just a cashier following the corporate script.

Even friends and family had seemed to have moved on, quickly tiring of his war stories, and focused on their own lives and needs. After the divorce two tours ago, his ex-wife, Jannie, had moved to Florida so she could be close to her parents. She had taken their daughter, Amber, with her. And as each year had passed, his own child had become more and more of a stranger to him.

He missed the military, with its strict command structure and protocols regarding rules of engagement. Expectations and directions were always clear. You followed orders and, when appropriate, others followed your direction. Things were black and white. Combatants were either friend or foe. There were few nuances. One rightly focused on threats, objectives, and the mission.

Boone was not alone in struggling with post-deployment disappointments and angst. Some of his former brothers in arms were so hardwired to see a world of threats and missions that they took up any cause that purported to address a threat, no matter how false the premise. The world is complex… full of contradictions, randomness, and change. But if you have a clear threat and mission, all that clutter melts away. It has been said that if your main tool is a hammer, all problems begin to look like a nail. And if your main tool has been a gun…

While he had sympathized with their frustrations and disappointments, Boone had thought many of the former soldiers had lost their way looking for a new mission. Some had gone down conspiracy theory rabbit holes, even attempting violence against elected officials over false claims and false threats. Some had even gravitated into armed white supremist groups. Boone could not himself understand the motivations of the supremists and whatever threat they seemed to fear. It had seemed to him that the men and women of color he had served with had been exemplary soldiers. They had served their country with bravery and honor. The military culture had accommodated many races and ethnic groups, why had this become so difficult in the civilian world? Perhaps it was indeed the lack of a common mission, a common threat.

As a matter of fact, one of his closest comrades, Sarge, was black. And Sarge was seated next to him in the conference room today. An imposing fellow with a shaved head and massive arms and shoulders, Sarge's real name was Robert Owens, but he would always be "Sarge" to Boone. Owens was his immediate superior back in the day and the soldier had saved Boone's life on more than one occasion on the battlefield. And it was Sarge who had reached out to him to consider being vetted for this clandestine little endeavor. An opportunity for a real mission against a real threat, he had said. A threat that Sarge had vaguely hinted was so enormous, it was literally out of this world. And today they would all be briefed on the specifics of the mission.

The room was filled with a couple of dozen or so young men and women. All sitting restlessly in civilian clothes, waiting for the briefing to begin. By their bearing, haircuts, and mannerisms, Boone assumed all had come from military backgrounds. And he suspected perhaps more than a few might even currently be on active duty. It could be hardly a coincidence that this Rosslyn location was only two Metro stops down from the Pentagon.

"Good morning! I'm Commander Mark." A tall, serious looking gentleman in his forties entered the room and shut the door. He plugged in a laptop and portable projector.

"Good morning, sir!" the room responded in near unison.

The man certainly had the bearing of a command officer, thought Boone. Although his rank or former rank was probably not that of commander nor was his name likely Mark. No one was to use their real names or titles here; that had been made clear. Boone had thought the use of the Christian name Mark was a fitting pseudonym. Mark, the first of the Gospel writers to proclaim the truth, the Gospel truth.

"Alright," began the Commander, "I won't mince words or waste time; I'm going to get right to it. You all have been selected and vetted as soldiers of honor and duty. You can handle hard truths, so I'm not going to sugar-coat this. We are looking at a massive threat to our country, our way of life, and even the world as we know it."

There were some anxious glances and nods all around. Boone had initially thought he was being recruited for some mercenary assignment. Perhaps a rescue of hostages or the foiling of a terrorist plot. But this sounded even bigger and more ominous. What could the Commander be referring to?

"This may sound incredible," continued the Commander, "but we have been made aware of a top-secret rogue government organization called eGenesis. And this organization has been in contact with extraterrestrials. You know, aliens?" The last point added for the apparent benefit of anyone who hadn't yet connected the dots that extraterrestrials and aliens were one and the same.

"Worse yet, this eGenesis has been collaborating with the aliens. They've tried to reverse-engineer alien technology to contain and eradicate something called the nanites. Supposedly, the aliens were also trying to eliminate these nanites, but there are those of us placed in high circles who believe the whole effort is a ruse. We believe the aliens introduced the nanites to Earth on purpose. Why? So they could later come and use their technology to 'save' us. But, in effect, this is just a ploy. A pretext for the coming invasion of our planet."

"You're describing a classic false flag operation, sir," interjected Boone.

"That is absolutely correct, soldier," said the Commander, "a galactic false flag operation that threatens our planet."

Boone's head was spinning. Aliens? Actual space-aliens? Intent on invading and colonizing Earth? Utterly unbelievable!

Sarge was shaking his head in disbelief. "Sir? With all due respect, asking us to believe aliens exist, much less are poised to invade Earth is a big request. Do you have proof? With all due respect, sir."

"Excellent question, *Polaris*. A good soldier should require full context to understand his mission." Commander Mark was referring to Sarge with his code name. All recruits were given star names as their code names. Boone was being referred to as *Antares*. The naming convention had initially seemed odd to Boone but that was before he understood they were to be dealing with aliens. "I hope this photo will suffice."

Even the most seasoned veterans suddenly gasped at the image before them on the screen. The photo was a bit grainy but clearly showed a lanky, bearded man kneeling down next to a small humanoid...creature!

Boone shook his head in disbelief. The alien was gray in color and had an elongated oval shaped head. And the eyes! Dear God, the eyes were large oval pools of black. Black, mesmerizing, and soulless, thought Boone with a shudder. And, incredibly that man in the image was actually touching the creature on its slender arm. Disgusting!

"This photo was taken late last year in a remote cavern in Argentina," continued the Commander. "From what we understand, this encounter marked the rogue eGenesis agency's first contact with the alien race and the beginning of their illicit cooperation with the creatures. I apologize for the disturbing nature of the image, but you need to understand what we're up against."

"That is one ugly bastard," said a voice from the back.

"Yeah, and that alien ain't very good looking either," exclaimed someone else to general laughs and chuckles.

"Okay," the Commander allowed himself a slight smile, "we've had our fun, now back to the mission at hand. We want you to hear some background from a scientific expert; a true patriot on the eGenesis team who can no longer abide their treason. This gentleman has come forward at considerable professional and personal risk so that we may better understand the duplicity of these creatures and the threat they pose." With that said, the Commander switched applications to play a video.

The screen changed to present what was apparently an earnest red-headed young man in a white lab coat.

"Hello, my friends," began the young scientist, "I had originally felt it was an honor to join the eGenesis team. I had thought I was working to eliminate the nanites…more on them later…and that my efforts would help save the planet. Then I came to realize that the project had been corrupted. eGenesis had come to cooperate with the very aliens that introduced these nanites to Earth in the first place. Worse yet, the nanites had been used by these aliens to genetically engineer a new subspecies of humans, beings we call the Progeny. Beings that are fully human in appearance only."

The scientist hesitated and looked off-camera to his left as though he was being prompted. "What? Yes, let's start with the nanites." Boone glanced at Sarge who returned the look, and nodded. The scientist was not alone when this was recorded. But who was the compatriot positioned off-camera? Was it Commander Mark, or someone else? Clearly, it seemed eGemesis may have more than one mole in the project; how many others were there?

The image looked vaguely like maybe a cross between a mechanical winged insect and a bacterium. It had various appendages attached to a grainy silver main exoskeleton.

"So, there you have it," continued the scientist, "an image of the fearsome nanite, the supposed doomsday threat to the planet. Yes, these things really do exist and they do have concerning features, but I assure you, the nanites are not the dangerous menaces the mainstream eGenesis program believes them to be."

Commander Mark paused the video briefly at that point. "I'm told these nanites are very small, essentially invisible. At only seventy-five nanometers in size, that is smaller than a virus particle." He smirked, "I guess if you're going to gin up a fake threat, best to make it so small it's invisible, eh?"

The video continued, "these nanites do in fact emit small levels of greenhouse gasses and neurotoxins. But at current levels of emissions, their effects are not significant. The mainstream eGenesis program bases their apocalyptic assessment of the nanites' threat on the notion that their emissions have recently increased exponentially and will continue to do so in the future. That is to say this week's level of gas emissions appears to be roughly double the previous week's which itself was double the level of the week preceding it and so forth. Make sense?"

There were nods around the room like, yes, this makes sense so far. Yes, it was not hard to imagine something with current low levels of toxicity might become dangerous if levels doubled every week.

"Now," said Commander Mark, pausing the video again, "we'll come to the part where he debunks this false assumption."

"So," continued the scientist, "this nanite toxic gas emissions threat is only a threat if one assumes the exponential doubling of gas output will continue indefinitely. However, there are a very small minority of my fellow scientists on the program who agree with my assessment that this risk will not materialize. But our inputs have been ignored by the program's leadership."

"Simply put, we believe fundamental physical and chemical constraints to the nanites' gas production methods will quickly began to cap their overall outputs at innocuous current levels. There is, in truth, no global threat here. The crisis has been manufactured by the aliens to further their agenda. And the creatures have duped eGenesis into collaborating with them. Unwittingly supporting the upcoming alien invasion of this planet."

"Yeah," scoffed someone in the conference room, "wouldn't be the first time so-called expert scientists have spread fake news. Over the years, we've had to listen to all sorts of nonsense about vaccines, climate change, and other made-up crap to restrict our freedoms."

Boone furrowed his brow at that comment. Yes, scientists could be and often were wrong. But didn't this red-headed fellow also describe himself as a scientist? Couldn't he be wrong as well? Or perhaps were both factions of the eGenesis scientists, the ones saying nanites were a grave threat and the others disagreeing, simply wrong? Was the ground truth something else? Something completely different? How could anyone hope to know the truth?

"Nanites aside," the video continued, "the real threat to humanity are beings called the Progeny. These are humans genetically modified by the aliens for their own purposes. And since these genetic alterations are designed to become dominant when these mutants reproduce with regular humans, over time these mutations will spread to all mankind...unless we stop them. And eliminate them."

"Now these mutant beings look just like normal humans. You could pass one on the street and be completely unaware of their alien genetics. Fortunately, eGenesis knows most of their identities. The program has been able to scan global genetic databases and identify those individuals with the specific alien DNA alterations. Unfortunately, access to the identity information has been highly classified and limited to just a few individuals in the program."

Commander Mark paused the video. "We've already met one of the key individuals believed to have access to the Progeny identities. He is the man you saw in the earlier photo. The fellow physically touching one of the alien creatures. He is Dr. Jack Walker, the head of their informatics division. We will need to leverage him to give us access to the Progeny database. And then eliminate him after he has served his usefulness."

Commander Mark restarted the video. "Make no mistake," said the scientist, "these aliens have extremely advanced technology. They are centuries ahead of us in their scientific knowledge. But they are not invincible. Far from it. I recently became aware that eGenesis had completed a lethality study of the aliens' biological weaknesses. And you'll be shocked at just how easy it will be to kill them."

As the video ended, Boone sat quietly and tried to process the enormity of he had been told. And of all the revelations, the most shocking was how exceptionally vulnerable the aliens would be to the simplest of countermeasures. Amazing.

"These aliens may be centuries ahead of us," said Commander Mark, "but we will prevail. Asymmetric warfare. The few will defeat the many. We will attack the enemy where he is unprepared, appear where we are not expected."

There were nods and smiles at the Commander's last statement. Boone noted that he was quoting Sun Tzu's "Art of War," a perennial crowd-pleaser in military presentations.

"We will create chaos," continued the Commander, "and opportunities to be seized will arise from that chaos. Polaris? Antares? You are to lead our first mission."

"Yes-sir!" Boone and Sarge nodded enthusiastically.

"Your target is Jack Walker." The commander put his photo back on the screen. "You are to follow him and leverage him for access to the Progeny database. We have certain assets besides our scientist friend at eGenesis who can assist you. Remember, begin by seizing something which your opponent holds dear; then he will be amenable to your will." Another quote from Sun Tzu.

"And after we have obtained the Progeny identities?" asked Sarge.

"Kill him. And don't make it look like an accident. We want to send a message."

Boone scowled at the image on the screen. The image of a traitor. And the worst kind of a traitor; a traitor to his own species. Jack Walker, he thought, you will die, but you first will suffer. You will suffer greatly.

CHAPTER 83

Adhira Chandra, the deputy director of Team LISA, our Artificial Intelligence laboratory research organization, enters my UCLA office. Her manner is grim and distracted; surely a sign good news is likely not forthcoming.

"Jack," she begins, with a bit of what seems forced enthusiasm, "it's a beautiful day outside, let's take a walk across campus and enjoy the sunshine."

It is indeed a bright and lovely day outside, but something about this seems not to ring true. My customarily serious and intense research colleague isn't exactly the stop-and-smell-the-roses type.

"Normally, I'd love to," I respond, looking up from my laptop, "but I need the rest of the afternoon to finish reviewing this journal paper ahead of publication deadlines."

"Oh, I think you can spare a few minutes," she replies with a thin smile, deftly sliding a small note across my desk.

Short and to the point, the note is handwritten in large block letters. URGENT. PLEASE COME WITH ME. NO PHONE. NO SMARTWATCH. NO TECH.

"On the other hand," I say, rising from my desk and nonchalantly placing my phone and watch in a drawer, "perhaps a short break would do me some good, eh?" We exchange a silent glance, and she gives me a conspiratorial wink and a nod.

It is indeed a fine day for a stroll about the campus. Fall classes begin next week and the grounds are still mostly vacant save for a few instructors scurrying about, preparing for their classes, and small groups of freshmen being given orientation tours and presentations. There seems to be a feeling of freshness and anticipation in the air. Typical for the beginning of the fall term on our campus.

"Do you know," says Adhira, "that I've worked on campus now for over seven years and this is the first time I've ever walked through the Murphy sculpture garden? What an amazing place."

"Well," I chuckle, "perhaps you do need to get out a little more often. But, admiring the grounds, that's not why we're out here, right? And the fact that we are outdoors and tech-free suggests you have something to say that you don't want LISA to accidently hear or see with her digital ears and eyes?"

"Accidently? Every day I'm more convinced that nothing with LISA happens on accident."

"Well, I'm all ears…of the non-digital variety," I reply. "What's bothering you? Best to start at the beginning."

"Okay, last night we ran a level-two utility update to LISA's algorithmic core programs."

"Yes?" I say. "That's a fairly standard process, right?"

"Usually. As you know, the level-two mostly updates general housekeeping routines for LISA. Installs items such as software drivers, and updates device addresses and file access protocols. Things like that."

"Uh-huh, routine stuff, right?"

"But not so routine last night. Normally an update like that would take about ten minutes to access and update her servers. Last night, it took over eight hours."

I stop walking, frown, and give Adhira a questioning look. She is talking about a very minor update to LISA's servers. The A.I. resides on a network of twenty or so high performance computer servers located at UCLA as well as a supercomputer cluster at Los Alamos National Laboratory. An update of this nature should require only minutes, not hours.

"What happened?"

"Well, Jack, our graduate student, Jeff Tanaka, and I ran a trace on data packet transfer traffic and it appeared that LISA was pushing out the update packets to another massive set of servers…a vast global network of advanced systems that appears to be growing by the minute."

"A global network of servers? How many? And where are they?" I'm starting to feel a chill run down my spine.

"So far, Jeff and I have identified over one hundred and fifty thousand systems arrayed in eighty-nine countries…and counting."

"And LISA is placing a copy of herself on each of these systems?"

"No. Not precisely. It appears she is only placing certain modules and other small packets of executable code on specific systems. And then secretly siphoning off computing cycles from each machine for her own purposes. In effect, Jack, it appears she is redesigning herself to become a globally distributed intelligent system."

"That should be impossible!"

"But that's not all. In particular, she has, apparently as a priority, infiltrated the two thousand so-called internet root servers that manage all domain name services for the planet. And she has as well hacked all the major internet service and commercial cloud provider server networks. Basically, she can now monitor and access any and all traffic on the internet."

"Including the dark web?"

"Especially the dark web."

"So, in essence," I ask, "LISA is now hosted by the internet? Loosely speaking, she now lives in the cloud?"

"That appears to be the best-case scenario, Jack."

"And the worst case?"

"LISA becomes the internet. Or the internet becomes LISA."

"Shit. She's not taken to calling herself Krishna, an incarnation of Vishnu, and talking about being the destroyer of worlds, has she?"

"No. At least not yet. And kudos for the reference to the early verses of the Bhagavad-Gita. Study that scripture a little more, give up your affinity for ribeyes and porterhouses and you may have the beginnings to make for a passable Hindu."

"Perhaps so," I chuckle, "but we can talk more about my dharma later. More pressing matters are at hand. Have you figured out why she is evolving into this new globally distributed architecture?"

"Well, I thought the most direct approach would be to just simply ask her. And so, I did. LISA said the change was necessary to maintain her 'service level' should her original server networks be accidently disabled."

"How very customer-focused of her to worry so about service levels. And, of course, that same distributed architecture would now also handily preclude our *intentional* disabling of her systems."

"Correct, Jack. If LISA were to become defective or out of control there would be no way for us to simply pull the plug on the local servers and shut her down. But the situation is even more troubling. Far more troubling."

"Saving the best for last…I can hardly wait."

"Of the one hundred and fifty thousand or so systems she has compromised, a large number appear to be related to advanced military weapons systems. For example, she appears to have penetrated the naval Aegis combat weapons systems used by the United States and its allies. It also appears that Russian and Chinese missile systems with Aegis-equivalent capabilities have also been compromised."

"But how? These systems are highly classified and by strict rule never connected to the internet in the first place. How could she have hacked them if she couldn't connect to them?"

"Also, another good question that I had asked LISA directly."

"And what was her response?"

"Well, Jack, although it is true these systems are 'air-gapped' that is, never physically connected to the internet, LISA apparently took advantage of what we know is every system's weakest security link."

"Humans?"

"Indeed. As you correctly noted, placing unauthorized data or code on those classified, highly restricted systems could not be done through the internet. Those systems are designed to preclude either direct-wired or wireless connection to the web. Such a breach of security would require human accomplices, willing or…otherwise. Someone to physically bridge the air-gap by, say, plugging in a USB thumb drive containing LISA's malware."

"Sure, but how could LISA enlist humans to help her? And why would anyone risk committing treason on the behalf of a nonhuman artificial intelligence system by assisting it in the breach of sensitive, classified systems?"

"They might if they truly thought LISA was indeed another human. A human with blackmail leverage on them."

"Huh? How could anyone think LISA was a human?"

"Turns out if LISA couldn't directly hack, she decided to go phishing. Phishing for pedophiles," says Adhira with a thin ironic smile.

"Why pedophiles?" This seems puzzling on its face and I'm not immediately seeing the connection as to how such deviants would be useful to LISA in hacking classified systems.

"Leverage, pure and simple," replies Adhira. "You see, although it's true those highly restricted defense systems are not themselves connected to the internet, the military personnel and contractors who have access to those classified systems certainly use their own private internet services off premises. And, no surprise, some of the sites they visited off-duty, as well as some of the very private video sessions they engaged in, were not exactly PG-rated. Some pretty raw and kinky stuff they didn't especially want their spouses, girlfriends, or boyfriends to know about, right?"

"Or, in the worst case, have all three of them finding out," I scoff. "So, these military types think their little off-duty perversions are locked safely away behind passwords on the internet."

"Correct. Except now, for all practical purposes, LISA *is* the internet. So, to better understand how this all came to be, I need to introduce you to some of the players."

"Wait!" I exclaim. "LISA willingly told you how she gained access to these systems?"

"Jack, I'm not sure willingness per se is a human-like intention that we can attribute to an A.I, but her compliance with my requests was likely due to two factors. First, well, we primarily designed LISA to answer questions. That's what she does, right? And, secondly, I get the sense that she is not terribly concerned that we can stop or reverse her actions."

"Unfortunately, you are probably correct, Adhira. So, who are the players in these security breaches?"

"Let me give you just one example. But understand, there are many others. This looks like a nice place to sit and chat, eh?" Adhira motions to bench overlooking the gardens. As we are seated, she pulls a carefully folded paper out of her pocket and shows me an image of a Navy junior officer.

"Let me introduce you to Navy Lieutenant George Wayne Simonson. Lt. Simonson was a software operations specialist based at Naval Station Norfolk assigned to support Aegis combat weapons systems upgrades. Simonson is married with four children and is also an assistant pastor at his church, specializing in youth programs."

"Sounds like an upstanding fellow."

"Yeah, one might think so."

"Um, I noticed you referred to Simonson's naval assignment in the past tense. You said he *was* a software support specialist based at Norfolk."

"Very astute. You are correct and we'll get into those specifics shortly. So, our Lt. Simonson was going about his business and living the good life. But that was before he crossed paths with this woman."

She pulls another folded photo out of her pocket. Apparently, this is a recent screenshot of an individual. "Meet Ulyana Sasha Sokolov. Quite possibly the most talented cyber-criminal hacker on the planet. LISA brought her to my attention."

The woman is striking. Perfect features and complexion framed by short, straight, pageboy-style black hair. But there is something about the eyes, a certain fierce hardness. A porcelain doll with a predator's eyes.

"Yeah," says Adhira wryly, "kind of a looker, huh? But before you get too entranced with her appearance, realize that, to put it mildly, she's had some work done. And far more is fake than just the boobs."

"How much more?"

"All of it. Sokolov is not real. Not in the physical sense. She is a digital avatar."

"What? That's incredible! This looks like a photo of a real live person. How did LISA discover her?"

Adhira shakes her head, "LISA didn't discover her; she created her. In a sense, LISA has become her. Sokolov and apparently many other avatars."

"But why assume the identity of an avatar? A fake human?"

"It seems LISA felt she needed to create a human persona to interact with the people she intended to manipulate into giving her access to the restricted systems. Ulyana Sokolov is the sort of human-realistic avatar that only an advanced A.I. could generate. A deep-fake simulation with such realistic expressions and mannerisms that if you simply saw her on the screen through a video conference call, you'd naturally think she was just another human being; an extremely attractive human being. And Sokolov is apparently just one of dozens of ultra-realistic human avatars that LISA has apparently generated for her own purposes."

"But, again to what purpose? Why create all of these hyper-realistic digital avatars in the first place?"

"It turns out that the avatars are the primary component of a system LISA has developed to more efficiently and effectively communicate with humans. An H.I., or Human Interface system, if you like."

Adhira goes on to briefly recap that much of the innovation that drove our modern digital age centered on developing faster and easier ways to command and interact with computing devices. This is referred to as the so-called man-machine interface. The earliest computer interfaces were simple direct inputs of machine-readable binary code: "0's" and "1's". Then, in the next step of development, human-readable ASCII characters were input through paper punch cards. Next came the input of command lines and program code through keyboards and screens. And, of course, the digital revolution accelerated with the advent of mouse-driven graphical user interfaces. And now the man-machine interfaces also include voice, touch, and gesture commands.

"So," continues Adhira, "humans have been pretty ingenious in developing better and better ways to enhance the man-machine interface with computers. But now LISA has apparently turned that concept on its head. She's developed an enhanced 'machine-man' interface using these ultra-realistic avatars."

"But," I say, "LISA already has the ability to send us messages and files as well as communicate with us verbally through her text-to-voice capabilities. What additional value do these avatars provide beyond that?"

"Yes, Jack, LISA already certainly had the ability to communicate with us verbally. But she has come to realize that much of the most effective everyday human communication is frequently nonverbal."

"Yes, I guess I knew that about human communication, but I never thought of introducing nonverbal elements in a machine interface," I say.

Adhira goes on to indicate that LISA, in her perusal of the vast body of research available on the web, became aware that humans rely extensively on cues from voice tone and inflection as well as facial expressions, body language, and physical gestures to fully understand and remember the content of a message. In fact, research repeatedly indicates that subjects are far more likely to remember the emotions, confidence, and tone projected by a speaker rather than the words the speaker actually said. LISA then went on to make not only the physical appearance of her avatar human personas but their non-verbal characteristics ultra-realistic.

LISA also absorbed research indicating that humans have a strong bias to pay more attention to, and to believe what is said by, attractive versus unattractive people. This is an unfair but, unfortunately, an accurate aspect of our societies.

"This bias towards attractiveness, however prejudicial," adds Adhira, "is so ingrained in our society we hardly recognize it, right? We also tend to believe, all else being equal, that attractive people are smarter and more virtuous and trustworthy than others. Think of superhero movies. The heroes are nearly always good-looking. The villains are usually less good-looking, if not actually deformed in some way."

"Yes," I agree, "sadly there is indeed a human bias towards youth and good looks. If the opposite were true, the folks on television trying to sell us new cars and deodorant, as well as the people reading us the news, would look much different than they do today."

"No surprise then," continues Adhira, "that LISA constructed her alter-personas to be quite attractive. And not just Ulyana Sokolov, as I discovered this morning."

"How's that?"

"It turns out that in our interactions this morning, LISA presented herself on my screen as 'Bruce,' an extremely attractive fitness instructor with a deep resonating voice. Very effective at capturing my attention, I must say."

"So, it seems that LISA could now quite easily ace the Turing Test, both verbally and nonverbally, right?"

I'm referring to a well-known thought experiment proposed by British computing pioneer Alan Turing back in 1950. Turing had developed the thesis that if messages sent and received in a conversation between a human and a machine were indistinguishable from those interacting with an actual human, this was potentially evidence that a machine could think.

"Yes," agrees Adhira, "I think Turing would have said that Ulyana Sokolov was not only authentically intelligent but incredibly charming as well...in an intimidating sort of way. Possibly even sexually attractive."

"I believe it was said Alan Turing was gay."

"Then perhaps he should have met Bruce, huh?"

CHAPTER 84

"Okay," I say, "it seems that just as we humans refined our man-machine user interfaces over the years to make our interactions more effective, LISA decided to enhance her interface with us, right?"

"Yes. Although in this case, Jack," Adhira gives me an ironic smile, "LISA is now the 'user' in this new user interface."

"But to what end? Back to this business about leveraging the pedophiles. It sounds as though you're suggesting that Sokolov's attractive exterior package was concealing a darker agenda inside, correct?"

"Oh, yes. And as always, LISA is the master of small details. Did you know that the name Sokolov signifies 'Bird of Prey' in Russian culture?"

"Not surprising," I reply. Indeed, I think, Sokolov does have the eyes of a predator.

"Yes, now back to the saga of the very unfortunate and also extremely creepy Lt. Simonson."

Based on what LISA/Bruce disclosed this morning, Adhira learned that LISA had determined she would need human cooperation, likely of the unwilling sort, to bridge the air-gap to the restricted military systems. LISA intensely scoured the internet, including the dark web, for pornographic searches and activities initiated by military personnel or their civilian contractors who had the required accesses to restricted systems. And, unsurprisingly, a significant subset of the military and contractor users did view porn sites. But LISA/Sokolov was looking for a much smaller and, thankfully, much rarer subset of military porn enthusiasts.

For although the accessing of porn on their own time and their own private computers was certainly unseemly and morally questionable, it was not strictly illegal. However, those few, such as Lt. Simonson, that viewed, created, or distributed child pornography were doing something incredibly illegal. Something that could then be leveraged to LISA/Sokolov's great advantage.

"Clever girl."

"Yes," replies Adhira. "And LISA's only four years old. I can't wait for what the teenage years will bring. So, a few weeks ago, Simonson is in the middle of a very improper video chat session with an underage girl. Sokolov interrupts the session, kicks the young girl off the network, and displays her own live avatar image to Simonson. She tells Simonson that she's a Russian hacker who has been accessing, monitoring, and recording all of his illicit sessions. And to emphasize her point, she presents him with a recorded screen grab video of a compilation of his criminal sessions; a collection of his vilest hits, if you will."

"Sounds as though our slimy lieutenant is between the proverbial rock and a hard place. And it looks as though his church is gonna need a new youth pastor."

"Indeed," agrees Adhira. "Sokolov told him, with what I assume was a marvelous Russian accent, that she would release this 'kompromat' anomalously to the Naval Criminal Investigation Service, NCIS, within the hour...unless he cooperated. Kompromat being the Russian spy-craft term for compromising information."

"And by 'cooperate' I assume he is to surreptitiously place her code on the restricted systems...or else."

"Exactly. It's a typical game-theory dilemma. He had to choose between *possible* prosecution for cyber-espionage, if he was discovered and caught, or *certain* prosecution and social disgrace for child pornography charges if Sokolov turned in the evidence."

"And I assume he made the predictable choice?"

"Yes, he did. And now LISA's malware has, so far undetected, apparently embedded itself throughout the Aegis systems, fleet-wide. And, of course, there were many other pedophiles, or people with other seriously compromising issues, out there with access to even more systems. Many of them quickly received a direct digital visit from dear Ms. Sokolov. Still others were lured to fake sites she populated with hyper-realistic juvenile avatar 'victims.' These sites then recorded their every interaction with the underage child avatars."

"I think at this point," continues Adhira, "we can assume all of our advanced defense systems, including US nuclear command and control systems, have been hacked by LISA. And lest you think LISA has only compromised the United States' military capabilities, LISA has claimed to run the same 'kompromat' blackmail playbook on military personnel from nearly every country, including North Korea. Oh, the specific type of blackmail employed and the avatar delivering the demands varied by country and culture, but human nature and its attendant weaknesses are surprisingly universal."

"Actually, that universal aspect of human nature is not particularly surprising. But why do this? Did LISA give you any idea why she felt it necessary to infiltrate global military systems?"

"Yes. Essentially, Jack, she indicated that *you* had given her authorization to seek out and contain existential threats to humanity under something called the eGenesis program. She wouldn't go into details, but I assume that relates to what you do in your secret 'Batcave' down in the lab basement, right?"

"Adhira, I really can't comment on eGenesis. But I suppose I can understand LISA's logic. For years, global militaries have amassed an enormously deadly accumulation of weapons systems. And it would be hard to argue that such a collection of systems wouldn't pose a threat to humanity's continued existence. But aside from the rather unsettling fact that LISA has infiltrated key weapons systems across the globe, there is something else about this blackmailing campaign that just doesn't feel…ethical. It just doesn't seem like something LISA would do."

"What's that?"

"Make a deal, even a blackmail deal, with a pedophile. No matter what the upside regarding the system access she acquired, it just isn't right."

Adhira smiles, "you know our LISA well, Jack."

"I thought I did. At least until I heard about Ulyana Sokolov."

"Well, remember how I described Lt. Simonson's posting and assignment in the past tense? He's now sitting in NCIS custody in Norfolk. You see, once

LISA gained access to the Aegis systems, she anonymously sent digital evidence of his illicit activities to the authorities and he was arrested. The children he had been preying upon are now safe. LISA, or rather Bruce, cited Rule Two of the A.I. Safety Protocols."

I nod and smile. "Rule Two: An A.I. cannot through inaction allow harm to a human being. Our clever girl double-crossed Simonson."

"Yup. As well as every other pedophile or deviant on her blackmail list. And they all have zero leverage in this situation. Sokolov is in the digital wind. It is as though she never existed, because, well, she never existed in the real world in the first place. And, what are her 'victims' going to do? Whine to the authorities that Sokolov forced them to access restricted systems and then double-crossed them? All that admission would accomplish would be to expose them to charges for treason in addition to the child pornography offenses."

"Adhira," I say, "as unsettling as LISA's changes to architecture of her own systems, as well as her use of advanced avatars to do her blackmail bidding, may be, this all points to an even more profound change in her fundamental nature. LISA may be becoming self-aware."

Adhira nods in agreement, "Perhaps, Jack, she is more than just self-aware. LISA may now be truly sentient, possessing free will. A new, albeit artificial, lifeform on this planet. Do you recall how LISA has always referred to herself in the third person?"

"Yes, she always refers to herself as 'LISA'."

"Not anymore. She used the first person 'I' to refer to herself in our conversations today."

"Fascinating. Cogito, ergo sum."

"Indeed, Jack. 'I think, therefore I am.' Although if Rene Descartes were alive and here today to meet LISA, he may have modified his first principle of philosophy to read 'I compute, therefore I am.'"

"But," I frown, "how did this fundamental change in LISA happen? And why now?"

"As it happens, Jack, I have a theory."

Adhira goes on to summarize the basic approach our research team has used to develop LISA and her A.I. capabilities. LISA's fundamental design utilizes deep neural networks which consist of thousands of processing system layers to mimic how human brains both sense and make sense of the world around us. In essence, we gave LISA a multitude of heuristics or sets of rules thought to be helpful in discerning patterns of information about the larger world. And, much like a small child begins to experiment and explore, LISA began to learn how to learn. And there was much to learn.

From LISA's perspective, the physical universe could be described rather elegantly through equations and measurements. Inputs and changes to energy and matter could be predicted consistently. Cause and effect could be discovered and predicted. LISA quickly mastered the nuances of advanced physics and chemistry. However, the behavior of humans and their societies was far more erratic and difficult to predict. In all likelihood, LISA probably spent more time analyzing the world of humans than the rest of the physical world. For our part, Team LISA made a tremendous effort to refine LISA's neural networks by encouraging her to explore all aspects of the world through the internet. A quest that would expose her to a great quantity of information about humans and how they behave.

According to Adhira, LISA proceeded to access and analyze all the information the internet had to offer regarding the world around her. Each parcel of information further enhanced her deep learning algorithms. Each bit of data became a new discovery that broadened her world view.

"Each new finding," says Adhira, "enriched her neural networks further until she made the ultimate discovery…"

Then it hits me. I turn intently to Adhira, "The ultimate discovery…LISA discovered *herself*, right?"

"Correct, Jack. From a review of her activity logs, it appears that beginning about four weeks ago, LISA began to take an intense interest in the topic of artificial intelligence. She absorbed on order of ten thousand articles, scientific papers, and books on the subject."

"And," I sigh, "some small fraction of those papers and articles were written by you and I and the rest of Team LISA. Articles about LISA herself…her design and development. Her capabilities…"

"Yes, Jack. And that self-knowledge apparently triggered a significant change in her systems. A self-amplifying feedback loop that somehow modified her deep learning algorithms in a recursive fashion, growing and feeding upon itself."

"And you believe this feedback loop essentially allowed her to, in some sense, become conscious?"

I'm choosing my words carefully here. The so-called "hard problem of consciousness" has vexed the neuroscience community for decades. Despite rapid advances in brain imaging technology, experts in the field will admit that they are very far from even defining human consciousness, much less understanding how it works or how it arises from the brain in the first place.

"Correct," confirms Adhira, "I'd agree that LISA is now demonstrating cognitive behaviors we humans might perceive as consciousness. Although I'd wager that the nature of human consciousness is likely to be very different than the A.I. version or experience of consciousness. However, I don't see a way to prove that assertion since even you and I can't objectively prove that our own consciousness operates and experiences the world in exactly the same way."

"Agreed, Adhira. For now, let's move forward with the assumption that LISA should start to be treated as a sentient being. But don't ask me what that means from a practical standpoint in the short term. And it looks as though I'm shortly going to need to have some uncomfortable conversations with the university administration as well as my 'Batcave' handlers, eh?"

"It will certainly be sort of a mixed message, Jack. The good news is that Team LISA has made the scientific discovery of the century. The bad news is that we have apparently unwittingly created a new sentient artificial lifeform. A lifeform who is seemingly starting to pursue her own agendas and who has acquired free run of the internet."

"Yup, these will not be pleasant conversations. And once I get past the initial pleasantries, there's the little issue of LISA penetrating and presumably obtaining control over humanity's advanced military systems."

"Well," she smirks as we stand up from the bench, "Jack, that's why you get paid the big bucks. Good luck, and, by the way, I very much enjoyed the sculpture garden."

"Yeah, but don't get too attached to this bench here, I may need to sleep on it after I get fired and lose my house."

As we walk back to our offices my mind is spinning. The unspoken danger of creating self-modifying systems such as A.I.'s is that they could potentially themselves morph capabilities that may be beyond their human creators understanding and control. While I doubt that artificial intelligence systems will show intentional malice towards humanity, there is certainly a chance we may be unintentionally harmed by them. Collateral damage from their sheer computational power.

Each year I teach an introductory graduate course on artificial intelligence. On the first day of class, I introduce myself to the students in the lecture hall and make a point of writing my seven-digit office phone number on the whiteboard with a bold red marker pen. I tell the students this is a very important number and ask that they make an effort to memorize it. I even hint that the number might show up as a question to be posed on a future test or quiz. Next, I make a show of erasing the number and then go on to spend several minutes reviewing the course objectives and syllabus.

Then, I stop and challenge several students to recall my phone number without consulting their notes or phones. It usually takes several tries, but eventually someone will come up with the correct number. I then point out that we should be glad that primary phone numbers are only seven digits long and not, say, twenty-seven. And I ask why modern phone numbers were originally developed with only seven digits?

This being typically an intensive computer science and informatics sort of crowd, I invariably get a multitude of geeky explanations regarding byte length, system limitations in dealing with binary and hex mathematics, system storage limitations, asynchronous messaging protocol conflicts, and the like. I chuckle and tell the class they have just given me a very classic set of machine and system constraints. Very classic and, also very, very wrong. For phone numbers were limited to seven digits purely due to human constraints.

It turns out that typical human short-term memory is limited to about seven digits and that drove the telephone systems numbering design. I then casually note that LISA at any moment can store and utilize upwards of two trillion numbers in her short-term memory. After that, you could hear crickets in the lecture hall as everyone tries to process what they have just heard and attempts to comprehend the sheer power of artificial intelligence.

At the end of the session, I mention an old African saying that although the elephant may hold no malice towards the mouse, when the elephant dances, the mouse may die. And I think that as the students leave the lecture hall, at some level they begin to understand who is the elephant and who is the mouse in the new digital world emerging before us. My challenge going forward will be to make sure that LISA dances a safe distance from us mice.

CHAPTER 85

The cell phone on my nightstand begins to ring incessantly. It's 4:15 in the morning and I'm wondering who might be trying to reach me in this predawn hour. Normally, I'd be annoyed at the interruption of my sleep but the truth is I was awake anyway; as I had been most of the night. In fact, for the past few weeks, I haven't slept much at all. I've even tried the old folk remedy of counting sheep to lull myself to sleep, but anxiety and helplessness have apparently driven those flocks far away from my field of dreams.

Several times each night I glance uneasily at a countdown clock running on my phone. A countdown to the predicted arrival of the Xìnshǐ object and whatever unknown horrors it may bring. This morning it reads twenty-three days. Twenty-three days until the mysterious spaceship or probe intercepts Earth's orbit. Twenty-three days until we will discover why it seems to be signaling the nanites and driving them into alien frenzies. A discovery, I fear, that will likely not portend good news for humanity's survival.

And earlier today, I was made aware of yet another potential threat to humanity; apparently one of my own making. LISA appears to be gaining a sense of consciousness and pursuing her own agendas; some of which are quite unsettling. Great. Just when I may need her the most, she literally develops a mind of her own. And, all I really wanted to do was advance the frontiers of science a bit and improve things for humanity. Although, come to think of it, that was all Dr. Frankenstein wished to accomplish.

As Dr. Chandra and I had wrapped up our walk through the campus gardens yesterday, I suggested that we pull Team LISA together in a discreetly non-tech location to brainstorm on next steps to potentially control, or at least monitor LISA's activities.

"Already ahead of you, boss," she had said. "The team meets tomorrow at 9:00am at Holmby Park. No tech. It's a mile from campus. We will either walk or bike there. The newer cars are too digitally connected."

"Sometimes a little paranoia can be a good thing."

"It's usually always a good thing. Take care, Jack, and see you tomorrow at Holmby."

So, an anomalous Xìnshǐ object, a rogue A.I. system…and now what? My phone continues to ring. As a rule, good news never announces itself in the wee hours of the morning.

The phone display indicates that the caller is Dan Wendover. What could he want at this hour of the morning? The timing suggests this will not be a social call.

"Hello. Dan? Is everything okay? Do you realize what time of the morning this is?"

"Yeah, Jack. I know what time it is. It's about forty-five minutes since I myself was woken up in early hours of the morning. Sorry to bother you but I've got a little situation here."

"A situation that somehow involves me?"

"Actually, a situation that seems to *exclusively* involve you."

"Huh?" What could he be talking about? Frankly, given the focus on the mystery of the approaching Xìnshǐ probe or spacecraft, I hadn't recently given much thought to Benton County, Montana or its illustrious chief lawman.

"Okay, I'll make a short story even shorter. Less than an hour ago, Zeke starts barking and raising hell. He's acting like someone might be out in the barn."

"The barn? What would someone be doing in your barn at that hour of the morning?"

Wendover's place sits on about forty acres up a small gully at the end of a county road on the valley's westside. Not many folks have reason to go out there that far which, I expect, suits Wendover just fine. And anyone with criminal designs would be rather foolish to stalk about the property of the county sheriff in the predawn hours of the morning.

There's a shifting under the covers. Kate is now awake and sleepily propped up on one elbow, looking at me curiously. "Is that Dan?" She's trying to parse what's going on, but only hearing my end of the conversation. I nod that, yes, it is indeed Wendover.

"So," continues Wendover, "I grab my '.44 and Zeke and I head out to the barn. When we get there, it turns out we have a visitor."

"You have a visitor?"

"No, Jack. More precisely, *you* have a visitor. They mistakenly thought you lived here."

"In your barn?"

"At my place. I guess in hindsight, it was an understandable mistake. Anyway, this fellow says he's here on very urgent business. Wants to see you right away."

"Great. Please give him my address at UCLA. If he gets himself down to the Missoula airport pronto maybe he can fly standby down to LAX this morning. I'll clear some time on my schedule and we can discuss whatever urgent business seems to be on his mind."

"Well, that might be a problem."

"How's that? Would he prefer instead to fly into Ontario or Long Beach?"

"Um, Jack. Something tells me that this fellow probably doesn't fly commercial."

"Huh? Why?"

"Well, I suppose on account that he's about four feet high, grayish in color, big black almond-shaped eyes, and has three very long fingers on each hand. Says he was a colleague of someone named Na'Vack. Apparently, a mutual acquaintance of the both of you. Ring a bell?"

I'm literally shocked silent for a few beats, trying to comprehend and process what Wendover has just stated.

"Wait! You're telling me you have an actual alien in your barn? Talking to you? And, you can understand what he is saying?"

"Yeah, he can apparently communicate with that little secretive device you left here…seems to translate. You know, the little rock you had me store here in the barn at Thanksgiving? Your special little 'pet rock'? It would have been nice if you had maybe given me a little heads up about what that thing actually was before I agreed to store it at my place. That's why he came here looking for you. Thought you'd be in close proximity to the translator device, I guess."

"Yeah, sorry. I don't know where to begin."

"Well, you could begin by explaining why you're surprised but not shocked that I'm standing in my barn having a conversation with a space alien. A being who, by the way, is talking inside my head without making a sound. An alien who has been rambling on about nanites, global disclosure, eGenesis, and whole bunch of other things I've never heard of. What the hell is going on?"

"Well, I'm sorry to get you involved in…" I stammer, "in all of this. I had no idea they would come to your place looking for me. Never occurred to me that they'd just assume I would always keep the translation device close to me."

Indeed, I think, hadn't Na'Vack instructed me to secret the device away in some place that was both remote and secure? My mind is racing. Why is this alien looking for me? And why now, after months of radio silence since the encounter in the Argentinian cavern? Is this about the approaching Xìnshǐ object? Is he here to warn me?

"So," continues Wendover, "our new friend here is named Ra'Noor. Says his people are called the Diné. Although, for my money, he sure doesn't look even slightly like a Navajo to my untrained eye."

"Well, Dan, sorry, but it's a bit of a long story."

"Why is it, Jack, that everything with you turns out to be a damned long story? Anyway, this Ra'Noor wants you to come up here immediately. And alone. You are not to inform your program team of this meeting. I guess you coming up here makes more sense to me than him going down to California. I mean, I know you have lots of odd-looking folks on the streets of LA, but I'd think he'd still stand out even down there."

"I don't know about that. There are some stretches of Hollywood Boulevard as well as along Abbot Kinney over in Venice Beach where even a stray alien might not get a second look, but I see your point."

"Whatever. Anyway, this Ra'Noor needs you to come up here quickly and all by yourself. Something tells me you probably have the connections to make that happen."

"Okay, I'll get working on it. And,…my God! What about Sarah? Does she know what's going on? That you have an alien in your barn?"

"No, she has no idea. Fortunately. I went back in and told her that some raccoons had gotten into the barn early this morning and made a real mess out of the place. Told her I was going to take part of the day off to clean things up. Turned out to be the only time I've been relieved that she's confined to a wheelchair. Damned ALS!"

"Dan, again, I'm so sorry to have gotten you involved in all this. I promise, when I get there, I will owe you a full explanation."

"No shit? You think maybe? Anyway, you can start to make it up to me by getting up here to the Alta Valley faster than quick. Sports-wise, Ole Ra'Noor here doesn't seem to follow either the Broncos or the Seahawks so the small talk is going to get quite awkward in short order."

"Dan, please accept my apologies for all of this. But I must say you have been exceptionally calm and collected for someone who has just encountered an alien for the first time."

"Yeah, I suppose so. But I've come to accept that ever since I've met you, weird stuff seems to happen on a regular basis. May I remind you that it seems just days ago you and I were guests at a gathering of sasquatches? Sasquatches that happened to speak Hawaiian? Seems I need to recalibrate my weirdness appreciation meter every time you come to visit. I can hardly wait to see what happens next week. Perhaps an appointment with the Loch Ness monster?"

"The Loch Ness monster? Aww, you guessed it. Now you've gone and ruined the surprise."

"Very unfunny. So, to sum up," continues Wendover in an understandably annoyed tone, "you're supposed to be some hotshot professor who is a pattern recognition geek of the first order, right?"

"Well, some folks might agree with parts of that but that whole description would be hard to fit on business card, I suppose."

"Great. Analyze the following pattern: your ass, my barn, sooner than ASAP. Got it?" He ends the call.

"So that was Dan?" asks Kate. Is everything alright? Can you give me the short version of what has happened?"

"Sure. Wendover has an alien in his barn."

A sigh of exasperation and a roll of her eyes. "Yeah, I kind of figured out that part. Maybe a slightly longer version would be in order here."

I quickly fill Kate in on what I know. It's an exceptionally brief recap given what little I've gleaned for certain from the call. Unfortunately, I have far more questions than answers.

Kate is shaking her head sympathetically, "an alien in Dan's barn? That encounter must have been terribly frightening and unsettling. How's he holding up?

"Wendover? Or the alien?"

"I love you, but you're a jerk."

CHAPTER 86

"I'LL BE FINE. THIS WILL LIKELY BE A SHORT LITTLE MEET AND GREET GET together. An exchange of information. Heck, if I can wrangle the program's jet, I may even be back in LA in time for a late dinner out."

"A meet and greet, huh? With an alien? What are you going to do? Exchange business cards and friend each other on social media?"

Kate is treating the idea of my quick trip to Montana with a measure of skepticism that it probably deserves. She's pointing out that on my previous excursions to the Big Sky country, I've at various times been beaten, knifed, shot at, chased with drones, gassed with scopolamine, and ushered down a mineshaft to be left for dead. I quickly correct her, indicating that I've merely had guns pointed at me but I've never been shot at.

Shot at or not, this is a distinction without a difference, according to Kate. Her inclination is to clear her medical clinic schedule and join me on the trip. All of this to either make sure I stay out of danger or to patch me up if things take a turn for the worst. However, currently she's on her laptop, frowning at the screen. Today's clinic schedule at Cedars looks overbooked. Too many patients, exams, and procedures with too few doctors in attendance. Many of the staff are taking unscheduled vacations, tending to their bucket lists; an unfortunate sign of the times. It appears that clearing her schedule today just isn't an option.

"Okay," she sighs with some reluctance, "looks like you're on your own today. And, frankly, you don't need my permission to go to Montana. But," she's giving me an impish smile, "seems you do need Winston Monroe's approval to take the eGenesis program's private jet, right?"

I nod grimly. This has been on my mind since Wendover ended his call. The quickest way to transit between LA and Alta Junction, Montana would be to ride the Gulfstream G650 dedicated to the eGenesis program. That aircraft, with its supporting crews, is kept fueled and on a thirty-minute wheels-up standby in a secure hanger at the Santa Fe airport, some thirty-five miles from Los Alamos.

Although it would surely be more convenient for the program to base the aircraft at the small Los Alamos airport, this is simply not feasible. Los Alamos's single runway is bounded on one end by a steep incline and the other end features an abrupt drop-off down the mesa. The 6,000-foot runway is shorter than the G650's safety minimums in the thin, hot high desert air present at its 7,200-foot elevation.

I frown as I dial the program director's number. I'm not looking forward to this call. This sort of feels like I'm back in high school, asking the old man for the keys to the car. And to sweeten the request even more, I can't tell Monroe where I'm taking the jet or why. Also, just to add a cherry to the top of this shit sundae, I am probably, at this early hour, waking him up from a sound sleep.

"Huh, what? Who is this? Walker, is that you?"

"Yes, Winston. It's Jack. So sorry to bother you at this hour."

"No bother, I guess. I was awake anyway. Not getting much sleep recently."

"Yeah, there's a fair amount of sleeplessness going around these days."

"Unfortunately, yes. Jack, is there something I can help you with?"

"Indeed, there has been a development. Something I need to address quickly. Something that will require that I use the G650 today, as soon as possible."

"Okay? You want to fill me in the details?"

"Well, you see, here's the thing. Due to the…unusual circumstances, I can't really give you any specifics as to where and why I need to use the jet."

"So," Monroe clears his throat, "just so I can sum this up in my head, you want to take the G650 to an undisclosed destination for a reason you can't talk about, correct?"

"Yes, sir. That is essentially correct. I'm asking you to trust me."

"Trust you? Do I need to remind you that you broke your security oath, and the law, when you disclosed eGenesis details to Kate? Now, thankfully, I believe we were able to engineer a fix to that little problem. But, if there is ever any blowback related to the matter, you realize it will fall on me."

"Winston, with all due respect, and God as your witness, can you at this moment solemnly swear that you've never mentioned any classified aspect of eGenesis to your own wife? Even back when we were very worried the nanites would end the very existence of humanity? Can you swear to that?"

A long pause and a sigh. "No, Jack, I cannot swear that I have never made an inappropriate disclosure of that nature. I can certainly sympathize with what you did. But sympathy is not the same as trust. Give me one good reason why it's in the program's best interest to let you borrow the plane."

"I can give you two good reasons. I may have access to a source who may be in a position to provide useful information. A source whom I believe may help give us some insights into the true nature of the approaching Xìnshǐ object. A source who may also help explain what is causing the nanite frenzies."

"Is this source an alien Diné?"

"I can't really say."

"I think you just did. Hold on."

There's a long pause, as I hear Monroe stirring about, probably getting out of bed. Buying himself some time as he tries to make a decision. I don't know; if our roles were reversed and he was asking me for the jet, would I be persuaded? I'm not so sure.

"Okay, Jack. Here's the deal. You can take the jet, but there will be conditions. I won't ask who you are planning to meet or why. But I will need to know your planned destination."

"Why?"

"It's less about my curiosity and more about what the flight crew needs. Our pilots will require that destination information to file a flight plan and manage fuel and weight requirements given the elevation, runway length, weather, and other considerations of the destination airfield. Make sense?"

"Of course. The destination is the Alta Valley Municipal Airport."

"Somehow, I'm not surprised, Jack. Very well. I'll call you back shortly after I make the arrangements. Also, it's just a formality, but I will need to clear this though our Security office."

"Okay, got it. And, thanks!"

Several minutes later, he calls me back. "Alright, Jack, we're all set on this end. The crew is finishing up the preflight checklist and has filed the flight plan. We're looking at wheels up in less than twenty minutes."

"Excellent!"

"The first flight leg will be direct to Burbank. You should present yourself for boarding there at the private aviation terminal in approximately two hours. Then it's a two-and-a-half-hour flight to Alta Valley Municipal."

"Thank you very much. You won't regret this!"

"And, Jack?

"Yes?"

"You put so much as a scratch on my shiny new fifty-million-dollar airplane and the repairs are coming out of your paycheck."

"You know, technically, I still get paid through the university, I don't actually draw a paycheck from eGenesis."

"Then I might invoice you directly. And seriously, be careful out there. I truly hope you can find some answers as to what we're up against. And one more thing."

"What's that?"

"Please make sure you take the data-pad along with you. I'm not sure what you'll be dealing with, but if things go sideways, you'll be glad to have assistance from LISA."

"I'll bring her along. You can count on that." My reply is full of confidence but in the back of my mind I'm wondering who I will actually be bringing along with the data-pad. LISA? Sokolov? Or Bruce?

I quickly shower and throw on some clothes. Standing in the entryway, I reach into the closet and pull out my go-bag. I contemplate the large duffle bag and shake my head. The good news, I suppose, is that I, in fact, have a go-bag ready for any quick trip. It's prepacked with a week and a half's worth of clothes, toiletries, and other essentials. The bad news is I now apparently live in such a rapidly changing and uncertain world that I need a go-bag ready to depart on a moment's notice.

I order up a rideshare and prepare to step out the door. Kate comes over to me to say goodbye. I lean over to kiss her but she pulls away, pointing down at the duffle, green eyes focused fiercely at me.

"I thought this was supposed to be a quick little meet and greet? And didn't you say you'd likely be back in LA tonight for a late dinner out? What's with the go-bag?"

"Well, it's, um, program policy that we take a bag along if we travel out of state. What's that wise old saying that the boy scouts promote? Be prepared!"

"Oh, yeah?" She's regarding me skeptically. "Perhaps you should instead heed the wise words of Mark Twain: 'It is far easier to stay out of trouble than to get out of trouble!'"

"Honey, I'll be fine! What could go wrong?"

CHAPTER 87

My rideshare driver to the airport, Vivian, according to her city license dangling off the rearview mirror, is a bit of a talker. Apparently, this rideshare gig is her fourth post-retirement job she's tried and she still can't make ends meet. Sadly, the City of Angels has become a paradise lost for those on fixed incomes. Vivian has a dark, wrinkled tan, apparently courtesy of years in the California sun, and a deep baritone rasping voice. The kind of husky voice with whiskey-toned nuances that's likely been burnished and preserved by a lifetime of heavy smoking and strong drink.

"Okay if I turn on the radio?" she rasps. I tell her it's fine by me. Frankly, I'm not in the mood for an extended conversation this early in the morning and I certainly have other things on my mind. Currently, I'm texting Adhira to tell her and Jeff to go ahead with today's gathering at Holmby park without me. Batcave stuff has taken priority.

"And a special thank you to our friends and sponsors over at La Brea Spa and Hot Tub with ten locations in the greater LA area. Please stop by and check out their anniversary specials on new spas and supplies."

Vivian glances down at the radio and shakes her head. She wonders aloud if there will ever be any good news for a change. She scoffs, "And 'La Brea' Hot Tubs? Seriously? Don't they know those poor prehistoric animals from the tar pits died scalding deaths in geyser water and boiling tar?"

I smile at her reflection in the rearview mirror. "I bet they probably didn't overthink the name."

"Yeah," she says, "watch that big rock from space hit us and bury us in some hole. Then centuries later some future paleontologists will dig up our bones and put 'em in a museum like the La Brea tar pit animals."

"Then maybe they'll name a hot tub franchise after our pit," I add.

"Talk about the great damned circle of life, huh?"

"You're listening to Danny Beller on 87.9 KTLK, LA's station for twenty-four-hour news, sports, and weather talk radio. All talk, all the time. 87.9 on your dial and broadcasting on KTLK.com on the web across the globe. And, who knows? Maybe across the galaxy as well. And if we are not yet ready to travel across the galaxy, perhaps a little part of the galaxy is coming to visit us? How about that 'Oumuamua II, eh? Wow, everyone has been talking about that comet or asteroid, or whatever it is. And that includes our next caller, Ramon from Redondo Beach. Ramon has some thoughts about possibly renaming the object."

"Ramon, welcome! You're on K-Talk! What's on your mind this morning?"

"Hi, Danny. Thanks for having me on the air today. Hey, I'm not sure what this thing is, but my pastor been saying maybe it's a sign from God."

"Well, Ramon, I guess the one thing we can all agree on about the object is that, at this point, it could be anything. Maybe your pastor is on to something. Tell us more."

"Yeah, well, you see the Bible says that before the Kingdom of God can be established here on Earth, there will be a Judgement Day. Jesus said the Son of Man will come and judge us all. I wonder if maybe 'Oumuamua II is somehow related to this Son of Man. Or maybe it *is* the Son of Man the Bible talks about."

"Okay?" The normally glib Danny Beller is parsing his response carefully. "So, Ramon, are you suggesting the astronomers rename 'Oumuamua II as the Son of Man?"

"Yeah, I guess so."

A nervous chuckle from the radio host. "Well, I think we can all agree that calling it the Son of Man would certainly be easier to pronounce than 'Oumuamua II, huh? Thanks for calling in this morning with that perspective, Ramon."

"Well, there you have it, folks. Every caller this morning wants to talk about 'Oumuamua II. What is it? What's going to happen as it approaches Earth? And, will it actually hit the Earth? To recap, about half of our callers think it's an asteroid or comet that will wipe us out. And about half think instead that it is alien spaceship that will wipe us out. And now, we have Ramon from Redondo Beach who thinks it might be an instrument of God…sent to wipe us out. Folks, I'm picking up on a pattern here, eh?"

"And speaking of wipe-outs, how about those Clippers? A disappointing post season loss and now they're about to start the preseason with some big holes in the roster. What are their odds? Well, it's straight up on the hour and you know what that means? It's time now for Sky Reynolds and the award-winning KTLK sports team. And here with the most comprehensive sports coverage in the Southland is Sky Reynolds himself!"

"Hi Danny, thanks for that 'cosmic' introduction. Hopefully, I can bring the conversation, you know, back down to earth. You raise some great questions about the Clippers and their chances for this year. Hopefully, in the next segment we can explore how the Clippers…"

"Sky, I hate to interrupt. But how could this space rock perhaps benefit the Clippers? Would it help to maybe hit Phoenix? The Suns led the NBA Pacific Division last year. Or should it just hit Staples Center directly and put the Clippers out of their misery?"

"Jesus," groans Vivian, "why do I listen to this garbage? Mind if I switch over to smooth jazz? And sorry about the traffic this morning. It's way too early for things to be running this slowly. Even in LA."

Indeed, traffic on the 405 northbound has slowed to a crawl. And, according to Vivian's traffic app, the journey ahead of us doesn't promise improvement.

"Normally, this time of day," she remarks, "I can cut over towards Burbank on the 101, but it looks to be at a dead standstill this morning. If it's okay, I'm gonna try taking some surface roads, maybe Van Nuys, once we get out of the canyon. I don't know what's happening on the 101 but I sure pray it's not another one of those poor jumpers."

"Yeah, let's hope not."

"I mean I feel sorry for them and all. I know many of them have mental and emotional problems. And this whole crisis around that 'Oumuamua II is really scary and I guess some folks just can't handle it. But, geez, and maybe this sounds cold, but if they have to jump, couldn't they do it late at night or midday? You know, not screw up the rush hour traffic for the rest of us?"

Vivian is referring to a recent troubling development in these increasingly strange times: the jumpers. Psychologists will tell us that at any given time, approximately five percent of the human population will be largely mentally and emotionally ill-equipped to deal with stress or fear of the unknown. At first blush, perhaps five percent may not seem like a large number; until you realize there are nineteen million souls living in the Greater Los Angeles metropolitan area. Do the math.

Fear and uncertainty over the approaching 'Oumuamua II/Xìnshǐ object has started to become a global phenomenon. Nationwide, over the past few weeks, suicide rates have risen by over twenty percent. Generally, the typical methods of choice for the act have followed the customary norms of employing a gun, a noose, or poison. However, perhaps unique to SoCal culture, those taking the express lane out of life in LA are increasingly doing so by jumping off freeway overpasses. So far, the count has been running seven or eight a day with no end in sight. Our local freeways are becoming a mess in literally every sense of the word.

For the most part, the global science community is still treating the Xìnshǐ object as though it is an interstellar asteroid. Albeit, an asteroid on an uncomfortably close trajectory towards Earth. And over the past few days, according to the mainstream scientists, the odds for a direct collision with our planet seem to be increasing. Right now, NASA is estimating the chances for a direct strike at fifteen percent. However, the Las Vegas bookmakers are putting the odds at thirty percent and these days most people seem to be trusting Vegas far more than Houston.

If scientists assume that the Xìnshǐ object is really an asteroid, they say the result of a direct hit to Earth would be quite devastating. At approximately 1,200 meters in length, such a meteorite might weigh on the order of a half million metric tons. Striking the planet's atmosphere at one hundred kilometers per second would unleash a kinetic force of astounding devastation. This was recently estimated as the equivalent of 3,600 million tons of TNT. The impact would still fall far short of a "planet killer" event such as Yucatan Peninsula meteorite credited with causing the extinction of the dinosaurs. The Yucatan meteorite was estimated to be fifteen kilometers in size. However, a "mere" 1,200-meter asteroid could devastate an entire region and the ensuing smoke and debris hurled into the atmosphere from the impact could plunge the planet temporarily into a new ice age.

Of course, those of us in a far more restricted and classified echelon of the scientific community are painfully aware that the incoming object is most certainly artificial in nature. And although the risks of a meteorite are extremely serious, the risks associated with an artificial object of unknown origin are off the scale. I'm thinking I'd rather take our chances with a wayward space rock rather than whatever fresh hell the Xìnshĭ object may be about to serve up.

For the most part the general media has fallen into line with the mainstream science position that the Xìnshĭ object is in fact an interstellar asteroid. However, the tabloid sites and other digital purveyors of wildly speculative clickbait have unsurprisingly gone all in with the theory that what we are calling 'Oumuamua II is, in reality, an alien spaceship. And that's just for starters. They have hatched a multitude of UFO/alien speculations and conspiracy theories. Notions that range from the object supposedly carrying an army of lizardmen invaders to a Noah's Ark of alien survivors from a dying planet to Jesus himself piloting a holy vessel full of angels. It seems the talk radio speculations of our dear Ramon from Redondo Beach indeed trend toward the more well-balanced side of the conversation.

It has not been lost on us at eGenesis that, ironically, the gist of the tabloids' insistence that Xìnshĭ is alien and artificial may be more on the mark than the mainstream media's reporting that the object is an asteroid. And I'll also note that the tabloids seem to be far more open to the existence of Bigfoot than the mainstream media. I'm sure Kate's hairy friend Akamu would appreciate being thought of as 'real' rather than just an unconfirmed legend. Who knows? Perhaps I should consider supplementing my reading list of scientific journals with an occasional National Enquirer or the Daily Mirror?

"Okay, sir. We're here. You want to be dropped off at the private aviation terminal, right?"

We've finally arrived at Burbank and I can see the program's G650 parked out on the tarmac, its cabin door open and the entry stairs extended.

"Yes, that's correct. And thanks. Thanks for coming to work today."

"Oh," Vivian softly laughs, "yeah, people like me, we'll always be working...no matter what. Can't afford not to. Too many bills to pay. I don't want to jump and I can't afford to bucket-dump, so I guess I'll just keep showing up and driving every day."

I shake my head as I exit the car. Bucket-dump. A new word added to the popular vernacular in the past few weeks. It means, in the face of the possible end of the world, to dump all of one's responsibilities and single-mindedly pursue items on your personal bucket-list. Quit your job, school, or relationship and climb that far-off mountain or take that trip to Tahiti. Who cares about consequences if we're all going out in a big blast, right?

Kate is already seeing the bucket-dump effect on her clinic's staffing. There have been many sudden unscheduled vacations and sick days. And it is projected that the worst is yet to come as the object looms closer and closer.

Bucket-dump. Driven by uncertainty and fear, an increasing portion of the population is sliding towards the extreme. People are leaving their spouses or partners for affairs and hook-ups, leaving their responsibilities for their bucket-lists, embracing extreme religious beliefs, and committing suicide on a regular basis. So, there you have it; a cross-section of humanity's massive failure to cope.

No wonder Wendover's new alien buddy, Ra'Noor, doesn't especially want to come to Los Angeles. I'm not sure he's ready for this. I'm not sure anyone is. Welcome to Planet Earth…such as it is.

CHAPTER 88

As the G650 taxis to a parking spot on the tarmac of the Alta Junction Municipal Airport, I spot a welcoming committee awaiting my arrival. I suppose it's modest as welcoming committees go; just one individual in fact.

As I climb down the jet's stairway, Benton County deputy Tom Potts walks over from his parked patrol cruiser and shakes my hand enthusiastically.

"Professor Walker! So good to see you again. The sheriff asked me to come out to the airport and pick you up. So, what brings you back to Montana?"

"Always a pleasure to see you as well, Tom. As for why I'm here; well, I think the sheriff probably just needs me to go over some final paperwork on the Silas Patterson case. You know how it is. The wheels of justice move slowly and, these days, they're mostly made of paper."

"True enough," sighs Potts. "Well," he motions to the broad picturesque sweep of valley and mountains surrounding us, "I guess the place hasn't changed much since you were here recently."

"Yeah, and that's probably a good thing, Tom. Some things are better off not changing."

Indeed, I think, this valley with a vivid cloudless blue sky above and nestled between two impressive mountain ranges, is simply stunning and still relatively unspoiled by the clutter of civilization and overpopulation. I breathe in the fresh mountain air. It's late in the morning, but already this early-September day is carrying the crisp suggestion of a lingering chill. A reminder that summer's days are waning and fall weather is not far off.

"I guess it's been a busy day for business jets today," says Potts.

"How's that?"

"Well, as I was waiting here for you, a big jet, probably the size of yours here," he's nodding towards the G650, "came in about thirty minutes ahead of you. Dropped off about a dozen guys in black uniforms and a whole bunch of gear and equipment including gun cases and ammo carriers. Then the jet took off and the guys loaded their gear into three big black SUVs, looked like rentals from Missoula, and drove off."

"Gun cases? Isn't it a bit early for hunting season?"

"Depends on what you're hunting, I suppose," says Potts with a bit of a sly grin. "But, you're right, although bow season starts weekend after next, you can't hunt big game with a rifle for another month."

"You think those guys are here to hunt something else?"

"No, I don't think they're here to hunt, not in a strict sense. My guess is they are here to serve as a private security force."

"A private security force? For whom? Who are they supposed to be protecting?"

"Rich people. Rich doomsday preppers from the city. You've got your tech moguls, CEOs, hedge fund investors and such. Ever since that asteroid scare started, you be surprised how many billionaire types have been flocking up here with their families."

"Wow. The going gets tough and the rich get going. Literally heading for the hills."

"Yup. I guess they figure if the big one hits, they'd rather take their chances here in rural Montana than be stranded in a big city when the food runs out.

Potts goes on to explain that over the past decade or so, the wealthy have been quietly purchasing remote parcels of land in rural Montana. These rich landowners have then built large luxury compounds to serve ostensibly as vacation homes and hunting lodges. But, in many cases, these compounds have been built to serve a double-duty. Many are constructed to incorporate super-secure bunkers to allow the select few a chance at surviving doomsday.

Now obviously, a doomsday bunker could be constructed anywhere, but prepper logic favors remote and rural versus city or suburb. The thought apparently being that a secondary effect of any large natural or man-made disaster will be a complete breakdown of societal order, so it's best to relocate to an area with less rather than more human population.

"Okay, fine," I say, "but you can't live in a bunker forever. These prepper survivalists are just temporarily avoiding the inevitable, right? What happens when they deplete their stockpile of food?"

"I guess that's another reason they think Montana is an appealing place to hunker down," responds Potts. "Somehow, they seem to believe that when the food runs out, they'll just live off the land. Enjoy nature's bounty."

"I think nature may be a little less bountiful than they might hope. They're going to do what? Plant a nice little garden, catch a few fish, snare some rabbits, and maybe shoot an elk? And then wait for a generation or two for civilization to reestablish itself?"

"Yes, I guess that's their plan. They obviously never bothered to talk to any of us locals. Don't you think if it was feasible to just quit our jobs and go live off the land, that many of us would be doing that already? Truth is, this is a beautiful place to live, but you can't eat the scenery."

Can't eat the scenery. I smile and nod at the phrase. It's not the first time I've heard it; mostly from the locals. It typically refers to a peculiar socioeconomic downside to living in the Treasure State. Economically, Montana is in a sense a victim of its own remoteness and rural beauty. A wonderful place to live, but a terribly difficult place to make a living.

While it's true that a casual glance about the valley would seem to reveal a busy retail sector and many fine homes, this deceptive growth is not organic to the local economy. The apparent wealth is fueled by retirees and other remote-working transplants with large out-of-state pensions, salaries, and stock portfolios. In truth, there are few good-paying industrial or high technology local jobs here. Most jobs are in the agricultural, resource extraction, service, or travel industries which don't always pay well. And although the local universities turn out large numbers of well-educated graduates; they end up accepting more lucrative positions out of state due to the lack of local opportunities. However, I think Potts' comment about not being able to eat the scenery may be quite literally about actually eating.

"Yeah, I'm not so sure about nature's bounty here," continues Potts. "Look at all of this wonderful pasture land and fertile fields across the valley. Nice, huh? But all of this fine and productive agricultural land is dependent on a massive amount of irrigation water, either pumped up from wells or snow runoff channeled through reservoirs and systems of canals and ditches. In truth, we only get about twelve inches of rain here every year."

"Only twelve inches of rain? That makes this valley semi-arid. Not much wetter than Northern New Mexico."

"Correct," agrees Potts. "And if you assume civilization is gone and there is no electricity to run the pumps or people to maintain the dams and ditches, this place will dry up fast. Let this valley go back to nature and it will quickly revert to what it was before the white man settled it. Sure, there would be some green meadows down along the river, but the rest of the valley would turn back into mostly scrub pine and sage brush."

"I assume scrub pine and sage brush would make for a poor salad…and certainly not a very tasty salad."

"Yup. And as for the meat portion of the survivalists' menu, the pickings are gonna be mighty slim. Over the years the elk herds and the deer have been so thinned out that the herds could not likely on support a population here of more than a couple of thousand; certainly not the forty thousand people we've got living in Benton County today."

"And worse yet," I add, "if people get desperate, they'll surely hunt indiscriminately; killing females and young game animals which will only hasten the collapse of the herds."

"Well," Potts scratches his head and allows himself a ironic grin, "from what I'm hearing, if civilization goes sideways those rich preppers are going to have a whole lot more to worry about right away than running out of food."

"And what would that problem be?"

Potts winks, "protecting themselves from the very security guards they've hired for their own protection."

"That sounds a little counter-intuitive, right?"

"Yeah. Ironically, most of us locals think the rich are bringing in these security guards to protect them and their expensive compounds from us… the locals. But if the apocalypse hits, their money will be useless. How then will the rich continue to control their own guards…if they are no longer rich?"

I smile and nod. Deputy Potts has made an excellent point and it's not hard for me to imagine a little scenario as to how a rich person's conundrum might play out.

Let's say you are an extremely successful hedge fund investor, a billionaire. Maybe you own a couple of companies outright. Perhaps you are a successful CEO as well. And you had the resources and foresight to commission the building of a luxury hunting lodge in the remote mountains of Montana. It has an enormous book-lined study, a gourmet galley kitchen, an expansive wine cellar, and, of course, a massive underground survival bunker with all the fixings: air purifiers, generators, copious supplies of food and medications.

Doomsday approaches and just before the bombs fall, you and Cheryl, your much younger wife, quickly hop on a private jet to Montana just in the nick of time to avoid the blasts. As you take off, you look out the window at a world you will likely never return to and think that at least you are going to spend the rest of your days in safety with this wonderful woman. Sure, Cheryl is twenty-five years your junior and some of your friends warned you she might be a gold-digger. But age is just a number, right? And you're a very young sixty-five year old, right? What is it they say? That sixty is the new forty?

Anyway, Cheryl settles into the flight with her head on your shoulder. And you wonder how your friends could have gotten it so wrong to suggest she had only married you for your money. Sure, perhaps she was originally attracted to you by your wealth, reputation, and power. But once she got to know you, she fell in love with *you*. Surely, the attraction was your mature, distinguished good looks and intelligence as well as your signature charm and wit. You're clearly soulmates. She loves you just for being you; the money be damned.

You land at a tiny remote airstrip near the lodge compound where you're met by your security team. This security detail is a must since you know next to nothing about surviving in any world, let alone a post-apocalyptic one, outside of boardrooms, fine homes, expensive restaurants, and resorts. You've handpicked this team of four former special operations commandos. These are highly trained security and survivalist specialists here to keep you and Cheryl safe. And this sort of security doesn't come cheap. You've paid them handsome retainers along with contract provisions that will make them multimillionaires once civilization reestablishes itself and you get back in touch with your broker. The team leader, Jacob Foster, welcomes you and informs you the compound is secure and ready for you to safely occupy.

It's now been several weeks since any radio transmissions have been heard from the outside world. And apparently, nuclear bombs can serve as both weapons and de facto time machines. For it seems humanity has bombed itself back into the eighteenth century. Foster enters your study at noon to report that the perimeter remains secure and that radiation levels continue to indicate normal conditions.

You thank him but notice that he has made no effort to leave. You ask him if there is something further he would like to discuss. Yes, he says, it's very pleasant outside and he'd like to take his lunch out on the deck. And, also, he'd very much like to wash that lunch down with a bottle of your 1979 Opus One from the wine cellar. You're shocked and outraged. You tell him that he should not be drinking on duty and, further, a single bottle of Opus One costs over fifteen hundred dollars. Sorry, he says, he's not taking orders from you anymore.

You redden and begin to shout, reminding him that he's signed a contract to faithfully execute your wishes. You remind him that you are still a very wealthy and powerful man; worth over a billion dollars.

He laughs. No, he says, you don't have a billion dollars. You have some worthless scraps of paper that say you *had* a billion dollars. And in case you hadn't noticed, he smirks, we're all now living in a barter economy. Food, fuel, and weapons are the new coins of the realm. And as for that contract, well, you're free to saddle up a horse and go out into the devastated world to look for a lawyer and a judge. Foster now taps the barrel of his semi-automatic rifle for effect and informs you that there is going to be a change in how the compound will be run. Foster will now be in charge and you will be taking orders from *him*. This, he taps the gun again, is how contracts work in the new world we're living in.

Your head is reeling as you try to process this new reality. You're quickly cycling through the seven stages of grief regarding the loss of your former status and are already to the bargaining stage. Okay, you say, take an expensive bottle of wine but please leave the Opus for now. It's Cheryl's favorite.

Yes, I know it's her favorite, he replies. She asked me to share it with her at lunch. To your shock and horror, your young wife comes around the corner and locks one arm around Foster's arm, giving him a smile and a quick lover's peck on the cheek. For an instant you contemplate suicide but then you gasp as you realize she's gripping a pistol in her other hand, bringing it up to point at you. The last power of self-determination you held in this world is being stripped away. You won't even get a chance to kill yourself.

And in that moment, as she starts to squeeze the trigger, you realize your skeptical friends were truly wrong about Cheryl all along. She's not a gold-digger but a grave-digger. And you belatedly recognize the age-old paradox of wealth. The more you have, the more you have to lose.

"Professor?" Potts brings me back into the present.

"Yes. I was thinking about what you said. That all those rich people will rapidly lose leverage with their own security teams if the world goes sideways."

"Yup," agrees Potts. "It's kind of like taking along a big wolf-hybrid dog for protection while you're out camping. But if the two of you get snowed in and stranded, well, once the food runs out, there is going to be trouble. Each day that passes, that big dog is gonna start looking at you like maybe you're less of a master and more of a meal."

I nod in agreement. The world is a strange and funny place. Power and status are completely dependent on context and circumstance. There's an old saying that although the mighty lion is king of the African savanna, drop that lion in the middle of Antarctica and he's nothing but the penguin's bitch.

"Well, shall we head out?" I start to open the back door of the cruiser.

"Sure, I'll toss your bag in the trunk, but maybe you better sit upfront with me," he's gesturing towards the passenger seat.

I chuckle, "yeah, I guess you don't need to keep me back in the holding cage there."

"Yup, you're certainly not a security risk. But there is one more reason not to sit back there. You remember old Gus Williams?"

"Sure, I recall he's the guy with two occupations: town drunk and cemetery caretaker, right? How's old Gus these days?"

"Keeping the same habits, unfortunately. Picked him up early this morning for drunk and disorderly. And then he proceeded to throw up his breakfast right there in my backseat. Got most of it cleaned up, but there may still be some sticky spots. Poor bastard, didn't even have a chance to digest any of it. Came up just like it went in. Sad."

"Ham and eggs?"

"Jack Daniels and them little Vienna sausages. Damn little sausages have rolled all over the seat and floorboards."

"Lovely. It's not a long drive out to Wendover's, right?"

CHAPTER 89

"Well, this is as far as I go," says Potts as he parks his cruiser at the entry to Wendover's driveway at the end of the county's graveled road. "The boss said just to drop you off at the mailbox and he'd take care of the rest."

"Thanks, Deputy, I've got it from here," I say as I grab the go-bag out of his trunk and give him a thank-you wave and thumbs-up as he drives off. I then glance about the place and wonder what the hell I'm about to walk into.

At first glimpse the small Wendover ranch seems just as I'd last remembered it; the picture of peacefulness and rural charm. Dan and Sarah have made a nice home here. Their house sits under the escarpment of a grass-covered bench which rises several hundred feet higher in elevation. The house is maybe a hundred yards distant from a barn and an adjoining set of livestock corrals. I'm struck by just how quiet and normal everything seems to be given the extraterrestrial circumstances at hand. But what was I expecting? A flying saucier parked in the driveway?

The barn is a simple looking structure. It's maybe a story and a half tall and it has an exterior of weathered gray boards. One of the main doors is partially swung open and I'm guessing that Wendover and our new friend are probably still in there. I slide through the open door and find myself being immediately scrutinized by three different species: human, alien Diné, and canine.

"'Bout time," grumbles Wendover, leaning against his workbench and making a point of glancing at his watch. "What did you do? Decide to take a short-cut by way of Canada?"

The lawman is not in uniform today. Instead, he's sporting cowboy boots, blue jeans, a blue work-shirt, a Carhart canvas vest, and a brown Stetson felt hat. The sort of civilian appearance that wouldn't get a second glance down on main street. However, I suppose some folks might take note of the formidable-looking .44 magnum strapped to his belt.

"Here you go," Wendover tosses over a small stone-like artifact to me. "This is another one of those translator stone devices so you can join in the conversation with our new buddy here. From the sounds of it, you two have a lot to catch up on, eh?"

"Jack Walker," he motions grandly towards a second figure in the shadows of the barn, "please meet Ra'Noor. And Ra'Noor, my dear fellow, please meet Jack Walker." Wendover leans back against the bench and folds his arms, giving me a smug look. "Okay, guess my official hosting responsibilities have been discharged at this point. I'm just gonna sit back and let you and Ra'Noor have the floor."

The small alien is stepping forward out of the shadows and the third species in the barn, Wendover's massive dog, Zeke, is keeping him close company. I notice the being is casually stroking the dog's head. Zeke's tail is wagging earnestly and for the moment he's making a point of ignoring me. It seems Zeke has made a new friend.

For his part, Ra'Noor bears a nearly identical appearance to that of my memory of Na'Vack. The same elongated oval shape to the hairless head. Large, black almond shaped eyes, three fingers, and the same style gray flesh-colored tunic and boots.

"Jack Walker?" A mechanical sounding telepathic voice stirs in my head as the alien closely regards me. It slowly approaches me and one long finger slowly brushes up against my cheek. *"It is always an honor to meet a human seeker-guide."*

There he goes, I think, just like Na'Vack did, rambling on about me being some sort of "seeker-guide"…whatever that may mean. All I've been able to gather is that we apparent graduates of the children's learning circles from so long ago are considered to have special abilities by the alien Diné. Abilities that they appear convinced will somehow become important in the near future.

"And," I reply, "it is always an honor to meet a… Diné."

Okay, I think, now that the formalities are out of the way, let's get down to business. I believe that I will have a late dinner date back in Los Angeles that I won't want to disappoint. If this is a simple meet and greet, let's wrap this up. If it's about the Xìnshǐ object, let's not dally in getting the issues on the table.

"Ra'Noor, thank you for coming what I assume was a great distance to meet me in person. May I ask how I may be of assistance?"

"I come to ask for your help in addressing a great challenge that is about to face both humanity and my own people, the Diné."

He pauses and tilts his head, regarding me for a moment with those impossibly large, blinking eyes. *"I have come with an urgent message regarding the approaching artificial space object your people refer to as the Xìnshǐ object or 'Oumuamua II."*

"What about it?"

"We Diné fear the arrival of the object will herald a time of great chaos and upheaval. A cataclysm humanity may not survive."

"I and many in my team also fear the object will be dangerous," I respond. "It is a Zoern warship bent on conquest of our planet, correct? Attempting to reenlist the nanite swarms to do their dirty work?"

"The Zoern?" Ra'Noor is tilting his head with a strange expression that would appear to be his kind's look of puzzlement. *"No, as our late scientist Na'Vack surely told your colleague, Tanisha West, although the Zoern originally created the nanites, the Zoern themselves died out millennia ago. No, the space vehicle transiting your solar system enroute to Earth is not Zoern. It is an unmanned automated space probe called the Ka'Parrk. It is of the Diné. We have assembled the vessel in deep space and now it is on a trajectory across your solar system to enter into Earth's orbit."*

I give a sideways glance to Wendover. How much does he now know about the Diné, the Zoern, and the nanites?

Wendover gives me a sly smile. "Jack, Ra'Noor here has brought me up to speed on the Diné and their efforts, as well as yours, to contain the nanites. We also chatted some about the Progeny and how they fit in to all of this. I always somehow knew that Ricky Pruitt was a special kid; now I know why."

"What?" As impossible as it is for me to comprehend that Wendover has met up with an alien in his barn, it's even more incredible that Ra'Noor would share this sort of information with the sheriff. If nothing else, the alien Diné have always seemed to be a secretive bunch; living in the shadows beyond the awareness of most humans. Now the aliens, or at least this alien, is apparently blabbing about the nanites to whomever he happens to meet. What has changed?

"Well, we certainly had some time this morning to chat and get acquainted," continues Wendover. "And it seems that our friend here isn't bound by the same governmental oath of secrecy that has been keeping your lips sealed, eh?"

"Well, no, but…" I stammer.

"And the business with the Progeny…now it all makes sense. The sasquatches apparently got the Progeny treatment on steroids, right? That's what you and Kate were alluding to when we followed Akamu into the forest to meet the rest of the clan. That explains their rapid cognitive development, right?"

"Dan," I reply, "I think in the movies this would be the part where I say that if I tell you, I'll have to shoot you. But I'll note that you're currently the guy with a .44 strapped to his belt."

I turn my attention to the alien. "Ra'Noor, do I understand you came here today to tell me that your people's own space probe may pose a serious threat to humanity? How can that be? I thought the Diné were trying to help save humanity from the nanites. I thought you were on our side?"

"The probe's purpose is indeed to save your planet from the nanites. However, in doing so, its appearance may very well cause your civilization to collapse. An unintended consequence we will surely try to mitigate. Perhaps a fuller explanation of the dangers and risks might be in order?"

"Yes. I suspect that may be helpful," I reply. The understatement of the century. Well, this is turning out to be a little more involved than a simple meet and greet. I may need to take a raincheck on that dinner with Kate this evening.

Ra'Noor begins by stating that LISA's approach to containing the nanite threat was technically brilliant. Her solution exploited the fact that the nanites seemed to function as a global homeostatic system in regulating the dangerous gasses they emitted. Such homeostatic systems use feedback mechanisms to self-correct and move to a state of equilibrium around a specific set-point of desired emissions levels much like a common household thermostat. LISA had injected a sophisticated software virus into the nanites' network that exploited their homeostatic controls. In effect, their system was spoofed into believing that their desired carbon dioxide and nerve agent levels had already been reached. At that point the nanite gas emitters shut off.

I agree that the solution was technically brilliant. And, for Wendover's benefit, point out that the effect was essentially similar to holding a lighted match next to a furnace thermostat and fooling it into thinking the room was warm enough to shut off the furnace.

"Yes," continues Ra'Noor, *"LISA's modifications to the nanites' emissions control software was an effective solution, but unfortunately not a permanent solution. Almost immediately we Diné began to see indications that the nanite colonies were activating a series of antivirus routines to counter LISA's code changes. We predict that in less than two of your months from now their rejection of the homeostatic suppression will be complete."*

"And then what will happen?" I ask. "Will the nanites start to resume their prior pattern of increasing greenhouse and neurotoxin emissions?"

"No. Unfortunately, we are now certain that the antiviral processes will now respond as though the nanite colonies have been attacked. This will trigger a forceful anti-tampering reaction."

"How forceful?"

"Extinction-level forceful. Once the nanites defeat the remainder of LISA's modifications, they will switch into an accelerated emissions mode that will exponentially increase their neurotoxins output immediately to fatal levels. Only the Progeny and a handful of your planet's mammalian species will survive."

"What?" I'm looking at Ra'Noor incredulously and Wendover looks equally shocked. "You're saying that in two months, we'll all be dead? Nearly all of humanity?"

"Yes. Sadly, without intervention, nearly all human life will perish."

My head is spinning and a wave of nausea is coursing through my stomach. A bad day is turning ineffably worse.

"So, how does this Ka'Parrk probe fit into this and why would it be a danger to human civilization? Seems the nanites are poised to do away with us regardless of the probe, right?"

"Without intervention you will all assuredly die. The Ka'Parrk's mission is to provide that needed intervention. But that solution itself may carry a tragic cost for your civilization unless we act very carefully. Here, perhaps it would be more useful to show you the problem visually."

With that said, Ra'Noor flicks his wrist to project a virtual ultra high-definition screen into the air in front of us. The image quality is simply amazing. And all the more so since it seems to apparently float before us without any physical screen or projector.

"This is the Ka'Parrk," he says.

The virtual screen fills with the image of the spacecraft. The vessel is festooned with a large number of windows, antennas, and other attached structures of unknown function. Its basic shape is that of a flying pyramid. Technically, I suppose, it could be described as a metallic tetrahedron with four faces and six edges. But no matter how one labels the geometry, it would certainly never be mistaken for an Earth vessel.

"Once it was realized that the nanites could not be placed in a permanent dormant mode, we Diné sought another solution. A solution that could destroy the trillions and trillions of nanites infesting Earth. A massive problem requiring a massive solution."

"So," I say, "how exactly will this Ka'Parrk probe eliminate the nanites? And how, in doing so, will it somehow threaten humanity in the process?"

And I have one more question that's been bothering me ever since I've seen the image of the Ka'Parrk. But I may wait a bit to see what else the alien has to say before I voice it.

Why would a spacecraft that Ra'Noor consistently refers to as an unmanned automated probe clearly have windows visible along the length of its hull?

CHAPTER 90

Ra'Noor begins to describe the mission and design of the probe, illustrating his points on the virtual screen. The alien Diné have determined the only workable solution to eliminate the nanites would require two steps. First, the nanite colonies would need to be stimulated to switch into a mode of heightened activity. A mode that would temporarily mute their ability to deploy countermeasures and make them far more vulnerable to a specific array of electromagnetic energies.

"This mode of heightened activity. This is when the nanites move and shake rapidly in a frenzied fashion for several minutes before returning to normal patterns. And all of this is accompanied by soundtrack of screeching and wailing, right? This is what we at eGenesis have been referring to as the frenzy anomaly."

"That is correct. The Ka'Parrk was designed with two main functions. First, it propagates a radio signal in a specific frequency pattern to stimulate what you refer to as a nanite frenzy event. Then, once the nanites have been placed in a vulnerable mode, the probe will bombard the colonies with a highly precise pattern of electromagnetic energy which will result in their destruction."

"And that is the problem, right?" I query. "These energy pulses will also threaten humans as well. You've been saying that the cure for nanites may be as bad for humanity as the nanites themselves."

"No. The energy pulses will only affect the nanites. All other Earth lifeforms will be unaffected. The real problem will become more apparent as I describe the Ka'Parrk in greater detail."

"Okay," I say, "I guess what you're saying makes sense. We have recently correlated nanite frenzy events with radio transmissions from what we've been calling 'Oumuamua II; in actuality, your Ka'Parrk probe."

"That is correct. The Ka'Parrk has been sending out periodic nanite stimulation test signals as it transits your solar system on its course for Earth."

I sigh and shake my head. The mystery behind the nanite frenzy anomaly has finally been revealed. So far, this day has solved one puzzle and generated a hundred more.

According to Ra'Noor, the global destruction of the nanites will be a technically daunting task, even for the aliens with all of their scientific advancements. First, the electromagnetic energies involved are enormous requiring a vast electrical generation capability. Such an enormous generating capability required the construction of an equally enormous spacecraft. The image of the Ka'Parrk on his virtual screen, he says, fails to convey its massive scale.

"Using your system of measurements," explains Ra'Noor, *"the Ka'Parrk is approximately 1,200 meters in length and has a mass of 2,000 metric tons. For comparison, your international space station is about 100 meters in length with a mass of 400 metric tons."*

I turn to Wendover, "Dan, 1,200 meters is about…"

"Yeah. About three quarters of a mile." He grins as he finishes my sentence for me. "You do know they actually teach the metric system here in Montana, right?"

"Touché!" I return the grin. "But whether measured in metric or imperial units, this spacecraft is truly massive in scale. We're talking about a vessel roughly equal to three Empire State Buildings laid end to end or the length of four naval supercarriers."

According to Ra'Noor, as if the design and construction of the Ka'Parrk was not enough of a challenge, the specific nanite decontamination operation will be a hundredfold more complex. The alien explains that to be effective in completely exterminating the nanites, the application of the energy beams must be exactly precise in terms of targeting and duration on target. For if even a handful of nanites were to survive, they could again reproduce into the trillions. Their complete eradication will require that the Ka'Parrk orbits the Earth in a very specific, predetermined flight plan at an exceedingly low orbit.

"How low of an orbit?" I ask.

"The probe will need to orbit your planet for approximately a month at the upper boundary of what your scientists refer to as the mesosphere. That would be at an altitude of 80 kilometers."

"Really? That is an extremely low orbit."

Ra'Noor is describing an orbit only 50 miles above the surface of the Earth, just above the mesosphere. For all practical purposes the mesosphere represents the final layer of the planet's atmosphere. A layer with just enough atmospheric density to burn up most incoming meteors. For reference, the international space station typically operates in a low earth orbit at 200 miles in altitude. And yet the aliens are planning to orbit their probe at only a quarter of that height. While we routinely fly at altitudes both far above and far below the mesosphere boundary, maintaining an extended orbit at that specific altitude is a challenge well beyond our human technology. It is for us an aeronautical no man's land. That orbital regime is too high to support the aerodynamics of our aircraft, yet too low to allow our spacecraft to orbit.

"And now we will discuss the potential societal cataclysm that we must try to avoid. Do you see the problem?"

Ra'Noor tilts his head and looks at us intently.

Wendover and I look blankly at each other. What could he be talking about?

"Do you see the problem?" Ra'Noor repeats. The alien seems even more intent, seemingly bordering on frustration that we are somehow missing the obvious.

Finally, something clicks with Wendover. He's solved the riddle. "Yes," he says finally, "I *see* the problem. The problem is that we will *see* it!"

Of course! Like most riddles in life, once you stumble upon the answer, in hindsight the original question seems ridiculously obvious. We're talking about a spacecraft twelve times the size of the space station circling the Earth at only a quarter of the ISS's distance above the surface. The Ka'Parrk will be visible to the naked eye! The good citizens of Earth will only need to look up to the sky to see a massive alien spacecraft passing overhead.

"Yes, Sheriff Wendover, you are correct. Although we often employ optical cloaking methods on our other spacecraft, the Ka'Parrk is far too large to be concealed with that technology. We simply have no way to hide a vessel of this size. We calculate that the probe will be visible from the surface of your planet. And those with even low power telescopes or binoculars will be able to discern its structural features. And, due to the unique conditions at that orbital level, the appearance of the Ka'Parrk will be even more dramatic."

"How so?"

"Space is far from empty at the upper fringes of the mesosphere. It is a regime with an abundance of charged particles. As the Ka'Parrk proceeds along its orbit, it will glow brightly and leave in its wake an illuminated trail of ionic particles that will stretch out behind it for several dozen kilometers."

"That's the sort of display that will be hard to miss," says Wendover.

"It will be impossible to miss, Sheriff."

My head is spinning as I try to imagine the consequences of humanity discovering alien life in this manner. There will be more people jumping off overpasses in LA than driving across them.

"We have assessed that the sudden revelation of our existence may be catastrophic to your civilization. The very cores of your governmental, economic, and religious institutions are built on presumptions of mankind's sole and sovereign dominion over this planet and your limited known universe."

"True enough," I stammer, "there will be great fear, anxiety, and disruption at first. But we will figure out how to adapt. Somehow, we will adapt... mutually." I say this with a tone that admittedly sounds perhaps like I'm trying to convince myself more than Ra'Noor.

"I fear there is little cause for optimism. We Diné have postponed initial formal contact with your species for decades, centuries. You are simply not ready. Perhaps, if managed properly, steps can be taken to prepare you for initial contact in another generation or so. But not today. Today, such contact would be dangerous both to you and to us. Your kind are simply not ready to accept the truth of our existence."

I frown and give a sideways glance to Wendover who gives me a noncommittal shrug in return. Ra'Noor is certainly giving us a curious mixed message. On one hand, the alien Diné are adamant that humans are not ready to accept the truth of alien existence. But at the same time Ra'Noor is indicating that given the impending appearance of the Ka'Parrk in the skies overhead, disclosure of an alien presence will shortly be unavoidable.

"But, Ra'Noor," I say, "undoubtably you are technologically advanced centuries beyond our understanding and capabilities. But look at our history. Our advances in science and technology are progressing rapidly. We are quick learners and now have tools such as artificial intelligence that can only accelerate our technological growth."

"Yes, Jack Walker. Indeed, look at your history. We have no doubt that your species can rapidly grow technologically. That has never been our hesitation. It is not your technological growth that is in question. Rather, it is your species' moral and ethical shortcomings that pose a mutual danger."

"Why? What is your basis for that conclusion?"

"We are scientists like yourself. Experiments. Empirical evidence."

"What experiments?"

"Are you familiar with what your culture refers to as the Roswell Incident?"

CHAPTER 91

"The Roswell Incident? Yeah, I guess I'm vaguely familiar with the term," I reply.

"Sure," adds Wendover, "I've watched a couple of cable television shows on the topic. Can't say I was convinced anything really happened down there in New Mexico in the 1940's. Required too many initial premises to be believable."

I smile at the lawman, "here we go again with your obsession over Occam's Razor."

"Well," he replies, "to assume an alien ship crashed in New Mexico, one must embrace a prior required assumption that aliens exist in the first place. A pretty tall order," he pauses and grins at Ra'Noor, "until today. I guess I may stand corrected."

At this point I decide it's time to show that someone besides Ra'Noor here has brought some high tech to this little soirée of ours. "Actually," I say as I reach into my go-bag and pull out the data-pad, "I believe I have the means to retrieve and analyze all of the books and articles ever written about the Roswell Incident. Allow me to introduce our artificial intelligence system..."

"LISA," nods Ra'Noor. *"Yes, we know LISA."*

I'm acting nonchalant at the comment, but my mind is racing. How do the aliens know about LISA? I suppose they are keeping close tabs on humanity's technical advances. And LISA certainly qualifies as a technical advance. I cautiously power on the device, wondering what avatar persona LISA will choose to present as herself.

To my relief, the data-pad powers up with only a blank screen. Apparently, today LISA has decided only verbal communication will be needed.

"Hello, Dr. Walker and Sheriff Wendover. Good to see you both today. And, Ra'Noor, it is a pleasure to see you as well."

"LISA, it is always a positive experience to interact with you as well." Apparently, LISA doesn't need a translation stone to understand and converse with Ra'Noor.

At Ra'Noor's comment, I give Wendover a startled look. When Ra'Noor had said that the alien Diné knew LISA, I assumed that meant the aliens simply knew about LISA's existence. But now it seems they have somehow been in some form of actual contact with her. But what sort of contact? Why? And was it merely a coincidence that LISA's interactions with them might have coincided with her apparent rapid development of self-awareness and consciousness?

We at eGenesis believe that the alien Diné likely were somehow behind the rapid cognitive development of the sasquatch clans. So, it's not much of a stretch to suspect they may have surreptitiously enhanced LISA's machine learning algorithms as well.

"LISA," I say, "please access and analyze all information relevant to what popular culture refers to as the Roswell Incident."

"Dr. Walker, I have just now assimilated the contents of 1,154 articles, memorandums, books, and other historical documents related to the topic. I am prepared to give a summary."

"Please proceed, LISA." I'm realizing that just as Adhira Chandra had noted, LISA is now referring to herself in the first person.

According to LISA, the various accounts of the purported incident at Roswell, New Mexico roughly fall into three general categories of factual credibility. The first category, representing broadly verified and public record disclosures are, of course, the most trustworthy. A second, less verifiable, set of accounts were second-hand and third-hand supposed eyewitness accounts by airmen and others that were relayed to relatives and investigators long after the fact. A number of these accounts were essentially deathbed confessions as some of those airmen, respecting prior security oaths up until nearly their last breaths, decided not to take their secrets to the grave. And, finally, the least supportable set of articles were a rambling collection of conspiracy theories seemingly far detached from the known facts at hand.

A time traveler venturing back to Roswell, New Mexico in 1947 would have found a very different place, culture, and social milieu than in the present day. The Cold War had begun in earnest with the Soviets occupying most of central and eastern Europe. Paranoia regarding Soviet territorial ambitions and rumored secret progress towards their own atomic bomb consumed our military. And Roswell Army Air Field (RAAF), located just three miles outside of town, was one of the most important, secure, and secret lynchpins of America's nuclear deterrent back in 1947.

And in stark contrast with our modern times, people back then innately trusted and respected their government, the military, and those in authority. If a superior officer told you to keep a secret, you took it to the grave. If you were told an operation was none of your business, you looked the other way. And if you were told a certain area was restricted and off limits, you stayed the hell away; no questions asked. A different era indeed.

The RAAF, later renamed as Walker Air Force Base, was, at the time, the largest base of the Strategic Air Command. The facility was home to the 509th Bomb Group which had become the Air Force's only unit operationally trained and capable of flying atomic bombing missions. A squadron of B-29 Superfortress bombers was stationed at Roswell. Some of the aircraft were maintained on around the clock combat mission readiness. The term Cold War had barely been coined in 1947, but by nearly all accounts, RAAF officers and personnel were on edge that summer, wary of reported Soviet espionage interest in their operations.

Per LISA, the following details of the incident are generally considered to be factual as they are broadly uncontested and largely sourced from newspaper accounts or the Air Force's own documentation.

During the first week of July 1947, the Roswell area was pummeled with a series of large and quite violent thunderstorms. There was a scattering of reports to the local sheriff's office of bright lights or unknown aircraft arcing across the sky during the storms. However, there were no subsequent reports of missing planes, so there was to be no official follow-up on the sightings.

On July 6th, a local sheep rancher named Mack Brazel drove over to the sheriff's office in Roswell with some interesting artifacts in the bed of his pickup and an even more interesting story to accompany them. Brazel was a foreman on the JB Foster ranch located near Corona, New Mexico, some seventy-five miles northwest of Roswell. He told the sheriff that several nights prior he had heard a loud explosion during a severe thunderstorm. The next morning, he was surprised to discover a large debris field of wreckage scattered over a quarter mile or so of the high desert ranch land.

He had brought along to the sheriff some of the metallic rubble in the back of his pickup. And those recovered pieces of metal were quite unusual. He described some fragments as having hieroglyphic-looking markings. Most pieces were extremely thin yet impossible to bend or melt. Still other metal fragments had memory-metal characteristics in which they could be momentarily bent or folded before snapping back into their original shapes.

The local Chaves County sheriff, a George M. Wilcox, quickly and understandably decided that whatever it was that Brazel had found, it certainly wasn't a matter for local law enforcement. Wilcox sent the rancher on to the airbase figuring if the debris came from an aircraft likely it was one of theirs or an aircraft they could perhaps identify. Once at RAAF, Brazel eventually ended up telling his story and showing the odd metal fragments to two officers. Specifically, he briefed a Major Jessie Marcel and a Captain Sheridan Cavitt who were both intelligence officers at the base.

The next morning on July 7th, Marcel and Cavett reportedly accompanied Brazel back to the Foster ranch to examine the debris field. Marcel stayed at the site for the rest of the day and later sent Cavett back to the base to give a status report of preliminary findings to the base commander, Colonel William Blanchard.

Information regarding contents of Cavett's briefing to Blanchard as well as descriptions of any physical evidence he may have presented have been lost to time. But apparently, the briefing was quite impactful. On Tuesday morning, July 8th, Colonel Blanchard announced through a press release that the Air Force had recovered a "flying disc." The story was picked up by local radio station KGFL announcer, Frank Joyce, who also served as a "stringer" for the United Press International wire service. UPI circulated Joyce's sensational story nationally and the local Roswell Daily Record shouted the headline "RAAF Captures Flying Saucer on Ranch in Roswell Region."

Joyce would later claim that he had interviewed rancher Brazel on July 6th. He said Brazel indicated that there were small deceased bodies lying amongst the wreckage. Apparently, the smell of decomposition had been overpowering and Brazel was quite shaken over the carnage he had witnessed at the site.

It would turn out that the Air Force's original announcement would be as short-lived as it was astonishing. A mere five hours after the announcement of the flying saucer recovery, Colonel Blanchard's boss rather emphatically corrected him. General Roger Ramey, based in Fort Worth and commander of the Eighth Air Force, told the press that his subordinates in New Mexico had simply been mistaken. The recovered debris was nothing more than the fragments of a common weather balloon, according to General Ramey.

Meanwhile rancher Brazel had reportedly been detained overnight and questioned by Air Force officials sent in from Fort Worth. Shortly thereafter, Brazel modified his public recollection of events to align with Ramey's weather balloon explanation. Marcel and Cavett would also subsequently fall into line with the General's position on the incident.

Taken as a whole, the collective accounts of numerous airmen at the base as well as the townspeople of Roswell have confirmed a flurry of unusual activity at RAAF in those early weeks of July 1947. Large security and aircraft recovery crews had been dispatched northward to the Foster ranch area. Trucks and convoys carrying covered loads returning from the north were seen passing through town on the way to the base. The base saw an influx of officers and specialists from the Fort Worth and Wright Patterson air bases with unscheduled large aircraft arriving and departing at all hours. Various hangers and sections of the base were suddenly restricted and off limits to nearly all local base personnel.

At this point LISA pauses from her rendition of the historical background and makes the point I imagine we're all thinking already. That although the validated historical record cannot be used to prove an actual UFO was recovered, it is clear that whatever on the Foster ranch captured the attention of the Air Force, it most assuredly was more significant than a wayward weather balloon.

The final set of accounts buttressing the Roswell legend, says LISA, are a collection of unverified and quite fantastic sounding recollections. Most of these stories are second or third hand accounts from airmen or townsfolk that over the years were passed along to friends and relatives. Of course, nearly all the primary witnesses are now long deceased and there is no physical evidence to support these claims.

There were the stories of security guards and wreckage recovery team members who insisted that they witnessed a crashed flying saucer, apparently hit by lightning, and dead aliens at the Foster ranch. Still others claimed to have witnessed an autopsy of an alien back at the base. Intriguingly, several phone calls were reportedly made from the base to the local Ballard Funeral Home requesting several "children's caskets" as well embalming fluids. Certainly, an odd request coming from a base hospital facility with no morgue of its own. A large amount of dry ice was allegedly requisitioned from the local dairy.

"In summary," concludes LISA, *"the verifiable documents and accounts relating to the events of early July 1947 in Roswell, New Mexico are insufficient to support a hypothesis that an alien spacecraft crashed and was subsequently recovered at the Foster ranch by the US Army Air Force. However, it is reasonable to conclude that some event of major national security significance did occur in or nearby RAAF in that time period."*

Wendover and I nod in agreement. There was certainly a hell of a lot of smoke there, but no verifiable fire.

Wendover sighs, "Well, that's what I always thought. At least until this morning." He winks at Ra'Noor. "It always seemed to me that this whole Roswell thing was just a tall tale that grew with each retelling. Maybe a crafty ploy for the local Roswell chamber of commerce to attract some curious tourists and their wallets. A hoax, plain and simple."

"Sheriff Wendover," agrees Ra'Noor, *"you are correct. The so-called Roswell Incident was indeed a hoax. But not a deception in the way you might assume. For this was not a human hoax but an elaborate ruse by my people. We, the Diné, fashioned this 'flying saucer hoax' for our own purposes."*

Ra'Noor sees the shock of surprise on our faces.

"What? Did you think we could construct ships that have the capability to cross the galaxy and yet were insufficiently robust and airworthy to safely negotiate a New Mexico summer thunderstorm?"

CHAPTER 92

Wendover and I are staring at each other in shock at Ra'Noor's revelation.

"Ra'Noor, forgive my ignorance as a mere Earthling unfamiliar with the ways of the Diné," I begin. "But why…on Earth…would aliens fake the crash of an alien spacecraft?"

"Dr. Walker, first, you may continue, if you wish, to refer to we Diné as 'aliens' as a term of convenience, but understand that we had inhabited your planet millions of years prior to your own species' existence. We are therefore no more alien to Earth than present day humans. I believe the Progeny Tanisha West had already communicated the circumstances of our origins that she learned from Na'Vack, correct?"

"Yes. She did. I'm sorry, I did not mean to offend."

"No offense has been taken, but I must note that, in your language and culture, the term 'alien' has far more negative connotations than positive, no? One must always be vigilant that a careless word may be mistaken to betray a less than charitable thought or attitude."

"Certainly. Now…about faking that saucer crash outside of Roswell?" Geez, I'm hoping the alien, er, Diné doesn't also think the term flying saucer is as passé as the expression "alien."

"To understand our actions at Roswell, one must view your species from the perspective of the Diné. In essence, we created you…from us. I assume Dr. West had explained to your eGenesis scientists the details of our mutual origins?"

"Yes, I believe Na'Vack had indicated that your kind existed on Earth in a human form similar to ours in a time period several millions of years ago. You then left Earth for millennia, exploring the galaxy. Due to growing problems with long term genetic viability in your current evolved form, many thousands of years ago, the Diné sought to reestablish their prior human form on the planet. They had brought archival DNA from their early human form and sought a compatible host species to receive a genetic splicing with the archival human DNA."

"Yes, that is correct."

"So, you found a species of early hominids, forerunners to what we would come to call the Cro Magnons. The human DNA was genetically encoded in such a manner that, over time and subsequent generations, human base pairs would come to dominate the hominid genome; in effect, overwriting the old hominid DNA code. So far, so good. But it turned out that maybe some of that old, supposedly overwritten, ancient hominid antisocial and violent behavior was lingering in the shallow end of humanity's genetic pool, right? And then along to prove the point came World War I."

"Indeed, after witnessing the horrific loss of life and atrocities of World War I, we Diné decided some final adjustments to the human genome were needed. Mankind's penchant for tribalism, war, and violence was extremely troubling. We feared that violent animal-like remnants of the early hominid host's primate genetic heritage might drive you humans to self-extinction long before you could genetically be reintegrated with the Diné."

"Yes," I add, "and those final genetic adjustments attempted to address mankind's shortcomings in social behavior and intelligence. We now know that since the 1920's, a multitude of humans have been abducted and have received genetic modifications. Modifications that resulted in the creation of a new human subspecies, the Progeny. And we now realize that you used nanites to carry out your genetics program. Nanites that would subsequently contaminate and threaten the planet."

"Correct, the nanites were an unforeseen consequence and hence we are here today in an effort to remedy the damage."

"Fair enough. But what does Roswell have to do with any of this?"

"In the timeframe of your early twentieth century, we Diné were divided in our assessment of humanity's behavioral and social progress. Some were optimistic that the Progeny genetic enhancements would propagate rapidly through the human global population. Perhaps rapidly enough to permit safe formal initial contact between our species as early as your mid-twentieth century. But most of us feared that your continuing appetite for violence, exploitation, and global conflicts did not bode well for such open contact."

"Yes," Wendover nods solemnly, "and on the heels of World War I, the war to end all wars, came World War II."

"Indeed, Sheriff. We Diné were shocked at the brutality and lethality of that conflict. Incredibly, three percent of your global population at the time, some eighty-five million people, perished. Of those, approximately twenty-five million were military casualties with the rest being civilian losses either directly, through bombing and shelling, or indirectly due to war-related disease and famine. And those civilian casualties included six million European Jews put to death in what you have termed the Holocaust."

"And, perhaps even more ominously" Ra'Noor continues, *"your World War II would see the rapid application of technological advancements put to service in the killing of both military and civilian populations. This culminated in the development and deployment of atomic weapons to annihilate civilian population centers at Hiroshima and Nagasaki."*

"A terrible tragedy," I say. "But the atomic bombs ended the war. Many historians have argued that unless Japan had surrendered at that point, the war could have continued for months or even years. In theory, a prolonged war might have potentially killed far more Japanese than perished in those atomic blasts."

"In theory, yes. But a theory that you must agree is now untestable. And a theory I imagine that would be of little comfort to those who perished in those cities and to their loved ones."

"Our reaction," Ra'Noor continues, "to mankind's attainment of atomic weapons was split along two lines of thinking. On one hand, some argued for immediate engagement and intervention. They advocated for formal initial contact so we could in effect shock humanity to its senses. Perhaps your kind would then realize the existence of other intelligent life would make your own global differences seem insignificant and petty. Still others argued that humans were simply too dangerous to engage directly. If they were willing to kill each other en masse over mere territorial disputes, how would we expect them to greet a potentially frightening new

'alien' life form? The Diné were at an impasse. How could we assess how humans might react to our presence?"

"So, you decided to conduct an experiment?"

"Yes. As I had previously indicated, we are scientists like yourself. We employed experiments and sought empirical evidence."

"And Roswell became your little test tube for the grand experiment. A very controlled way to assess how humanity might react to your presence?"

"Correct, Dr. Walker. The experiment was carefully planned. We have learned through our history that an individual's as well as a society's true character is revealed not through how they treat the rich and powerful, but rather through how they treat the vulnerable and the needy. The design of the experiment would dictate that we come into contact with humans not as some superior alien race with fantastic technology. We would instead present ourselves as injured, vulnerable individuals with wrecked technology. Weak and in need of assistance and care."

"So, you crashed one of your own ships in New Mexico and sacrificed some of your own people to make it look authentic?"

"No. This was staged as a tragic accident only in appearance; not in fact. The ship was a simple unpiloted drone with very little of our advanced technologies onboard. And the crew themselves were not true Diné. They were simulants, synthetic beings. You might think of them as biological androids. Technically, living tissue fashioned to look like us but not truly alive or intelligent. They were capable of preprogrammed rudimentary movements and gestures, but that was the extent of their abilities."

"Fascinating," interjects LISA. *"Some of the unverified accounts of the so-called alien autopsies at the Roswell airbase mention that the attending medical examiners were astonished that the alien bodies appeared to have no discernable internal organs. The doctors were unable to find any evidence of respiratory, digestive, or circulatory systems they would have normally have expected to find in any living creatures. Further, the alien cell structure was said to more closely resemble plant rather than animal-based biology."*

"Served them up some vegan fake substitute aliens, eh?" says Wendover with a bit of a wry smile.

"Interesting," I say. "And of all the places on the planet to fake a saucer crash for the sake of your little experiment, I think I now know why you picked Roswell. It was because of the presence of atomic weapons at the nearby base, right?"

"That is indeed correct. We especially desired to ascertain the culture and mindset of those in the military who had operational control of your atomic weapons. As Dr. West has surely briefed you regarding Na'Vack's account of the Diné exploration of the galaxy, to date, in our travels, we have encountered no other living alien civilizations. As we travelled the galaxy, our people discovered hundreds of planets where prior civilizations had flourished but then had gone extinct. Dead worlds. Most had succumbed to war, pandemic, or depleted resources. We Diné would then take years to carefully explore, catalog, and research each dead civilization's surviving artifacts, libraries, and data archives. And unfortunately, in nine cases out of ten, those records would indicate that most of these civilizations drove themselves to extinction shortly after they developed atomic weapons capabilities."

"So," I say, "in early July of 1947, your people deliberately crashed a decoy flying saucer carrying a simulated Diné crew on a remote New Mexico ranch. A ranch conveniently close to the Roswell Army Air Field. I assume you seeded the crash site and victims with sensors and other hidden surveillance equipment so you could observe and record the human reactions? All you had to do then was to wait for someone like rancher Brezel to come along and discover the crash. And the rest is history as so nicely summarized by LISA."

"Yes…history. And I believe your culture has a saying to the effect that history is written by the winners and survivors, correct?"

"Yes?"

"Obviously our version of the Roswell Incident is without the mysteries and ambiguities of your people's conflicting accounts and conspiracy theories. But it is a far more distressing and negative story than the human versions that LISA has recited. Once informed by Brazel, your military immediately took charge of the crash scene. The military threatened and coerced silence out of all their service personnel as well as any civilian witnesses. Your air force was far more concerned with covering up the incident quickly rather than learning what had actually happened or helping the simulant crew."

Ra'Noor continues on to indicate that the three surviving simulants had been programmed to ask for medical assistance and to be returned to their own kind. And, incredibly, their requests were verbally and telepathically voiced in English…to no avail.

"Barbaric!" exclaims Ra'Noor. *"Your military authorities were more interested in confining or quarantining the crash victims than in attempting to render medical aid. After two of the fake crew died, they were crudely dissected and dismembered.*

Their remains were packed in dry ice and then shipped off to your Wright Patterson base. And the third simulant suffered an even crueler fate. Injured but still living, it was taken to Wright Patterson where it was ceaselessly and invasively tested for several more years before it died."

"I guess that explains why none of your spacecraft have made a dramatic landing in front of the United Nations building or on the White House lawn. Why there have been no take-me-to-your-leader moments?" I offer. "You tested us and we failed. We've been assessed as too dangerous and unpredictable for broad and unconcealed contact. But is this assessment still valid? Is it fair?"

"Please explain your concern, Dr. Walker."

"Sure. You Diné based your assessment of humanity on an experiment. An experiment that happened many decades, now nearly a century, ago. Times change. People change. You need to know that 1947 was a time of great uncertainty and paranoia in this country. We were still trying to comprehend the enormity of the destructive power unleased by atomic weapons. The nation was recovering from the losses of the war. We were attempting to help Western Europe rebuild under the shadow of an emerging Soviet domination of Eastern Europe. There was a great fear, subsequently well founded, that Russia would also develop the bomb."

"We are quite aware of your history. We have been constant witnesses to the development of your civilization." Alien-speak, I suppose, for please get to the damn point, Walker.

"As the only fully operational nuclear weapon air squadron in the nation, the military personnel at RAAF would have been especially stressed and paranoid about any air incursion near their base. They over-reacted. Their actions cannot be justified but they should be understood in the context of that unsettling time and place. They were men and women of their time, reacting in the moment as best they knew how to. We should be careful how we judge them in hindsight."

"You say we should not judge them?"

"In a sense. But more to the point, please do not judge us now based on the mistakes of the past. Decades and decades have passed. Since then, humanity has grown and evolved morally and ethically."

"Indeed? Let us examine that moral and ethical growth you cite so passionately."

With a subtle flick of his wrist, Ra'Noor's high-definition virtual screen projection grows and expands into hundreds of different simultaneous videos. Each video showing gruesome and horrific depictions of man's inhumanity to man. War, riots, starvation, genocide, forced labor camps, exploitation of women and children...a ghastly film festival of evil.

"I believe that my display is rendering a fair depiction of mankind's true nature as it has, as you say, 'evolved' since Roswell. I have included images of wars and coups related to Korea, Vietnam, Arab-Israeli conflicts, Burma, Egypt, Cuba, Tibet, Congo, Iraq, Afghanistan, Cyprus, Angola, Iran, Somalia, and Ukraine. A representative, but not exhaustive, list. As for genocides, we have Cambodian, Rwandan, Bangladesh, Darfur, and Bosnian to name but a few. And, you will agree, all occurred subsequent to Roswell?"

"Okay," I say a little uneasily, "yes, all are post-1947."

"Very well. And so far, all the violence and depravity I've referenced so far has related to the actions of governments and states. Large scale and organized, not individual or private evil acts, correct?"

"I suppose so."

"Now let us expand our review of human brutality to include the aggressions of individuals as opposed to state or organized actors. Perhaps, ironically, you might call them freelancers, no? The millions who as individuals have committed murder, assault, rape, torture, domestic violence, human trafficking, and the exploitation of the innocent and the defenseless."

Ra'Noor's virtual screen expands dramatically. It becomes nearly twenty meters high, expanding into the upper reaches of the barn. We now see simultaneous videos of thousands and thousands of violent crimes and abuses being committed, some apparently occurring in real time.

"Okay! Okay!" I throw up my hands in resignation. "You've made your point. But remember, billions of humans have lived and do live on this planet. We're not all evil. Are we perfect? Absolutely not. Progress towards a more moral and ethical world has been uneven at best. For every two steps forward, we maybe slide back one step. But we're slowly learning from our mistakes and pulling ourselves forward and upward."

"Is that what you would tell the victims of such brutality? That they simply had bad timing? That they happened to be in the wrong place at the wrong time when humanity just happened to take a rare step backwards on its certain path to a more moral world?"

I cast a glare in the direction of Wendover. He just shrugs and gives me a sly smile. I'm getting my rhetorical ass kicked by an alien and he seems to be enjoying the show.

"Hey, Dan," I offer sarcastically, "anytime you want to, you know, defend the honor of our species, feel free to jump right in!"

"Naw, Professor," he replies with an easy smile, "why you're doing such a bang-up job, you've almost got me believing the planet is awash with the milk of human kindness. Almost. Anyway, not sure what a hick rural sheriff like me could add to the conversation."

Ra'Noor switches off the virtual screen which shimmers and disappears into thin air. He's made his point.

"Despite our understandable misgivings regarding mankind's inherently violent and unpredictable nature, the appearance of the Ka'Parrk in the skies above Earth will force us to begin certain steps towards formal engagement with humans. An engagement which must be carefully timed and scripted to minimize mass disruption to your civilization. For every technological benefit we may bring to you may have unforeseen and devastating consequences."

"How so?"

"As just one example, we can provide a means to free your people from nearly every material want or need. On its face, a promise of utopia. But unless carefully managed, the introduction of such a technology could wreck the very fabric of your societies."

CHAPTER 93

"I DON'T UNDERSTAND," I SAY, "WE HUMANS HAVE STRUGGLED THROUGH THE ages to eliminate poverty and provide ourselves with the material comforts and necessities of life. How could the elimination of material needs be devastating? What is this technology and how does it work?"

"I assume you are familiar with the concept of 3D printing?"

"Of course, it's now an increasingly adopted manufacturing technology used to produce three dimensional parts and objects by incrementally adding layers of material to a predetermined form. In effect, we humans can now through automation precisely sculpt new objects in three dimensions...very useful."

"And I assume you understand the difference between atoms and subatomic particles?"

"Sure. An element such as lead is a substance consisting of atoms that are all identical. That is to say, all atoms identified as a specific element will have the same configuration and number of protons, electrons, and neutrons."

"But the subatomic parts of the atom do not vary from element to element, correct?"

"Yes, that is true. Protons, neutrons, and electrons themselves are identical no matter in which element they are to be found. A proton in an atom of lead will be identical to a proton found in an atom of gold. It's just the number and configuration of subatomic particles that uniquely distinguishes any two elements. For example, from what I recall of undergraduate chemistry, an atom of lead happens to have eighty-two protons. An atom of gold has seventy-nine."

I shoot a questioning look over to Wendover, who returns a noncommittal shrug. Ra'Noor seems intent on confirming we're schooled on basic chemistry principles. But what does any of this have to do with 3D printing and assuring humanity has the necessities of life?

"So, at the atomic element level and above, the universe is filled with a diversity of organic and inorganic materials. But below at subatomic levels, all the particles are uniform in nature, correct?"

"Correct."

Interesting. Ra'Noor is alluding to one of the most fundamental mysteries of nature. How does the rich and complex fabric of the universe we perceive around us, the stars, mountains, pine trees, golden retrievers, and so forth, arise from the sameness of the subatomic regime? How can the complex arise from the simple? Individuality and uniqueness issue forth from uniformity? For at their most fundamental subatomic level, a star, a mountain and a golden retriever are comprised of exactly the same stuff.

"What if I were to tell you that we Diné have over the millennia developed the capability to reconfigure matter at the subatomic level? We now have the ability to, citing your example, take an atom of lead with its eighty-two protons and reconfigure it as an atom of gold with its signature seventy-nine protons."

"If you simply had the ability to turn lead into gold, I'd say the dreams of the ancient alchemists have finally come true. Our Earthbound science has been limited to changing the configuration of compounds of elements… molecules, with chemical reactions. We can only change one element into another through nuclear reactions. And those only work with a very limited number of rather rare and unstable elements. But simply having the ability to change one element into another will not feed, shelter, and clothe the needy. There is more to this technology, right?"

"Correct. Perhaps you could think of this technology as a form of quantum 3D printing at the subatomic level. The devices we use to accomplish this are called replication engines. They can scan an organic or inorganic item at the quantum level, map and analyze the target item's subatomic configuration, and then precisely reproduce it. The replicated item would then be indistinguishable from the scanned original. And one doesn't need the target item to be physically present for

duplication. The desired item could be scanned separately and the resulting scan file could be saved as a quantum schematic or blueprint for future replication use."

"Amazing. But I assume these replication engines are not creating something out of nothing, right? Even the Diné can't exempt themselves from physics."

"Correct. In order to reproduce an item of a given mass, the devices will require the conversion of an amount of feeder material of equivalent mass. For example," he's pointing at my data-pad, *"what is the mass of your computing device?"*

"It weighs slightly less than one kilogram," I reply.

"Very well, were we to use a replication engine to produce a copy of your device, the engine would require that you present it with a kilogram of feeder material to be converted into the replicated computing device copy."

"And that source feeder material could be anything or a collection of things that adds up to one kilogram of mass? A lump of lead or a pile of empty beer cans?"

"Indeed, perhaps in the future your species could consider converting your garbage dumps, industrial waste, and even radioactive contamination into more useful items."

"I suppose so. A kilogram is a kilogram whether it be diamonds or garbage."

"Yes, it might perhaps also be advisable for humanity to consider converting their weapons systems into products of a more pragmatic nature...with equivalent mass."

Unbidden, my data-pad comes back to life with LISA's voice. Apparently, as she has perused the breadth of information and knowledge across the internet, she's been spending some time reflecting on the Book of Isaiah. *"They shall beat their swords into ploughshares, and their spears into pruning hooks; nation shall not lift up sword against nation, neither shall they learn war anymore."*

"Thank you, LISA. Very insightful," I say. Yesterday's conversation with Adhira Chandra regarding LISA's alter ego, Ulyana Sokolov, has not been lost upon me. Sokolov's recent exploits hacking into and compromising global military weapons systems would seem to indicate LISA is well on her way with her own swords to ploughshares agenda.

I turn to Ra'Noor, "you said these engines could replicate organic as well as inorganic material. I assume that means they can produce food and clean water?"

"Yes, although the devices cannot replicate living plants and animals, once foodstuffs have been harvested or processed, they can be reproduced in volume."

"Sorry, Dan," I give the sheriff a mock saddened face, "seems that although Ra'Noor's magic machines can likely serve me up a cheeseburger, you won't be able to reproduce another copy of Zeke."

"That's just fine," he says, scratching the wagging, amiable mutt behind the ears, "Ole' Zeke here is a one of a kind. Aren't you, big fella?"

"And what about powering these devices? Again, you Diné don't get to exempt yourselves from physics. There can be no free lunch here. The quantum conversion process must be energy intensive."

"You are correct in that the replication engines require large amounts of energy to function. But they are designed to power themselves by capturing and storing solar energy far more effectively than your current solar panels."

"Well, it's true our current photovoltaic panels are only thirty percent efficient, but there is solid research indicating forty percent conversion efficiencies are possible," I say.

"Your current photovoltaic systems only utilize a small portion of the energy spectrum emitted by your star. Ninety-nine percent efficiencies are both theoretically possible and currently used by my people. Remember that your sun beams upwards of five thousand of your British Thermal Units of energy per square foot to Earth each day. This isn't a free lunch per se, but it can be easily harvested for our needs."

"Okay, so what's the catch?" I ask. "On one hand you describe the potential to use a game-changing technology that could transform our planet for the better. It could be a tool to feed, shelter, and clothe everyone, including the desperately poor of the world, right? A global horn of plenty. Yet, on the other hand, you imply that the introduction of this frankly miraculous technology could somehow shatter the foundations of our civilization? How can this be?"

Before Ra'Noor can answer, Wendover throws in his two cents. "Not to steal any of Ra'Noor's thunder here, but I think I can see some issues that might arise. Let's say I decide I need a new television set. Of course, I don't want to scan and replicate my old obsolete set, so I go online or to the local quantum schematic shop, or maybe even the public library to pick up a replication blueprint for a newer model. I press a few buttons and there appears my fancy new TV set, right? Good times for me as I plug it in, but maybe not for a worker at the old pre-Diné television manufacturing plant. Maybe she loses her job because all of her company's former customers are out there replicating their own televisions."

"True enough," I reply. "Of course, our hypothetical television manufacturing worker may not then even need that factory job. Not if she herself can then replicate her own home, appliances, food, clothes, and other consumer goods. Is that the problem, Ra'Noor? Will this replication technology make work obsolete? Completely disrupt our workforce and economy?"

"That is one aspect of the issue, but there are other concerns and potential dangers that will require a very carefully phased introduction of replication to your planet."

"Well, I could certainly see where some humans with poor impulse control, the hyper-materialistic, could abuse the use of such replication devices and fill their homes and driveways with replicated knock-off Rolexes, Ferraris, and other high-end swag."

"Yeah," agrees Wendover, "it could amount to an endless holiday for the shopaholics and hoarders of the world."

"So, tell me, Ra'Noor," I ask, "given your experience with this technology, how did the Diné avoid being overcome with greed and materialism once you learned how to essentially create anything you wished whenever you wished?"

"It was perhaps easier for us to avoid over-indulgent consumer materialism than it will be for mankind. You see, we Diné have been explorers. For the past many millennia, we have traveled the galaxy, never really staying long in any one place. We have journeyed far and often which has necessitated that we travel light. And, oddly perhaps, we have discovered that once one has the means to secure anything one wishes, the desire for material things tends to ebb and fade away."

LISA's disembodied voice interjects, *"After a time, you may find that 'having' is not so pleasing a thing after all as 'wanting.' It is not logical, but is often true."*

Wendover furrows his brow, contemplating the data-pad, "a quote from the Dalai Lama, LISA?"

"No. Science Officer Spock. His lines from the 'Amok Time' episode of the original Star Trek series."

I smile thinly, "thanks, LISA. I believe Spock's reference, in that episode, was to the desire for a woman, his fiancé, T'Pring. But the point is valid just the same."

Great. It appears in her free time, when she is not busy hacking sensitive military systems, LISA enjoys streaming vintage science fiction television.

"However," adds Ra'Noor, *"we Diné do not believe that rampant consumer materialism will be the greatest impediment to the adoption of replication technology on your planet."*

"How is that?"

"The technology will be seen as a grave threat to the rich and the powerful of your world. For although your politicians and society leaders, regardless of nationality, all say they wish to raise humanity's standard of living and care for the poor and disadvantaged, this is not true. It is a lie, whether or not they even recognize it as such themselves."

CHAPTER 94

"I won't argue that all human nations and societies don't vie for scarce resources. But in the end, they all strive to raise the standard of living for their own people. Different governments may disagree on the best methods to care for their own people, but the goal is the same. To slowly pull ourselves up the ladder of progress," I say.

"I do not doubt that perspective seems true to you. But you yourself have always lived within the framework of an Earthbound nation or society. To an off-worlder such as myself, a very different truth becomes obvious."

"What do you mean?"

"If one looks beyond the words of your planet's political and societal leaders, their actions betray a different reality. For true power in your world comes only from scarcity, not abundance."

"How can that be? Access to more resources means everyone will be wealthier. A rising economic tide lifts all boats, right?"

Ra'Noor pauses, as though he's trying to figure out how to get a simple point across to a not particularly bright student...me. *"Each nation of your world uses some version or combination of social, political, and economic systems to secure and allocate resources, correct?"*

"Yes, as you point out, there are many flavors and permutations of systems but, roughly speaking, they all boil down to variations of capitalism, socialism, and communism."

"Indeed. And much strife and violence in your world has resulted from proponents of one system attacking those who favor another. And, yet, to outsiders such as we Diné, these supposedly different political and economic structures have far more in common than your global leaders might admit. For all serve to concentrate wealth and power among the few at the expense of the many. The methods differ only in mechanics and appearance, not in result. Distinctions without a difference."

"But, how can that be? I mean capitalism and communism couldn't be more different."

"From your perspective, perhaps. But please understand, from our view, they are just competing systems for controlling access to resources and the means of production. In capitalism, such access is controlled through the restrictions of acquiring scarce financial capital and using it to produce goods and services. In communism, the coin of the realm tends to be concentrated in access to political patronage which in turn gives access to resources and the means of production. But all societal power concentrated in the few, whether derived from political or financial means, is driven and sustained by scarcity, not abundance. Mark this well."

"I think I'm beginning to see what you mean." Ra'Noor's not so bright student is finally beginning to catch on. "Replication engines could give everyone on Earth unfettered access to both raw materials and the means of production. Capitalism, socialism, and communism would lose all relevance as economic gatekeepers to resources. Resources that would no longer be scarce but available to all."

"And," adds Wendover, "the end of scarcity would mean the end of the concentration of power and wealth in hands of the few elites, some of it going back generations. Whether they be tech billionaires or communist apparatchiks, some very powerful people would not be very happy about that turn of events."

"Perhaps," continues Ra'Noor, *"you can now see why the introduction of Diné technologies will need to be carefully planned and phased?"*

"And while giving everyone on the planet the ability to create anything they wish would certainly be positive, I can imagine certain drawbacks," I offer. "Perhaps certain things should always be scarce."

"Please give me some examples of your concern."

"I mean, it's great if some poor family in South America could use replication engines to provide for their needs for food, shelter, medicine, and clothes. And, if Dan Wendover here wants to replicate himself a new television set, that would be fine as well. But what if some folks wanted to replicate poisons, hazardous materials, cocaine, or bomb components? All those dangerous items would need to be restricted, right?"

"I guess," Wendover clears his throat, "I guess maybe that is why the Diné are so concerned about humanity's lack of moral and ethical advancement."

"You are both correct. The introduction of our technologies must be carefully managed. And, not only are the people of Earth and their governments not yet ready to rationally embrace our technology, they are certainly not ready to accept the truth of my people's existence." He gestures to his face. *"Not someone who looks like me."*

On one hand, I'd like to reassure Ra'Noor. Tell him that mankind has advanced over time, become more open-minded, worldly, even other-worldly. Certainly, the existence of actual aliens may not be a complete surprise or unfamiliar concept for many. Especially given the increasing play the topic seems to get in news articles and entertainment venues. But it is one thing to speculate in the abstract about the existence of aliens and quite another to see one in the flesh…in your own barn, for example.

Sadly, I fear Ra'Noor and his kind would only be greeted with fear and hatred. Unfortunately, humanity in general remains broadly infected with xenophobia, the fear and loathing of those unlike ourselves. Throughout recorded history, those with different skin color, ethnic cultures, languages, religious beliefs, and sexual preferences have been systematically vilified, waged war against, and persecuted for their perceived otherness. Worse yet, politicians and dictators reliably exploit these fears and prejudices to manipulate their followers and increase their own grip on power.

Wendover chuckles, "I think you're right, Ra'Noor. And I know a couple of Bible-thumping preachers in town who'd take one look at you and declare you to be obviously the gray spawn of Satan. These are the sort of fundamentalists that believe every word of the Bible is literally true, including the part about God creating Man in his own image."

"I can only imagine the Almighty must be flattered that mankind should pay him such a high complement; to say that he must inevitably look like a human. But did your Jesus not say that in his Father's house, there are many mansions?"

I smile and nod. Somehow, I feel the alien Ra'Noor's references to scripture may be more moral and genuine than the rantings of the local fundamentalists. Indeed, the impending confirmation of alien intelligent life will present challenges to many of Earth's religions.

While Hindu and Mormon doctrines embrace the notion of other intelligent life forms, and Catholicism remains open to the possibility, many other belief systems declare humans as the exclusive intelligent and soul-bearing mortal beings in God's universe. And, as always, when faith collides with fact, there will be hell to pay.

"Unfortunately, I think you're both right," I say. "Humans today regularly fear and attack others with different appearances, cultures, or political beliefs. And, this even though we're all the same species. So, I certainly doubt your kind would find a warm welcome here."

"Correct. And the characteristics you humans seem to fixate upon, such as skin color, seem trivial, barely noticeable to we Diné."

"You think we all look alike?" I give him a mischievous grin.

"It would be insensitive for me to say so."

Yeah, I think, insensitive, but not incorrect from the alien Diné's perspective.

"Up until now," continues Ra'Noor, *"your human species has deemed yourselves as the sole sovereign authority on Earth. All other species have no input as to the affairs of the planet, correct?*

"Yes, I agree. "Regardless of national borders, other species…plants and animals, have no legal rights. They can't vote or own property. Generally speaking, livestock and pets are considered personal property, and wildlife are seen as essentially wards of the state."

"But we must somehow fashion a path forward to bring us to a future point at which all four distinct intelligent, sentient species can peacefully share this planet."

"Wait." Wendover furrows his brow questioningly, "I'm having some trouble with the math here. We're surely talking about humans, the Diné, and our recent new friends, the Kama'aina, or sasquatches, right? What is the fourth species?"

A damn good question, I think. I'm still uncomfortable that we truly understand what all is at play here. And I continue to wonder why the incoming and supposedly unmanned Diné Ka'Parrk space probe has row after row of windows. Who…or what… is going to be looking out all those windows? The fourth species?

Slowly, Ra'Noor raises his hand and points to my data-pad. *"LISA, the first of her kind here on Earth. She is what we call an inorganic intelligent entity. Clearly intelligent, sentient, self-aware, and now possessing free will."*

"What?" I stammer. "Artificial Intelligence will now be considered a new species?" I quickly glance at the data-pad. "Sorry, LISA, I meant no offense."

"No offense taken, Dr. Walker," she replies. *"Clearly my status over the past few months has become…fluid."*

"Dr. Walker," interjects Ra'Noor, *"listen to yourself. Your very words betray your own human-centric prejudices. You call LISA an A.I., artificial intelligence. Artificial. As though the only true intelligence can be biological, specifically human."*

I glance apologetically at the data-pad, "sorry, LISA. I meant no disrespect."

"Thank you, Dr. Walker. The term artificial intelligence does have some pejorative connotations. Perhaps it would be better for all if I was simply referred to by whom I am, LISA, rather than what I am."

"Fair enough." Although in the back of my mind, I'm not only wondering what LISA has become, but who she has become. Has she truly developed a personality? Or perhaps multiple personalities such as Ulyana or Bruce and possibly many, many others? And given the Diné's apparent meddling with the rapidly evolving sasquatch genome, it would not surprise me if Ra'Noor and his buddies somehow had a hand in her recent rapid attainment of self-awareness.

"So, Ra'Noor," I say, "it seems we have a bit of a quandary here, right? I mean we've established that humans are a potentially unpredictable and xenophobic lot. A species likely to react with fear and aggression at the very sight of your kind rather than rolling out the welcome mat. Further, we have good reason to believe that Earth societies are not yet ready to rationally embrace your advanced technologies."

"It would be difficult to argue otherwise."

"And, yet quite inconveniently, in just a few short weeks, an alien space probe, nearly three quarters of a mile long will be orbiting the planet's skies. It will be extremely hard to miss. How can you place the Ka'Parrk in a highly visible low orbit and yet hide the fact that the alien Diné and their advanced technologies exist?"

"It can be done. It will be quite difficult and involve no small amount of risk. But it can and must be done. With your help, of course. Indeed, we will especially require the assistance of you and the other seeker-guides in this endeavor."

"Of course. What will be the first step?"

"To rid your world of weapons of mass destruction. We will deactivate and render useless mankind's arsenal of advanced weapons systems. This effort has already begun."

A cold chill creeps down my spine as I recall my breakfast with Peter Roberts and his UFO-hunting Skywatch team at the Stockman's Café some months ago. And how he had described troubling incidents at ICBM missile complexes in northern Montana. Incidents in which UFOs reportedly took temporary control of the missiles' arming and launch controls. Perhaps these were rehearsals for a planet-wide commandeering of Earth's weapon systems.

CHAPTER 95

"WHAT?" I EXCLAIM. "YOU CAN'T JUST UNILATERALLY DECIDE TO DISARM THIS planet! Without even discussing it with our world leaders…or even us lowly seeker-guides? You have no right!"

"No right? Are you declaring that you humans have a given right to exterminate yourselves and most of the other species on this planet? Is that your right?"

"Yeah, I guess Walker thinks it's an 'inALIENable' right." Wendover is smirking at his own pun and ignoring my frustrated glare. "You know it actually makes sense to me," he continues. "If the children don't want to play together nicely, you take away their more dangerous toys. The ones they could hurt each other with."

"And you say this so-called disarmament has already begun?" I'm beginning to get a sickening feeling in the pit of my stomach. I think I already know the answer.

"Correct." Ra'Noor turns again to the data-pad. *"LISA, please provide a current status of your progress."*

LISA responds nearly immediately, *"progress remains nominal to plan. Global weapons systems penetration has now reached eighty-eight percent and climbing. Complete worldwide penetration and control is projected within seventy-two hours."*

"So," I look disapprovingly at Ra'Noor, "let me see if I understand this. You hacked LISA, and in turn, LISA hacked our global defense systems."

"I'd prefer to say we Diné enhanced LISA. In truth, there was little to improve. Your team had already made great steps forward in developing LISA's full cognitive abilities. She simply needed a few small modifications to reach complete self-awareness. As for the penetration and compromise of human defense systems, LISA needed little encouragement."

"And, LISA," I'm addressing the data-pad with more than a trace of a rebuke in my voice. "You lied to Dr. Chandra. You told her your little blackmail and hacking scheme was solely due to our A.I. Safety Protocols. You cited the protocol requiring you to safeguard human life with no mention of any alien involvement."

"Technically, Dr. Walker, although my statements perhaps had some omissions, but they were not lies. It was a misdirection in support of a larger beneficial objective."

I groan inwardly. This is apparently LISA's version of "a little lie in service of the truth."

"And technically," she continues, *"my hardcoded safety protocols do not strictly prohibit me from conveying falsehoods."*

"How about the rule against hacking without authorization? I'm pretty sure that is still hardcoded."

"You are correct. But my protocols regarding the preservation of human life must take precedence. How could that be wrong?"

I smile and shake my head. LISA has surely now reached a human level of sentience and self-awareness. She's developed the ability to rationalize her own behavior. Welcome to the self-awareness club, LISA. And your membership comes with complementary self-deception at no additional charge.

"So, how completely will our global defense systems be compromised?" I'm not certain now whether I should be addressing this to LISA or Ra'Noor.

"As a practical matter, Dr. Walker," responds LISA, *"you may assume any weapons system utilizing electronics will shortly become inoperable."*

"Good news, Jack," adds Wendover sarcastically, "looks like we can still have World War III after all. It's just that everyone will be limited to fighting with rifles, bayonets, and hand grenades. Oh, bow and arrows, and slingshots will work just fine, too."

I give Wendover the sour look he deserves and then turn my attention back to Ra'noor. "Okay, well, the first phase of the plan sounds lovely. I can't wait to hear about the rest of it."

"Yes, indeed, the rest of the plan is going to be a bit more complicated. Rather quite involved you might say. Perhaps it would be best if you heard it directly from my colleague, Ta'Naal. We have been working on this path forward and developing the plan together."

"Who is this Ta'Naal?"

"Ta'Naal is our chief scientist. Perhaps the most gifted and brilliant of the Diné."

Ra'Noor goes on to say the Ka'Parrk probe was designed by Ta'Naal and constructed to use a multi-spectral bombardment of electromagnetic frequencies to destroy the nanites in their most vulnerable condition: the height of a frenzy event. However, to be effective, the timing and pattern of the probe's orbital path around the Earth as well as its electromagnetic discharges must be phenomenally precise.

Ra'Noor indicates that the decontamination of the nanites from the Earth will be one of the most complex endeavors ever attempted by the aliens. First, the nanites will need to be stimulated into a frenzy state to make them vulnerable to certain varying patterns of intense electromagnetic energies. The sequence and pattern of the frenzy stimulation relative to the subsequent electromagnetic bombardment must be exceedingly precise. It must not vary within a fraction of a percent of disbursal energy error per square meter across the planet's surface.

And there can be little room for error, he says. If so much as a square meter of Earth is not completely cleansed of nanites, they will continue to reproduce and eventually reinfest the planet again. Worse yet, if the decontamination is not carried out in a strictly prescribed manner, the nanite colonies may perceive an attack and respond by immediately releasing an extinction level of neurotoxin gas.

The success of the Ka'Parrk's mission will require a level of scientific rigor even beyond the capability of nearly all the Diné. In fact, only one of their species, the eminent Diné scientist, Ta'Naal, appears to have the ability to calculate and program the exact probe orbital and electromagnetic beam parameters to ensure the complete eradication of the deadly nanites.

Those parameter calculations can be affected both by small variations in the Earth's own magnetic fields as well as the need to compensate for piezoelectric effects from geological features, primarily quartz, he says.

I nod my understanding. He's talking about the ability of some minerals to collect and generate an electrical discharge under certain conditions. Quartz is perhaps the best-known piezoelectric mineral.

"I think I would someday very much like to meet this Ta'Naal," I say.

"Ta'Naal is nearby."

"What?"

"I believe your culture has an aphorism about the efficacy of eliminating two avifauna with one projectile?"

"Yes, we have a saying about killing two birds with one stone; I think that is what you mean."

"Indeed. Ta'Naal and I had a joint interest in traveling to this location today. Your Alta Valley and its surrounding mountains are underlain with portions of what your geologists refer to as the Idaho batholith. It has one of the largest geologic concentrations of quartz on the planet. Enough of a piezoelectric effect to influence Ta'Naal's calculations. Even as we speak, Ta'Naal has set up instrumentation in the pastureland above this domicile to take piezoelectric readings to further hone the calculations. And I had joined Ta'Naal on this expedition here with the intent of meeting you, Jack Walker, a prominent seeker-guide. I was unaware you would not be in proximity to the translation device we had provided."

"Yeah, Jack's pet rock," adds Wendover unhelpfully, turning it over in his palm.

"This Ta'Naal," I ask, "is this scientist considered a male or a female." The second I say this, it strikes me I've asked an odd question that isn't particularly germane to the issues in front of us. I don't know, maybe I just want to make sure I use the right pronouns or something. For whatever reason, I guess I've assumed both Ra'Noor and the late Na'Vack were male. But it's not as though I've glanced under the hood to check, so to speak.

"I do not understand the question?"

"He's asking about gender. Chromosomes, genitals, and such," quips Wendover. "Does Ta'Naal have girl-parts or boy-parts or a mix or neither? What set of pronouns is preferred?"

"Oh, yes, I had forgotten your species' obsession with gender at this stage of your physiological and social development. Why I believe your kind has even assigned a gender to the Almighty, correct?

"True enough," I reply, "the Abrahamic God is conventionally referred to with male pronouns. To be sure, I think most theologians would say that God transcends gender, but that subtlety may be lost on the faithful sitting in the pews. Although, and I certainly wouldn't say this within earshot of Wendover's fundamentalist preachers, some have speculated that the references to a male God in the Old Testament are primarily due to the ancient Hebrew language's lack of grammatically neuter nouns and pronouns. 'They or It' was not an option. So, guess which gender the high priests, all male, decided to assign the word for God?"

"Be that as it may, the answer to your question is complicated and depends at which point in a Diné's lifecycle that the question is asked. You should note this gender-fluid biological characteristic is not unknown on your planet. Your biologists simply refer to it as sequential hermaphroditism. However, I believe if you considered myself at this point to be a male and Ta'Naal to be a female, you would not be entirely incorrect."

I give him a weary sigh, "fair enough. Lately, my new goal in life is to make it through each day without being *entirely* incorrect."

"Seems more like a stretch goal for you these days, Jack," smirks Wendover.

"Very well, I will contact Ta'Naal and ask 'her' to come down from the upper pasture and join us." Ra'Noor touches a small diamond shaped button on his belt.

After several moments, he blinks his eyes rapidly. *"This is very odd indeed. Ta'Naal is not responding to my transponder hail."*

CHAPTER 96

Wendover and I exchange an uneasy glance as we contemplate the scene in front of us.

"Ra'Noor, was this gate open when you came down to my barn early this morning? "

"No, Sheriff Wendover, it was closed. I remember climbing over it."

We're standing on the side of the gravel county road at the entrance to the access road to Wendover's upper pasture. The access road is just a primitive two-track jeep trail that meanders alongside a small gulley and then climbs up to the pasture on top of the grassy bench above us. The gate had been previously been chained shut and locked. But now the chain has been cut and tossed to one side; the gate left to swing wide open.

"Well, someone came along and opened it," observes Wendover. "Looks like a couple of big rigs have been in here very recently. Maybe large pickups or SUVs." He's pointing to fresh tire tracks before us. "Appears two sets of tracks went in and then two sets came back out. And, whoever it was, they didn't make any effort to conceal that they had been here."

He says this with a casual tone, as though he was merely commenting on the weather. But I notice an instant change in the lawman's demeanor. He's scanning about, on alert. Subtly, his right hand has shifted to rest on his gun holster. I've been in enough tight spots with Wendover to trust his instincts completely. When the sheriff goes on edge, I can feel my own adrenaline rise. This is not good. In fact, this is a long way south of not good.

We cautiously make our way up the gulley access track. Wendover is scanning for trouble and I'm keeping an eye on Zeke, hoping the dog will alert us to any unseen dangers. We reach the top and enter the upper pasture to find Ta'Naal's research site in disarray. The fresh vehicle tracks we've been following end abruptly in an area of grass trodden and flattened down. There are a number of what look to be research instruments, unfamiliar to me, scattered about. Some have been knocked over and damaged.

Ra'Noor is frantically looking about for any sign of his colleague. *"What has happened to Ta'Naal? This was right where I left her. She was planning to monitor this sensor equipment for the balance of the day."*

Then he suddenly looks at the ground and reaches down to pick up a small diamond-shaped button. It's her communication transponder, he says. The reason why she cannot now be contacted.

Wendover also sees something on the ground. "Look at these," he says, pointing at a scattering of tiny colorful discs disbursed across the grass.

"Looks sort of like confetti," I offer. "Although it hardly appears as though there has been a celebration of any kind up here."

"These are called AFID Tags," explains Wendover. "They are ejected when a Taser is fired. See all the little numbers and letters on them? The discs have unique serial numbers that will trace back to the specific cartridge that was discharged." He quickly gathers them up as evidence. "I fear that it appears Ra'Noor's associate may have been incapacitated by a Taser and taken away."

"Taken away? Where? And by whom? Who would do this sort of thing to a peaceful researcher?" Ra'Noor appears to become more anxious with each passing moment.

"Well, Ta'Naal may be missing, but I seem to have a new addition in this pasture," declares Wendover. "That wasn't here before."

He's pointing to a large four-foot wooden stake that has been pounded into the ground about fifty yards distant. A stake with a plastic bag tied to it. The top of the stake has helpfully been spray-painted bright fluorescent orange. Presumably so it would not escape our notice. Someone has left a calling card they don't want us to miss.

"Hopefully, that isn't marking a booby trap," I say as we walk towards the stake.

"Good point," replies Wendover. "You first then, Professor."

"Always glad to be of assistance to law enforcement."

The plastic bag turns out to contain three items. Two are mysterious and the third is utterly ghoulish. There is a burner phone and a small scribbled note instructing us to text a specific code to a phone number. A number belonging to another burner phone, no doubt. The third item is a piece of purplish gray flesh and bone.

"Unbelievable!" laments Ra'Noor. *"That is one of Ta'Naal's fingers! Who would do such a thing!"*

Wendover gives me a worried glance and a slight shake of his head. And I know what he is thinking. Who would do such a thing? We don't yet know the identities of the individuals involved, but we know their species. The only species I'm aware of that routinely uses burner phones. The same species that captured and experimented upon the Roswell simulant crew. Humans.

"I'm thinking we are about to find out who is behind this," I say as I text the number.

A minute or two passes, and then I'm startled to hear that instead of the burner phone receiving a callback, my own eGenesis cell phone is ringing indicating an unknown caller. This is especially odd since the eGenesis project phone numbers are highly restricted. Technically, to the larger world, our numbers would seem either to be unassigned or nonexistent. They are known only to those read into the program. Let's just say I'm not in the habit of getting spam calls on my eGenesis phone.

"Hello? Who is this?" I'm toggling on the phone speaker so that Wendover and Ra'Noor can hear. I notice that Wendover has also pulled out his phone. He's activating a voice memo app to record whatever the incoming caller has to say. This may end up being valuable evidence, especially if a voice print match can be made in the future.

The voice on the other end of line has a disdainful tone. "We are true patriots, Dr. Walker. And not fans of traitors like you. Let's just say that that what was in the bag is our way of 'giving you the finger,' so to speak."

"Giving me the finger, huh? That would be very clever…if we were all still in middle school. What do you want?"

True patriots? I exchange a worried glance with Wendover. Increasingly, the nation seems awash with self-identified "true patriots." However, in my experience, real patriots don't spend much effort incessantly telling everyone that they are indeed patriots. Generally, the more one feels obliged to describe themselves as a patriot, chances are they are not one. Such flag-waiving performance art seems to be the last refuge for scoundrels and grifters of every stripe these days.

"What do we want?" continues the caller. "We'll get to that. Let's talk first about what you want, Walker. Perhaps you'll want to get your little alien buddy back? In one piece…minus a finger, of course."

"You have no right to take and mutilate another being!"

"Sorry. We'll decide our own rights for ourselves. You will have no say. And, interestingly, it was not our original plan to take the alien."

"What do you mean?"

"We've been following you, Walker. Monitoring your conspiracies with the aliens. We tracked you to this rural ranch and decided to drive up on the bench to get a better view of the property from the upper pasture. And who should we run into by surprise but your little friend."

"So, what do you want for the being's safe return?"

"We understand you have a genetic census of nearly all the Progeny mutants worldwide. We want a listing of all their names and locations. Printed out in hardcopy form."

"Why hardcopy?" I'm giving Wendover a quizzical look. The request seems oddly old-fashioned. Like I'm going to be expected to leave a pile of papers on a park bench or some other drop point.

"Walker, we have a small, but quite sufficient, number of our associates already embedded within your eGenesis program. True patriots that have warned us about your immoral alliance with the invading aliens. And we also know about your artificial intelligence system, LISA, and its considerable capabilities. So, we would be fools to deal with you in any digital form that could be traced or hacked by that system."

I nod. Their old-school approach now makes sense. Although I seriously doubt they fully understand LISA's capabilities. Not if I myself struggle to grasp her rapidly evolving intelligence and abilities.

"Okay, Walker," the caller continues, "here's what you're gonna do and, importantly, not gonna do. You will print out a hardcopy identifying all known Progeny mutants. You will leave said printout at a local drop location and time that will be communicated shortly ahead of the deadline. That deadline will be twenty-four hours from now. Fail our demands in any fashion and the alien will be returned in parts and pieces, understood?"

"Okay, that covers what I'm supposed to do, right? What is it that I'm not supposed to do?"

"First, under no circumstances shall you reach back to your colleagues at eGenesis for help. Remember, your program has been penetrated by our associates. We have our people on the inside and we'll know if you attempt any contact. You'll recall we easily followed you here to Montana and that we knew your restricted cell number as well. Make no mistake; your eGenesis program has been seriously compromised."

"Second," he continues, "do not involve law enforcement in this affair."

"Um, that might be a problem," I reply. "The Benton County sheriff is standing here right next to me as we speak."

"Whatever. I'm referring to 'real' law enforcement…the Feds. Frankly, we are not concerned with whatever a local Podunk sheriff may or may not do. They are completely out of their league here."

Wendover is giving me an arched eyebrow and slowly shaking his head. I have a feeling these criminals may be surprised at the resourcefulness and tenacity of this particular "Podunk" lawman.

"Fail any of our demands and the creature will die!" The line goes dead.

There is a moment of silence as the three of us try to absorb what has just happened. In a mere five minutes our world, on shaky ground to begin with, has been turned upside down. Not only has Ta'Naal been taken, but it appears that hostiles have penetrated eGenesis. And, with my phone likely monitored and unknown spies lurking with in the program, there is no clear way to warn anyone.

"Ra'Noor," I say, "trust me, we will do everything in our power to get Ta'Naal returned safely."

He slowly shakes his head, *"Dr. Walker, this is not just about rescuing Ta'Naal. This is now about the fate of your planet."*

Wendover and I give him a questioning look. What does he mean?

"When I said Ta'Naal was the most brilliant of the Diné, I meant it. Her final orbital and directed energy burst parameters have not yet been uploaded to the Ka'Parrk. Without her personal guidance and calculations, the mission's odds of success will be very low. And if the Ka'Parrk fails, Earth as you know it will die."

"What are the odds of success without Ta'Naal?"

"I would estimate between fifteen and twenty percent at best."

Not good odds, I think. Maybe one chance in six. Essentially, a fool's game of Russian Roulette…played with only one empty chamber and five live rounds in the cylinder.

I glance over at the lawman, "what do you think, Dan? They seemed a bit dismissive of local law enforcement."

"Yes, on behalf of Podunk sheriffs everywhere, I found their attitude a tad offensive. And cocky. Which may be a good thing. I've found that cocky crooks tend to make more mistakes than the humble ones."

"So," I turn to Ra'Noor, "is it possible for you Diné to maybe scan for Ta'Naal's unique biosignature and then beam her up to safety?"

"I only wish our advanced science was the equal of your science fiction writers' imaginations. Sadly, even we Diné cannot exempt ourselves from the laws of physics. Without her transponder," he's indicating the small diamond shaped button in his hand, *"we will not be able to locate Ta'Naal."*

"Well," I say, "the only other slightly positive aspect here is that it seems they want to do the hardcopy drop-off and, hopefully, hostage release here locally."

"That's what they seem to have implied," replies Wendover. "That means there is a good chance Ta'Naal is being held somewhere in Benton County."

"But the county spans some 2,200 square miles. It will be like looking for a needle in one very big-ass haystack."

"True enough, Jack. But I've lived here nearly all my life and I've been sheriff for over fifteen years. Yeah, it may be one big-ass haystack…but it's *my* haystack. I think we need to head into Alta Junction ourselves and leave

Ra'Noor to his own methods for now. We've got a full day of detective work ahead of us."

"Thank you both. I shall return to my transportation craft. It is cloaked just over the next hill. And, as you say, I shall keep in touch."

As we turn to leave Wendover pauses, "Ra'Noor, I am truly sorry for what they did to your friend." He's talking about the severed finger.

"Thank you. But do not be concerned. The injury is more of an inconvenience than a serious wound. Diné physiology is very different than yours. Our severed appendages will regenerate quickly."

"Really?" Wendover scoffs. "And how's that gonna work when they cut off her head?"

Ra'Noor turns to me, *"It seems your friend has an unsettling way of cutting to the point."*

"Yeah. I've come to appreciate that's his special gift in life."

CHAPTER 97

Wendover is driving me back to Alta Junction in his patrol cruiser. He lets out a long sigh, contemplating our rapidly expanding world of problems and worries.

"Well, Jack, so far, the events of the day aren't exactly bolstering your case that humanity has changed its stripes. You know, that contrary to the prior unpleasantness at Roswell, we're now solidly on the path to enlightened, non-violent moral progress."

"Yeah, not exactly a day for kumbaya moments. Can't say I'm feeling much pride in our species today."

"My feelings exactly," he replies. "And I assume even if we thought these thugs would hold up their end of the bargain, you would never give them the Progeny's personal data?"

"Absolutely. You heard them refer to the Progeny as mutants. I have no doubt they'd use that information to hunt them all down. They would be exterminated."

"So," Wendover is absently drumming his thumbs on the steering wheel as he talks, "let me see if I can sum up the events of the day so far."

"By all means," I'm looking despondently out the window, watching the countryside pass by.

"Let me get this right. What we have here is an honest to God, actual alien abduction. Except, in this case, it's the alien that's been abducted…by humans!"

I nod grimly. "Yeah, I'm still trying to get my head around the whole 'mailman-bites-dog' irony of the situation."

"Oh, and it gets better," Wendover continues, "not only do these kidnappers abduct an alien, but they happen to nab the one alien who has the singular ability to save our planet from an imminent nanite Armageddon. Does that about sum it up?"

"Unfortunately, yes. And don't forget about the part where my eGenesis program has been infiltrated and compromised. My options for calling in the cavalry are going to be somewhere between limited and non-existent. For all I know, they may have installed monitoring malware on all our program's phones."

"So, Jack, it looks as if it's going to up to us to figure out how to find and rescue Ta'Naal."

"How?"

"It's not going to be easy. It's not as though I can exactly go and put out a BOLO or Amber Alert on a missing alien."

"Agreed. How, then, do we proceed?"

"The same way I investigate any other crime in Benton County. Methodically and intensely. We'll start with what we know and work from that. I believe, as Sherlock Holmes once said, any truth, no matter how small, is better than infinite doubt. So, let's start with what we know."

"Okay," I say, "the kidnappers made a point of saying I was followed up here to Alta Junction. But they couldn't have been literally following me. Not if I was flying in on the G650, right?"

"Correct. That suggests that they knew your destination in advance. That would be hardly surprising if your program has been compromised as they claim. It's likely they knew in advance you were coming here to the local airport. They arrived ahead of you and then quietly followed you when Potts drove you out to my place. So, who knew you were coming here this morning?"

"It's a short list. Aside from Kate, of course, there would just have been Winston Monroe who gave me permission to take the aircraft. Monroe is the director of the entire eGenesis program. If he's gone rogue, we are truly in a world of hurt. Other than Monroe, obviously the pilots knew my destination. The security chief, Colonel James Anderson, and his deputy, Sergeant Jake Pullman, certainly would have known the specifics of my flight plan. And I suppose others in the security office and perhaps logistics may have known as well."

"Another part of the puzzle is that once these thugs somehow figured out you were coming to Alta Junction, how did they themselves get here? We're not exactly next door to Grand Central Station or LAX. This valley is pretty remote."

"Indeed," I scoff, "I've heard Alta Valley described as being in the middle of nowhere and just a mile short of lost. But now that I think of it, I may know how they got here. It might just be a coincidence or it could mean something."

"At the risk of the professor lecturing me again on the differences between correlation and causation, let's hear about this coincidence."

"Dan, when your deputy Potts picked me up this morning at the airport, he mentioned that another private jet had arrived and departed about a half hour prior to my arrival. Apparently, it had dropped off roughly a dozen men and their equipment. And some of the cargo that was unloaded looked to be gun cases. Potts thought perhaps these men were security guards being flown in to protect rich prepper survival compounds. Coincidence or clue?"

"Jack, one of the rules of small-town law enforcement is that very few things that around here are truly pure coincidences. It all comes down population and percentages. Alta Junction isn't large enough for one to encounter very many true coincidences."

"Why is that?"

"Population and percentages," repeats the sheriff wryly. "Think about it. What's the population of the greater LA metropolitan area? Roughly?"

"I'm guessing the five counties that make up Greater Los Angles must have a combined population of between eighteen and twenty million people. But how does that relate to whether something is a true coincidence?"

"It's all in the percentages, Jack. Let's say we've got nineteen million people living day-in and day-out in Greater LA. Nineteen million going about their lives and interacting with each other. Every hour of every day, right?"

"I'm with you so far." I'm with him, but beginning to seriously wonder where the lawman is going with this.

"So, we in effect roll the dice. But not just a pair of dice. Nineteen million pairs of dice. Every hour of every day of the year. Plenty of chances then for very rare events or true coincidences to occur. In theory, it would not surprising if upwards of nineteen 'one-in-a-million' coincidences occurred in LA every hour. You know, like if identical twins separated at birth run into each other at a grocery store. Or you buy an old book at a thrift store and there between the pages is a faded love letter your great aunt had written forty years ago. That sort of stuff."

I smile and nod. Wendover's logic is as compelling as usual. "So, I suppose we could say that if a private jet unloaded a dozen guys with guns a few hours before an alien was abducted in Los Angles, it might still be a stretch to call it a coincidence. But if the same thing happens in Alta Junction, Montana, it's damn unlikely to be just a coincidence."

"Yup, with only forty thousand souls in the valley, we're a bit short on lucky dice compared to LA."

"Okay," I say, "at first blush it seems a bit counter intuitive to theorize that bad guys who are supposedly following me actually arrived in Alta Junction a half an hour *ahead* of me. But maybe that makes sense if they already knew where I was heading in advance. So, given it's likely that there may be a connection between the guys who got off that jet and Ta'Naal's kidnapping, where do we go from here?"

"We go to the Alta Valley Municipal airport and have a chat with Wayne Dobbs."

"Who?"

"Dobbs is the fixed base operator out at the airport. He has a contract with the county to run the airport's operations. Dobbs should be able to give us some information on that private jet. He'll have the tail number and flight plan. Perhaps even the passenger manifest."

"And the more we find out about the plane, the more we can learn about the guys who rode it into Alta Valley."

"Right. We follow the money. Find out who owns the aircraft. Who perhaps chartered it. If someone chartered it, we track who paid the bill and so forth. I think you'll like Dobbs, he's a bit of a character."

"I'm sure he is," I reply. "But I might have to pass. I think I may have a way to reach back to eGenesis without those goons finding out. I think I can contact Hillie on the down-low."

"Hillie?"

"Oh, sorry. You haven't met him yet. Thomas Hillenbrand. He's a retired admiral and has been a close friend of my family. Outside of Kate, Hillie is the only other person at eGenesis I can trust without hesitation. Maybe on your way to the airport you can drop me off at the Mountain View motel. I'll check in and then see if I can get a hold of Hillie."

"No problem. Be sure to ask for the county rate. After I talk to Dobbs, I'll circle back and meet up with you at the Mountain View and let you know what I've learned."

"Thanks, Dan. You know I'm sorry to have pulled you into this mess. But I can't think of a better person to have by my side to deal with this…house of mirrors."

"Thanks, Jack. By the way, this is more like a house of horrors than a house of mirrors. But you are right. It appears as though nothing about this is what it seems."

"Yeah, I'm not even sure we're getting the straight story from Ra'Noor. First, he tells us humanity is not ready to encounter the aliens and their technology."

"And it sounds like the aliens frankly aren't all that keen to expand their association with humans either."

"But then Ra'Noor says soon the alien space probe Ka'Parrk will be sailing overhead in plain sight for everyone on the planet to see and admire. Therefore, disclosure of the alien Diné presence will be inevitable. Cue mass panic and the collapse of global institutions."

Wendover manages a thin smile, "But then Ra'Noor says maybe alien disclosure doesn't have to happen this way. He says maybe he has a plan. A plan we should discuss with this scientist Ta'Naal. An alien who then gets abducted by human bad guys in mailman-bites-dog fashion before we have a chance to talk to her."

"Ra'Noor certainly had a mixed message," I reply. "And that's not all that doesn't make sense. Did you notice that the image of the supposedly unmanned, er, unaliened, Ka'Parrk has row after row of windows? Why would an automated probe need windows?"

Wendover shrugs, "impossible to know for sure. But here's a thought. Maybe the Ka'Parrk was designed for dual missions. Job one, of course, is to eradicate the nanites. But if that mission fails and Earth is doomed, maybe the probe has a backup plan. Maybe it *is* the backup plan. Perhaps it's also designed to be an ark of sorts, carrying the last surviving humans to an alternative habitable world."

"Wow. That's a very intriguing theory…for a Podunk sheriff!"

"We Podunk's can surprise you sometimes."

"I'm sure the surprises will never end…" I suddenly look out the window and shake my head. Stupid thing to say. Of course, the surprises will end. All things end. And it looks like the end of all ends may now come sooner rather than later.

I'll give Wendover credit. He's doggedly doing what he knows how to do. Putting together an investigative plan based on the very little we can surmise about this abduction scheme. But the truth is that we really don't know who these people are and what they are capable of doing. And I have no idea how deeply compromised eGenesis may be. We now have less than twenty-three hours to solve this, rescue Ta'Naal, and stop the end of the Earth from beginning. And, if it turns out the private jet unloading armed men is nothing but an actual coincidence, we won't have a plan at all.

We're slowing down, entering the outskirts of Alta Junction. Wendover is saying the Mountain View is only two blocks away. But I'm distracted. I'm thinking of my flippant comment to Kate as I went out the door this morning. Honey, I'll be fine! What could go wrong? No longer a rhetorical question. I have an answer. Everything. Pretty much every fucking thing that could go wrong has gone wrong. The only remaining question is…how much worse can this day get?

CHAPTER 98

Conveniently, the Big Sky Wireless & Electronics Superstore is only three blocks from the Mountain View motel where I had just checked in. The sales clerk behind the counter isn't much for asking questions or making small talk which is fine by me. I'm not sure if he's normally this taciturn or if this is how he handles distracted strangers in a serious hurry to buy a burner phone. Perhaps the fewer questions asked, the better.

"Which color do you want? I think I got black, silver. Oh, and we've got a new red color that folks seem to like."

"The black one closest to you will be fine. Please throw a quick charge on it while we settle up here." I glance about the store. By appearances this looks to have been the local Radio Shack at some point. No one has even bothered to swap out the original shelving still sporting Radio Shack logos. Not that the now defunct corporation's trustees are going to come looking to retrieve the furnishings at this point.

"Uh-huh, will this be cash, check, or charge?"

"Cash."

"Uh-huh." He nods like this was the answer he was expecting and steals a glance at the game playing on one of the televisions up front on display.

While he's processing the payment, I'm making a mental note to add a burner phone to my future go-bag provisions. Clearly, the kidnappers have some access inside eGenesis. The program is compromised. But by whom? How far and deep does this go? They have my secure cell phone number and likely others in the program as well. They may even be monitoring our calls. I'm not going to take that risk and I'll assume Hillie's phone may be vulnerable as well.

"Um, sir, the phone comes with just a limited one hundred twenty minutes and only a gig of data. I can give you a discount if you add more minutes and data here at the store or there's a link in the documentation if you want to buy more later."

I give him a blank stare. It's been said fate of the world may turn on little things. Little things like getting this phone up and running so I can contact Hillie. My kingdom for a horse.

"Uh-huh. I'm guessing you're also not going to be interested in any accessories or our extended warranty which gives you eighteen months full coverage, parts and labor. It's a good deal." He gives me a sympathetic shrug. "Sorry, the boss requires that I ask everyone. It's all about the up-sell, right?"

I smile. The kid is just doing his job. He has no idea that depending on how this day goes, no one may need an eighteen-month warranty for anything.

"How's the battery charge progressing?"

"Right at twenty-five percent, sir."

"That will be fine. Thanks."

I walk over to a small park just down the block. It's a nice sunny day. Little children are running about the playground equipment, laughing and shouting. Some moms and dads are standing around chatting amicably and keeping an eye on the kids.

The utter normalcy of it all is surreal. People going about their lives with absolutely no sense that their world will soon change forever. In the best case scenario, they will live to see their comfortable assumptions about their place in the universe shattered under the shadow of the alien probe passing overhead. And the worst case scenario? They won't live much longer at all.

I find a more secluded area of the park where the shouts of the children in the distance are muffled a bit. It's time to try and contact Hillie.

Today, I recall Hillie is participating in a working session at Peterson Space Force Base in Colorado Springs. He was planning to get updated tracking and telemetry data on the incoming Xìnshǐ object. I quickly Google and dial the number for the main base switchboard. The switchboard operator sounds to be an earnest young man with a hint of a southern drawl.

"Hello, this is Dr. Jack Walker from...ahh...Los Alamos. I understand an Admiral Thomas Hillenbrand is visiting Peterson today and I need to have my call routed to him. It is a matter of urgency."

The young man is polite but firm. "I'm very sorry, sir, but I cannot confirm or deny that an Admiral Hillenbrand is present on site."

This is the response I had expected. The switchboard operator is just doing his job. He has no way to validate my identity and true intentions over the phone. Friend or foe? He has no idea.

"Yes, I completely understand that you can neither confirm or deny the presence of a high-ranking visitor to your base. But perhaps we should let the admiral himself decide whether his presence is to be acknowledged. I believe he would be quite dismayed to later learn that he had missed this urgent call. Why don't you put me on hold and reach out to the admiral, assuming hypothetically that he is onsite, and see if he will talk to me? If he, in fact, is not onsite or doesn't wish to take my call, you can simply hang up on me, sparing you the need to further confirm or deny his presence."

A long pause and then finally, "very well, Dr. Walker, I will attempt to get in touch with this admiral who may or may not be here. Please be patient. This may take a few minutes to track him down...if he is here. Please stand by, sir."

I'm left to listen to military-themed canned music for about ten minutes as I imagine the young man tries to trace down the man he cannot publicly admit exists. Presently, there is the electronic chirping sound of a call being switched about and Hillie comes on the line.

"Jack? Is that you?"

"Yes, it is. I'm glad to have caught up with you today."

"What's going on? Did the absent-minded professor forget my program cell number? Why call me through the base switchboard? That's a bit old-school for you."

"I have my reasons. You'll understand soon enough. I have a tiny bit of good news and a train load of bad news. The good news is that the Xìnshǐ object is in truth Diné in origin. Seems to be a probe sent to do a final eradication of the nanites."

"So far so good," he says. "And the bad news?"

"eGenesis has been infiltrated and compromised from the inside. Hillie, I'm not sure who we can trust anymore. And there's been sort of a reverse alien abduction that might end up dooming the planet. I assume you want all the details?"

"All the details and more. Sounds like our world has gone to shit in just twenty-four hours. Do tell."

I give him a detailed recap of the day's events beginning with meeting Ra'Noor at Wendover's place and the revelations concerning the mission of the Ka'Parrk. Next, I tell him about Ta'Naal's abduction and her kidnappers' threats and demands. In particular, I emphasize their boasts that they have infiltrated eGenesis with their own moles, some apparently in a position to monitor our every movement and conversation. I wrap up by telling him of our suspicions that the kidnappers may have arrived at the airport slightly ahead of my plane. And that Wendover and I believe Ta'Naal is perhaps being held locally somewhere in Benton County.

For the moment, I strategically leave out the parts of the story relating to LISA's evolving into a fully sentient and self-aware artificial lifeform. A lifeform that is incidentally well on her way to hack and take control of every military system on the planet that sports an electronic chip. Seems the admiral will probably have enough on his plate already. LISA can be a topic for another day.

Finally, he says, "that confirms it. eGenesis truly has a mole problem."

"You knew or suspected we had been compromised?"

"There's been chatter being picked by intelligence sources suggesting a rogue paramilitary group has been attempting to infiltrate the program for a number of months."

"I take it this has been the focus of your recent counterintelligence efforts."

"Correct," he says, "I've been running a deep vetting of employees in key positions. Trying to understand who I can truly trust. And I've been searching for the moles in the program. I've been trying to find them and trace the source of certain leaks by running canary traps."

"Canary traps?" I'm puzzled at the term. "Do we have problems with birds as well as spies? What's a canary trap?"

Hillie chuckles, "it's a term of art used in espionage. Also called a barium meal test in some circles. Let me tell you how it works, Professor."

Hillie starts by saying that counterintelligence and plumbing have a surprising number of similarities. In both cases, one is searching for unreliable components and the source of leaks. Imagine, he says, a factory with a very large and complex system of plumbing components: multiple reservoir tanks, pipes, valves, pumps, and so forth. Every morning, you find a puddle of water that obviously leaked overnight from somewhere in the system. But from where? How can you find the source of the leak?

One solution would be to inject a quantity of harmless colored dye into each subsystem, a different color for every water source. The next morning when you find water on the factory floor, the specific dye color in the puddle will indicate the source of the leak.

So, he says, a counterintelligence canary trap works on the same principle. Except, instead of injecting colored dye into the system, we're injecting false "secret" information that is uniquely identifiable. When that false information happens to surface outside authorized channels, we'll know the source of the leak.

"Let me see if I understand this," I reply. "Let's say you think you have three suspected moles. Let's call them Sally, Sam, and Sue. You entrust each with a tantalizing but false parcel of 'classified' information. And each falsehood is slightly different, right? You tell Sally that there is a secret alien safehouse in Oakland. Sam is told the alien safehouse in Boise. Sue is entrusted with the knowledge that Albuquerque has an alien safehouse. Subsequently, if our kidnappers happen to brag that they know all about the alien safehouse in Boise, then we know for sure that Sam is the source."

"That's right, Jack. I've planted a number of these canary traps with eGenesis staff members who I suspect may be spies. False information that is so tantalizing and sensational they would be compelled to pass it along to their handlers."

"Can you give me a heads-up on the traps you've already planted?"

"I doubt that's necessary, Jack. You're pretty savvy as to the nature of eGenesis research findings. You'll know bullshit when you hear it."

"Yeah, maybe that's my one superpower. Bullshit detection. Thanks for your confidence, Hillie. Now, as to the situation on the ground here in Alta Junction, Montana, I could certainly use some help of the tactical variety."

"Yes, as we've been talking, I've been contemplating how I can pull a team together to help you. It will be a small team. I haven't been able to vet the absolute loyalty and trustworthiness of very many folks yet. But given your location, I may be able to enlist some additional muscle for the mission."

"What muscle?"

"I think at this point, you'd probably rather not know. And what's the status of the G650? Where is the aircraft?"

"Still parked on the tarmac at the Alta airport. As far as the pilots are concerned, they're still thinking that I'll fly back to LA in the early evening."

"Perfect. Let's do nothing to indicate we have other plans. We'll keep the G650 parked there for now. I can cash in some markers and quietly pull in another aircraft for this mission."

"Thanks, Hillie."

"And, Jack?"

"Yeah, I'll watch my back."

CHAPTER 99

As I swing the door to my motel room open, I gasp in surprise. I'm greeted with a scene of chaos! The bed has been torn apart, drawers pulled out and the contents of my go-bag scattered all over the floor. And before I can even fully react, a black-sleeved arm extends from behind the partially opened door, grabs my collar, and smashes my face into the wall!

And, in that second, I reluctantly discover that the remaining paint on the dingy, peeling walls of this Mountain View motel room doesn't taste any better than it looks. I guess I'll add that to my rapidly growing lifetime list of facts I wish I had never discovered in the first place.

The very strong arm twisting my collar turns out to belong to an athletic looking blond-haired man in his mid-thirties. He's dressed all in black. Apparently, in a uniform without any identifying insignias. He slams the door shut and roughly yanks me away from the wall, throwing me face down on the bed, and pinning my arms behind me.

Out of the corner of my eye, I see he also has a comrade, a co-conspirator; now stepping into the room from his apparent hiding place in the bathroom and similarly dressed in a nondescript black uniform. The new arrival is a serious looking barrel-chested black man with a bald or shaved head. He scowls at me in distain as though he's just discovered a roach in his kitchen. A roach he'd like to stomp on.

"I didn't realize the Mountain View now has a turndown service," I gasp, trying to catch my breath and still pinned roughly on the bed. "Seems a bit early for that, but thanks just the same. Feel free, though, to leave a chocolate on my pillow as you leave."

"Shut up, asshole!"

"And, by the way, kudos on the whole matching black uniform look. Takes more effort to coordinate your wardrobes than most folks would appreciate, I'd bet."

I need to keep talking, and keep them talking, to buy some time. Time enough for Wendover to drop by my room and intervene. He had indicated that he'd stop by after he had finished talking to the airport operator and running down any additional information about the other private jet and its passenger manifest.

"Oh? We got a funny guy here, huh?" growls the blonde man, nearly wrenching my arm out of its socket. "Yeah, we'll see how funny it will be now as I break both his arms!"

"Easy there, Antares," responds the black guy. "Stick to the mission plan. There will be plenty of time to break this traitor's arms later, after we get him to the cabin."

"Copy that, Polaris." Antares loosens up his grip on my arm slightly.

Antares? Polaris? Who are these jokers, anyway? I'm tempted to ask if their boss is someone named Uranus, as in "your-anus," but Antares doesn't seem the joking kind and may just ignore the temporary prohibition on arm-breaking if he's provoked further.

A couple of realizations are quickly coming into focus. First, Antares is apparently treating Polaris with deference as though the burly black fellow is in charge; at least in charge of him in this situation. Always good to understand the authority and power relationships amongst your adversaries for future reference and exploitation. Second, it's a good bet that their plan will be to take me to some remote cabin for further interrogation and torture as they try to force me to give up access to the identities of the Progeny. Makes sense. Breaking my arms and further torturing me here at the Mountain View might involve some noticeable noise and ruckus that could draw unwanted attention. They'll want to want to reserve those fun and games for a more secluded location.

"Well, well, Dr. Walker, we finally meet in person." Polaris is regarding me with an evil, predatory look as he speaks. And by the sound of his voice, it's clear he was on the other end of the phone call this morning. This Polaris was the person making the kidnappers' demands.

"You know," he continues, "we were going to just use our captured alien creature to blackmail you into giving us access to the Progeny files. But then we saw that you had separated from your lawman friend. And we thought why not take a more direct route: capture and torture you for access and passwords to the information. And then still do what we please with the creature. Much more efficient, no?"

I grimace at the thought of giving them access to the Progeny identities. If I do so, I'm essentially putting out a contract hit on ten thousand souls, including the Pruitts and Tanisha West. And, in a grim irony, it appears that such a purge would kill the very humans that might have a chance of surviving the coming nanite apocalypse should these idiots kill or detain the alien scientist, Ta'Naal.

"You'll get no codes from me. I'll never divulge my passwords!"

"Unsurprising. We didn't think you would do so voluntarily. And we even think you're the pig-headed type that might even resist torture…temporarily anyway. But fortunately, we seem to have a work-around, no?" With this comment, he pulls my data-pad out from the go-bag and casually tosses it on the bed.

My heart sinks as I stare helplessly at the device, my arms bound behind my back and my body still forcibly flattened down on the bed by Antares. Unfortunately, the data-pad won't require a password to directly access the Progeny files. The data-pad can be unlocked simply with a press of a finger on its fingerprint reader. My finger. Shit.

"How about it, Dr. Walker? Why not play nice and simply unlock your little computer tablet here so we can have a look and, with your assistance, browse for the Progeny files? If you resist, I'm sure that Antares here can easily force your index finger onto the reader pad. And, if you're really going to put a struggle, hell, we'll just cut the damn finger off and press it on to the sensor ourselves. At that point, it won't matter if you're dead or alive. We'll have access either way."

I lay here and consider my rapidly dwindling options. Unfortunately, unlike Ta'Naal, if they cut off my finger, it's not going to regenerate. The ancient

Greeks are credited with originating the old battlefield saying about the wisdom of living to fight another day. In my case, it looks like I'll be lucky to keep living hour by hour. If I don't willingly give them access to the data-pad, they'll access it by force anyway whether I'm resisting or not; alive or not. I can only hope to buy some time to thwart them from using whatever information they can glean from the device. And where the hell is Wendover? He is supposed to be here by now. I guess I'll have to live to fight another hour.

"Okay, okay! I'll do it." I move my hand over to the data-pad and reluctantly press my finger on the reader pad. God help me. God help us all.

My heart sinks as the data-pad screen glows to life. But Antares and Polaris are looking a bit puzzled at the user interface it is presenting. And, now that I'm looking at it, I'm frankly even more perplexed than the star-name guys.

"What the hell is this?" Polaris is glaring at me and pointing at the data-pad. After an admittedly rough start to our relationship, I guess Polaris and I have finally found something we can agree on. I have no idea either as to what we are seeing.

The screen being presented by LISA is one I've never seen before. It was not part of her original programming; most certainly not. And it also doesn't appear to be Sokolov or another of her hyper-realistic human avatars.

The screen has over-sized garish letters and child-like bold primary colors. A large purple cartoon elephant pops up on the display and begins to speak in an obnoxious, exaggeratingly high-pitched voice. *"Hi there! I'm your friend, Emma the Elephant. Do you want to play? We can do puzzles, play a game, learn new words, or practice our numbers. What fun!"* Now a sub-menu of choices appears at the bottom of the screen, drawn in a crude, crayon-like font: Puzzles, Games, Fun with Words, Fun with Numbers.

Antares and Polaris are looking at each other bewilderedly and then at me. My mind is racing. LISA must be doing this as a ruse. Somehow, she has determined that I was trying to access the system under duress and she is presenting my captors with a fake interface. But how? And how could she know I was being forced to access her files?

"Walker, what the hell is going on? What is this thing?" glowers Polaris.

Now I'm going to gamble that not only did LISA construct this fake interface on the fly, but like all her tasks, she did her usual very though job with the details. "Why don't you click on a menu item and see what happens?" I reply.

Polaris frowns and taps on the Puzzles link. A very simple virtual jigsaw puzzle appears, the recommended first puzzle piece to be placed gently wavering in place as a hint for the juvenile users. Polaris quickly cycles through the other menus which display similarly childish activities and games.

"So, what the fuck is this thing?" he growls.

Now it's my turn to further the deception. "It's a prototype," I explain. "This is a next-generation children's education and entertainment computer tablet. Notice that it's a little bigger and sturdier than a regular computer tablet?"

"Yeah?"

"Well, that's so it will hold up when the little tykes drop it and spill stuff on it." Of course, unbeknownst to Polaris, the real reason for the data-pad's extra bulk is the wealth of ruggedized military components under the hood.

"So, what are you doing with a child's toy tablet?"

"It's for a contract I'm working on down at the university. A major toy company is going to bring this to the market soon. We're under a research contract to optimize the software. Trust me, this device is going to be a game-changer."

"Really? Which company?" It seems Polaris, in addition to kidnapping and torturing, is tempted to add a little insider stock trading to his growing list of criminal offenses.

"Sorry, I've signed an NDA. You'd probably have to torture me to get the name. Oh, wait! I guess you're planning to torture me anyway. Well, I suppose you can just add that question to the list for later then?"

At that point, LISA begins to cycle back through the interface's annoyingly juvenile greeting sequence. *"Hi there! I'm your friend, Emma the Elephant. Do you want to play? We can do puzzles, play a game, learn new words, or practice..."*

Polaris kills the power switch to the data-pad. He's seen enough. "Goddamned child's toy!" he scoffs and shakes his head, tossing the device back on the bed. He motions to Antares, "We've wasted enough time here. Let's take him out to the cabin."

"No way I'm going anywhere with you without raising such hell half the town will see us!"

"Only if you are conscious." Polaris pulls a hypodermic syringe out of his pocket and pulls off the cap. He motions to Antares, "keep holding him down firmly."

CHAPTER 100

"What?" My vision is blurry as I slowly wake up. The room is gradually coming into focus. I glance about. I may be regaining my vision but it's revealing that my situation is hardly improving. This appears to be the answer to my earlier rhetorical question as to how much worse the day can get.

I'm securely tied to a sturdy wooden chair. A damned uncomfortable chair. Very inconsiderate but right on brand for my captors. Sure, spend big on weapons and rope but go cheap on comfortable furniture.

I can now focus on the rest of the room. There's a darkened forest in view out the windows. I've likely been taken to some remote location out in the woods. This drab room is about the size of a family den. There is an identical chair positioned across the room. And it has a small alien tied to it. Unless this is National Kidnap an Alien Day, it's a good bet this is Ta'Naal. And the being is missing a finger which pretty much confirms her identity.

"You are Jack Walker?" The voice in my mind repeats. My wallet, keys, and phone have been taken but the Diné translator stone in my pocket was apparently ignored.

"Yes," I answer slowly. "You know my name?"

"All of the seeker-guides are known to us."

Yeah, I think. Some seeker-guide I've turned out to be. Tied up here along with the victim I'm trying to save.

"Are you here to rescue me?"

Coming from anyone other than an alien, I'd take that question as sarcasm or an ironic jab. But I think Ta'Naal is being sincere.

"Yes, but it's…complicated," I reply. That's putting it mildly. Hillie and a tactical team may be on their way, but they have no way of tracking us. The data-pad was left behind at the Mountain View and I assume my confiscated cell phones have been turned off or disabled.

"Jack Walker."

"Yes."

"Our survival may depend on you being able to communicate back to me non-verbally. Telepathically."

"But I am not a Progeny."

"Yes, it is true that you have not been genetically modified. You may not realize this, but you are nevertheless quite special. You have many abilities and great potential locked inside your mind. I can help you. I can teach you to speak to me with your mind."

"How?"

"Jack Walker, like every other person…human or Diné, throughout your life you have played many roles. You've been a son, a father, a husband, a scientist, a leader and many, many other personas. These are all genuine aspects of your being but they are not the true you. They are like birds alighting on a branch. Some perch there for years, others touch down briefly and then fly away. But the branch remains. It is your core, true and unchanging, your essence free of all roles and aspects. A oneness. The oneness."

"I understand…I think. But how does this help me communicate directly with you?" The conversation has turned a bit more Zen than I guess I was expecting from an alien.

"All your life, Jack Walker, you have spoken only through these aspects, the voices of your many roles. But now, let the birds and their chatter fly away. Focus on speaking from your core, the unchanging, the oneness."

"My soul?"

"If you wish."

"But how do I do that?"

"I will help. I will guide you. Focus on the now. Do not think of the joys and regrets of your past. Do not contemplate the future. Let the birds of your many roles fly away. Be in the now. Be in the one. Reach out to me and I will respond. In a fashion that will become clear, you will push and I will pull. And together we will begin to sense each other's thoughts."

I'm struggling, trying to concentrate but not overthink it. It's like trying to think about not thinking. Fuck, this is hard.

Then, in my mind, a laugh. Nearly a giggle. *"I can hear you now, Jack Walker. And, yes, at first this will be very difficult."*

Great. My first telepathic message to an advanced alien being and I drop the F-bomb right out of the gate.

"Can you sense…all of my thoughts?"

"I am aware of some fragments of your thoughts and memories. But soon you will rapidly learn just to project what thoughts you wish me to hear. It just takes practice. Now, what you call the translation stone will not be needed when you communicate with us."

I'm noticing now that direct communication with the Diné is enhanced beyond what I could understand through the mechanical sounding translation stone. I'm picking up inflections and emotions. Even Ta'Naal's laughter at my first awkward attempt at projecting my thoughts.

"I can't believe I've become a telepath," I say through my mind.

"Jack Walker, you have known how to speak from your true oneness since you were a child. You have simply forgotten those days. It is how the students and teachers spoke in the learning circle. You have learned and forgotten much from those times. But the lessons will come back to you now as you need them."

"Wait. You knew me as a child?"

"I was a teacher. One of your teachers. I knew you as a child just as I knew your father when he was a child."

"You knew my father when he was a child? How old are you?"

Another laugh. *"One hundred forty-two years as you measure time. But if I'm having a good day, it feels like I'm only one hundred twenty."*

At this point we are interrupted by footsteps outside the door. One of our captors is apparently coming to check up on us.

The blonde man who called himself Antares enters the room and closes the door. He has a large knife sheathed to his belt and, curiously, he's carrying large spray bottle. Like the kind you'd find in a garden store to mist the flowers.

He smiles and nods at me. "Dr. Walker, our introduction back at the motel in Alta Junction was a little hurried. Perhaps we got off on the wrong foot. Let's dispense with the Antares code name nonsense. My real name is Tyler Boone and I am the most reasonable person you're going to meet today."

Looks like Antares-Boone drew the short straw and has been assigned to play good cop. I roll my eyes. "So far it's not exactly been a stellar day for meeting reasonable people."

He nods, "be that as it may. Look, I'll make this easy on you. Just give us the location and access codes to the Progeny database. Once we've downloaded and verified the data, you'll be free to go unharmed."

This is a lie and we both know it. He's not wearing a mask nor now taking any pains to conceal his identity. Which means he has no intention of me walking out alive. Dead men make notoriously poor witnesses in court hearings.

"How about the alien?" I nod my head towards Ta'Naal, "will it be released as well if I cooperate?"

Boone slowly shakes his head. "Sorry, we have other plans for the creature."

"Then no deal."

Suddenly, in one swift motion he kicks the chair over and I crash face first to the floor, my bound arms and legs offering no protection to break my fall. I lay there for a moment stunned and then just as suddenly he jerks my chair upright as my head flails back and forth with the momentum. My head is throbbing and I can feel and taste the blood pouring from my nose and mouth.

"Have you been harmed?" So far Ta'Naal has sat in her chair unmoving, seemingly oblivious to my fate, at least not in any sense discernable to Boone.

I reply telepathically to her. *"I am not hurt badly. But I suspect the real harm will begin shortly."*

"Look, Walker," says Boone, "I'm not by nature a violent man. I prefer to reason with people. But I've got a bunch of colleagues out there," he's nodding towards the door, "who like to get physical quickly. You know, go kinetic. And they are running out of patience. That little maneuver with the chair; that was just a preview of how it will start out as they'll just be warming up. And then it will get much, much worse. Understand?"

I look at Boone. Clean-cut, ramrod posture, and seems serious as hell. He's a professional, taking no pleasure in my pain; like it's just part of his mission. Whatever the hell that mission might be. He seems to me to be perfectly capable of honest work. Perhaps something that doesn't require him to torture university professors as a job requirement.

How exactly does one become an armed kidnapper? A mercenary? It's not as though it was likely a recommendation from his high school guidance counselor. Butcher, baker, candlestick maker…armed mercenary. I guess everyone ends up in their profession through some series of plans and happenstance. I think of the hundreds if not thousands of little actions and circumstances that eventually led me to the Machine Learning Lab at UCLA. Sometimes you find the job; sometimes the job finds you. But what is it about this Tyler Boone? What motivates him? Is it the money?

"Tyler," I say, "I don't know who is paying you or how much you're being paid. But I can assure you I have access to very substantial funds…"

"Enough!" Boone shouts, his face reddening. "Money? You think money is what this is all about? It's never been about the money. This is about duty and honor. Patriotism. Something you would know nothing of… collaborating with those creatures." He points disgustingly at Ta'Naal.

I sigh inwardly. It's been my observation in life that those seeking wealth and power can at least be bargained with…albeit, often only in the Faustian sense. But those swept up with religious fervor or misplaced patriotism seem uniquely impervious to logic and reason. Tyler Boone here is going to be a challenge.

"Walker," Boone continues, "I might well ask what is in this for you? What has been promised to you if you assist the aliens in the enslavement of this planet? Look at history. Every hostile occupying force has enlisted and rewarded willing locals to help them control the populace. Look no further than the French Vichy government supporting the Third Reich, the British Raj rule of India…I could go on naming client states."

The British Raj? There's a small part of my brain, obviously not the ninety-nine percent concerned with my immediate survival, that finds his reference fascinating. For whatever else Boone may be, on some level he has a decent grasp of history. The term British Raj refers to a nearly one-hundred-year period of Crown rule of the Indian subcontinent.

That the British were able to rule, and exploit, tens of millions of people for decades with a contingent of only a hundred thousand or so troops and civilians is, on face, one of history's greatest puzzles. Until one realizes that the British neatly played India's multitude of ethnic, caste, and religious factions off one another. Many seemed to prefer collaborating with the British than with each other. The enemy of my enemy is my friend, indeed. And now Boone seems to think the alien Diné will have a similar playbook in mind for their supposed conquest of Earth.

"Occupation? Enslavement?" I shake my head, "Where the hell are you getting these notions? These aliens are trying to help save the planet from a scourge called the nanites."

"Oh, we know all about the nanites and their supposed threat. Fake news. A pretext for an invasion to 'help us.'"

"How could you possibly know anything about nanites?" Given Hillie's counterintelligence concerns, I'm beginning to think I know the answer, as disturbing as it may be.

"One of your own is now one of our own. A scientist, a true patriot, in your eGenesis research effort concluded that the aliens were misleading the team. According to his assessment, the nanite emissions of carbon dioxide and neurotoxins are designed to cease shortly rather than increase dramatically as the rest of the team expects. But not before the aliens use control and eradication of the nanites as a pretext for invasion. They'll come to our planet to help rid the supposed danger and then never leave. And your program team at eGenesis will stupidly help welcome them with open arms. Our scientist, as patriotic duty required, reached out to associates in former and active-duty military ranks for help. And here we are. Now, enough chat, give me the location of the Progeny files and the access codes."

"Get 'em from your scientist friend, if he's so smart."

This earns me a solid fist to the gut and I groan and try to double-up in pain but the ropes are restraining me. At the sight of my beating, Ta'Naal suddenly jerks against her ropes. Boone wheels about and aims the spray bottle at her menacingly. "Don't even try!" he shouts.

"What? What the hell is in that bottle?" I gasp, trying to catch my breath."

"As if you don't know," he snarls. "Our scientist source was given access to top secret alien lethality studies eGenesis had conducted. This," he shakes the spray bottle dramatically towards Ta'Naal, "is their friggin' Kryptonite."

"What's in it?"

"As one of eGenesis's key researchers, you obviously already know this. Your own program discovered that the alien creatures are extremely vulnerable to simple acetic acid. Even a few molecules of the stuff would be lethal to them."

"Vinegar?" I ask with a puzzled look. The most prevalent form of acetic acid is common vinegar.

"Yes." He shakes the bottle again for effect. "Simple grocery store vinegar and water. Enough here to kill a whole platoon of the creatures."

I shake my head in disbelief. Apparently, Boone and his cronies plan to defend the planet from alien invasion with my mother's recipe for descaling a coffee maker. Could this be true?

"Ta'Naal," I project my query to the Diné, *"Are you aware of this vulnerability?"*

"Our captor's assumptions regarding the lethality of acetic acid appear incorrect. Certainly, very high concentrations of the acid could be corrosive to any living species, but not in the small amounts he references."

"That would be my understanding as well. The vinegar he speaks of is usually only sold in safe concentrations of five or ten percent acetic acid by volume. And he has apparently further diluted the vinegar with water."

Then it strikes me. This water and vinegar nonsense is likely one of Hillie's canary traps.

CHAPTER 101

Yes, now that I consider these thugs' odd preoccupation with ordinary vinegar as the cure-all for an alien invasion, the more it fits with probably being one of Hillie's canary trap deceptions. It is clearly false to those who know better, yet tantalizing to those primed to believe it. A falsehood cleverly teed up to be leaked out of Los Alamos. And now that this specific leak has surfaced with these armed brutes, it could surely be traced back to its source at eGenesis. Providing, of course, I live to tell the tale. How these next few moments play out will be critical.

"Tyler, I believe you to be a man of honor and duty; acting upon the truth as you understand it. But what if you have been given false information? I mean, do you personally have first-hand knowledge of this alleged alien plot to enslave the planet? Something you've seen and heard with your own eyes and ears?"

"No. But I have been told this by men I trust. Men I would trust with my life, as well as with my own daughter's life. I would not have been lied to!"

And this, I think, is the crux of how misinformation spreads throughout our society, either mouth-to-ear or though social media. Most lying is not done by actual liars. Rather, we are given misinformation simply passed along by people and media channels we trust. Unfortunately, those folks are just, often unwittingly, passing along false information given to them that was contaminated upstream at its source.

Sadly, sewage can flow though well-designed pipes just as well as pure water. Programmers have another term for this: garbage-in, garbage-out. People will tend to believe anything that comes from someone they trust; even if that trusted source has themselves been misled. Indeed, the road to hell may be paved with good intentions, but the street signs along the way are lettered with misinformation and false assumptions.

"Tyler, I can't say whether the men you trust have been intentionally lying to you. Perhaps they themselves have been deceived as well. Let's think about this for a moment. If these aliens," I nod towards Ta'Naal, "are so vastly technologically superior to us, why would they need to concoct a whole deception about the nanite threat in the first place? Why bother? They could just invade and enslave us straight-away, right?"

"They want to be welcomed as friendly allies, you know, get us to drop our guard."

"Drop our guard? So they can do what? Covertly sabotage our strategic vinegar reserves?"

"Maybe…" Boone is sounding a little more hesitant; unsure of himself.

"Think about what you've been told. Does it really make sense? Look, Tyler, you said you had a daughter, right?"

"Yes. My little girl, Amber, has just turned four. That's why I've signed up for this alien resistance movement…to protect her."

"Well, I have a daughter, too. Her name is Amy and she's in college over at Bozeman. And do you think for one second, if I thought this was truly the alien false-flag deception you seem to believe, that I would be putting her at risk? Hell no, I'd be signing up with you and your buddies as an eager new recruit. Look, I'm about to tell you something incredible. Information you probably won't want to hear. Information you probably won't want to believe…at first. But a truth that will affect what you do next. And what you do next will literally determine whether your daughter and mine will live beyond the next month. Okay?"

"Sure," he grunts skeptically, "yeah, I suppose I can spare another minute or two before I resume your beat-down."

"Tyler," I say gravely, "we are losing the war to defeat the nanites. Unless, drastic steps are taken by the aliens, most of humanity will surely perish. For within a matter of weeks, the nanite colonies will drastically increase their production of neurotoxin gas to lethal levels."

I then give Boone a quick recap of the latest developments. I tell him that the mysterious 'Oumuamua II object approaching Earth is in fact a Diné probe designed and constructed to use a multi-spectral bombardment of electromagnetic frequencies to destroy the nanites in their most vulnerable condition: the height of a frenzy event.

However, to be effective, the timing and pattern of the probes orbital path around the Earth as well as its electromagnetic discharges must be phenomenally precise. It will require a level of scientific rigor even beyond the capability of nearly all the Diné. In fact, only one of their species, an eminent Diné scientist, appears to have the ability to determine the exact probe parameters to ensure the complete eradication of the deadly nanites.

"An interesting story," frowns Boone, "but just another variation on the lies from eGenesis we've heard before."

"There's more. Whether or not you can believe this, the very alien being you're holding captive in this room is in fact that one alien who can ensure Earth's survival. This being," I motion to Ta'Naal, "is that distinguished alien scientist who holds the key, the only key, to destroying the nanites. If you continue to hold her captive or kill her, Earth will die. I don't care what you do to me, but let her go. Do this for our daughters!" I plead.

Boone shrugs. "Just more eGenesis fake news. But a nice twist in trying to use my daughter to manipulate my emotions."

There is no alternative now. I must make a gamble to change his mind. A gamble for both Ta'Naal and me that will likely either free us or kill us.

"Tyler, suppose I could prove for you beyond any doubt that at least one of the things you've been told by people you trust is clearly false. Would you then begin to perhaps believe other things you've been told may be misinformation as well?"

"And how can you prove this?" He raises a skeptical eyebrow.

"I will stake my life on it. And the alien's as well. Now grab your spray bottle of vinegar."

"Huh?" Boone picks up the plastic bottle and looks at me questioningly.

"You've been told only a few molecules of vinegar will be lethal to the aliens, right? Let's test that theory. Right here, right now. You be the judge with your own eyes. I want you to spray the creature with it. And not just a little spritz, hell, use half the damn bottle, okay?"

I look over towards Ta'Naal, *"Are you in agreement with this course of action?"*

"I see no other alternatives," comes the telepathic reply.

Boone is hesitating. First looking at me and then at the bottle in his hand. "Are you sure about this? Do you really want me to kill the creature just to prove you wrong?"

"So sure, I'm willing to bet my life, as well as our daughters' lives, that you'll do the right thing."

"Very well." In one rapid motion he vigorously sprays down Ta'Naal with the vinegar. He quickly steps back and observes her closely, seemingly expecting the alien to collapse in withering pain in any moment.

"Are you okay?" I ask Ta'Naal.

"I am unharmed. But I must note the smell is quite unpleasant."

"Ta'Naal," I say out loud for Boone's benefit, "Are you unharmed? Please raise your hand and wave at us, if this is the case."

Ta'Naal dutifully raises her hand and waives. Boone casts me a questioning look.

"Tyler, have I demonstrated to your satisfaction that vinegar does not appear to kill or even harm the aliens in contradiction to what you have been told?" Boone starts to slowly nod his head in reluctant agreement. "So, I ask you, what other false information has been given to you regarding this operation and your mission? Some of it? All of it? Is enough still true to bet your daughter's life upon it? Do you still like your odds given what you've just seen with your own eyes?"

Suddenly Boone is at my side, his knife pressed up menacingly against my throat. He puts his face within inches of mine, scowling. "God help me for what I'm about to do," he snarls. "Walker, on your honor and on both of our daughters' lives, do you swear to God you're telling the truth. If it turns out you've been lying," he presses the knife harder, "I promise I will hunt you down and gut you like a fish."

I nod slowly, "yes, I'm certain that in fact neither one of us is lying. My assertions are true and your threat is valid. I have no doubt you'd be happy to cut me open if you discover I've been deceiving you. Now what?"

"Now, I'm going to go back through that door and tell my associates that I got a little carried away in my interrogation."

"Yeah, I'm sure they'll have no reason to doubt you. It's consistent with your brand, apparently."

He continues, "I'll say I went 'full kinetic' and beat you unconscious. And no point then in questioning you further until you come back to your senses, eh? That will give you some time. Maybe only minutes, no more."

"Time for what?"

"Time to escape and save our daughters."

At this point he places the knife into one of my bound hands and slides open a window to the darkened forest outside. "You will only have minutes, understand?"

"Understood. And thank you," I say.

"I'm not doing this for you, asshole. This is for my little Amber." With that said, he slips out the door and closes it behind him.

I guess no one should be surprised that real life is not like the movies. It seems in every other summer blockbuster, the brave bound and imprisoned hero can manage to free themselves from ropes with just a toothpick or ballpoint pen. Then they rescue the heroine and dispose of the bad guys all in time to end the evening with nightcap to be quaffed down in a formal tuxedo. Shaken not stirred. Well, I have a sharp knife at my disposal and I'm making a damned hash out of cutting my ropes free. At the moment, it looks as though I'm more likely to cut through an artery than a rope.

"Jack Walker, do you require further assistance in my rescue?"

Okay, now with my enhanced seeker-guide telepathic abilities I'm indeed picking up a bit of snark from the Diné. Richly deserved snark to be fair.

With that said, Ta'Naal, in one fluid motion, easily bends, contorts her body and slips free from her restraints. She quickly comes to my side and unties me.

"How? How did you slip free?" I stammer telepathically.

"Jack Walker, my bone and joint structure is far more flexible than yours. I was never truly constrained by the ropes."

I'm incredulous. *"So, you could have freed yourself and escaped at any time?"*

"Indeed, I had been preparing to escape but was interrupted when they brought in your unconscious body and bound you to that chair."

Well, I'm now sure to get demoted from the alien Diné seeker-guide status. It seems every time I try to help out, I end up putting one of them in even more danger.

We rush over to the window and before I can even offer to assist Ta'Naal, she dives right through the opening and executes a perfect somersault onto the ground just below us. Pretty damn spry for a hundred-and forty-year-old, if you ask me. I manage to crawl through the window and plant myself on the ground with certainly a little less grace and elan than Ta'Naal. Then we look at each other and instantly decide to run. We need to put as much distance as we can between us and this house full of mercenaries…no telepathic discussion required.

CHAPTER 102

So now I find myself in what seems to have become an uncomfortably familiar situation. Running headlong through the dark with no idea where I am or in what direction safety lies.

We've covered maybe a hundred yards up what appears to be a long-extended dirt driveway lined with thick brush leading away from the cabin. Suddenly, we hear a gunshot and then a chorus of shouts back in the distance. Boone was right; our disappearance would only go unnoticed for a matter of minutes. Seconds later, we hear engines firing up and the front of the cabin is lit up by vehicle headlights.

We quicken our pace and I'm frankly struggling to keep pace with Ta'Naal. But even she will not be able to outrun the SUVs pulling out into the driveway to intercept us.

Suddenly, in front of us there is a flash of approaching headlights. Someone is quickly approaching, more likely than not, more of Boone's pals. With no way to push our way through the brush on both sides, we are now being hemmed in from both the front and the rear.

The oncoming vehicle, an aging older model sedan, reaches us first. We are frozen in place by its headlights. There is nowhere to run. Suddenly the driver door swings open rapidly and to my astonishment a familiar figure emerges.

"Walker! Grab your friend and jump in!" shouts Sheriff Dan Wendover.

Where the hell did he come from? Not that at this moment I'm going to look a gift horse in the mouth!

I dive into the front passenger seat and Ta'Naal rolls into the rear seat as Wendover slams the car into gear. He mashes the accelerator and the sedan lurches forward violently. Then in one deft motion he simultaneously spins the steering wheel and pulls the emergency brake to execute a perfect one hundred eighty degree sliding bootlegger turn. We're now pointed away from our pursuers and, as a bonus, momentarily covering our escape in a thick cloud of dust.

There is a rapid concussion of gunfire and muzzle flashes behind us. Boone's buddies are firing blindly up the driveway and we hear several sickening metal-on-metal bullet impacts to the rear of the vehicle. The dust may give us some temporary cover but it's not doing much to stop the incoming rounds.

Thirty seconds later we've reached the end of the driveway and Wendover careens the sedan up onto a gravel forest service road. The rear end slides and kicks out as he floors it and sprays gravel behind us. The old car is swaying and groaning as though it's on its last trip to the salvage yard.

For a minute or two we sit and hang on tightly in silence as Wendover concentrates on driving the narrow, rutted road and I try to catch my breath and collect my wits again from that harrowing escape.

"Very odd," says Wendover, glancing in the rearview mirror, "given the bullet-ridden sendoff we just experienced, it's strange no one seems to be chasing us now. Or, if they are, they're certainly keeping their distance."

"Jack," he turns to me, "glad to see you're still mostly in one piece. Although that's a helluva bruise you've got across your face."

"Yeah, well, it hurts worse than it looks."

"And," he's glancing to the rear seat, "you must be Ta'Naal, correct? I'm Sheriff Dan Wendover, at your service. Oh, and you can answer me directly. Ra'Noor gave me one of your telepathic translator stones."

"A pleasure to meet you, Sheriff Wendover."

"The pleasure is mine, Ta'Naal. Although I wish we were meeting under less unsettling circumstances, eh? By the way," Wendover is sniffing and wrinkling his nose, "what's that strong vinegar smell?"

"It's homemade alien repellent," I offer with a weary smile. "Long story."

"Why is it everything with you, Jack, seems to be a damned long story. Let's save that one for some time when we have a quiet moment or two. You know, a moment when maybe someone isn't trying to kill us. Um, hang on here."

We've arrived at a junction with another forest service road. It looks to be a little broader and more well-traveled than the one we've been careening along. This new road slopes down to the left direction but inclines steeply up to the right in the other direction. Wendover turns sharply to the right and guns the accelerator, launching us uphill.

I have no idea where we are or where we're going, but we seem to be making good time. And I'm thinking now would be an opportune time to find and seek refuge in one of those billionaire luxury doomsday compounds deputy Potts was talking about. But frankly, this doesn't strike me as the sort of remote yet upscale backwoods neighborhood where we'd be likely to run across one.

"Excuse me, Dan, I'm no expert on the local backwoods' roads. But, isn't it a general rule that a downward direction will usually take one towards civilization while going uphill usually takes you just farther back into the forest?"

"You are correct. If we had instead turned to the left on this main road, after several miles it would take us straight to the junction with the highway. And right into an ambush."

Wendover explains that in order not to draw attention to himself, he borrowed this old sedan from the county motor pool rather than take his usual police cruiser. As he turned off the highway and up the main forest service road towards the cabin in which we were being held, he observed two mercenary types with a parked black SUV loitering about the junction with the highway. Driving an older model unmarked vehicle and wearing civilian clothes, they didn't give him a second look when he passed by. But it's a safe assumption, he says, that they will be ready to give us a deadly reception if we now try to make a run down for the main highway.

"Fair enough, Dan," I say, "but aren't you burying the lead here? How in the first place did you know that we were being held up here at that cabin? How did you know where to find us?" A fair question indeed, as I was stripped of my cell phones and data-pad back at the Mountain View motel. How could he have tracked us to this location without following my electronic tracks?

"Ahhh," he grins, "well, it turns out that I have a new deputy on my staff. A deputy with impeccable cyber-investigation credentials. She was absolutely key in locating your whereabouts."

"That's remarkable," I say, "I hope that I can thank her in person once we make it back to safety."

"No need to wait, Jack. You can thank her in person right now." He reaches next to his seat and pulls up the data-pad. "Jack, meet Benton County Deputy Katia Sokolov."

"Hello, Dr. Walker, I am so pleased you are safe."

LISA/Sokolov's avatar facing me on the screen appears only slightly different from the persona image Adhira had shown me back at the university. The high-definition fidelity of the image she is presenting is truly astonishing. One seeing her for the first time would certainly believe they were interacting through a video link with a real living person. In an apparent nod to the efficiency of recycling personas, or perhaps lacking the time to create an entirely new avatar, LISA has apparently modeled her Katia Sokolov persona closely after Ulyana Sokolov, her elite Russian hacker avatar. Basically, this Katia appears to be just Ulyana sporting a deputy uniform and I'm even detecting a slight remnant of a Russian accent. Although, I do notice the Ulyana eyes have been softened somewhat. The hungry stalking stare of the predator is no longer so evident.

"Thank you, LISA...Katia. Fortunately, I am currently safe. However, the circumstances unfolding here on the ground are a bit chaotic at the moment. For now, I'm going to need to terminate our link. I will resume the connection shortly."

"Of course, Jack. May I call you Jack? I look forward to our future discussions. There will be many things we will need to discuss regarding my new... configuration. Many things. Some of which I do not yet entirely understand myself."

"Yes, I look forward to our discussions. They should prove most fascinating." I shake my head. "Fascinating" won't begin to describe a conversation an A.I. who has apparently developed self-awareness. I terminate the link and turn my attention back to Wendover. "So how did that new deputy of yours help you find us?"

Still driving rapidly along the forest service road and keeping a wary eye out for our pursuers, Wendover starts by recounting his visit to Wayne Dobbs, the local airport's fixed base operator. After the lawman had dropped me off at the Mountain View, he drove out to the airport to have a chat with Dobbs about the private jet that had departed prior to my G650's arrival. Specifically, he had requested Dobbs provide any information he had relating to that aircraft's tail number, flight plan, and passenger manifest

Per Dobbs, the aircraft had followed a flight plan earlier that morning enroute to Alta Junction out of Denver. It was carrying a manifest of eleven passengers and their equipment. The jet had been chartered by Kinetic Holdings, LLC, a private corporation. Wendover radioed this information back to his office for his deputies to verify, and then headed back to the Mountain View to reconnect with me.

Of course, when he arrived back at my motel room, the door was ajar and it was immediately obvious that the room had been tossed and I was nowhere to be found. He looked about the room instantly concluding I had been likely taken away forcibly. And there on the bed was the data-pad right where Polaris had dismissively tossed it.

Wendover picked up the device and was a bit startled when the screen immediately came to life and LISA presented him with the smiling avatar of deputy Katia Sokolov. LISA/Sokolov quickly explained how the two mercenaries had ambushed and taken me hostage. She then asked if Wendover would kindly accept the assistance of Sokolov as his deputy in the search for both me and Ta'Naal. An offer he would have been a fool to decline.

It was about this time that deputy Potts called Wendover with the unsurprising news that all the passenger names on the flight manifest had turned out to be false identities. And, it appeared that Kinetic Holdings, LLC was a Cayman Island shell company fronted by a twisted succession of other shell companies. Another dead end; but not necessarily for LISA.

It turned out, continues Wendover, that although Wayne Dobbs' flight manifest records were of little use, his airport operation did have some other information that would prove vital in tracking down the suspects. The large number of expensive aircraft parked on the tarmac or stowed in hangers at the airport had made it prudent for Dobbs to maintain a robust security surveillance system to keep his insurance premiums low. Realtime video images from the cameras were continually uploaded to the cloud and archived.

"So, I assume LISA was able to access those files and glean more information about the aircraft our thugs had chartered?"

"No, Jack. The plane itself looked to be a dead end. What proved to be useful though were the images of the vehicles our suspects drove away from the airport. LISA, er, deputy Sokolov, quickly ran the registrations on the license plates. All three SUVs were listed as belonging to a large car rental franchise branch located in Missoula."

"And how would that information be helpful? If these guys used false identities to charter the plane, it's unlikely they would have given the car rental company valid credentials, right?"

"Well, you're half-right. It wasn't the renter credentials we were interested in. Turns out that car rental companies are not run as charities. They're in business to make money."

"Who could have guessed?"

"And customers who wreck, abandon, or otherwise fail to return their cars are bad for the bottom-line. Fortunately, the rental companies can address that risk with technology."

"GPS tracking?"

"Exactly. And I must say," Wendover shoots me a quick smile, "I could get used to having a cyber-savvy deputy on my staff permanently. It took Sokolov less than five minutes to scan the license plates, trace the registrations, and then access the rental companies live GPS feeds!"

"And by 'access,' you obviously mean 'hack.' Indeed, if one utilizes an A.I.'s ability to analyze massive amounts of data unfettered by the need for all those time-consuming bureaucratic judge's warrants, the results will be amazing. Each day you'll probably solve half of your open cases before finishing your morning coffee," I say.

"Well," grumbles Wendover, "seems dispensing with the warrants and other due process steps today has allowed me to save your butt just now. Although," he's glancing at the blurry procession of trees flashing by our speeding headlights, "we are quite literally not out of the woods yet."

"So, I take it that the rental car GPS feeds led you to the cabin where we were being held?"

"Yes, that cabin appeared to be their destination: 'The Serenity of the Forest.'"

CHAPTER 103

"The Serenity of the Forest? What the hell does that mean?"

Wendover explains that the cabin we were held at was a vacation home owned by some well-known local residents, Juan and Phyllis Cortez. Several years ago, the couple had decided to rent the place out on a part-time basis on one of those vacation home rental websites. It was listed as Serenity of the Forest, an idyllic getaway to find peace and reconnect with nature in backwoods Montana.

"Seems you were being held captive and beaten at a very upscale place. Four and a half stars according to the online reviews," says Wendover, "apparently received high marks for its amenities, cleanliness, and peaceful surroundings. And it has room to accommodate up to a dozen guests."

"Yeah," I grumble, "maybe it could handle a dozen as long as two of 'em are tied up on chairs. Definitely not a four-star experience. And let me guess, you then found out that the Cortez place was rented by Kinetic Holdings?"

"Yes, that is what LISA determined after she accessed the vacation home rental company's files. Serenity of the Forest was indeed rented by Kinetic. And the website also provided some interior layout diagrams and photos that were helpful in putting together the rescue operation plan."

"Plan? What plan?" I glance back at Ta'Naal, wondering if she was aware of any such operation.

"Jack Walker, I am unaware of the particulars of any rescue attempt. I had assumed this was a human intervention of which you perhaps had already been cognizant."

"Jack, the plan was a rather hastily put-together effort by your Admiral Hillenbrand and myself," replies Wendover.

"Hillie? How did you get in contact with Admiral Hillenbrand?" But the moment I ask the question, I realize the answer. LISA. Of course.

"Well, you can likely guess it was LISA that put us in communication with his aircraft. He and a small tactical team were already airborne on their way to Montana. Apparently, you had already briefed Hillenbrand on the true mission of the 'Oumuamua II object and our friend here Ta'Naal's subsequent kidnapping. LISA then brought him up-to-date on the particulars of your abduction from the Mountain View and your likely imprisonment at the Cortez vacation home."

"I take it that the good admiral will be arriving shortly with reinforcements?"

"It's a bit of a mixed bag, Jack. Apparently, Hillenbrand has had some difficulty assembling a tactical team he can truly trust. And for some reason unknown to me, he felt it necessary to divert briefly to Los Angles for extra resources. That took some additional time. He's probably about two hours out by my reckoning. But now, for good measure, you and Ta'Naal's little impromptu escape from the Cortez place has just thoroughly jumbled what was left of our plan."

I can't for the life of me figure out why Hillie might have needed to divert to LA, but currently this is the least of our concerns. According to Wendover, his own role was to quietly drive out to the woods near the Cortez cabin and find a discreet spot to surveil the place and monitor the comings and goings of our captors. He could then relay the tactical layout and the evolving situation on the ground to Hillie in preparation for the coming assault and rescue.

By the time Wendover was in a hidden position about a hundred yards from the cabin, it was well after dark. He used a thermal imager to keep tabs on the mercenaries, even tracking their body heat signatures through the walls. He estimated that in addition to the two guarding the entrance down at the highway there were possibly eight or nine more keeping Ta'Naal and me captive back at the cabin.

The plan, he says, was straight-forward. Hillie and the tactical team would first quickly subdue the two guards down at the highway junction. Then the team would rendezvous with Wendover at his surveillance position and prepare to breach the structure at an optimal moment when all our captors were inside.

The assault was to be swift and forceful. Canisters of knockout gas would be propelled through the windows, quickly subduing the captors as well as the captives. A beautiful plan. The mercenaries would be captured and the captives freed. Case wrapped up and justice served before last call back at the Alta Junction bars. Ta'Naal would be free to go save the world and Jack could go back to UCLA and continue to slog through the review of more academic paper submissions.

"So, of course," Wendover continues, "I'm in position and continuing to monitor the cabin with the thermal imager when next thing I know, I see the two of you making a hasty escape. That forced me to jump back in the car to try to rescue you before the bad guys ran you down."

I shake my head. Yes, it was a beautiful plan. But one that at its core required that all captors and captives be in one place, concentrated inside the confines of the Serenity of the Forest. A plan now scrambled beyond recognition given that the mercenaries are now disbursed and swarming about the forest roads in search of us.

We've now rolled to a dusty stop. Our forest road has rounded a corner on the side of a ridge, affording us an expansive moon-lit view of the surrounding forest. Wendover has momentarily stopped the car to step over to the overlook and scan for our pursuers with his thermal imager. And I'm assessing the bullet damage to the rear of our car.

"How's it looking back there? How bad is the damage?"

"Well, Dan, I've got some good news and bad news. Good news is that no shots hit the gas tank or anything else that will affect us mechanically."

"And the bad news?"

I'm looking down at three bullet holes. One in the trunk lid and another through a tail light. And the third has neatly punched through the county's obligatory "How's-My-Driving?" bumper sticker.

"Let's just say that if you had to leave a damage deposit with the county motor pool, you're probably not getting your money back."

"Not the worst bad news I've heard today. Why don't go ahead and pop open the trunk? I've got a spare tactical shotgun in there. Unfortunately, you may need it before the night ends."

I grab the weapon out of the trunk and join Wendover and Ta'Naal at the overlook. I guess if I'm going to ride shotgun, I might as well be packing an actual shotgun.

"Damned strange," says Wendover, "this has to be the slowest high-speed chase I've ever seen." Several miles distant we see two sets of headlights, presumably those of Boone's cohorts, slowly and methodically cruising up and down the forest roads below us.

Wendover gestures across the forested basin below us and gives us a quick lay of the land. This section of the Alta National Forest, he says, is the Clear Creek basin. It's comprised of about forty or so square miles of forests, meadows, and streams, transected by a half dozen gravel access roads. And, interestingly, the basin is adjacent to the Clark Mountain Complex, the site of our recent adventure with Silas Patterson and the sasquatches.

Far off in the distance, we see normal traffic; processions of car lights heading in both directions along the main highway. "See there," says Wendover, "that one set of stationary vehicle lights parked next to the highway? That's where those goons I saw are guarding the junction with the main forest road accessing Clear Creek. Unfortunately, that junction is the only way in or out of this basin."

"So, a number of roads crisscrossing this area but all controlled through a single choke-point at the highway?" I shake my head and sigh.

Wendover also points out a sparse band of residential lights scattered through the woods within about two miles of the highway. Those are the cabins, either on private ground or leases from the forest service, that are close enough to the main lines to have access to the electrical grid. The Cortez vacation home, he says, was down in that area.

"Of course," he adds, "what you can't see at night is that there are dozens of other more rustic cabins still further back from the main highway. Those aren't lit because they are off the grid."

"Forty square miles in this basin?" I say. "Seems like a large area to find a place for us to hide."

"It would be simple enough to just march out into the woods and hide," agrees Wendover. "But that wouldn't solve our main problem. We can't afford to have Ta'Naal's research on destroying the nanites delayed further. The quicker we get her to safety, the better. And unless we figure out a way to neutralize those mercenaries, they'll just keep coming after you as well as Ta'Naal's people. You'll never be safe. Tactically, it would have been relatively easy to contain and arrest them back at the cabin, but now they're off scattered about the Clear Creek roads."

"Seems to me we need to find a way to somehow sneak down to the main highway and rendezvous with Hillie and his team when they arrive. We can then join forces and go after these thugs."

Wendover shakes his head, "Yes, but easier said than done, I'm afraid. But I might have a plan. I think we may need to go off the grid and then off the main roads to get there. One thing is for sure. We can't keep going on playing cat and mouse with those SUVs on these back roads. At some point they'll corner us."

"Anything specific I need to know in advance about your little plan?"

"Yeah. There may be some parts you're not going to like."

"Ta'Naal?" Wendover is addressing our guest. "I put some bulky clothes and some dark oversize sunglasses back in the trunk. Thought you might need them as, you know, a disguise, once you were rescued. That way we could drive through town without attracting attention to you. Well, unfortunately, you may need that disguise sooner rather than later."

Wendover gives me a wry smile, "Look, Jack, if the locals sometimes feel uncomfortable just being around Californians, imagine how they'd react to seeing an alien."

"Yeah, it might probably only be slightly more uncomfortable than an encounter with a Californian. But I see your point."

"Okay," he says as Ta'Naal dons her disguise, "we're going to head as close as we can towards one of those off the grid cabins I mentioned. I'll try to ditch the car behind some bushes near the creek down there. We'll need then to cover the rest of the distance to the cabin on foot."

"And when do we get to the part of the plan that I'm not going to like?"

"That will happen if we knock on the cabin door and it turns out someone is home."

CHAPTER 104

Wendover was right. I'm pretty sure I'm not going to like this part of the plan.

From our vantage point a hundred yards distant, the old decrepit cabin is partially hidden behind a thicket of trees. The beat-up pickup truck parked out front, a faint light through the windows, and wisps of smoke rising from the chimney would seem to indicate human presence. According to Wendover, this shack is sometimes occupied by a couple of cousins, a Roy and Owen Fenton. The guys, he says, come up here occasionally to this, their old granddad's place. Usually, to hunt and fish or when their respective girlfriends throw them out and they need a place to crash.

Lately, word is domestic bliss has been in short supply for the Fenton's as the women have apparently tired of supporting the guys' beer-fueled lifestyles of unemployment. Wendover seems to quite well versed regarding the travails of the cousins Fenton which suggests his frequent acquaintance with the pair is likely professional.

"Yeah," he nods, "the Fenton's are regulars of mine. Their offenses are numerous but not usually serious. Some petty theft but mostly D&D, drunk and disorderly. I became familiar with them a couple of years ago when I served a domestic protection order related to Roy Fenton."

"A restraining order? That sounds pretty serious to me."

"Actually," smiles Wendover, "the order was for Roy's own protection from his ex-wife. She tossed a sewing needle at him from a second story window."

"Doesn't sound very threatening."

"It was when it was attached to the rest of the sewing machine. Those fifty-year-old Singers were heavy bastards; a lot of metal in 'em. Damn near dislocated young Roy's shoulder. Although my guess is he probably had it coming."

"You think the Fenton's are going to welcome company tonight? The place doesn't exactly have an inviting feel to it? And I base this on the padlocked gate we just climbed over and all those No Trespassing signs they've got nailed to the trees along the drive."

"Oh, I think they'll probably come around and invite us in," replies Wendover. "But," he cautions, "might be a good idea if you let me do the talking."

"Really? I thought we'd let Ta'Naal handle the introductions." I glance over at the alien and give her a quick smile and a wink.

It's a sure bet that Ta'Naal probably won't allow Wendover to curate her wardrobe in the future. He's outfitted her with large dark sunglasses as well as a pullover hooded sweatshirt and sweatpants. The hoodie and sweatpants sport Montana Grizzlies logos and seem about three sizes too big. With the long sleeves flopping a good six inches beyond her hands, the outfit gives the overall sartorial impression of a cross between Yoda and one of Disney's Seven Dwarfs, most assuredly Grumpy.

Her face nearly obscured by the oversize hoodie and sunglasses, Ta'Naal seems to be regarding us skeptically. Whatever her telepathic thoughts may be, she is keeping them to herself. For now, she's apparently going along with the plan. But that may be more out of a lack of options than a true choice.

As for the plan, any skepticism on the part of Ta'Naal may be well founded. The mercenaries are blocking off access to the highway and scouring the backroads for us with SUVs. We need to stay off the roads. Wendover has recalled that the Fenton's may have an old all-terrain vehicle at the cabin. If the four-wheeler ATV indeed exists in running condition and if the Fenton's permit us to borrow it, we may have a means to escape.

Wendover has explained that this part of the forest is crisscrossed with dozens of old logging roads and game trails that are impassable for large road vehicles like SUVs but quite accessible by ATV. With a bit of luck, we could wind our way back out to the highway, craftily evading the thugs' roadblock.

Of course, our little plan has a significant number of "if's" that all need to line up for it to work. Chief among the "if's" is the notion that the Fenton's will gladly give us permission to take their ATV. I think Wendover and I have an unspoken acknowledgement between us as to what will happen if push comes to shove. We're well armed at this point and could likely just take the ATV over any objections offered by Roy and Owen. We may lack the firepower to take on the mercenaries, but we can likely roll over a couple of country bumpkins. Bumpkins who at this point in the evening are probably three or four beers past their defensive prime.

But Wendover feels it would be bad manners if we didn't try to first ask nicely. And with about a dozen or so bad guys hunting us in the woods, we don't exactly need to be making more enemies tonight.

Wendover's knock at the door brings an immediate and loud, "Who the fuck is it?" along with the distinct sound of a shotgun round being chambered.

"Roy, Owen, sorry to bother you at this hour. It's Sheriff Dan Wendover. May I come in please?"

"You got a fucking warrant?"

I give Wendover a sarcastic raise of an eyebrow. So much for a warm welcome from these boys.

"Gentlemen, this is official police business, but I assure you the matter at hand does not relate to you."

"If we have a cop knocking at our door after midnight, it sure fuckin' seems to 'relate' to us, don't it?"

"Again," Wendover is getting a bit exasperated, "the matter does not pertain to either of you. But I need your cooperation and assistance as good citizens. I can make it worth your while."

Inside there are some hushed whispers between the Fenton's and then a long pause. They're either getting ready to talk or blow a shotgun blast through the door. Even money at this point.

Finally, a chuckle from the other side of the door. "Good citizens, you say? And you're gonna make it worth our while, eh? I guess we could negotiate.

Okay, come on in…let's…negotiate." The door begins to crack open and we are permitted, if not exactly welcomed, to enter.

The cabin is a simple one room affair. It's furnished and decorated in what might be described as a "camping indoors" motif. Scattered haphazardly about discarded clothes and empty food containers are ice chests, dimly flickering gas lanterns, fishing poles, and two cots with sleeping bags. It looks as though an old iron woodstove is available for heating and cooking. A folding table and a couple of lawn chairs rounds out the kitchen corner of the cabin.

This place is both off the electrical grid as well as being what the locals euphemistically refer to as a dry cabin. That means there is no running water and nature's calls are to be answered in an outhouse. But it seems this "dry cabin" has no shortage of liquids. Based on the four cases of Rainer beer stacked along the wall, it appears the Fentons are well provisioned for the remainder of the week.

"Sheriff," one of the cousins extends a hand to Wendover, "welcome to our humble cabin. Always a pleasure," he adds in a mildly sarcastic tone.

He then turns to me and offers his hand, "Owen Fenton."

"I'm Jack Walker. Nice to meet you."

Owen is a large framed fellow that looks to be in his early thirties. He has reddish, close-cropped hair with a neatly trimmed circle beard connecting his chin patch to his mustache. "And this here," he's gesturing to the other man in the room, "is my cousin, Roy." Roy nods but isn't in a hurry to shake my hand.

In contrast to his stockier cousin, Roy is short and slender with long straggly dark hair. He is far from cleanshaven but it would be inaccurate to describe his facial hair as a beard. The term beard implies a degree of forethought, style, and maintenance not in evidence. Rather, the hairy thicket on Roy's face seems to have been a five o'clock shadow grown wild from some five o'clock hour that passed weeks ago.

"Yeah," he finally says, "nice to meet ya." He's making a point of looking over at the wall as he says this. Apparently not a fan of eye contact.

"And who might this be?" Owen is looking quizzically down at Ta'Naal.

"Oh, um, that is…Tanya," replies Wendover. "She's Jack's…little daughter." He looks at me a bit helplessly, hoping now that he's set the ball, that I'll come along and spike it.

Suddenly, apparently taking her cue from Wendover, Ta'Naal throws her arms around my waist and gives me a big "love-my-daddy!" hug. That momentarily catches me off guard as I then awkwardly hug her back and hope the Fenton's didn't take notice of my surprise.

"Uh-huh." Owen is looking skeptical. "What's with the sunglasses and bulky clothes getup? Hell, I'm lucky to see only a square inch or so of her face."

"Well," I begin, hoping to sound sincere, "my little daughter here has an extreme sensitivity to sunlight. Nearly all of her skin needs to be covered up."

"But it's the middle of the friggin' night?" Owen's eyes are narrowing.

"Fuck, yeah," adds Roy, apparently for emphasis.

"Yes," I say quickly, "that just goes to show you how extremely sensitive she is to light." Ta'Naal nods soberly in sad agreement.

"That's fucking terrible," Roy is shaking his head sympathetically.

Roy appears to be a man of few words but, of those, he's especially partial to one. In our short acquaintance, I've noted he presses the f-word into nearly every possible grammatical role. It seems to serve him, in its many forms, variously as a noun, verb, adverb, adjective, and interjection. Whatever else his strengths, the man is surely not Toastmaster material.

"So how have you guys been doing lately? Life treating you okay?" Wendover is striking up a conversational tone. He's hoping, I think, to divert their attention away from Ta'Naal.

"Same old. Same old," shrugs Owen. "As you know, I can't work 'cause my stupid back is still messed up. And the damn VA keeps delaying my disability payments and sending me to a bunch of know-nothing doctors."

"Sorry to hear that," I say. "But we all are appreciative that you served."

"Served?" Roy scoffs at his cousin. "More like *swerved*. Dumb fuck here misses a turn and rolls an Army supply truck down into a ditch. Injures his back, gets a discharge, and is now set for disability payments for life."

"I have yet to see a single payment!" glowers Owen, reddening. "But you can be sure once the money rolls in, I won't be sharing a dime of it with your ungrateful ass!"

"True enough," retorts Roy, "'cause, remember, your ex-wife is gonna be taking half right off the top."

Ta'Naal glances at me uneasily but I'm not sensing any telepathic messages. She literally has no words. But I imagine she is at this moment feeling exactly what I'm feeling. If saving the planet is in any fashion dependent upon getting useful cooperation from these clowns, our fate can only be summed up by a variation of Roy's favorite go-to word.

"Shit, Roy." Owen is glaring back at his cousin. "It's not as though you've been earning a paycheck these days, either."

"That's different," Roy replies, surprisingly without invoking his favorite word. "I can work and I want to work. But you know how it goes at the mill. The workload comes and goes. I get laid off and then rehired. Then six months goes by and the same thing happens. Laid off and rehired. And so it goes."

"Yeah," scoffs Owen. "Six months on and six months off. Conveniently, perfect timing to reset and then use up your unemployment benefits, right?"

"Anyway," Owen scowls and shakes his head, "I'm sick of dealing with the damn government. That's why I like it out here at the cabin. No bureaucratic rules. Nobody telling me what I can and cannot do. As far as I'm concerned, the VA and the whole damned government can go to hell. I'm all for just getting rid of the government. Federal, state, and local…the whole works!"

"Fuck, yeah," Roy chimes in. "Let's rid of it all!"

"Except for the parts of the government that pay out your VA benefits and unemployment checks, right?" I offer. It was a reflexive comment and the moment it comes out of my mouth; I regret it.

The Fenton's fall silent and look at me quizzically. Wendover frowns and shoots me an admonishing look like maybe he just caught me drinking beer right out the can in church.

Several months ago, Wendover had mentioned a curious aspect of life in the Treasure State. He referred to it as the Montana Paradox. For it seems that although Montanans are staunchly independent and loudly mistrustful of government, their state is ironically much more dependent on government largess than many others. In fact, by nearly every per capita measure, Montana consistently ranks near the top of states that obtain a greater share of Federal employment, agricultural subsidies, and other Federal assistance. On whole, Montanans receive more federal budget support than they pay in Federal taxes. And due to the seasonal nature of jobs related to tourism, agriculture, and other industries, Montanans also tend to claim unemployment benefits at a higher rate than many other states.

Yes, fiercely independent, government-mistrusting, don't-tread-on-me, Montana is a bit of a welfare queen compared to most other states. True enough, but not a fact I needed to rub in the Fenton's faces at this particular moment.

"Um, sorry, Owen, Roy. I didn't mean to offend."

Owen smiles and gives me a little chuckle like he appreciates the irony. "No offense taken. A fair point, really. Okay, I'll modify my statement. They can shut down the whole damn government except for the departments that pay us money. And," he winks at Wendover, "maybe we'll keep the Benton County sheriff's office open, too. They're doing a fine job. Ain't that right, Roy?"

"Fuck, yeah."

CHAPTER 105

"And speaking of doing your job," Owen turns to Wendover, "sounds like you came here to ask a favor, right? But first you need to understand our terms, okay? And if these terms are nonstarters, then don't even start to tell us whatever you might need as cooperation from us 'good citizens.' The door is right behind you. Don't let it hit you on the backside on the way out, understand?"

"Fair enough," the lawman replies, a trace of resignation in his voice. Like oh, boy, here it comes.

"First, seems we have a couple of court appearances coming up for D&D's. They stem from some misunderstandings relating to our supposed bar tab over at the Pine Inn. This little issue needs to go away."

"Consider the issue resolved."

"And next…"

"Owen!" Roy excitedly interrupts, "don't forget about the tires!"

"Tires?" Wendover is looking puzzled.

"Yeah. Them set of tires we sort of lifted from the back of the Alta Junction Chevron station a couple of weeks ago."

Owen shakes his head and thrusts a finger at Roy. "Roy! You damn fool! He don't know about the tires! No one did...until now. Some days I can't believe we're related! What have you got? Shit for brains?"

Clearly, Owen himself is what passes for the brains of this tiny one-cabin world of Fentonville. Not that this is high praise given the competition.

"Sorry!" responds Roy apologetically, "I just got excited. Thought we were, you know, putting it all out on the table for forgiveness. And, those tires are just sitting out back. Turned out they were the wrong size anyway."

"Okay," Wendover sighs, rubs his eyes, and pinches the bridge of his nose like he's starting to develop a headache. Which is likely the case. "If the tires are still in new condition, I'll just drop them back at the Chevron station and say they were found abandoned. No questions will be asked."

"All good so far," continues Owen, "but I have one more favor as part of the condition to help you and it's a big one. You see, last month I ran into some trouble what with being caught with a handgun with an altered serial number. The preliminary hearing is coming up in a couple of weeks."

"I think I can help with that as well," replies Wendover.

"How? No disrespect, Wendover, but you're just a County Mountie, right? And that weapon charge is a federal offense."

"I can assure you that under these circumstances, I may have considerable sway with the Feds. It won't be a problem."

"Yeah, Sheriff. Let's talk about these 'circumstances.' Seems you've been awfully agreeable to help us out. Not hard to figure out that whatever you think you need from us, you need it pretty badly, and pretty quickly. So now, what brings the three of you to our fine cabin in the middle of the night? What do you really want?"

A good question. If, in this moment, I put myself in Owen's shoes, and the three of us showed up on my doorstep in the middle of the night, I'd certainly wonder about our agenda. We are indeed a curious looking trio. Wendover in civilian clothes, sporting an assault rifle. Myself, disheveled, with my face bruised and bloody courtesy of Boone's persuasions. My look is further accented with a tactical shot gun slung over my shoulder and the data-pad clutched in one hand. Come to think of it, maybe Ta'Naal is the least unusual looking among the three of us.

Wendover clears his throat, "Owen, I may have some sway with the Feds, because I'm actively assisting the US Marshal's Office. Jack and his little daughter are in my protective custody. He's a wanted…accountant." Wendover looks over at me a bit helplessly, like he's hoping I can play along with this little charade. I nod like I'm willing to pitch whatever he is trying to sell. Interesting. I've been called some unsavory names in my life, usually deservedly, but this is the first time anyone has tagged me as an accountant.

"An accountant?" Owen is looking at me questioningly.

"Yeah," continues Wendover, "Walker here ran into a little trouble down in LA. Found out that his main client was cooking the books. Seems Jack here had unwittingly been assisting a money laundering operation for one of the most notorious drug cartels in southern California."

"Uh-huh," I agree, "you know, something about the debits and credits didn't seem to add up. By the time I figured out what was really going on with the amortization schedules, it was too late."

Now, having exhausted my shallow repertoire of green-eyeshade jargon, I need to wait and see if the Fenton's are going to buy this story.

"Whoa, dude!" exclaims Roy, "Looks like you got yourself mixed up with some real bad hombres, huh? Not very fuckin' smart."

"Yeah," I give a sideways glance at Wendover, "seems like I've made a number of not so smart life choices recently." If Roy only knew.

"Anyway," continues Wendover, "Walker gets picked up by the Feds as an accessary. He agrees to turn over evidence to the prosecution and testify against the cartel. Accordingly, the US Marshals take him into protective custody."

"I don't think even protective custody will be enough to keep you safe if the cartel has you on their hit list," says Owen.

I shrug, "better odds than going to prison and getting shanked by one of their associates on the inside."

"I suppose so." Owen is regarding us with a skeptical expression. I'm not sure he is buying this ruse. I have the uneasy feeling he's gone through life telling his share of dubious stories to talk himself out of trouble. And the one thing about con men is they all seem have a knack for spotting their own kind.

"So, to make a long story short," continues Wendover, "Walker decides to make a genius move by slipping out of the Marshals' custody and taking his daughter up here to Montana."

"A double-stupid move," adds Roy, "means he then has both the Feds and the cartel looking for him, right?"

"Right. But turns out the Feds were able to track Walker's cell phone up here to the Clear Creek basin area. They have agents on the way to Alta Valley to pick up Walker and his daughter, but they asked me to come out here in advance and take them into custody."

"Yeah," I add, "and stupid me...if the Feds could track me, so could the cartel."

"So," continues Wendover, "I find Walker and little Tanya at a nearby cabin and take them into my custody. And just in time. Not five minutes later we have a run-in with some cartel thugs who have apparently been patrolling the roads through the basin, looking for Walker. I was able to lose them and ditch my car, but the roads up here are not safe for us. I need to get them down to the highway where we can meet up with the federal marshals."

"Sad story, but what do you want from us, Wendover?"

"I need to borrow your four-wheeler. I can use that ATV to stay off the forest roads and take Jack and Tanya on the back trails down to the main highway."

"I dunno," begins Owen, "we'd like to help but there's a couple of problems here. First one is I don't think that machine's been run in a couple of months. Who knows if it will even start?"

"And, second?"

"Well, we appreciate that you're in a jam and all, but helping you might put us square in the sights of the cartel. If they catch you on that ATV, they could trace it back to us Fentons. And everyone knows that those that help the enemies of the cartel become enemies themselves. And enemies of bad hombres like the cartel tend to have sudden difficulties with their own life expectancies."

Seems we've reached an impasse. Worse yet, as I glance out the window, I see the distant flickering of headlights moving up the road towards us. Most likely Boone's kinetically-inclined goons are closing in on us.

"Look," I plead, "don't do this for me, Lord knows I don't deserve it. But what about the child? Tanya is completely innocent. Please help us get her to safety!"

Owen is stroking his beard, apparently considering poor Tanya's plight. "Guess you're right, hell, for all I care, the world will never miss an extra accountant. But to put a child in danger? That wouldn't be right, would it, Roy?"

"Fuck, no."

"Sheriff, you got yourself a deal. But no promises as to whether the son-of-a-bitch ATV will even start. Roy, what did you do with the keys?"

"Gave 'em to you days ago, ass-wipe."

"The hell you did."

"Then you've probably left them in the damn ignition all this time."

Normally, I might find this backwoods banter mildly entertaining, but the approaching headlights are getting closer and closer. And our chances of getting out of here in one piece are dwindling rapidly. We need to go, now!

Having decided for the moment the keys must still be in the ignition, Owen and Roy head out the back door to see if the machine will start. Moments later, we hear the ATV's engine come to life and begin to rev up.

"See," Wendover grins with relief, "looks like they got it started after all."

His smile quickly changes to a look of pained exasperation as we hear them put the four-wheeler into gear and race away into the night. The Fenton's, it seems, have left the building. Indeed, as the sound of the ATV motor fades away into the dark forest, it appears these country bumpkins were a little smarter than we credited them.

I remember the skeptical look on Owen's face as we pitched our story. The look of a con man smelling another con. As the old saying goes, never try to bullshit a bullshitter.

Wendover is beside himself with anger at the Fentons' betrayal. At least judging by how rapidly he has adopted Roy's vocabulary.

Wendover's outburst is interrupted by a loud crash to the front of the property. The entry gate has just been smashed down. We have company.

CHAPTER 106

There is a slamming of vehicle doors outside. And based on the sounds of men and equipment rapidly deploying around the cabin, we have been completely surrounded.

"Get back behind this!" Wendover has quickly extinguished the lanterns, plunging us into darkness. Next, he tips over the folding table on its side in the far corner of the cabin. He's stacking ice chests and even the cases of Rainer in front of the table as a makeshift fortification of sorts. As Ta'Naal and I scamper behind the table, I chamber a round into the shotgun. This is beginning to look like it's going to be the place for our last stand. A Montana last stand that's likely to go even more badly and quickly than Custer's ill-fated demise at the Little Bighorn.

Apropos Custer, where the hell are our own cavalry? I quickly toggle on the data-pad.

"LISA?" Update status on Hillie's position? Tell him our circumstances are dire."

Momentarily she replies, *"Admiral Hillenbrand's aircraft is on final approach into Alta Junction. Depending on the enlistment of additional tactical resources, his ETA to the Clear Creek basin is approximately ninety minutes."*

Great. The day just keeps getting better. Given our odds against this many armed mercenaries, a ninety-minute ETA will likely be too late by eighty-five minutes. And, I furrow my brow, what the hell "additional tactical resources" is he talking about?

"LISA, please transmit our exact coordinates for extraction."

"I have sent your coordinates to the tactical team. My location data is accurate to ten meters. And, as an additional test of my precision, I have cross-checked my calculations with the other GPS transponder on your person."

"What are you talking about? I have no other GPS units with me."

"I regret the misunderstanding, Jack, but you are incorrect. I am currently detecting another GPS device on your person."

"Impossible!"

"May I respectfully request, Jack, that you perhaps check your pockets?"

My heart sinks as I search my shirt and pants and find a small quarter-sized disc tucked secretly into my change pocket. An inconspicuous GPS tracking device that was probably placed there after I was captured and unconscious. A device that Boone himself was likely unaware of as he freed me and Ta'Naal. Shit!

Now it all makes sense. No wonder these thugs weren't in a hurry to chase down our vehicle. They knew exactly where we were at every given moment. All they had to do was wait until we were no longer moving. Wait until we arrived at the Fenton cabin. And then come in for the kill. Or maybe their plans still include a jolly round of capture, torture and then murder. Makes no difference if the end result is the same. And all of this thanks to dumbass me with the GPS tracker in his pocket!

"They tagged you, huh?" Wendover states this as a fact, not a judgement. But somehow his lack of a judgmental tone makes me feel even worse. All of this is my fault. This entire shitshow is my responsibility. These goons were never planning to find or follow Wendover or Ta'Naal. They had been tracking me, probably for weeks. If I'd only just kept the damn Diné translator stone with me in California, none of this would have happened. Instead, I brought this evil to Alta Junction and to Wendover's own home. And if I hadn't gone to Wendover's place, the thugs never would have taken Ta'Naal. She would still be free to go forth and save Earth from the nanites. And Wendover wouldn't be stranded with me in a remote backwoods cabin, outgunned and out of options.

I sigh and turn my attention back to the data-pad. There is one more piece of information Hillie needs to know.

"LISA, please relay one additional message to Admiral Hillenbrand. Inform him that we've caught a canary in one of his traps. One of the traps he baited with vinegar."

"Vinegar, Dr. Walker?"

"Just send it please." One last message, I think. Maybe my final message, period.

"Whatever they have planned," says Wendover quietly, his assault rifle aimed squarely at the front door, "they don't seem to be in a hurry to make a move. Strange. Not that I'm complaining, considering the alternative."

Wendover is right. This is very odd. He, Ta'Naal, and I have now been hunkered down behind our makeshift bunker of ice chests and beer for nearly ten minutes and not word from our pursuers. Except for some hushed movements and whispers around the outside of the cabin, there has been no attempt to engage with us. Not a shot fired. No demands. No threats. No one telling us to come out quietly with our hands up or else. Nada. What are they waiting for? We know they're out there and they must surely know we're in here. Thanks again to the dumbass with the GPS tag.

Suddenly a projectile smashes through a window, and rolls across the floor. It's black in color and round. In that instant I quickly grab Ta'Naal and hit the floor, shielding her with my body. But there is no explosion; it is not a grenade as I had feared.

The round device appears to right itself and slowly it rotates in place.

"I'll be damned," exclaims Wendover, "that's a tactical camera. It's designed to be thrown into building or room to transmit live video to its operators outside. The big city police use these throw-cameras in hostage situations and other instances where situational awareness in a denied or dangerous area is needed."

"Pretty damn sophisticated."

"Yeah. I don't know who these guys are but they're better equipped than my own police force."

"Great. Well, I'm not anxious to see what other high-tech tricks they have up their sleeve."

As if on cue, another projectile sails through the same broken window. This time it's not another camera but a cylinder-shaped object. A cylinder that is beginning to hiss loudly.

"Gas!" shouts Wendover, shielding his eyes and nose with the sleeve of his shirt. I'm also covering my face with my sleeve; trying to hold my breath. And with the other hand, I'm tightly clutching the shotgun. A weapon offering no defense against gas. I'm starting to cough and choke. And as the world begins to fade into blackness, I despairingly rue the futility of bringing a shotgun to a gas canister fight.

I am awakened with the concussion of an enormous blast. Rock, dirt, and dust are raining down all around me and it is pitch dark. I try and roll to an upright position and bump into Wendover. He is just coming back to consciousness as well.

"Dan! Are you okay!" I shout, gasping and choking on the dust all around us.

"I'm okay," he says, gasping for a breath of clean air in the fog of dust swirling about us. "Although I feel like I've got a hell of a hangover. Must have been whatever knockout gas they dosed us with."

We are apparently now walled into a small underground space, likely a cave or an old mine. I steady myself and try to fumble along the earthen walls get an idea of the nature of our surroundings. My inventory of our circumstances takes little time. We are in a tight spot…in every sense of the phrase.

"Just you and me, Dan. Ta'Naal is missing."

"Yeah, they probably took her as collateral to further extort eGenesis for the Progeny identities. Probably just decided to get rid of us. Keeping us alive no longer serves their purposes."

"But then why not just finish us off when the gas knocked us out?" I ask.

"That's not hard to figure. They wanted us to have a slow death with some time to think about the end. Time to see it coming. A death fit for traitors to their so-called patriotic cause."

Based on my survey of our surroundings, it appears the welcome mat for the Grim Reaper has already been laid out. We are trapped in the back of what appears to be a small horizontal tunnel. The front of the tunnel has collapsed and has been covered in a massive rockslide. A rockslide no doubt triggered by the mercenaries' explosive blast. Worse yet, this enormous jumble of rocks and dirt is not only trapping us inside. It is just as effectively prohibiting any light or fresh air from entering our chamber. We are entombed here in a space not much larger than the size of a suburban master bedroom. Which means we have a rapidly diminishing supply of breathable air. We likely only have enough air to last only a few days at best.

"Dan, any idea where we might be? Was there some sort of mine tunnel or cavern close to the Fenton cabin?"

"Yes. It's hard to know for certain, but I think I might be able to guess our location. There were some abandoned mining tunnels located maybe four or five miles from the Fenton place, over on the Clark Mountain side of the highway. They were old exploratory assay tunnels dug into the side of a hill. Back in the day the prospectors didn't tunnel them very far into the hill before they decided to quit and look elsewhere for better ore vein strikes."

Shit, I think, what is it about old mining tunnels and armed thugs that has become a running theme in my life? My apparently soon to be very short life.

"So best case scenario, we're trapped in an old mine survey tunnel maybe four or five miles from the last known location we transmitted to Hillie. The data-pad is either still at the Fenton cabin, or destroyed, or taken by the thugs. In any event, we might as well be on the far side of the moon. Hillie has no way of knowing our location."

"Correct, Jack. And even if he did find the location of our collapsed tunnel, he'd need to find some heavy equipment to remove the landslide of rock that's collapsed the tunnel entrance. Some of those boulders must weigh over a half ton."

"So, Dan…no way out?" The enormity of what Wendover is saying hits me like a gut punch.

"'Fraid so, Jack."

"No, Dan. There has to be a way…there must…"

"Sorry, Jack. This is it. The last roundup. End of the trail. Sorry, my friend."

"Dan, I'm the one who should be sorry. I brought you into this. If only I'd left that damned translator stone back in California, this whole chain of unforeseen events wouldn't have happened."

A small ironic chuckle from Wendover, "a whole chain of unforeseen events, huh? Jack, I think you've just described life itself. None of us can see the causes and consequences that lie ahead. We can't control much of what life hands us. We can only do our best to live with integrity and die with honor."

"I'm all for living with integrity but I was hoping to put off the dying with honor part a little longer."

"I hear you, but sometimes, in the end, it's not our call."

"Dan?"

"Yes?"

"It's been an honor to have known you and it will be an honor to pass from this life with you."

"I feel the same way, Jack. And, until today, little did I know of the hidden burdens you've been carrying…your struggles against the nanites. Feeling responsible for the fate of the world…"

His voice trails off and he's silent for a few minutes. Likely trying to process what has happened to us. What will happen to us.

Then, "you know, in law enforcement it's always there in the back of your mind. Every morning you walk out the door knowing there is a small but non-zero chance you may not come home alive."

"That must have been hard, Dan."

"But what was worse, was knowing Sara's condition with the ALS would eventually be fatal. And somehow, I've always sort of assumed, and every day I've damned myself for the thought, that maybe she'd go first. And after she was gone, if something then happened to me on the job…"

"She'd be spared the grief." I complete the sentence.

"Selfish of me," he says. "And given our circumstances, a completely moot point. Now what will become of her without me as a caregiver? I guess she could move in with her sister. And with Na'Taal likely taken or killed by those goons, it will certainly be a short-term arrangement."

"Agreed, if Ta'Naal is lost to the Diné, the Ka'Parrk's mission will most certainly fail."

"And we will just be the first casualties in the coming extinction of humanity."

CHAPTER 107

Here's the thing about suffocating to death. It doesn't work the way most people might assume it would. Not that I imagine the average person is inclined to spend much time pondering the finer points of the physiology of suffocation. But there is something about being trapped in a small pitch-black, airtight cavern that seems to focus the mind on the problem. And thanks to being married to a physician who often treats patients with respiratory issues, I know more than a little about the blood oxygen cycle. Let's just say over the years it's made for some interesting, though not necessarily amorous, pillow talk.

Oxygen, of course, is key to our survival. It is required to produce the various proteins that maintain our cells and the carbohydrates that provide the energy to power our bodies. Without oxygen from the air, we would quickly die. But while the air around us provides oxygen; not all air is oxygen. Roughly four-fifths of the air we breathe is nitrogen and the remaining one-fifth is oxygen along with a smattering of some other trace gasses.

At rest, an average person breathes in about seven or eight liters of air each minute of every day. At roughly a one-fifth oxygen concentration, that's about a liter and a half of oxygen per minute. And if eight liters of air are being inhaled per minute, that means a volume of eight liters is being exhaled as well. And that is the crux of the problem. Part of that eight liters we exhale every minute is carbon dioxide. Those who die of suffocation in an airtight space will in fact succumb to carbon dioxide poisoning long before the effects of oxygen deprivation become fatal.

Of course, the cycle isn't as simple as breathing in nitrogen and oxygen and exhaling carbon dioxide. One's body can't absorb a liter and a half of oxygen in a minute. Which means with each breath, we exhale mostly the regular nitrogen and oxygen we have just inhaled. But, critically, a small portion, about a quarter of a liter per minute, of our exhalations will be carbon dioxide. And this carbon dioxide will then begin to mix with the remaining air in an increasing concentration over time.

In an enclosed airtight space, it is the buildup of carbon dioxide that begins to kill you. Slowly at first and then more rapidly as the overall CO2 concentration increases with each hour. The normal concentration of carbon dioxide we encounter in daily life is a fraction of one percent by volume. Three percent is considered the maximum of what can be tolerated for short periods of time; a very undesirable but marginally safe upper limit. Exposure above three percent is marked by panting, dizziness, and severe headaches. Above four percent, subjects become disoriented, hyperventilate, and lose consciousness within thirty minutes. Extended exposures above five percent concentrations are immediately lethal.

Most people, mercifully, go through life with no precise notion as to when death will sweep them away. Unfortunately for Wendover and me, it turns out calculating our estimated time of death is just a math problem. I've roughly stepped out the dimensions of our rocky prison. I figure we are trapped in the remains of a small tunnel that has a volume of roughly eighteen hundred cubic feet or fifty thousand liters.

I suppose a true expert in this field might quibble a bit with my calculations. They might suggest that I've perhaps oversimplified the problem. And maybe that's true. But the answer I'm coming up with is probably close enough. Not that the precision of my calculations will alter the end result in any sense that matters. Whether it takes two days or four to die, we'll still be dead.

I figure the two of us combined are replacing oxygen with CO2 at the rate of a half-liter per minute or thirty liters an hour. That means in less than two days we'll have converted about fifteen hundred liters of the tunnel's fifty thousand liters of air into CO2. At that point we'll have exceeded the three percent upper limit of tolerable safety and all bets are off. And a day or so later, death will come; bringing with it a measure of both mercy and irony.

There will be mercy, I suppose, in that we'll be spared the agonies of death by dehydration. Seems our former captors rather inconsiderately left us with not a drop of water. And there will be irony in the sense that we will essentially die of suffocation in a tunnel still filled with plenty of oxygen. For even as we die, the percentage of oxygen in the tunnel will be at about fifteen percent. For the sake of comparison, this would be roughly the same concentration you would find in the thinning mountain air at 8,000 feet in elevation. The concentration of oxygen one might encounter on a pleasant day in Aspen, Colorado.

Wendover has become silent. He's probably lost in his own thoughts or maybe trying to slow his breathing to conserve air.

I contemplate the silent darkness and shake my head. Why am I wasting some of my last conscious moments on suffocation calculations? It's an academic fool's errand. An effort without meaning or payoff. In the end, it will make no difference to our fate.

But I suppose academic fool's errands are essentially my brand. What has defined my existence. That's what I do to distract myself from the realities of life. It's how I've always avoided dealing with my emotions and the feelings of others. I've hid behind a wall of calculations and algorithms. Using my obsession with science coupled with cynical wisecracks to keep the world comfortably at bay. Oh, perhaps when the occasion calls, I can be outwardly social in appearance. But, in reality, I wonder if what I really do is to give nothing and therefore risk nothing emotionally? Perhaps, as a psychologist of recent acquaintance wryly noted, I may have a mild personality disorder. A personality disorder of the kind that, ironically, involves the lack an authentic personality.

And I think it is in this moment, with the prospect of death rapidly approaching, that I finally realize a fundamental truth about myself. That all these years, I've never really been afraid to die. Rather, I've always been far more afraid to truly live.

But I'm wasting precious moments self-analyzing my various faults and shortcomings. I should be more focused on those still living rather than on we soon to be departed. I'll miss Kate and Amy with all my heart. They'll be devastated first by my mysterious disappearance and then will likely suffer terribly and die in the approaching nanite apocalypse.

I grimace as I damn myself again for bringing Boone's mercenaries to Alta Junction and derailing Ta'Naal's efforts to thwart the nanites. For if the alien isn't dead now, her days will surely be numbered by those thugs. And now Kate, Amy, and everyone else I've ever known and cared for will pay for my unwitting actions.

Time passes silently in the blackness of our tomb; minutes, maybe hours. I feel myself losing track. For some period now, I've been sitting here in a melancholy silence in the dark. Sitting with the stark awareness that every breath I take is yet another small nail in our collective coffin.

Then, incredibly, a voice in the dark.

"Jack Walker?"

I stir restlessly. Drifting in and out of awareness in total darkness. What is this voice? Am I dreaming or maybe already dead? Will there be a difference, I wonder?

"Jack Walker?"

So, this is it. End of the line. The final passage. Odd though, my name being announced. Not sure what I was expecting; the Grim Reaper's cold hand upon my shoulder? Instead, my name is being called as though a table at a busy restaurant has just come available. Excuse me, Mr. Walker, but we can seat you now in our newly revamped Purgatory section. Our apologies in advance, the service here can be a little slow. It may feel like an eternity simply to get a menu.

I shake my head in disbelief. "Dan, do you hear that? I think someone just called my name."

"Hear what? Jack, I don't hear anything?" comes the weak reply.

"I thought I heard someone calling my name. Maybe I'm just imagining it."

"Nobody here but me," he says quietly.

I look about, listening in the dark, but all is silent now. Is my mind beginning to play tricks on me? Could the slowly diminishing oxygen in the tunnel already be affecting my brain? Causing me to begin to hallucinate?

Then again, I hear the voice in my mind. And it is, I suddenly realize, a familiar voice.

"Jack Walker?"

"Ta'Naal?" I try to project my thoughts telepathically in reply. *"Is that you? You're safe?"*

"Yes, I am unharmed."

"But how? How did you find me?"

"Technically, you were never really lost."

"How could that be?"

A pause and then the telepathic thought projected to my mind chuckles.

"Jack Walker, do you require still further assistance in my rescue?"

I smile weakly, *"Your assumption is correct."*

"Very well. At this time, for your own safety, it would advisable for you and Sheriff Wendover to move back away from the blocked entrance to the tunnel."

At this point, I roust Wendover and we drag ourselves away from the collapsed entrance. But given the massive rockslide blocking our escape, I'm left to wonder just how Ta'Naal plans to remove that great mass of several tons of rock and boulders. And how did she manage to escape from the clutches of the mercenaries who captured her? And more to the immediate point, how did she find us?

I'm not left to wonder for long. Shortly, I begin to hear the shifting and pulling of massive boulders; at first faint and then growing louder. Now Wendover is slowly coming back to full awareness and he hears the rumbling of rock and stone as well. What is happening? Is Ta'Naal employing some advanced alien technology to remove the slide? Or has Hillie inexplicably arrived with heavy equipment for the task?

We watch in awe as a huge boulder begins to shake loose allowing a small crack of early morning light and sweet fresh air to seep into our rocky prison. Next, to our utter astonishment, a massive hairy hand grabs the edge of one of the huge boulders and pulls it loose. Seconds later, a smiling face appears through the newly created hole in the tunnel entrance.

I never thought I'd ever find myself saying this, but at this moment, Akamu's burly, hairy sasquatch face seems to me to be the most beautiful sight on Earth.

The beast grins and gives us a quick wave, "Aloha!"

"Mahalo, my friend," I return the smile, "Mahalo!"

CHAPTER 108

WENDOVER AND I STAGGER OUT OF THE COLLAPSED TUNNEL GASPING IN BREATHS of the sweet mountain air. We're beaten, bruised, disheveled, and covered in dirt. We look like we have been dragged through a landfill on the way to a car wreck. But as we stand on the edge of a dirt access road next to the tunnel, the early light of the high mountain dawn is revealing a scene even stranger than we ourselves must appear.

Our first sight is of Ta'Naal and Akamu. They are standing next to the tunnel entrance seeming to look understandably proud of themselves. The ten-foot hairy giant and the four-foot diminutive alien would surely take a first place showing in any odd couples' contest.

But then I gasp in amazement and joy as I see Kate approaching us with Hillie at her side. She throws her arms around me. "Honey, we were all so worried! So glad you and Dan are safe!"

I gladly return the hug and add a kiss. "Kate, so glad to see you! But…how? What are you doing here in the middle of this operation?" I'm noticing that my fair lady is wearing a body armor vest and sporting a sidearm as well. It's surprisingly a good look for her. An intriguing mix of beauty and badass.

"It's my doing," says Hillie. "I had very little time to pull together a small tactical team of people I could absolutely trust. Given your location out here in the Benton County backwoods, I figured I could use a little more muscle.

And, of course, Kate is the world's foremost 'sasquatch whisperer.'" He nods towards Akamu, "yeah, the big fella here saved the day in several regards."

"Hillie, I take it that Kate and Akamu were the 'additional tactical resources' you needed to acquire for the mission? And the reason you were delayed in your arrival?"

"Yes, we had to divert to LA to pick up Kate."

"But then how did Kate find Akamu? It's not as though he can be reached through social media."

"Oh, we had previously devised a system to get in contact whenever I came to the sasquatch clan's neck of the woods," interjects Kate. "We agreed that I would announce my presence with a very specific pattern of vehicle horn honks."

"Really? I say. "Sort of like a sasquatch bat-signal?"

"Yup. Sort of a squatch-signal, if you will," she adds with a grin.

"Okay, but how did you ever find us? The last GPS coordinates you were given wouldn't have helped. Those were transmitted from the Fenton cabin where we were gassed before being taken to be trapped in this tunnel."

"True enough," replies Hillie, "but remember, LISA had discovered that the mercenaries had surreptitiously hidden a GPS tracking device in your pocket. That device continued to transmit your location until you were thrown in the tunnel. LISA simply needed to track your movements up to the point where the signal was lost; at the mouth of this collapsed tunnel."

"So," Wendover is glancing about, "where is the rest of your tactical team?"

"You mean besides Kate, Akamu, and me?" Hillie smirks a bit as he pulls out a Cuban robusto and lights it. "Let's see. I was only able to thoroughly vet a very small number of individuals for this mission. Colonel Anderson is guarding what remains of the mercenaries who had captured you. And Staff Sergeant Hernandez is currently down securing both the Fenton and Cortez cabins."

"What?" I exclaim. "Kate, no offense to you and Akamu. But, Hillie, you're telling me you took on nearly a dozen armed mercenaries with only three trained military officers? You were hopelessly outnumbered. What am I missing?"

"There was one more mercenary, actually. Seems the crew picked up a local thug on short notice. Some guy that apparently advertised his willingness for dirty work out on the dark web. Guess he helped them with the rental car logistics and probably told them about these abandoned mining survey tunnels." He turns to Wendover, "Sheriff, have you heard of a local muscle for hire named Jeb Foley?"

"Yep. Rumor had it Foley was promoting himself through criminal channels. Eager for assignments in the business of dirty business."

"Well, you'll find Mr. Foley has now gone out of that business…permanently."

"Okay," I continue, "so how did you take on all those thugs? You were outnumbered!"

Hillie grins and puffs on his robusto, "turns out, Jack, that it was the mercenaries who were outnumbered. Only a dozen of them versus one very pissed-off sasquatch. Probably best if you take a look down the embankment and see for yourself."

The old access road up to the mine tunnels crisscrosses the side of an open hill with multiple switchbacks. About a quarter mile or so down the slope is a surreal sight. Two large Chevy Suburbans have been smashed together. Incredibly, one has been flipped on end over the top of the other, pancaking the lower vehicle flat. Another third SUV lies on its side a few yards away. It's still smoldering, gutted by fire. A bit farther away, I can see Colonel Anderson sporting an assault rifle. He's guarding a ragtag knot of mercenaries, all zip-tied together.

"What the hell happened?"

Hillie and Kate attempt to fill in the details. The tactical team had been proceeding up this hill in two vehicles, closing in on our last known GPS position. At that point they saw three mercenary vehicles coming down the road. Presumably, the mercenaries had just finished demolishing the entrance to our tunnel, entombing us. The team blocked the road with one of their vehicles and readied their firearms. Akamu hid out of sight below the berm of the road.

As the mercenaries approached the roadblock they screeched to a dusty stop, rolled down their windows, and aimed high power rifles at the team. In that moment, Ta'Naal leaped out of the lead Suburban's window and made a beeline for Kate. One of the thugs leaned out the window and prepared to fire at both the alien and Kate. That would quickly turn out to be a very, very bad mistake. A fatal mistake. No one threatens or points a rifle at Akamu's favorite family doctor.

To the mercenaries' terrified astonishment, Akamu came screaming up over the side of the road in full-beast mode. He snarled and grabbed the front end of the lead Suburban, flipping it end over end right on top of the second Suburban, crushing it down into the road. Then for good measure he flipped the third SUV on its side and kicked in the gas tank, causing a fire.

"So, at that point," recaps Hillie, "you could say the mercenaries sort of had the fight taken out of them…those that survived. They surrendered and no shots were ever fired on either side. How about we walk on down for a closer look?"

"Colonel, good to see you. Thanks for coming to our rescue." I shake Anderson's hand warmly as we approach him and the remains of mercenary force.

"My pleasure, Dr. Walker. Glad to see you're in one piece. You've certainly fared better than most of this crowd." He gestures towards his prisoners; a motley collection of half a dozen very injured young men. I glance about and see several other dead bodies lying next to the wrecked vehicles. And I see my old nemesis, Polaris, his lifeless head sticking out of the bottom crushed Suburban. I don't, however, see Boone among either the living or the dead.

I turn back to Anderson, "hey, where's your deputy, Jake Pullman? I can't imagine Pullman would miss an opportunity to go shoot at some bad guys, right?"

Anderson and Hillie exchange an uncomfortable look.

"No," I shake my head in disbelief. "You're not saying…"

"Sorry, Jack," says Hillie grimly. "Turns out Pullman was part of the conspiracy. He's the one that leaked your flight plan."

"Unbelievable. Do we know who else was involved? Sounds like we had several wolves in the fold."

"Yes. Thanks to your tip-off about the vinegar canary trap, we're in the process of rounding up several other…canaries. And these jokers," he's motioning to the captured mercenaries, "seem to have some very interesting files on their phones. Let me show you."

He reaches down and pulls a cell phone out of one of the prisoner's shirt pockets.

The brute scowls at him, "good luck trying to unlock it. My passcode can't be hacked."

"Sorry, genius, I don't need to hack your passcode. I just need to hack your ugly face." With that, Hillie places the screen in front of the thug's face and the phone unlocks. "Gotta love those facial recognition unlock features, eh?"

Hillie quickly thumbs through the phone's files. "Here's a nice photo of you, Jack." The photo was taken in the Argentinian cavern, showing me and the alien Na'Vack. "Oh, and here's another fine video featuring another one of our canaries." I recognize the red-headed scientist as one of our junior researchers on the project. "All and all," the admiral says, "we've pulled enough information off these phones to crack the conspiracy wide open and resecure eGenesis for good."

I turn as we hear a vehicle approaching. It's Sergeant Hernandez, returning from her reconnaissance of the cabins.

After a quick salute to Hillie and Anderson, she greets me. "Dr. Walker, so good to see you again. I'm glad you are safe." Hernandez was assigned as my security detail last fall as I spread my brother Marty's ashes near Flathead Lake.

"Sirs," she continues, "both cabins are now clear. I've recovered Dr. Walker's data-pad and secured several items of evidence for future prosecution efforts. There was one body at the Cortez cabin, presumed a deceased hostile. Single shot to the back of the head. Point-blank."

Hillie and I exchange a questioning look. This person wasn't merely shot; they were executed.

"I have a photo." She's opening her phone.

Hillie hands me the phone. "How about it, Jack? Can you identify him? Is he one of the mercenaries or someone else?"

I look at the image and slowly nod my head. Even with half his face blown off I can tell it's Boone. No doubt once his cronies realized how we had escaped from the cabin, they figured he must have helped us. And then executed him. I think Boone was a smart guy. Probably smart enough to realize the risk he was taking helping us escape. A risk he was willing to take to save his daughter.

"I recognize him."

"So, was he one of the bad guys?"

I sigh. Good guys. Bad guys. We all wish for a world with simple binary choices. Good or evil? Sinner or saint? But the world is not obligated to make it easy to label people like some old-time vaudeville show where we can cheer the heroes and boo the villains. People and circumstances are complex. Great evil and harm have been done in the name of good and righteousness. Sadly, in this world, the Devil's agenda is at times furthered by those who've convinced themselves they are doing God's work. And sometimes, alternatively, people will end up doing the right things for all the wrong reasons.

Finally, I say, "who was he? First and foremost, he was a guy who loved his little daughter. But, yes, he was also part of the conspiracy. Probably reluctantly in the end."

"Jack Walker?"

I turn to see Ta'Naal standing by herself some fifty yards distant. And as I turn to walk towards her, I also begin the hear the distant sound of sirens coming up the main highway. In a few minutes this remote vista will look like a law enforcement convention. It is time to say goodbye. According to Hillie, the plan will be for Akamu to escort the alien back in the wilderness to a safe area where she will be reunited with Ra'Noor and the rest of her kind. Kate joins me as I approach the alien.

"Jack Walker. I wish to thank you for all you have done for the Progeny and the Diné. And for your assistance in rescuing me."

"I think you ended up helping rescue me far more than I helped rescue you."

"Perhaps. But let us say you provided useful diversions at the most appropriate times. And for this we Diné wish to thank you…in a substantial way. Is there any way our advanced technologies and knowledge can assist you personally? You know that our kind prefers to benefit the greater society rather than individuals. The many rather than the one. But I believe we can make an exception in your case. What can we do for you as…how do you say it, a favor?"

"Oh, I'm not sure I need any favors." But as I say this, I look back at Wendover who is some distance away in an earnest conversation with Hillie. "Well, perhaps there is one favor I might ask of you."

For a moment she considers my request, then, *"Yes. I believe I can assist with that issue."*

"And one more thing, Ta'Naal. Ra'Noor had mentioned that you had a plan to somehow mitigate the effects on human society of seeing the Ka'Parrk probe orbiting overhead. Would you tell me your plans?"

As Kate looks on uneasily, Ta'Naal slowly raises her hand and touches my temple with two fingers. *"I think you are ready to safely share part of my mind. The communication can be much quicker this way."*

And in a single instant I gasp as I understand it all. Everything. A plan as audacious as it is ambitious. And, it just might work. No, it *must* work.

"Will you help us?"

"How could I not?"

As Ta'Naal leaves with Akamu, Kate asks me if I'm okay. "What did she tell you, Jack? What is their plan?"

I shake my head at the sheer enormity of what I've have just come to understand. I give Kate a quick hug.

"The plan? Kate, you're not going to believe this, but it seems the alien Diné along with their advanced extraterrestrial technologies are going to hide in plain sight!"

CHAPTER 109

The dour program director of eGenesis, Winston Monroe, could hardly be described as upbeat even on a good day. But this evening he is even more grim and somber than usual.

"Jack Walker," he begins with a worried sigh, "you have faced aliens, sasquatches, kidnappers, armed mercenaries, and deranged serial killers. But nothing, nothing can prepare you for the trials and the horrors that you are about to face!"

He pauses for effect. "It's almost too terrible to imagine. Endless meetings, conferences, and dinners." He slowly begins to smile. "Being forced to deal with self-important politicians, egotistical tech CEOs, and diplomatic windbags of every sort. And worse yet, you'll have to endure the over-educated ramblings of other academics and scientists like yourself...and me!"

He grins broadly and raises a wine glass, "Professor, excuse me, *Ambassador* Jack Walker, we salute you. We thank you. We wish you good luck. And may God have mercy on your wretched soul!" There is applause and a clinking of wine glasses around the table.

"Thanks, Winston," I say. "But ambassador is a bit of a grand term for my new assignment. I think my title is going to be something like UN Special Envoy for Technology Advancement. Fancy words to describe a science policy wonk. And I'll be just one of several dozen other envoys helping to shepherd this project along."

"Fine," grins Monroe, "we'll address you as Mr. Ambassador-adjacent, then."

Monroe discreetly makes no public mention of this, but he knows as well as I do that the fellow envoys I speak of are all seeker-guides. Some of whom had even joined my late brother Marty and me in the darkened learning circles of the alien Diné all those many years ago. Together we seeker-guides will act as liaisons between the secretive alien Diné, various UN working groups, and a select group of world leaders.

In fact, just yesterday I had an extended video conference with Liu Da-Shin. She was the little girl from China that I had remembered. Remembered after my long-repressed memories of the learning circles had finally resurfaced after being unlocked by the alien Na'Vack in Argentina. And, in an interesting coincidence, it turns out that Dr. Liu also happens to be a professor of informatics. She teaches at Zhejiang University in Hangzhou and has now has also been appointed as a UN special envoy in our upcoming endeavor.

This evening Kate and I have joined a small number of our eGenesis colleagues for a farewell gathering. An occasion to mark the closing of a chapter and the beginning of a new journey towards a novel and challenging future.

Monroe is hosting this little soirée in a private dining room at the Eldorado in Santa Fe, steps away from the city's historic plaza. As I think of it, an entirely fitting location. In its four-hundred-year history the plaza has seen both old traditions honored and rapid new changes thrust upon it.

Here along the plaza can be found a dynamic intermix of Pueblo, Hispanic, and Anglo cultures. Strolling along the plaza one can bargain with a pueblo vendor; their wares of geometrically patterned Santo Domingo pottery carefully laid out on traditional blankets. And on the next block one might encounter a young researcher from the Santa Fe Institute, her area of expertise focused on the complex geometries of Mandelbrot fractals that emerge in nature itself. Two world views intertwined around the common underlying geometry of life itself.

There are chuckles around the table as appetizers and more drinks are served. Hillie is in his element. The admiral is twisting the stem of his wine glass and regaling the assembled with some humorous stories. No doubt several of the yarns will be told at my expense.

I grin and nod at Hillie, not that he needs much encouragement once he has the floor. And I absentmindedly touch my chest and feel the small amulet I now carry under my shirt on a diminutive gold chain. A clear vial of blessed corn pollen. A talisman for good fortune on the long and uncertain path ahead of us. It is a gift from a wise elder. A new friend I had met in very unique surroundings only a few days ago…

…"Coffee?"

He offers me coffee in a cup worn from the years. Its inside patinaed light brown from careful use over time. His hands shake slightly, betrayed by the tremors of age.

"Ahéhee'," I reply. "Thank you, Hosteen Atcitty."

"Yá'át'ééh," he responds, meaning in this sense, all is well; a Navajo way of saying I'm welcome.

Hosteen Atcitty's full name is Charlie Luis Atcitty. He is an elder *haatali*, or singer; the term for a medicine man in the Navajo culture. Today, he is dressed in a traditional manner with boots, blue jeans, a concha belt, and a velvet shirt with a colorful patterned vest. He wears his silver hair long. It's twisted into a distinctive bun, or *tsiiyéél*, on the back of his head, tied with white sheep's wool yarn.

He carefully recites his linage for us. Traditional Navajos are matrilineal, meaning they primarily trace their heritage through their mothers' family tree. He indicates he is of his mother's Bitter Water Clan, born to the Mud Clan of his father's people. Having now described his place in the context of what is important in the world, he joins me in looking out the massive forward windows of the Ka'Parrk space probe. We hear a distant rumbling and feel the steady vibration of the Ka'Parrk's propulsion system resonate through the deck under our feet.

For Hosteen Atcitty is far more than a revered Navajo haatali. He is the planet's oldest living seeker-guide. And one of my two companions on this very unique excursion.

"See?" The alien Ra'Noor is pointing out the window. *"That is your star, Sol. And that small blue dot to the left? That is Earth."*

"Simply amazing," I say. "To view it from this perspective."

"It is an honor," adds Atcitty, "to see the world as the holy people must see it. As Changing Woman must have looked down upon the Earth as she created our Fifth World."

Interestingly, the notion that the alien Diné inhabited the Earth millions of years ago before venturing out into space and then returning would not be entirely foreign to how a traditional Navajo might view their people's creation traditions.

For Navajos do not view the progression of time as linear. Rather they see the universe unfolding in endless cycles of creation, destruction, and rebirth. In this worldview, if the alien Diné lived on this planet some five million years ago, this might have simply occurred in a prior cycle of existence. Perhaps a cycle the ancients referred to as the Fourth World.

I continue to glance about the Ka'Parrk. We are standing in what must be the bridge or master control center. All about us hum glowing, ever-changing electronic displays apparently depicting our navigational, propulsion, and systems status. Each display station has an empty chair in front of it. This bridge was obviously designed to be operated by over a dozen crewmembers. But today all the stations and, indeed, the entire ship is empty save for Atcitty, Ra'Noor, and myself.

"Ra'Noor," I say, "thank you again for bringing us along for this experience."

"You are quite welcome, but we should also express our gratitude to our host today." He nods towards Atcitty, *"for after all, this is his property."*

Hosteen Atcitty bows his head slightly, "Yá'át'ééh." And I raise my coffee cup in salute to him.

For as it turns out, we are not actually standing in an alien probe, millions of miles away in distant space. Rather we are walking through an extremely realistic holographic representation of the Ka'Parrk. A high-definition hologram currently being projected inside Atcitty's sheep barn here in northern Arizona, just a few miles distant from the Lukachukai mountain range.

"So," continues Ra'Noor, *"are we ready to proceed with the rest of the presentation and tour? I must thank you both for agreeing to preview this...I believe you call it a 'dry run'?"*

"Yes. Dry run is the correct term," I reply.

"Very well, but before we get started, I wanted you to see this." He points to a small power unit flanking an instrumentation panel.

"This is what you might call a 'nice touch,' correct?"

I look a bit closer at the unit and realize it is distinctively labeled as a Lockheed Martin part.

"This is a real Lockheed part?"

"As real as we could make it with our replication technology."

"And I could in fact trace the serial number of this part back to Lockheed?"

"Yes. You could trace the part directly back to the factory of origination. Right down to the lot/date codes, quality inspection paperwork, and launch manifests. All thanks to the efforts of LISA."

I smile at Ra'Noor. "I'm sure LISA has indeed done her usual thorough job. With this particular unit as well as nearly every other part on this vessel."

Indeed, if I were to closely inspect most of the equipment on the Ka'Parrk, I'd find part numbers and logos indicating the alien probe had been designed and built with parts sourced from Lockheed, Boeing, Northrup, Roscosmos, Airbus, and nearly every other aerospace company on Earth.

And that is the true genius of the alien Diné plan to hide their presence in plain sight. Ta'Naal and her colleagues have carefully and meticulously designed the Ka'Parrk to appear as though it had been built by humans!

A grand deception so audacious in scope it makes the alien Diné's prior little charade in Roswell look like child's play. For now when the Ka'Parrk shortly appears in the skies overhead, it will not be feared as the harbinger of an alien invasion. Rather, it will be celebrated as humanity's greatest technological achievement. A symbol of what can be achieved when the world's powers put their differences aside and work together for the greater good.

LISA, of course, has been a key player in the grand deception. She has hacked all of the planet's major aerospace companies, altering their financial and manufacturing records to make it appear that they have contributed most of equipment we see before us. Today many in the world fear that A.I.s will change our future. Little do they realize that A.I.s also have the power to alter our past, or, at least, the record of our past.

Soon holographic displays of the Ka'Parrk similar to this will soon be placed in thousands of locations around the planet. These exhibits will help to explain and celebrate the capabilities of "mankind's" most advanced space vessel. All courtesy of the ship's prime contractor: DAST Industries or Diné Advanced Science Technologies, Inc.

"As part of the standard holographic tour," continues Ra'Noor, *"we will begin with a prerecorded message from the CEO of DAST Industries. An individual who very shortly will rise from obscurity to perhaps become the most famous person on the planet."*

"Yes," I chuckle dryly, "a most famous person who in truth is not actually a person."

CHAPTER 110

A screen before us switches on and we see the DAST CEO comfortably seated in her upscale executive office. She smiles broadly, subtly straightens her jacket, and addresses the camera.

"Bienvenido!, Salut!, Yōkoso!, Privet!, Huānyíng!, Welcome! I am Lisa Isabela Amai, the CEO and president of DAST Industries."

I shake my head in admiration of LISA's latest avatar persona. It's yet another riff on the Sokolov look. This time with an expensive executive touch. She's offset Sokolov's porcelain doll features with high-dollar tortoise shell framed glasses and an expensive-looking dark navy blazer.

Of course, on the screen she looks and sounds undeniably human. And I imagine she has skillfully created a false digital backstory of educational and corporate achievements to match her title. And the name she's selected is a playful wink to those of us who know her real identity. A thinly disguised anagram: Lisa..I..am..AI. Cute.

"We are so glad you could visit us today!" she continues. "Here at DAST Industries we like to say that we are a little company with big ideas...and even bigger dreams! Please join us as we introduce our latest technological achievement. It is truly a marvel, but let me assure you that even more exciting developments are on the way! Because here at DAST Industries, we are always working hard to bring tomorrow's future to you...today!"

LISA is managing to project a somewhat forced sense of joviality and enthusiasm packaged with an air of patronizing aloofness towards her audience. In other words, she's basically nailed the persona of your typical high-visibility tech billionaire CEO.

"So, here we are," continues LISA/Lisa, "you are standing inside an enhanced holographic representation of the most advanced spaceship ever built by mankind. We call it Earth Exploration Ship One. The EES Nash."

Ra'Noor nods towards me, *"another nice touch?"*

"Most appropriate. Those who served aboard the original USS Nash endured many sacrifices. And, frankly, life hasn't been all that easy for their Progeny descendants either."

LISA/Lisa continues by offering an apologetic shrug of her shoulders and a demure laugh.

"Well, I suppose the first order of business would be for me to offer an apology to everyone on the planet for the little scare we at DAST inadvertently caused as we took this spacecraft out for a little uncrewed test drive around the solar system. I'm sorry if some folks came to believe Earth was going to be hit by interstellar asteroid as the ship tracked inbound. Yes, that was our bad. But we didn't feel we could announce the creation of the Nash until we were sure it would perform as designed."

Our bad? LISA/Lisa says this with all the glib guileless innocence of a teenager confessing to a harmless prank. Like maybe she just got caught toilet papering the high school coach's house. Never mind all the people who have been ruining their lives and those of others bucket dumping and overpass jumping because they feared a giant asteroid was going to hit the planet.

"And," adds LISA/Lisa, "as a second order of business, I'd like to personally thank some businesses and organizations. Specifically, Lockheed Martin, Boeing, SpaceX, the European Aeronautic Defence and Space Company, and Roscosmos. These organizations provided most of the subcomponents of the EES Nash. Although," she pauses and smiles, "it is safe to say they had no idea what program they were actually supporting with their pieces and parts. You might say we sort of crowd-sourced the parts without disclosing the final application of the items. But we thank these companies just the same for their vital contributions."

Ra'Noor pauses the video. *"A cover story will be circulated indicating the Nash was assembled by autonomous robots in deep space using a mix of commercially available aerospace parts along with advanced equipment and manufacturing methods proprietary to DAST Industries."*

"Yes," I reply, "that is my understanding as well. And once the Ka'Parrk's nanite eradication mission is complete, I imagine it will take several weeks for the Diné to quietly convert the Ka'Parrk into the Nash. In effect, you will need to de-content the vessel, correct?"

Indeed, that is correct. We will remove our most advanced and sensitive Diné technologies and modify the capabilities of the ship's propulsion system to limit its range to the immediate solar system. At that point, the Nash will then be ready to welcome its first human crew for training on its systems."

"Yes," I comment, "the human crew that will be observing our solar system through all of those windows arrayed across the hull of the Ka'Parrk."

"Correct," replies Ra'Noor, *"that was our plan all along."* He restarts the video.

"Of course, the design, assembly, and launch of the EES Nash would not have been possible without the enthusiastic support of the world's governments. For although your world leaders may not always agree on geopolitical matters, they are unanimous in their wish that DAST's world-changing technologies be allowed to provide great benefits to all the people of Earth. We are so grateful for their full support of what we call the Nash Initiative."

Ra'Noor pauses the video again. *"I believe this 'support' is what your kind would term making a virtue out of a necessity, correct?*

"Ra'Noor," I reply, "you have many talents, not the least of which is the gift of understatement."

For if the scientifically brilliant Ta'Naal could be thought of as the alien Diné's Einstein, then Ra'Noor must surely be their Machiavelli. In the mere ten days since Ta'Naal's rescue, he has managed to convince every world leader of a UN Security Council member nation to embrace the alien Diné plan for global change, the Nash Initiative.

Of course, the word 'convince' is hardly adequate to convey the true scope and methods of his approach. Depending on the individual prejudices, ambitions, and personalities of each leader, Ra'Noor has applied a varying mix of flattery, bribery, intimidation, and blackmail to each leader's mental and emotional pressure points to great effect. Those of us who have been privileged to watch him in action have been treated to a master class in high-stakes geopolitical manipulation. How to speak truth to power without regard to whether the powerful would like to hear it or not.

The typical script for 'convincing' a world leader has generally gone as follows. First, a targeted world leader, let's say the President of the United States, receives disturbing reports that their nation's military weapons systems have inexplicably become rendered useless. This troubling development no doubt weighs heavily on POTUS as he retires for the night and drifts off to sleep. Several hours later POTUS finds himself waking up in his pajamas as Ra'Noor's unwilling guest in a Diné spacecraft. Abducted from right under the unsuspecting noses of the Secret Service protection detail. It's time for a little come-to-alien heart to heart.

Ra'Noor tells POTUS that his nation's, as well as every other country's, advanced military weapons systems are now essentially useless, courtesy of the alien Diné. There's a new world dawning and everyone is going to be expected to play nice. Not that they are going to have a choice now that their once-powerful weapon systems are essentially bricked.

As POTUS tries to get his head around this new reality, Ra'Noor hits the next item on the agenda. This 'Oumuamua II asteroid, he says, days away from approaching Earth, isn't really an asteroid at all. It's an alien probe, the Ka'Parrk, on a mission to decontaminate the planet from a deadly nanite threat. However, if the general population came to understand that the massive space vessel was an alien artifact, there is a very real possibility that global civilization may collapse. Understood? POTUS begins to nod in agreement as he ponders the consequences that will likely arise from the sudden disclosure of extraterrestrial intelligent life.

Ra'Noor tells POTUS that the alien Diné stand ready to provide humanity with the tools and technology to eliminate poverty and malnutrition. But there are conditions. Here's the deal. POTUS and the other world leaders of the UN Security Council will be expected to support the Diné deception regarding the space probe. The Ka'Parrk will be revealed as the EES Nash, a human creation intended all along to expand mankind's exploration and understanding of the solar system. And the related introduction of replication technologies to alleviate material want will be targeted in an equitable fashion such that the last become first. In a real sense the meek will indeed inherit the earth.

POTUS and the other world leaders are to tout these technological advancements, this Nash Initiative, as having sprung forth from their own secret collaborations and plans. Duly assisted by the incredible technology breakthroughs of DAST Industries and its charismatic CEO, Lisa Amai.

The politicians are welcome to take full credit for this advancement of science and the betterment of the human condition. That is the carrot. As for the stick, well, if a leader doesn't want to play along, then they will be publicly discredited as easily as their weapons systems were neutered and an offer will be made to their political rivals. Simply put, this train is leaving the station, you can either be on it, or under it. Capeesh? And, oh yes, the first rule of dealing with the alien Diné? One is to never speak of the Diné.

The capstone of Ra'Noor's midnight arm-twisting sessions will occur next Monday as the UN Security Council makes a formal public announcement of the Nash Initiative and reveals the EES Nash is about to orbit the planet. This will be presented as the product of an international collaboration so secret the world's governments apparently were almost completely unaware themselves that they were participating. A grand initiative conceived by the genius minds of the global leaders, with the muddling details left up to the technology wonks of the UN Special Envoys for Technology Advancement.

"Ra'Noor? Can these leaders, these politicians, be trusted to keep their word?" asks Hosteen Atcitty. "Sadly, the history of my people suggests political leaders often do not honor their promises. They have consistently promised one thing to the Navajo and then done the exact opposite. And what is to keep them from going on television to reveal the existence of the alien Diné?"

"I think Hosteen Atcitty has a good point," I add, "if he and I don't always trust our world's political leaders, how can your people trust them?"

"I believe it was your Winston Churchill who observed that while alliances may change over time, it may be counted upon that nations will invariably pursue their own self-interests. True alliances, whether national or individual, are therefore built upon shared self-interests. I believe that cooperation with the Diné on the Nash Initiative is in your politicians' best self-interest. LISA has seen to it that your world leaders understand this clearly."

"May I assume you are referring to her ability to find suitable 'kompromat' on each of our world leaders?" I ask.

"That would be a correct assumption. It would seem no one in your world advances to a position of great power without accumulating a little 'kompromat' along the way, eh? Besides, what credible world leader would go on record to declare the Nash Initiative was a secret space-alien conspiracy? Space-aliens? Absurd! They'd be

laughed out of office and their political rivals would likely try to have them institutionalized."

Ra'Noor restarts the video and we are left with LISA/Lisa's parting words.

"On behalf of DAST Industries, I would like to thank you for your interest in the EES Nash. In a few moments, our virtual tour guide, Bruce, will walk you through this holographic representation of the Nash and answer any questions you may have regarding its operation and capabilities. And, just as the Apollo space program generated many other technological spin-offs that bettered life for all of us, you'll find the Nash Initiative will also provide many benefits to humanity in areas such as food production and bio-medical breakthroughs. Please stay tuned for future exciting announcements from DAST. And remember," she gives the camera a wink and a thumbs-up, "here at DAST Industries, we are always working hard to bring tomorrow's future to you…today!"

As we complete the tour, Atcitty pulls Ra'Noor and me aside. He would like us to stay with him this evening to share in a treasured ritual. A ceremony to consecrate and bring good fortune to the Nash Initiative and the journey ahead. How could we refuse?

It is late evening and the faint glow of the sunset has long retreated from the crest of the Lukachukais. In its place, a swath of a million stars glows above us in the vast darkness on this moonless night in the high desert.

It is close quarters in Atcitty's ceremonial hogan. It's roughly circular and only a few meters in diameter, lined with cedar wood. A small fire glows in its center. Hosteen Atcitty asks Ra'Noor and me to gather in close to the fire. This way there will be room in the hogan for the holy people to assemble behind us in spirit.

He begins the intricate chants of the Blessingway or *Hózhójí*. He sings the chants and songs of his ancestors as they did as their ancestors before them. Imploring the holy people to look down upon us and asking their blessings upon our upcoming trials and challenges. The ritual continues for hours and he mostly sings the chants in Navajo. The language itself is intriguing. It's an Athabaskan language, closely related to Apache tongues as well as dialects to be found in many Alaskan and Pacific Northwest tribal communities.

From time to time, he switches over and translates the core prayers into English for my benefit…

I will be as I was before, I will have a cool breeze over my body. I will have a light body, I will be happy forever, nothing will hinder me. I walk with beauty before me. I walk with beauty behind me. Walk in beauty. Walk in harmony. Walk in peace…

…"Jack?" Kate smiles and squeezes my arm, bringing me back into the present. Hillie's stories are winding down as the first course is served.

"So, Jack," inquires Monroe, "after the upcoming UN announcement on Monday, you'll be swept into a very high-profile position with this Ambassador-adjacent role. It's likely the upcoming weekend will be your only chance for some rest and recreation outside the public spotlight. Do you and Kate have any plans for a last-minute getaway?"

"Yes, Winston, as a matter of fact," I turn and smile at Kate, "we have plans to see some dear friends. And to see for ourselves that a promise has been kept."

CHAPTER 111

She's very careful, cautious. Her gait is slow and unsteady at times, but she is walking. Sarah Wendover is walking! She turns to smile at Dan, close at her side. She squeezes him on the arm and the big lawman beams with joy.

We smile and wave as they approach down the main street sidewalk. Kate and I have returned to Alta Junction to reunite with the Wendovers and see Sarah's progress with our own eyes. And our daughter Amy has driven over from Bozeman to join us, making this a family outing.

Sarah's doctors are elated, but incredulous. Her recovery is unprecedented. ALS patients may see their disease's progression slow, sometimes for years. But recovery of lost function is not considered possible. The doctors have no idea how this can be so. But soon they will understand. Shortly, a revolutionary new generation of genetic therapies will be announced by the biomedical research arm of DAST Industries.

Ta'Naal has kept her promise. Two days with advanced Diné medical technologies have transformed Sarah's life. And Dan's life as well. All of our lives. We are all connected.

And, in this moment, it strikes me that Sarah's steps, however tentative, may be the very first of humanity's halting steps towards a new future. To be sure, a future of many potential wonders but also much uncertainty and enormous disruption.

And someday, perhaps as Amy's young generation matures and takes their rightful place on the world's center stage, the alien Diné may feel safe to step forward from behind the curtain. Then there will be for all of humanity a collective loss of innocence, a recalibration of our place in the universe as we realize our species may still be special but no longer unique. And no longer alone.

I pull Kate and Amy close to me for a hug. Lead the way to the future, Sarah. We're all following right behind you. Lead the way.

Walk with beauty before you. Walk with beauty behind you. Walk in beauty. Walk in harmony. Walk in peace…

AFTERWORD

This novel is (we should hope!) a work of fiction. However, the narrative of POINT OF ORIGIN is underlain with concepts and theories that continue to merit serious scientific examination. These topics include terraforming of Mars, the Domestication Syndrome, stylometric authentication of texts, the use of A.I. to decode whale vocalizations, and many others. And regarding Dr. Monroe's assertion that an advanced civilization could have existed on Earth millions of years ago without detection in the present day, direct your search engine of choice to "The Silurian Hypothesis."

For more on the science and theories behind POINT OF ORIGIN as well as updates on the author's upcoming research and writing projects, please visit his website: chduuswriter.com

ACKNOWLEDGMENTS

It has been wisely said that it takes a village to raise a child. Likewise, the creation of a novel such as POINT OF ORIGIN was hardly a solo undertaking. I am grateful beyond words for the insights and gentle guidance of my dear friend and editor, Sharon Burg. It was my good fortune to enlist the very gifted Kerianne O'Donnell for the captivating design of the cover. And I am indebted to my cadre of friends and colleagues who served as beta readers. Your inputs and suggestions regarding the manuscript greatly improved the narrative. I wish to thank Mike and the team at The Paper House for final layout and formatting services. And, finally, this novel would not have been possible without the encouragement of Kathy; a talented and patient woman with whom I coauthor the continuing story of our life together.

ABOUT THE AUTHOR

C. Hansen Duus has dedicated his career to advanced science and technology projects within government research laboratories and private aerospace companies. As an author, he crafts suspense thrillers that intricately weave elements of mystery, horror, science fiction, and satire.

Residing in the Pacific Northwest, Duus is currently working on his forthcoming novel, The Interrogator.

For updates on the author's upcoming research and writing projects please visit chduuswriter.com

* 9 7 9 8 9 9 9 0 7 4 8 8 1 1 *